THE COMPLETE TRILOGY

BY ZACK ARGYLE

SYL PUBLISHING LLC

Copyright © 2022 by SYL Publishing

All rights reserved.

This is a work of fiction. Any resemblance to reality is coincidental.

No part of this book may be reproduced in any form or by any electronic or mechanical means, including information storage and retrieval systems, without written permission from the author, except for the use of brief quotations in a book review.

www.zackargyle.com

Cover illustration by Ömer Burak Önal

BOOK BLURB

A protective father with a voice in his head.

A sheltered young woman addicted to threadlight.

A reckless young man whose life changes after he dies.

Together, they will change the world—whether they intend to or not.

While preparing for the birth of his first child, Chrys Valerian is tasked with uncovering the group responsible for a series of missing threadweavers—those able to see and manipulate threadlight. With each failure, the dark voice in his head grows louder, begging to be released.

As he learns who is responsible, they come for him and his family. He must do everything in his power to protect those he loves, even if it means trusting strangers or, worse, the growing voice in his mind.

★ *Indies Today 2020 Best Fantasy Award*
★ *SFF Oasis Indie Book of the Year 2022*
★ *2020 Book Bloggers' Novel of the Year Finalist*
★ *2020 SPFBO Finalist*
★ *A FanFiAddict Favorite Series*

PRAISE FOR THREADLIGHT

"Zack Argyle wowed me with this story."
—*Fantasy Book Critic*

"The Threadlight trilogy and author have quickly become one of my favourites to date."
—**Kay's Hidden Shelf**

"I laughed, I cheered, I gasped and I even got a little teary at the end...One of my favourite series of all time."
—**Indie Accords (Lana)**

"A thrilling ride from start to finish...one of the best series I've read in ages."
—**Bookwyrm (Craig)**

"The main takeaway I had when closing the last page is 'This is how you end a trilogy!'"
—**Under the Radar SFF (Blaise)**

"This will leap to the top of many lists, and it deserves to be at the top. The trilogy is concluded in a surprising but very satisfying way...I could not have asked for anything better."
—**Escapist Book Company (Justin)**

"I would highly recommend this series to anyone that is a fan of epic fantasy, especially fans of John Gwynne and Brandon Sanderson. *Threadlight* is a riveting, action-packed, compelling fantasy story that will have the reader turning the pages from start to finish...I will definitely be picking up whatever Argyle writes next!"
—**Library of a Viking**

For Hillary, who supports me endlessly

BOOK 1 OF THREADLIGHT

VOICE of WAR

BY ZACK ARGYLE

SYL PUBLISHING LLC

Chrys Valerian had seen the insides of men displayed on their outsides, he'd seen the life fade from limbless soldiers, but something about a child's discomfort unsettles a man's soul.

He stood beside his wife, Iriel, his hands behind him, his back straight, and his head tall, as a priest placed a glove over each of his hands and reached out to the child on the altar.

"May the will of the Father be manifest."

Chrys looked over to his best friend, Luther, whose chest heaved up and down with each fear-filled breath. Only a few paces away, Luther's wife, Emory, stood with a tremble in her legs. Chrys couldn't imagine what they must be feeling. The Rite of Revelation was stressful for every parent—determining whether or not your child was a threadweaver could change their life—but this was their third child, and the law was clear.

The priest gently felt his way over the curves of the child's face, finding and opening the lids of the child's eyes. He lifted a vial out of his robes and forced a drop of clear liquid into the left eye. The child squirmed but did not cry as the liquid settled over his iris.

Beneath the ritual chamber's domed ceiling, intricate stained-glass windows graced the walls and a hint of lavender lingered in the air. The room spread out in a wide circle. At the center stood a solitary marble altar with a hand-span-high lip protruding from its four corners, forming a protective barrier for the squirming infant laying on its padded surface. To the side, a large veil masked a temple worker set to record the events.

On the stone floor, an intricate design swirled around a painted gold triangle, the altar centered on the far edge. Luther and Emory each stood at separate ends of the triangle. Chrys appreciated the symbolism, but even more so he appreciated the order.

"What is the will of the Father?" the priest asked, his own eyes closed as he held the child's eyes open.

Chrys watched Luther and Emory step toward the altar.

Iriel reached over and gripped his hand.

The room grew still.

Emory choked on her breath and began to cry. "Brown," she exhaled, trying to hold back her emotions. But that single word—so colorless, so ordinary—was a herald from which she could not hide.

Achromic.

Chrys squeezed Iriel's hand as they soaked in the revelation. Having brown eyes wasn't the end of the world. It simply meant that you were not a threadweaver. Most people weren't. But Luther and Emory were, their Emerald eyes a sharp contrast to their dark, Felian skin. And their first two children were, too.

Emory buried her thick hair into Luther's chest. He gripped her fiercely, his eyes burning resentment. Slowly, he led her away from the altar. What came next would not be something any parent would choose to witness.

Iriel's hand trembled against Chrys'. He glanced over to see a tear falling down her cheek. She was a warrior, not one to cry, but pregnancy had a way of amplifying her emotions, especially in familial matters. He steadied her hand with his own.

As they walked through to the waiting room, he grabbed Luther and embraced him, cursing the law under his breath. In Alchea, families were only allowed to have two children, according to the Book of Alchaeus. If, however, a third child was born, it was given to the church to be raised in the priesthood—unless that child was a threadweaver. If the rite revealed blue or green eyes, the couple could keep their third child. It was a risk Luther and Emory had known beforehand and, still, foresight dampens loss only the slightest.

Chrys held his friend tight. It felt wrong to see a soldier cry. If only he could convince the Stone Council to let them keep the child. Or perhaps he could convince the Great Lord to grant an exception. Doubtful on both counts. They'd known the risk.

As they left the room, the sound of the recorder's pen scratching at parchment from behind the veil reverberated off the vaulted ceilings. It was done.

Cursed to darkness. Blessed to serve.

Was that the priest's voice? Chrys glanced back as the door closed behind them. The priest was holding a different vial now.

A solemn echo carried through the hallway and into the waiting room as the door slammed shut.

"What were we thinking?" Luther asked. He ran his hands over the bare skin of his head as he fought back tears.

"You knew, and still you tried," Chrys said. "That's damn brave if you ask me."

"I don't know." Luther took a steadying breath and looked to Chrys. "Thank you...for being here."

"You know I'll always be there for you. You've had my back more times than I can remember. Two threads; one bond."

"Two threads; one bond," Luther repeated as they clasped arms. "I should go. Emory's parents are waiting."

Chrys looked him in the eyes. "Take some time. Spend it with your kids. Take care of Emory. She'll need you more than you need her. I'll make sure your shifts are covered."

"No," Luther said strongly. "The last thing I want to do right now is sit at home all day thinking about this. Promise me you'll let me know if anything comes up. If we can catch the Bloodthieves—"

A blood-curdling scream thundered out from the ritual chamber. Every person in the waiting room turned to the door, terror-stricken. One by one, they each dropped their head. *Cursed to darkness.* Emory fell to her knees wailing. Luther sank down with her. He squeezed her as they embraced the truth. The child they had known was no longer theirs.

Chrys could picture it in his mind. The priest injecting a few drops of acid in each of the child's eyes. The liquid entangling with tears as they bled down his face. A lifetime of divine blindness. It was cruel. It was horrid. It was commandment. All priests were blind in accordance with the Book of Alchaeus.

"And they shall shed off the light of the world for the light of Alchaeus, for it is greater to see truth than light."

Chrys and Iriel stepped away as Emory's family surrounded the couple. They walked silently, hand in hand, to the top of the temple's stone steps where Chrys could see a broad view of the Alchean landscape. The temple was nestled against the Everstone Mountains near the top of a large hill. A river flowed down from the mountains through the valley to the south.

Three central buildings loomed to each side, forming an elaborate tapestry of shadows where stone pillars and protrusions battled rays of sunlight. A spiraling dome capped one of the buildings. The top of the dome bloomed like a rose into two figures adorned in floral robes representing the Heralds, a remnant of the old religion.

A pity such lovely buildings were given to the blind.

Iriel winced as they descended the stairs. "We're never having a third."

"Stones, no," Chrys said.

"If anything happened to ours—" she paused, glancing down at her stomach.

"If anything happened to either of you—" Chrys added.

"—It would destroy me."

Once, when he was young, Chrys' mother had found a leafling and let him keep it as a pet. He'd named the small creature Shelly. It had been his first charge, and he'd taken the responsibility seriously. When a neighbor boy had tried to break its shell, Chrys had broken the boy's finger.

A manservant waved to them from atop the carriage. His big brown eyes were flanked by deep wrinkles that shone brightly when he smiled. "Lord Valerian! I always forget how short the Rite of Revelation is. Any shorter and I'd swear it was an Alirian wedding! Ha! Seems like something that determines the rest of your life ought to be dragged out a little longer. Then again, I suppose it's the kind of thing you don't really want to drag out. Well, come now. I'm stepping on stubble. Was the little one a Sapphire or Emerald?"

"Achromic," Chrys said. From the corner of his eye, he could see the word sink in. The word used for those born with brown eyes. Like it was some kind of disease.

"Well. Well, well, well. Even with two threadweaver parents and two threadweaver siblings?" The manservant shook his head. "I suppose that's why most people don't even try. Like they say, the Lightfather saves whom he will. Still, heartbreaking."

Iriel squeezed Chrys' arm. He knew that with a child inside her, the pain of their friends' loss was a pain to her. They stopped, and he kissed her head. She hunched over with her hands on her knees and puckered her lips as she took in shallow breaths.

"Are you okay?" he asked.

"I don't know." Her eyes squinted shut as she groaned in pain, both hands now clutching at her stomach. She leaned forward and simply breathed, waiting for the pain to subside. She nodded to him and stood up straight once more. She doubled over again as a storm wall of pain crashed into her. She screamed out and nearly tripped down the remaining stairs.

Chrys steadied her, eyes wide with fear. What was happening to her? It wasn't too early for contractions, but they shouldn't be this painful at the start. He'd read as much as he could about the birthing process, enough to know that something wasn't right. He helped her down onto the stone steps. She grabbed his arm and squeezed with a fierce strength as she arched her back and fell back onto the steps. A soiled red patch surfaced far below her stomach.

No. Chrys scrambled around looking for something, anything that could help. He had no idea what to do. He knew how to stitch wounds and care for broken bones, he knew how to *deliver* a child, but this was beyond his knowledge. He checked beneath her dress and found more red spotting. "GEOFFREY!" he screamed out. "Get inside and find a doctor!"

The shocked manservant jumped off the carriage and sprinted up the steps and into the temple while Chrys continued comforting Iriel. "It's going to be okay. We'll find help. Breathe. Breathe." He found himself unable to follow his own advice.

He sat waiting, his blood boiling as anger awoke inside him. His knuckles ground into the stone steps and his jaw clamped tight. There was something he could do. There had to be. He thought hard about everything he'd read, but this wasn't birth. This was something else. He closed his eyes, the skin of his knuckles breaking open as he ground them deeper into the stone.

Mmmm, a voice echoed in his skull.

No. Chrys closed his eyes and shook his head. *I am in control.*

As he opened them again, a man with a wide-brimmed hat came running from the other side of the carriage. He rushed forward while opening a large leather bag. "Chrys Valerian? I am a doctor and, if you want Iriel to live, you must trust me." He began poking Iriel's torso. With each forceful prod she cried out in pain.

"What are you doing? Get away from her!" Chrys shouted.

He reached out a hand to push him aside, but the man caught his wrist. "I am the only one that can perform such a surgery. Step aside and let me save her."

Chrys saw the man's face for the first time. His skin looked like he'd soaked in a pool for too long, thick wrinkles from ear to ear. And yet, his eyes had a healthy air of youth about them.

He couldn't possibly trust this man with Iriel's life. But what choice did he have? He had no idea what to do, and there was no one else. If he truly did know how to help her, and Chrys didn't let him, he could never live with himself. He looked back for Geoffrey but the servant still had not returned. He hated the helplessness. He hated himself for not making her stay home. He never should have let her come.

The man must have seen the resolve in Chrys' eyes. "Good. Help me lift her into the carriage. Quickly now!"

Shaking his head clear, Chrys succumbed. Together, they lifted Iriel into the carriage. The man shoved himself between the two of them and pointed back. "Give me space to work and I promise you she will live. There's more at stake here than you know."

Chrys jumped off of the carriage and looked back inside. The last thing he saw as the door closed was the shimmer of a long, thin device being extracted from the leather bag. His chest burned.

He should be in control.

A minute later, her screams stopped and the carriage went silent. Chrys rose to his feet just as the door to the carriage swung open. The man looked down, took the few steps to the ground, and turned to Chrys, though his eyes stayed low.

"They will be okay," he said.

Again he saw the man's face. Unblemished, yet sickly. Old, yet young. Instinctively, Chrys reached for the knife in his boot.

"The recoil will happen any moment. Chrys, you must listen to me. Your child is the key. They will come for it. You cannot let them have it."

A dark feeling grew in the pit of Chrys' stomach.

"Whatever it takes, you must protect the child."

Chrys felt his pulse quicken. "What the hell are you talking about?"

"You will need this," he said, pulling out a gleaming black dagger from his bag. He tossed it over to Chrys. "Use it to break the threads that bind you. Relek, forgive me."

Chrys caught the knife as it arced through the air toward him. He looked down at the gleaming obsidian and, when he looked up, the man with the wide-brimmed hat was gone.

Where had he gone so quickly? Was he even real, or had Chrys' mind finally given way to the madness? And what had he done to...Iriel.

Chrys ran over to the carriage and looked inside. Eyes closed, her chest rose up and down, each breath flowing like nothing had happened. Were it not for the red stains spotting her dress and thighs, he could have believed that was the case. A piece of fabric covering her stomach had been slit, revealing a small hole that had been sewn up. What had the man done? Had it worked? He felt the knife in his hand and eyed the shimmering reflection. He'd never seen an obsidian blade before.

"Lord Valerian!" The manservant had returned, sprinting down the steps two-by-two, a crowd of people following close behind. "I found the temple doctor, sir!"

Chrys looked through the open carriage door, his eyes an exhausted shade of red matching the blood on his knuckles. He spoke, more for himself than for the others. "Lightfather, let her be okay."

A BRIGHT SUN crept over the Everstone Mountains, the peaks of Endin Keep casting long shadows over the Alchean city streets. Winding walkways crisscrossed between home and shop with the exception of Beryl Boulevard, a wide, well-groomed street leading from the western borders of Alchea proper directly to the archway of Endin Keep. A straight fixture amidst a city filled with unplanned growth.

The sight from the highest tower of Endin Keep was breathtaking, with sweeping panoramic views of the landscape. Yet Chrys sat staring into a book. He'd been there for hours, a melted candle flickering in the dim light of morning. Hundreds of notes written down meticulously onto dozens of parchment papers, stacked in ordered groups, surrounded him. Charts and diagrams and sketches. His eyes were filled with exhausted passion, but he was driven by a profound thirst for knowledge. Never again.

"Good morning, General."

Chrys startled. He hadn't noticed the Great Lord Malachus Endin entering the briefing room. "Good morning, sir." He gathered his notes, arranging each of them meticulously, and placed them in the sleeve of the leather book.

Malachus approached him. "How long have you been awake?"

"A while, sir." Chrys sat up straight. He adjusted the book so that it was lined up with the edge of the table.

"Is this about Iriel? I hear she is recovering well."

"She is, sir. We were very fortunate." Chrys looked up and met eyes with Malachus. The bichromic gaze of the Great Lord never ceased to unnerve. One eye a deep cerulean blue and the other a bright minty green. The colors were accentuated by the long, black hair falling on both sides of his bronze face. Light gray brushed carelessly across a well-trimmed beard. Malachus reveled in eye contact, knowing well how it reminded people of his dual threadweaver nature, and he respected those who were willing to keep his gaze when he spoke.

"I'm glad to hear it." Malachus rounded the other end of the table, looked at the leather book, and laughed to himself. "Chrys, do you know why I chose you to be high general?"

One year had passed since Chrys had accepted the position: one of three high generals to the Great Lord. He had been twenty-nine at the time, young for the prestige of the highest office, but well-respected for his leadership in the War of the Wastelands. Many discounted his achievements and saw him only as the boy who had lived in Endin Keep during his early years. Malachus' wife had taken in Chrys and his mother when they'd first arrived in Alchea from Felia. They'd lived in Endin Keep until Chrys was eight years old, and in those years Malachus had grown fond of the little fighter. Even after two decades, the fondness remained.

"There are many practical reasons, sir. The political…"

"No, no, no. Come now. Politically it was an awful choice. Rynan had more years of experience, had spent time in both Felia and Alir, and is possibly the best swordsman in Alchea. Jurius thought I'd gone mad when I chose you instead. It wasn't completely mad, of course. You were a legend after the war. *The Apogee.* For me, that was nothing but a convenient selling point. Even still, some considered it a form of nepotism when I promoted you. But, do you know the real reason?" Malachus gestured to the book and papers. "This. You sitting there with your head in a book is why. When you find a weakness, you wake up with the sun, grab it by the stones, and bring it to submission. Self-betterment is the rarest form of ambition. I admire it greatly."

"I wouldn't call it ambition, sir."

"Sure, it is," Malachus said, his brows furling. "You know, sometimes I look at you and wonder how it's possible. On the one hand, you're this." Malachus gestured to him. "A man completely in control. And on the other hand, we've all heard the stories."

"That part of me is gone, sir."

Malachus huffed. "No, it's not. I know you too well. That fire you get in your eyes. Some fires burn so bright you spend years finding unbridled coals. One of these days, if you're not careful, one of them will catch fire."

"I'm managing." The truth was that Chrys had struggled ever since the war. He still had nightmares of his hands dripping red while hundreds of wastelanders lay dead around him. Women and children. Even some of his own men. The Apogee they'd called him. The man who turned the tide.

"Don't shy away from ambition, Chrys. It's a tool as useful as any other. I was once overflowing with it and it won me a nation. These days, I'm afraid I find it in short supply. I like to tell myself that I'm just waiting for the right opportunity but, when decades pass, you start to doubt your own lies. If you'd known Jurius and I thirty years ago, you'd have seen pure ambition personified." He relaxed back in his chair.

In many ways, Chrys looked up to Malachus. His cunning rise to power. His peace treaty with Felia. He had been ruthless in those days, but somewhere along the way he'd grown softer. Chrys had never understood what had brought about the change, but "diminishing ambition" was as good a reason as any.

A knock at the door broke the moment. A man and woman entered and Malachus gave a wide smile. "Speak of the old stone."

High General Jurius, an older man with well-trimmed dark hair and a beard that was dusted with gray, frowned as he entered. Deep bags lay beneath his bright green eyes. "What are we talking about?"

"Ambition." Malachus smiled.

The white-haired Alirian woman, High General Henna, raised her brows. "From Chrys? I've seen more ambition from a fish."

Malachus laughed.

Chrys rose and greeted her with a handshake. "I'll take that as a compliment."

"It's not," she said with a smirk.

High General Jurius took a seat and noted the book in front of Chrys. "What is 'Late-stage Obstetrics'?"

"It's a..." he looked to Malachus.

"The handsome one is a doctor now?" Henna interrupted.

"...weakness." Chrys finished. "I don't like to be caught off guard twice."

Henna ignored him. "That *is* rather serendipitous; I'm due for my next lady checkup." She smiled. Despite having been born in Alchea, it had been a scandal when she'd been named high general. Angry commoners cursing and calling her a spy. As far as Chrys knew, she'd never even been to the Alirian Islands. "I'll have Geoffrey schedule it."

Malachus pointed at the book. "Knowledge is the foundation of every victory. Rather than mocking Chrys, you both would do well to follow his example."

The room grew quiet. The other high generals hardly tried to hide their disdain. Both were many years his senior, and neither had earned the title so easily. He hoped it would fade sooner rather than later, but a year had passed and the aversion remained.

"Henna." Malachus leaned forward. "Why don't you give me your report."

She nodded. "Of course, sir. The mountain passes have continued to receive pressure from the wastelanders, but only reactively. They appear to have greater numbers than our original estimates, but we've managed to force them completely out of Ripshire Valley and down into the swamps. We've set up an outpost at the choke point and should be able to sustain control of the passes with minimal manpower.

"A small skirmish broke out south of the pass, but we were able to dispatch them easy enough with a small force of threadweavers. We've still yet to see any threadweavers among the wastelanders—probably because they aren't human—so it should be safe to man the outpost with achromats going forward."

Henna was achromic herself, but she was one of the fiercest fighters in all of Alchea and her knowledge of historical battle strategies was second to none. Chrys had started to believe the stories about her. Supposedly, when she'd first joined the Alchean army, a group of sloven soldiers had approached her on her way home. They had surrounded her and tried to convince her that, although she wasn't the prettiest, her Alirian hair and fit frame were enough to find her a special "someone" to take care of her. When one approached with grease in his gaze, she caught him off guard, pinned him to the ground, slipped out a knife and cut his thumb off. Before the others understood what had happened, she held up the finger and told them she'd already found her *special thumb-one* and wouldn't be needing their services. Everyone left her alone after that. A guard had once claimed to Chrys that there was a thumb framed in Henna's living room. Chrys didn't doubt it.

"Proceed to man the outpost as you see fit." Malachus nodded. "And keep me informed of any further advancements. Especially if they become more proactive. At some point, we may want to send scouts deeper into the Wastelands to get a better read on their numbers but, if things have settled for now, do as you wish. Was there anything else?"

She raised a finger. "There is one thing. While scouting the mountain peaks, one of our men discovered a cave. There were etchings found at the mouth of the cave and it appears to go deep into the mountain. He traveled and never found the end, but he did find mining tools and a few weapons along the way. Looked fresher than they would have expected. They are exploring further at my request."

"As long as the wastelanders are kept at bay, you may use your resources as you see fit, though I would not personally spend time exploring caves. Thank you." Malachus turned to his longtime friend, High General Jurius. "And what news from Felia?"

"The roads remain clear of bandits on our side of the border. I've heard reports of trouble on the Felian side but, for now, it's nothing but hearsay. The Empress doesn't care about us so long as we stay east of Shay's Meadow." General Jurius hated his assignment. When Chrys had been tasked with weeding out the Bloodthieves, Jurius had about jumped over the table and strangled him. But for good reason—his son was the first threadweaver who had gone missing.

Malachus nodded. "Good. Any word from the spies?"

"Nothing new." Jurius paused. "There is little to worry about and little to do. I would be happy to help in other areas while my duties are light."

"Jurius," Malachus exhaled. "It's not a matter of qualification or workload. This needs to be handled carefully, and you are too emotionally connected to it."

"It's been more than a month and we have nothing! I don't care how emotionally connected I am. We need results, and we're not getting them!"

Chrys shifted in his chair, his hands clasped atop the book. The words were an attack on his abilities, but Chrys understood. Jurius wanted his son back. As a soon-to-be father, Chrys couldn't even imagine what Jurius must be feeling. While the Bloodthieves were out there, kidnapping threadweavers and selling their blood, none of them were safe. The doctor who'd performed surgery on Iriel the previous day had said something about stopping the Bloodthieves and stopping them from taking his child. He wished he could ask the man why he would say something like that.

"I'm following up on a lead later this morning," Chrys responded. "We're doing everything we can."

"That is well. I want Chrys to focus all of his efforts on rooting them out." Malachus nodded to Chrys then turned back to Jurius. "In the meantime, I would like Jurius to take over the training of the Sapphire threadweavers until the Bloodthieves are dealt with."

"But, sir—" Chrys started.

"It's not up for debate. There is nothing more important than stopping the kidnappings before it gets even more out of hand. Thank you, Jurius. Chrys, what updates do you have?"

Chrys composed himself. He knew Malachus well enough to know when his mind was set in stone. Even more frustrating was the smirk on Henna's lips. He ignored her. "We received a report that the Bloodthieves have a base of operations in the lower westside. The source gave us directions to a warehouse. I plan on taking my team to investigate later this morning."

"What kind of source?" Henna asked skeptically.

"Someone from the area who said they saw a brown-eyed man go into a warehouse and come out with his veins tinted green."

"Someone?" she pressed.

"A boy," Chrys said.

"A boy? How young?" She wouldn't let it go.

"I don't know, Henna. A young boy. Maybe twelve? A source is a source."

Henna frowned. "How much are you paying him for the information?"

"The most recent missing threadweaver was an Emerald. The boy saw green veins. It could have merit. Every source is worth confirming."

Jurius shook his head. "You can't be serious. This is the only lead you have? A deadbeat off the street looking to make a few shines? How could this possibly be the best lead you have after a month?"

"Enough!" Chrys exploded. "We're on the same side. I understand that you want your son back. I want them *all* back. Malachus trusts me. If you doubt his judgment, then speak up."

Silence.

"And if not, then keep your mouths shut and let me give my report." Chrys felt a familiar anger boiling inside him, a voice in the back of his mind.

Mmmm, the voice spoke to him. *You don't deserve to be disrespected this way. Let me help. I will* make *them respect you.*

Chrys shook his head.

For the last five years, ever since the War of the Wastelands, Chrys had heard the voice. Like a shadow living inside him, a reminder of the day he'd slaughtered hundreds. The world believed that Chrys was the Apogee, that they were one and the same, but Chrys knew better. And he knew how dangerous it would be to lose control once again. No one knew. Not even his wife. Insanity isn't high on anyone's list of leadership qualities. But Chrys had controlled it for years, and he wasn't about to let his guard down now.

He spoke back to the voice. *No, I am in control.*

But you don't have to be.

Malachus scowled. "It appears that matter has been resolved. Chrys, please finish your report."

"Of course, sir." Chrys took a breath. "As I said, I will be taking my team to investigate the warehouse later this morning. Whatever the outcome, I'll report back as soon as possible."

"And what of the missing threadweavers?" Malachus asked. "I assume I would have heard if we'd found any bodies?"

Chrys shook his head and sighed. Four had gone missing, but the body of one had been found the prior week. Bruised and pale, with marks all over his body from cuts they'd used to drain his blood. "Still no sign, sir. This afternoon I am heading to the temple to get a complete list of threadweavers. I am going to see if there is any pattern with those who have been kidnapped in an attempt to predict the next target. It's a long shot. The Bloodthieves have been careful."

"If you find them," Jurius said, scowling, "rip the heart out of every last one of those cowards. They don't deserve a trial. They don't deserve a chance to explain themselves. They deserve a swift death."

"I would prefer to capture them alive."

Henna leaned forward. "I say we drown them in blood. Pour it down their throats and let them choke on the irony of it."

There were rumors that Jurius and Henna had been lovers in the past while Jurius' wife was still alive. Chrys didn't believe it. They respected each other; friends maybe, but certainly not lovers. Jurius was older and reclusive, and Henna had other interests.

"Your creativity is inspiring, Henna." Malachus leaned back in his chair. "I will ponder on a befitting punishment for our transgressors after we find them. Thank you all. You are dismissed."

Chrys gathered his things and left the room, glancing back to see Malachus deep in thought and the two high generals talking as they walked out behind him.

"Chrys." Jurius ran forward and stopped him.

"What do you want, Jurius?"

"I wanted to apologize...for everything. You were placed in a tough situation, and you don't deserve the way I've treated you. I just hate sitting back while my son is in danger."

Chrys looked at Jurius, and the man seemed sincere. "I appreciate that."

"If you ever need help with the investigation," Jurius added, "I'm here and I'll help in any way that I can. I would do anything for my son."

The words sparked a memory in Chrys. He recalled the odd man who'd saved Iriel, and his words of caution. *Your child is the key. They will come for it. You cannot let them have it.*

"Of course," Chrys nodded. "I'm not a father yet, but I know I'd do anything for my child. I promise I'll find them."

Jurius thanked him and walked down the spiral staircase. Chrys was surprised by the unexpected apology. The high general was smart; he must have realized that the only way Chrys would ever let him get involved was by smoothing over the relationship.

Chrys walked forward and made eye contact with two guards posted at the top of the stairway. He stepped forward and fixed the collar on one of the guards. "Soldiers."

"High General," they said in unison.

"Thank you for your vigilance. You are prime examples of professionalism." Chrys turned to the female guard. "How's your uncle?"

"Much better, sir."

She stood a little taller and Chrys was sure that, for a brief moment, he'd caught a smile forming in the corner of the woman's mouth.

A tall, wide window lay just a few strides from the top of the stairs, looking out over the keep's courtyard. Chrys stepped forward, opened the window, and nodded to the guards. His veins began to glow a bright blue as he opened himself to threadlight. Then, as if he'd stepped into a higher plane, brilliant strands of colorful light burst forth into existence all round him, a tapestry of pure energy connecting him to everything around. Below him, a dense, bright thread ran from the ground up into his body. His corethread. His connection to the world itself.

Then, he jumped.

The wind rushed through his dark hair and his cloak flowed high up overhead as he fell to the distant ground. He focused on his corethread and, as he approached the ground, *pushed* energy through it. His veins burned hot, adrenaline mixing with the power of threadweaving. As he *pushed*, it pushed back and his eyes glowed bright blue. He *pushed* harder until gravity no longer had hold of him and, just before he hit the ground, he gave a final *push* on his corethread, stopping his fall completely. He landed with the smallest thud. The veins in his arms radiated a strange, luminescent blue light that seemed to pulse brighter with the beat of his heart.

In a world where Chrys had to be in control, he cherished such moments of ungoverned freefall. He stood up straight, smiled, and clasped his hands behind his back.

His manservant, Geoffrey, bolted upright from his seat on the carriage. "Stones be damned," he let slip. "My apologies, Lord Chrys. My tongue curses quicker than my mind can stop it. Really should keep my eyes up, like the priests are always telling me to do. Again, apologies, my lord."

"No apology needed," Chrys assured him as he walked toward the carriage. "I need you to send out runners to fetch my crew. Have them meet me at The Black Eye. I'll meet them at noon."

"Even Luther, sir?" he asked.

"Yes," Chrys confirmed. He'd thought about what Luther had said about not wanting to be sitting at home with his thoughts, and he was right. If Chrys were in his position, he wouldn't want that either.

Stealing a quick glance up at the high tower window that was still open, Chrys was sure he heard another "stones be damned" under Geoffrey's breath as the manservant rode away to notify the others.

THE BLACK EYE was empty save for the scarred-up barkeep and his daughter. Chrys sat in silence for a time thinking about Iriel, hoping that everything was okay with her and the baby. After studying each of the medical books he'd had procured from the keep library, he was fairly certain he understood what had happened to her, but he still wasn't certain what the doctor had done. None of the methods he'd read about required surgery. But whatever the stranger had done seemed to have worked.

Luther walked in the door first, Reina and Lazarus walking in behind him. Chrys greeted each of them as they entered. "Luther, how are you, friend?"

"I've been better. Thanks for letting me come. I needed this." Luther's eyes were sunken and dry. He looked fitting for a man who'd lost his son.

"Let's take it easy if we need to."

Luther nodded.

Chrys turned to Lazarus, a hulking Sapphire threadweaver with bright red hair. Next to Luther's dark complexion, looking at Laz was like looking at the surface of the sun. "Laz, today may be your lucky day."

The big man smiled a toothy grin. "Is bath time?"

"If we're lucky."

The first day Chrys met Laz, the big oaf had made a joke about the city being a child. "Kids are dirty and show no respect," Laz had said. "Sometimes you must take out back, give whack, and give bath." He claimed that when he slid his blade through a criminal, he was simply "giving city a bath." Lovely man.

"We received some intelligence about a warehouse that may be a Bloodthief hideout. No guarantees but, if it's true and we're not careful, it could become a bloody bath indeed. Now, let's see your arms." They were accustomed to this. Chrys always checked their veins to make sure they had not been threadweaving. Too much in a day was dangerous and, if things went south, they'd need to be ready.

One by one they rolled up their sleeves, extended their arms, and let Chrys examine their veins. Laz was a Sapphire threadweaver, but his veins didn't radiate the bright blue they would if he had been threadweaving recently. Reina was a capable Emerald threadweaver whom they affectionately referred to as The Alirian Spider. Her veins were clean. Professional as always. Luther looked at Chrys and rolled up his sleeves. Chrys could see a slight green discoloration in the veins.

"Stones, Luther," Chrys swore.

"For what it's worth, this *was* kind of last minute," Luther said impassively. "My son was taken from me. Threadlight helps."

Chrys took a deep breath. He was starting to wonder if letting Luther come had been a mistake. "That's a conversation for another time. It's not enough to delay things, but next time I want you clean."

He nodded.

"The plan is to approach the warehouse," Chrys explained, "careful to observe any comings or goings. Be wary of windows and lookouts. We don't want them alerted. If this is real, it could be a huge win for the city. Luther will come with me through the front entrance. The two of you will approach from the rear."

"Won't be the first time Laz approached from the rear." Reina smirked as she clapped the big man on the back.

"Huh? Ah! Ha!" Laz let out a bellowing laugh.

Chrys stared at them, his eyes emotionless. "Thank you, Reina. Are you finished?"

"Wouldn't be the first time Laz finished—" Reina started, unable to hold it in. "Sorry. Please, continue."

Laz and Reina smiled at each other. It was always a sound strategy to pair a Sapphire with an Emerald. Complimentary threadweaving. *Push and pull.* Chrys and Luther had been working together since the War. Laz and Reina had started working together since Chrys had become high general. They trusted each other.

"This may be nothing, or it may be more than we can handle. If it's too dangerous we'll pull out on my signal. Any questions?"

"I assume non-lethality is the goal here?" Reina asked, eyeing Laz.

Chrys nodded. "Yes. A nice, soothing bath. Not a blood bath. The more we capture alive, the more we have to question."

The two of them were so different both mentally and physically that it was surprising how well they worked together. Laz was thick. There was no better word to describe it. Huge muscular arms under a trunk of a neck, topped with well-cropped red hair and a stylish beard. Reina was lithe and short, with the white hair of the Alirian island natives. Luther kept his head shaved.

"Bath is bath as long as you scrub few stains."

"Right. I'll take that as a confirmation."

Reina raised her hand, her tattered arm leathers swaying with the movement.

"Yes?" Chrys asked.

"Who was your informant? If someone saw something, then others probably did too. Chances are they've already moved. What if we're walking into a trap? Four threadweavers sauntering into the warehouse of a group that's been kidnapping threadweavers? Could be awfully convenient for them." She folded her arms and her long hair bunched up at the shoulders.

Laz gave them a sadistic smile. "If is trap, I get the soap."

THERE IS nothing like the smell of stale sewage for masking crime. As Chrys watched Laz and Reina start down the shadowed alleyway, a foul stench lingered in the air. The lower westside of Alchea was far from the city center and had significantly less foot traffic. Chrys and Luther passed by a man who looked like he was days away from death. He was lying on the corner of an alleyway that smelled like urine. If he'd brought any shines—the tiny gemstones used as currency—Chrys would have tossed the man a few, but instead he walked on.

"Come on." He nodded down toward the opposite road. Luther followed without a word. "Keep your eyes open. We stand out here."

They moved slowly through the streets, peeking around each corner before rounding it. After a few minutes they reached their destination, a large warehouse squished in between decrepit houses. There were no windows on the ground level, but there were a few on the floor above. From a distance they all looked covered.

They stayed hidden for a few minutes, watching the windows and door. There was no movement, and no passersby. Chrys gestured to Luther and they moved forward.

They approached a large, nondescript wooden door. Upon closer investigation, they noticed specks of blood at the base of the handle. Luther pulled out a whistle and blew into it. The noise was so high pitched that it was hard to hear unless you were listening for it. Laz and Reina would be listening on the other side of the building.

Chrys tested the door; it pushed open with a creak. He signaled to Luther and they prepared for a quick entrance. He thrust his boot into the door, and it splintered near the hinges as it shot open from the force. Dust kicked up in the air, swirling in the misty sunlight shining down through holes in the roof. A partially broken staircase led up to an open second floor that wrapped around the outside of the room. The ceiling was high enough for a third floor, but was left open, exposing beams and a curved, arching roof. Soot and dirt lined the walls and railings.

From the back of the warehouse another loud boom reverberated through the empty air. Laz and Reina came bursting through the doorway, axe and daggers raised, veins lit with threadlight.

Chrys turned to Luther. "It's either a trap or the intel was bad. Either way, proceed with caution."

He signed for the others to do the same. They each made their way through the vast room. Silent, save for the sound of creaking floorboards. There were two rooms along the eastern wall; both were empty. After a few minutes of quiet investigation, they came back together.

Laz lowered his axe and hiked up the bag on his back. His toothy grin broke the silence. "Looks like place needs different kind of cleaning."

Reina laughed. "You've been smiling to yourself for the last minute. I bet you've been waiting this entire time to say that."

"Oh, come on, was good one!"

Chrys leaned against a railing. This was his only lead, and he desperately needed answers. Not to mention how Jurius would react if they came back empty-handed. "Luther and I saw some blood on the door handle out front. Make another sweep and see if you can't find any more.

There has to be something in here. Luther, try the roof." He paused. "And Laz. That *was* a good one."

Luther ran toward the north wall, the veins in his arms radiating green threadlight, and he leapt. If an Emerald threadweaver *pulled* hard enough against a wall or ceiling, they could overcome the gravitational pull of their corethread, allowing them to walk up the wall. Luther, a well-trained Emerald, ran up, shifting the base of the thread he was *pulling* as he ascended.

The other three spread out and stared at the ground as they looked for anything suspicious, moving from the center into the four corners. Chrys approached the southwest wall where the decrepit staircase began and examined the railing, unsure what he was looking for, still finding nothing out of place.

Luther leapt back toward the ground after checking the roof, *pulling* on the ceiling to slow his descent. It groaned under the weight and Chrys cringed at the idea of the roof collapsing. Luther's boots hit the ground hard, and he looked down, surprised.

"Aye, Chrys," Luther shouted from across the room.

"What do you have?"

"Nothing." Luther looked confused. "The walls and beams and crates are all covered in dust and dirt, but the floors have nothing. This place isn't abandoned. Lots of people have been walking around here recently. I'd bet they even swept it."

Nothing is better than nothing. Chrys looked down at the ground and was mad that he hadn't seen it earlier. Luther was right; the floors near the wall were dirty, but the rest of the floor was nearly dust-free. He walked around, eyes glued to the floor, searching for anything unusual. He ended up near the west wall and stopped on a dirty, ripped-up rug. The floor beneath his feet creaked.

"Well, looks like we got some bad intel." He emphasized the word as loud and clear as he could, then brought a finger to his lips and signed for the others to join him quietly. He continued his lie. "Stones, Malachus is going to be furious."

As the other three made their way over to Chrys, he pointed to the floor, brushing aside the rug with his boot. Beneath it was a large trap door. He signed for the others to prepare themselves, and hoped that if anyone was listening from below, they would be thrown off by his words. Laz was smiling from ear to ear as they moved into position.

Chrys opened himself to threadlight, the veins in his arms and neck beginning to glow with Sapphire threadlight. Luther's veins glowed with Emerald threadlight just before he *pulled* on the trapdoor. It ripped open, revealing a long ladder leading to a dark basement. Adrenaline pumped through Chrys' veins as he prepared for anything, but nothing happened.

Laz dropped to a knee and opened his bag. He pulled out a torch, a bottle of alcohol, and a flint kit. Pouring the alcohol on the torch, he struck the flint on the steel of his axe. Sparks flew and the torch blazed to life. He tossed it down the hole into the basement. The echo of the torch hitting the ground reverberated back up through the trapdoor and a small pool of light lit the ground below.

Still nothing.

Laz bent down to get a better view and almost fell in the hole as Reina's foot nudged his side. He turned and glared.

Reina smiled on the verge of laughter. "You are very kickable."

"You are very mean." Laz turned back around and continued looking down into the fire-lit basement.

"Looks empty, but we should be careful." They all turned at the sound of Chrys' voice. "Who's first?"

Reina smirked. "Is the Apogee scared of the dark?"

"The Apogee is dead."

She raised a brow.

Luther stood up and shook his arms out. "I'll go first."

The veins in his arms pulsed with bright green threadlight as he prepared to drop down the gap. He stepped forward and dropped down, threadlight blazing in his veins as he *pulled* on the floorboards above him to slow his descent. He landed with a slight thud and took a defensive position as he scouted the room. After a few moments, he gave them a thumbs up.

The other three dropped down the hole one by one into the dark basement. The fall took longer than Chrys had anticipated, the basement ceiling easily reaching two stories high with thick exposed trusses across its surface. Large crates and dusty furniture lined the outer rim of the massive room. A small tunnel, barely visible in the dim light, led around the far corner. Laz picked up his torch and held it out in front.

A strange sound echoed down the tunnel. Chrys turned to the others and whispered. "There is someone here. Laz, be careful with the torch, it's the only light we..."

A gush of water splashed on Chrys as it poured over Laz. A sound like wind rushed past him before the light went out. Footsteps poured in from all sides. A small amount of light trickled in from the trapdoor in the ceiling, but by the time Chrys' eyes adjusted he had three men tackling him down to the ground. A hard fist cracked into his ribs. He struggled to fight back, but there was no light, and he was pinned.

Three lanterns lit. A dozen men held down Chrys, Laz, and Luther as a gangly man with a tattoo on his neck approached. "High General Chrys Valerian. The Butcher of the Valley. The Apogee. I would have expected you to be taller. And older. I'm underwhelmed."

Chrys stared at the man, scanning the room in his peripherals for anything he could threadweave, but there was nothing useful for him to *push*. "So am I. I want to speak to your boss."

"I'm in charge."

"Maybe so, but you're not the boss."

The man frowned. "I bet we can sell your blood for double, funny man."

"No one on this rock would consider me a funny man," Chrys said, shaking his head. "But I am smart. And you're not. Minimum requirement for being the boss is knowing how to count."

Reina Talfar, the Alirian Spider, dropped down from the ceiling, *pulling* on her corethread as she fell to accelerate the descent. She crashed down onto the confused leader, her boots connecting with his head as he crumbled under the force. Luther *pulled* on two large crates at the sides of the room and they flung toward the men pinning them down. As they flew through the air, Reina *pulled* against the wall and launched herself toward the nearest enemy. The Bloodthieves dove out of the way of the crates. Chrys and Laz *pushed* on the crates before they smashed into them, and Chrys saw a sadistic smile on Laz's face as the melee began.

He felt the rush of warmth flow through his veins as he let more threadlight flow through him. Dim threads of light swirled throughout the world around him. It was dark, and his ability to see threadlight was connected to his ability to see real light. Threads linked him to the wall, to the crates, to the broken pieces of wood on the far side of the room. Finding the thread of the wall behind him, Chrys *pushed*, launching himself toward the Bloodthieves at an inhuman speed. His eyes blazed blue.

Mmmm. The Apogee awoke. *There are too many of them. Let me out and I can help you. I can protect you.*

Chrys ignored the voice. They needed to capture these men alive. To his left, he saw Luther bury a knife into the chest of an attacker, screaming with a savagery Chrys had never seen from his friend. The rage of losing his son to the priesthood. Stones, he shouldn't have let Luther come. Laz took the kill as a suggestion and brought his axe down into the neck of another. So much for non-lethality. *Keep one or two alive, that's all we need.*

Reina was a blur to his right, and Luther was now somewhere behind him.

Sliding the obsidian knife out of his pocket, Chrys rushed forward. When he'd let the Apogee take over during the War, people said he fought like a god or a demon. But Chrys had been trained his whole life, and he didn't need the Apogee to win. Three men approached him and attacked without hesitation. He sprinted toward the first, sliding down at the last minute and burying his knife deep in thigh tissue, tearing as he slipped past. He ripped it out, spun, and stabbed twice into the back of each of the man's thighs. A knife flew through the air and caught the man in the chest. Chrys looked up and Reina nodded.

A boot connected with Chrys' shoulder as he rolled away. He *pushed* off the ground, blue veins blazing, and brought his knee up into the second Bloodthief's chest. An audible *crack* reverberated from the man's ribs. The last Bloodthief, surprised by the quick defeat of his two comrades, found himself on his heels as Chrys leapt up onto his chest. His knees straddled the man's shoulders as they fell down onto the stone floor. The familiar adrenaline of war coursed through his threadlight-infused veins. It felt good. The anger he'd let simmer inside boiled out, and he twisted the man's neck until it popped.

Stones.

Mmmm.

The man with the broken rib rose to his feet and darted toward Chrys, but before he made it far, Laz's axe buried itself into the man's back from across the room, hitting him like a boulder.

Chrys surveyed the surrounding chaos. Seven dead, two in combat with Luther and Reina, one in the corner. The gangly leader was limping around the corner into the tunnel. Chrys rushed forward, intent to capture him alive. They'd already been careless enough as it was. He rounded the corner and found the man grappling a young girl by the neck with a knife at her back. She was chained to the wall. He met eyes with Chrys and smiled. Next to him lay another man, chained to the wall and pale as a winter moon.

Two *thuds* behind him signaled the fall of the last Bloodthieves.

"Move a muscle and the girl dies." The tattooed man's lip curled into a snarl as his free hand worked the locks on her chains. The heavy steel linking her to the wall fell to the ground leaving only her wrist bindings. The girl was blindfolded and gagged, dressed in dirt-stained clothing with her hands bound behind her back. It didn't look like she'd been here long.

"No one else needs to die," Chrys said with a warm tone.

The man smiled. "For once we agree. You're going to let me walk right—"

Before the man could finish his thought, the girl kicked her heel up into the man's groin. In one smooth motion, she rolled forward, moving her bound hands in front of her and lifting the blindfold off her face. Her veins blazed a bright blue and the knife in the man's hand blasted back into his own shoulder.

The man groaned painfully and ripped the knife out, his left arm limp at his side. He hid the knife behind his back and surveyed the room, but there was no one left to help him. His comrades had fallen. His collateral set free. He was trapped.

Chrys walked forward. "It's over. Come with us, cooperate, and I promise you will not be hurt. Now drop the knife."

The man breathed frantically, deep gulps of sporadic air. Then, as if a storm had passed, he calmed. "My life for yours," the man whispered.

Mmmm.

Before Chrys or the others could think to stop it, the man sliced the blade through his own neck, choking as blood dripped down his chest.

He stumbled and fell. The girl turned away, but the others stared on in awful numbness.

Chrys ran to the man, squeezing against the crimson stream. Blood soaked his hands, but it was too late. The man sank down against the basement wall, life gone from his eyes. Chrys found a small towel and used it to wipe his own hands and jacket. He took a moment to fix one of his buttons that had come undone during the fight.

Everyone stared at him, but he turned to the girl. "Are you okay?"

She nodded, eyes examining him with reservation.

"My name is Chrys." He reached out a hand, but she did not return the offer. He looked down at his hands, remembering the bloody stains. "Right. Well you're safe now. We'll take you up to the keep and make sure you're taken care of. I can't imagine what you have gone through. I'll save the rest of my questions for later. Reina. Luther. You two investigate the area. We don't know how many there are, so I want to know if this was all of them. And be careful in case others come. Laz, come with me and the girl.

"Do you have a name?"

She looked him in the eyes but did not respond.

"Fair enough."

They began their ascent up the long ladder to the trapdoor with Laz leading the way. She was young and tall, with long blonde hair running down her thin frame. While climbing he glimpsed what looked like a tattoo on her upper back, hidden mostly by her shifting hair. Tattoos were uncommon in Alchea, but in the western countries they were becoming increasingly more popular. Her veins still radiated a dim blue from her use of threadlight.

When they reached the top, she looked around the room like a predator, sharp eyes scanning as if looking for something.

"It's okay. There is no one here," Chrys thought out loud, knowing she was unlikely to respond. "I have to give it to them, an ambush in the dark was their best chance against four threadweavers. If they'd put blindfolds on us faster, we'd likely still be down there."

Her gaze turned to the ceiling, noting the holes in the roof that let in the afternoon sunlight.

"You can relax now," he said, trying to relieve some of the tension.

She turned to look at him and opened her mouth as if to say something, but paused. Then, she took a deep breath. "Sorry, flower boy, but I can't go with you."

Déjà vu struck him like a storm cloud.

"Little flower, fetch me some turmeric from the garden. Supper will be ready soon." His mother's voice called out to a young Chrys playing outside in the dirt. She always called him her little flower, even if he hated it.

In his moment of confusion, she sprinted and leapt, veins a blistering blue, eyes lit with threadlight, launching herself high up into the warehouse rafters. Chrys shook his head and jumped up after her. Laz ran toward the back door. Before Chrys landed in the rafters, she had already shot out of a hole in the roof and into the sky, flying high above the building.

Chrys ran toward the gaping hole in the roof and *pushed* out into the open air. He looked out and caught a glimpse of her falling below the next building over. He jumped as high as he could, gaining a bird's eye view of the greater westside, but already knew what he would find. Nothing. Streets filled with men and women carrying food and clothing, winding pathways, and shadowed back alleys. But there was no trace of the girl. The first person who knew anything about the Bloodthieves… and he let her get away.

SHADOWS RIPPLED over Laurel as the afternoon heat burned hot over broken cobblestone. The back alley was far enough away from the warehouse that she felt safe to pause and catch her breath. She pulled her dirt-stained clothing tight to cover her tinted veins. Her body felt far too warm, a collaboration of magic burning her from the inside and sunlight beating down from the outside. It felt amazing.

She moved northwest following the sun, but the streets were a winding labyrinth, and it was hard to maintain her direction. It was also the first time she had set foot inside the city, having been specifically ordered *not* to enter the city during her trips to the temple. The grounder city was far larger and far more confusing than her own home.

As the adrenaline faded to a dull buzz, she felt utter fatigue wash over her. Even without the looming threadsickness, she had been through an experience that would send any sane person to sleep for days. Memories of her capture flooded over her.

Walking from the temple into the city. Adrenaline knowing she shouldn't be there. A fork in the road. A man down one path—weird hat; she took the other. Eyes watching. Danger. Threadlight to look for an ambush. Too late. A bag over her head. Ropes around her legs. Laughing. Whispers. "Young...transfusers...Sapphire." Kicking and screaming. Thud. Darkness.

Then the soldiers had arrived. The one with the dark hair. There was something about his eyes. Not the blue; Laurel was used to people with blue eyes. It was the intensity. Even when he'd tried to calm her down, it frightened her. A sharp blade feigning dullness. Even so, he'd given her the opportunity to escape. She needed to get back home, away from the grounder city. The elders would never forgive her if they found out what had happened.

She paused for a moment and laughed. Had she really done what she remembered doing? Kicked a grounder in the groin? *Pushed* his knife into his shoulder? Escaped from her rescuers?

Bay would never believe it.

Laurel stood up, keenly aware of how much threadlight she'd let burn in her veins, and began walking. In the next alleyway, she found a clean shirt hung out to dry and traded it for her own dirt-covered top.

She walked for hours, exiting the city, passing farm-filled countryside, until finally she reached the edge of the Fairenwild.

Home.

The sun was setting, and bulbous multicolored photospores dangled off the ends of long reeds, emitting a phosphorescent spray that glowed in the darkness. The eerie depths of the Fairenwild were illuminated by the dull light radiating from the bulbs. High above, a drove of skyflies drifted in the wind, their long bodies curling under flowery heads.

Then there were the feytrees. Gigantic trunks sprawled across the grassy floor. Their branches refused to form until high into the sky, then sprouted forth like thick lines of yarn knitting ferociously with the branches of their neighbors. In the afternoon, the interlacing branches were so dense that they blocked out all sunlight to the forest floor, leaving it to be lit only by the light of the photospores. At night, were it not for the glowing fungus, the forest would be dark as the core.

Laurel looked longingly up to the treetops; her eyes dark with fatigue. She wondered why the wonderstone had to be in the middle of the forest, still so many hours away. Awfully inconvenient.

She stepped forward into the trees, careful to give them a wide berth in case a treelurk was nesting there. She reached out and grabbed a handful of photospores, ripping them from their stems. Light emanated before her, providing a small amount of visibility to areas with fewer naturally occurring spores. The occasional puffing noise nearby accompanied her as she began her journey deeper into the forest.

There was a good reason her people were left alone—the Fairenwild was dangerous. Between the darkness, the eerie ambience from the photospores, treelurks, hugweed, and the howling of chromawolves echoing from afar, outsiders gave it a wide berth. But the Zeda people, Laurel's people, gave it their hearts. To the grounders, her people were a myth, a tall tale, and they were happy to keep it that way.

Laurel trudged forward using the yellow roses to guide her. She was physically tired from walking, mentally tired from being kidnapped, and tired to her core from all of the threadweaving. How was she going to explain what happened to the elders? Messengers were forbidden from entering the city. She was to skirt the outside, meet her contact at the temple, and then return the same way. It was made very clear from the beginning: do not engage with the grounders. What would they do when they found out that she'd not only entered the city, but been kidnapped by a group that sells threadweaver blood like wine? The winds were not blowing in her favor.

After what seemed like an eternity of walking, she recognized the flora around her. Berries grew on thick vines and moss covered the base of the feytrees. She could hear the chromawolves howling. Always best to be careful. A chromawolf would blend into the forest and tear you apart before you had a chance to breathe. She knew the creatures well enough to avoid them. Not all were like Asher.

Off in the distance was a wide clearing filled with colorful flowers. In its center lay a large circular slab of white stone, glyphs carved across the entirety of its surface. Her people called it the wonderstone. The steppingstone of Zedalum. She was glad to see it not only because it meant she was home, but also because the chromawolves refused to set foot near it.

She relaxed her eyes and let threadlight seep into her vision. The wonderstone burned brilliant as the sun. The bright corethread of each living person was but a dim flame beside the majesty of the wonderstone's threadlight. She stepped up onto it, feeling its pull on her. Not a physical pull, but a mental one, urging her to use her power. Fortunately, in this very moment, that is exactly what she intended to do.

With a rejuvenated spirit, she *pushed* down onto her corethread, the wonderstone amplifying her abilities. It launched her like a catapult up into the air. Wind rushed past her face as she approached the high branches of the feytrees. She passed through a man-made opening and turned, *pushing* on the thin thread of a large wooden plank opposite her. It redirected her momentum toward the other end and out onto a wooden balcony built into the branches. Her boots slid across the wood as she landed. A pinch of vertigo mixed with threadsick dizziness came over her as she looked over the ledge back down.

A Zeda guard sat opposite the landing pad and looked up wearily; brown robes flowed over his seat. There was always someone posted at the entrance to Zedalum, but it was not a coveted position. There had never been an attack on the treetop city, nor had there ever been an unexpected visitor. Their secrecy had paid off.

"Stop! Identify yourself!" The Zeda man blinked, his eyes adjusting to being awake. The moonlight illuminated them both through the wooden stairway leading up to the treetops, but the feytree shadows obscured her face.

"Alder. You know you're a terrible guard, right?"

He stepped forward, getting a better look at her. "Laurel! You're back! Your grandfather's been worried sick. Almost left the city to find you."

"I know. I know."

He gave her a sheepish grin. "Do me a favor and don't tell Rowan about this?"

Laurel laughed. "Of course not."

"I owe you," he said. "May the winds guide you."

"And carry you gently home," she finished. The wooden steps were built securely into the thick mesh of tree branches. She ascended them one by one until she stepped out into the open air. A refreshing breeze fluttered about her, rejuvenating her after a night of musky, spore-filled air.

Alder was a good guy. Not the smartest, but he was always kind to her. At nineteen, just two years Laurel's senior, he'd already married. Again, not the smartest.

Laurel looked out over her home. Zedalum. The city of wind. Moonlight trickled down like rain over the treetop metropolis, illuminating the carefully plotted walkways that connected homes, centers, and the colossal Zeda stadium. The size of each building was a testament to the strength of the intermingling feytree branches that served as the city's foundation. Towering, heavy threadpoles were scattered throughout the city, many with faces and intricate designs carved into them, providing a quick means for threadweavers to get around. Laurel was tempted to use them, but she was exhausted already. Instead, she let a bit of threadlight seep into her veins and walked along the wooden path toward her home.

The wooden streets were empty as she moved toward her family's house. Before long, she could make out the distinct figure of her elderly grandfather seated in his rocking chair on their porch. When her parents had passed away, he had embraced the "protective parental figure" role wholeheartedly. At this point, he was the second most elderly Zeda in the entire city, having survived two passings of the Gale. The elders had only given him a pass because both Laurel and her brother Bay were still underage at the time. This year there would be another Gale; she worried what would become of him.

As she approached, he stood as if he knew she was coming. Wild, white hair draped over wrinkly, bronzed skin. His mid-length beard danced as he spoke. "You look tired." He smiled wide and opened his arms to embrace her. She fell into them with a smile. "And what is that shirt?"

Gale take me. She'd forgotten about the grounder's shirt she had stolen. She would need to swap it out before going to the elder's lodge.

"My other one got dirty," she laughed, hoping to ignore the question.

Laurel was old enough to be considered an adult in Zeda society, and she did her best to act like one, but her grandfather was her refuge. A firm root in the tempest. When the world demanded flawless maturity, he loved her as she was.

"You can tell me if you'd like. Or not. I was worried about you."

"I can tell," she said, laughing. "It's not like you to be awake past sunset."

He smiled but his brows pressed tightly upward. "Now don't make me feel older than I already do, Laurel. I was very worried. You were supposed to be back last night. I spent almost all of today at the lodge trying to convince Rosemary to let me go ground-side looking for you. They act like my heart would give out if I did any kind of threadweaving. I spent the entire evening sitting in this chair convincing myself not to disobey. If I were a few years younger, I'm not sure I could have stayed put, permission or not."

"I know. I—" she paused, realizing that she probably shouldn't tell him everything that had happened. "Sometimes these errands take longer than expected. Your old friend says hi, by the way."

"Pandan, that old fool. Is he coming back yet?"

She laughed. He knew the answer before asking. "He said to tell you that he is still 'waiting for his sun to rise'."

Grandfather Corian shook his head with a look of bemusement.

"He's more patient than any man I've ever met. Although, he'd probably have been taken by the Gale years ago were he not so valuable. I suppose he's having the last laugh after all."

The comment brought a solemn tone to the conversation. "I'm the one that should be worried. Maybe I can convince the elders that we need you here. Parenthood is a good reason to pass, and you're the only parent we have."

"Oh, you will be fine without me, and they know that. Bay on the other hand...that boy has shallow roots. But you're both of age now and, to be honest, I think I'm ready. You're both grown, and there's not much left to me but memories. And even those are fading fast. Odd as it is to say, I think it's about time this old bag of bones lets the wind take him home."

Laurel frowned. "I don't accept that. There has to be something we can do."

"Some winds have no counter," he replied.

Without the threadlight coursing through her veins, she'd be in tears. She hugged him again and looked up. "I should go report to Elder Rowan. I'll see if I can put in a good word. It's not over yet, old man."

They exchanged nods, and she headed to her room to change her shirt, then walked back down the wooden path she'd arrived on. A light breeze rustled the thick floor of leaves to either side of the walkway. Her feet followed a familiar path, but her mind entered a state of hollow serenity. Time passed in a blur.

She arrived at the door to the elder's lodge. There were five of them. Elders, not lodges. Each selected by the others when one passed away, generally young enough to survive at least three Gales. Together, they governed the affairs of all of Zedalum.

Laurel approached the door and gave it a hard knock, the thick wood reverberating out into the quiet night.

An old woman opened the door. Elder Rosemary. Laurel relaxed. The old woman's blue eyes were bright and warm, even in the fading moonlight, and she smiled as she saw who was at the door at such an odd hour. A long pendant hung down from her neck, draped over a green robe and flanked by strands of long gray hair.

"My dear Laurel. It is always a pleasure to see you."

"You as well, Elder."

Elder Rosemary motioned for her to enter. "I'd ask you why you're here, but you've made quite a commotion with your absence. I presume you're here to report to Rowan?"

"Yes, Elder." Laurel stepped into the lodge, the faint smell of incense still lingering in the large entry room.

"Let me give you some opportune advice," she said, bringing her voice down to a whisper. "Rowan is not a morning person. Nor is she a night person. Start with the good news, then sweet talk her a bit, let her wake up a pinch, and then go into the bad parts. And if all else fails, she loves the smell of north Felian oranges."

Elder Rosemary lifted an orange off a side table in the main hall, tossed it to Laurel, and winked. "Trust me."

"Thank you." Laurel remembered her grandfather. "Can I ask you something?"

"Of course."

"My grandfather." She paused. "The Gale is coming soon, and I'm worried about him. I know what you're going to say—I'm an adult now—but I still need him. And Bay needs him even more. Is there anything you can do?"

Elder Rosemary sighed as if recalling a conversation that had happened a hundred times before. "The Gale takes whom it will in the time that is right. It is not the decision of any one person. It is what's best for us all."

Laurel wanted to say something to convince her, but from the look on Elder Rosemary's face she knew it would serve no purpose. "I understand."

"Can I ask you something in return?" Elder Rosemary's eyes pinched in at the ends.

Laurel raised a brow.

"Do you ever let go of the threadlight?"

Laurel looked down at her arms and noticed that her veins were glowing just the slightest. She immediately stopped the flow of threadlight in her veins and it hit her like a windstorm. A deep thirst awoke inside her that could only be quenched by the taste of the magic.

Elder Rosemary looked at her, concerned. "One can never be too careful. Powerful feelings demand powerful fealty. You wouldn't be the first to become dependent."

"I'm not," Laurel scoffed. "I'm just tired."

They ended their walk in silence, stopping at a large door around the corner with the sign of the elders stenciled into the wood—a large circle divided into five segments with unique designs in each. Elder Rosemary gave her a gesture of good luck and walked slowly back down the hall. Laurel took a deep breath and knocked three times.

The lodge was so quiet that Laurel could hear the bed creaking as the Elder stood up, followed by the light pitter-patter of footsteps. Her heart started beating faster. She fought her instinct to embrace threadlight, knowing well how Elder Rowan would respond. Something about the old woman made her nervous, despite them having worked together for the better part of a year.

The door opened. Elder Rowan was wearing a brown robe and a scowl. Her typical leather headband graced her forehead, partially covered by a mess of wavy gray locks. Laurel remembered what it was that made her nervous. The crescent shape of Elder Rowan's mouth was an eternal grimace, and she wielded it like the sharpest of blades. Her green eyes were creased with a lifetime of disappointment and sharpened to a terrifying point.

Without a hint of emotion, the old woman spoke. "You look rotten, but you smell wonderful. You can leave the orange on the nightstand. Come in." She turned and walked over to a rocking chair without turning to see if Laurel had followed.

Laurel smiled as she closed the door, the fragrant Felian orange still in her hand. She took the second chair opposite Elder Rowan and placed the fruit on the table.

"It's an ungodly hour. Please do not waste my time. Give me your report and tell me why you're a day late in returning to us."

So much for small talk. Laurel remembered Elder Rosemary's advice. Good news. Sweet talk. Bad news.

"Yes, Elder. I made it from the Fairenwild to the temple with no problems and approached the temple cautiously." The events replayed in her mind. She had a sharp memory which was one of the reasons she'd been chosen as messenger. It also helped that she was a Sapphire. *Drifting* made the trip go faster. "I waited for sunset and found Pandan on the bench he always sits on. We talked a little, he told me a story about my dad, and then I asked him if he had anything to report.

"He told me about some concerning developments within the grounder city." If she lied, there wouldn't have to be any sweet talk or bad news, but if they ever found out what happened she'd never be able to leave the Fairenwild again. "There is a group of people that the grounders are calling the Bloodthieves. They are kidnapping threadweavers and selling their blood. Apparently, if someone who is not a threadweaver drinks threadweaver blood, they can see threadlight temporarily. They can't *push* or *pull*, but people will pay a lot for the feeling. Pandan doesn't think we need to act, only that we should be aware in case things get worse. The grounders have men out trying to stop them."

"Despicable," Elder Rowan remarked. "Barbaric, the things the grounders do. Heretics *and* imbeciles. Next time you return, we'll ask Pandan to dig deeper. Any group that defiles the honor of threadweaving must be watched carefully."

Laurel nodded. "Of course."

Elder Rowan sat staring at the wall for far longer than Laurel was comfortable. "Well, and what of the delay? Looks like you have a brand-new shirt on, old one get dirty?"

The old treelurk was smarter than Laurel gave her credit for. More than anything, she should have planned out the lie ahead of time. Laurel racked her brain for something believable. An idea popped into her head. "I know I shouldn't have, but I went out looking for the pack." She hung her head in shame, only partially an act. She hated that she was using her dead parents as an alibi, but Laurel was sure the elders had lied to her anyway. Her parents hadn't died from a pack of chromawolves, but no one would tell her the truth.

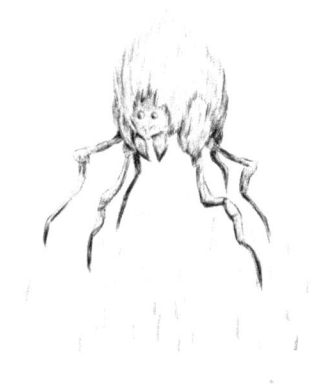

"You did what?" Elder Rowan choked out a horrid sounding cough. "You think to get revenge? Fool child. It's been years. The pack has moved on, and so should you. You think to kill a pack of chromawolves all by yourself? You're as self-aggrandizing as your father was." She paused, thinking through the story. "So, you slept in the woods? Explains the dirt. Surprised you're not dead. For your own sake, I hope it was grim and uncomfortable. That's what you deserve for such senselessness."

"I'm sorry, Elder." Laurel kept looking at the floor in defeat. She always found self-deprecation to be the key to a good lie. If others feel sorry for you, they're less likely to scrutinize your story.

"This is your one warning. If you ever do something so stupid again, I'll find myself another messenger. I've a mind to do it right now. Can't have such poor judgment roaming the ground. Do you understand?"

Laurel nodded fervently, sniffling as if her emotions were rising. "Yes, Elder."

Elder Rowan kicked Laurel's chair. "Well. Get out. I've at least an hour of sleep left before sunrise."

Without lifting her eyes from the floor, Laurel turned and left. The adrenaline of deceit raged through her shaking body. She couldn't believe that she had lied to Elder Rowan. And more so, she couldn't believe that the Elder had believed it!

She passed through the main hall and saw no sign of Elder Rosemary. Next time she saw her, she'd have to thank her. Laurel opened the door and burst out into the open night. She looked back into the candlelit lodge and smiled. No one needed to know what had happened to her in the city. She'd learned her lesson on her own.

Like Rowan said, it's better to move on.

5

LAUGHTER FILLED LAUREL'S HOME, spreading forth like an obnoxious weed from the family kitchen. She'd tossed and turned all night despite her overwhelming fatigue. A nightmare had taken her back to the Bloodthieves' basement, and then her mind refused to relax in fear that she might return yet again. She looked down and noticed that the veins in her arms were tinted blue; she must have been threadweaving unconsciously while sleeping. At least she'd been able to get some rest.

She slipped on day clothes and stepped out of her room, quietly treading down the hall toward the kitchen. Her brother, Bay, and her grandfather, Corian, were smiling and talking about the latest Threadweaver Games. Corian loved taking Bay to the stadium to watch the Sapphire Long Jump tournaments. While many Zedas idolized the competitors, Laurel had always found it monotonous.

"No way!" Bay coughed as he laughed. "Euca is for sure going to take the Long Jump this season. She's so reed-thin that the wind basically does the work for her."

Corian smiled. "We'll see. Dogwood has the best form. On a good day, I think he could win it all."

"Don't get him started on Dogwood again," Laurel said, smiling and picking up a strawberry off the counter. "You've been waiting for him to have a 'good day' for three years. There's no chance he steals it from Euca."

"Oh, what do you know?" Corian took his spoon and scooped out a bite from his ripe, blue fyrfruit.

Bay's eyes lit up. "You're awake! I knew you were okay. What took you so long to get back?"

Laurel nervously glanced at her grandfather. "Just took a little longer than expected."

"Oh, come on. Is it secret? For the elders' ears only? I bet it is." Bay leaned back in his chair triumphantly.

"Something like that."

Her grandfather stood up and threw his finished fyrfruit out the window and into the feytrees below. "Before I forget, Cara was looking for you yesterday. You should head down and pay her a visit if you have time this morning."

"Will do." Laurel took a bite of strawberry.

Corian stepped out of the kitchen and walked down the hall to his room. He had left a bowl of feyrice pudding on the table for her; it was her favorite. The feyrice they grew in Zedalum required less water than normal rice, but it was also not as soft. She still loved a bowl of it with strawberries and a pinch of white clover mixed in.

She settled into her chair and scooted in closer to Bay. "Want to know the truth? The part I didn't tell the elders?"

She grimaced looking at the bruise on his chin. Bay had a blood disease—he'd had it since he was young. Some days were better than others, but usually it meant that he tired easily, bruised easily, and sickened easily. His skin was pale even when he felt well, and his muscles were atrophied from a lifetime of careful living. Even his long Zeda hair, shaved to the scalp on the right side, was thinner than most. And to pluck the last fruit from the tree, he was the only one in the family who wasn't a threadweaver.

He pulled his hair up into a low ponytail in the back. "Tell me everything."

"Elder Rowan sent me to the grounder temple again to check in with Pandan. It was fine. I've run the route half a dozen times before. But I was bored, so I took a detour into the city."

His eyes widened. The grounders were off limits. Which is exactly what made the city so hard to resist.

"I know. I *know*. You can't even imagine what it's like. Huge roads of stone twice as wide as our streets. Hundreds and thousands of houses, and people. *So many* people. I kept to the edges so I wouldn't get too far off course, but even still it was overwhelming. But then..." The flashback replayed in her mind.

"Then what?"

"I was kidnapped." Her heart beat faster remembering it. "Blindfolded. By this group of grounders who steal threadweaver blood. They sell it and others drink it. They were going to drain me and sell my blood."

Bay's eyes were wide as plates. "Gale take me. You can't be serious."

"Dead serious."

"Father of all," he swore. "But the elders would never let anything happen to you."

"What could they have done? They didn't even know I had gone off course. I was *underground* in some broken-down building. No one could have found me. I froze. I just sat there in the dark waiting for them to steal my blood. I didn't do anything."

"Of course you didn't! It would have been stupid to try and escape." Bay paused. "What did the elders say? I bet they were furious!"

"I may have told them a different story."

Bay almost fell out of his chair. "You *lied* to the elders?"

"They would have stripped me of my assignment! What was I supposed to do?"

"I don't know." He slouched back, shaking his head. "Wait, if you didn't fight back, then how did you get away?"

"Some other grounders showed up and killed them all. One minute I was blindfolded and bound, the next the sounds of fighting and screaming. Then there was a knife to my back. You should have seen it. I kicked him, rolled away, and *pushed* the knife in his shoulder. Then I got away and ran. *Drifted* as fast as I could 'til my veins were burning, but I got away.

"I know it sounds crazy, but it was the most fun I've had in years! Bay, you have to promise me you won't tell anyone."

After a few moments of silence, Bay took a deep breath and closed his eyes. "I won't tell anyone. But lies are dangerous, Elle. Things like this can't be tucked away and forgotten. They fester. You're my sister, and I'm here for you always, but I'll judge you if you make stupid choices, and this was top-of-the-tree stupid.

"But I'll always love you no matter what. You know I live my adventures through you, and I don't want you getting killed over it. So, if you promise me that you won't go back to the grounder city, I promise you I won't tell the elders."

Laurel hugged him tightly. "I don't deserve you, little caterpillar."

"No, you don't, little wolf." Bay stood up slowly.

"That reminds me," Laurel said. "I need to get down to Cara. Thanks for understanding."

He smiled and shook his head as she stepped out of the house.

Zedalum was much different during the day. People crowded the wooden walkways, young threadweavers leapt between threadpoles, floating through the air like dancers. Laurel preferred *drifting* down the runner lanes.

She *pushed* a small amount of energy down through her corethread and shifted the thread to be slightly behind her. It gave gravity less of a hold on her and helped propel her forward as she started to run. Her speed picked up quickly. It was a trick all Sapphire threadweavers learned early on. With it they could jump higher and run faster. There were tradeoffs of course. Try turning a tight corner without the added friction of gravity to lean into. Many new Sapphires could be seen tripping over themselves as they learned to rely less on that most basic force of nature.

The designated drifter path was open, and she took off like a wolf. She passed by the marketplace, with dozens of stands selling all manner of food collected from the farmlands that were built on the treetops outside of Zedalum. Beans, carrots, tomatoes, spinach; any vegetables with shallow roots did well in the Zeda farms. She rushed past a group of people standing in line for use of one of the dozens of wells built to pump water up from the streams and ponds below the city. Each well ran down the base of a feytree toward the nearest water source. Some people had begun building water basins outside their own homes to catch the rainfall. She understood the concept, but thought they looked absurd. Far in the other direction she could see the elders' lodge and the towering stadium. But she was headed back to the ground.

As she approached the entrance to Zedalum, she was greeted by an older Zeda guard. Alder must have gone home to rest. The woman wrote down her name in a log and let her through. They kept detailed records of each Zeda who descended to the surface. Of course, anyone could drop down between the branches if they wanted, but the only sure way back up was using the wonderstone, especially for a Sapphire. Some of the more rebellious Emeralds were known to drop down between the trees, and then run back up the feytrees to return.

She descended the steps and approached the ledge of the landing pad. Without a second thought, she leapt. The ten second freefall ended as she used the wonderstone to slow her descent. She landed with the faintest thud.

Light trickled in from the gap in the canopy, providing more useful light than the glowing photospores. Whenever she stood here on the wonderstone she'd always get the distinct urge to *push* off the ground and fly, as if the curious amplification that it provided could not only boost her higher but could give her wings. There were stories about the windwalkers who could stay airborne indefinitely. Of course, there were also stories about people who could breathe underwater, kill you with a glare, and topple mountains.

Because the fauna stayed far away from the wonderstone, the flora thrived. Especially the roses. Blue, green, yellow, and white. The roses of the Fairenwild were unique, each variety useful in their own right, opening and closing their petals in their own time. The green dayroses and the brilliant, white threadroses were all fully bloomed around her as she stood atop the wonderstone. Further away, she spotted some wild green laurel, her mother's favorite.

As she drifted farther away from the wonderstone she heard the sound of birds chirping overhead. She couldn't see the birds, but high above her she saw a drove of skyflies darting back and forth, their wispy green tails floating in the spore-illuminated canopy.

A few minutes later she arrived at the large wooden enclosure to the nursery. Reaching over and moving the latch, she entered. The nursery was a training ground for young chromawolves, and the only settlement below the treetops. The Zeda people had learned early of the dangers of these Fairenwild natives and looked for ways to tame them. What they learned was that young wolves, when exposed to humans early on, would be less likely to attack later in life, and the individual bonds made during those formative years would stay forever. The couple that currently served as their caretakers, Cara and Mace, had bonded dozens of wolves over the years. Of course, the chromawolves weren't the only danger in the Fairenwild.

After three years of life within the nursery, when Cara deemed the time was right, the young chromawolves were brought back to their packs. The reintroduction had a high success rate, but there were times when the packs no longer accepted them, or the chromawolves did not want to return. Mace had an elderly chromawolf, named Leadpaw, that never returned to its pack and still lived with him.

The chromawolves here were young, but still strong. Best to be careful. Laurel entered through the gate and saw Cara's house right next to the entrance, a single-story log cabin built with thick wood that had dozens of deep scratches along the exterior. A few pups wrestled on the ground nearby, snarling and biting playfully. On the front porch, Leadpaw lethargically watched the younger wolves. The old wolf reminded Laurel of her grandfather.

Off in the distance she saw Asher coming—he always knew when she was nearby. The young chromawolf dashed toward her at an incredible speed, howling all the way. His dark green fur was dusted with curling white strands, like roots running down his back, that shimmered in the light of the photospores. Laurel took off toward him at a run, two astral bodies bound for an earth-shattering collision.

As they closed the distance, Asher leapt high up into the air, front paws extended, and Laurel followed suit. They collided hard. Asher tackled her to the ground and they rolled. He jumped back up playfully and danced around her with his twin tails whipping back and forth, snarling and growling with the fierce energy she'd come to love. She laughed and snarled back.

A year after Laurel's parents had died, her grandfather had asked Mace to let Laurel raise one of the new pups. It had seemed cruel at the time, forcing her to confront the beasts that took her parents. But as she came to be with the chromawolves, she no longer believed that that was how her parents had died. She was sure the elders were keeping the truth from her.

Laurel and Asher had bonded quickly, two high-energy creatures cut from the same branch. She spent too much time with him—she knew that—but it felt good to spend time with someone that didn't lie or judge or expect anything from her.

Cara walked out of the cabin. Nearly the size of her behemoth husband, broad shouldered and fit, she managed to maintain an air of femininity through the rough outer layer. Like many Zeda, she kept the side of her head cut close, but the rest of her light brown hair she kept braided and pulled back. Cara was the closest thing that Laurel had to a mother now.

She spotted Laurel wrestling with Asher. "Laurel! Tempest take you, girl. You gave me a right fright not showing up yesterday. You know them grounders are dangerous."

"I'm wrestling with a chromawolf and you're worried about the grounders?" Laurel laughed as she swiped down at Asher. "You should know I can take care of myself."

"Spendin' too much time with them wolves, girl. And that's coming from me! One of these days you're gonna bite off more than you can chew." She was only half joking. "So, what's the story? Find yourself a grounder boy and plannin' an elopement?"

Laurel gave her a look of pure ice, but then she realized the horrible truth: she couldn't use the same lie she'd told Elder Rowan. Cara would know it was a lie. But she also couldn't tell her the truth. Yes, she was like family, but she was more like the family that tells on you for your own good. She couldn't risk it. It had been a single day and she'd already trapped herself in her own web. She tried to think quickly.

"Want to know what I told Elder Rowan? Or do you want to know the truth?" Her mind raced, still unsure what she was going to say. Maybe a partial truth?

Cara raised a brow. "I'd like to know both, but you can start with the truth."

Laurel took a deep breath. "I was walking down the big hill at the grounder temple, and it started to rain. Not a lot, just a light sprinkle, but I didn't want my clothes to get soaked to the core, so I left the path and ran toward a little house not far off. It smelled terrible and there were all kinds of strange animals inside."

"You went into a grounder's house? Tempest take you, girl. You're walking a narrow path."

Laurel cut her off. "It was a house for their animals. It wasn't a big deal."

Cara turned away covering her ears. "Don't tell me another word. I don't want to know. The grounders find you out and you'll be tortured. The elders find you out and you'll be exiled. Nothing good will come of this. I don't need this kind of weight on my shoulders, girl. You were smart not to tell them what happened. But wait, that couldn't have taken a whole day? Nope. Don't want to know. If you don't tell me, I can't tell them. Whatever you did, promise me you won't do it again?"

Laurel nodded.

"Good enough for me." Cara walked toward the gate shaking her head. "Come along now. We gotta go take Asher back to his family."

"Wait, what?" Laurel's heart was beating rapidly from the lies, but then it stopped. The words buried deep into her chest. She practically whispered the next. "Take him *back*?"

"Why did you think I wanted you to come down here? This wasn't a social visit, girl. The pup's too big to stay any longer. He's fully grown. Could probably jump the fence now if he tried. Too dangerous to keep around."

Cara was already walking, her whistle beckoning Asher to follow. Laurel watched in shock as the two passed through the gateway. Her feet trailed without thought, the forest blurring in her vision as the world spun around her. She was going to lose her grandfather to the Gale. She was going to lose Asher. And she was going to lose her position. Everything she held dear swirled around in a dark cloud, slowly dissipating into the darkness of the Fairenwild. It felt as if the Father of All was punishing her for disobeying the elders. But it was only one mistake. What were the chances she'd be kidnapped the one time she went into the city? Deep down she knew what she was doing when she stepped onto those stone streets.

She let threadlight run through her veins and calmness washed over her.

They walked for what seemed like an eternity, her sense of direction lost in the endless glow of the Fairenwild. A duskdeer ran past on her right, jet black legs hopping over a small creek running across their path. Asher moved to chase, but Cara commanded him to stop. And he did.

After a short time longer, Asher roused. Recognition kicked in, and he bolted forward. Cara had always said the chromawolf pups had an uncanny memory for their old homes, but Laurel had never seen it until now. Cara ran after him, Laurel still following silently behind. A minute later they came to a clearing with a small pond. Dozens of photospore reeds grew out of the water, their bulbs emitting their luminescent spray. A rock formation was built up along the far side of the water with a pack of chromawolves standing atop at attention, staring fiercely at Asher. He watched boldly in return.

Laurel had only ever seen the docile pups; these creatures standing in front of her were something different. Their eyes seemed to growl along with their mouths. The alpha wolf leapt off the rocks with its chest puffed up and walked toward Asher. It had the characteristic green fur of the chromawolves with chunks of white hair weaving throughout its coat like vines over moss, but its paws were far wider and larger than Asher's. The fur split apart at the rear into two distinct tails, each a brilliant white where they weren't covered in dirt. She thought Asher was large, but this alpha stood even taller. The lithe muscles in its legs rippled as it approached, its paws poised to pounce.

Despite the time away, Asher knew what to do. He stepped forward, keeping his posture low and unassuming, then approached. He stopped within an arm's length and dropped his head as if bowing to a more formidable elder. The alpha stepped forward and sniffed him, weighing and measuring who he had become. He paused, considering his verdict, then roared. A powerful swipe of his paw crashed down onto Asher's head. The young chromawolf was thrown down to the ground, whimpering in pain.

Something broke in Laurel. Threadlight exploded in her veins, and she ran at the alpha with blood in her vision. Anger rose like a swelling wind and drove her forward. She refused to sit idly and watch her friend be hurt.

Cara saw it too late. "Laurel, no!"

The alpha saw her coming and snarled a deep, nasty growl. The other chromawolves stayed put on the rocks, watching their leader. It compressed its legs and pounced.

Hot, burning rage rose to a boil, bubbling out of her. She screamed a feral battle cry and *pushed* with all the energy inside of her against the nearest feytree. The thread between her and the tree seemed to expand with force, and then exploded out both ends. She crashed into the alpha like a cyclone crashing into a mountain and drove her elbow into its stomach. They both fell to the ground.

A thick vine snaked its way around Laurel's leg and started to squeeze. Hugweed.

The alpha howled and it started to rise, but its left hind leg was injured from the collision. Still, it pushed forward with surprising speed toward Laurel who lay trapped on the floor with her foot constricted by the vines. The alpha lunged toward her, clawed paws extended, teeth quivering with hunger. She tried to *push* against the hugweed, but nothing happened. She was trapped and the alpha's thick teeth flashed in front of her.

Just before it reached her, Asher sprang forward, blindsiding the alpha and knocking it off course. The alpha was stunned and confused. Asher was family, and he would protect her. He bore down on the alpha with a savagery she'd never seen from him, teeth clamping down on green fur, paws digging deep into flesh.

The alpha kicked Asher off. Bloody and furious, it stood on all fours and growled. It sprang forward. Its back leg buckled from the effort, but Asher was still recovering. The alpha swiped a second time at Asher's face, gnarled claws connecting with tender nerves that ripped out hair and skin. Blood sprayed from the open wounds.

Asher howled out in pain and launched himself forward, headbutting the wounded alpha between the eyes. An audible crack reverberated through the air. Asher wasted no time. He dove back on top of the larger beast, swinging uncontrollably. A wild claw swiped through the alpha's neck, and blood sprayed out onto a bright photospore. Red-stained light projected out over the Fairenwild floor and washed over the motionless corpse of the alpha.

It was dead.

Laurel shook her pounding head, the blood in her veins burning hot, her chest ready to burst. Threadlight still danced brightly in her vision; she couldn't make it go away. It was too much. Bright threads of light danced in every direction, exciting her already overstimulated senses. She couldn't focus the light.

The young chromawolf nuzzled her gently. His blood-matted fur brushed her cheek, leaving a smeared stain. He moved to her leg and tore into the hugweed, releasing her from its grasp, then lifted up his head and howled. The other chromawolves, still watching from the rock formation near the pond, howled in return, then jumped down and wandered over to Asher. He stood tall to match their stature. One by one each of the chromawolves bowed their heads to their new alpha. He brought a gentle paw to each of their noses, recognizing the gesture of submission. He was family now.

Laurel's eyes glazed over with tears as she watched Asher embraced by his pack. She was happy, but still she cried. Would she ever see him again? Part of her wished they wouldn't have accepted him. Everyone else seemed to find their place in the world, but she was yet to find hers.

6

"Luther, we should talk about what happened," Chrys said as he walked through the dark basement.

"What are you talking about?" Luther's eyes were cold.

"I said we wanted to capture them alive."

Luther turned away and walked toward one of the crates. "It's not like I'm the only one who killed somebody."

"Yeah, but you were the first. The feel of a fight changes when men start dying. Every death spurs the likelihood of the next."

"You're right, okay?" Luther raised his hands in defeat. "Is that what you want to hear? You're right. I shouldn't have come. I should have stayed home and drank myself to sleep thinking about my damn son. Thinking about those damn priests that took him. I should have sat there and yelled at my wife because I'm no good at dealing with emotion."

"Luther—" Chrys started.

"No. You're right, Chrys. I'm a damn fool."

Chrys knew that Luther was in a sensitive place. He would spiral if Chrys let him. "Stop it. This situation, it's on all of us. It's not all on you. I killed a man today. We all did. Two threads; one bond. Do I like it? No. But it is what it is. Now clear the rocks out of your head and let's see what we can do to fix it."

Silence floated through the air of the warehouse like a storm cloud. They each knew they'd bungled the mission in their own way. Not a single Bloodthief alive. The captive escaped. The pale threadweaver they'd found chained up was Harlon Brandock—one of the missing threadweavers—and he was dead too.

They wandered the basement scouring the crates and tables for clues. A small fire had presumably been used to burn evidence. On the tables, boxes of equipment were ready to be moved. One crate held a collection of extraction equipment, bloodied bowls, and binding kits. If they'd had any doubts that these were Bloodthieves before, those doubts were gone.

Chrys picked over the bodies. It was everyone's least favorite job, so he felt like it was his responsibility. Besides, his hands were already red with blood. There was little to be found save for a few weapons and some shines. There should have been more equipment, more something. This wasn't everything.

He kept replaying the phrase the Bloodthief had said before he killed himself: "My life for yours." He'd heard it before. It was an old Felian religious phrase, spoken to the Heralds. Were the Bloodthieves from Felia?

What frustrated him more was the feeling that they had been prepared. How had they known? Was it a coincidence that they'd packed up already? The two prisoners were still there, so if they'd had a warning, they hadn't had much of one. It nagged at the back of his mind, wrestling with the thought that maybe he was making excuses for his failure.

Reina was on her hands and knees poking at the embers with a stick. She spoke up as she pulled a partially ripped paper out from under a charred piece of kindling. "Hey, I might have something here."

The others all stopped what they were doing and approached her. Laz was still clutching his arm from an arrow that had struck him, and Luther was quietly staring at the aftermath of the brawl, his chest moving with long, deep breaths. Chrys watched intently as Reina squinted, trying to read what was left of the note.

"...cular mineral craft?" She looked up to Chrys. "It's a little smudged but pretty sure. Anyone know what the stones that means?"

They all shook their heads.

Laz snorted. "We're fighting necklace-making old women!"

"Take it seriously, Laz," Chrys snapped. "This raid is a disaster enough as it is. If we have nothing to bring back to Malachus, he's going to lose his mind. Let me see the paper."

Reina handed it to him. It did look like it said *cular mineral craft*. Stones. But it was a little smudged at the start of the last word. "Could this be a *d* or a *g*? Mineral craft. Mineral draft. Mineral graft? Any of those ring a bell?"

"It might not be anything. My old teacher used to say the obvious answer is usually the right one." Reina shrugged her shoulders.

Chrys stared down at the paper. Crafting. Drafting. Grafting. This was the only clue they had; it had to mean something. "Maybe. I'll bring it to the Great Lord and get his opinion. Maybe he knows something we don't. How are the rest of you doing with the sweep?"

"There's nothing here," Luther mumbled.

"Agreed," said Reina.

Laz smiled, big teeth showing through his red beard. "The city has taken warm, soothing bath this day. I think it is our turn. We all stink."

Even when they were standing in the bloody basement of a decrepit warehouse, Laz was always able to think optimistically. Dead bodies scattered around them? Crack a joke. Chrys wasn't sure if it was a gift or a sign of insanity but, knowing Laz, it was probably a bit of both.

"I'm going to head up to the keep to report to Malachus. He'll want a full recounting of what happened. I'll send back a crew to clean this up, but we need at least one person to stick around and wait for them to come."

They all looked at him blank-faced.

"What? Do you want to carry the bodies up to the keep yourselves?"

They all looked at each other, waiting for another to speak up. No one wanted to spend their afternoon standing in a warehouse full of dead Bloodthieves. After a few moments of uncomfortable eye contact, Laz raised his hand. "I will do this thing. But only if Luther and Reina buy drinks tonight!"

Reina jumped on the offer, "Deal!"

"Bring deep pockets, friend. Staring at dead bodies all day will give me great thirst!"

A look of disgust crossed Reina's face. "That is incredibly disturbing, Laz. Even for you."

"What?" Things clicked in Laz's mind. "Oh, stones, no! Real thirst, not sexy thirst! Gross, Reina! I will not have thirst because of the bodies. I will have thirst from long time of waiting in dusty warehouse!"

Reina laughed. "They did just take a bath after all. Always want your lovers to bathe beforehand."

Laz slapped her on the shoulder. "You are terrible person, but I love you."

"Alright, Laz. Stay up in the rafters just in case, but it looks like they were done with this place. I'd be very surprised if any Bloodthieves came back." Chrys turned to Luther and Reina. "The two of you are off duty. And Luther, get some rest.

"Here's to hoping Malachus is in a better mood than I am."

It was nearing sunset by the time Chrys reached Endin Keep. The warmth of the sun faded below the western horizon. He was starving, but he was also parched, which made him smile as he thought of Laz.

As he approached the keep, he passed a pair of guards, waved to each of them, and greeted them by name. They were well-poised and alert, even though their shift was almost over. Standing guard in a low-traffic area was mentally exhausting, and Chrys liked to reward men who stayed vigilant. He tossed them each a few spare shines for their diligence.

It wasn't the first time he'd done this, and word had gotten around that High General Chrys would give shines to guards on occasion. At the start, it had been purely out of good will, but then he realized that it both improved his standing with the guards and made them better at their jobs.

He gazed up at the keep, sitting like a lapdog at the base of a mountain range that spanned from the northern sea all the way to the deserts of Silkar. The positioning gave it away as a wartime fortification. Great Lord Amastal had built it two hundred years before, during the Binding War. He'd started the work the same year the wastelanders had first been defeated. Chrys could still picture their beady eyes and small frames attacking with a brutal savagery. People called them cannibals, but Chrys had never seen any proof to the claim.

A short way south of the keep's outer wall was the only real pathway through to the other side of the mountains. It was brutal, snow-covered at times, and rife with dangerous wildlife. The map in Malachus' study had a big blank space for the Wasteland; Chrys had always dreamt of exploring the region and completing the sketch.

As he took his first steps up the winding staircase of the north tower, a familiar face greeted him. Eleandra Orion-Endin, the Gem of Alchea. The Great Lord's wife. But, unlike him, the people loved her. She had pale blonde hair wrapped up in a perfect chignon atop her head, her elegant neck covered by the high collar of her dress. The color of her hair came from her mixed descent. Her mother was a white-haired Alirian and her father was from Felia. She was the perfect compromise—though her skin tone was far more Alirian. If she'd been born with colored eyes, she'd be empress of the entire Arasin continent, but instead she subtly guided the most powerful man in Alchea, the nation's first bichromic Great Lord.

She lifted a hand in greeting, beautifully manicured furs resting over narrow shoulders. "Chrystopher!" She smiled knowingly.

"Lady Eleandra," he replied, smiling and giving a slight bow. Many years ago, she'd asked if Chrys was short for Chrystopher; he'd told her it was not. She found it so peculiar that she'd been calling him the incorrect name impishly ever since.

Half the city-state was in love with her, and it wasn't hard to see why. Her light brown eyes were shaped like almonds, and the sweetness with which she looked at each person she met was intoxicating. To Chrys, she had always felt more like a mother.

Iriel, on the other hand, was the spell that bound him wholly.

"What brings you to the keep today? Should you not be taking care of your lovely wife? She is due any day now, isn't she?"

The conversation was a timely distraction. His shoulders relaxed as he stopped thinking about the warehouse. "She is. But you know Iriel, she's a mind not to be coddled. I'm here to talk to your husband. He asked me to oversee important work, and I am not one to forgo my promises."

"Indeed, you are not. An attribute more would do well to adopt. And are your families planning to help after the birth? I'd be happy to help or have someone sent if you need anything at all."

Chrys smiled. "That is a very generous offer. My mother will be around to help, and Iriel's will as well. We should be well cared for."

Eleandra lit up. "Oh, I just adore your mother so much. She must be ecstatic to have her first grandchild. And, tell me, what is the count up to now?"

Chrys' mother, Willow—despite being a threadweaver and quite fetching—had turned down dozens of marriage proposals. Willow and Chrys had arrived in Alchea when he was a toddler, two foreign threadweavers escaping a broken life. They had been the talk of the whole city for months. Every eligible bachelor in town had tried his best to pursue her, but she'd systematically turned them all down. Over the years, the efforts had decreased, but never ceased. Eleandra had always looked at Willow's independence as a badge of feminine honor.

Chrys scratched the back of his head. "Sixty-seven? Unless another delusional man has tried his hand at the Valerian gambling table in the last few days."

"I reckon the odds at that table are not so good."

"Hard to win when the dealer won't play the game!"

"Yet hard not to play when the prize is so lovely." She cocked her head to the side and winked. "When you see her, tell her I miss her dearly and that she needs to come visit."

Chrys gave her a small bow. "Of course, my lady."

With that, Eleandra wished him well and headed off. Feeling renewed, Chrys began the ascent up the winding staircase. His footsteps were muffled by a black rug that ran the entire length of the stairs like a stripe down its center.

After climbing multiple stories in the tall tower, he finally arrived at Lord Malachus' study. Two fit guards flanked the large mahogany door, each nodding to Chrys as he approached.

"Gentlemen."

They both stood at attention and spoke in unison. "High General."

"How's the shift?"

"Boring, sir," the taller guard said.

"Boring is good."

"Boring is good," they repeated.

Chrys gave them a nod of approval before moving forward to open the door. It opened with a loud groan, like the seal of a crypt. Inside was the definition of Alchean finery. The north wall was a two-story library of ancient and modern works. The south wall was an enormous map of Arasin, with three dimensional representations of the Everstone Mountains east of Alchea and the Malachite Mountains south of Felia.

A dark mound of green representing the Fairenwild covered a section of land between Alchea and Felia. The Alirian archipelago floated in the sea west of Felia, and the islands of Kulai could be seen south of the Alchea-Felia border. A rough, rust-colored material covered a huge swath of desert south of the Everstone Mountains. Silkar. East of the Everstone Mountains the map faded to black with a single calligraphed word written in a murky green: Wastelands.

Scholars claimed that it was the most to-scale representation of Arasin ever made. But such hyperboles are typical of scholarship and impossible to verify. Whether or not it was true, the massive depiction of continental landscape was beautiful in its own right.

Toward the west wall, past a sprawling silk rug, the Great Lord Malachus Endin sat behind a walnut desk, back turned, looking out over the city far below with a book in his hand. A small lamp burned brightly on a side table. The sun had dropped below the western skyline, casting a scenic orange glow into the sky. He glanced over his shoulder and motioned for Chrys to come over.

"Have you ever been in this room during sunset?" His eyes still focused out over the streets of Alchea.

Chrys stepped forward, getting a better view of the scene. "I'm not sure, sir. I've been in the briefing room below, but the view from this altitude is far more impressive."

"It's the shadows. The mountains cast sweeping shadows over the city in the morning. But at night, there is nothing but flatlands to the west."

This odd beginning nearly caused Chrys to forget the bad news he'd come to report. "Sir, I have news from the raid this afternoon."

Malachus brought a finger to his lips. "Shhhh. It's beginning." He extended that same finger out toward the city, pointing toward the residential district.

Small lights flickered into existence. Lamps, candles, torches. One small light would pop, and, like a rippling pond, dozens of others nearby would follow suit. After a few minutes of silence, tens of thousands of lights were burning down below them.

"A flame is a fickle fortune," Malachus said as he held up the book he was holding. "Thoralan. One of my favorite scholars. I always think of that quote this time of night. Have you heard it?"

"I have not."

"Oh, come now, Chrys. You really do need to read more philosophy. You're too grounded in the hard sciences. It would be good for your soul, although I'm not sure either of our souls have much chance at redemption."

"Redemption isn't something that can be obtained or withheld," Chrys replied. "It's a commitment you make."

"Perhaps for you, Chrys, but I'm not interested in the warmth of redemption." Malachus turned back to the window. "Life itself is a flame. Fickle as any. Some burn brightly and die swiftly. Some burn dimly and live far past their need. In the end, all flames die. Look out there; in a few hours, all of those lights will die and the city will be lost to darkness. But in the morning, it will be reborn. More flames will burn, and they too will be forgotten the next day.

"I've spent a lifetime looking down at those lights and it seems that the only flames that are remembered are the ones that burn the world. Do you want to burn the world, Chrys?"

Chrys shuddered, thinking of the War of the Wastelands. His memories of the war were a blur, but he preferred it that way. Leave the past in the past.

"Do you want to do something so drastic the world will remember you forever?" He didn't wait for a response. "Thoralan called it a *Legacy Complex*, people who become overly fixated on leaving a lasting impression on the world. I find it hard not to feel that way when the only social ladder left to climb is that of historical relevance."

Chrys often felt kinship with Malachus, a paternal bond from his time spent living in the keep, but in this thing they were opposites. He wanted nothing more than for the stubborn flame of the Apogee to be forgotten. "Five years ago, maybe, but I was a different man then."

Malachus smiled. "I'm not so sure. I think that man is still there, hidden under a brittle layer of self-control. Every once in a while, a crack breaks through the armor and that man comes out. It's a bit refreshing to be honest. As a leader, I like the new you, but I must say that as a man there are times when I wish the Apogee lived on. That kind of man has his uses too."

It was true. It *was* a brittle layer, but it was growing stronger over time. Chrys had never told anyone that he heard a voice in his mind. It started during the war, the day he'd butchered hundreds in Ripshire Valley. Now the Apogee spoke to him daily, begging for Chrys to let him out. But the one time he had, death had flowed like a landslide and Chrys couldn't recall any of the events. "I fear that, no matter how hard I try to change, the world will always see me as the Apogee."

"It's fascinating to me that your greatest fear seems to be yourself." Malachus breathed out sharply through his nose with a smile pricking the corner of his lips. "What's even more fascinating is that I actually believe you. It's refreshing to be honest. I have always appreciated that about you. Fearless candor. Unlike the leeches I spend most of my time with. Now, enough of an old fool's ramblings. You came here to brief me on the warehouse raid."

"Yes." Chrys squirmed. "The good news is that the reports were true. It was a Bloodthief hideout."

"That's wonderful news. So, why does your tone make it sound like bad news?"

Chrys went on to explain how the four of them had carefully walked the streets and seen nothing suspicious. When they'd entered the warehouse it was empty, bare. They were ready to call it when Luther had noticed the peculiarity in the floor's dust patterns which led them to the trapdoor. An ambush, Reina's sly trick, and a brutal fight. He hesitated as he described the prisoner.

"She was young, tall, blonde hair. Blindfolded and gagged, hands bound behind her, with a knife to her back. She got away from him, I told him it was over, and he slit his own throat before I could stop him. Which means that despite the intel being good, all we have is ten dead Bloodthieves and no more information."

"Unbelievable. Almost like they knew you were coming."

Chrys nodded. "Possibly. But we have no evidence."

Malachus leaned back in his chair, deep in thought. "Yes, only a fool lays blame without proof. There are many who knew of the operation, but little time for them to warn someone all the way on the westside. And what of the girl. Who is she? Has she told us anything helpful?"

"I've never seen her before, sir. A young Sapphire. She played like she was coming with us and then...she escaped. I tried to follow her but lost her in the lower westside alleys. It's my fault she got away. I never should have trusted her so quickly. But, stones, I did not expect someone so young to have such skill." Chrys straightened up. "Of course, that is no excuse. I take full responsibility."

Malachus slammed his fist down onto the table. The force of the pounding shook the wood with such force that it displaced the clean organization. "She just...got away? From a team of my most skilled threadweavers? Stones, Chrys, you're not making this easy on me."

One of the guards burst into the room to check on the noise.

"Leave," Malachus dismissed him, and the guard left.

Here it came. Chrys braced himself for impact. The moment he'd been preparing himself for all afternoon. Every step down the cobblestone streets had felt like the countdown to a concussive blast, the heat of it already tangible across his nervous skin. Malachus was likely to give Henna or Jurius control over the investigation, or if Malachus was really furious, he might dismiss Chrys from his duties altogether.

"Unbelievable." Malachus rubbed his temples, all sense of joviality wiped clean from his face. "The closest we've come to uncovering their operation and we come up with nothing. If Jurius finds out about this, you're done. He'll revolt unless I give him control of the investigation, but there's no way that ends well. Chrys, I trust you. Probably more than I should. If you say you did everything you could, but she got away, I believe you. Jurius won't. You know he came to me after I gave you charge over the Bloodthief investigation? Told me all the reasons it should be him instead of you. He was absolutely furious.

"He can never know about this failure. In fact, no one can. There *was* no girl. Understand? There was a group Bloodthieves that you efficiently dispatched, one that killed himself rather than be questioned. Can you make that happen? More importantly, can we trust your team to keep the secret?"

Chrys was in shock. Rather than demoting him, Malachus was going to lie for him. "Yeah...yes. Yes. We can trust them. Luther would do anything for me, and we should be able to trust Reina and Laz."

"*Should* isn't good enough. Make sure they're on board," Malachus demanded. "We need to find out who the girl is."

Chrys had been so busy worrying about telling Malachus the bad news, that he hadn't even thought about trying to find the girl. "Absolutely. I can pull records from the temple and look for any Sapphire girls between the ages of fourteen and twenty-two. The list should be small, and that bright blonde hair is uncommon enough that we should be able to filter it down even more."

"Perfect. Do it discreetly." Malachus grabbed a quill and jotted a name onto a small slip of paper. "If anyone bothers you, find Father Jasper and tell him you're on assignment from me. He's on the Stone Council and I've known him for decades; he'll be discreet."

This was not how Chrys had expected this conversation to go. Malachus had every reason to be furious. Stones, he'd killed men over smaller mistakes. But here and now, he was putting his own credibility on the line to protect him. If the others ever found out, they would not only depose Chrys, but the integrity of the Great Lord himself would be damaged in their eyes. Perhaps he could find new high generals, but it was less work for Malachus to keep the ones he had happy.

As if on cue, a knock on the door revealed the white-haired high general peeking into the room. The twinkle in Henna's eye made Chrys uneasy.

Malachus raised a finger, and she retreated back into the hallway with the guards. "My brain is telling me that this is a poor decision, Chrys, but my gut says to trust you, and it's never led me astray. Tell me you can handle this."

"I can handle it." Doubts flooded his mind as soon as he'd said the words. So many uncertain variables: Luther, Laz, Reina, the Sapphire girl, the temple workers, or even any passerby who saw the girl's escape. This was a dangerous lie, but at least he had Malachus on his side. "You can trust me, sir. This will be the last time you hear anything about it."

"Good. You're dismissed. Send Henna in after you. And Chrys," Malachus said with a voice of warning, "don't let me down."

Chrys walked away from the desk feeling both lighter and heavier at the same time. The entire encounter had taken a different turn than he'd expected, and mostly for the better...at least for the moment.

He reached the door and opened it.

High General Henna was outside, still with big, excited eyes. As soon as she spotted him, she smiled and greeted him. "Chrys. What was that about? He looked pretty serious."

"Nothing important."

"Good, because you won't want to miss this." She slid past him beckoning him to follow. A small bag swung below her hand, weighed down by its contents.

Well now he *was* curious.

Malachus stood up, still not having shaken off the irritation from his face. "General. What is this about?"

"Great Lord..."

Malachus interjected. "What is *this*? Why do you look like *that*?" He waved his hand out gesturing to her face.

"Sir?"

"Like a bad card player with a good hand."

She laughed. "I've never been good at hiding a winning hand. And I'm not positive yet, but I think that's exactly what we have here." She raised up the small bag and bounced it around a few times.

"Go on." Malachus leaned forward.

Henna dropped it on the desk, drawstrings still closed tight. "Remember that cave my men were exploring? They found something. At first it looked like it was just the remains of an old miner settlement, some rusty century-old equipment, a few broken-down wagons, some cracked support beams. But then we found one of these."

She untied the bag and pulled out a small shard of black mineral. "Some of the engineers think the mine has obsidian deposits."

Malachus raised a brow. "This is your winning hand? A deposit of a low-demand mineral buried deep in a mine in the mountains?" The look of irritation chiseled deep into the wrinkles of his eyes.

She grabbed the piece and stepped a few paces back, still smiling like she knew something they did not. Without explaining, and before anyone had a chance to ask, she threw the rock right at Chrys' torso. His eyes and veins flared blue as he *pushed* it away.

But it didn't work.

The obsidian struck him hard in the chest—the force nearly knocked him off of his chair—and it fell down onto his lap.

"Stones, Henna!" Chrys rubbed at his ribs.

"Henna!" Malachus roared, stepping forward. "What is the meaning of this? Petty revenge? This kind of behavior is unacceptable!"

She waited, saying nothing, the same obnoxious, knowing smile pasted on her face.

Chrys broke the silence, an earth-shattering realization forming in his mind. "Stones."

Malachus turned to him.

Henna smiled something wicked.

"That's not possible," Chrys said.

"Quit with the theatrics."

"Malachus, look. In threadlight." Chrys held up the chunk of obsidian in his left hand.

Malachus' veins swirled with green and blue energy as he glanced into the realm of threadlight, his left eye glowing green and his right eye glowing blue. "That's impossible." He walked over and pulled it out of Chrys' hand.

Henna finally spoke. "Exactly what I said, sir. I had two different threadweavers verify it. For some reason, this obsidian is different. It's thread-dead." The crass slur was common among threadweavers when referring to those who could not threadweave. The more acceptable name was *achromat*. Despite the word coming from Henna, an achromat, in this moment the word seemed appropriate.

"Henna. Do you realize what this could mean?" Instantly, Malachus' eyes took on the same excited look as hers. "If we could mass produce weapons that threadweavers could not influence...Imagine a threadweaver assassin with one of these weapons. They'd be unstoppable; not even other threadweavers could stop them. A threadweaver with a blade against an unarmed threadweaver. Gah! Tell me everything, Henna."

Chrys didn't like it. The world had rules. As a Sapphire threadweaver, he had the power to *push* on anything around him. An arrow coming toward him? Send it away. The idea of something with no thread was frightening. A volley of thread-dead arrows raining down toward him? He would be helpless. If they found more of this, and mass-produced weapons, the safety that threadweavers had come to expect would be gone.

Henna went on to explain that she'd sworn the few who knew to secrecy, and then had sent the expedition further into the cave to look for more obsidian under the guise that Lord Malachus wanted an entire table built of the mineral. They were exploring even as they spoke.

"Well done, General. This could change everything. I have much to think about. Do not share this information with anyone else, and keep me up-to-date with any further findings in the cave." Malachus sat back down, smiling to himself, and stared back out the window down at the candlelit city. He turned to Chrys and smiled. "Looks like I may have found the kindling for that wayward ambition."

CHRYS TOSSED AND TURNED. Sleep taunted him within sight but never within grasp. As Iriel returned to bed after her fourth trip to the toilet, he kept his eyes closed so she wouldn't think she'd awakened him. The truth was that the whole situation didn't sit right with him. He'd been ready to receive his punishment—he deserved it. He'd failed. And yet, Malachus had let him off the hook. He'd realized while lying awake that his own failure could be seen as a failure in Malachus' judgment for entrusting him with the task in the first place. If Chrys could make the failure disappear, it would be better for Malachus as well.

The morning passed quickly and, now, he stood in front of the great temple of Alchaeus, eager to find information on who the mysterious threadweaver girl was. If he could tie up that loose end, he was sure things would be easier with Laz, Luther, and Reina. At some point he'd need to send for them, and he was hoping to have more information before asking them to lie for him. They didn't need an explanation—they were loyal enough—but it would put Chrys' mind at ease.

The dual spires of the temple's eastern building loomed over him, eclipsing the rising sun over the mountains. The vast library was the only part of the temple he regularly visited. Over the years he'd read hundreds of books, most relating to medicine, biology, or history, though Malachus' influence had caused him to pick up a few philosophical works as well. The books by Gauxin about threadweaver physics were some of his favorites. In them, Gauxin attempted to apply mathematics to explain the effects of *weaving* threads. There was, of course, a religious aspect to the text that covered some of the more esoteric aspects but, overall, he found the text to be quite enlightening.

Chrys wasn't particularly devout himself, but he did believe in the

Lightfather, Alchaeus. Chance and luck were poor explanations for too many of life's questions.

Being back at the temple reminded Chrys of the terrifying incident with his wife only days before. He could almost hear her screams as he looked out toward the steps leading up to the temple. The mysterious doctor who had saved her. *Your child is the key.*

He reached down and pulled the black blade out of the sheath strapped to his leg. Looking down at its surface, he thought of Henna and her thread-dead obsidian. What if...he relaxed his eyes and let threadlight wash over his vision. Dozens of brilliant, pulsing threads flowed between him and the world around him, but there was no thread connecting him to the knife. *Stones.* He muted the rest of the threads and focused harder on the obsidian knife, searching the other realm, but he found nothing. This knife too was thread-dead.

How had he not realized it before? He was carrying one of the most valuable weapons in all of Arasin, given to him by a stranger. The final words of the man sprang back into his memory. *Use it to break the threads that bind you.* The man knew exactly what he'd given him. A weapon with a broken thread. The priests told stories about the Lightfather walking the earth in the form of a man...what if they were right? He shoved the knife back into his boot sheath. If it had been the Lightfather, then he had all the more reason to find the girl and stop the Bloodthieves.

He walked up the steps into the library, greeting several temple workers, a priest, and a group of priestesses. They all knew who he was—something he was still getting used to after a year as high general—and let him through. He exchanged pleasantries but was happy to evade more in-depth conversation.

The library itself was enormous, built centuries before and maintained with the utmost care. Even during decades of brutal warfare, the temple was left alone—a prize for the victor. There were two levels of shelving, four rows of books on each, with stairs leading up to a walkway that bordered the entirety of the library. The ceilings arched high overhead with large windows letting in bounties of morning sunlight. Dozens of aisles spread out across each room like silken rows of a great web. Each aisle was labeled meticulously by the temple workers and organized by the priestesses.

The blind priests were the religious leaders of the temple, but the seeing priestesses were the operational leaders. The priests performed the ceremonies and served as liaisons with the congregations, but the priestesses organized it all.

Chrys turned a corner, looking for one of the private sections that contained records of the populace. Information about each family: number of children, homes, debts, alliances, education, etc.

The priestess on duty led him into the records room. Chrys had never entered the room before and found himself overwhelmed by the size. There must be a hundred thousand records, all in alphabetical order.

Seeing the letter "v", he walked forward and thought how interesting it would be to see what his own family record looked like. There would be a page dedicated to the Apogee, and the family section would be small. It was just him and his mother, Willow. He had no aunts or uncles in Alchea, and no father. His mother refused to talk about him, calling him a coward. As a kid, Chrys had always wanted to meet his relatives.

A priest wandered into the room, walking slowly with a white cane tapping gently out in front of him, probing for collisions. He heard Chrys' footsteps and lifted his head. "Ryana? Is that you?" His voice was low and tired.

"Good morning, Father. Just looking through some records, maybe you could help me."

The old man scrunched his brow and pursed his wrinkled lips. "Perhaps I can, my child. Perhaps not. Tell me who you are, and what you need, and I will do my best to assist you."

Chrys felt distinctly absurd asking a blind man for help searching written records. "My name is Chrys Valerian, I'm looking for some records."

"Chrys," he repeated, smiling. "Valerian is a unique name. Did you know the valerian plant has asymmetric flowers? Something the blind do not fancy so much. We much prefer symmetry and predictability over uniqueness, as you can imagine. And if I'm not mistaken, the plant also has medicinal usages?"

"It does. It is supposed to help you sleep." Chrys had learned that from his mother.

"Indeed." The priest smiled as if he knew it were untrue. "Your mother has taught you well. To be truthful, I have wanted to meet you for quite some time. Perhaps not in this way. I wish I had known you were coming. You have made quite the name for yourself."

Of course, everyone knew about the Apogee. The bloody butcher of the valley. He couldn't even hide from the blind.

"They call me Father Xalan."

"It is very nice to meet you," Chrys lied. He gestured over to the wall of records with his left hand. "Not to be curt, but I'm on assignment from Lord Malachus. I need to find some records. Do you know if the threadweaver records are kept separately? Or here amongst the rest?"

Some blind men kept their eyes open, which Chrys found quite unnerving. But Father Xalan kept his closed. Chrys looked at him and felt grateful for that small detail. "I believe that, in general, they are kept here with the rest of the records. However, my dear friend Father Jasper had a collection of threadweaver records pulled just a few moments ago. I can only assume he was more prepared for your arrival than I. The records were taken to his personal study. You can find it in the west wing, first floor, third door on the left."

Of course, they'd known he was coming. They must have spies in the keep. Well, perhaps not spies. Malachus technically headed the church's Stone Council, though his participation was more for show than anything. If the church had spies—if he could even call them that—inside the keep, it would have to be with Malachus' blessing.

"Thank you, Father. I'll head there right away."

"I believe we will be meeting again soon. Your wife is with child."

"She is."

Father Xalan grinned again. "Will your mother be attending? She is your only family, I believe?"

"She is, and she would tear down this temple before letting us come without her. For the ceremony itself, though, it will just be Iriel and I."

"That is..." The priest smiled and shook his head. "I look forward to seeing you again. A word of advice. The most sacred moments in one's life are also the most vulnerable. Childbirth most of all. Be kind and patient and loving. Iriel will need you. May the Lightfather bless you and your child. I pray we both find what we seek."

Something about his tone struck a chord in Chrys' mind. That's why he looked so familiar. Father Xalan was the same priest who performed the Rite of Revelation for Luther's child. Which meant that he was also the priest who took their child away from them. A flash of anger toward the priest passed over him as the thought entered his mind, but he knew it was irrational. It wasn't the priest's fault. The rite and its laws were predetermined. He was just doing his duty. Chrys could respect that.

"Lightfather bless you as well, Father."

They parted ways and Chrys headed toward the west wing. Getting there was the most difficult part. The campus seemed to be a winding labyrinth of unplanned expansions. Even with directions, it took him some time to find the west wing.

The entire corridor was lined with private study rooms, each door marked with inset carvings to set them apart. He found the third on the left and gave it a hard knock. A door down the hallway opened up and a woman looked out toward Chrys. She was dressed in the temple robes of a priestess. She started to walk toward him but then the door in front of him opened. She stopped and returned to her room.

In front of him stood an unnaturally old man. The most surprising thing about him was that despite the deep wrinkles of his face, and the sagging bags under his eyes, his long, gray hair was quite luscious.

"Good morning," he said. The wrinkles near his eyes shifted as he turned his neck.

"Good morning, Father."

"Ah, a voice I do not know. Humor me." He smiled and extended his neck a bit, as if trying to see through his blindness. "You've a knock of authority yet waited for me to speak first. Nobility but not by birth. Male voice, deep but not profound. I'd venture mid-thirties. I hear no one else with you, which means you've been given permission to wander the temple or have a face recognizable to most. Tell me, child. Are you clean-shaven?"

Something about the question made Chrys smile. "I am not. I have a short beard, well-trimmed."

The old man stepped forward and extended his hand. "In that case, High General Chrys Valerian, it is my honor to finally meet you. I am Father Jasper."

Chrys smiled as he reached out and shook the priest's hand. "The pleasure is mine, Father. For a man who has almost certainly been waiting for my arrival, you really struggled to come up with my name."

"It seems my wit has aged less gracefully than the rest of me."

"I had an advantage, of course, knowing that you had pulled the records. If I hadn't known, I'm sure the trick would have amazed and astounded. Which reminds me. I wanted to thank you for gathering the records. The Great Lord said you'd be helpful; I can see why he holds you in such high regard."

"Oh, come now. I'm too old for flattery. I know very well that I am but an arrow in the quiver to that man. He's less religious than the last Great Lord. I imagine he'd get rid of the Stone Council altogether if he could. After all, arrows in a quiver can still be a thorn in your side.

"But that is beside the point. You came for the records of the threadweavers, possibly to find a connection between the kidnappings. More likely it is for another, more covert, purpose conveniently disguised behind the other." He paused, waiting to see how Chrys would react. "We have eyes everywhere but in front of ourselves." He left the explanation at that.

"Nothing nefarious, I assure you," Chrys said. "It's true that we're looking for connections between those abducted by the Bloodthieves."

"Good, good. I hope you find them."

"I hope so too. But if it's as difficult as it was to find your study, don't hold your breath. And that was *with* the help of Father Xalan's kindness."

"*Kind* is too bland a word to describe him. That man is a warm fire in the winter woods." Father Jasper smiled, thinking of his friend. "Now that you're here, what can I do to help?"

Chrys thought for a moment. It would be nice to have someone help look over the records with him. Unfortunately, a blind priest was not the best resource for that sort of aid. "Do you know how the records are organized? Birth year, gender, threadweaver classification?"

"Ah yes. That would be useful. They are sorted simply by birth year. Sapphires and Emeralds are not partitioned separately, and neither is gender."

"And this is all of them? No records have been omitted?"

"None that I am aware of."

"Good," Chrys said. "I think that is all the help I need. I can handle the rest on my own if you need to be somewhere."

Father Jasper coughed a light laugh. "This is my study, child. The only time I leave is to eat and sleep. And when my bones are too tired to make the trip, sometimes I sleep in here as well." He pointed over his shoulder with his thumb and Chrys saw a small cot tucked into the far corner of the room. "I'll be doing my own studies. Don't worry about being quiet, my hearing is poor enough that, unless I'm talking to you, I'll probably forget you're here."

The next hour was spent pulling records for every female blue-eyed threadweaver between the ages of fourteen and twenty-two. There were only a dozen, but it took significant time to continue filtering. There were, of course, no portrait drawings associated with the files, but by using familial nationality he was able to filter the list down to who he thought might have blonde hair. He also knew most of the names from his time running training for young Sapphires over the years and could cross many off of the list. By the end he had one unknown name that he thought might be a blonde threadweaver, and one other unknown name that was more likely brunette based on her northern Alchean ancestry.

He turned to the blind priest. "Father Jasper?"

"Yes? What is it?"

"Do you happen to know anything about either of these names?"

Father Jasper sat up and turned, raising his brows.

"Anna Coramine and Jessa Saltar?"

"Hmm." Father Jasper brought his hand to his forehead and rubbed as he thought. "If I am not mistaken, Jessa Saltar is a pseudo threadweaver. She does have blue eyes, but they are a murky mix of brown as well. I believe she can see threadlight but does not have enough power to effect change on those threads."

Chrys had heard of that happening, but it was extremely uncommon. Generally, the world thought of people as threadweavers or achromats; in reality, there was a spectrum of power. On rare occasions some could only *see* threadlight, and others had blue or green eyes but could not. It was hypothesized that these people could affect change on the threads were they able to see them—the complement of Jessa's condition.

"Interesting. Would that information be..." He looked through Jessa's file and saw the note. *Unable to threadweave.* "Ah, yes. Thank you. I see that now."

The records were incredibly detailed. They had information about when and where they were born, relatives, education, jobs, likes and dislikes, and myriad other seemingly mundane notes about their lives.

Chrys assumed that such detailed reckoning was saved for the threadweavers. There was no way the temple had this much information about every person in the city.

How detailed were his own? Was it possible, through some mistake of his own, that they knew the truth about the Apogee?

Father Jasper grunted. "And Anna Coramine, you said?"

"Yes."

"If she is who you are searching for, you may have some troubles. Anna passed away last year of a blood illness." He nodded his head with a look of sadness. It was not uncommon for threadweavers to have issues of blood. A lifetime of threadlight coursing through your veins took its toll. Some died young of a blood disease, often from overusing threadlight, and others lived into their fifties and died of a heart attack. No threadweavers lived much longer than that. Some threadweavers, like Chrys' mother Willow, abstained from all threadweaving in order to prolong their life, but it only ever gained them a few years in the end.

The worst part of Anna's death was that it left him back at square one. He was pretty confident he knew the rest of the Sapphire threadweavers in the list. So, who was she?

"That is unfortunate to hear. Do you know if there are any other records missing from this list? I'm looking for the record of someone I met recently, but I'm not sure who she was. Maybe you'd have an idea." Chrys was wary to share more information with Father Jasper, not knowing who he'd share it with, but Malachus had said he was trustworthy. "Young girl, somewhere between fourteen and twenty-two, I'd guess. Blonde Sapphire. Fairly tall and thin."

Father Jasper thought for a moment, rummaging through the vast library of knowledge he'd gained over his long lifetime. "Anna would have fit that description. Jessa is a brunette amongst the other classification issue. Do you know the Tarata girl?"

Chrys sighed. "I do. It wasn't her."

"Unfortunately, I cannot think of anyone else that fits that very specific description. But, as you can imagine, a blind priest might not be your best resource here. Perhaps many years ago when my mind still held its edge. It is possible that she's not Alchean. I'm told that, so close to Alir, the light-skinned population in Felia is almost all blonde haired. Visitor, perhaps?"

That was exactly what Chrys feared. There had been something exotic about her. He remembered a small detail. "Are tattoos popular in Felia?"

The priest looked surprised and excited by the question. "I do not know. I'm told the people of Kulai are fond of tattoos, but I do not believe that blonde hair is common on those islands."

Chrys thought hard, picturing her hair waving back and forth as she climbed up the ladder out of the dimly lit warehouse basement. He was pretty sure it was a tattoo. Large. Maybe multiple. "Perhaps. Anyway, I should be on my way. Father Jasper, you have been a wonderful help today. I can't thank you enough for having all of these records gathered for me beforehand. I'm sure it saved me half a day's work. Still not sure how you did it, but thank you. May the Lightfather illuminate the threads before you."

"And may they never grow dim, General Valerian. It has been my pleasure to meet you. You are, as I've been told, an honorable man of great respect, and I pray the Lightfather bless you for that." Father Jasper gave a small bow to Chrys, his long hair shimmering in the daylight. "Maybe you'll humor an old man and pay me a visit when you come for the Rite of Revelation for your new child."

"Of course, Father."

Chrys left the room, pleasantly surprised by the easy conversation with the priest, but displeased with the lack of information he'd gained. Who was she?

The tattoo was the only thing he had left. It reminded him of the stories he'd heard when he was young. Stories meant to scare children. Stories of when gods walked the earth, and the corespawn fed on the minds of men. He'd loved the stories as a kid, each night asking his mother to tell a variant about corespawn attacking and a hero protecting the people. She'd made all kinds of variations. They ate minds. They ate hearts. They ate souls. The heroes could fly. They could turn to stone. They could disappear. In the end, the heroes always won, and they tattooed themselves, so they'd never forget the dark history.

Telling bedtime stories was one of the things he looked forward to doing with his own child. Unfortunately, he worked late most nights with his new position. He would have to figure out how to better balance that once his child was born. Though if he didn't find the Bloodthieves soon, he might not be a high general much longer. There had to be something he could do. He was starting to believe that Jurius was right. Maybe Malachus had chosen the wrong person to lead the investigation.

Chrys needed help.

He didn't want to admit it but, with no leads and no plan, he only had one choice. Jurius. He was well-connected and cared deeply about stopping the Bloodthieves. As long as his son was missing, Jurius wouldn't be sitting idly by. Chances were high that he'd been running his own covert investigation, which meant that he might have information that Chrys could use.

Before he realized it, Chrys was out of the temple and well on his way to Jurius' home. He spent the long walk rehearsing the conversation—he would start by telling Jurius what happened in the Bloodthief warehouse —and trying to predict how Jurius would respond to the request for help.

The sky dimmed as the sun began to set for the day. Chrys was only a few streets away from Jurius' home when he saw the high general walking down the street. Chrys ran to where Jurius had been walking, but he'd already disappeared down another road. Chrys jogged up the road and caught another glimpse of him as he darted down a side alley. Odd. He was heading west.

Chrys knew he shouldn't—if Jurius found out there would be hell to pay—but he followed him anyway.

Voice of War

8

At first, Chrys thought Jurius was headed to the lower westside, but then he turned south. He had almost left the city proper, with nothing but farmland as far as the eye could see, when he finally slipped into a building. Chrys had never been to this area before.

What was Jurius doing?

He moved with caution around the side of the building, observing bricks, windows, and possible blind spots. Each window was locked tight and boarded up with no way to see inside. The building was small enough that, if he entered, Jurius would know. He doubled back over each of the windows, checking for any gaps he could see through, periodically looking over his shoulder to make sure no one was watching. But then he noticed a bit of smoke rising up from the top of the building.

Chrys opened himself to threadlight and leapt, *pushing* hard on the thread that bound him to the earth. His meager jump turned into soaring flight as he shot up to the rooftop.

It was late, and the dark red brick glowed softly with the falling sun. The building was shaped like a huge box, each side equal in width to the others. On the roof, a large chimney released smoke from a fire, and two small windows lined the rooftop floor to let in sunlight below. A bright fire blazed in the hearth below him, and candlelight flickered in the increasingly dark ambience left over from the setting sun.

There were three people in the room. A woman, Jurius, and...his son.

Chrys backed away from the window. Jurius' son was alive. But he'd been kidnapped by the Bloodthieves. What did that mean? Was this woman a Bloodthief? Was Jurius bargaining with her to get his son back? Or worse, was Jurius working with the Bloodthieves? Had he been working with them all along? No, Jurius' emotions had been real. He hated the Bloodthieves. Chrys peeked back over the window and into the building.

The woman was in her late thirties, with dark hair slicked back behind her ears. Black pants and a tight-fitting tunic of curious design, like raven feathers, partially covered her collarbone. The shadows accentuated a strong jawline and high cheekbones.

Jurius and the woman spoke to each other, their mumbled words reverberating through the window. They were unintelligible by the time they reached Chrys' ears. Jurius walked over to his son and embraced him with a sense of desperation.

He needed to hear what they were saying.

Chrys moved to the latch on the window. He laid on his stomach and slowly twisted the handle. When it started to groan, he paused, looking down at the three below him. None of them shifted their attention upward. He twisted the handle even more slowly, pushing down slightly to release the pressure. It stopped as he reached the end. But then, the pressure he'd been applying popped the window's seal and it flung wide open below him.

Chrys reflexively opened himself to threadlight.

All three of them looked up.

Threads, like hungry tentacles, burst forth from the ground toward the ceiling. Chrys had never seen anything like it before. He dove out of the way, but they were too fast. The threads latched onto his body and *pulled* on him, multiplying the force of gravity. He tumbled down through the window toward the ground. Mid-flight, he gained his bearings and *pushed* down hard on his corethread, counteracting the wild threads, launching himself back up toward the ceiling. But then he stalled, suspended in the air like a drifting cloud. He *pushed* harder, but the opposing force grew stronger. When he looked down, he saw the woman staring up at him, dozens of tentacles of threadlight fastened onto his body, each one pulsing with profane energy. He *pushed* harder, but the sheer number of threads increased until he crashed to the floor, pinned down like a nail in wood.

It was impossible. What she was doing defied the primary law of thread physics: thread permanence. Somehow, this woman was *creating* threads.

His hands were bound near his feet, his legs trapped in a deep crouch. He couldn't move, but he could still threadweave. As she approached, he *pushed* a chair at her, but a single thread appeared and fastened the chair to the floor.

"What have we here?" the woman asked. She walked around him, observing him with a wicked smile.

"Jurius! What the hell is going on?" It took all of Chrys' strength not to collapse to the earth beneath the weight of the threads.

Mmmm. A foul voice rose in his mind. *She should not be. Let me out! You cannot fight her. But I can.*

He tried to ignore the voice, but it was right. There was no way to fight back.

Jurius clenched his jaw. "You shouldn't have followed me."

"You know him?" the woman asked.

Jurius nodded. "High General Chrys Valerian."

The weight of gravity applied through the threads faded. Not completely, but the pressure was lessening over time. Chrys took a deep breath and turned to see Jurius' son. He stood tall, a strong Emerald threadweaver like his father, but his eyes were so deeply set they were hard to see in the twilight. Jaymin. That was his name. He should be dead, or close to it.

"He's strong. Good blood," she mumbled as she finished a circuit around Chrys. He finally got a good look at her. Her eyes were yellow, like bright amber dancing near a subtle flame. They radiated, along with her veins, as if she were a threadweaver, but threadweavers were either Sapphire or Emerald, blue or green. There were no other kinds of threadweavers. *Push* and *pull.* The two halves of the Lightfather.

"Don't get too close to him," Jurius advised. "He is not one to be underestimated."

"The boy is yoked. Until the threads fade there is nothing he can do."

"If Chrys goes missing," Jurius thought out loud, "Malachus will blame the Bloodthieves. He'll send the entire damn army into the city searching for him. But, more importantly, he will almost certainly give me charge of the investigation. That would simplify things for you."

She smiled, full lips parting like honey. "Pity to kill him. His blood would sell for a high price."

Stones. Jurius *was* working with the Bloodthieves. But why? It explained how the Bloodthieves had been tipped off at the warehouse. It also explained why Jurius wanted to be in charge of the investigation. But, stones, his anger and worry had seemed so real.

Chrys fought against the threads holding him down, but they held him fast. His blood boiled as he strained against them, anger rising like a tide.

Mmmm. Don't be a fool! Let me out!

For a moment, he considered it. It was foolish to leave a tool unused. He was outclassed. Overpowered. Like a thread-dead soldier fighting a threadweaver.

The spark of a memory lit in his mind. *Thread-dead.* He didn't need the Apogee. He had another tool. The obsidian blade. If she couldn't threadweave the knife, maybe he could surprise her with it. It was in the sheath on his lower leg, right next to his bound hand. If he could kill her, the threads might release him. He felt confident he could handle Jurius if it came down to it.

"You know, general, you ruined a perfectly joyous moment just now." She stared down at Chrys. He continued reaching down toward his boot. "Jurius made two important realizations today. First, he realized that I am not the enemy. It was a long road, but the truth is that we all do what we must for a better future. And second, he realized that your Great Lord is unfit to rule."

In that moment, the truth dawned on Chrys. Despite Jurius being one of the most powerful men in all of Alchea, this woman was in charge. After seeing what she could do, Chrys understood. What hope did Jurius have against someone with her power?

Chrys waited patiently. He could feel the force of the artificial threads continuing to ease, his arms and legs almost free. He tested the threads, pressing against them.

"How heroic of you," the woman said with a smile. The yellow glow in her veins pulsed brighter, her eyes glowing like the sun. Chrys could see the jungle of threads morphing into each other, forming five thick threads attached to each of his limbs, and his head. "There, that ought to make you a little less bold."

LET ME OUT! the Apogee screamed in his mind. *SHE MUST PAY!*

The strength of the fused threads was unreal, like his body was being sucked into the earth, each of his muscles straining to stop it from taking him under. The thread attached to his head pulled him back into an unnatural arch that he worried would break his neck if he didn't resist. There was no escape. There was no hope.

But then he realized that, although his arm was bound, his hand was free.

He slipped the knife out of his boot and kept it hidden behind his wrist. With the blade in hand, his mind flashed to the steps outside the temple, the voice of the man in the wide-brimmed hat echoing in his mind. He remembered the words.

Use it to break the threads that bind you.

He thought of General Henna and her discovery, the thread-dead obsidian. Thread permanence dictated that no thread could be created or destroyed. Each thread was a permanent entity indicating the celestial bond between two terrestrial constructs. But this woman had just proven that it was a lie. She had *created* threads from nothing.

What if?

Chrys opened himself to threadlight and slid the knife toward the root of the thread latched onto his arm. Out of the corner of his eye, he watched as the blade slid weightlessly through the pulsing line of light. The thread popped out of existence just as the knife passed through its end. Then, like a chain reaction, each of the sibling threads burst apart in an explosion of threadlight.

The woman inhaled sharply, as if she could feel the destruction of her creations. She turned to Chrys and saw him freed from her yoke. "Heralds be—"

Moving before she could react, Chrys *pushed* with all his strength onto his corethread, launching him back up into the air toward the open window on the roof. Tentacles of light flung up toward him again, attempting to latch back onto his body, but he sliced through them with the obsidian blade. Her threads burst apart and disappeared in a mist of light. The woman hissed from below and Jurius came running up the wall after him, his veins surging with green threadlight.

Chrys landed on the roof's edge and immediately *pushed* back off toward the inner city, leaping from roof to roof, his heart and veins burning. He turned back to see Jurius standing on the roof watching him, fists clenched.

After a dozen rooftops, Chrys dropped down into an empty street and ran, *drifting* with a light *push* on his corethread. He ran and he ran, his heart beating like a thunderstorm. Finally, he collapsed into an alley, vomiting forcefully. His head was pounding in concert with his chest, and the entirety of his skin sizzled with a deep heat.

    He stood back up and forced himself to move. He had to get back to Iriel. A reckoning was coming. They were no longer safe.

9

YOU SHOULD HAVE LET me out! the Apogee thundered in his skull. *She is too dangerous to keep alive. She will come for you, and there is nothing you can do to stop her!*

After an hour of running, vomiting, and vain attempts at muting the Apogee, Chrys finally arrived at his home. It looked so peaceful in the moonlight, but all he could see was red. The small garden blossomed against the cottage-style architecture, and candlelight flickered in the windows. He stumbled forward, still looking over his shoulder, sure that the woman, or Jurius, would appear at any moment. He had to get Iriel out. Somewhere safe. He had no idea where they would go. His mother's? No. It had to be somewhere Jurius wouldn't look.

"Chrys, is that you out there?" Iriel's voice sang out from the kitchen window, her pregnant silhouette standing in the lamplight.

Chrys pushed the door open, the bright lights inside burning his threadsick eyes.

Iriel caught sight of him and hurried over. "Chrys, are you okay? You look terrible. And your eyes! How much have you been threadweaving?" Her hands moved across his cheeks and his forehead, feeling for temperature and signs of sickness. She used her fingers to look deep into his eyes, blue veins breaking out of a Sapphire iris.

He practically collapsed into her as they moved into the living room. Everything was spinning. The room. His thoughts. Their entire life was spinning out of control and Chrys couldn't stop it. "We have to leave, Iriel. It's not safe here."

"Chrys, you're scaring me. Tell me what's going on."

"They're coming for me." He couldn't think straight. How could he possibly explain what he saw—what he experienced. It was impossible. And the more she knew, the more danger she was in. That was the last thing he wanted. "The Bloodthieves. I know who they are, and they know that I know. They'll come tonight and I don't think I have it in me to fight."

"How much time do we have? I can help fight. Stones, no I can't. You're sure they're coming now? Can we send for help?" she asked, rambling until she broke down into tears. "I can't deal with this right now. Not with the baby so close."

Chrys had no idea what to do. Iriel was always his balance. When he was upset, she was calm. When she faltered, he was her firm foundation. Pregnancy had taken that away right when he needed it most. "Gather your things, we need to leave now. We'll get you somewhere safe and then I'll figure out what to do."

This answer did not satisfy Iriel. She buried her head in her hands as she fought back tears. He hated doing this to her, but there was no other way. Her face paled. She choked on her breath, gasping as she tried to contain her emotions. She shivered, then went still. Her mouth dropped in shock as she looked down between her legs. A puddle of water on the floor, pooling up on the beige rug. She brought her hands to her mouth, terrified at what had happened.

"Chrys."

"Stones," he said knowingly.

"I'm having the baby."

Stones. Now? Of all times. They needed to leave. They had to get somewhere safer. Anywhere but here.

"Can you hold it until we get somewhere safe?"

Her eyes were cold fire. "Can I hold it?"

"Sorry. You're right. Stay here. I'll figure something out."

He sprinted out of the house, adrenaline fueling his movement despite the profound exhaustion that permeated throughout his body. He ran to his neighbor's house and told them to go fetch their midwife, Mistress Amarra. It was all part of their birth plan, so the neighbors knew exactly what to do.

Chrys stood staring down the road, time passing like a dream. Every well-laid plan crashing down around him. Every bit of his perfect life crumbling to dust, suffocating him as he held tightly onto any semblance of order that remained. But there was none. It was over. His perfect life, their perfect plans, nothing but smoke in the night.

Then he saw the first shadow.

He counted four stalking down the dark road. He lifted his chin high and stood with his hands behind his back. He was tired and threadsick, but he knew the power of appearance. There is no greater motivator than to see your enemy's lack of confidence. On the other hand, it is a sobering experience to approach an enemy that has been waiting for you.

The Bloodthieves walked forward in lockstep, trained predators in the night. They looked behind and scattered off of the road and into the trees. Two other figures followed behind, running up the road toward Chrys' home. As they approached, he recognized them as his neighbor's son and Mistress Amarra, the midwife.

The older woman was always serious, and no more so than she was now. "Chrys! The baby is coming?"

Chrys nodded his head and surveyed the tree line behind her. "Her water broke. I don't know how long it's been, but she is inside."

A scream of pain echoed from within the house. Mistress Amarra rushed toward the door and opened it. "These things usually take time, but if her water broke, it's possible the child could come quicker. That didn't sound like a woman with time to spare. What are you waiting for? You need to be inside comforting her."

"I..." Stones. He couldn't. Could he? Was he going to miss the birth of his child? Iriel needed him. But what choice did he have? Go inside and risk their whole family being slaughtered by the Bloodthieves, or stay outside and miss what was supposed to be the most joyous moment in a man's life? His jaw clenched tight. Iriel needed him, but he would have to serve her in a different way. "I need to speak to the neighbors first. You go in. I'll be right there."

He watched as Mistress Amarra hurried inside with a scowl. Chrys could hear Iriel's deep breathing until the door swung shut. Then silence. He turned, eyes probing the tree line for any sign of the Bloodthieves. He slipped out the obsidian blade from the side of his boot and spun it in his hands. This wasn't supposed to happen. He was supposed to be settling down with a family.

Deep within himself he could feel the familiar rage that had engulfed him so many times as the Apogee.

Mmmm, it said. *She is in danger, and you are weak. Let me out. I can protect you. I can save you both!*

Chrys couldn't let it take over him. He couldn't lose control. The Apogee was friend to none. Would it kill the shadows? Almost certainly, but, in the war, the Apogee had killed friend and foe alike. He couldn't risk it.

But...he was so tired.

No. I am in control, he replied.

Threadlight ran through his veins, bright blue radiating across the skin of his arms and neck. He relaxed his eyes, waiting for signs of movement. There. To his right, he caught sight of a figure prowling in the shadows. He knew better than to let them get in position. Never let an enemy choose the grounds. Chrys took off toward the shadow.

An arrow flashed in his vision just in time for him to flare his threadlight and *push* it out of the way. He continued running toward the shadow. They must have known he was a Sapphire but, even still, an unexpected arrow always had a chance at landing.

The shadowed man walked forward. Chrys paused, surprised to find glowing veins peeking out from beneath the dark mask. The other three Bloodthieves stepped out into view, surrounding Chrys from all sides. All four were threadweavers, and each had their face obscured by a strange mask.

"Our mistress is merciful and offers you your life if you'll come with us. We bind your hands and eyes, and you live. If you haven't noticed, you are outnumbered."

"If you haven't noticed," Chrys spat, "you're outclassed."

The Bloodthief smiled beneath his partially veiled face. "Can't say we didn't try. Kill him. Then we kill the wife."

Iriel's voice screamed out from inside the house. Chrys' lip quivered. He knew what he was missing. And he knew the stakes. They would never have his family.

The four Bloodthieves settled into the stance of well-trained Felian combatants. Chrys had trained enough to know what to expect but, more importantly, he had an advantage they couldn't possibly expect. He kept the black knife concealed behind the joint of his wrist as he shifted onto his toes and watched the Bloodthieves' movement. Two Sapphires and two Emeralds.

As if on cue, all four rushed him in unison. Adrenaline burned alongside threadlight as Chrys wasted no time. He leapt forward toward the Bloodthief he'd seen in the trees and crashed hard into him. But the man didn't move. It was like charging into a stone pillar. The Bloodthief's veins were lit with green threadlight as he *pulled* against his corethread, increasing his weight ten-fold. *Stones.* A thread-*pulled* elbow came crashing down on Chrys' shoulder from behind, knocking him to the ground. Chrys *pushed* hard on his corethread, launching himself back up into the air. He slipped the knife out as he rose, and let it slice through the first Bloodthief's chest. Blood sprayed out across Chrys' face as the Bloodthief dropped to the ground.

Mmmm.

The other three were on him before they could see what happened. The Emerald came barreling down onto him with an unnatural descent, threadlight burning in his veins. Chrys turned and threw him off to the side as he thrust the blade forward at one of the Sapphires. The Bloodthief *pushed* at the blade, but instead of diverting it, he watched as it buried deep into his chest. Chrys jabbed twice more through the gap in the man's rib cage before the Bloodthief fell.

Let me out. I can finish it!

Chrys turned and hurled the knife into the second Sapphire's stomach, then rushed him, pulling the knife out, and slit his throat. The last Bloodthief—the second Emerald—rolled to his feet and stared at Chrys holding the thread-dead blade with his three companions motionless at his feet. He cursed under his breath before he sprinted for the trees. Chrys ran and *pushed* off the ground, sending himself in a high arc toward the Bloodthief. While in the air, he threw the black blade at the man's back, but it hit hilt-first. It did little damage, but it did knock him off balance, sending him tumbling into the dirt. Chrys was on him like a wolf, rage boiling inside him. His fists rained down like hellfire onto the Bloodthief's face. Fist after fist, fueling the hot fury inside.

The stranger's words filled his bloody mind. *They will come for it. You cannot let them have it.*

He'd stopped them, but he was losing control.

Inside, he could feel the Apogee squeezing through his defenses. He caught himself. He shook his head and looked down at the disfigured face below him and lost his breath as he understood how close he'd come to releasing that *thing*. He collapsed onto his back, the moon staring back at him as if it were the judgmental eye of the Lightfather.

I am in control, he lied.

He breathed on his back, bloody and broken, and remembered Iriel. A foreign sound rang out in the night. The sound of a child. *Stones.* He forced himself back up, putting the bloody blade back in its sheath, and lifted the Bloodthief's body over his shoulder, and dragged it back behind his house. Then did the same with the other three. By the end, his face was covered with dirt, blood, and sweat. He washed his face and hands in the water basin behind his house. Iriel and Amarra didn't need to know what had happened.

Chrys ran back to the front door, stripped off his outer shirt, and opened it. His red eyes filled with emotion as he saw Iriel holding the newborn child. Not because of love—no, he felt that too—but at this very moment, he felt a profound emptiness where a beautiful memory should have lived. He'd missed the birth of his child. This was a night he would never forget, for reasons that should not be. The tainted frame of a perfect moment.

At least they were safe...for now.

"I'm so sorry I missed it. I—" Chrys closed his eyes. "I'm so sorry, Iriel."

She looked up at him, lips quivering with emotion. But it wasn't anger in her eyes. It was resolve. "Did you kill them?"

"I—"

"Are we safe, Chrys? Tell me we're safe."

Chrys broke. A stream of heavy tears poured down his face. He didn't deserve her. He didn't deserve to be a father. He was nothing but a broken man with rage in his heart. He'd already broken the first promise he'd made when he found out Iriel was pregnant. He had promised to be to his child what his father had never been: present. He'd failed on day one.

The midwife came back in and gave Chrys a disapproving scowl as she helped him lift the towel-wrapped infant. "I need to run back to my home to pick up a few more things. If the baby gets fussy, he's probably just hungry."

He. It was a boy. The realization struck Chrys like freezing rain, rattling his bones, and sending a shiver down his spine. The clouds of death and danger clashed with joy and possibility. He'd wanted a boy.

But not like this.

After Mistress Amarra had stepped out, Chrys turned to Iriel. Her breathing was calm. Even now she was more beautiful than anything he had ever seen. Her pale complexion was blushed and shimmering with sweat from the effort of delivery. Her brown hair draped down, accenting her bright green eyes. He would do anything to protect her. "Thank you for not being angry."

"I *am* angry!" she said. "But not with you. We're parents now, sacrifice is part of the job."

Chrys looked at his son. She was right. Sacrifice is the core of parenthood. But while others were sacrificing time or wealth, Chrys had sacrificed a memory. An irreconcilable sacrifice. And, somehow, Chrys knew deep in his heart that it was nothing compared to the sacrifices he would have to make in the future. Tonight, they were safe, but as long as Jurius and the woman were out there, it wasn't over.

10

THE NEXT MORNING, Chrys awoke to the sound of a crying child. When had he fallen asleep? He'd stayed up most of the night staring out the kitchen window, watching for the next wave of attacks. Every hour or so he'd go outside and take a loop around their home to check for Bloodthieves. The bodies of the four threadweavers lay motionless not far from the well. No one had come. He knew he should eat, but the threadsick nausea and fatigue took away any semblance of hunger he should have had.

As Mistress Amarra finished cleaning the newborn, Chrys walked over and picked him up. He felt clumsy with the child in his arms. Undeserving. He felt like an almost-hero who held the fate of the world in his hands yet knew that someday he would fail. If he could make Aydin a better man than himself, he would consider it a success. Stones, if he could keep their family alive through the week, he would consider it a success.

Mistress Amarra moved quietly to the other side of their bedroom and picked up a piece of paper. She read it over, and then pulled out a quill and stopper of ink. Her brush strokes were quick and precise, a professional in all of her midwife duties.

"Have you chosen a name for the child?" Mistress Amarra asked. "If not, you'll need to make sure you have one by tomorrow."

"His name is Aydin." Iriel turned to Chrys after saying the words, and there was a moment of mutual agreement. Chrys nodded, looking down at his son, a worthy memory of Iriel's grandfather whom Chrys had only met once before he'd passed.

"Aydin. A beautiful name." She wrote it down in her records. "I'll have this sent to the temple to have it recorded. Though there may be some leftover disarray with the passing of Father Jasper."

"Wait, what?" Chrys asked, shocked. "Father Jasper passed away? I just talked to him yesterday."

She seemed discomforted by his words. "He had a heart attack last night. He's been in the temple for so long that it's hard to imagine the place without him. And they'll have to find a replacement on the Stone Council."

Chrys didn't know how to respond. The old priest had been so lively and happy when they'd met. Unfortunately, everyone is lively until they're not.

Mistress Amarra put the birth record into her satchel. "In the spirit of being healthy, Iriel, you should stay in that bed as much as you can for the next week. I know how you threadweavers think that you can heal faster than you actually can, so take it easy." She turned to Chrys. "You don't look so well yourself. But whatever you're feeling, it's nothing compared to what your wife is feeling. Take care of her. Food, pillows, anything and everything she needs for the next week. She will be fragile and in need of a little patience and tenderness. There are some notes by the bedside. I trust you can handle the task?"

Chrys nodded.

"Well in that case, I'm going to go rest up a bit myself. Make sure to keep the child well nursed. I'll be back later this afternoon to check on you." A twitch in the corner of her eye said she would rather not return prematurely.

"Thank you," Chrys responded. "We are forever in your debt."

She grunted. "If every family was in debt that I helped midwife, I could amass an army to rival the Great Lord himself. Just doing my job, General. Take care now. And don't forget, tomorrow is Andia. They will be expecting you at the temple."

As she left, Chrys saw the worry on Iriel's face. "Iriel. It'll be okay. If someone like Girtha Dimwater can have eight children, and none of them ended up deformed or dead, an intelligent, careful person like yourself will be able to figure it out."

"Girtha. Ugh. She's the worst."

He moved over to sit by Iriel on the bed. Her jaw moved up and down as she chewed on an herbal root Mistress Amarra had given her to quench the pain and exhaustion. Chrys held out Aydin in front of them so they could take a good look at their child. He touched Aydin's closed eyes. "Blue or green?"

"Green if he's lucky. The less he takes after his hideous father the better."

Chrys almost laughed. "Misshaped head, discolored skin. I'd say he's taking after *you*."

A knock came at the door.

For a brief second, Chrys panicked. He should have been watching the window. Stones. He looked down at Aydin, bundled up and sleeping quietly in his arms, and handed him over to Iriel. Cautiously, he stepped to the door and opened it.

At the door stood a woman. Blue eyes under brown hair that ran just past her shoulder blades. Part of her looked young and beautiful, but a closer look revealed a weariness only gained by age and bitter experience.

"Mother," Chrys sighed. He fell into her embrace. He needed her there to help with the baby, but the last thing he wanted was to put her in danger as well. It took all his willpower not to unload his burdens on her. He would tell her everything, but not yet. Instead, he turned to her and introduced her to the littlest Valerian. "Say hello to Aydin. Healthy and happy."

Willow Valerian was an odd woman. Harder than most, but soft as a feather when it came to Chrys. And despite her being a threadweaver, Chrys had never seen her use her abilities, claiming the health benefits of a life free of threadweaving. She was immovable when it came to her resolve. Every opinion she held was carefully thought out and firmly held. In her roots, she was a protector, and had passed that along to her son.

"He's beautiful." She reached out to take the child, smiling as his weight shifted to her hands. "So small. I remember when you were this small, my little flower."

The phrase triggered a memory of the blonde Sapphire calling him *flower boy*. He still needed to find her, but that need was drowned out in the cacophony of bitter reality that surrounded him. Not to mention how tired he was. The physical drain of heavy threadweaving mixed with a sleepless night and emotional turmoil all weighed on him like an anchor in the Terecean Sea.

"Everything okay? You look worse than Iriel, and she just gave birth!" Willow laughed, unaware.

"I..." Chrys wavered. He wanted so badly to tell her everything, but was it safe? The last thing he needed was for his mother to be in danger as well. Unfortunately, the truth was that if she was here with them, she was already in danger. "I killed four Bloodthieves last night. Their bodies are behind the house. It's not safe for us to be here, but I don't know what else to do."

Willow's eyes grew wide. She opened her mouth to speak, but stopped, turning toward the back of the house as if she could see through its walls. "Tell me everything."

He did. He told her about Jurius' missing son. The Bloodthief warehouse. The woman with the Amber eyes. The obsidian blade. About the four Bloodthieves come to slaughter their family. And through it all, Willow sat emotionless, same as Iriel had the night before. They were blank slates, absorbing each mark as Chrys penned his story. The two women were similar in many ways.

Willow stood at the end, clenching her jaw. "You were right. It is not safe for us to be here. Give me an hour and I'll come up with a plan."

"There's nowhere to go. What Jurius doesn't already know is most likely available in our records at the temple."

"They don't know everything about us."

A creaking sound rang out from the street, followed by the pitter-patter of hooves. Chrys ran over to the kitchen and gazed out the window into the street beyond. A familiar carriage trudged up the street toward his house. Stones. Two stallions led forward at a steady pace.

He turned back to the others. "Malachus is here."

Chrys hid himself as he kept an eye on the carriage through the window. Black boots exited the carriage door. Stones, no. General Jurius, face ripe with bitterness, stepped out onto the street. He bolted back out of sight, scrambling, terrified at the realization of his greatest nightmare. He had hoped to talk to Malachus in private, but now that wouldn't happen. He reached down and grabbed the obsidian knife from the sheath on his lower leg and hurried over to Iriel and Willow.

"Both of you, take Aydin and go to the back. Lock the door. Keep the back window unlocked in case you need to go. Jurius is with him."

A minute later, a loud knock came at the door. This was it. The two women had gone to the back of the house, and Chrys prepared himself for battle. As he opened himself to threadlight, his stomach churned with discomfort. He fingered the black stone dagger in his hand. If anything was going to give him an advantage against Jurius, it was the knife.

He walked over to the door and opened it.

The Great Lord Malachus Endin and Lady Eleandra Orion-Endin stood in front of him, dressed in full regalia and flanked by both High General Jurius and High General Henna.

Malachus was grinning like a fool until he saw the knife in Chrys' hand. After a second of confusion he laughed. "'Welcome! Now I'm going to assassinate you! Stones, Chrys. Put the knife away and let us in. The breeze is chilly out here. Eleandra thought it would be nice if all of us came together to support you and Iriel."

Chrys backed up, hand still clutching the knife. His eyes fixed on Jurius' every movement. What had he told Malachus? The snake must have whispered something nasty before they'd come. Some smooth lie to convince Malachus that Chrys was the enemy, maybe even switching their roles and persuading him that Chrys was one of the Bloodthieves. He wanted to drive the knife into Jurius' chest and be over with it. Rage boiled in his core.

Mmmm. He will lead you to her. Let me out and I will kill them all.

Chrys shook the voice away. *No. I am in control.*

Malachus grimaced as he looked at Chrys. "You look like you spent a week starving in a Kulaian monastery studying the ancient art of insomnia. Is that what childbirth does to a man?"

Eleandra slapped his arm then glided through the waiting room. "Is Iriel sleeping? We were hoping to meet the child this morning."

He wasn't sure how to respond. Eleandra was a good woman and, if she was there, it most likely meant that they weren't there to kill or imprison him. Perhaps Jurius had said nothing. If the Bloodthieves were smart, they wouldn't want Jurius connected to Chrys' disappearance.

Chrys turned to the Great Lord. "You and Eleandra are welcome to come say hello. They should be awake, but I don't want to overwhelm her." He turned to Henna. "I hope you don't mind staying out here. I really do appreciate your visit."

Henna nodded and Jurius clenched his jaw.

Malachus and Eleandra followed Chrys back toward the bedroom, leaving the other two in the main room. They reached the door and Chrys knocked. "Mother? Lord Malachus and Lady Eleandra are here. Just the two of them. Can we come in?"

"You didn't tell me Willow was here!" Eleandra whispered excitedly; she had always been enchanted with his mother.

The door opened and Eleandra practically burst through the gap, pulling Willow into a tight embrace. "Oh Willow, it has been far too long. We have so missed you around the keep."

"And I you, my lady." She eyed Chrys out of the corner of her eye, unsure how she was supposed to react to the situation based on his previous comments.

Chrys added, "Jurius and Henna are in the waiting room. I told them we want to keep the visits small for now."

Willow nodded, making room for the Lord and Lady to enter. Smiles were in surplus as the bedroom filled with people. Eleandra found her way to the bedside to see the child, like a root to a water source. She had always wanted children but was unable. Rather than succumbing to jealousy, she had appointed herself the Mother of Alchea and taken great pride in the stark contrast of her compassionate care to Malachus' cold rule. None who had met her questioned the self-prescribed title.

"He is absolutely beautiful," Eleandra said with tender eyes.

Iriel looked up to her. "Thank you. Would you like to hold him?" She lifted Aydin toward Eleandra and gave a nod of encouragement.

"I would love to." The Lady took off her gloves and reached over with gentle hands. She lifted the child, bringing him to her chest as if she had been a mother many times before. "I am glad you trust me enough to hold him while he is still so frail. I washed my hands carefully before coming just in case."

"If anyone deserves our trust, it's you." Iriel knew she had spoken well when the corners of Eleandra's mouth curved up.

Malachus stepped over to Eleandra to look at the child who slept soundly in her careful swaying cadence. He moved to feel the child's cheeks with the back of his hand. After a single stroke he seemed satisfied with the softness and his index finger moved toward Aydin's eyelid.

Eleandra slapped his hand like a mosquito. "And what do you think you are doing?"

"Just one little peek," he said. "With Chrys and Iriel as parents, Aydin will surely be the greatest threadweaver of his generation!"

"I don't care if he is the next Drayco the Fearless, his eyes will be revealed in the temple. Even you cannot circumvent the commandments of Alchaeus. And anyhow, the color has likely yet to settle. Even if you managed a glimpse, you'd likely know as much as you do now." Her voice was passionate. Somehow, despite the innate nobility that Malachus exuded, Eleandra could still put him in his place. Some wives are trophies, some are burdens, but others are the very heartbeat of a man, so beautifully harmonized that without her, the man would fade to naught.

Malachus withdrew his hand, feeling sufficiently chastised. A mischievous grin crossed his face, warning of the deep temptation to disobey. In his younger, more brash, years, he likely would have done it to spite her. The recklessness had faded, but the boldness remained. Eleandra turned from him and handed the child back to Iriel before he had a chance to reconsider. They exchanged a glance that seemed to say, *husbands, a necessary evil.*

Knowing he'd lost the battle, Malachus reached into his suit jacket and pulled out a small box. "As diverting as is your company, we have come here to present the child with a gift."

"Oh, you really don't have to," Chrys said.

Malachus gave him a bright, wide smile. "Friends do things they don't have to all the time. It is the gulf that divides acquaintance and friendship. A gift from all of Alchea, to your son." He handed Chrys the box.

Friends? It was the first time Malachus had said it. Chrys had always seen him as a master, a mentor, but friends? Chrys wasn't sure if he agreed. He hadn't even known it was an option.

The box was small but heavy. Should he open it now, or wait until they left? He hated receiving gifts. He would much rather choose something out for himself. What if he hated it? He was a terrible liar. Fortunately, it was for Aydin, not him, and newborns tend to be less judgmental.

"Go ahead and open it," Malachus said. "It's more for you than it is for the child."

Great. Chrys untied the ribbon that held the lid fast to the box. He lifted the top and set it on the nightstand. Inside was a...what was it?

The confused look on Chrys' face seemed to be the cue Malachus was waiting for. "They call it a pocket watch! The lines along the perimeter of the face represent the times of the day, and the thick line that starts from the center moves at the same speed as the sun. You don't have to go outside to tell the time of day!"

"That's incredible," Chrys whispered, turning over the device. "I've heard of the grand clock in Felia's city center, but this is so small. How does it work?"

"It's from that famous Alirian craftsman. He just invented it, and there are only a few that have been made because he refuses to teach people. He's charging a kingdom for a single watch, but he made a deal when I said I wanted a second one." A hint of pride pricked in his voice. "Anyway, congratulations on the child. I hope you like it."

"Of course," Chrys said. "It's incredible. Malachus, thank you for everything. You have been so good to us." He turned to Iriel and the child and held out the gift. "Aydin, what do you think of the pocket watch?"

"It's beautiful," Iriel responded for the sleeping child.

Malachus looked to Eleandra, who motioned to the door. "Enjoy the rest of your day and, if you need anything, you know where to find us."

Chrys' face grew serious. For a moment, he reconsidered telling Malachus everything. He'd covered for Chrys once, proving his trust, but still...Jurius had been there with Malachus since the beginning. The two of them, hand in hand, took over Alchea together. Without proof, would Malachus trust Chrys over Jurius? What risk would it pose to Iriel and Aydin?

And what had Malachus said? *Only a fool lays blame without proof.*

Not yet. Chrys needed evidence. But he also wasn't going to sit by and let the Bloodthieves win. He couldn't tell him everything, but he could tell him enough to keep his family safe.

"Actually," Chrys said. "There is one thing."

. . .

"Henna!" Lord Malachus came bursting out of the room followed by Chrys. "The Bloodthieves attacked Chrys and his family at their home last night. How have I heard nothing about this?"

The high general choked on her words. "I...it is the first I've heard of it, sir."

"You are supposed to be my eyes in the city. I should not discover things before you. While Chrys is here, I want a dozen guards posted out front for protection. At least two of them should be threadweavers. And Chrys says there are bodies out back behind the house. Get it cleaned up and let's see if we can identify any of them. Can't have my high generals getting murdered in their homes now, can we?"

Jurius' jaw clenched tight. "The Bloodthieves attacked him at his home? That seems very unlike them, sir. Are we sure it wasn't something else?"

"Chrys says it is Bloodthieves, and he would know better than anyone else. He says all four attackers were threadweavers as well."

"Threadweavers? We've seen no evidence that the Bloodthieves have threadweavers on their side. I'm not convinced. Isn't it possible that it was just a group of miscreants from the lower westside?"

"We have no reason not to believe Chrys. He is a good man."

"Tell that to the children of the Wastelands."

Great Lord Malachus lifted a hand but restrained himself. "Watch your tongue, Jurius. Good men do what must be done, even if it is dark. Henna, send for the guards. Jurius, take over the Bloodthief investigation while Chrys is home with Iriel. Don't make me regret the decision."

Jurius suppressed a victorious smirk alongside his injured pride. "Of course. I was out of line."

As Henna and Jurius moved toward the doorway to leave, Chrys stepped forward and grabbed Henna's hand. "Thank you for coming. It was exactly what I needed. I know I may not show it often, but I have always respected your judgment."

She gave him a strange look as she glanced down at their clasped hands. He'd slipped a folded-up piece of paper into her hand. She nodded, acknowledging the secrecy. "Glad we came all the way here and were able to enjoy your living room."

Henna and Jurius made their way to the carriage as Malachus and Lady Eleandra prepared to leave. Eleandra nodded to Chrys. "If there's anything else we can do, let me know."

"Protection is more than enough. Thank you."

"Stones," Malachus laughed shaking his head. "You killed four threadweavers last night—the night your son was born. If that isn't fitting for the Apogee then I don't know what is."

"Malachus!" Eleandra shoved him out the door. "Apologies for my husband. You two get some rest when the guards get here. Congratulations again. I'm sorry it was clouded by such gloomy circumstance."

Chrys stood in the doorway and watched the four visitors climb into the carriage. Jurius was last, holding the door open for the others. A pure image of traitorous chivalry. He looked back to the house and saw Chrys standing in the doorway. He didn't smile. He didn't scowl. He stared. Chrys might be safe for the moment, but a storm was coming.

DURING HIGH HEAT, the children of Zedalum were hired to sprinkle dirt across the main walkways. The hot, wooden pathways, encouraged by the light dusting, cooled to a dull warmth for the Zeda people traveling barefoot. At sunset, the same children would sweep the dirt into buckets to use again the following day.

Laurel walked across the soot-sprinkled path leading back to the Elder's lodge, a place she had spent far too much time at in recent days. Her thick, leather boots—a requirement for all messengers with ground-side assignments—left curious lines in the dirt with each step. It was midday and the streets were filled with foot traffic. Congestion was a real issue, especially near the markets where people would carefully step off the wooden paths and onto the tree branches to avoid others. This, of course, was highly discouraged, and a few particularly congested intersections had added standing pads. They were meant to get conversations off the main road so that foot traffic would not stall. In reality, they were more often used as a quick shortcut around corners.

Laurel chose the quickest option: the threadpoles. She opened her eyes to threadlight and *pushed* on her corethread, launching herself high into the air toward a wooden beam a short distance from the side of the road. A large spherical chunk of wood hooked onto the top and a dozen support beams branched out from the center like a wooden mushroom with multiple stems. She landed atop the top sphere, wood groaning under the pressure, and immediately *pushed* back off toward the next threadpole. She smiled as she rode the wind, a bird in the sky above the busy streets.

The threadpoles were designed to be used in emergencies but, in reality, people used them whenever they wanted. Since she was headed to the Elder's lodge, she didn't expect anyone to question her. It also felt good to threadweave again. Her grandfather, Corian, had told her not to, but it relieved some of her stress to let the energy flow through her veins. The headache she'd had since waking up promptly disappeared.

She reached the lodge and found Elder Rosemary sitting on the porch with a warm cup of tea in hand. Her old teeth shined bright as she smiled at the sight of her young friend. "Well hello, my dear. Once again, I find myself painfully aware of why you are here. It's becoming quite the pattern, I do believe."

"I hope not," Laurel mumbled.

"Oh? Us old people are such a toil to be around, are we now?" Elder Rosemary peaked a brow.

"That's not what I...I'm sorry, Elder. I..."

"Come now. I was playing. We're not all bones and blood here. Some of us even have a, dare I say it, youthful spirit. Now, go get inside before you catch a case of old age."

Laurel rushed away from the awkward encounter, leaving the elder on the front porch. She was sure that old people liked to joke about their age as a defense mechanism. Her grandfather did it all the time too. Or maybe they did it to remind her how young she was? Laurel planned on dying in some dramatic fashion long before she was as old as Elder Rosemary.

She started to threadweave, *drifting* as she walked through the halls of the Elder's lodge. She felt lighter, stronger, faster. She felt ready to take on whatever Elder Rowan could throw at her.

Down the hall, she found the lodge's council room and knocked on the door. Muted voices mumbled from the other side. Elder Rowan was generally nicer when she was giving assignments, which is what Laurel presumed this meeting was about, but part of her wanted to go find a Felian orange and try Rosemary's trick again. Just then, Elder Rosemary walked down the hall behind her, catching up just as the door to the council room opened.

Elder Rowan, living up to high expectations, wore a frown. Unexpectedly, each of the other elders were there too. Elder Ashwa, pretty and rotund, sat to the right of Elder Rowan's empty seat. Next to her was the eldest member of the Council, Elder Violet. She should have been taken by the previous Gale, her mind already showing signs of wear; over the last five years it had continued to decline. This year's Gale would surely take her. Last, in the seat next to Elder Violet, across the circular table from Elder Rowan, was the youngest member of the Council. Elder Ivy was in her early forties, and her fair skin was a constant reminder to the other elders of their age.

But why were they all there? Laurel's mind raced with possibility. Maybe it had to do with the Bloodthieves. Some kind of super-secret mission with the future of Zedalum at stake. Or maybe she was finally going to get to travel to Felia in the west. The port city sounded fascinating. An endless sea of water as far as the eye could see. That was the kind of adventure she wanted.

Elder Rowan made no attempt at a greeting. "Have you been weaving, girl?"

Laurel looked down, realizing that her veins were pulsing with a light blue aura. "I took the threadpoles. I didn't want to keep you waiting."

"I'm sure." Elder Rowan motioned Laurel and Elder Rosemary to enter and close the door behind them. The two elders took their seats at the table and they all stared quietly. "Laurel, we heard about what happened with the chromawolves. First, we are glad that you're still alive. You did a very stupid thing and are lucky they didn't tear you apart. Though Cara commended you for your bravery, our position on the matter is quite different. We don't need to be losing any more of our people to those blasted creatures."

Elder Violet, skin sagging and wobbling with every motion, nodded her head as she spoke. "You of all people should know how dangerous those beasts can be. This is Corian's fault for letting you spend so much time at the wolf nursery. Gives you a false sense of reality."

Laurel wanted to defend herself, to defend her grandfather. All she had done was protect Asher. When someone was in danger, you helped them. It was simple. Why were they being so harsh about it? Was she supposed to just watch as Asher got mauled and killed by the alpha? That's not the kind of person she wanted to be. Asher was her friend— one of her only friends— and she wasn't going to lose him.

You of all people. The words infuriated her. They claimed her parents had been killed by chromawolves, but Laurel knew it wasn't true. They'd covered up the truth and refused to tell her what really happened. She wasn't as naïve as they believed.

Elder Rowan continued the lecture. "Secondly, there is the matter of why you were a day late in returning home from your last assignment. It was completely inappropriate behavior for someone with such a vital role in our community. And lastly, Laurel, we believe that you've become addicted to threadlight and are no longer in a good state of health. We've discussed it at length and, effective immediately, you are relieved of all duties pertaining to serving as a messenger to the council."

The wind flew from her lungs as the words seared into her soul. She felt like she was falling. Her worst nightmare realized in the flicker of a moment. It couldn't be happening. Everything she'd worked for. Everything she'd cared about. She wanted to scream. Run. Fight. Everything about it seemed unfair. With all her heart she wanted to weave a thread so hard it shattered in an explosion of pure force. She couldn't breathe.

No longer in a good state of health? Addicted to threadlight? These women were fabricating problems to fit their narrative. They were conspiring against her. She didn't deserve to be treated this way.

Elder Rosemary leaned forward. "We like you, girl. We really do. But until you learn to rein in whatever it is that's driving you to such brashness, we can't trust you with matters of such import."

Part of her wanted to spit the whole truth about the kidnapping at them—in pure spite—just to prove some point that she knew didn't need proven. But she also knew that, if she did, the chances of ever becoming a messenger again would be gone. Did she even want that? Did she want to be beholden to the whims of these *blasted creatures* seated in front of her? They clearly didn't understand her, or respect her, or even care about her.

No. She realized in that moment that she didn't want to be a messenger. Gale take them and their rules. If she wanted to visit the grounder city, she was going to visit the grounder city. If she wanted to visit Asher, she was going to visit Asher. If she wanted to go ride on a boat at the ports of Felia, what could they do about it?

"Well?" Elder Rowan piped. "Do you have anything to say?"

Laurel looked at all five of the elders and smiled, though her eyes said otherwise. "It is what it is." She started to walk out, then turned back before rounding the doorway. "And I hope the Gale takes you all."

She could hear the shocked gasps of each and every one of the old hags as she walked away feeling invincible. It was horribly rude—a nasty

Zeda curse—but they deserved a moment of real honesty from her. After all the lying she had done recently, it was the least she could do. She felt strong. She felt purpose. She was going to go back to the grounder city. She was going to explore and discover and learn. She was going to stand up for herself.

As she exited the lodge, she prepared to *drift* until she made it to the threadpoles, but realized she had already been weaving. She wondered if she could increase the threshold for her threadsickness like a muscle. Slowly stretch it to its limits, or even reset her body's expectations of what was normal. What if she could change her natural state to one that was open to threadlight?

Laurel knew exactly what her grandfather would say. "Life is more valuable than threadlight." Was she going to tell him her new plan? Probably not. He only had a week left to live anyway; no point in ruining those last few days. But she would tell Bay. He would understand. He'd be jealous because he didn't have the health to join, but he would understand.

She took off down the wooden walkway, kicking up dirt as she *drifted* along, then launched herself up toward the first of many threadpoles on the path home. People looked up at her with disapproving frowns—which was stupid. For all they knew she was rushing toward an emergency. She was starting to realize how judgmental her people were. Surely the grounders were more open-minded. The thought made her even more excited to learn about their culture and customs.

She reached her home in no time, sweat dripping down her temples from the exertion and the heat. But it felt good. She felt alert and alive.

Her brother, Bay, was in his room reading. He was always reading. It was his way of experiencing the world. For someone who'd never left the treetops, let alone the Fairenwild, he knew more about the grounders than anyone.

She couldn't help but smile as she approached the room, giving a small knock on the door and peeking her head in. "Hey, little caterpillar. Whatcha reading?"

Bay smiled as he set his book down. "I know that look. You've either done something mischievous or have a mind to. Go ahead. Spill it."

"You know me too well." She sauntered over to the bed and hopped up next to him. "There is bad news, and there is good news. What do you want to hear first?"

"Bad. Best to get it out of the way."

"Bad news is that I am no longer employed as a messenger by that pack of old, shriveled beans."

Bay shook his head rapidly like he was trying to shake something off it. "Wait, what? Are you serious? Laurel! I'm so sorry! I can't imagine…wait, why did they do it? Is it temporary? Is this about Asher? I can't believe it. Wait, why are you smiling? What is the good news?"

"I'm going to the grounder city." She said it proudly, as if it were a divine mission from the Father of All himself.

"You're what?"

The voice did not belong to Bay.

Behind her stood her grandfather, Corian, concern plastered over his wrinkled face. He walked forward faster than she would have thought possible and loomed over her. She forgot how tall he was when he stood up straight.

"Did I hear you say you're going to the grounder city? The week before the Gale?" Corian could light a candle with the fire in his eyes. His usual level-headedness gave way to a rage that frightened her. "I can't have you going off and getting yourself killed by a bunch of miserable grounders. Who is it, Laurel? Who gave you the assignment? Rowan? I've a few words to say to her."

This was exactly what Laurel was hoping to avoid. She looked to Bay, who looked more confused than Corian. Her first instinct was to spin some elaborate story about a secret mission, but she knew Corian would find out the truth. She wished that the Gale was farther out; it would make the situation much less complicated.

She took a deep breath and stood a little taller. "No one. I'm going because I want to go."

"Out of the question! You know the laws. They'll have you killed, Laurel. This is not some game. There's a reason why we stay away from the grounders. The elders take containment very seriously."

Something about the way he said it made her blood boil. What gave the elders the right to control them all? She had no plans to divulge the location of the Zeda people. Laurel could feel the energy burning hotter in her veins, a hint of blue radiating across her arms. "So, we're slaves?

To a few grumpy, old women? I don't think so. They can't stop me any more than you can. The winds take us where they will."

"You're as stubborn as your mother. I told her not to go out on the hunt that killed her, but she wouldn't listen to me. And look what happened! I won't sit idly by and let that happen again. You're not leaving this house. I forbid it."

She choked out of amusement. "You think you can keep me here?"

"I do." The way he looked at her, she knew he believed it.

Laurel accepted the challenge. She reached deep into her core and *pushed* against the wall next to her. The weave launched her to the side in a blur. Corian turned and his arms lit up with green. He staggered against the wall.

"Stop it!" Bay screamed. "You're going to kill him!"

Corian fell to his knees. His hand clutched at his chest. His breathing grew sporadic and irregular. Bay moved to his side. The two of them coughed in concert, a pair of weak, sick men who wanted to control her.

"I'm done being told what I can or can't do."

Laurel walked away from her family out onto the hot wooden streets of Zedalum and *drifted* toward the exit. A warm, dry breeze brushed past her as she ran. Adrenaline coalesced with the hot energy burning in her veins. Each jump from threadpole to threadpole heated her on the inside as the sun heated her from the outside.

Sweaty and angry, she reached the exit. The guard waved to her as she dropped down through the man-made hole in the feytree branches. She *pushed* down on the wonderstone and floated down to the ground like a leaf in the wind.

The call of the wonderstone was strong. It spoke to her raging soul, urging her to release the energy inside of her in one wild *push*. But even in her adrenaline-fueled rage, she knew better than to succumb.

One of the first things Zeda messengers learned when they visited the ground was that the wonderstone was dangerous. Every once in a while, someone would return from the ground threadsick, or worse, because they'd succumbed to its seduction. It felt physical, like the wonderstone had its own gravitational pull, drawing her in toward it.

Legend was that the stone could not be broken, but Laurel figured that, if she could *push* with enough force, it would almost certainly crack. Everything breaks if you push hard enough.

She'd asked her teachers how it was built, or even why it was built, but none of them seemed to know. They gave vague answers like "the Father of All helped them." But when she asked why, they would say "he loves us" and "to protect us." Nothing about their answers felt satisfying, or even intelligible. Maybe the grounders knew the truth.

She turned away from the wonderstone, clearing her head of its cloudy enticements. Before heading to the grounder city, she needed to make a quick stop to visit a friend.

A drove of skyflies floated overhead, translucent wings fluttering in the dim light of the photospores. The green, insect-like creatures never surfaced above the treetops, but some people would capture them, bring them up, and sell them as pets. Their thin, coiling bodies were fascinating to watch as they moved through the air.

She took the path she'd taken the previous day and, after a time, found herself at the pond with rocks built up around its edge. There was no sign of the chromawolf pack. Scuff marks painted the ground where the alpha had died. Blood still littered the forest floor where they'd fought. The alpha's body was no longer there, but there were bloody drag marks to the east. She hoped Asher was still okay. Memory of the alpha swiping down at Asher's face still gave her anxiety. She was glad the alpha was dead.

The drag marks ended not far to the east near a rock formation. Fascinating. It was a boneyard. Laurel had never heard of such a thing, but surely Cara knew something about it with all the years she'd spent among them. The chromawolves gathered their dead. It seemed such an odd thing for a beast to do. It gave her more respect for them and proved that they were far smarter than most gave them credit for. She'd always sensed it with Asher, the feeling that he understood her when she spoke.

As she walked the chromawolf boneyard, she noticed a collection of fresh prints headed farther east, which she followed for quite some time before finding the pack lounging near a small stream. She set down the photospores she'd been carrying like a lantern and stalked forward, looking for Asher. He was flanked by two females. She pictured the other chromawolves bowing to him after he'd killed the previous alpha, accepting him as their new pack leader.

Among the Zeda people, women were the leaders. It seemed wild to have your leader chosen by physical strength alone when there were other attributes so much more important. The grounder nation to the east was ruled by a man, but that solidified the Zeda perception that they were fools. To the west, a woman ruled. Another reason to visit. Her grandmother used to say that true leadership is not taken by brutish means, but is earned by exemplary service to others. Men have a hard time with the latter. The idea that her culture was different than the chromawolf culture made her feel good about the matriarchy. Sure, life at Zedalum had its issues, but at least they weren't living like animals.

The trick now was getting Asher's attention without calling down a pack of chromawolves on herself, some of which were even bigger than her friend. She wondered if some day one of the larger wolves would try to dethrone him, but qualification and aspiration are often at odds, especially in leadership. Maybe she *had* spent too much time in the chromawolf nursery; she was starting to analyze their political motivations.

She snuck around the perimeter until she was closer to Asher's position. Then, she nudged him by subtly *weaving* a rock on the ground in front of him. He looked at it, confused, and then perked his head up excitedly. Without a second thought, she stepped out from the big feytree she was hiding behind and snarled.

Asher seemed like he'd already grown in the time they'd been apart. He ran forward and they leapt at each other, colliding in an explosion of laughter. It felt good to wrestle. Fortunately, the other wolves did not make a movement, and as her eyes met theirs, she could tell that they recognized her. Did they consider her part of their pack?

They tumbled on the ground for a few minutes before they were both panting of exhaustion. "I have to go away for a few days, but I'll be back. Stay safe. Maybe I'll bring you back a leg to gnaw on."

In the far distance to the east, the clear howl of a chromawolf echoed in the twilight. Then another, and another. Asher jumped to his feet and let out his own raucous howl. He looked to Laurel and gestured with his head, as if beckoning her to follow.

Together, they raced toward the sound.

12

It was just after high noon and the sun was drifting from its peak, scattered by clouds that danced over the curves of the Everstone Mountains. The white marble of the temple reflected a brilliant light that acted like a beacon for the rest of the city.

Every noise in the night had awoken Chrys, including the constant crying of their newborn when he grew hungry. Even still, he felt refreshed. His family was alive. They might just live through the week. The bad news was twofold. First, they'd had to leave their house for Aydin's Rite of Revelation day. Second, the Alchean soldiers accompanying them couldn't watch over them forever. Time was not on his side.

Chrys, Iriel, and Willow traveled up the road toward the temple accompanied by a dozen Alchean soldiers. It was a quiet journey despite the distance. The gentle rumble of the carriage put Aydin to sleep early on. Chrys walked beside the carriage; he needed the walk to distract his mind. Iriel had joined him for a very short time, wanting to stretch her legs without putting undue strain on her body. Threadweavers recovered faster from injury—the threadlight in their blood provided a small amount of healing—but not so much as to nullify childbirth after a day.

They traveled alongside the Jupyter River that ran from the ravine at the base of the Everstone Mountains all the way to Lake Landrian south of the Fairenwild. The trade route followed the river all the way from Alchea to the lake, where it split west toward Felia. It was the best way to get between the countries and, near the border, a favorite spot for bandits.

The grass was bright green against the backdrop of the wide cerulean river water, and it had Chrys wondering about the eye color of his newborn. The Rite of Revelation was such an important event for a parent, but would a parent really love their child less based on the color of their eyes? Love is not a calculated result of features and faults. Love is the unseen thread binding two souls together no matter the externalities.

He found himself at ease knowing that he would love Aydin regardless. While the rest of his life burst into raucous flames, at least he knew that. It sickened him that they were in danger because of him. He would fight the Lightfather himself if it meant they would be safe.

After another mile of walking, they reached the front steps of the temple. Iriel paused halfway up, taking in the architectural masterpiece and catching her breath. Huge columns lined the steps up into the waiting room, where white chairs sat next to old-world mosaics lining the wall. High above the entrance arch was a pale blue stained-glass window that added to the already ethereal ambience. It was also where she'd almost lost the baby.

Chrys looked around to make sure there was nothing suspicious but saw only hills and a few temple workers. He turned to the soldiers. "You may wait out here. We'll be safe inside. And thank you."

They hadn't invited any friends or additional family. Chrys knew that at least one of Iriel's sisters would be offended, but it was better than adding more risk into the mix.

Iriel's head propped back in awe at the statuettes lining the high domed ceilings. Some things inspire wonder no matter how frequently they are experienced. A young priest sat at the front desk, eyes closed, yet keenly aware of the visitors. His hair was cut short, and he had the characteristic black robes of a priest of the Order. Beside him sat an older woman.

"Welcome, friends," the boy said. "How may I help serve you this special day?" With so many people in the city, dozens of children were brought in each week on the first day, Andia. There were three smaller temples in the city for those unable to travel up to the great temple, each with rooms set apart for performing the Rite of Revelation.

"We are here to present our child to the Lightfather," Iriel said.

"May Alchaeus bless your child." The young priest tucked his chair back and stood. "If you follow this hallway to my left, you will find a room with a few other couples waiting. Please take a seat and join them. The servant will instruct you when it is your turn." He smiled and motioned to the left. "Alchaeus bless you both."

They nodded before realizing that nodding to the blind is as effective as yelling at the deaf.

"Thank you," Chrys muttered.

The boy ironically nodded in return.

They walked through the hallway, feeling the warmth of the candles that lit the walkway. Before long they walked into a large waiting room that could have easily held twenty-five couples. Fortunately, there were only three others waiting. Some periods of the year tend to have more births. This season must have been the trough in the wave.

The other couples looked nervous and stressed. All six of them were achromats from what Chrys could tell, and he could almost hear their silent prayers begging the Lightfather to bless their child. The chance for a privileged life.

Iriel sat first, giving a courteous nod and smile to the other couples as she sat straight backed and confident. She understood that there was more to life than the color of your eyes. Of course, there was an unavoidable pride that came with giving birth to a threadweaver, much like a baker pulling a perfectly formed pastry out of the kiln. We sit and wait, hoping that our creation will come out lovely.

Time passed and the temple worker standing at the door ushered in the first couple, and then the second, and then the third. Half a dozen other couples entered the queue, keeping a steady flow. With each new couple, Chrys' unease grew. He watched them carefully, looking for any sign of duplicity. It was eerily quiet. Seven infants in a strange room should have been disastrous. The world was funny that way. Silence can calm and silence can unnerve, but it's never the one you're expecting.

The temple worker glanced behind for a moment as if he had heard something. "Brother Valerian. Sister Valerian. The priest is ready to see you now. May Alchaeus bless your path." He opened the door and gestured for them to pass through. As Willow rose to follow, he added, "Parents and guests may wait in the room to your left."

Chrys could have requested her company like Luther had, but it was more common for the couple to go alone. Willow exited left and handed Aydin over to Iriel, but not before giving the temple worker a dirty look. As they passed through the doorway, they found themselves in the enormous ritual room. A beautiful mural covered the domed ceiling, and huge mosaics, stained glass, and ornate tapestries covered the walls.

Chrys couldn't help but remember the Rite for Luther's third child and the horrible outcome. If nothing else, at least the church couldn't take his son.

To the right there was a man dressed in white seated behind a wooden desk. He smiled at them as they entered. Directly in front of the desk was a large white veil blocking his view of the rest of the room. The recorder had a pen in hand and began scribbling down notes into the thick book in front of him. Chrys thought of the detailed records of each of the nation's threadweavers. Today they would begin Aydin's.

Directly in front of them stood a waist-high stone altar. It was covered with a white brocade fabric and curved in a manner to firmly hold whatever was placed atop. Standing at the side of the altar was a priest, dressed in an immaculate white robe in contrast to the stark black of their daily garb.

It's Father Xalan from the library, Chrys thought.

The priest beckoned them to bring the child forward and place him on the altar. Iriel moved slowly, placing Aydin down atop the soft temple linens. She had bags under her eyes, but she was indomitable.

"Welcome, and congratulations. It is just the two of you, I'm told. Willow is in the waiting room?"

"She is."

"That is well." The priest's lips curled into a smile. "I should very much like to meet her. I try to meet the families of all who come through."

"Of course, Father." Chrys realized that the statement wasn't completely true. He hadn't met with Luther's family. But it would be quite uncomfortable to meet the relations of a child you'd just blinded and taken away.

Father Xalan lifted his hands, palms up. "Again, congratulations. There is great beauty and knowledge that can be learned from the Rite of Revelation. I pray you are humble enough to see the hand of the Lightfather this day. Chrys, it is wonderful to be with you again. As patriarch you may take your place at the left point of the triangle. And Iriel, as matriarch you will take your place at the right point." His hands spread out, motioning to the ground.

They took their places. There was a knock on the floor, and they turned to see the recorder poking his head from behind the veil with a metal staff in his hand. It was the sign given to let the priest know when the parents had taken their places.

Father Xalan dropped to his knees at the altar and raised his hands high above his head. "Father of light. We come before you this holy day to present this child. Open our hearts as we open these eyes. Glory and power are yours, let us be but small conduits of your supremacy. As you will, let it be, and let our will be a thread bound only to you."

There was a reverent air of silence after the prayer as Father Xalan rose to his feet using the altar to lift himself.

"The will of the Father be manifest in this child."

He placed white gloves over each of his hands, then reached toward the child's face, seeking through touch the insets marking Aydin's eyes. Slowly, the lids were lifted, and he placed a few drops of the clear liquid he held in a small vial. The priest opened his mouth to speak but said nothing.

His hand dropped to the side and his face washed over with stern solemnity, brows furling in thought. After a moment of silence, he turned away from the altar and walked toward the veil, reaching out a hand to motion Chrys and Iriel to wait, anticipating their confusion. He made his way across the room and disappeared behind the veil.

Glancing toward the altar to make sure that Aydin was safe lying there alone, Chrys turned to see if Iriel had any idea what was happening. There was no similar interlude during the Rite for Luther and Emory's child. But then again, that was their third child and a whole different situation.

There were whispers from behind the veil, and then the room echoed with the sound of something heavy hitting the floor. Chrys and Iriel turned to each other confused.

Father Xalan walked back around the edge of the veil into view. But something had changed. His posture was stronger. His head was higher. His eyes were open.

Eyes that were not blind.

Eyes that were not murky from acid exposure.

No. They were bright eyes that shined like Sapphires in the daylight.

"We need to talk," the priest said.

VOICE OF WAR
13

A CHILL SHOT THROUGH CHRYS. Father Xalan wasn't blind. Which meant that he wasn't really a priest. And that almost certainly meant...Bloodthief.

They were in danger.

Chrys reached instinctively for a weapon. Finding the obsidian dagger at his side, he left his corner of the triangle and jumped into position between the priest and his family even as Iriel jumped forward to grab their son. Rage boiled inside him.

Mmmm. Let me out! I can protect you!

Chrys focused. *No, I am in control.*

He balanced himself, feet wide, ready to intercept the priest. He let threadlight pour over his vision and waited only a moment before his anger sent him charging toward the false priest. Xalan was not as fast as Chrys and took a blow to the chest after dodging the hilt of the blade.

"Chrys!" The priest leapt back out of range. "You must listen to me. I am not here to hurt you."

"You cannot have my family!"

Chrys leapt forward again slashing with his dagger. The priest extended his hand, expecting the dagger to redirect as he tried to *push* the thread that was not there. The knife sliced across his palm, bright red blood staining the sleeve of his white robes. The priest stumbled back, clutching his cut hand to his chest.

"Open his eyes!" the priest shouted, backing up and placing his hands up in the air. "Open your son's eyes and tell me what you see. I am not your enemy! The farthest from it. The truth is...just look at the boy's eyes."

It took all of Chrys' control not to heave the knife into Xalan's chest then and there, but it was clear that the man was too old to escape.

"You move, you die," Chrys commanded.

It could be a trick. He backed up, walking toward the altar where Iriel held Aydin, then turned, reached down, and opened Aydin's eyes.

Staring back at him was...impossible. They were not blue like Sapphire. They were not green like Emerald. They were not brown like an achromat. They were a piercingly bright yellow. The same color as the woman, like the pollen of a daisy had been suffused over the iris.

Chrys' eyes widened, and he took a step back. A thousand questions flashed through his mind as he took in the information. He looked back to Xalan. "What did you do to him!"

The priest shook his head. "I could not do this if I tried. There are stories of people with such eyes. Let me bring you to those who can answer your questions. We can keep the child safe, and they will have answers for you."

The stranger who'd saved Iriel once again came to mind. He'd said, *"Do not let them take your child."*

Chrys snarled. "If you think I'm so easily deceived, you've misjudged your standing. Do you work for Jurius or the woman? You'll find that killing me is a much more difficult task than you're prepared for."

"I'm fifty-two years old, child. Not a prime choice for an assassin."

Chrys' lip twitched. "The veil worker disagrees."

"He's not dead. And it doesn't matter; we need to get your son out of the city. I had far different plans for today, believe me. But if we don't leave now your child will be taken from you. They will kill him, imprison him, or worse. The way I see it, you have two choices. You can come with me, or you can burn the color out of his eyes."

"Or I can leave with my family and figure it out on our own."

Just then, the recorder limped out from behind the veil holding his head. He looked to Chrys and the priest and his eyes grew wide. Father Xalan wasted no time, slipping a pen out from under his robes and sending it surging through the air with a strong *push*. It ripped into the recorders neck and buried itself deep into his artery.

Chrys wasted no time, lunging forward and holding Father Xalan with the black knife to his neck. "I should kill you."

Mmmm.

"The world will think it was you," Father Xalan said stoically. "You gave me no choice."

Thoughts raced through Chrys' mind. Was he right? No. Chrys was reputable enough that people would believe him. Except for one problem: Jurius. This would be the perfect opportunity to paint Chrys as a murderous traitor. He'd be the Apogee once again. And if Jurius ever found out about Aydin's eyes...

"Tell me the truth. Who are you?"

"That is more complicated than you know."

"Simplify," said Chrys.

"It is easier if I show you. May I?" Father Xalan pinched at his robes. "I promise there are no weapons—or things that could be used as weapons—beneath my robes."

Chrys released him but kept the knife at the ready.

Father Xalan peeled off his ceremonial garb, down to his blacks. "My name is Pandan. I am from Zedalum in the Fairenwild. I came here many decades ago as a spy in hopes of finding...that is not important. It is my duty to send reports to the elders of Zedalum about the happenings in Alchea. I was not here for your son, but I think the Father of All may have had this in his plans all along. I promise you on the wind that I will do everything in my power to protect him."

The room spun. Chrys had heard of the Zeda people. They were supposed to be deformed, dark creatures that lived in the Fairenwild, feasting on the raw flesh of animals. The Wasteland savages of the west. A scary story to discourage youth from going into the forest. No one actually lived in the Fairenwild. The dank darkness was less inviting than a sewer. Not to mention the chromawolves. This liar claimed to be a Zeda. But what if he was telling the truth? If there was truly a city in the Fairenwild, what safer place could there be for his family?

"Prove it."

Pandan hesitated. "Our people mark ourselves when we come of age." He pulled the black robes off his shoulders, exposing his bare back as he turned. A feytree was tattooed between his shoulder blades, roots growing over a large circle. The branches...the girl.

A vision swam before his eyes, a girl climbing a ladder, her hair swaying to reveal a tattoo on her back. The tattoo he'd seen; this was it. She too was a Zeda.

"Are there others of your people here in Alchea?"

"No. Just me."

"Was there a young, blonde Sapphire here last week?" Chrys hoped to have at least one answer to the thousand questions piling up.

"Laurel?" Pandan looked concerned. "How?"

That was it. "She and I had a brief encounter. I saw the same tattoo on her back. We'll need more answers when there is more time but, if you'll lead us to Zedalum, we'll go with you."

"What?" Iriel exploded, her eyes smoking fury. "Are you insane? Stones, Chrys. We can't go with him. He just killed an innocent man!"

Chrys turned to her. "Jurius will pin the murder of the recorder on me. If he's telling the truth—and I have reason to believe he is—then we found our safe house while we figure things out with the Bloodthieves. I understand how it sounds, but do you trust me?"

Iriel's jaw clenched tight. "Yes."

Pandan started walking toward a door on the far end of the room. "I promise more answers will come, but now is not the time. The temple workers will be checking on us soon. We need to leave."

"I still think this is a bad idea," Iriel reiterated.

"You'd be crazy not to, but Aydin's eyes are the same as the woman I told you about. Whether what he says is true or not, we're in even more danger than we were before." Chrys moved closer and whispered to her so that Pandan couldn't hear. "I believe him, but I don't trust him. Keep an eye out."

They ran through a sunlit corridor that curved to the right, taking them further into the vast temple interior. Pandan moved swiftly without looking back, assuming that their decision to follow him still held true. The way he moved was slightly off, like a warrior returning to the battlefield after a time away.

They came to a door and Pandan stopped. "Follow my lead. If anyone asks, I am giving you a tour. Only priests are allowed in this part of the temple, but your status and name should grant some leniency. They can punish my disobedience tomorrow."

No one smiled at his joke.

He closed his eyes and pushed open the door. "This building is often referred to as the Dreams," Pandan announced loudly. "Home to many of history's greatest prophecies and dormitory for the vicars of the Lightfather."

There were upward of twenty people in the room, three of which were priests, a handful of temple workers tending to their needs, and a dozen priestesses. It looked to Chrys like some kind of common room, with large circular tables, bookshelves, and storage containers filled with tools.

An older priest rose from his chair and stepped toward them.

"Father Xalan?" the elderly priest asked. "I thought you were leading the Rite of Revelation today. I presume there to be a good reason that you bring a tour through our sacred halls?"

"Of course, Father Andrum," Xalan said humbly. "The Great Lord has asked me to show High General Chrys Valerian, and his lovely wife Iriel, the inner sanctuary of the temple. For anyone else I would have denied the request. I'm aware it is quite unusual. If it displeases you, I will end the tour early and send word to the Great Lord of the misunderstanding."

Father Andrum stood thoughtfully with his lips pursed. "It is our solemn duty to observe the commands of our blessed ruler. Please, continue, but next time be sure to warn the brethren, so as to avoid interjections. Apologies for the disruption, Lord, Lady. May Alchaeus bless you all."

"Thank you, Father."

Chrys sat back and watched Xalan, or Pandan. Stones. How long had he lived here among the priests, the only one able to see? The only one able to read facial expressions and body movements.

There was something morally wrong about manipulating the blind, blasphemous even. Pandan was a professional counterfeit. How long had they lived with a traitor in their midst? Unaware.

Apparently, they were blind in more ways than they knew.

A loud bell rang out from across the campus. They moved across the room and Pandan opened a door, ushering them through, eager to be away from the other priests. Chrys saw two guards burst through the other door and into the common room just as their door closed.

"They must have found the body." Pandan continued walking. "There is an exit close by, and it should be guarded by no more than three men. That shouldn't be a problem."

"We are not killing more people," Iriel said. "One is more than enough. We still don't trust you, and a flippant suggestion of murder isn't helping your case."

"I agree. The guards are good men and shouldn't be harmed," Chrys said. "Can we not just walk past?"

"I was not suggesting...it does not matter. The bells are a complete lockdown of the temple. I was hoping to reach the exit before it sounded. We should obviously try to get past them without violence if possible." Pandan hesitated. "But if they refuse, then we may need to try an alternative approach."

They all understood his implication and nodded. Pandan led the way through a long corridor. A servant ran past them going the opposite direction and stopped in his tracks as he realized that Pandan was running with his eyes opened. They slowed to a walk and turned a corner, out of sight of the servant, Pandan closing his eyes as they rounded the bend.

At the end of the hallway were two guards in front of a large wooden door. They stood strong with their hands on the hilts of their swords, alert and ready for action. *Stones*, Chrys thought, *any other day and I'd give them a few shines for their vigilance.*

"Father," the left guard spoke as they approached. "The doors are sealed until the bell chimes again. I apologize for the inconvenience."

"There is a time for obligation, and there is a time to set it aside. We are the reason the bell rang." Pandan spoke with authority, as if his word was law. "You may recognize High General Chrys Valerian. This is his wife and son. They are in danger. A guard was murdered during their Rite of Revelation, and I am leading them away to safety. Your duty is not to protect a door. It is to protect the people inside. Let us pass or raise your blades. I am taking this family through that doorway."

The guards looked to each other, unsure how to respond to the imposing priest. They both waited for the other to make the call, scared of the repercussions. Chrys wasn't sure what he would have done in their position. *When promise and purpose differ, which do you choose?*

"We probably report to the High General anyway," the left guard said. "Father, keep them safe."

Chrys let out the breath he'd been holding.

"Thank you, brother," Pandan said. The comment was more than a simple thank you. Most priests, when speaking to others, referred to them as son or daughter. In calling the guard *brother*, Xalan had given him an acknowledgement of respect. The guards parted, and they passed through the doorway.

Iriel paused. "If we turn back now, Chrys, we can tell the guards what happened. We can take Aydin and go home. If we go with him, we're complicit. *He* killed the recorder. *He* lied about who he was. *He* made a mockery of our religion." Her skin grew redder as she continued. "You saw how easily he lied to those guards. Who's to say he hasn't done the same to us?"

"I assure—" Pandan started.

"Quiet!" Chrys snapped. He felt the fire burning within him. His mind raced back and forth, weighing the realities of their situation. If they left with him, there was no doubt he'd be tied to the murder of the recorder, never able to return to Alchea safely. If they did not leave with him, he might still be tied to the murder and his son's eyes would put his family in even greater danger than it had been. Either way they needed to leave Alchea.

Jurius and the Bloodthieves were a guaranteed danger. There was still a chance that Pandan was not.

Iriel stood staring at him, trying to discern his expressions while waiting to hear his thoughts. It was a gamble, but following Pandan was the best move. "I trust you, Chrys. If there were another way, you would have thought of it. Say the word, and I'll stop questioning."

Chrys nodded, turning to Pandan. "It is the best choice we have. Lead the way."

14

OFF IN THE DISTANCE, Chrys could see a few of the Alchean soldiers still surrounding their carriage near the entrance to the central building. The rest must have rushed inside when the bell rang. Soon, Chrys would be the enemy.

Pandan stole three horses from the front steps and brought them around the corner to where they were hiding. They helped Iriel up and gave her Aydin to hold. He saw a hint of green in her veins as she promised Chrys that she could handle the ride. It was common practice not to threadweave while your child still nursed—some claimed that it caused the milk to go rancid—but it was just a superstition.

Pandan and Chrys jumped up onto their own horses and they headed toward the city.

The journey was long, but they made good time. Not long before sunset, they reached their home. Pandan took point watching outside the house while they gathered their things.

"Take only necessities, we need to move quickly. We have to get to the Fairenwild before we're followed."

They all jumped at a rustling in the bushes not far off, but nothing appeared.

Chrys gathered a large bag of clothing and other supplies, then paused. This was the only home they had ever known. This could be their last chance to see it. Years of memories were being put to rest out of fear. Fear for their son. Fear of the unknown. Was he making the right decision?

When he got to the doorway, Chrys saw his elderly neighbor, Emmett, waddling over toward their house. He was the oldest man

Chrys knew, far older than he had any right to be. His eldest son looked after him and was the one who'd run to fetch their midwife.

He was intercepted by Pandan.

"Good evening, brother."

"Huh?" Emmett squinted at him. "Oh yes, you must be the estranged half-brother my father told me about all those years ago. Pity you lost your manhood in that fight with a frisky Felian."

Pandan's jaw dropped and a strained smirk crossed Chrys' lips.

"Unless of course you're the half-brother from my wife's side. The one with three nipples and a mole larger than the lot. Or perhaps you're just in my way. Do move, young man. Chrys and I have a matter to discuss."

"Young man? Chrys is...he's helping with the baby. Can you come back another time?"

The old man scowled at him. "I can see him standing in the doorway. Are you blind? Now, this is important, and won't take long. So why don't you roll your stones out of the way before I test their resolve."

Without giving Pandan a chance to respond, Emmett ambled down the path and up the porch to the front door. "Chrys."

The old man was one of the nicest people Chrys had ever met. Quirky as a crystal, but soft as silver. They had become genuine friends over the last few years. "What can I do for you, Emmett? We're in a bit of a hurry."

"Your mom asked me to keep an eye on the house. Said some strange folk been showing up and to let you know if I saw anyone. Well, when you were gone, I saw someone sneaking around your house. You tell your mom I let you know. She's a fine woman she is."

Ignoring the disturbing conclusion, Chrys thanked him and rushed back to the bedroom.

"Iriel, we need to go."

She was at the bedside table, nursing Aydin in one hand and holding the pocket watch Malachus had gifted them in the other. "If we can get to Felia, all we have to do is sell this and we'll be okay."

Chrys watched as she packed it away and tightened the drawstring on her sack. For a moment he stood quietly in the bedroom doorway staring at the bed, eyes glazed over as he stored away the precious image for what might be the last time. He was leaving behind a piece of himself.

He walked out of the house. Pandan still waited with the horses. Chrys helped Iriel back up into the saddle and lowered his voice. "Someone was here earlier, and they very well could be watching us right now. No more stops. We go straight to the Fairenwild. Stones, but I wish we could have grabbed my mother. She'll be in danger because of her connection to us."

"Your mother can take care of herself," Iriel said, looking down at him from the horse.

"I too would love nothing more than to wait for Willow," said Pandan, "but the first place the guards will look is where we are. The elders will let us come back for her at a better time."

As much as Chrys hated it, Pandan was right. They took off back down the road, galloping as fast as they could. The journey through the fields west of Alchea passed in a blur, the group only stopping for a few minutes to give Iriel time to find a position where she could nurse the child while they rode. The perpetual movement of the galloping horse helped lull Aydin into a deep sleep.

Finally, the top of the Fairenwild came into view.

Chrys had only been there a few times, and only when he was younger. Some youth found it entertaining to see how deep they could go before turning back. An appalling brand of childish machismo. No one made it far. Between the eerie darkness, hugweed, treelurks, chromawolves, and tales of the Zeda, no one dared venture far.

The trees looked like they were made for the gods. Huge lumbering structures taller than most buildings in Alchea, without a single branch growing until their highest peaks. Limbs sprouted forth every which way, fighting and clashing with their myriad neighbors, creating a curtain of darkness overhead that draped the ground in shadow. The branches, so dense in their mesh, formed a single structure, like a roof held up by thick support columns.

It was wonderfully quiet, which was exactly what they needed. With all of the commotion and intensity at the temple mixed with the hovering cloud of danger, the silence was refreshing. They slowed to a walk, the tree line only minutes away, and Chrys looked up at Iriel and their new son. No other woman could have endured so much so near childbirth, but Iriel was a fighter. If he lost his home, his position, and his friends, he knew that it would be okay so long as he had her.

Chrys wondered how they would navigate the Fairenwild. If Pandan wanted to spring a trap, it would be the perfect place. Chrys still didn't trust Pandan, and there were surely dangers in the Fairenwild waiting for them, but at least Jurius was behind them.

"Run!" Pandan shouted, snapping Chrys out of his reverie.

Chrys looked back over his shoulder and was terrified to find a troop of twenty soldiers riding warhorses toward them. The Fairenwild was close enough that they might be able to reach it before the soldiers overtook them. He slapped the horse to move and they all galloped as fast as they could.

The wind grew stronger as they drew closer to the trees, the pounding of horse feet growing louder and louder behind them. The angry flame in the pit of Chrys' stomach grew stronger, but this time he didn't want to suppress it. Twenty soldiers? Not impossible.

Just then Pandan stopped. "Keep going! I'll hold them off. You have to get to Zedalum. Head toward the center of the Fairenwild. Follow the yellow roses."

Chrys scowled. The soldiers *would* catch up to them; it was only a matter of when. In the dark of the Fairenwild they could hide, or fight. On the green fields, the warhorses would put them at a much greater disadvantage. Pandan might be able to slow them down long enough for his family to hide, but finding a secret city in the middle of the Fairenwild without a guide was highly unlikely.

"Not an option!" Chrys kicked Pandan's horse in the rear and it took off running.

The beating of hoof on dirt grew to a roar, like a wave crashing overhead. Chrys' heart beat fast, burning hot with adrenaline and threadlight. They were almost there. He turned around just in time to see an arrow falling toward him. He *pushed* its thread, sending it off in another direction, then realized that Pandan had stopped once again. Arrows streaked down toward the Zeda spy, but he swatted them out of the sky like flies, his veins glowing Sapphire blue.

There was no time to go back for him, so Chrys made a decision. He ran. The old man was going to die for them. It was in that moment that

Chrys understood. Pandan had been telling the truth. Somewhere in the Fairenwild were the Zeda people, and they had answers.

PANDAN HADN'T FELT this way in decades. His blood sang with threadlight as his horse charged toward the oncoming soldiers. He jumped off as soon as he grew near and danced between the enemy's horses. He *pushed* spears out of the way, spun around rearing hoofs, and dodged incoming arrows. His body wasn't as sluggish as he would have expected, but threadlight had a way of making up for lost years.

A thick boot thrust toward his head, but he dropped low, moved in close, and *pushed* hard on the ground. He launched up in a monstrous uppercut that knocked the soldier off his horse, dropping his spear to the ground. Pandan picked it up and used it to stab into the thigh of a second horse. It crashed forward causing two others to collide.

He'd been a guard once upon a time—before he'd convinced the elders to let him go—but nearly thirty years had passed since those days in the Fairenwild. His breath was heavy and his muscles sore after only a few moments of combat. At least half of the soldiers had stopped to deal with him; the rest were led by a copper-colored stallion that chased off toward Chrys and his family. Hopefully it would be enough. He smiled because he knew that this very moment was the reason he had been at the grounder temple all those years. It wasn't for her—she was just who the Father of All had used to keep him there. It was for Chrys. For the child. The Gale should have taken him long ago but today, with the wind in his face, he would die knowing that he'd served a greater purpose.

He prepared himself for the soldiers that charged him, but then his left arm went numb. His heart was too old for so much threadlight. It was giving out. He fell to the ground, clutching at his chest just as a soldier tackled him from behind. Dust rose from the ground as his knees hit. He could feel the threadlight in his chest, it was too much for his aged heart.

Just before the world faded away, Pandan caught one final glimpse of Chrys at the edge of the Fairenwild.

And smiled.

As Chrys and Iriel reached the edge of the Fairenwild, their horses reared back, neighing wildly, refusing to enter even a step. Iriel was almost thrown from the beast before Chrys helped her dismount. They left the horses hastily and dashed into the forest. Strange, bulbous spheres swayed back and forth glowing from the end of long reeds. Photospores.

Chrys glanced back. A familiar man rode a familiar stallion. Jurius. Fewer than a dozen soldiers followed close behind. Chrys ran deeper into the forest. From behind, he heard the whinnying of the warhorses as they reached the edge of the Fairenwild, refusing to step foot inside.

They rounded a small hill and Chrys whispered to Iriel. "We can't outrun them. We need to hide."

"But Aydin."

Stones. "Feed him. Pat him. Rock him. Whatever you have to do to keep him quiet."

From the small hill, he could see a group of large bushes with relatively few photospores nearby. He pointed to them and started moving forward. Iriel followed close behind. Pulling out his dagger, he cut his way into the shrubs, creating a small pocket for them to burrow into. It was uncomfortable, tight, and hardly provided enough cover to hide but, in the dark forest, it would have to do.

They sat in silence, Aydin cuddled up to Iriel, and Iriel cuddled up to Chrys. Sharp, jagged branches pricked from every angle. Jurius and the guards rounded the hilltop. It took all of his willpower not to break out of the bushes and charge forward in fury. Chrys' stomach churned with hate.

Mmmm, the Apogee whispered. *Let me out! I can protect you! I can protect them!*

Chrys closed his eyes and shook his head back and forth. *No. I don't need you. I am in control.*

For a split second his mind lingered on the idea. The Apogee had killed far more men by himself during the War. Was it more dangerous to let him out, or to keep him in? No. He couldn't become that man. Never again.

Far in the distance, a deep howl echoed beneath the vaulted canopy.

Stones.

Eight soldiers prowled like predators, each footstep a muffled echo on the mossy dirt. Chrys held Iriel tight. Jurius yelled something, pointing every which way. The guards fanned out to search. One of them veered right and set his trajectory directly toward their hiding spot. His eyes peered into the darkness, searching, but the lack of spore luminescence made it difficult to see.

He moved, now only ten feet away from the bushes. His attention diverted as he looked back toward his companions. They were widespread and the quiet intensity told that none had yet found their quarry.

He moved, now only five feet away from the bushes. They could hear his breath as they inhaled and exhaled through their hands to mute the sound of their own.

He moved, now only two feet away from the bushes. Dangerously close. His boot brushed up against the twigs at the base of the shrubs. His eyes brushed over the bushes but then looked away.

They held their breath.

Another howl echoed in the distance, drawing the attention of the soldier.

He moved, now five feet away from the bushes. They exhaled. He kept walking forward, oblivious to their location.

Little Aydin, understanding only the cold and his hunger, let out a small screech. The guard turned around. It was loud enough that several of the others turned to face the source of the noise, including Jurius, who came sprinting.

Iriel clapped her hand over the infant's mouth, aware that such a dangerous action was the only choice. It successfully muted the noise, but the closest guard could still hear the faint whining. He approached, squinting to see better.

Chrys' chest seethed with fury. This is not how they were going to die. He wouldn't die hiding in some brush like a coward. He would die fighting.

Mmmm. Let me help!

"I don't need you!"

Chrys screamed as he kicked his foot out of the brush into the guard's stomach. He ripped himself out of the hiding place, twigs and leaves cutting deep into his skin as he exited. He got low and tackled the guard to the ground, yanking the dagger out of its sheath. By the time they hit the ground, he'd already thrust it deep into the guard's breast.

Yes! Let me out! Let me finish it! You cannot protect your family alone!

The other guards saw him and sprinted forward.

As Chrys rose to his feet ready to make a stand, veins burning blue and soul filled with anger, death flashed before his eyes. He imagined Iriel, run-through, bleeding out. Pandan, trampled, rain falling on broken corpses. And Aydin, dead, lying on a table. He knew what would happen if he failed. He couldn't fail. He was going to kill them all.

Mmmm. I will kill them all.

"Get out of my head!"

An arrow flew through the darkness and slammed into Chrys' shoulder. He stumbled back, shouting as he ripped it out of his arm.

Mmmm. You will fail!

"No, I will not!"

Jurius appeared, leaping forward while Chrys wrestled his demon. His fists blurred in the dim light, cutting low, swinging wide, testing boundaries. Chrys reacted in turn, blocking and swatting aside each attempt. Jurius kicked hard and Chrys caught a foot in mid-flight, rotating and throwing Jurius down to the ground. The older man launched himself back, *pulling* recklessly against the base of a feytree. He blasted forward into Chrys' body. The black knife broke free of Chrys' grip and tumbled to the ground.

Chrys looked to the knife, but Jurius was on top of him before he could move, pummeling his face and chest with ruthless savagery. Years of aggression released in moments of unadulterated brutality. The forest grew darker and darker with each primal punch. Slam. *Iriel.* Slam. *Aydin.* Crack. *Pandan.*

As Chrys' consciousness fled from his broken body, he had a sick realization.

He *did* need the Apogee.

Mmmm.

"No!" Iriel screamed out from the bushes.

A massive shadow burst out of the darkness and crashed into Jurius. Enormous canine teeth clamped down onto his shoulder. Jurius flared the threadlight in his veins and *pulled* hard against the nearest feytree, tearing his body away from the chromawolf's jaws.

More chromawolves crept out of obscurity and pounced on the Alchean soldiers. Tendons and ligaments ripped away from their mortal frames.

Chrys lay panting on the ground, watching the photospores bobbing back and forth, shadows dancing on dying men.

Jurius scuttled away, rebuffing another advancing chromawolf. He took off to the east, leaving his men behind, desperate to escape.

Chrys was barely conscious—his sight blurred in and out—but he could hear everything. He lifted himself to his feet, groaning as his broken rib jutted into tender flesh. He walked in circles trying to make sense of the chaos, but all he could hear were screams, and all he could see was a family of dancing shadows and shades of red.

Iriel. Where was Iriel?

A low growl drew near. Chrys' blurry eyes sharpened, and he turned to see a massive creature standing in front of him. Thick green fur mixed with cords of white running down its back. Two tails, like a scorpion's barb, danced high above it as it bore its monstrous fangs.

He'd failed.

They were all going to die.

He fell to his knees and closed his eyes. If only he'd let the Apogee take control.

"Asher! Stop!"

He tried to open his eyes, but they'd gone black. A blurry figure stepped forward. A girl's voice. She spoke to the beast. It bowed its head to her. His mind spun along with the world around him.

"Gale take me, it's you!"

15

Alverax lifted a hand to shade his eyes from the beating desert sun. He groaned. A deep soreness throbbed in the muscles throughout his shoulders and neck. As he tried to sit up, a searing pain ripped through the flesh of his chest, drawing his eyes to a complex weave of fresh markings and a large scar over his heart. He fought through the pain and stumbled to his feet before realizing that the unstable footing below wasn't sand. It was bones. His head swung on tender hinges as he took in his surroundings.

Heralds save me.

He was knee deep in decayed human remains. The smell hit him like a scorpion, inserting its stinger down his nostrils and tickling his throat. He heaved but managed to keep himself from vomiting. Most of the corpses had finished their course, but a few scattered throughout the crater still clung to their hollow shells. The freshest of them had festering wounds across its chest. The sight of it terrified him; he had never seen a dead body before. His heart pounded in his chest and his head pounded in his skull as he tried to recall how in the hell he'd got there. He was alive, wasn't he?

Pain answered the question quite regrettably.

He looked down at the source and remembered the marks on his chest. His finger traced a single line of raised flesh that arced under his collarbone and circled over his heart. It was tender, but the wound was sealed. He was no stranger to scars after a careless life, but this was no simple scar. It reminded him of the large line of scarred flesh on his upper back. At least now he was symmetrical.

His eyes darted back and forth over the dozens of skeletons baking in the pit around him. What was he doing there? He had no recollection of dying, but then again, most people don't.

Breathing was difficult as he took careful steps toward the edge of the crater. He tried his best to use femurs as stepping stones, their wide surface area lending well to the task.

It is a curious thing to experience horror. The mind has a way of dulling such moments to preserve its own sanity.

Bones crunched under foot as he traversed the pit. A rib jutted upward from the force of his step and cut into his heel, leaving a red stain on the ivory landscape. It's not good to be naked in the desert. The thought brought a smile to his lips. He knew he shouldn't laugh, but the sun was blistering and his mind was swimming with pain and confusion.

The first step was to get out of the crater. He laughed as his foot crunched down on bone. *Technically, the first step was a pelvis.*

He climbed up over the rim of the pit, awkwardly maneuvering to avoid pressure against his chest. When he got out, he counted like his grandfather had taught him. *One. Two. Three. Four. Heralds calm a troubled core.* But it didn't work. As he looked out into the desert beyond, he knew where he was, and he was starting to remember what had happened to him.

"SUBJECT THIRTY-ONE. *With a focus on insertion strategy four—pertaining to specific placement within the left ventricle—and incision process six.*"

Alverax lay next to the surgeon, eyes closed, counting over and over again as his toes shivered on the cold bed. His arms and legs were double strapped to the table with another band across his forehead. He was shirtless, his chest covered with ink marks that the doctor had applied. Four others watched over him, one of them taking note. Amongst them was a woman with jet black hair and eyes the color of the sun.

She stepped forward to get a better view. "Proceed with caution. We're getting low on material."

He felt sick. Of course, it was either this or be fed to the necrolytes, and he'd watched that happen before. Heralds knew he wasn't going to die that way. The tingling of his toes had spread to the rest of his body, each limb now numb.

Whatever they'd given him was working. They'd told him that he had to be alive, and he had to be awake.

It hadn't gone well.

Alverax's body shook like an earthquake, vicious spasms sending his chest and limbs straining against the straps, his body rejecting whatever they'd done to him. His veins turned black, then pulsated a dark, radiant energy as he let forth a blood-curdling howl. His eyes opened wide, irises black as night, twin voids of pure darkness.

The woman cursed the response, and Alverax succumbed to the pull of death.

So, he *had* died.

That meant he was free! No one comes looking for a dead man. Debts? Gone. Justice served. He laughed out loud, a naked mad man in the middle of the desert. Better to be naked and mad than dead.

Alverax stumbled toward the entrance to Cynosure, the desert hideout for a growing group of anti-establishment rebels. It had been around for nearly one hundred years. Everyone knew about its existence, but no one cared. It was far enough south into the deserts of Silkar for its reality not to matter. Alverax had lived there his whole life, like many others. As he walked closer to the entrance, he hoped his friend was on duty, otherwise he'd have to make up some elaborate lie about how he got there. It was the only useful thing he'd ever gotten from his father: the gift of guile.

A small leafling scuttled past his feet. Stepping on its jagged, leaf-shaped shell would tear his foot apart, but otherwise they were harmless little lizards. Some people ate them, but Alverax preferred fish.

He rounded a shaded rock overpass and found himself face-to-face with the entrance, a tall, wide gap in a massive sandstone mountain. At first glance it looked like a deep cave, but he'd been there once before and knew it for what it was. One of the three entrances to Cynosure.

Two guards were posted inside, and neither of them were his friend. They looked at his nakedness with cautious curiosity.

"Gentleman!" Alverax laid on the charm.

The guards put their hands to hilts. The taller of the two spoke first. "Who the hell are you?"

"Alexander Grant. But let's cut to the part where you ask why I'm naked. As much as I'd love to chalk it up to some form of skin therapy I learned in Kulai, the truth is that I lost a bet with Jelium. You know how he is. Not the type of man to let you keep the clothes on your back." He lifted his hands to the side, palms up.

Everyone was terrified of Jelium. His fat face, his fat hands, and his fat head. The man was a big pile of lard who controlled everything. Commerce. Women. Gambling. But neither his prestige nor his girth was what was most terrifying about Jelium.

The taller guard raised a skeptical brow. "What the hell happened to your chest?"

"Torture is a psychopath's favorite pastime."

The other guard, who had been silent up until then, slapped the other on the shoulder. "Heralds. Just let him in. He looks like death."

"Alexander Grant, you said?"

"From head to toe, and every bit between."

The guard shivered, still standing face-to-face with Alverax's dangling indecency. He wrote something down in a ledger and let Alverax through the wide passageway. They all but turned away completely as he entered. He was so happy to be out of the sun that he almost forgot. "Either of you have a towel I can borrow? Err...that I can have?"

They shook their heads, still facing forward, neither wanting any further exposure to his exposure.

Alverax had been out the front gate once before with his father and had a good memory for directions. If he took the first fork to the right, it should take him directly to the city. Then he needed to find Jayla so she knew he wasn't dead. She'd always been fascinated with the scar on his back, her hands tracing it over and over as they kissed. She was going to love the new additions. And that meant...his feet moved a little bit faster.

The pain in his chest throbbed with each step, but he was used to it now. They had done something to him, but it had failed and killed him. Almost. His grandfather was right. *Us Blightwoods don't die easy.* Of course, his father had also said the same thing the night before he was executed. Thieves were always optimistic until they were dead.

He wondered what they would do if they found out he was alive. The whole situation was infuriating. He'd been framed, and because of who his father had been, everyone believed it. They'd never told him where their "intel" had come from, but it was almost certainly Jelium, the man who looked like the human version of a sandhog. Someday he'd pay.

Alverax rounded a corner to a panoramic view of Cynosure. The city was a sprawling metropolis, tucked away under a sandstone mountain in the southern deserts of Silkar overlooking the Altapecean Sea. Thick, portable tents and sprawling pavilions lined the lower division's marketplace. Towering stone buildings were spread across the upper division, their styles stolen from modern Felian and Alchean architecture. Alverax needed to get to the lower division but, first, he needed some clothes.

He slipped past what looked like a small caravan preparing to leave. A few empty wagons were watched over by a few tired men lounging on small cushions. One of them leaned over and vomited. Oddly, it reminded Alverax how hungry he was.

Light crested over the city, finally casting off the morning's shadows. The northern quarter of the city, where Alverax stood, was always covered in shadows. A massive sandstone lip protruded out over the city like a half-built roof. The rest was open air out to Mercy's Bluff overlooking water as far as the eye could see. He'd always loved the sea, the water, the freedom. He was yet to find someone who could hold their breath longer than him, and that victory—however small it was—had always felt significant.

He ran from building to building, surprised with how stealthy one could be while nude. The next building over was a clothing shop, but he had no money and no way to walk through the front door without being seen. He walked around the back and found an open window. It was small. The sill rubbed against his scarred chest as he squeezed his way in, and it took everything in his power not to curse out loud. As he flopped over the ledge, the sill scraped him in even worse ways. That time he did curse.

He looked around for some clothing and found a black shirt and tan pants that he slipped on as fast as possible. A large wooden box in the corner held a collection of leather sandals; he borrowed a pair, then exited through the same window, but this time it was less painful with the help of a crate to give him a bit of a lift.

After another thirty minutes of walking, he found his way back to Jayla's house. It was just outside of Jelium's fortress where he kept all of his children. Close, but not within his own walls, a reminder that they were of him but not with him. Father of the year.

He rushed to the back door and let himself in like he had done a hundred times before. This time, he was careful that no neighbors saw him as he entered. If he wanted to be free from Jelium, he needed everyone to think he was dead.

Inside, the house was free of the sand that riddled the city roads. It was a tremendous effort to keep a house clean in Cynosure, but Jayla had cleaners that would come each week and painstakingly purge the floors. Alverax took his sandals off out of habit, not wanting to muck up the floor, and walked in. He stopped himself before calling out to her, knowing that others could be in the house. With his luck, Jelium would be there visiting daughter number sixty-three.

There were whispers coming from down the hallway. He started to turn around but wanted to see who it was. There were a few others he wouldn't mind knowing he was alive, like his best friend Truffles. Inching forward, he tiptoed barefoot across the rug that ran the length of the hallway until he came to the bedroom.

What the hell?

Jayla lay beneath silk sheets, entangled in the arms of his best friend, Lariathoralan, whom everyone called Truffles. They'd been friends for almost a decade, and here he was, the snake, making love to *his* woman. The sounds and movement coming from the bed didn't stop as he stared in horror. It appeared that his friendships had died alongside him.

Alverax was not an angry person. His father had taught him that it was better to wit than hit, so he'd grown up outthinking bullies rather than sparring with them. Even so, his broken heart pounded in his chest, rage bubbling up in his arteries. He tried to count—*One. Two. Three. Four. Heralds calm a troubled core*—but the pain of a beating heart against his bruised ribs made him even more angry. He closed his eyes. His body felt like it was on fire. The veins in his arms and neck itched under his skin. The darkness behind his closed eyelids filled with a bright white light. When he finally opened his eyes again, the world had changed.

Hundreds of thin strands of multicolored light pulsated around him, overwhelming his senses. Tears streaked down his cheeks as his eyes darted back and forth taking in the ethereal vision in front of him. The world was the same, but different. It was like some kind of spiritual realm was overlaid on top of the physical one but, unlike in the physical world, each thread he could see called to him, whispers in the chaos.

He looked down and saw a thick, bright thread below him. It seemed to give off a ghostly mist as energy darted back and forth across its surface. Like the others, its connection points moved erratically, the base swaying across the ground as if it were trying to find something. He reached down to touch it, but his hand passed through unimpeded. Still he felt it calling. His mind ordered an unspoken command to it, an attempt to connect with it.

But then, it popped. Like a knife to a bubble.

Weight lifted off of his shoulders. Every care, every pain, floated away from him. He coughed out a laugh as the sensation overwhelmed him.

Jayla looked up at the noise and saw him standing in the doorway, no, floating in the doorway. Alverax was suspended in the air, veins dark as night, eyes black as the abyss. An angel of death come to reap his reward. She screamed, squeezing tightly against the sheets away from Truffles, as if realizing for the first time the injustice of what she'd done. Truffles cursed and reached for a knife in his belt on the floor.

Alverax didn't care anymore. They were nothing to him. They were worms, and he was a bird in flight. The silence demanded he speak, but he just stared. His black-eyed gaze bearing down in deific judgment.

Tears bubbled up in Jayla's eyes. She coughed out a babble of desperate words. "You're dead! They told me! This isn't possible. They told me you were dead!" She buried her face in her hands sobbing.

Alverax looked down at them. "Us Blightwoods don't die easy."

He floated back down to the ground and walked away.

Every vein in his body pulsed with blackness. He looked down at his arms as he walked away from Jayla's home. He had been reborn. He was a threadweaver. He'd heard descriptions of threadlight enough times to recognize it, especially from rich acquaintances who'd taken transfusers. But he was different. He'd *broken* that thread. Not a *push* or a *pull*. He was something different.

He'd spent his whole life trying to be more than his father was, but everywhere he went he was "the thief's son." Never quite able to escape the stain. This was his chance. With this new power he could become someone. He could be anything.

But first, a little payback.

16

Laurel watched as a woman climbed out of the brush, dozens of tiny lines of blood scattered across her forearms.

Gale take me, Laurel thought. *She's holding a baby.*

Tears flooded down the woman's cheeks as she gestured to the grounder man. "Please, help him."

Laurel didn't know what to do. She recognized the man from the Bloodthief basement. He'd saved her life once; the least she could do was return the favor. But how? Take them to Alchea? If there were any more soldiers, that would not go well. There was only one other option and, if she took it, the elders would be furious. She smirked. That she could deal with.

She turned to the chromawolf. "You're not going to like this, buddy, but I need you to carry that man."

Asher huffed, but bent low so Laurel could lift the grounder onto his back. He was heavy, so Laurel *pushed* against the ground to ease the process. Her veins were alive with threadlight by the time he was safely draped over Asher's back. She tried to remember the man's name. It was a common name. Fenn? Cardam? Chrys? That was the one.

"Thanks, buddy," Laurel said, scratching behind Asher's ear. She turned to the woman. "Can you walk?"

"How far?"

"A ways. You're an Emerald, yeah? You can use the canopy to *drift* if it helps."

The woman looked to the dark awning above and nodded. "Thank you for helping us. My name is Iriel, and that's Chrys."

Laurel smiled. "I know."

Iriel raised a brow.

"We need to get moving. I'll explain while we walk."

They walked silently for hours. Laurel kept her hand raised high, carrying a bouquet of photospores to provide additional light as they walked through the Fairenwild. Fortunately, with Asher as their guide, they wouldn't be in any danger traveling through. Chrys was in more danger than the rest of them, and not only because of his injuries. Iriel's eyes were daggers.

The uncomfortable silence was broken only by the sounds of creatures skittering through the brush, birds chirping high overhead, or the occasional puff of photospore luminescence. Laurel wasn't sure what to say, so she didn't speak. After she'd explained how she knew Chrys, Iriel had grown gravely quiet.

Chrys was in bad shape. His face was battered and bruised, his eyes swollen shut, and dirt smeared together with blood covering his left cheek. Asher had complained less than she had expected, which made her wonder if he'd ever let her ride him like the grounders rode horses. Cara said a chromawolf would never allow it but, watching him carry the wounded grounder, Laurel had her doubts.

She still couldn't believe it was the same man who had rescued her. Climbing up the ladder out of the Bloodthief basement. Reassuring her that everything was okay. Even now, there was something different about him. It was anything but reassuring. Iriel looked like she hadn't slept in days, her arms speckled with blood, and yet she walked without complaint while carrying their sleeping child.

Laurel wasn't sure she ever wanted kids. They seemed like more trouble than they were worth. One messenger she knew had retired after having children because she didn't want to be away from her family. That kind of familial chain was not something Laurel was interested in. She wanted to be out in the world exploring, adventuring, discovering. Her people siloed themselves off so much that they were missing out on an entire world that was ripe for exploring. Of course, there were some bad grounders—she would need to be careful—but there had to be good ones, too.

Iriel flinched as shadows flitted back and forth across their path.

Laurel smiled. "It's just shadows. When the spores move, sometimes the shadows move too. You get used to it. It's the treelurks you have to watch out for."

"What is a...treelurk?"

Laurel pointed to one of the feytrees. "There's one right there."

"Where?" Iriel asked. "I don't see anything."

"They change their color to blend into the feytree bark. It's dark, so the shift in color is really effective. Once you know what to look for, it's pretty obvious."

"I see something toward the base. Is that it?" Iriel took a step toward the feytree. "Stones! It's a spider!"

Laurel laughed out loud. "Pretty much. A really big, color-shifting spider. If you get too close, they jump out and sink their fangs into your arm. It's venomous, but treatable with the right salve."

Iriel frowned. "I hate spiders."

"Same, but they hate light, so if you have some photospores with you, you'll probably be okay."

"Lovely," Iriel said. "I hate to ask, but how much longer? I'm surprised Aydin has gone this long without crying, and I don't want him giving us undue attention."

"Not much longer. If you get bored, I like to count the skyflies." She pointed up high overhead. A drove of green and white colored insects floated about near the high canopy.

Iriel eyed Asher as they walked, still unsure of the creature. Finally, she let it out. "I have to ask? I watched some of those ripping people apart, but this one seems to defer to you. Why? Am I missing something?"

Laurel laughed, her blonde hair shaking as she looked to Asher. "We're family. I helped raise him. Chromawolves are much smarter than you grounders give them credit for."

"I swear I saw him nodding to you earlier. Not the bloodthirsty monster I grew up hearing about. And what's a grounder?"

"Oh, that's just what we call your people. Because...well, it'll make more sense when you see it for yourself."

"So, you really live in the Fairenwild?"

Laurel looked for a yellow rose to follow. "We don't really live *in* the Fairenwild. Just trust me, it'll make a lot more sense when we get there."

"How can you even tell we're going the right way? It all looks the exact same. You can't even see the sun to reorient yourself."

"That," Laurel said, "is a great question. The roses in the Fairenwild are not the same as yours. There are four types: dayrose, stormrose, threadrose, and the Zedarose. The last one we named after ourselves, but it's really more like a trailrose. Our people planted them a long time ago to remember the way, and they've grown naturally ever since. I've been following them the whole time."

Iriel was drifting off into her own thoughts, but Laurel was ready to get her own question answered. "So, what happened back there? Who were those soldiers?"

Her distant eyes grew cold. "It's complicated."

"What's so complicated about someone trying to kill you?"

Iriel stopped walking. "Is there anything more complicated than someone trying to kill you?"

"I guess not. I just thought we should talk about it before we get to the elders. You're going to have to tell them anyway."

"Fine," Iriel snapped. She held out the baby toward Laurel. "You want to know why they were trying to kill us? Look for yourself."

Laurel cocked her head, confused, but walked over to Iriel. The young mother was probably a decade older than her, but a few inches shorter. "What? The baby? Is it someone else's or something?"

"Look." Iriel took her fingers and opened Aydin's eye. The bright amber in his iris glowed in the darkness.

Laurel jumped back, startled. "What's wrong with his eye? Is he sick? Am I going to be sick now?" She looked back up to Iriel. "Sorry. I'm not so good at this. Why are his eyes yellow?"

"We were hoping you could tell us."

"Why would I know anything about that?"

Iriel sighed. "Not you, your people. The priest said that your elders could tell us more. We're hoping that's true."

"Wait, what priest?"

Iriel frowned. "The one that was from Zedalum. Father Xalan, I think. He killed a man in the temple and basically forced us to follow him. Said that the Zeda elders could give us protection and answers. He's the reason we came this way."

Excitement pulsed inside of her. "Did he head back to the temple? Why didn't he come with you? Seems like a bad decision to send you both into the Fairenwild by yourselves. Especially with an army after you. I thought he was smarter than..." Then it dawned on her. He *wouldn't* send them on alone. Especially if he thought that their son was important enough to break Zeda law and take a grounder to Zedalum. "Is he dead?"

A small bunch of photospores moved back and forth in the breeze, causing the shadows of a small fern to vacillate over their path. Iriel looked to Laurel and nodded. "He saved our lives. When the soldiers were arriving, he stayed behind to stall them. I never trusted him. Not until that moment at least. Anyone willing to sacrifice themselves for a stranger is either completely mad or perfectly trustworthy. Did you know him?"

Laurel nodded.

"I'm sorry. We owe him our lives. And you as well. If not for you, the chromawolves would have eaten us. So, thank you. We owe you a life debt, Laurel."

Laurel was silent the rest of the journey, mind captivated with the idea of coincidence. Was there such a thing? The only two Zedas in Alchea, both in the right place at the right time to protect these people. Her arriving at the very moment the one wolf that would heed her voice was about to attack the man who had saved her life. It was as if coincidence was a unique point in time that had been pulling each of their lives toward it, like an immense force of gravity, until finally they came to a brilliant intersection.

Asher whimpered as they approached the clearing where the wonderstone lay. He was afraid. It seemed to speak to the wolves differently than it spoke to her. It drew her in and begged her to threadweave, to amplify her own power through the power that churned beneath its surface. It repelled the wildlife.

She ran her hand across Asher's green fur and nodded. Only problem was that Chrys was still passed out. There was no way she was going to carry him the rest of the way. She turned to Iriel. "Can you help me wake him?"

His eyes were bloated masses of skin and dry blood. Laurel noted the look of sadness that knit together across Iriel's lips. Whatever grief Laurel felt for the man was nothing compared to Iriel. She put her right hand on his cheek, left hand still clutching tightly to Aydin. She whispered something into Chrys' ear and his face contorted in pain as he awoke.

"Take your time," Iriel said. "You're hurt."

After a minute of struggling to slide off of Asher's back, and realizing he could only see well out of one eye, Chrys finally stood on his feet ready to walk. He looked up and saw Laurel for the first time. "You."

"Me," Laurel responded playfully. Asher nuzzled Laurel and licked her cheek before he dashed off back in the direction they had come. His fur quickly blended into the dimly lit greenery in the background. "I already explained how we met."

"You did?"

"She did," Iriel repeated, her eyes a storm of judgment. "And I don't appreciate hearing about dangerous events from a third party."

Chrys winced as much from pain as from the jibe. "Where are we?"

Laurel gestured forward. "Almost to Zedalum. Asher doesn't like this place, but neither do the treelurks. We'll be safe. Do you think you can walk?"

He nodded.

They moved slowly along the grass until they arrived at the clearing where the wonderstone lay. Bright flowers dotted the floor surrounding it. As they approached, Chrys and Iriel both stared at the circular white stone slab in front of them. It was thick, almost up to Iriel's knees in height, and wide as a room.

"Stones." Iriel's eyes grew wide. "Chrys, look at it in threadlight."

They walked forward in reverence. The wonderstone shone like a multicolored sun, but its light did not illuminate the physical world around it. Threadlight did not increase the light in the world but overlaid a higher form of light that transcended the physical realm.

Small gaps in the feytree branches overhead let in tenacious rays of sunlight. They approached together, and Laurel watched as Chrys stepped up onto the raised platform, his eyes fixed to the bright threadlight of the stone. He bent his legs as if preparing to jump, and Laurel rushed up to him, grabbing his arm.

"Chrys!" she said, clapping. "I should have warned you. I'm sorry. I've never shown someone the wonderstone before. It has a way of making threadweavers want to threadweave so much they die. Seriously, it's happened before. You'll get your chance though. Not to die—gale take me—to threadweave. For now, just try to ignore it."

As Iriel approached the wonderstone, Aydin grew increasingly fussy.

She rocked him back and forth and hummed a song in vain attempts to keep him from crying. Unfortunately, music can't fill an empty belly.

Laurel looked up above the wonderstone, high up into the gap in the feytree branches. As her eyes adjusted, the wooden landing pad came into view. From the distance, and backlit by sunlight, it was hard to see what it was unless you already knew.

"I'll show you how to do it, then I'll come back down, and we'll send you up. Iriel, you're an Emerald, so you can't get up by yourself. I'll take the baby up to Chrys once he gets up, and then I'll come back and we'll make the jump together." She made her way to the center of the stone, glyphs chiseled into white stone beneath her feet. "Careful not to get off center, otherwise you won't make it to the platform."

Chrys sneered at her words. "You're telling me you are going to jump all the way up there? That's impossible."

"Scared, flower boy?"

He gave her a strange look, but she didn't wait for him to respond.

"Impossible is my specialty." She exploded off the wonderstone like a streak of lightning rising up toward the break in the branches. Her speed slowed as she rose higher into the air, up, up into the vaulting branches of the feytrees. After a few moments, she came soaring back down through the air, her blonde hair flailing in the wind, her feet landing with hardly a sound.

"What, you can't do that?" The look on his face was worth the whole experience. "All Zeda Sapphires can do it. Maybe you grounders just aren't as powerful."

Chrys stood silently staring into the canopy.

"Okay, okay. I'm just fanning your chimes. It's the wonderstone. It amplifies your ability to threadweave without making you threadsick. It lets you use its energy to fuel your own *push*. I promise you can do it too. Zedalum is up there."

"It's up there?" Chrys stepped into the center. "Stones, I can feel the stone's power in my veins. Feels like I could fly. So, I just jump and *push*? That's all? And I'll soar as high as you did?"

"There's a threadpole on the left side when you get to the top. Push on it to position yourself onto the platform on the other side."

Chrys focused, bending his knees and looking up into the break in the branches. His veins lit with threadlight and then he *pushed*. Laurel watched as his eyes blazed blue just before he launched up off of the wonderstone. She was sure she saw a smile on his face. As he reached the top, his body took a sudden horizontal shift, and he was out of Laurel's sight.

Iriel stared at Laurel. "There's no way I'm handing you my son to do that."

"It's perfectly safe," Laurel said. "I've done it a thousand times. There's nothing to be worried about."

"Sorry," Iriel repeated, "but I just met you, and that's not a risk I'm willing to take. Tell Chrys to come back down. He can do it."

"I didn't say anything before but, in his condition, I wasn't even sure he'd be able to get up once himself. You make him do it again and who knows if he makes it." Laurel looked up to the opening high above. "I promise you it's more of a risk to make him do it than me."

Iriel thought for a moment, then begrudgingly handed the baby to Laurel. "I swear if anything happens to Aydin..."

It took all of Laurel's self-control not to reply with something snarky. Of course she would be careful. Laurel held fast and *pushed* off the wonderstone, sending her and the child soaring up into the air. The shock of it actually stopped the screaming for a moment. It was glorious.

She rose higher and higher, leaving behind the darkness below, rising up toward the gap in the branches. She *pushed* off the threadpole opposite the platform and sent herself off to the side, landing gracefully on the platform.

Laurel handed Chrys his son—who was still quiet—then remembered that they weren't alone on the platform. A Zeda guard looked at the two of them with confusion. He had his ledger in hand but didn't need it to see that Chrys wasn't a Zeda; his high general uniform made that very clear. Laurel lifted a finger to the guard, smiled, and jumped back off the platform, leaving Chrys and Aydin.

Somehow, she'd forgotten about the guard at the entrance. How was she going to convince him to let them through when his sole purpose was to disallow just that? If she was lucky, he wouldn't know that she was no longer Elder Rowan's messenger to Alchea. She could work with that.

Laurel landed back on the wonderstone and gestured to Iriel. "Ready? Hold on tight."

When threadweavers use threadlight to *push* themselves into the air, it is not like a regular jump. *Pushing* against their corethread diminishes the force holding them to the surface. If they *push* hard enough, the force becomes like a magnet repelling them from the surface. The threadweaver becomes weightless. The person they are carrying? Not so much.

Laurel's veins burned with threadlight as she *pushed* harder than she'd ever *pushed* to offset Iriel's weight. Luckily for her, the wonderstone made that much less painful. They reached the top—though the landing was a bit less graceful than her own—and made their way back over to Chrys and Aydin.

"Laurel, what is this?" the guard asked. "These are grounders! It is forbidden!"

"It's not forbidden. It's highly discouraged. And the elders asked me to bring this family to them. Elder Rowan specifically. And you know how she gets. Obviously, this isn't a normal situation. I'm taking them directly to the Elder's lodge." She held up her hand. "Swear it on the wind."

The guard looked nervous. "Why don't you go get the elders and I'll watch over the grounders here."

"There's not a chance the elders are coming all the way out here."

He bit the inside of his lip. "If they won't come here, then I'm coming with you. And we go straight to the lodge. No stops."

"Fine by me. Let's go."

She nodded to Chrys and Iriel and they followed her up the wooden steps built into the thick branches until finally they stepped out onto the windy treetop haven.

Laurel watched as awe spread over Chrys' face. She'd never had a good look at him in the sunlight. His jaw was strong, though hidden behind a short beard. His hair was pushed to the side, but long enough to cover his eyes. He stood with his hands behind his back, straight-backed and strong, despite the myriad bruises.

She looked out over her home. The sunrise cast a warm glow. She had a pretty good idea of what Chrys and Iriel were feeling. It was the same thing she'd felt the first time she traveled to Alchea. The contrast. The otherness. His was a city of stone, hers was the city of wind.

"My grandfather has a saying: Wonder is the passing wind. In other words, you'll get used to it." Laurel wasn't sure they'd heard her. Their eyes were still glazed over, staring. "I'm taking you to see the elders. If anyone knows about the yellow eye thing, it'll be Elder Rosemary."

Chrys' eyes grew wide. "It's amazing. My whole life, I've seen the Fairenwild peeking out over the western horizon. And all the while this was here? Unbelievable. I have so many logistical questions. Do you know why they did it?"

"Did what?"

"Why did they build a city here, on top of the Fairenwild?"

Laurel kept walking. "Well, I never really thought about it. I guess because they want to be left alone. Don't get many visitors here. And it wasn't safe to build a city down there. Up here, it's just us and the wind."

They walked down idle streets, crowds walking farther along on an adjacent street near the marketplace. The guard trailed close behind, watching intently as they moved toward the elder's lodge. When they arrived, the sweet smell of incense wafted out through an open window near the entrance.

Laurel opened the door and walked in. There were several people in the large entry room, all lounging around and talking. All but two had one side of their hair shaved close to the skin. They stopped as Laurel entered, then stood when they saw her guests. Iriel's face was speckled with dirt and her hair was a ratty mess, but Chrys looked worse. One of the Zedas rushed away down the hallway.

"Is Elder Rosemary in?" Laurel didn't address it to anyone in particular but asked the group in the entry room.

One of those standing in the room was a curly blonde Sapphire named Meg who was currently serving as Elder Ashwa's messenger assigned to Felia. It was the most coveted messenger position of all. The exotic port-city was a melting pot of culture and information, everything a girl from a reclusive treetop city could want.

Meg walked over to Laurel and pulled her to the side whispering. "Are those who I think they are? I heard what happened to you yesterday, and now this? You're going to get yourself exiled!"

"Don't be so dramatic. I'll be fine. It wasn't my decision anyway. Sometimes you have to break the rules for the greater good."

"Laurel, this isn't breaking the rules, this is burning them to the ground! There has *never* been a grounder in our city. And you brought three!"

"More like two and a half." If Meg was looking, she would have seen a slight tint of blue in Laurel's veins. "Why does it matter if we bring grounders to our city? Do you just blindly follow everything the elders say, or do you think for yourself on rare occasions?"

It was harsh—Laurel knew it—but she was tired of everyone treating her like she wasn't thinking through her actions. Meg had no context for the situation or who these people were. She had not even asked her why she'd brought them, and still she felt entitled to tell her it was wrong.

A moment later the man who'd run off down the hall returned and summoned Laurel, Chrys, and Iriel, gesturing for them to follow him farther into the lodge. Laurel held onto the threadlight coursing through her veins. It felt like a warm embrace.

They were led to a familiar door. The man knocked and opened it. Laurel shifted from one foot to the other. She had been so sure they would understand—especially since Pandan had been bringing them—that she discounted the power of tradition. What if they did banish her? Did she even care?

Inside sat five women, scowls at the ready, fire burning in each of their colored eyes. She could see it in that moment—they were tired of seeing her. They had already preconceived her guilt. She should have thought beforehand how she was going to explain it all. Should she start with an apology? Or by talking about Pandan? She was no good at these types of political maneuverings.

Chrys stepped forward, beaten and weary, and addressed the elders. He must have read the room because he spoke humbly and reverently. "We are honored to be here. My name is Chrys Valerian. The girl, Laurel, has warned us that this is quite unusual, but this was not our decision, nor hers. It was the decision of an Alchean priest whom we knew as Father Xalan, but I believe you know him as Pandan."

As soon as he spoke Pandan's name, the air in the room changed. The elders sat taller and listened more intently. Laurel felt grateful that Chrys had spoken first. Rowan and Rosemary whispered to each other, eyes darting back and forth between each of the Valerians. The question now was whether Pandan had been compromised voluntarily or not.

Elder Rowan, eyes sharp as knives, leaned forward. "If that is true, why would he want you to come here? Every Zeda knows well the law restricting such actions." She eyed Laurel at the end.

"He said you had answers. That if we wanted to keep our son safe, you could help us. Stones, he killed an innocent man because he believed it."

"He killed someone? We will need a full recounting of this." Elder Rowan glanced down to the child. "Tell me, what kind of danger threatens your child?"

Chrys looked to Iriel, who nodded her approval. "It is easier to show than to explain." He walked forward and set Aydin on the table in front of them with his hand cupping Aydin's head. Laurel had no idea how the elders were going to respond. She had thought the baby was sick. Would they think the same thing? Or was Pandan right that they knew more? The baby fussed and wiggled as Chrys opened its eyelid to reveal the bright yellow iris.

Every elder gasped in turn, hands springing up to cover their mouths, shock pasted across their faces as if they'd seen a ghost. The oldest of them, Elder Violet, whispered loud enough for them all to hear. "It cannot be."

Elder Rosemary, kind and gentle as ever, looked to Laurel and said, "Our apologies for presuming your guilt. You have done well, Laurel. Chrys, you said? The three of you are welcome to stay as long as you like. Our home is yours, and our protection will forever be open to you. Fenn, take them to the empty room at the end of the hallway. Laurel, you will give us a full report of what happened. I imagine the child needs food and a good cleaning. I will send someone to help and to provide ointments for your wounds. You all would do well to get some rest. The five of us have much to discuss."

17

Willow Valerian—mother to the most wanted criminal in all of Alchea—sat in a quiet room with High General Henna Tyran. The general was as cold as the room; Willow rubbed her arms to keep warm. When she'd set out that morning, she hadn't expected to be detained and questioned by the Alchean guard.

They had shown her the evidence, but Willow knew Chrys too well to believe that he was guilty. At his core, he was a good man. Of course, she'd never fully accepted the stories of the Apogee's murderous rampage during the War of the Wastelands either. The man she'd raised would fight to protect, but never with glee.

General Henna sat across the table, her white Alirian hair messily covering the side of her face. Her eyes were red with fatigue, but she continued the questioning. "Willow, you have to give us something. You were there with them at the temple and spent the previous night in their home. There's nothing I can do for you if you won't help."

"Maybe you should ask Jurius," Willow said.

"And what is that supposed to mean?"

"Chrys is innocent." Willow was steel.

The truth was that it looked really bad. A dead temple worker and two guards who testified that Chrys left with the priest willingly? If she didn't know Jurius' secret, she might have been convinced. But she did know, and she knew that she couldn't trust anyone. Chrys was worried for his family's safety and for Willow's in turn. And now here she sat, being interrogated by one of the Great Lord's high generals under suspicion of aiding a criminal. There was a connection, but she couldn't figure it out.

A knock came at the door.

General Henna walked over to answer. There were whispers and confusing hand gestures as the man on the other side explained something to the high general. She turned around, closing the door again as she walked back to the table. "They found Chrys. He's dead."

Willow flinched.

"Tell me who Father Xalan really is and why they were going to the Fairenwild."

Willow stared, unable to process the words. "He's not dead."

Henna sighed. "Jurius caught up with him at the border. There was a fight. They captured the priest, but Chromawolves came out of the trees and started ripping men apart. We have ten men unaccounted for. Chrys, Iriel, and the baby were right next to those men."

"LIAR!" Willow screamed, slamming her fists down on the table.

"Sit down." Henna rubbed her eyes. "I'm not here to feed you lies. I just want to know why. Why did he kill the temple worker? Who is the priest? Where were they going? You've been a respected woman for many years, but you have to understand that your life is on the line for collusion. Malachus wants answers. He liked your son. Trusted him more than the rest of us. A betrayal like this is as deep as they come. So, whether you tell us the truth or not, the priest will. His questioning will be far less diplomatic."

Willow gathered herself. Fury bubbled wildly below the surface. If Chrys was truly dead, she would slit Jurius' throat herself. She didn't know how, but this was his fault. Father of All knows she had reason enough.

"Well?"

Willow clenched her jaw. "I have nothing to tell. Clearly if I had known what was going to happen, I would be with them right now. Chrys is too smart to leave such an obvious loose end. So, unless you're going to place me in a cell, I think we're done here."

Henna took a deep breath and stared at her for a moment. "We're not going to lock you in a cell, but you should know that all of the keep guards have been ordered to keep you within the walls. I'm sure you understand. A security precaution. There is a room prepared for you on the third floor. I believe you've been there before."

It was the same room she'd stayed in when she came to Alchea thirty years ago. It felt like another life. Just her and little Chrys walking into

Alchea. If it weren't for the fact that they were both threadweavers, they would have been living on the streets. Instead, a young Lady Eleandra had taken a liking to them, and offered to put them up in the keep to protect them in case her husband came looking.

By the time Willow reached the room on the third floor, her wrists had finally stopped hurting, and the rage in her blood had faded to a dull ire. She would never sleep tonight. The truth was that they couldn't really make her stay; she was a Sapphire threadweaver after all. But she hadn't done any threadweaving since she'd moved to Alchea. It was part of a renunciation of her former life. It had all been lies, of course. Threadweaving draws far too much attention and that was the last thing she wanted when she'd arrived in Alchea. Better to be a woman running away from an abusive marriage, in need of help to hide. Lady Eleandra had been all too eager to save the damsel in distress. In all her years in Alchea, she'd never let anyone get close enough to discover the truth.

What she needed now was to talk to the priest. Henna said they'd caught him, which meant he was down in the dungeons below the keep. Even if she wasn't allowed to leave, she was still a threadweaver with political influence. The dungeon guards might let her speak with him. On the other hand, it would make her look even more guilty if the high generals found out. She didn't care. If Chrys was dead, it didn't matter; if he was alive, she had to go to him. The priest was the only one with answers.

Later that night Willow made her way down to the kitchen, passing a few guards that eyed her warily. A friend from her time living at the keep was still the night chef. Most nights the woman would sit reading while everyone else slept, waiting for someone to order something. Willow embraced her and they talked for a few minutes. She then grabbed a loaf of bread and headed down the eastern staircase toward the dungeons. The elegance of the keep faded to a dreary ambience as she reached the entrance to the dungeon. A guard stood at attention on her side of the gate and placed a hand on his sword as she approached.

"No one is allowed past here, my lady. General's orders." He did his best to avoid eye contact with her as he spoke.

Willow continued her approach until she was right next to him, uncomfortably close. "Lady Eleandra asked me to bring the prisoner some food. But I'm also a threadweaver, which means that you can either believe me and let me in like a gentleman, which I highly recommend, or I can let myself in. The latter would surely tarnish people's opinions of us both."

His hand rested on the hilt of his blade, but a sense of understanding seemed to wash over him as he finally looked up into her blue eyes. "The Great Lord's wife, you say? I suppose her orders would take precedence over a general's. Be quick about it. And be careful. He's blindfolded, so he can't threadweave, but they say he's still dangerous."

"You are wise for your age." She walked forward as he unlocked the gate.

As soon as she was through, he locked it behind her. "Nothing personal, my lady."

Willow nodded. "No offense taken."

As she looked out into the dark dungeon, she couldn't help but smile. She was finally going to get some answers. What would she do if it was true? What if Chrys was dead? No, not possible. But who was the false priest, and why were they traveling near the Fairenwild? She had an unlikely suspicion, but she had to be careful in case she was wrong.

A dank musk filled the dungeon, filling her nose with the stench of sweat and worse. She grabbed a torch off the wall and used it for light as she traveled deeper. There must have been two dozen empty cells she passed before finding the priest bound, gagged, and blindfolded. Dry blood stained the rag in his mouth, and his shirtless chest was marked with bruises and pain. He looked dead. So still. So calm. She was worried she wouldn't be able to wake him.

"Hello," she whispered. "Hello!"

He didn't respond.

She tore off a piece from the loaf of bread and threw it at his face. He winced as it struck and started mumbling through his gag. It was working. She tossed in three more chunks of bread. One missed, but the other two struck him across his bruised face. Each time he grumbled louder until his head was up and he mumbled something through his gag. She looked around for something she could use, like a broom, to reach in and dislodge the bloody rag from his mouth, but there was nothing. The dungeon hallways were bare stone, flickering shadows, and torchlight.

"Can you hear me?"

He nodded.

"Good. Do you know Chrys Valerian?"

Nothing.

"I'm his mother, and I need to find him."

He started shouting through his gag and shaking wildly against the chains that bound him. If only she could understand him. After a few moments he settled down. His chest rose up and down with each painful breath.

When he finally calmed down, Willow spoke. "I'm going to ask you a series of questions. There is no one else here but me. Please, I need your help to find my son."

He nodded.

"Do you know where he is?"

Yes.

She smiled. "Is he alive?"

No answer.

"Was he alive when they caught you?"

Yes.

It was difficult; she needed to ask *why* questions. Why had they gone to the Fairenwild? Why had they killed the temple worker? Why had they left her behind? But he wouldn't be able to respond. How could she obtain useful information with a simple yes or no?

"Did Chrys kill the temple worker?"

No.

She nodded and smiled. It felt good to know that she had been right about his innocence. If he hadn't though, that meant...

"Did *you* kill the temple worker?"

Yes.

"Why were you at the Fairenwild?" Stones, she needed to ask something else. "Was the Fairenwild your destination?"

Yes.

"And you know there are chromawolves and other dangerous beasts inside?"

Yes.

"Is there something else in the forest?"

Hesitation. Yes.

"Were you headed to Felia on the other side?"

No.

It must be. The implications were troubling, but the possibility that she had been correct also invigorated her. How could she ask without asking? If she was right, then she knew exactly where they were headed. "There are four types of flowers in the Fairenwild. Yellow. Blue. Green. And white. Do you know them?"

Yes.

"Which of the four should I follow?"

She thought she saw a smile through his gag.

"Green?"

No.

"Blue?"

No.

"Yellow?"

A vigorous yes.

Her heart was racing. She had to be sure. He was still shaking his head excitedly when she finally asked him. "Are you from Zedalum?"

His body relaxed. *Yes.*

She wished she could run in and hug him, blood stains and all.

He lifted his head and smiled through the gag.

Memories of her old life flooded over her. The wind rushing through her hair as she ran along the wooden streets of Zedalum. Aqueducts. Threadpoles. The wonderstone. The Gale. The elders refusing to listen. Her husband refusing to believe. A young mother giving up everything for what she believed. That girl was gone. She'd taken her son and left, then she'd spent the last thirty years trying to forget, as if accepting its existence proved her fallibility. But here it was, bloody and broken, kneeling in front of her in a dark dungeon, beckoning her to return home. And she had no choice but to succumb.

"Thank you. I wish I could help you, but I have to go to him. I'll make sure your family knows you were brave. May the winds guide you and carry you gently home."

The priest dropped his head and Willow thought she saw tears running down his swollen cheeks. She considered trying to help him escape, but it was too dangerous. So, she turned and left. As soon as the guard opened the door, she sprinted up the stairs, around the corner and up several more staircases. As she slowed to catch her breath, her chest ached and her mind raced. She didn't care that it was the middle of the night, what better time to slip away. Her legs moved faster than they had in years, but it felt right.

As she rounded the stairs to the third floor, her path was blocked by a familiar face.

Lady Eleandra Orion-Endin.

Not now. Father of All, please not now.

"Willow?"

She didn't have time for this. When Jurius and Henna found out that she'd spoken to the prisoner, she knew what they would do. And now she had a place to be, even if it was many hours away. She had no time to talk to her old friend.

"Eleandra. As much as I would love to stay and chat, I'm afraid today has not been the best of days. I could really use some rest."

Eleandra kept her head held high as she looked at Willow who was only slightly her senior. "We've been friends for a long time, Willow. I know you better than anyone, and I feel like I hardly know you at all. You've always been a guarded woman. Chrys is the same, but he has always been honest. He never offers more than requested, but his motives are clear as quartz. What do you know about this business with the priest? There is something off about it."

Willow gave no response.

"I don't know what I expected, coming up here to speak with you. Even if you knew where Chrys was, you would never divulge it." Eleandra cocked her head and looked deep into Willow's eyes, reading her expression. "So, I was right. You do know where he is. Don't tell me. I don't want to know. I want you to bring him back. Malachus needs someone like him by his side. Henna and Jurius are bad influences, but Chrys sparked a paternal side of my husband that I cannot let go. Please, Willow, bring Chrys back."

Tears formed in Willow's eyes. She stepped forward and hugged Eleandra. "Thank you."

She truly was the Gem of Alchea.

Willow headed down a long, dark hallway until she arrived back in her room. She slipped out of her dress and into a pair of light gray pants and a long-cut blue jacket.

Purpose fueled her every movement. There was nothing to bring where she was going but stale memories and regret. She stepped over to the high window near her bed and opened it. A vicious night wind blew over her, tossing her black hair out behind her. She threw her hood up and stared out into the sky. The moon shone high overhead, illuminating the keep's fields.

The blue in her eyes, like a sleeping dragon, awoke in brilliant fury. Threadlight washed over her vision, overwhelming her like it had so many years ago. It took her breath away. Her feet swayed with the wind, and she grabbed the windowsill for support. Hundreds of threads of vivid, prismatic light pulsed around her, each competing for the attention of her aging mind. It felt so natural. So familiar, like friends reunited. She focused, relaxed, and let the many threads fade away, all but the thick corethread pulsing beneath her.

It felt amazing. It was invigorating, intoxicating. Her heart pounded harder than it had in years. The blood rushing through her veins warmed to a dull heat, but she could feel it flowing out from her chest to the edges of her hands and feet. She'd forgotten the feeling, the craving. She would be happy letting threadlight keep her warm for the rest of her life. And that terrified her. She almost shut it out, but she needed to do this.

For Chrys.

She leapt. Gravity grabbed hold of her corethread and pulled, sending her falling toward the field below her window, but she *pushed* back with the power running through her veins, altering the force pulling her down. But not enough. She hit the ground hard and rolled into a somersault as she landed.

There were no guards nearby; they would be staggered across the keep's wall. She found her way toward the northwest wall where she expected there to be less of a guard detail. In the distance, she saw two pairs of guards staggered, walking along the field below the wall. Maybe twenty years ago she could have fought her way through them, but her bones were frail now, and her anger kindled only for one man.

There was no good way to get to the wall without being seen, so she took her hood off and walked over, trying to do so in an unthreatening way.

One of the guards saw her. He stepped forward and yelled, "Hey! Who goes there?"

Acting a fool is the wisest way to fool the wise. Willow herself was in her late fifties, far older than the guards in front of her. She hunched over and gave her voice a scratch. "Oh boys, please help me. I've lost my cat! I saw her run this way. I swear it on the Lightfather, she did. She's an inside cat. Cute as can be. She'll die if I don't find her. Please, boys. Please help me find my precious little Luker!"

She was able to close the distance with the guards, now only a short walk from the outer wall. One of the guards spoke. "Ma'am, you can't be out here. The fields around the wall are off limits, especially at night time. If we see your cat, I promise we'll bring it back inside. What's your name? We can send for you if we find it."

"Her. Luker is a her, not an it. And she does so love playing with her yarn. You should see it, her cute little paws swatting the ball back and forth. I need to find her. Wait! Was that her?" She waddled closer to the wall, leaning over as if she were going to catch something. "Luker, is that you Luker?" When she was close enough, she released an explosion of energy into her corethread, sending her blasting up into the night sky. She landed on the top of the wall chest first. She'd be bruised in the morning, but it was good enough.

"Sound the alarm!" The guards pulled out their bows but were too late. Neither of them were threadweavers. There was nothing they could do.

She ran and jumped off the other side, feeling the familiar burn in her veins. Far off to the west somewhere was the Fairenwild. She threw her hood back over her head and walked. She had a long way to go if she was going to make it to Zedalum before sunrise.

18

A LOUD CRACK reverberated off the walls of the Great Lord's study. High General Jurius spat blood into his hand and wiped it across the thigh of his pants. He didn't deserve this kind of treatment. All that he'd done for Malachus over the years, and the only reward was a bloody lip.

The entire keep had awoken an hour earlier to the sound of belltower alarms, only to find that it was not some enemy threat entering their walls, but Willow Valerian escaping. Henna was questioning the guards to figure out what had happened. It was easy to forget that Willow was a Sapphire; she had always refused to use her abilities. Apparently, that was no longer true. On the bright side, it made Chrys look even more guilty.

"This is unacceptable. I am done with failure, Jurius. First Chrys, and now his mother? I gave you the benefit of the doubt the first time—Chrys is resourceful—but now I'm starting to believe that you may have lost your touch."

Jurius stood tall, his mouth still bleeding from the discipline. "Henna's the one who questioned Willow, not me. I was busy at the time not getting eaten by chromawolves."

Malachus rolled his eyes. "I admired you, you know. All those years ago when we first took down Great Lord Larimar. I thought to myself, 'That is a useful man.' Lately, it seems all you have are pretexts. And it is quite unbecoming."

"Respectfully, I have done more for you than any single person in this damn country. If it wasn't for me, you wouldn't have taken the throne and the wastelanders would be pouring down the passes."

Malachus fumed. "Without *you*? You think I couldn't have achieved all this without you? *You* are nothing without *me*, Jurius. Not the other way around. You are nothing but pride and pretexts. Don't forget your place."

Jurius was trying hard not to lose his temper, but the Great Lord was making it damned hard. Through clenched teeth, he feigned humility. "You're right, of course. I apologize for overstepping. We do still have the priest. He will tell us everything we need to know to find Chrys. No one stays tight-lipped forever."

"I hope you're right." Malachus sat back down in the large chair behind his desk. "We don't have time for pleasantry. Whatever it is they're planning, we can't give them more time to prepare. Go down, and don't leave until you have answers."

Jurius nodded. His tongue licked at the blood in his gums as he walked away. It was the middle of the damn night and Jurius had other orders. He should have rammed a knife into Malachus then and there, but Alabella had made him promise not to do anything rash. A chill ran down his spine thinking of her.

Their first meeting would be forever seared into his memory.

"Ah. My dear general, I have been very much looking forward to meeting you."

Jurius was bound to the ground, eyes covered with some kind of fabric. The woman's voice was smooth and warm, but sharp in its pronunciation. He thought he heard a pinch of the Kulaian islands in her accent. Despite not knowing where he was, he was painfully aware of how he'd gotten there. He'd been walking to his son's house when a group of men had jumped him in a dark alley. It happened so fast. They'd pounced on him and he'd fought back, snapping the neck of one of his assailants; that had earned him a nice pair of bruises on his chest later.

The woman removed his blindfold and looked deep into his eyes. A trick of the light made them look a sickly, pale-yellow color. "What do you want?" *he snapped.*

She smiled, cocking her head to the side as she studied him. "I've a feeling you haven't yet grasped the gravity of the situation." *Her eyes gestured to his hands.*

When he looked down his eyes grew wide. Where he expected to see rope, his hands were bound together by nothingness. He tried to pull his hands apart, but they wouldn't budge. He looked down to his waist and feet, finding both bound by some invisible force. But there was only one invisible force he knew of. He opened his eyes to threadlight.

A dozen strands of light bound him in impossible ways. A short, thin thread ran from one wrist to the other, with another linking that thread to the floor, somehow feeding it with gravitational energy. Half a dozen ran from his torso down into the ground like inverse supports. Two at his feet. Two at his knees. He looked back up to the woman, her full lips curling into a devious grin.

"Perhaps now you understand."

Jurius felt a drop in his gut but did his best to keep his resolve. She wanted him to feel helpless, but he wouldn't give it to her. "What do you want?"

The woman had jet-black hair, slicked back and running down her neck like a pitch waterfall. "The first thing you must understand is that I will never lie to you. As you can see, I have the power to create threads. In short, it means that at any moment I could crush you with the weight of the world. But, my dear General, that's not why I've brought you here. You see, you are not the only one here with us."

She gestured behind him. His son was chained and blindfolded against the far wall with guards on either side of him. After his wife had passed away, Jurius' son was the only thing he still loved in the world.

"Please, not him."

She smiled. "Cooperation is the key to abdication."

AT FIRST THERE wasn't much of a choice: obey or watch them drain his son's blood before they drained his own. He'd betrayed the Great Lord, his old friend, in the name of survival, but somewhere along the way—perhaps to justify it to himself—he'd begun to see the lack of appreciation, the coldness, and the outright disrespect that Malachus offered him. Disrespect deserves no loyalty.

He descended a flight of stairs and reached the dungeon gate, finding a guard with his hand on his hilt looking at him. The guard relaxed his hand but tightened his stance as he saluted Jurius. "High General."

"Your shift is over. Leave."

The guard furrowed his brow, confused. "But, General, my shift doesn't end for another hour. And if you go in, protocol is for me to lock the gate behind you."

"Damn the protocol! Who do you think created it? Give me the keys and get out."

The guard grabbed the chain around his neck, hands shaking, and handed it over to Jurius, keeping his eyes fixed to the floor. Jurius opened the gate and walked into the dungeon, blood on his lips, and fire in his eyes.

The table outside the false priest's cell held all of Jurius' tools. Torture was a dirty business—he loathed the process—but he'd seen its effectiveness. At the base was an empty bucket that he filled with water. He picked it up and walked over to the prisoner. With one hand he grabbed the back of the man's neck and, with the other, he poured the bucket of water over his head.

The prisoner inhaled a gasp of air, choking as water trickled in past his gag. It ran down his face, a sick intercourse of blood and water where one of Jurius' captains had taken a blade to split his nostril earlier.

Jurius threw down the empty water pitcher and released his grip on the man's neck. He stepped back toward the table and picked up a thin blade with dry blood speckled across the hilt. Up above the table, the word *fortune* had been carved and painted into the wall.

The prisoner looked pathetic. Blindfolded, bound at the ankles and wrists, drenched in water and blood, and deathly pale across his naked chest. But he'd fought bravely at the border of the Fairenwild and had not revealed any secrets when the captain had questioned him. Impressive, when you looked at the slice marks down his upper arms, the swollen clamp marks on his fingers, and the torn flesh of his nose. But time is the master negotiator. The most stubborn of men yield to her words.

Everyone breaks.

He stepped forward and pulled the gag out of the man's mouth. "Wake up."

The first step to breaking a man is breaking his hope. Jurius knew this well. He stood in front of the shivering prisoner. "No one is coming for you. That is a reality that you cannot change. Not Chrys. Not Willow. You are alone. Well, you do have me."

Jurius took his knife and traced it over the man's cheek. "I know you're a Zeda—the tattoos give it away. I need to know how to get to Zedalum, and I need to know why you were taking Chrys there."

"I will not betray them." His head bowed humbly.

"Yes, you will!" Jurius shouted. He calmed himself and spoke to the false priest in a way that he would understand. "No man can stand against the wind forever."

Jurius shoved his knife through the man's cheek, ripping through skin and tissue. The old man sobbed. His eyes squeezed shut as he tried hard not to move his head. Jurius spun it in a circle, grimacing as the sharp edge stretched raw flesh. The false priest's hands were bound; the blood, spit, and dripping water drooled down into his beard. Jurius took a deep breath. He was getting too old for this.

He wiped the blood off his knife on the man's other cheek. "Let me ask again. Why were you taking Chrys to Zedalum?"

The old man laughed, once, and then again, his cheek still running with his blood. "The breeze is pleasant down here."

Footsteps echoed from the distant stairwell, stopped, and then continued.

"The winds have only begun to stir, Father." Jurius' eyes grew colder. "Have you heard the metaphor of the sticks? Grab a stick at both ends, you bend it, and it breaks. Gather a bundle of sticks together, grab it at the ends, and you cannot break them. The problem is that sometimes there are stubborn sticks that refuse to break, even on their own. No matter how hard you twist and bend, they refuse to snap. I have an eye for identifying those sticks. When I find one, I don't waste my time on it. I grab another from the same tree and make the stubborn stick watch as I break its brother."

The footsteps grew louder as a guard came into view. A second hooded figure walked slowly beside him. He understood the false priest's resilience, respected it even, but Jurius had two masters that both wanted answers, and he had no time for games. He stepped forward and pulled off the priest's blindfold.

"Why don't you say hello to Dalia, priestess to the ever-absent Lightfather."

The guard lifted the hood off the figure revealing a terrified woman with long dark hair and skin pale as a pearl. Tears streaked her face, and garbled sounds sat masked behind a thick rag in her mouth. The man's eyes grew wide.

"To be honest, she doesn't deserve this—I take no joy in the process

—but I don't mind breaking a few dishes for a good meal. So, why don't you tell me why you were taking Chrys to the hidden Zeda city?"

The old man shook his head, face filled with resolve. "I'm sorry, sister. Some truths are greater than any one of us."

"How unfortunate."

Jurius drove his blade through the woman's stomach.

"No!" The false priest fought against the chains that held him, screaming at the top of his lungs.

Jurius stepped forward and met eyes with the prisoner. He then leaned in and whispered to him. "If you have a bundle of sticks, breaking them all at once is pure foolishness. One at a time is far more satisfying. It makes it easier to save the stubborn stick for last. Turns out, the temple is full of sticks."

The man said nothing.

The guard nodded to Jurius and walked out of the dungeon. After a few minutes, the woman finally stopped moving. Her lifeless eyes stared forward into the darkness. Tears stained the old man's cheeks.

Jurius shivered. He wished he could have made someone else do the torturing, but the answers he needed were for Alabella, not Malachus.

"If my information is accurate, then you know our next guest very well. Perhaps too well."

The guard returned with another hooded figure, moving more slowly than the first. He pulled the hood off to reveal a shriveled old man with a long beard. He looked malnourished and frail, but the lines of his face still held some semblance of grace.

"Impossible," he said as panic washed over his bloodied face. "Jasper?"

When Alabella had discovered that the church's Stone Council had begun to investigate the Bloodthieves, she'd ordered a false death for the old man. They'd kept Jasper alive for days now, collateral in case of some catastrophic failure in their plan. Today, Jurius was glad they hadn't killed him. Supposedly, the two priests had had a particularly intimate relationship.

The guard led Father Jasper over to Jurius, who placed him in the cell directly in front of the false priest. As he put the chains on him and cranked the gear to lift him up, Xalan begged him to stop.

"Please, don't."

"Oh, trust me. He will last much longer than the first. She was the appetizer, but Father Jasper here is the main course. I'll make sure—for old time's sake—that you savor every morsel."

Xalan slumped in his chains, bloody and defeated.

"I'm afraid you'll be needing to watch this next part." He turned to the guard. "Watch over him. If he turns away or closes his eyes, we'll clamp his head and pin his eyelids. Understood?"

The guard's eyes darted from Jurius to the prisoners. He nodded, but Jurius saw a hint of fear in his eyes. Not all men are made for dark places.

"Please, don't do this," Father Xalan begged.

"You had your chance to plead for mercy. We've moved on to a harsher reality." He brought his knife to Father Jasper's feeble arm and let the tip scrape against skin as he dragged it lightly from wrist to shoulder.

"Please, I beg you. Not him."

Jurius walked over to his table, and perused the instruments laid out across it. "Now typically, I would start with removing a finger, but I just can't help picturing a blind man with no arms." He lifted up a hacksaw and nodded.

Jurius walked over to Jasper and placed the saw on the crook of the old man's arm. "Shall we count? Three."

"No, please."

"Two."

"Stop it!"

"One."

"I'll tell you how to find it!"

Jurius paused. "So, the rumors are true. You and old Jasper here were closer than friends? I must say I didn't believe it at first. I suppose gender matters less to the blind. It's a pity really. He'd have made a fine-looking amputee. Now to start, tell me why you are protecting Chrys?"

Xalan leaned forward, his arms held up by the shackles that bound them. Tears dripped down into the hole in his cheek. "It's not about Chrys. It's his son."

"The child? What about the child?" Jurius leaned forward.

"It shouldn't be possible."

"What?"

The old liar shook his head. "They aren't born."

"Enough! Tell me what it is about the child!"

The prisoner, defeated and broken, looked from Jasper to Jurius. "The child has Amber eyes."

Jurius opened his mouth, then closed it. He stared down at Xalan. Was it possible? Could there be another like Alabella? Did he mean for Chrys' son to be a weapon for the Zeda people? "What else?"

"That is all. I performed the Rite of Revelation. When I saw the Amber eyes, I knew I had to take him somewhere safe."

"What are you not telling me?"

"Nothing! I was taking him to Zedalum to protect his son. I swear it on the Lightfather."

"On the Lightfather? Seems you've spent too long in another man's skin." Jurius walked over to Father Jasper, the hacksaw still swinging in his hand. "I actually believe you're telling the truth."

Jurius was tired, but at least he had what he needed. Both Malachus and Alabella would be pleased. He stepped back toward the table and traced his fingers on the wall where the word was carved. "You haven't asked why it says 'fortune' here. It's to remind you that the power is in your hands. With two strokes of a pen, any man can change *torture* into *fortune*."

The man's eyes were closed.

"We have a lot in common, believe it or not. We're both willing to sacrifice others to protect those we love." He turned to the guard who was frozen in the corner of the room. "Go get something to clean up this mess."

The guard wasted no time in retreating.

"Now all that's left is for you is to tell me how to get to Zedalum."

Jurius walked away from the dungeon annoyed at the stains on his hands but pleased that he'd learned all he needed to know. Malachus would neither understand nor appreciate the implications of an Amber-eyed child—Jurius would have to feed him some other lie—but more importantly, he needed to play his cards in proper order.

Both of his masters were waiting.

But the lady was much more dangerous.

19

Light afternoon clouds diffused the sunlight as it beat down high overhead. More and more, Jurius hated the sun. After such a long morning, the clouds seemed a more appropriate compliment. The general ruckus of the previous evening had settled and the grounds of Endin Keep had quieted, though the guards remained on high alert.

A large marble gazebo covered in budding flowers lay surrounded by a team of threadweaver guards as the Great Lord ate lunch with his friends. The structure was large and white with a myriad of pink and red flowers blooming across its surface. Beautifully trimmed greenery surrounded its borders, and inside there was a light oak table with an elegant white runner down its center. Flowers and a smorgasbord of food were laid out with care.

At the table sat a variety of people close to Malachus. The luncheon was a weekly scheduled occurrence, but the invitees changed for each event. Today, as always, to his left sat Lady Eleandra Orion-Endin. Her blonde hair curled and ran down across the neckline of a flowery white dress. She laughed with joy as her nephew, Fain, along with her brother and his wife, Kent and Brooke Orion, told a story about a pilliwick and a lonely widow.

On the other side of the Great Lord sat Henna followed by Jurius. It was a slight to his recent failures; he knew that. Next to him sat a beautiful, dark-skinned, black-haired woman. Some would call her nothing but the companion of a lonely man, but Alabella was much more dangerous.

There were eight other guests in attendance including the illustrious Tyberius and Mirimar Di'Fier, and a popular artist who went by the name Alexandrite. Jurius had never liked the woman. She was too prideful for the quality of her work.

Servants brought out platters of desserts. Sunlight reflected feverishly off the silver. Mirimar—a purveyor of privacies—turned to Eleandra, a mischievous smile on her lips. "Now that dessert is here, how about some conversation that is a little bit...tastier. Tell me, dear. What is this I hear about Willow Valerian being a fugitive?"

"Mirimar, come now."

She ignored her husband. "Was she involved in the death of the temple worker? I've so many questions but, quite honestly, I always found her to be a particularly curious woman. You know, some say that her and Chrys are scheming to take the throne. The scandal! Can you even imagine that woman in charge? A disaster, surely."

Eleandra sighed. "Nothing so dire, I assure you. She simply wanted to go out searching for her son, and my husband wanted her to remain in the keep."

"So, she did sneak away." Mirimar smirked. "The mother of the most wanted man in Alchea slips out from under your nose? You know, the people are quite distraught that General Chrys hasn't been found. He is the Apogee after all. We worry for our own safety. Surely you all are getting closer?"

She directed the last question to General Henna who nodded in response. "He's most likely lying face down in the Fairenwild."

Alexandrite, wearing a layered dress that shifted from red to green depending on the light, gave a slight puff of disregard. She spoke with an unnatural air. "That man is as hard as his name. I would not write him off so quickly."

They all looked to her, but Tyberius nodded his head as if he understood.

"Chrys. As in chrysoberyl? The way he spells it, I presumed he was named after the precious mineral. It is known for being quite difficult to break, you know. Of course, the name could very well be in reference to chrysocolla or chrysoprase, but I find those two minerals far less interesting. Alexandrite is a variety of chrysoberyl. I must admit the connection may give me a bit of a bias. Yet still, I make it a point never to trust a man who's as handsome as he is hard." She blushed as the insinuation dawned on her. "Unwavering that is."

Jurius scoffed. He looked down at his hands, bits of blood still crusted under his nails. "The boy is nothing. A murderous traitor and a mistake."

He knew he'd misspoken when Malachus shifted in his seat. No one insinuated the Great Lord's fallibility.

"That's not what I heard," Fain said. The boy paled as soon as he spoke.

"Oh? And what is that?" Henna asked.

Mirimar perked up. "Yes, do tell."

His father gestured for him to go on. "Down at the shopping district, I heard people saying he was the rebel leader, and that this whole time he was undercover, planning to bring down the entire Alchean government!"

"That's absurd," Jurius spat.

Malachus laughed out loud. "Rebels? It is nothing but a dozen angry farmers. The last thing Chrys wants is to lead a nation. Henna once said he had the ambition of a fish. It was hard enough to convince him to become a high general. No. There is another reason. It's not power."

"Hmm. A small taste of power *can* intoxicate the soul." Alabella's lips curled up at the ends.

Stones. The damned woman had promised she would stay quiet if he brought her with him. Introductions only. Play coy. Meet Malachus. It wasn't like he had much of a choice in the matter, she'd wanted to see the nobility of Alchea, and Jurius was one of the few invited to the table.

Malachus looked at her. They were the first words she'd spoken since Jurius' introduction. Her jet-black hair was slicked back behind her ears, falling across her collarbone, and brushing against small black feathers adorning her light summer dress. Jurius had introduced her as Lady Sia, an old friend from Felia. She wore lightshades over her eyes, quite popular among the Felian people, and convenient for hiding her secret.

"Is that so?" Malachus cocked his head to the side. "I suppose a Felian would know a little of intoxication."

Forced laughter broke out across the table, led by Tyberius, whose jowls tossed back and forth like a ship at sea.

Alabella looked back at Malachus, an uncomfortable look of hunger in her posture. "Intoxication, not so much. Power, now there is a taste my tongue has savored."

"But have you tasted these poached pears? The ginger and cinnamon with the red wine and mulberry. Stones. This is the most wonderful thing I've tasted in years!" Tyberius shoved another bite of dessert into his mouth. His wife looked at him cheerily and slapped his shoulder with a smile.

From the other side, Lady Eleandra glared at Alabella.

Malachus stared at her. "A story for another time, perhaps. Tell me, Lady Sia of Felia, as an outsider, what do you think of our country? What do you think of Alchea?"

She smiled, white teeth contrasting with her mahogany skin. "Felia is beautiful and diverse, white spires and ocean blues. But Alchea is a rarity. You can feel it in the air. Look around this table. Almost every one of you is a threadweaver. That may seem normal to you, but not to most of the world. I've traveled far, and never have I seen so many threadweavers in one place. So, what do I think of your country? I think it is lucky. Or blessed. Or both. It is certainly memorable. But if I had to boil it down to one single statement, I would say that Alchea is the future."

"Well said, my lady. To the future!" Malachus held up his goblet, looking at her with profound interest.

"To the future." They all pitched back their goblets and drank to the toast.

"To the pears!" Tyberius raised his glass again, drinking before anyone had the chance to ignore him.

Lighter conversation ensued, and Malachus continued to steal glances at Alabella. Damn her but she knew how to leave an impression.

Jurius eavesdropped as Lady Eleandra started up a conversation to distract Malachus. "Have you thought about what these rebels are saying? I know they are few, but I think they accurately express real concerns that the people have."

"Fanatics do not speak for the masses. We cannot let those who speak loudest do so for those who do not. Besides, what is it they want? They want me off the throne, but they would want the same for any other."

"They just want to know that you think of them, of their well-being. People yearn for acknowledgement, even if it is artificial. Surely there is something you can do to appease them."

Malachus rubbed his temple, closing his eyes as he thought. "Do you have a suggestion? You always end these conversations with a suggestion. So, let's have it."

"What about the Festival of Light?" She smiled. "What if we opened the keep to the commoners, invite everyone in. It would mean a lot to the people if they felt like you were letting them be a part of your life. It would make you more relatable and accessible. We wouldn't let them into the main tower, of course, but we could put a big event together at the central fountain. Just imagine how beautiful it would be to have the fountain surrounded by all those people."

He turned to her. Her light brown eyes stared back into his bichromatic gaze. He let out a sigh of defeat. "General Henna, work with Eleandra and see if you can make it work. Security will be a nightmare. I'm not going to risk my life for it, but I am open to the idea."

Eleandra leaned forward and kissed his cheek, whispering something into his ear. He smiled something devious, then stood up and patted himself down. "Thank you all for coming. As always, the pleasure is ours. Fain, keep practicing your threadweaving. Tyberius, leave some pears for the rest of us. And Lady Sia, it has been an immeasurable pleasure. Please tell us you'll be staying in our city a little while longer?"

"Oh, I do think so. I'm quite taken with your city, and I mean to return the favor."

He nodded and turned to the others. "Friends. Stay. Drink. May the Lightfather bless you all."

Alabella leaned into Jurius and smiled as she whispered in his ear. "To the future."

20

"You cannot recover if you do not try." Staunch-faced Elder Rowan hardly glanced up as Chrys stepped out of his room. She had a leather strap across her forehead and green eyes that pierced in the early morning light.

Chrys had not rested much. He'd found it hard to sleep with the sporadic pains across his face and a headache that seemed to rise with the sun. One eye was black, and his nose was a little more crooked than it had been, but he was a threadweaver. His body would recover quickly. What kept him up the most was knowing how he'd failed to protect his own family.

He feigned a smile for the old woman. "I'm well enough."

She shook her head. "I've known men like you. Stronger than most. Rugged. Handsome. Those tricks don't matter to an old woman like me. Sit your arse down and don't get out of that bed until you're better."

Chrys wasn't sure if he should be offended or grateful but, either way, he was too exhausted to fight. He slipped back into his room without responding and imagined the old woman smiling to herself in the hallway. The other elder had been much nicer; he hoped the rest were more like her.

A light breeze brushed against the walls outside, causing the occasional creak as he went back into his room. Iriel lay asleep in a rocking chair in the corner of the room. She'd been up feeding Aydin on and off throughout the night.

He walked over to a window and pushed back the wooden slats so he could look out over the city. It felt impossible, an entire city built atop the feytrees, and yet the ground was sturdy as stone. The branches of the feytrees were so thick and twisted together that they created an immovable foundation. From the forest floor you couldn't see the sky or the city overhead. The audacity to build such a monument was commendable.

He had so many questions. What was the genesis of the city? And the matriarchal government? The curious relationship with the chromawolves? The hair? Why did they all shave one side? He found his eyes wandering back to the basket of vegetables on the side table. Stones, where did they get their food?

The rocking chair groaned as Iriel stretched out atop it. She reached her hand over her shoulder and arched her back. Little Aydin was swaddled tightly and nestled up in the crease of her other arm. Her lips arched upward as she caught Chrys' eye.

"Good morning my winter rose."

She coughed into her hand and laughed. "Your winter rose? That's a new one. A little mushy for my taste, but not your worst."

Chrys smiled just the slightest as he walked over to her. "Something my mother used to call me whenever I came out the other end of something hard. She said any rose that could live through winter was something special. And stones, Iriel, if we haven't lived through winter these last few days, I don't know what we've done."

"When you explain it that way, I kind of like it." She smiled through a bit of pain. "I changed while you were sleeping. I'm still bleeding a lot from the birth. As much as I want to go explore, I need to relax. I'm worried my body won't heal properly if I don't. Frankly, I'm worried even if I do."

It was incredible how much she'd managed to do the day after giving birth. Sure, threadweavers healed faster than others, but no one healed that fast. The pair of them were a mess. Both so beaten and broken that they were hardly recognizable from the man and woman they'd been only days before. Yesterday, they were nobility. Today, they were nothing.

Chrys took a seat on the bed. "The elders offered to help with Aydin. I wasn't sure what to tell them, but it sounds like it might be a good idea. Give you more time to rest."

She looked down at their child, sleeping peacefully in her arms. "If they have silksap milk, a night nurse would help so I could get some uninterrupted sleep."

"I'll ask around, but we're in the middle of the Fairenwild. I'm not sure they have many food options."

"It is quite strange."

Chrys nodded, looking around the room. "It's even more strange to think that this is home now."

Iriel stared at him, silent for a moment before she spoke. "No, it's not."

"It's not as bad as it seems, and we're safe here."

"Not that bad? We're living in a forest like a bunch of savages."

"Come now, Iriel. There's nothing savage about these people."

Her voice rose. "Have you forgotten that I just had a child? I don't want to raise a baby in the forest!"

"You think *I* want to?" he asked. "Of course, I'd love to be back home! But the reality is that our child is different. We don't have the luxury of choice."

"There's always a choice," she replied.

"And where would you have us go?"

"A small town outside of Felia? A quiet island in Kulai where no one knows us? Anywhere else! I don't understand why you're acting like the Bloodthieves won. We got away. We can do whatever we want."

Chrys took a breath, kneading his temples in a vain attempt to rub away the headache. "And how would that work out for Aydin? You think in Felia or Kulai they'll treat an Amber-eyed kid any better than the people back home? At best, he'd be bullied his whole life."

"And you honestly think that it will be better here? Aydin will be different no matter where we live. We might as well live somewhere we're happy."

"We could be happy here."

"That's where you're wrong. Maybe you don't care because you don't have to take care of a baby but let me make this very clear: I will never call this place home."

She was infuriating. Unreasonable. Stubborn as stone. They were safe in Zedalum. Aydin would be accepted. She wasn't thinking through the consequences of leaving. He wanted to scream that she was being foolish. And, stones, his head was pounding. The pressure near his temples had been rising ever since he woke up. He wanted to take a pin, jam it in, and let it all out.

Mmmm. I can be quite convincing. Let me speak to her.

The pressure intensified with each word. He leaned forward, grabbing his head. *Leave me alone! Not now!*

"This is on you, Chrys. Figure it out, because I'm not staying here."

Mmmm. I can help.

"Are you even listening to me, Chrys?"

Mmmm.

"Get out!" Chrys yelled, his hands still clutching the sides of his head. His fingertips were white with pressure as he squeezed tight against his skull.

"Are you serious? I'm your wife, not a damn soldier you can send away because they displease you. You need to figure this out," Iriel exhaled in disbelief, anger flashing in her eyes. She opened her mouth to speak again but, when she looked at him, she knew something was wrong. "Chrys, what's happening right now? Are you okay?"

He was a dam on the verge of collapse, and the voice of the Apogee was the last tap. He broke. Tears poured like a river down his bruised face. It was too much. After everything they had been through, after everything they had lost, he couldn't deal with the Apogee anymore. He couldn't keep the secret to himself. He couldn't do it alone.

Chrys looked up, his eyes red with agony. "Iriel, something is wrong with me."

She placed Aydin on the bed and grabbed hold of Chrys as he cried onto her shoulder. "Talk to me, Chrys. What is wrong?"

He wanted to tell her—he'd wanted to tell her for years—but the fear of letting her see the darkest parts of his soul was too much.

"You'll think I'm crazy."

"Never."

He knew it wasn't true, but he wanted to believe it. He wanted to believe that if anyone could see past his problems and still accept him, broken as he may be, it was her. But the world is cruel, and people act rash when expectations misalign with reality. What if she didn't accept him? What if she thought he'd gone mad?

But, then again, what if she didn't?

"It started during the war. I don't know when, maybe after the first battle. A voice. I started to hear a voice." He let the words sink in, expecting a deluge of questions, but instead she sat quietly, listening. His voice shook as he continued. "It's the Apogee, Iriel. *I'm* not the Apogee.

There is something inside me, or someone, that begs me to hand over control. But when I do, it kills everything. I don't even remember the slaughters they say I committed in the war. The battles I'm said to have won are cloudy at best. By the time I understood what was happening, I'd killed some of our own men. I swore to never let him out again, but his voice is there. Every time I get angry, I hear him. 'Let me out. Let me out. I can help if you let me out.' I thought I could control it, but I've lost control of everything else in our life. I just don't know if I can do it anymore."

"Oh, Chrys."

He shouldn't have told her. It was foolish. If ever she needed him to be strong, it was now. He could see it coming. The pity. The shame. She would never look at him the same. Every piece of insecurity and fear that had built up over the past five years came rolling through him like a ghostly tremor. There was no turning back now that she knew the truth. Her husband was broken. Unstable. A clay pot turned dry, cracked to the core, fit to be cast out.

But her eyes, soft as silk, met his own. "You've fought this alone for all these years? I can't imagine how exhausting that must have been. You should have told me."

"I couldn't. I..." He trailed off.

They both sat, neither speaking. Chrys stared at the floor, feeling the weight of the silence as each moment passed. His chest was a boulder dragging him into the ground. Pressure continued to build up in his head. What did he expect? That she would be happy? That she would smile and tell him "It's okay"? It wasn't. He wasn't. None of it was okay.

"I had a neighbor when I was a child." Iriel finally broke the silence. She nodded her head as she recalled the memory. "His garden was beautiful, full of bright colors and exotic flowers. People from all over the city would come to see it, but they were careless. They stepped on his grass, picked the flowers, and muddied the walkways, so, he closed it off with a wall. But people still came. He added decorative stonework and ivy that bloomed in the springtime. It took all his time to care for the wall, but everyone admired him greatly for it. One winter, the people stopped hearing from him, and when my father went to his home to check on him, he saw the garden for the first time in years. It was dead. All of it. He walked on cracked stone, over thriving weeds and dead flowers. The neighbor had been neglecting the garden to care for the wall. My father walked into the house, and you know what he found? The man had taken his own life.

"Chrys, it doesn't matter how beautiful the wall is if the garden inside is dying. No one can live like that forever."

He struggled to breathe. She'd seen his withered garden and she accepted him, nonetheless. In that moment, his load lightened. The weight remained, but a weight held by two is easier to bear.

Her hand rubbed away his tears. "It's you and me, Chrys. You don't have to fight this alone."

21

Iriel lay asleep on the bed as Chrys snuck out of the room. She'd spent the last hour holding him as he'd let out five years of bottled-up emotion. The relief was tangible. Oddly enough, if none of this had happened—if they were still back in Alchea in their quiet home—he wasn't sure he would ever have told her. At least one good thing had come of it all.

As he peeked out of the room, he looked for any sign of the grouchy, elderly woman. She was gone, so he meandered down the hallway. He passed a young Zeda boy and couldn't help thinking of his friends back home. His mother. Luther and Emory. Laz and Reina. Even their crazy, old neighbor, Emmett. The thing that sickened him the most was knowing that Jurius was working for the Bloodthieves. Henna was smart but, if she couldn't piece it together, who knew what the Bloodthieves would do? And Malachus. The Lightfather only knew what the Great Lord would do when he discovered the betrayal.

Chrys looked down at the wooden floor as he walked, rubbing at his sore ribs. No give. A lodge on top of the trees and the floor felt more solid than an Alchean home. What about when a rainstorm struck? Winds must have done a number on the city.

He found his way to the lobby where a young girl sat alone. Both sides of her head were shaved and the top of her hair was pulled back into a ponytail. She was reading a book. Stones. They even had books. He thought about talking to the girl—children are often great at sharing things they shouldn't—but instead moved toward the doorway.

He imagined the sprawling treetop metropolis before the door even opened. The bright sun would be beating down over the wide-set buildings, and people would be bustling back and forth across busy wooden paths.

But the door opened before he reached for the handle.

Willow Valerian, tired and covered in dirt, nearly crashed into him as she entered.

He took a step back, bewilderment plastered across his face. "Mother?"

She was the last person he'd expected to see. The tightness in his chest loosened, and the flares of pain seemed to subside.

Her fatigue changed to joy as she threw her arms around her son. Tears ran down her cheeks. "Oh, Chrys." She squeezed him with maternal ferocity. "I knew you were alive." She spoke the words quietly, personally, as if she had been doubting their truth for some time.

Chrys held her close, then pulled back for a moment. "We're all okay, but how are you here?"

"I'm a stubborn woman. Is Iriel well? I can't imagine."

Chrys nodded. "Tired, but well."

"And Aydin?"

"Sleeping."

She exhaled. "There is so much to tell you, Chrys. But I really must speak with the elders. Come with me. I imagine many of your questions will be the same as theirs."

Willow turned and gestured to a Zeda man standing behind her. Chrys hadn't seen him, but assumed he was a guard similar to the one who had followed them to the lodge.

She led Chrys down the hall toward the elders' council room. They passed a side table that held a bowl of Felian oranges, the sweet scent filling the air. Finally, they reached the council room, and Willow knocked. Without waiting for someone on the other side, she pushed the door open.

Inside, Elder Rosemary sat conversing with Elder Rowan and, quite surprisingly, it was Elder Rosemary that donned the frown. As the door opened, they both turned and looked. After a moment of confusion, disbelief took over.

"Gale take me. It cannot be. You're alive!" Elder Rosemary smiled wider than a feytree.

Willow walked into the room. "I could say the same about you." She smiled and hugged the older woman with a love that Chrys couldn't understand. "Less surprised about you, Rowan. You've always been as stubborn as stone. The winds couldn't take you if they tried."

Elder Rowan smiled, something Chrys had not yet seen from the woman. "Second only to you, my old friend."

"I see you've met my son," Willow said, gesturing to him. "Chrysanthemum."

Elder Rosemary laughed, shook her head, and laughed again. "Of course, he is. He has your eyes. I should have known. The Father of All has a wicked sense of humor, hasn't he? I suppose the age lines up. And Chrysanthemum? A good Zeda name."

"Chrysanthemum?" he asked. Chrys' head was spinning. His mother was acting like she was from Zedalum, but was that even possible? They were from Felia.

Willow gestured to the chairs at the table. "Everyone, please sit. I imagine we could all use a little explanation.

"Chrys, I was born in Zedalum. I was raised here and fell in love here. You were born here."

Chrys' mind reeled. He was born here? He was a Zeda? All these years believing he'd been from Felia, escaping an abusive father. Was none of that true? He could feel each beat of his heart pounding against his bruised ribs.

"Two days after you were born, before we'd given you a name, I had a vision. It was me, but it wasn't me. I told myself to take you away. That a storm was coming and the Fairenwild wasn't safe. When I told your father that I was going to take you away, he didn't believe me. No one did. He said I was being foolish and irrational, and that the pregnancy and birth had confused my mind. He had guards watch my family's house to make sure I did not leave. I waited a few days for emotions to settle and, when the opportunity arose, I took you and we left. You are not from Felia. You have Zeda blood and a Zeda name. This place is your birthright."

Chrys closed his eyes. He tried to process her words, but his mind was so exhausted that he felt like a man trying to catch the sun. "Why would you lie to me about this?"

"I always meant to tell you, but by the time you were old enough to understand, it was a life so distant from us that it would have made no difference."

Chrys' eyes were cold, a myriad of emotions stewing in their depths. "It would have made a difference to me."

Willow took in a slow breath. "You have every right to be angry. If I could go back, maybe I would do things differently. But there is more. When you disappeared from the temple, I was taken to Endin Keep for questioning. They think you are planning to overthrow Malachus or some nonsense that Jurius has planted in their minds. That's when I heard that they'd captured the priest that you'd escaped with."

"He's alive?"

"As far as I know, yes."

Elder Rowan shook her head and smiled. "Pandan that old dog."

"Pandan?" Willow choked on the word.

"You didn't know?" Elder Rosemary brought a hand to her cheek.

"I spoke with him. Surely I would have recognized him."

"You spoke with him?" Elder Rosemary and Elder Rowan both said.

Willow stared down at the table as she spoke. "It was dark. His eyes were covered, and his mouth was gagged. He'd been tortured. He only spoke to me through gestures. If I'd known…"

A fire inside of Chrys ignited, embers of truth flickering deep in his soul. Was it possible? After all the time he'd spent with Pandan, could it be? He barely uttered the words. "Is he my father?"

Before Willow could answer, Elder Rowan blurted out, "Your father's dead, boy. Pandan's your uncle."

The room warped in Chrys' vision, spinning and growing in surges. It was hard to focus on any one thing. He looked to his mother, but her eyes were vacant. Chrysanthemum? Flower boy? Stones. He should have made the connection. Every Zeda he'd met had a name derived from nature. Laurel. Alder. Rosemary. Rowan. Willow. His mother was a Zeda. *He* was a Zeda. The man who'd saved him was his uncle. The man who'd sacrificed himself was his uncle. And he was being tortured by Jurius.

"My little brother," Willow whispered. Chrys could see the pain in her eyes. She'd spoken to her own brother and hadn't recognized him.

Chrys straightened his back. "We have to save him."

The others turned to him. Elder Rowan huffed out her disapproval.

"You grounders are far too hasty. It's dangerous, and Pandan knew what he was getting himself into."

"He sacrificed himself to save us! And he didn't even know who we were! We owe him our lives. We have to do something."

"Calm yourself, boy," Elder Rowan sneered. "He knew the dangers when he left. He's been in Alchea for nearly twenty-five years. You don't think he knew exactly who you were? He did what he had to do to protect his nephew and the child. Take the gift he's given you, and let him pass with honor."

He knew. Of course, he knew. The priests had records of everyone; it must have been simple for Pandan to figure it out. But why hadn't he contacted them? It didn't matter. He'd saved them. It was time to return the favor. "I refuse to rest while a member of my family is killed on my behalf."

Willow looked to Chrys and smiled, shaking her head. "You may have met your match, Rowan. Chrys, we'll figure something out, but you and I are the most wanted criminals in all of Alchea, and two of the most recognizable. Even with your current disguise," she gestured to his bruised face, "it's suicide."

Elder Rosemary nodded. "The priority is your son. We still haven't figured out what to do with him yet."

"Aydin?" Willow raised a brow. "What about Aydin? Did something happen to him in the Fairenwild?"

Elder Rowan and Elder Rosemary both looked to Chrys. They each dared the other to explain. With puckered lips, Elder Rowan nodded. "The child is an Amber threadweaver."

The moment lasted forever as the words sunk in. "I thought that was just a myth."

"We'd be better off if it was." Elder Rosemary rubbed her temple. "There are only two types of naturally occurring threadweavers, Sapphires and Emeralds. Our people know of two other types, Amber and Obsidian, but these are not naturally occurring. They are created, so far as our records say. But how, we do not know. The last known Amber threadweavers died centuries ago. No one has seen one until now."

"I have."

"Excuse me?" They all turned to Chrys.

"Aydin is not the first Amber threadweaver I've seen." The memory replayed in his mind, tentacles of light grasping up from the ground onto his legs, pulling him toward the earth. "The leader of the Bloodthieves is a woman with eyes like the sun. She was able to somehow create threads."

Elder Rowan frowned even more profoundly. "This is very troubling. Two Amber threadweavers in a generation." She turned to Willow. "If children are being born as Amber threadweavers now, Gale take us if children are born as Obsidians. It seems you may have been right about that storm after all, Willow."

Chrys needed more answers. There was something they weren't telling him. The texts they spoke of must have more information that could help him understand. "What else do you know about Amber and Obsidian threadweavers? What do your texts say? I want to know everything."

Elder Rosemary started to speak. "A long time ago—"

"Rosemary!" Elder Rowan looked furious.

"Silence, Rowan! If there has ever been a time to discuss this, it is now." She looked fierce. Elder Rosemary had such a kind face that it was easy to dismiss her. But in that very moment, Chrys saw the true power of the woman. "Our people are the descendants of the last recorded Amber threadweavers. They used their power to protect the world by creating what we call the coreseal. They were so worried that something would happen to the seal that they built this city—sequestered from the rest of the world—and spent the rest of their lives protecting it."

The look on Willow's face was indiscernible. "How have I never heard of this? What is the coreseal? And why don't we teach these things to our people?"

"Our ancestors were clear that great danger would befall the world if anything happened to the seal. Our people are its guardians, and the best way for us to keep it safe is to keep it secret. The elders keep the secret, as do some of our most trusted advisors, and we pass along that knowledge, so it is never lost.

"So, while we may not know everything, it is clear that the Father of All has brought your Amber grandson to the home of his heritage. This is no mere coincidence, and it gives me hope to know that we have divine providence on our side."

Chrys scoffed at her words. "Divine providence? That my wife may have permanent health issues because she had to run for her life the day after giving birth? That my ribs and nose are broken? That an innocent man was killed in the temple by my uncle who is almost certainly being tortured by a traitor? That my mother is a wanted criminal? You have a skewed view of reality if you think the situation we're in is *divine providence*."

Mmmm.

Chrys stopped himself. The last thing he needed now was the Apogee whispering in his ear. *I am in control.*

"Are you done?" Elder Rowan stared blankly, unimpressed.

Chrys was tired and frustrated and, as his blood cooled, he saw the rationality of it. "You're right, of course. I apologize for my temper."

Both Elder Rosemary and Elder Rowan raised their brows.

Rosemary turned to Willow. "Well that was unexpected. An apology? It seems you have raised him well. Courage is the core, but humility is the foundation."

Willow smiled. "Elder Sage used to say that."

"She did." Elder Rosemary tilted her head, smiling. "More importantly, we should discuss this business with Pandan. You said he is still alive? Tell us everything."

Together, Chrys and Willow explained it all. Chrys started with the discovery that Jurius had been working for the Amber threadweaver, then skipped to the birth. He related the happenings at the temple, of the escape and subsequent flight to the Fairenwild. While Chrys told them of Pandan's heroic stand against the oncoming horsemen, Willow teared up. Chrys' voice shook as he explained the vicious battle in the forest that ended with the arrival of the chromawolves. He told them how they would have eaten him and his family if not for Laurel. Willow took over from there and explained Pandan's imprisonment, her interrogation by High General Henna, and how she conned her way into talking with the prisoner. It was hard for her to talk about it, knowing now that she'd stood mere feet away from her estranged brother and could have done something to rescue him. Finally, Willow told of her escape from the keep and journey back to the Fairenwild.

"This Jurius," Elder Rowan grumbled, falling back into her chair. "He is not a good man?"

Chrys shook his head. "I thought he was, but he's working with the

Bloodthieves now. What I don't understand is why the Amber woman is working in the shadows. She has Jurius in her pocket, and he's one of the most influential men in Alchea, right hand to the Great Lord. She could kill Malachus and take the throne, and there's nothing anyone could do about it."

"What makes you think she could kill the Great Lord so easily? She couldn't kill you. Are you greater than he?" Past the façade of amiability, Chrys caught another glimpse of Elder Rosemary's cunning mind.

"Divine providence?" he said with a smirk.

The elders did not look amused.

Chrys knew he had to tell them the truth. If for no other reason so that they could help him find it. "I was only able to escape her because of a stranger's gift. An obsidian blade."

Elder Rosemary raised a brow. "An obsidian blade?"

"Yes. And as unbelievable as it may sound, the blade can sever threads."

The sound of wood creaking echoed from the hallway outside the door.

LAUREL'S HEART QUICKENED. She pulled away from the doorway, the floor creaking under foot. The whole conversation was unreal. And just when she thought it could not get any more unbelievable, she found out that the blade she'd picked up in the forest could "sever threads." What did that even mean? Part of her felt like she should get rid of it, as if its power would somehow contaminate her. But she wasn't that stupid.

She crouched down and peeked through the crack in the doorway. They were still sitting and talking. Footsteps came from down the hallway around the corner. She pulled back from the door and leaned against the wall like she belonged. An older woman smiled at her and nodded as she passed. Laurel recognized her from her time spent as messenger for Elder Rowan. As soon as she passed, Laurel shoved her ear up against the crack in the doorway to continue listening.

"That's not possible," said the muddled voice of Elder Rowan. "Physical objects do not interact with threadlight."

"This one can."

"You said you dropped it near the eastern edge of the Fairenwild? We need to send scouts down to the site to find the blade immediately. If you are telling the truth, it could be an invaluable tool in the oncoming storm. Let's pray that we find it before someone else."

"Agreed," said Rowan. The legs of her chair scraped against the wooden floor. "I'll go gather a group straightaway."

Laurel was just about to run down the hallway when Rowan's footsteps stopped, and she spoke again. "Chrys. Where, again, did you say you obtained this blade?"

"The doctor who helped my wife when she was sick. I wish I knew more. It happened so fast and my mind was occupied by other things. Trust me, I wish I could tell you more."

"Divine providence, indeed," Elder Rosemary muttered.

The slow, elderly footsteps started back up and Laurel raced down the hallway, slipping around the corner just in time to avoid the Elder's view. Her heart was pounding, but not from the effort. She was definitely *not* supposed to have heard any of that conversation. And to think, she'd almost knocked when she'd arrived.

Her whole life she had been told that the grounders were heathens and should be avoided. The reality was that the hermetic Zeda culture had nothing to do with the grounders and everything to do with some ancient oath to protect the coreseal. What even was that? The reason the elders didn't tell anyone was probably because they knew no one would believe it. How many hundreds of years had they spent isolated from the rest of the world protecting an old tradition?

Laurel found the veins in her arms glowing faintly. The pulsing threadlight was mesmerizing, like waves flowing back and forth in a bowl. The Zeda people needed to know the truth. They *deserved* to know the truth. Part of her wanted to run out and scream it for everyone to hear—so that they all knew the elders had been lying—but she needed proof. Maybe then they could finally open their world to the grounders.

She ran outside, the light breeze tossing her blonde hair. Every bone in her body wanted to take out the blade and figure out how to make it work. Her hand shook with the desire, but she fought it. First, she needed to get to a quiet place.

She used threadpoles to travel quickly to the entrance platform. She slipped down the stairs, winking at a young guard, and leapt off. She descended fast and landed hard against the wide surface of the wonderstone.

She ignored the enticements and jumped down onto the dirt, surrounded by dozens of roses. The brilliant white threadroses slowly closed their petals as Laurel stopped threadweaving.

Laurel headed toward the base of a nearby feytree. She pulled the black blade out of her pocket and held it up toward a group of photospores. The shaft shimmered in the pulsing light. As she opened herself to threadlight once again, her veins pulsed and the nearby white roses opened their petals once more.

She smiled and focused on the thread that ran from the center of the photospore bulb down to the earth. Slowly, delicately, she slid the obsidian blade through the thread. As soon as it passed through, the thread popped out of existence and the photospore shifted upward.

Gale take me.

She grabbed the reed and broke it in two. The bulb, still pulsing with luminescent light, floated up into the air. It rose higher and higher, up into the vaulted darkness of the canopy. She watched in awe until...

Pop. A thin thread of light reappeared, connecting the photospore to the ground. Gravity took hold once again and it fell back down to the forest floor.

Amazing.

She gathered a dozen photospore bulbs, pulling them from their reeds, and laid them in a small pile. Opening her eyes to threadlight, she focused on the corethread for each of the spores. One by one she let the knife slide through their thread, each time a silent *pop* as the thread burst out of existence. Grinning from ear to ear, she watched as each photospore rose up into the dark canopy. Floating balls of luminescence spread out above her like stars under a coniferous sky.

Then they fell. It felt surreal watching as each of the photospores descended to the ground. She looked at her own corethread, a brilliant strand of pulsing light beneath her, and had a wonderful idea. A terribly wonderful idea.

What would happen if she cut her own corethread?

With a newfound hunger, she brought the blade down and carefully brought it toward her corethread. Thoughts of flight took off in her mind before she'd even severed it. Without gravity to pull her down, she would be able to soar into the sky. A bird in flight, walking the winds.

As she pressed the blade up against her corethread, her hand shook wildly and the blade seemed to blur in the air. Her corethread fought back like a magnet resisting its match, refusing to let it pass through. She tried harder, but her hand continued to vibrate back and forth. The muscles in her arm strained against the force. Furious, she hacked into the open air over and over again trying to sever her corethread. It felt like she was trying to chop down a tree with a spoon.

She started to tear up. Not for any good reason, but she did.

Her eyes closed and her arms sprawled out to either side of her as she dropped to the ground. Another failure. One more opportunity dangling overhead as she leapt and failed to snatch it from the tree.

She took a deep breath and let the sweet nectar running through her veins feed her emptiness. With threadlight, she would never be alone.

22

ALVERAX HAD A GREAT IDEA.

He walked away from Jayla's house, numb inside and out, and yet, despite the pain, he felt thrill. The thrill of freedom. The thrill of power. The thrill of purpose. He'd not only been given a second chance, he'd been given something more. And he was going to use it to get a little payback.

The dank shed behind his grandfather's house was a perfect hideout. He could spend the night there and no one would know he was alive. Even with the door closed, moonlight broke through slits in the wooden doorway, lighting the inside. Because the city was only exposed to the sky at its southern and western borders, some areas of the city were pitched in shadow throughout the night; however, his grandfather's house was far enough south that the moon's glow bathed it in dim light. Massive fire-lit beacons spread throughout the city providing light and warmth throughout the night.

There was so much to learn about what he could do. His abilities seemed to be different than what he'd heard about threadweaving growing up. Threadweavers should only be able to *push* or *pull* on a thread, and that surge would affect whatever item was on the other end. It was balance. So why was he able to make the thread vanish altogether?

And why the hell was it called *threadweaving*? Push. Pull. Break. No one was actually *weaving* anything. But, then again, do strawberries look like straw? Does one really rest in the restroom? The world is full of poorly named things.

He sat down on an old pile of blankets and tried to open himself to threadlight. The world stayed dark. He flexed his whole body and squeezed with all the power he had inside himself. The world stayed dark. He cursed the Heralds under his breath. He'd done it once; it should be easy to do again.

He closed his eyes and thought about how he had felt just before it happened in Jayla's house. His mind's eye filled with bright light as if he were staring up into the sun and, as he opened them again, dozens of threads of pure light burst into his vision. There were fewer than there had been at Jayla's house, but even still the quantity was overwhelming. His mind raced trying to take in each thread.

He shut his eyes and willed away the threadlight. When he opened his eyes, the shed was dark again. It was unnerving when he realized that the pulsing threads did not actually illuminate the real world at all. It wasn't dark *again*; it had always been dark. The physical world and threadlight overlaid on top of each other. Seen by the same eyes but disconnected. It didn't matter that the threads represented connections between real objects with real mass, their glow stayed separate from the real world.

The only way this was going to work was if he didn't get overwhelmed every time. He closed his eyes and let threadlight flood his vision once more. If the threads weren't pulsating, maybe he could focus. With the subtle movement of hundreds of strands of magic throbbing all around him, it felt impossible.

He stared at the thread that connected him to a shovel in the corner of the shed. As his mind fixed on the shovel, all of the other threads that had been bombarding his vision faded away. Only the thread between him and the shovel remained.

That will be useful.

He squeezed his fist as he stared intently at the thread, as if to break it physically. Nothing happened. He squeezed harder. His body shook with the exertion. The thread vibrated for a moment and then returned to its previous state.

"Break!" he yelled before he could stop himself.

The thread did not comply.

He quieted himself. Making noise while hiding was...not ideal. As his mind calmed, he looked again at the thread and instinctively touched it with his mind. His veins turned black as threadlight pulsed through his body. The force he exerted on the thread burst it asunder, a small mist of light puffing out as it disappeared entirely.

His body felt warm while looking at threadlight, but his chest burned hot when he *broke* a thread. It was like drinking hot tea; the heat flowed to the ends of his fingertips. He experimented, *breaking* thread after thread of various tools and knick-knacks, finding it harder to *break* the threads of objects at a distance. Same with objects in shadows. His ability to see an object affected his ability to *break* it. That lined up with what he knew; if you cover a threadweaver's eyes they can't threadweave.

As he experimented, he found that threads had no breaking point. No specific amount of pressure that would cause it to *break*. Any amount of pressure broke it. Soft. Hard. The words felt strange in his mind, because the action wasn't physical. Either way it was true. If he focused, he could vary the pressure that he applied to the thread, and that dictated the length of time a thread disappeared. If he broke it gently, it was gone for a few moments, but if he let threadlight flare inside of him as he broke it, it might be gone for a few minutes.

He stopped filtering out the myriad threads and stood in awe at the beauty of it. Beautiful lines of light sprouted forth from him as if he were the sun itself. Below him, he saw the thick thread that bound him to the core of the world. It was how Sapphires could launch themselves into the air and how Emeralds could become immovable. For Alverax, it was what had made him float. The corethread was much thicker than the rest. Different somehow. Something about it drew him to it. Urging him to threadweave. He reached his hand inside, as if he could touch it, and swore that he could feel a warmth emanating from within.

When he pulled his hand out, he learned the final lesson.

Threadweaving too much made you sick.

After hours of *breaking* threads, he'd hit some kind of tipping point. He vomited every last bit of fluid from his body, and dry-heaved for another half hour after that. The motion tore open a bit of the scar on his chest, and he bled all over his shirt.

Exhaustion finally took him and he passed out in the corner of the shed, lying in a bed of blood and vomit.

When he awoke, his grandfather was standing over him, a shadowed vignette of relief and disappointment. The shed smelled horrid. Alverax couldn't imagine what his grandfather thought of him in that moment.

"This must be real." The old man loomed over him. "If I were imagining you were still alive, this is not how I would have pictured it. When I heard noises out back last night, I thought it was that pesky pilliwick again. Core-spawned creatures. Never expected to find my dead grandson covered in vomit. Well, let's get you cleaned up and we can talk after."

HE LIFTED Alverax and hauled him to the house and into the bathroom. The clothes were unsalvageable, so they were tossed out. His grandfather drew him a salty bath and left him with a few towels and some soap to scrape off the blood and debris.

Alverax had never understood how his grandfather, the most selfless man he'd ever known, had raised his father, the most selfish man ever to walk the desert. He saw himself somewhere in between. Alverax was decent, skewing toward good. At the very least, he was a better man than his father had been.

After his body was clean, Alverax left the bath and put on some new clothes. His room hadn't changed. Then again, he hadn't been dead for long. It would be weird if his grandfather had removed everything. He found some clean clothes and got dressed. If there was a way to avoid talking about what had happened, he was going to take it. The last thing he needed right now was to explain how he'd died and been resurrected as a new breed of threadweaver.

He left the bathroom and his grandfather was sitting cross-legged on a plush rug in the living room. An unavoidable location. *Well-played grandfather.* "Thanks for the help this morning. Didn't mean to scare you."

His grandfather looked deep into his eyes. "I know I'm old, and you think I couldn't possibly understand, but you *can* trust me. I won't make you—Heralds know I'm not one to force a man against his will—but you won't find a more willing ear than mine."

If he thought that meant Alverax was going to tell him everything, he was wrong. This was just the out he was looking for. "I'm just not ready to talk about it yet. I need a little time to process. Tomorrow. I'll tell you everything tomorrow." He glanced outside and noticed the sun was already starting to set. Heralds. He'd slept most of the day. If it wasn't tonight, he'd have to wait another week. "I'm going to take a walk, maybe a swim in the geysers. Tomorrow."

The old man nodded. "Be careful. I'd prefer not to mourn your death twice."

Alverax didn't wait for any more conversation. Back in his room he opened the hidden hole in the corner under his rug and pulled out a bag of shines. He'd need some money to initiate his plan. Tying it onto his waist, he grabbed some food and went outside into the darkening desert city.

As he walked through sandy roads, the sun passed down below the western horizon. The southern edge of the city was a miles-long steep cliff face overlooking the Altapecean Sea, called Mercy's Bluff. Because the cliff curved around the western edge, the sunset lasted until the light fell below the sea itself.

Towering stone buildings cast long shadows over the eastern half of the city where the Three Darlings were found. Owned by Jelium, the multi-part complex was home to the vilest citizens of Cynosure, and that was saying something. The three sections were called the Veil, the Nest, and the Pit. The most famous section was the Pit. During the day they raced camels and sandhogs, but at night they raced necrolytes. The stakes were high and the danger was undeniable.

That was his destination.

There were two paths to get to the racetrack. The first was a straight shot through well-lit roads where he was likely to be recognized. The other was through the Nest. He'd only gone there once; his friend had convinced him to go try a pinch of lytemare. It had given him hallucinations for two days and he'd vowed *never again*. The Nest was where people went to lay mindlessly in smoke-filled rooms with strangers and poor friends.

He took off down the second path with a hood pulled up over his face, darkening his already dark skin. His coarse black hair was cut short with a small strip down the center grown out longer than the rest. He'd inherited his father's infectious smile—perfect for a conman—but he hid it behind patchy facial hair.

After a time, he arrived at the entrance to the Nest. A pair of able-bodied giants stood guard at the archway. They stood staring down at Alverax and his average height. Part of him wanted to flaunt his new abilities to show them that he was more than what he seemed, but when they nodded him through without question, he changed his tune. What was he going to do? Make them float?

Inside the Nest was a huge stretch of sandy path flanked on both sides by stalls of various concoctions. Some were more popular during the day, general herbs and roots that were helpful for healing. At night, the lines shifted to the back. He could see at least four large lines farther down and a few smaller, with some stragglers vending at the "more savory" shops.

He kept his hood cinched tight and walked forward as he passed the first of the major lines. The next two lines were harder drugs: necrotol and lytemare. They were both harvested from live necrolytes and had major hallucinatory effects while providing certain levels of serenity. As hard as he tried not to remember his experience, passing the lytemare vendor made him shiver. He had no interest in the other three, but the last line, smaller than the others, was something he'd always wanted to try but never had the funds. It was also the most controversial.

Transfusers.

In Cynosure, threadweavers were not only rich because of what they could do. They were rich because of what they could provide. Blood. Threadweavers were paid richly for donated blood. If an achromat drank it, it allowed that person to have a taste of threadlight. As amazing as the feeling was supposed to be, Alverax was sure it was nothing compared to the real thing. He walked past a few eager, rich kids and remembered the tears streaming down his face the first time he'd seen threadlight.

"It's ridiculous how expensive it is," one said.

A well-dressed woman tending the stall replied to the young man. "While other solutions can make you imagine things, at the end of the day they are merely imaginings. Threadlight is real. Transfusers open your eyes to the *reality* that is all around you. Seeing it will change you. It will change how you see the world. A change of perspective is priceless, my boy."

Alverax scoffed as he pushed his way to the end of the Nest's long walkway. *I wonder how much they'd pay for my blood.* He felt like a god walking among children. No one here knew that he was a threadweaver.

No one knew the strange power coursing through his veins. Part of him wanted them to know, but he knew it was good to be underestimated.

He slipped out the other end of the Nest and walked through a wide corridor leading to the back side of the Pit. Thousands of people were packed into the outdoor stadium, chanting the names of their favorite racers and mumbling prayers under their breath for a lucrative win. Alverax pushed past a gang of Alirian men, and a circle of friends that must have smoked a tub of sailweed by the look on their faces.

There were three kinds of people in Cynosure. First were the *lifers*, those born and raised in the desert city. Their numbers were growing each year. Second were the *believers*. Somehow, they'd learned about the city—likely from the recruiters who were sent out across the continent—and they'd traveled far to join the anti-state. The last were the *defectors*. Exiled, or run out, or outcast, they didn't have anywhere else to go. Cynosure let everyone in but fewer back out. Looking at the Alirian gang, Alverax guessed they were of the latter.

"Hey, pretty boy." A sparsely dressed girl approached, her dark skin a perfect match to his own. "Looking for some company tonight?"

Alverax ignored her but bumped into a giantess of a woman as he walked. She looked down at him, her muscles rippling as she glared. His feeling of godhood shriveled faster than his manhood. He kept his head down and hoped she wasn't going to pummel him down. When he peeked up, she smiled...lasciviously.

That terrified him more.

He slinked away as fast as he could. It's good to know your strengths, and Alverax knew that strength was not one of his. He steered clear of the Masked Guard moving toward him, and edged closer to one of the money changers, a stick-thin man, pale as a full moon. He was collecting bets on the next race and yelling out the odds for each of the necrolytes and their jockeys. This was exactly what Alverax needed to know. He had a plan after all.

"Odds for the next race go as follows. White Thorn/Jani, 16 to 1." He provided the name of each of the six necrolytes, their rider, and the odds that they would win. They'd use these numbers to pay out winners after the race was over. "Sandstalker/Antonin, 16 to 1. Shadow's Eve/Feather, 12 to 1. Calibra/Brandonian, 8 to 1. Xanaphia/Althea, 6 to 1. And last, the crowd favorite, Spectacle/Sir Kenneth Wheeler, 2 to 1."

Alverax had heard of Ken, the pompous, bald-headed stump who changed his honorifics so frequently it was hard to keep up. What he hadn't expected was how much of a favorite the man was to win. There are some people born with such pomposity that an axe would chip trying to break them.

Heralds save me. He was even wearing Felian lightshades at night.

Alverax could see all of the racers below on the dirt track, saddling up on their creatures. The necrolytes were the least docile creatures in the desert—perhaps the world—which is what made the races so exciting. The hard plates that lined their giant, snake-like bodies worked perfectly as saddles. The riders used special gloves and grabbed tightly onto the ribbing of the black spikes on their backs. Their mouths were harnessed shut, and the ribbed tusks that wrapped down from ear to chin were partially blunted in an attempt to provide at least a small measure of safety. If a rider fell off, and wasn't impaled in the process, he would most likely asphyxiate while a necrolyte wrapped itself tightly around him.

Every rider who crossed the finish line became a legend. As far as prestige went, it didn't matter who won. As far as the vast pile of shines went, it was winner take all.

There was one important rule that gave hope to many a young man: no threadweavers. Anyone could ride, so long as they were a registered achromat. That had been Alverax's first idea, but he realized it was a terrible one. Riders had to be wickedly strong, and he...was not. He'd be dead in seconds. Plus, the last thing he needed was more people looking at him. If they noticed the black tint to his veins, or how truly dark his irises had become, he'd be strapped down to another table.

Alverax glanced around the Pit. It was built like a grand stadium but dug below the surface. Flat rings of sandstone descended gradually down the outsides, stairs leading from level to level, all the way to the bottom. In the center of the Pit was the track, a huge weaving maze of sandy pathways and hills decorated with the bones of failed racers. Or so they claimed. Smooth lines marked the path where the necrolytes moved, their weight compressing deep into the sand.

Screams rang out into the night air. Angry fans losing shines. Happy fans winning some. Drunken thugs in drunken fights. And every other baggy-eyed sinner shouting at their neighbor just to be heard. The commotion and overwhelming nature of it all reminded him, in a small way, of the first time he'd seen threadlight.

As the thought drifted away, he saw a throne perched down near the track surrounded by dozens of women. A small barricade was erected around the area setting it apart from the rest of the chaos. The throne overflowed with clothing, jewelry, and stomach.

Jelium. The unofficial Lord of Cynosure burst into a fit of hideous laughter, his jowls rocked like tidal waves beating against the shore. His wives lazed about him, contempt shadowed by riches, sisters bonded together by a cruelly dealt hand. Each of them was an immaculate beauty. Old, young, dark, light, but each thin as reeds—a sick juxtaposition to their husband. Gelatinous Jelium. His graying hair was slicked back and his teeth were slicked forward in an unfortunate overbite. Nothing about the man oozed supremacy...except his eyes.

Jelium was one of two and, though Cynosure had no true ruler, the two of them owned it all. Jelium Kirikai and Alabella Rune. Amber threadweavers. Even from the distance, Alverax could picture the pale yellow that radiated from Jelium's irises. There were countless rumors about their power. Some said that they could control others, make them do whatever they wanted.

Alverax had heard another theory, and he'd soon find out the truth.

"RIDERS READY!"

Alverax watched as a short man with a deep, booming voice called out for the race to begin. Each of the six riders leapt atop their caged necrolytes, settled into their saddles, and gripped tightly onto the ribbed spikes. Watching them mount the creatures gave Alverax anxiety, and an odd respect for them. They may be insane for doing it, but the fact that they didn't all die in the process was impressive.

He watched Sir Kenneth Wheeler leap onto his necrolyte, Spectacle. It reared its head back and forth against the steel bars on either side, but they held firm. Spectacle was the largest of the pseudo-domesticated necrolytes. Its tan scales, covered by charcoal plates all along its back, wrapped around to the length of a mid-size boat. Its head, flanked by huge downward cresting tusks, was topped with additional scales and spikes. Its mouth, mostly harnessed shut, contained six rows of sharp teeth, though only the upper two canines were venomous.

A horn blew, followed by a man yelling, "GATES READY!" Well-armored helpers scrambled toward the gates containing the necrolytes, fumbling over large mechanical bars. Each of them raised a hand to signal their ready state.

"THREE." The riders settled into their makeshift saddles and clutched savagely onto the spikes.

"TWO." The crowd counted along.

"ONE." Latches lifted from the gates.

"GO!"

All six necrolytes burst forward out of their cages and onto the sandy track. Riders dug spiked boot heels into the creatures to steer them—a horribly imprecise method. The beginning was a straight shot until the first curve. The monstrous reptiles slithered down the track with terrifying speed, predators unchained.

As they rounded the first curve, one of the riders ripped free of his saddle and soared out onto the track. He'd dug his heels in too hard and couldn't handle the torque of the turn. He scrambled about in danger of being trampled.

Alverax shook the distractions out of his mind. This was important. He relaxed himself and let threadlight bathe his vision. He focused his attention on Jelium's rider. In threadlight, Alverax could see dozens of threads coming off him in different directions, including the thick corethread below him, but he was looking for something different. There. Small tendrils of light latched themselves to Sir Kenneth Wheeler as he rounded the next bend, binding him to the saddle.

Ha!

He was right! The old crustacean *was* cheating. The rider could take sharper turns and bigger risks with less fear of falling, because Jelium was binding him to his mount. *Heralds, but it is clever.* And only a threadweaver, focused intently on the rider, would ever know. And even then, who in their right mind would say anything? Never slap a happy hog.

Did he fix every race? That might be too obvious. But maybe the pudgy sandhog didn't care. Alverax didn't see Jelium as the kind of man to feign innocence if it'd cost him a shine. No, he was the kind of man who would build a racetrack, make it perfectly acceptable for the owner to place bets on races, and wield the power to fix each one. And then do it with a smile on his fat face.

This also meant that he'd been correct. Jelium's ability was the compliment to his own. Alverax could break threads, and Jelium could make them. No wonder nobody could kill him. If he could bind a rider to a saddle, he could bind any attacker as well. Unfortunately, that seemed way more useful than his own ability.

An enormous bonfire lit the winding racetrack and the necrolytes as they continued along the switchbacks. They raced up over a large hill and one of the riders was almost bucked off, but he stayed attached by the knife in his boot. One necrolyte lashed out at another, nearly throwing both riders from the force of the impact. The crowd cheered for more.

The necrolytes rounded the final bend, five of the six still battling it out for the victory, with Sir Kenneth slightly leading the pack. Sandstalker, a necrolyte with a fiery red tint to its scales, lunged forward with its tusks. Spectacle slapped its long tail at the enemy's eyes and launched its rider from his seat, sending him flying toward Jelium's subdivision. If he kept going, he would crash right into him. Alverax smiled. Mid-flight, the rider's arc stopped, and he dropped straight down to the ground like he'd fallen from the sky, as if all horizontal momentum had been stripped away.

In threadlight, Alverax saw it for what it was. Dozens of threads of light, like hungry eels, reached up and latched onto the rider's body. As he hit the ground, he clutched his leg, screaming in pain, bone jutting out from his shin. Medics rushed toward him as the other riders finished the race.

Four out of the six had finished, a fairly standard outcome. Sir Kenneth Wheeler took the victory. Alverax watched as the money changers handed a bag of shines to Jelium.

Supposedly, when Jelium had first arrived in Cynosure, he was thin and handsome and happy. In an attempt to propagate his gift, he'd taken one hundred wives and had even more children. None of them had Amber eyes. Oddly enough, none of them were threadweavers at all. Over the years, he'd created an empire and lost his soul. Alverax had plenty of reasons to hate him, not the least of which was that he'd ordered Alverax's death for dating Jayla. As if he truly cared about daughter sixty-three.

Minutes passed and Alverax continued watching. Money changers took new bets. Drunkards swung heavy fists. Young fools smoked sailweed trying to impress their friends. And Jelium's Masked Guard patrolled the stadium. Alverax watched them carefully.

The Masked Guard were Jelium's elite. Each of them was a threadweaver. In fact, almost every single threadweaver in Cynosure was a Masked Guard. Alverax watched to see if there was a pattern to their patrolling, but it seemed random. Best to avoid them if possible. The last thing he needed was a Masked Guard questioning his black irises.

The horn blew once more. Alverax pulled his hood forward, obscured his face, and moved down closer to the track. He needed a good line of sight if this was going to work. Unfortunately, he had no idea which rider Jelium had bet on for this race.

A bellowing shout rang out as the announcer called out that the gates were ready, and then initiated the countdown. A rough group of dark-skinned Felians—who looked like they could be Alverax's cousins—stood next to him, each of them shouting out the countdown. He moved closer to them, trying to blend in.

The race began.

Six new riders burst forth out of the gates, necrolytes thrashing back and forth as they slithered down the sandy racetrack. He looked at the riders. Alverax opened his vision to threadlight and examined each of the riders before finding Jelium's threads. They surrounded a thick tree of a man who had taken an early lead. The spindly threads of pulsing light latched onto him, fastening him securely to his mount.

Alverax waited for the final switchback. As all six creatures rounded the turn, he ran his experiment. All he needed to know was if he could break a thread at this distance. He squeezed gently against the smallest thread and gasped as every single one of Jelium's threads burst apart in an explosion of threadlight. The sudden shift in gravity surprised the rider, and he was thrown off his necrolyte as they finished rounding the corner. Panicking, Alverax grabbed onto the man's corethread and squeezed right at the pinnacle of his ascent, hoping to save him from the same fall as the earlier rider. His corethread burst asunder and he started to float in the air, like a wayward bubble.

Heralds save me.

The necrolyte thrashed out at the other necrolytes around it, gauging a tusk deep into the body of its nearest neighbor. A beastly howl rang out from under its harnessed mouth and it reared back, tossing its rider off into the sand. The two necrolytes fought fiercely, dashing in and out of each other's striking distance. Their tusks tied together, and they came crashing to the ground. The tusks of the larger necrolyte rammed down through the plated scales of the other and its body went limp.

The crowd exploded in applause, but Alverax stood still as death.

What had happened? He was sure he'd only broken the one thread. Not the whole lot! He looked around, terrified that the Masked Guard would find him. Jelium was standing and yelling at people as he raised his hand and stilled the last, raging necrolytes. Two guards near him nodded and surveilled the stadium.

Gasps and curses surrounded him as fans watched the man floating in the air above the track. Alverax needed to get out. One of the Masked Guard moved in his direction. He turned and walked as fast as he could up the stairs toward the exit. It was a struggle to push past the gawking crowds. Rough men cursed him as he bumped his way through. After crashing into a fully tattooed Kulaian, apologizing, and melting away, he made it to the top of the stairway.

A masked guard stood staring at him. Alverax looked into the man's green eyes. The guard looked back. "What in the—"

Alverax shoved a thin girl into the guard and took off. He rushed through the overcrowded street, crashing into dozens of people, until a short, angry man grabbed his arm.

"Watch it, pal!" When the man saw Alverax's eyes, he cursed and let go, backing away. "I didn't mean nothing!"

Alverax looked over his shoulder, but the Masked Guard was nowhere to be seen. He ran, continuing toward the exit leading to the Nest. He could see the tunnel going in and out of view as he dodged around people.

Two masked guards dropped down from above, eyes burning blue in the bright moonlight. They were cutting off his path to the Nest. He turned in a full circle, looking for a way out. The crowd stared at him, curious why the Masked Guard was so interested.

"On your knees. Hands behind your back." They moved forward. "Jelium would like to speak with you."

His hands shook as they moved toward him. He couldn't go back to Jelium. There was no way he'd be as lucky a second time. He looked to the guards and *broke* their corethreads. His veins burned hot as fire. He needed water. He needed to jump off Mercy's Bluff and into the ocean to cool his skin. Instead, he watched as the guards both took their next step, launching themselves in a slow ascent up into the air with puzzled looks on their faces.

Just then, he was tackled from behind by a third guard. He didn't fight back; he was terrible at it. Instead, he simply complied.

The whole thing had been a terrible idea. Every time he had a chance to make something of his life, he ruined it. Maybe he was more his father's son than he wanted to admit.

He dropped to his knees and put his hands behind his back. The guard tied a thin rope around his hands and placed a blindfold over his eyes.

Tears built up in his eyes. He was so stupid. He'd been given a gift and the first thing he did with it was to cheat a king. He should have run. The desert was only so big. If he'd run north, he would have made it to Alchea eventually. He could have started a new life. Become something more than the thief's son. Instead, he was going to die...for the second time in a week.

The guard lifted Alverax's hands high behind his back as they pushed him forward. He tripped on a rock and they beat him for it. He could hear everyone whispering as he passed, mocking him under the dull roar of the crowd. He must look so pathetic. Some poor sod. A nobody.

After a few minutes of walking, they finally stopped. With his eyes blindfolded, he had to rely on his other senses. There was no breeze, so they were likely indoors. It was quiet, which meant they were far enough away from the Pit for the noise to fade. But the most intense sensation of all was the smell. He recognized it but couldn't quite figure out what it was. Horrid, surely, but there was something familiar about it.

A door opened, and heavy footsteps passed through. Dread washed over him. He had flashbacks to the week before, but this time he was actually guilty.

No one spoke. And even though Alverax knew he shouldn't, a small part of him started to hope.

"I don't surprise easily," a familiar tone said.

Oh, Heralds, why?

Jelium's voice was gravelly, as if he were gurgling a pinch of saltwater while he spoke. "Yet here I stand...quite so."

Alverax knew he shouldn't, but he did. "I'm surprised you can stand at all without help." He cringed, cursing his tongue, preparing for a brutal response, but it never came.

Jelium ignored the jibe. "You know, people with not only the will but the ability to survive can be quite useful. I think you could be useful to me but, knowing your lineage, I've a feeling you would be much more trouble than you were worth. We have much to discuss, and it would be more efficient if I didn't have to extract the answers from you manually. So, do behave, and we can have a pleasant rest of the evening."

Did Jelium already know? Maybe he had a suspicion but needed to confirm. And what would Jelium do if he found out that Alverax was a threadweaver now? Run experiments on him? He already had scars from the last one. That's when he realized what the smell was. It smelled like the pit of bones he'd awoken in. The smell was death.

He'd been so focused on what he could do now that he was a threadweaver that he hadn't thought to ask how. They did this to him. Whatever they'd done on that operating table, it was what had given him these abilities. How was that even possible? Could you *make* a threadweaver?

Jelium ripped off the blindfold. "Let's have a look, shall we?" Alverax kept his eyes on the ground in front of him. "Oh, don't be shy, little thief."

The insult cut deep. Jelium knew well who Alverax's father was. He'd executed the man. And he would always see Alverax as the thief's son. He looked up defiantly, black eyes meeting a pallid yellow. "I told you before, I am NOT a thief."

"Oh, you are." Jelium smiled, tilting his head as he stared at the black irises and thin black veins pulsing in Alverax's eyes. "But you are also much, much more now."

Jelium sat down in an oversized chair in the corner of the room, smiling to himself. The rest of the room was empty. A large door with no handle to the left of Jelium's chair. A slight breeze wafting down from the open roof. Flickering torchlight barely peeking over the high walls. Just the two of them.

"I suppose the right thing to do would be to hand you over to the lady," he said with a rhetorical tone. "But, then again, you would be a powerful tool to hold onto for myself. It would infuriate her if she ever found out. You are her proof. But plans change.

"The greatest irony of it is that my most worthless daughter has unintentionally delivered me a most priceless treasure."

Alverax lunged forward, a primal defensive rage burning in his soul. He shouldn't care for Jayla after what she'd done to him, but the deepest wound doesn't cause love to fade any faster. He had barely moved before

Jelium's veins lit up with Amber threadlight. A dozen tendrils of light crawled out of the earth, latching onto Alverax like vipers.

"I will break you personally. And I will enjoy every last moment of it. By the end, you will be mine, mind and body. Everyone breaks, little thief."

Everyone breaks. It made it sound like he wasn't already broken, but he was. He didn't deny that. Alverax was broken. Perhaps in time—much like threads—the broken parts of him would heal. But not if he was dead.

The thought gave him an idea. Threadlight burned inside of Alverax, his veins glowing with black effervescence, and he grasped onto the unnatural threads holding him down. He poured every ounce of hate, every scrap of pain, every fragment of his soul into the threads. They burst apart into millions of incandescent specks of threadlight. At the same time, his corethread exploded in a brilliant spray of light and the weight of the world lifted from him.

Jelium gasped in his chair, as if he could feel the breaking threads. He pounded on the door. "Open the damn door! Now!"

Alverax took a step forward, rising up just the slightest off the ground. Jelium had no power over him. As the door opened, Alverax smiled. "Goodbye, little beef."

He leapt off the ground, launching into the air with no gravity to stop him. A bird with no need of wings. The wind flowed over his body, cooling the burning in his veins. Slowly, but surely, he continued to rise. Then, looking down at the cityscape below him, he realized his mistake.

He had no way to land.

24

It was an odd feeling, weightlessness. Floating. Wafting in the wind. With how bad the situation stunk, Alverax was trying hard not to apply the obvious metaphor.

He'd drifted far away from the Pit but could still see the little room in the distance. He couldn't see Jelium down there, which surprised him considering the girth. A cloud passed high over the city's southern quarter. The view was captivating. He'd once climbed to Lover's Lookout with a "friend," but his current view from the sky made the other seem like a guest room in a palace.

The desert city sprawled out beneath him. To the northeast, he could see Jelium's palace with a complex of apartments for all of his children. He could see Alabella's more humble home beside it. The city center was a ghost town, filled with empty tents and quiet streets that would fill to the brim in the morning.

And, Heralds, the horizon. He'd grown so accustomed to the view looking out over the Altapecean Sea that he'd forgotten how magnificent it was. Mercy's Bluff at the southern edge of the city was an abrupt drop-off, a cliff that plunged hundreds of feet down into the sea. Down below was a collection of ships that floated in the ocean surf. Cynosure itself was miles wide and partially covered by a sandstone mountain arcing overhead like a half-completed ceiling. It's what caused darkness to constantly cover the northern quarter.

After the wind drag had stopped his initial horizontal momentum, he floated helplessly in the air, a light breeze carrying him along. He knew it would happen any moment. When he broke threads, it was temporary. But what if it wasn't this time? What if he was stuck up in the air forever? He'd already floated longer than he'd expected to. Either way, he was probably going to die. The thought was oddly reassuring. He'd already died once. What was one more time?

Then it happened. His corethread reappeared, popping back into existence, becoming brighter and thicker over the course of a few moments. The world pulled him, and he fell. Slow at first, but he knew it would accelerate until he was falling at terminal speed. An image of himself splattered over a sandy walkway flashed in his mind. He panicked. He did the only thing he *could* do. He grabbed onto his corethread. His veins filled with dark threadlight, and he *broke* it. It shattered apart into a thousand particles of threadlight and faded away.

He was still falling, but gravity no longer pulled. As he descended, he realized that the friction of the air itself was slowing him down. He'd felt a host of new feelings over the last day, but a freefall that slowed as he descended had to be the strangest. He was going to live! The Blightwoods *were* hard to kill after all.

"WOOO!" He screamed out into the open air, pumping his fists over his head. Unfortunately, it threw him off balance, and he began to rotate. Despite being alone, he was horribly embarrassed. Hours ago, he'd felt a god, and now, he was a floppy, floating sky fish.

As if on cue, his corethread reappeared. The sudden jerk of gravity pulled him down. He crashed into a tent in the city center, rolling head over heels until he was flat on his back in a large box that smelled like stale wolfberry. He picked himself up and hopped down out of the box. His first steps felt odd, like he'd stepped off a ship onto dry land. His mind matched his dizzy feet.

It was dark in the empty market. Feeling brilliant, he opened his mind to threadlight to better navigate the world, but quickly remembered that his own vision was tied to his ability to see threads. The world stayed dark, only a few dim threads appearing. As he let it fade, he had to place a hand on a large tent pole to keep himself from falling. Not all of the dizziness had come from flying. The veins running through his arms and neck were warm to the touch.

Not again.

He vomited.

A stranger passed by on the other side of the market and Alverax remembered that the Masked Guard would be looking for him. He needed to be discreet, and, Heralds, he needed to warn his grandfather. Then, he needed to get out of town. For good.

His feet guided him home, his mind and body still dealing with the overuse of threadweaving. His grandfather's house had candles lit inside, but it was too late for him to still be awake. Alverax's heart beat faster. What if they were already there? Would they hurt him? He was old. They wouldn't. Would they?

He ran forward and almost knocked the door off its hinges as he burst into the small house. His grandfather startled awake, sitting cross-legged on the floor in the living room, eyes filled with exhaustion and worry.

"You're safe," his grandfather said.

Alverax smiled something fierce. "Me? I was worried about you, old man."

"You've never been a good liar, Al. It was obvious you were going out to do something reckless, and I was worried you'd come back deader than you were last night."

"I'm fine," Alverax said, the nausea still a dull pecking in his stomach, "but I have to leave. For good this time."

His grandfather nodded, unsurprised by the revelation. "You do what you have to do, son. Your father used to go on trips. He always came back. Just promise me you won't be gone for too long."

Alverax's heart broke. He knew what his grandfather was implying, and the thought of his grandfather passing seemed so distant. He'd always been the rock Alverax came back to when things got rough. What would he do when the man actually was gone? But if Alverax left, what was the difference? Everyone in Cynosure may as well be dead. He wouldn't see them again either way.

"I...I'll try. Jelium is looking for me, and it won't be a happy ending if he finds me." He moved toward the hallway leading back to his room. "They'll come here. It would be safer for you to hide out for a while as well."

His grandfather laughed. "I'm too old to play games. Let 'em come. Us Blightwoods don't die easy. You take care of yourself. You're a better man than your father. Wherever you end up, act like it. You're the only good thing he ever did."

He disappeared into his room before the tears came. If anyone should get credit for any semblance of goodness Alverax had, it was his grandfather. He was just too humble to admit it.

Alverax packed a bag of clothes while he thought about his grandfather's words. It felt strange knowing that whatever he didn't pack, he would never see again. In general, he wasn't a sentimental person, but extreme times call for extreme feelings. He still wasn't sure how he was going to get out of Cynosure; they weren't keen on letting people freely leave. But he could fly now, sort of. He was sure he could figure out something.

He returned to the living room and gave his grandfather a hug before walking to the door.

The old man sat nodding his head and smiling. "I should have done it myself a long time ago. The world is so much more than the sludge of taractus turds in this core-rotten city. Go, and don't look back. Be better. I'll be just fine."

It wasn't the right time to laugh, but he let out the whisper of one. He was going to miss the old man. "Thanks for everything."

Alverax walked away from the small sandstone home he'd lived in his whole life, but he'd died this week, so it felt fitting. As he walked in darkness toward the northern exit, he thought about what he might do when he got out. Alchea felt like the obvious choice. It was the closest metropolitan city. There were smaller farming towns on the way, but if he was getting out of this place, he wanted to see more than farmland. In all honesty, he had no idea how far Alchea was from the desert, or even how far it was to get out of the desert. Was it true that there were wild necrolytes? And sandhogs? If they came at him, he could just float away. The thought put a smile on his face. He needed to invest in a really good pillow he could use for soft landings.

Being able to *glide*—he'd finally settled on the word for it—was going to be awfully convenient. As long as he didn't do it too much. The nausea was real.

As he approached the exit, he was surprised to find it populated with all manner of caravan equipment. The few wagons he'd seen the day before had grown to dozens of partially packed wagons. People moved around, coming and going and loading travel goods and food. Two women were trying their best to wrangle a taractus. Its green, prickly skin and slow-moving stoutness made it quite difficult to subdue. A cluster of the creatures were chained up near the exit with harnesses already attached, ready to haul the wagons.

The company was completely blocking the exit. He looked up and thought about trying to glide over them, but the ceiling in this section started to recede as it formed the tunnel leading out. The passage was tall, but not tall enough for a floating man to glide through undetected.

While he watched, he saw a woman who appeared to be in charge. She had a thin reed of sailweed in her mouth and hoop earrings dangling down the side of her head. Her hair was a long, warm brown pulled back in a tight ponytail. She wore a backless shirt with thin straps that wrapped around the sides of her neck. Short sleeves revealed tattoos flanking a leather strap around her upper arm. A thin, brown silk collar curled around her thin, brown collar bones.

Right about then he decided that he had a new plan.

He gathered his belongings and walked forward confidently, putting on an air of authority. He kept his head high while he passed two workers who looked at him curiously. He pursed his lips and ignored them as he approached the woman.

"Pardon, my lady. Are you not the one in charge here?" He tried speaking like one of the rich idiots in Jelium's household.

She nodded, looking him up and down, and cocked her head as she looked into his eyes. She opened her mouth to respond, but he beat her to it.

"Good. Good." One thing he noticed from the rich was that they spoke over each other constantly. "Alexander Grant, at your service. Lady Alabella has just asked me to bring a package to Alchea. It is very important I do so in a timely manner and without incident. You know how she is. Quite particular and unforgiving of failure. Now, I assume by the hullabaloo that you're leading this team up north. I'll be needing to tag along until we exit the desert. From there, I can continue the journey on my own. Any questions?"

It was audacious and presumptuous, two factors that made a great lie. But the girl didn't even respond; she simply stood still staring at him.

"Are you done?" She raised a brow and smiled something devious. "That was cute and, to be honest, you're cute too…for a dead man."

A shiver ran up his spine. Not good. Definitely not good. This was a terrible plan. He needed to get out. His eyes wandered toward the exit. Maybe if he ran, he could get past the guards on the other end. In an ideal world, Jelium wouldn't know about his departure but, in an ideal world, he wouldn't have been recognized by the first person he approached.

He flinched as she slapped his shoulder. "Relax, Al. Alvie? Ew. Axe? That's not bad. Name's Farah, daughter forty-four. Jayla and I are close. I've heard stories" —she winked— "including the one about how our father had you murdered."

He still had no idea how to respond, so he stood there with stiff hands down at his sides, fiddling precariously with the strings on his bag.

"Shyer than I'd imagined."

He puffed out a laugh and scratched the back of his head. "Guess I'm just not used to being called out so thoroughly."

"For what it's worth, it was well-executed. Pompous, presumptuous, and peckish. The three P's of the privileged." She offered him a puff of her sailweed but he declined. She shrugged and took another drag herself, letting the smoke out in one long breath. "Problem is that I recognized your face from Jayla's drawings. That and Alabella is in Alchea so there's no way she could have 'just asked'."

"Heralds save me," he whispered under his breath. "I'll take that sailweed now."

Her laugh caught him off guard. It was loud and obnoxious—ill-paired to the rest of her. She passed him the sailweed, and he took in a deep breath of it. He hadn't smoked in a while, but he handled it well.

"So, father must really hate you."

He looked at her and nodded as he handed the sailweed back. "More than stairs."

"How dare you!" she said with a look of impish shock on her face. "Don't you think he has enough on his plate as it is?"

Alverax snorted louder than he ever had in his life. The workers all stopped and looked at him while he composed himself. "You are a terrible daughter."

She winked. "We leave in an hour. One of our workers went home sick, so you can take his place. Any enemy of my father is a friend of mine." She stretched out a hand. "Welcome aboard, Sam."

She had a strong grip for a thin woman. "Sam?"

"All personnel leaving Cynosure are approved ahead of time, and Sam is the guy who got sick. Pretend to be him, and the guards won't look twice. I'll let the crew know."

"Sam it is!"

"Sam was a worker." She leaned down and grabbed a large bag and tossed it to him. It was much heavier than he'd expected. He stumbled as he caught it. "What? This can't be totally out of the malice of my heart. There's not much to load but food on this end, but we'll have some heavy lifting for you at the pickup. After that, if you want to disappear, or head to Alchea with the others, choice is yours. I'll tell the guards you died."

"Thank you," he said. He moved to put the bag away, but then stopped and turned back around. "Hey, forty-four."

She smiled. "Yeah, corpse?"

"Where do I put the bag?"

25

Long before the sun rose, the caravan was prepared and ready to embark on its journey northward. Each taractus was hooked up to a wagon with a metal harness wrapped around its neck and a driver who held long ropes for guiding its movement. The creatures moved as though they were walking through sludge, each step carefully placed on the sandy rocks. Somehow, they were still able to provide a smooth ride for those in the wagons.

Alverax was paired with a man who was either a mute or incredibly rude. Together, they rode in silence for hours, staring blankly into the desert through iron bars. He could appreciate the desert more now that he was clothed and sheltered, even if it felt like he was in a portable prison cell. Looking out over the sandy ocean reminded him of nights he'd spent staring out over the Altapecean Sea, legs dangling from Mercy's Bluff. That was where he'd had his first kiss.

Even though he knew he shouldn't, he missed Jayla. Could he blame her? She'd thought he was dead. *Ugh, but why Truffles?* Cored by a mushroom. More than likely, he'd taken advantage of the emotionally unbalanced depressive state that Alverax's death had caused. If Alverax should hate anyone, it was the traitorous toadstool. The human fungus. The philandering spore-bearer. Not Jayla. He'd come back for her someday.

The wagons began heating up and the Mute started mumbling under his breath. Even in the shady comforts of the wagons, there was no respite. Alverax was sure he was going to die of heat stroke. The constant, all-encompassing warmth felt like swimming in a sea of fire. He decided that he would have rather died from the Masked Guard.

Somehow, in spite of the audible groans, he survived the day. The sun set over the caravan as they made camp. There were only a dozen people in the group, each moving about silently as they settled down near a large fire. Now that the world had cooled off, Alverax decided that the journey wasn't so horrible after all. In fact, the temperature was nearly perfect.

Farah approached from the center of the caravan, her large hoop earrings gleaming in the light of the campfire. She brought him a bowl of the soup they'd made for supper. "How you holding up, corpse?"

"Only half dead," he said. "The heat nearly finished me off."

"You're lucky you have dark skin. Check out Kase over there."

An older woman with broad shoulders sat staring into the fire. The firelight made it look even worse, but Alverax could tell the woman's pale skin had turned bright red.

"Heralds. That can't be healthy."

Farah laughed. "I told her to wear a jacket, but she said it was too hot."

Just then, the Mute passed by. He was bald, but he wore a wide-brimmed hat to protect his skin from the heat.

"That guy always so talkative?" Alverax asked.

"The mechanic? Not sure I've ever heard him say more than a few words that weren't curses. Damn hard worker though. I'd take him over any two."

"I talked to him for five minutes earlier today before I realized he wasn't going to respond." Alverax took a step toward the fire. "For future reference, a warning would have been nice."

"And spoil the fun? Not a chance."

Some of Farah's movements were eerily reminiscent of Jayla. The way her lip curled when she was being sarcastic. The way her left eyebrow raised more than the right. Part of him wanted to run away, but being near her felt like home. Her carefree spirit helped him forget about everything that had happened.

"Okay, corpse. The game is called *crockpot*. Wait right there."

She jogged off and returned with a bowl and a bottle of whiskey the size of a small barrel, which she opened and emptied into the bowl. She placed a ladle inside and looked up at him. "I'm going to tell you something, and you have to decide if I'm lying. If you think I am, say 'crockpot.' If you're right, I'll drink a swig from the bowl, but if you're wrong, you will. Easy."

Alverax nodded. He'd played plenty of drinking games before, but never in a one-on-one scenario. "What if I want to drink the whisky every time?"

She leaned in close. "You might like me better with a few drinks in me."

Heralds save me.

"First one," she announced. "My mother is one of the original Hundred Brides."

Ugh. Why did it always come back to Jelium? The man was about sixty now, and he'd come to Cynosure about forty years before. He'd married the Hundred Brides all in the first year. Looking at Farah, she could only be a few years older than Alverax, so, maybe twenty-two? Timeline was feasible. Jelium did like them young.

"True."

"Wrong!" She smiled wide while handing him a ladle-full of whisky. "Of father's original one hundred brides, eighteen have passed away and been replaced."

"He probably ate 'em," Alverax mumbled.

"Ew. That is disgusting, but not totally impossible. My mother was actually the very first replacement. Lots of rumors about what happened to the eighteen, illness, murder, suicide, you name it. At this point I wouldn't put anything past him."

Alverax nodded. "No kidding."

"Alright, drink up." She waited for him to finish the ladle. "Second truth. I was offered a seat on the Council of Heralds."

"Ha!" he laughed. She was too young to be offered a seat on the council. They were all lifers well into their fifties, selected because of their influence. Of course, by the time Alabella had arrived—ten years after Jelium—the ruling authority of the council had been forcefully diminished. It felt like a trick question. Maybe she *had* been offered a seat, but as a scribe or assistant. "Can I clarify something?"

She raised a brow. "One question."

"Was this seat on the council itself?"

"Yes," she said with quick confidence.

He looked deep into her eyes, looking for the deception, but there was none. It seemed like such an obvious lie, but if it *had* happened it would make a great truth for the game. Her dark eyes stared right back. "Heralds save me, but I think you actually *were* offered a seat."

She burst out in laughter. "You are terrible at reading people. It's actually rather impressive how bad you are. That was supposed to be an easy one."

"That's the problem! It was *too* easy. Heralds, you're a good liar."

"I have one hundred and forty-seven siblings. What do you expect?"

He shook his head. "I can't even imagine."

She filled the ladle with whisky and handed it to Alverax. It tasted better the second time. He looked back to Farah and about choked on the last drop. The way she was looking at him. He knew that look. He'd seen it in Jayla's eyes a hundred times.

"Last one." She inched toward him, her eyes searing into his own. The heat of the bonfire was nothing compared to the burning inside him as she moved in. Her lips parted like ocean waves. "I've a taste for dark skin."

The urge to run exploded throughout his body. His heart beat fast as a flickering flame, each beat a powerful rhythm. Thud, thud. *Heralds save me.* Thud, thud. *Look at her.* Thud, thud. *Those lips.*

She moved in closer and closer until he could feel the warmth of her skin. She paused. He hesitated. His insides felt exactly the same as when he was threadweaving, like his veins were filled with the heat of the sun. He leaned forward and kissed her, his lips igniting with every powerful emotion he'd let build up inside. He was reborn for a second time.

Her hands squeezed tightly against his back, crawling up his spine, over his neck, and up into his hair. He knew it was a bad idea, but he didn't care. His own hands drifted over the curves of her ribs and along the sides of her abdomen, pulsing with each beat of her heart. He'd needed this. This raw release of careless passion. They pressed hard into each other, their shadows flickering against the caravan.

In the heat of the moment—when he certainly wasn't supposed to— Alverax thought. Was he becoming his father? Was he going to leave Cynosure, get a woman pregnant, and return home with a baby? What was he doing? *Shut up, brain.* He tried to let it go as his hands drifted lower and lower.

"Stones!" One of the other members of the caravan stumbled across them. "Sorry, sorry. Don't mind me. Just, uh, passing through. You, uh, just, uh, continue on, I guess..."

The man started to leave, but then paused and turned back to Farah. "While I, uh, have your attention. You wouldn't happen to know where the whiskey is? The others were looking for it." He scratched his head and coughed.

A mischievous grin crossed Farah's lips as she pulled away from Alverax. "I know where it is. I'll grab it and meet up with you all in a minute."

"Good, good." The man continued walking, clearing the lane between the two carts faster than a leafling running from its shadow.

Farah turned back to Alverax and smiled her devilish smile. "I know you're planning on disappearing, but at least stick around another day. I think I might have more work for you to do tomorrow."

Before Alverax had the chance to compose himself and respond, she'd already left with the whiskey. He slumped down onto the ground and laughed at himself. What had his life become? A series of insanity. Dead. Alive. Cheated on. Cheated. Chased and seduced. Somehow through it all, he'd ended up in the best possible scenario. He had a free ride out of Cynosure, and companionship.

After things settled down, Alverax thought about walking over to the rest of the group, but he was exhausted. Instead, he climbed up into his wagon and nearly died of fright when he found the Mute awake inside staring out the wagon window. The man said nothing. It took some time, and a bit of trust, but finally Alverax drifted to sleep beside the smallest sliver of hope.

THE NEXT MORNING, the entire camp awoke with the sun. Alverax learned that they were to reach their pickup location around midday to receive a shipment from another caravan that they would bring back to Cynosure. When he asked others what the shipment was, they told him that it was mostly expensive ingredients that were hard to gather in the desert.

With that, they set back out northward toward the border of the

Alchean city-state. Each taractus trudged forward unimpeded by the weight it pulled behind, and the workers lounged in the shade of the wagons while the air still remained cool. A few of the workers had drunk too much the night before and were moaning about the sun's reflection on the sand.

Alverax sat daydreaming about what he would do next.

One thought he had was to join up with the caravan team that they were meeting. If he worked for them, every so often he'd get to meet up with Farah. But if word got out that he was showing up at all of the pickups, Jelium would send the Masked Guard to kill him. There was no getting around it. This afternoon he'd have to say goodbye. He wanted to invite her to come with him but thought it might sound desperate.

As the morning wore on, Alverax could see the peaks of a mountain range to the east. They were less impressive in real life than they were in drawings—at least from that distance.

He trapped a small leafling he found on the side of the wagon and watched it try to escape. Its hard, rigid body left scratch marks against the wood. The leaf-shaped shell on its back looked brittle and gave Alverax the crude urge to grab hold of both ends and break it in half like a wafer. Instead, he let it go and opened himself to threadlight.

Alone in the wagon, he practiced *breaking* threads.

He drifted in and out of sleep, overheated and dehydrated, until the caravan came to a halt. He sat up, rubbed his eyes, and found himself alone. It felt nice not to have the Mute staring at him.

Muddled voices conversed outside as he stretched his arms. Farah had told him that he could trust the people in the drop-off caravan, but he wanted to stay hidden in the wagon just to be careful.

He peaked out the barred window and counted eight large wagons sprawled out over dry grassland. Some of Farah's men were unloading crates from one of the wagons, hauling them back over onto their own. Alverax thought he saw a hand reaching out from between the barred windows of the farthest wagon. Farah was in a small group talking to a woman with jet black hair slicked back behind her ears. The woman smiled and put a hand to Farah's cheek. She said something, and Farah turned and pointed toward the wagons.

Toward Alverax.

She was pointing at *his* wagon.

Heralds save me. He rushed to the back door and tried to push it open, but it was locked. The Mute stood outside the door holding a bag of tools, staring at him with the same emotionless gaze he'd had since they had left. The wooden box Alverax sat in *felt* like a cage, because it *was* a cage.

Farah had betrayed him.

His blood boiled. Threadlight seeped into his veins and they swirled with blackness. He looked for any threads he could *break* that might help, but there was nothing. He moved forward and kicked at the lock over and over again. There was no way out.

The group Farah had been talking to was walking toward his wagon. He scuttled toward the back, angry at himself for trusting her—she was Jelium's daughter after all. The worst part was that he was so close. He could see the Alchean grass. Freedom was right there.

They reached his door and the Mute unlocked it. Farah stood next to the black-haired woman as the door swung open and Alverax got his first good look at her. He knew that face. He knew those eyes.

Alabella Rune.

She looked younger than he knew she was. Her movements, her stance, her gaze, every piece of her emanated a self-assured understanding of her place in the world. And it was nowhere near his own.

"I remember you," she said, nodding. "Subject twenty-three. Jelium's petty grudge. I watched you die."

Alverax's mind flashed back to the moment he lay chained to the operating table. She was there. This was not the first time he had been near her, and the last time had not ended well.

"Imagine my surprise when young Farah here told me what she'd caught. Do me a favor, boy. Take off your shirt."

He was going to die. It was the story of his life. Every time he found any semblance of happiness or hope, it was ripped away, leaving him even lower than he had been to start.

Farah stared at him, trying hard to hide her guilt, but he knew it was there. He pulled his shirt up over his head, for the first time realizing that the scars on his chest had completely healed. The bruising had faded to reveal a web of black veins spread out across his chest.

Alabella's lips crept upward as she eyed the scars. "Are you what I think you are?"

Heralds. He'd forgotten his only advantage. He opened his eyes to threadlight, and *broke* his corethread, preparing to launch himself into the air—it was his only chance—but as soon as he *broke* it, a barrage of threads popped into existence and latched onto him, holding him fixed to the ground.

"I'll take that as a yes," she smiled. "Let's do ourselves a favor and assume that you cannot escape. Now, again."

Before the words had left her lips, a weight unlike anything he'd ever experienced flushed over him. Dozens of threads latched onto him, each one increasing the sum. They were the same threads that Jelium had used to fasten his riders to their necrolytes, but stronger. He grabbed onto one of the threads with his mind and squeezed. The whole collection burst in an explosion of threadlight. He gasped as the pressure lifted.

Alabella turned without speaking and talked with two of her companions. After a minute of quiet deliberation, she turned around. "No one, especially Jelium, can know we have the boy." She tossed a pair of shackles to Alverax. "You, my young friend, are going to help us change the world."

26

Laurel had nearly spent the night camped out under a feytree but, in the end, Cara had let her stay at the chromawolf nursery for the night with the promise that she would help with the next morning's chores—Laurel knew that Cara would let her stay regardless. The year after her parents had passed away, she had spent the better part of a month living at the nursery, and often helped with chores during her visits.

Breakfast was divine. Cara's husband, Mace, had pounded out a vegetable puree to eat with some bread and fruit. Like most Zeda men, Mace was an expert with herbs and spices, and the tastes hit Laurel's tongue like a summer rain. It was the perfect meal to prepare her for a morning of hard labor.

"Okay, Elle. Let's head out. Grab that leash and meet me outside." Cara brushed a few strands of wild auburn hair out of her eyes and back into the rest of her mane. Her naturally olive skin was pale from a life in the forest, and her thin-strapped shirt showed plenty of it.

Laurel grabbed the leash and ran outside. A small chromawolf ran up beside her as she was jogging to the other side of the clearing. It jumped from side to side as it ran, taunting her. She sped up into an all-out run. The wolf sped up to meet her speed, no longer playfully moving, but intensely focused on the race. They ran all the way to the far end of the clearing where a wheelbarrow and shovel lay.

A minute later Cara caught up with them. The energetic pup still danced around happily.

"Ah, I see you met Racer!"

Laurel was still catching her breath. She wouldn't have been able to keep up with the little chromawolf if not for the threadlight she'd used to *push* herself faster. "I'm pretty sure you just made that name up."

"After decades of raising these pups, it gets hard to think up new names. One of these days, people will start giving human names to animals. Mark my words. Either that or the names will start gettin' real specific." She paused and pointed over to another chromawolf, limping as it walked. "Names like Infected-Toe-Nail, or Droopy-Right-Eye. Or He-Who-Eats-His-Friend's-Turds."

Laurel choked as she burst out in laughter. "I like him. He's got spunk. You can tell he's smart."

"Definitely has spunk. Would've been a real killer if he grew up in the wild. Chromawolves with that much energy don't know what to do with it. End up huntin' all day." Cara leaned down and gave Racer a scratch on his back, then gestured back to the den. "Get back home, Racer."

The little wolf sped off obediently with his twin tails dragging along the dirt.

"Alright, let's get this over with."

The chores took less time than Laurel remembered. An odd part of her wished they'd taken longer. By the time they were done, the chromawolves were all fed and ready for an afternoon nap. She pushed the wheelbarrow out of the gate to dump the soiled dirt and looked back with a pinch of pride.

She ran over to the pond at the edge of the camp, dipped her hands, and washed off the dirt and fur. This was exactly what she needed. A distraction from everything. Physical labor had a way of masking a bleak reality.

Cara joined her at the pond. "You've been awfully quiet this morning, even for you. Want to talk about it?"

She didn't, but she did. Cara had helped her through the death of her parents, not because of her words, but because she knew when she needed to be silent. Laurel was the closest thing Cara had to a daughter, and Cara was high on the list of the people that Laurel most cared for.

"Have you ever learned something," Laurel said, "some truth that made you want to just get up and run away?"

Cara sat down on an overturned tree stump. "Oh, yes. The truth is often infuriating, but you should never run from it."

"But what if you found out someone had been lying to you your whole life? And you would have done everything differently if you had known the truth."

"Your whole life? That's a long life for a lie. I suppose my first question would be, why? Most people wouldn't put in that much energy to something they didn't think was important. The truth is that not all truths are safe to share. Maybe they were trying to protect you."

"I don't need protection."

"I know that better than anyone. I've seen you fight a full-grown chromawolf. It's not like you to run from something. Is that what you're doing here? Trying to avoid something, or someone? We all lie, Laurel. The world would be worse if we didn't, but it's also more brittle because we do. Intent may not remove the impact, but it's important, nonetheless. You have to try to give people the benefit of the doubt. Most of us mean well."

Cara was right, of course. Laurel knew she was being unreasonable, and that was the most frustrating part. She wanted to be angry at the elders for keeping their secrets. How could she trust them if they couldn't trust her? *Try to give them the benefit of the doubt.* It's possible to understand someone even if they're wrong.

They did seem spooked by the color of Aydin's eyes. An Amber threadweaver? What did that mean? If something bad was happening, they should want to warn their people rather than keeping them in the dark.

"I don't know," Laurel said, shaking her head.

The older woman stood back up. "It's also possible that they don't care about you."

"What?"

Cara's lips curled. "If I told you that I saw the future and Bay was going to fall to his death at the edge of the Fairenwild, what would you do?"

Her brother had a blood disease. Ever since he was a kid, he'd had spells of intense vertigo and dizziness, among other things. The doctors thought he wouldn't live past his twelfth birthday, but here he was at eighteen alive and well. "He knows it's dangerous for him. He always stays close to home."

"Humor me. If I saw the future and knew this was how he would die."

Laurel didn't like the idea of losing her brother. Especially since she'd already lost her parents, and her grandfather wasn't far from riding the winds. "I don't know. I'd forbid him from going near there."

"And what if he didn't listen?"

"I'd convince him."

"By lying?"

Laurel scoffed. "No, I'd tell him the truth."

"That a crazy old woman who lives with chromawolves told you he would die there?"

A dawn of understanding rose in Laurel's mind.

"If a lie would convince him to stay away from danger, does that justify it?" Cara leaned down and pet one of the little chromawolves that had approached.

If the elders truly believed that protecting the coreseal was important, then they would do everything in their power to keep it safe. Even if that meant living in the Fairenwild, isolated from the rest of the world, with an artificial contempt for other cultures to dissuade leaving. But it had been hundreds of years. If the coreseal wasn't real, or if it wasn't actually in danger, then the whole reasoning fell through. She needed to talk to Elder Rosemary. If any of the elders were going to tell her the truth, it was her.

"I've got to go," she said, picking herself up. "Thanks for letting me stay here last night."

Cara laughed. "You know you're always welcome here. One of these days you're going to have to unload all them worries you have boiling up inside you. I'll be here when you're ready."

"I know."

Laurel started running back toward Zedalum. She should have stayed outside the elder's door and listened to more of the conversation. There were so many questions to be answered. How was she going to convince Elder Rosemary to tell her more? She'd already told the grounders, maybe she'd be more open to sharing it now.

The grounders. They owed her for saving their lives. Maybe she could convince them to tell her what they'd learned. They weren't sworn to secrecy. That could work.

After summiting the entrance to Zedalum from the wonderstone, and *drifting* through the city, Laurel made her way back to the Elder's lodge. She knew that her brother and her grandfather would be worried about her because she hadn't returned home last night, but that was the least of her worries.

Her feet carried her into the large wooden building. A group of her old friends, young women she'd grown up with, sat inside the lobby in a circle talking. They stared at her as she walked past. It wasn't until that moment that she realized how she must look after a morning of doing chores at the nursery. But it didn't matter. They had all unfriended her when she'd become a messenger for Elder Rowan—mostly out of jealousy—but she wasn't jealous of their bland lives.

Laurel walked down the hall and knocked on the grounder's door. The older woman answered, but Laurel could see both Chrys and Iriel inside staring at their child. Laurel never understood why people stared at babies so much.

"Can I help you?" Chrys' mother asked. Her dark hair was in wild disarray, and the fatigue on her face seemed a fitting match.

Laurel looked past her, hoping that Chrys would look up. "I need to talk to him."

His mother opened the door the rest of the way. "Chrys, it appears you have a visitor."

Both parents looked up from the baby and saw Laurel standing in the doorway. It only took a moment for Chrys to light up at the sight of her. He rose to his feet and approached her. "The one that got away."

Chrys' mother stepped aside. "The one that got away?"

"It's a long story. I don't think you've met my mother, Willow. You two should chat sometime. I think you'd have a lot in common." Chrys stepped toward the doorway. "I would like to say that we're even, but I'm quite sure you did more for us than I did for you."

"Well, I did owe you," Laurel replied.

"You overpaid."

The way he said it made Laurel feel an odd kinship with him. He was older, and from a completely different world but, somehow, she felt like he understood her.

"Did you hear?" Chrys asked. "Pandan is alive and, apparently, he is my uncle."

Gale take me, I'm not supposed to know any of that. Laurel hesitated, then forced her eyes to enlarge as she feigned surprise. "No, I had not.

That's unbelievable. How is that even possible? You've never been here."

A snort burst out of Willow. "Apologies! It's refreshing to be around such a terrible liar. I've been around nobility far too frequently over the last thirty years."

"What?" Laurel's cheeks grew red as an apple.

"No need to lie about it. You obviously knew about Chrys and Pandan already. Unless, you weren't supposed to know." Willow gave her a sly wink.

Laurel stood in the doorway, feeling a fool.

"Give the girl a break, mother."

The rocking chair creaked as Iriel rose to her feet. Her clean, dark hair tickled the baby's cheek as they moved toward the doorway. "Hello, Laurel."

"Hello," Laurel said. "So, what's the plan? Chrys is a Zeda. Does that mean you're going to stick around here for good? Probably as good as any place for keeping a kid safe."

Iriel turned to the others. By the look they gave each other, it was clear that they had been discussing it, and those discussions had left an uncomfortable residue. "Chrys and Willow want to go rescue Pandan."

"We can't just let him rot in prison," Chrys said. "Who knows what Jurius is doing to him?"

Iriel scowled. "You're in no condition to go. Not to mention you're the most wanted man in Alchea, one of the most recognizable, and I don't want to be a widow with a newborn."

"I know Endin Keep better than anyone. We could be in and out without anyone noticing."

"That's assuming you could even make it into Endin Keep unseen. And even if you made it into the keep, you think a man in your condition is going to make it out lugging a man in his condition?" Iriel's voice grew louder as she spoke. "Willow agrees with me."

Willow nodded. "I agree that Chrys should not go, because I'm going alone. One is less conspicuous than two, and a woman even more so."

Chrys scowled at her, upset that everyone was against him. "You're not going back alone. That's absurd."

Willow kept her composure. "What's absurd is looking like you do and thinking you can infiltrate Endin Keep. No one will question a woman and, when I arrive, I can find someone to help me carry him out."

Without noticing, Laurel had begun to threadweave. Her veins came alive with a slow simmering energy. She wanted to go with her. She wanted to be knee deep in the action. She held her tongue because she knew that she had more important matters to figure out. Still, she could imagine herself, teamed up with a grounder, infiltrating their massive fortress, rescuing one of her own. It would be dangerous. It would be challenging. It would be an adventure.

Willow folded her arms, annoyed with her stubborn son. "Do you have a better idea?"

"If you had help, it could work, but that's asking a lot from someone. You'd need to be able to trust them completely." Chrys' eyes lit up. "Luther, Laz, and Reina would do anything for me, and I'd trust them more than anyone else."

"They're already used to taking orders from a Valerian," Iriel interjected.

Willow's arms fell to her side. "I've met them before, so they would recognize me, but why would they do it? Besides loyalty, there's no reason for them to risk their necks going against the Great Lord and Jurius."

"They're probably being watched as well, and whoever is tailing them would likely recognize you." Chrys thought to himself. "There's got to be a way to contact them without arousing suspicion."

He paused, then he looked to Laurel.

No, no, no. She was here to get answers, not to get roped into their rescue mission. But...it wouldn't hurt to hear him out.

"The one that got away." He cocked his head to the side, brows raised, taunting her. "They would both recognize you."

Laurel shook her head back and forth. "No way the elders would allow it."

"Gale take the elders," Willow cursed. "They're old bags of dirt. I knew each of them when they were younger, and there's nothing special about the lot of them."

Something about Willow insulting the elders felt good, as if Laurel's own truths had been suddenly validated.

Chrys took a step toward her. "When I found you in the basement of the Bloodthieves, I didn't see a hint of fear in you. There aren't many people in the world who react that way when they're in danger. Trust me, it's my job to find them. I'm that way too. That look in your eye right now, I know that look. So, go ahead and protest as much as you want, but you and I both know that there's nothing in this world you'd rather do than run toward adventure."

Laurel's veins were on fire. With each word he spoke, she felt seen. Chrys understood her, heart and soul, and he was right. As much as she wanted answers from the elders, the truth wasn't going anywhere. The coreseal could wait. They needed her, and she needed this.

"Gale take you all, but I'm in."

Willow perked up. "It's settled then. Laurel and I will head out first thing in the morning and we should make it to Alchea by nightfall."

Chrys and Iriel looked at each other, both understanding that Iriel had won but neither letting it show on their face. Chrys turned to Willow. "Luther will be home. Laz is usually at The Black Eye tavern. He loves their milk stout. If he's not there, you can ask around. I've never actually been to Laz's place. Reina may be at The Black Eye as well, if you're lucky. Otherwise, she's living with a guy off Beryl Boulevard near the orphanage. And you already know where Pandan is."

"Yes," Willow added. "Unless they've moved him."

Laurel already felt the rush of anticipation. She was going deep into grounder territory to rescue a spy. A huge smile crossed her lips. "So how do we get in?"

Willow smiled. "Ever heard of a skysail?"

27

Dark clouds passed overhead as the sun set on the treetop metropolis. It was early in the year for rain, but not uncommon to have spouts of cloud coverage and light mists of rainfall. Laurel had spent the evening in one of the guest rooms of the elder's lodge. After the arguments last time she'd been home, she still had no desire to return and try to smooth it over. They could come to her.

She awoke early to the sound of knocking at the door. Willow Valerian stood tall outside, clean again and brimming with nobility. Her dark hair seemed longer somehow now that it was clean. Laurel grabbed the bag she'd packed the night before and followed Willow away from the lodge. The sun was still rising far to the east, which gave off a blinding glare as they followed the wooden walkway.

A guard had been posted just outside of the city to make sure Chrys and his family didn't leave. Technically they were not Chrys and his family so, with a little convincing, the guard let them pass and told them he'd deal with the consequences.

Laurel had wanted them to *drift*, but Willow was against the unnecessary use of their power. She understood the reasoning, especially for an older threadweaver, but their pace felt sluggish and lifeless compared to her normal speed. She'd been using her threadweaving a lot over the past few months, and the world was starting to feel dull without it.

She was most grateful for the quiet. Nothing but the sound of the passing wind and the occasional bird's song as they followed the long wooden path to the edge of the Fairenwild. Laurel had been worried Willow would want to talk the whole way, but the older woman appeared to have her own thoughts to digest.

When they reached the edge of the Fairenwild, they dropped down to the surface, *pushing* on their corethreads to soften the landing. The Alchean countryside east of the Fairenwild flaunted varying shades of green as far as the eye could see. Far to the east, the Everstone Mountains peeked their crests over the distant horizon.

Laurel thought about what it would be like to live in Alchea. The sheer number of people made it hard to imagine. Living in a city where you knew less than one percent of the population? It would be overwhelming. In Zedalum, she was one connection away from everyone. If she didn't know someone personally, she knew someone who did. Something about the inherent anonymity excited her. She could be whoever she wanted. No one would judge her. No one would expect anything of her. She'd be free.

Willow broke the long silence without breaking pace. "Just so you know, after we've convinced the others to help, you are free to leave. The last thing we need is you getting stabbed by a stray blade."

Laurel wasn't sure how she should respond. Mothers were supposed to be soft and gentle, but Willow was hard. Maybe motherhood was different in the grounder city, or maybe she was just focused on rescuing Pandan. It made sense; he was Willow's brother. If it were Bay in that dungeon, Laurel would do anything to get him out, no matter the consequence.

After passing a stretch of farmland, they reached the outer rim of Alchea proper. Small homes littered the barren streets. They passed by an elderly couple happily chatting as they hung wet clothing out to dry. Ominous rainclouds threatened to sabotage the process.

Laurel had never considered settling down. The world was too vast, she was too young, and her dreams were too grand to be dammed by a boy. It didn't help that she had never had someone in that way but, even if she had, she wouldn't throw away her dreams for it. She had everything she needed: ambition and threadlight.

Empty streets filled as they entered the westside markets. Inns and taverns nestled up next to barbers and clothing shops, all bustling with residents and guests. Laurel found the variety of clothing among the grounders quite strange. Some dressed like her in beige and browns, but others wore bright colors, flamboyant headwear, or dresses that seemed insufficient for the cold weather.

Laurel and Willow traveled with their hoods up. They followed

Chrys' directions toward a small tavern. Willow posted up in an alley out back, and Laurel stepped inside.

The Black Eye was full of drunken men, and men who were well on their way. It was nicer inside than she'd expected, especially given the name, but, then again, she'd never been to a grounder tavern before.

She spotted them immediately. Laz's bright red hair stuck out like a bonfire in a field. The Alirian woman, Reina, sat on the far side of the table, straddling the line between drunkenness and sobriety. Three rough looking men and a pretty brunette barkeep sat at the table with them. One of the men, a scrawny man with a snarl to his lip, ranted about the whiskey having gone bad while the woman argued that it was impossible for whiskey to go bad. Laz sat back laughing as he sipped away at a mug.

She started making her way over when she overheard two drunkards at a table to her right, speaking as if they each were deaf.

"...swear it. I heard it from Gill who was posted in the temple when it happened. The General went into the altar room and slaughtered the recorder in cold blood! Then he snatched a priest and escaped out one of the back doors."

"I still can't believe someone would do something like that. Guess they called him the Apogee for a reason."

"Aye. And I heard from Jaysin that they got the priest, but the general got away. Can't 'spect they are going to make it far in there, 'specially with a baby in tow."

"Wait, he escaped from Gen'ral Furious with a baby in his arms?"

"You're an idiot. Ain't no one gonna start callin' Jurius General Furious. Ain't no one else dumb enough to risk their neck when he hears you say it!"

"Shut it. Let's see what happens if Gen'ral Furious comes after me! I ain't scared a' him."

"You should be if you know what's good for ya. Old or no, he's still a weaver."

Laurel snapped her head back away from the table. She needed to focus. The first step was to get Laz and Reina to meet up with Willow outside so she could explain the situation.

She approached the table confidently and nodded to them all. "Good evening."

One of the men at the far end of the table looked Laurel up and down. He was a scrawny gentleman with a smile far less charismatic than he believed. "Well, hello. Always room at the table for a precious gem like yourself."

"Calm yourself, Roy."

Before Reina could finish, Laurel had opened herself to threadlight, grabbed hold of the thread between herself and a half-full mug of ale, and *pushed* it. The cup catapulted itself across the table, colliding with Roy's chest and soaking him with lukewarm fermentation.

He stood up, appalled. "Stones, girl. What's your problem!? Are you insane!?" Dripping with ale and embarrassment, he grabbed his things and stormed off in a rage.

"Ha!" Laz's deep, guttural voice burst out in laughter. "I like this one! Come, come. Anyone that offends Roy is friend of me. I am Laz. Please, please. Take seat."

As they sat down Laz and Reina studied her. Laurel caught them both eyeing her pockets and inspecting her lower legs. When she realized that they were looking for weapons, it made her feel respected. They knew she was dangerous and awarded her the appropriate level of scrutiny. When Laz's eye returned to her leg for a second time, she wondered if maybe he was just...ew.

"Do I know you?" Reina cocked her head to the side, bringing her hand up to her cheek as she observed Laurel. "Not many threadweavers I don't know. You do look awfully familiar."

Laurel turned to the other two men and the barkeep. "Would you three excuse us? I've a rather personal matter to discuss with these two."

The two men stood up hesitantly, eyeing Laurel as they made their way toward the other side of the tavern. The barkeep scowled, rolling her eyes as she looked down at the mess made from the spilled ale under Roy's seat. She left without a word.

"Stones." Reina's eyes lit up as reality dawned on her. "Lightfather be damned. You're her."

Laz looked to Reina. "Who? She is who?"

"From the warehouse."

Laz whipped his head back toward Laurel and his eyes grew wide. He opened his mouth to speak but nothing came out. He pursed his lips and swore. "Stones."

Laurel took a seat and raised a finger to her mouth. "Never had a chance to thank you. Reina and Laz, right? Chrys sent me. Said we could trust you. His mother is outside. We need your help."

"Chrys' mother?" Laz asked. "Ha! Is great news!"

Reina slapped his arm. "The guards are still watching. Don't act suspicious. Where is Chrys?"

Laurel wasn't sure the red-headed man was sane. There was just something about him that she didn't trust. She continued to let threadlight swim through her veins, prepared for anything. The tavern had fewer than a dozen people inside spread out across the large room. Laurel watched each of them.

"Chrys is safe. Willow will tell you everything."

Laz eyed the guards. "Problem is guards. Follow us everywhere."

Reina nodded and looked at Laurel. "If you can distract the guards for a minute, Laz and I can sneak out and meet you out back. I think they've had a little to drink themselves. Shouldn't be hard."

Laurel looked at the guards, both taking occasional glances their way. "Just tell me what to do."

Reina laughed. "You're a pretty girl. And with blue eyes like that, just flirt a little. Those two will eat it up."

Flirt? Threadlight ran through Laurel's veins. Theoretically, she knew what she needed to do. Realistically? It couldn't be that hard. "I can do it."

No one moved. Reina and Laz sat staring at her with a twinkle in their eye.

"Wait." Laurel paused. "Now?"

They both nodded.

Laurel rose from the table and took a breath. As she took a step toward the guards, she was grateful that they were both rather plain looking. They were also both much older than her, probably mid-twenties.

As she approached, one of the guards looked her up and down and nudged the other. She smiled and took a seat on a stool next to them. She opened her mouth to speak and realized she had no idea what to say or what to do. She froze.

"Can I help you?" the first guard asked.

"A drink maybe?" asked the other, leaning forward.

Laurel panicked and raised up two fingers.

"Two drinks? Stones, girl. With a frame like that?" He laughed and raised a hand. "Hey, Barb. Two drinks for my friend."

The other extended his hand. "And what do I call you?"

"Laur—" She responded without thinking of using an alias. She switched mid-name and used the first alternative she could think of. "C—"

She stopped. Corian was a boy's name. They'd never believe that.

After an uncomfortable pause, the first guard looked at her and raised a brow. "Lork? Like a Fork?"

"With a waist like that, I'd say she fares better as a little spoon."

It took all of Laurel's willpower not to grab the nearest fork and stab them both. She'd distracted them long enough, right?

With the warmth of threadlight in her veins, she made a decision. Laurel stood up, grabbed her stool, and *pushed* it as hard as she could at the guards. It launched from her hands and crashed into both of their heads. They fell to the floor, and their drinks exploded into the air.

Laurel turned to the barmaid and smiled. "I'm...sorry about that."

Then she ran.

Once outside, Laurel rushed around the building into the alley. Laz and Reina were waiting for her, and she led them around the next corner.

"What was that loud noise before you came out?" Reina asked.

Laurel kept her eyes forward. "They spilled their drinks."

Around the next corner, Willow stood waiting for them. Her eyes lit up when she saw them. Laurel hadn't seen Willow smile since they'd left Zedalum, but Willow knew that if she wanted to rescue her brother, she'd need Reina and Laz on their side.

Willow embraced them both. "It is good to see you."

"We're just happy that Chrys is okay," Reina said. "We knew none of that nonsense about him rising up in rebellion was true."

"No. There's a lot we have to discuss," Willow agreed. "I'm just glad you recognized Laurel. We worried the guards would know who I was."

Laz gave a toothy grin. Laurel wasn't sure the man had ever stopped smiling since she'd arrived. "I knew Chrys would find her! He is resourceful man."

"Actually, I found him," Laurel countered. "Half-dead and about to be eaten by my chromawolf."

"Hold on a second," Reina said, cocking her head to the side. "*Your* chromawolf?"

"Not now," Willow said. "Chrys said you could help us."

"With what?" Reina asked.

Willow leaned forward and smiled. "We need to break into Endin Keep."

28

There was something comforting about incarceration. Over the last few weeks, Alverax had grown accustomed to the warmth of cold steel and cold shoulders. His optimism wasn't completely unfounded. If Alabella had wanted him dead, he'd be dead. In the end, it always came back to his grandfather's prophetic words, "Us Blightwoods don't die easy."

Before they'd locked him away in his windowless cage, two people had been pulled out of Alabella's carts. Even from a distance, Alverax could tell that both were threadweavers. Bulging, colorful veins lined their necks, arms, and chests. They were deathly thin, and their skin was an unnatural, pallid color. They were loaded into one of Farah's carts.

He overheard some of Alabella's crew talking about taking the pod of taractus and heading back to Cynosure just before a man's scream cried out at the desert's border. Alverax had no idea what was happening, and he was afraid that he might not want to. Finally, after some time, they left.

The journey north was uneventful. Alverax tried his best to eavesdrop, but the noise of the horse-drawn carts was enough to dampen their voices. The horses were disturbing creatures. He'd only seen them in paintings, but their mannerisms in person were much more unnerving. Every time he glanced at one, he was certain it gave him a judgmental eye in return. He'd prefer to be pulled by a dumber creature, like a taractus. Something that didn't stare back.

They covered his window and told him to stay quiet. He wasn't interested in disobeying. By the clanking sound of horseshoes and wheels on stone, he assumed that they had arrived in a city. He heard the occasional muffled voice as they wheeled down streets until finally the cart stopped.

A pair of men opened his door and let him out. They manhandled him through a large, thick door and into a sprawling warehouse crawling with people.

Alverax wasn't sure what he had expected, but this wasn't it. There had to be a hundred people in the warehouse lined up in rows washing, dyeing, hemming, and sewing a variety of clothing. The workers faced the northern wall on the other end of the building, and not one of them registered his entrance over the bustle of the job.

The men ushered him into a tight room in the corner where he found Alabella seated at a desk. She paid no mind as Alverax was led past her. The wall opened up into a hidden room with a staircase leading down into a dark, cavernous hole.

Heralds save me.

"Wait." Alabella looked up from her papers and squinted her eyes. "Come here. We should talk before you see what's down there. And take his shackles off. He's to be treated as one of us from now on. He's no slave."

The men released Alverax and gestured to a chair on the other side of her desk. He reached a hand behind him and rubbed his back as he got a better look at the room. Three crates lined the northwest wall. An open box full of used parchment paper. A thick, black rug compressed under his feet as he took his seat. Across from him, a full-sized mirror was fixed to the west wall. He looked at himself and was shocked by what he saw. For the first time, he saw his eyes, and a shiver ran up his spine.

Alabella touched the end of a pair of Felian lightshades, lining them up with an ink bottle next to them on her desk. "I want you to tell me everything."

Alverax rubbed at the stubble on his cheek. "Can you be a little more specific?"

She leaned forward, eyes bright with excitement. "How did it happen? What did it feel like? Does it still hurt? Heralds. You're the first person to survive a ventricular mineral graft in Heralds know how long. The ramifications are immeasurable. If it is reproducible—which I believe it is—it could change everything!"

Alverax leaned back in his chair. Her excitement was unnerving.

"I—" she stopped herself. "Have you been outside of Cynosure before?"

He shook his head. "Almost made it on a ship to Felia once, but they kicked me off when they found out who my father was."

"A father should leave his son more than a tainted name. Very few know that Alabella is not my given name. I changed it many years ago. Like yours, mine was tainted, and I found myself in need of something more...stately."

He'd never considered it before—Cynosure was small enough for it not to make a real difference—but changing his name was probably a good idea.

"Alverax, I need to apologize for everything that has happened to you. Starting with Jelium, you have been the recipient of so much undeserved suffering. I want you to know that from this moment onward, I will do everything in my power to protect you. You needn't fear Jelium anymore. You are an Obsidian threadweaver, Alverax. A singularity. Not one person in this world will be able to guide you. I've been where you are. It's not an easy place to be. You and I are the same."

Never in all his years at Cynosure would he ever have imagined comparing himself to Alabella, let alone her making the comparison. And she was right. An Obsidian threadweaver? He'd never even heard of such a thing. No one would be able to guide him, teach him, warn him. And that's exactly how it must have been for Alabella—and Jelium, but to hell with him. If anyone could understand what he was going through, it was her.

"But enough of that," she continued. "Tell me. When did you realize you had become an Obsidian threadweaver? Start from the beginning."

"Well," he thought. "I woke up in the boneyard with scars all over my chest."

She smiled. "Threadlight must have sustained you. How long were you dead?"

"I don't know. Less than a day."

"Incredible."

Remembering that day gave him phantom pains in his chest. He rubbed at his ribs, knowing full well that it wasn't real. "I didn't know that I had become a threadweaver until that night. I got angry at someone, and it just happened."

"What exactly happened?" She relished every detail, nodding along as he spoke.

"Threads of colorful light popped into existence all around me. I'd never felt anything like it. Like the entire world knew that I existed, and I was the center of it all. And the thick thread beneath me, it called to me. I reached out to it and it popped like a bubble. Then I started to float."

"Ha! Yes!" She slammed an excited fist down on the desktop. "You can break your corethread! Sarla is going to be furious. She was so certain it wasn't possible. Ah! This is thrilling. She'll want to study you thoroughly. Heralds, she'll probably want to marry you to keep you close."

Alverax twinged.

She laughed. "Don't worry. I'll keep away the chaff. And trust me, there will be many in your future. Queens will beg for you to take their hand. The first Obsidian threadweaver in centuries. Can you show me again?"

"Here?"

"Of course, you don't have to," she said. Her veins lit up, radiating a bright yellow as she opened herself to threadlight. "But what you can do is a beautiful thing. You should never be ashamed of it."

She was right. He shouldn't be ashamed. Afraid, maybe—it could easily put a target on his back—but not ashamed.

He let dark threadlight flood his veins and filtered out the noise. Below him, his corethread shone with a welcome intensity. He reached out with his mind. The thick thread burst, and the weight of the world faded away. He took a deep breath and tapped his toe to the ground. His body began to float upward.

The feeling was euphoric. Pure freedom. Not even the world could hold him. Despite a life of being constantly dragged down, he was weightless.

"Extraordinary," Alabella said, staring at him. "Absolutely extraordinary."

A short moment later his corethread reappeared. Gravity grabbed hold of him and pulled him back to the ground.

"So short," she said, disappointed.

"I can control the length of time it's gone."

"Of course. It only makes sense that yours would work similarly to ours. Sit, sit." Alabella grabbed a pen and wrote something down on a sheet of parchment paper to her right. "I could spend hours studying this with you—and maybe someday I will—but we should discuss some grim realities that may make you uncomfortable. I am not one to apologize for my actions, but some brighter futures require a darker present."

She stood and moved toward the hidden room behind her, waving for him to follow. They headed down a wooden staircase into a lamplit chamber. It was larger than Alverax would have expected, but not so large that he couldn't see the man tied up at the far end. He looked just like the two that Alverax had seen in the desert, starved, with skin the color of pale moonlight. Flickering flames fed the shadows dancing over his sunken eyes. Alverax shivered. A chill crawled up his spine.

Two large glass containers half-filled with wine lay next to strange equipment. *Heralds.* It wasn't wine. It didn't take long for Alverax to realize what was happening here. Much like the Nest in Cynosure, they were extracting threadweaver blood, but this was not a willing participant.

Alabella reached the bottom of the stairs after him. "Do you understand?"

He shook his head.

"If I were a brilliant engineer, perhaps we could have done things differently, though that too would have brought unwanted attention. We need local capital to fund our endeavors."

He turned around at the last line. "What endeavors?"

Alabella smiled at him. "If you had asked me this question yesterday, it would have been much less ambitious. But you, my sweet boy, enable so much more. I'm being presumptive, of course, on several accounts. Come with me and I'll explain."

There was something about the way she looked at him. It wasn't distaste, or cynicism. It was empathy. She understood him in a way that no one else could. He didn't know what to think. It was as if she were two separate people. The woman with unfaltering ambitions, willing to drain a man's blood for shines, and the woman who looked at him with motherly adoration. He wanted her to be the latter, but he couldn't discount the other.

She led him back up the stairs and through the office, out into the vaulted warehouse floor. The workers continued their duties at the rows of tables before them. Alabella guided him up a flight of stairs that led to a second story balcony where they could look down over the workers. He recognized the style of clothing being manufactured; Felian garments were popular in Cynosure as well.

Alabella leaned over the balcony and smiled. "Can you see it?"

He looked for whatever it was she was alluding to, but he saw nothing out of the ordinary. One of the workers leaned back and yawned, covering her mouth with a partially crippled hand. "They're tired."

She looked to Alverax and laughed. "As am I. But why are they tired?"

"I don't know. Probably because they're stuck doing an awful job."

"Exactly!" she shouted. "They're bored! And do you know why? Because the fount of madness is filled with monotony! This life...it's a collection of dreary moments one after the other in an endless cycle of fatigue, each day a proverbial tap on the forehead until at last you can't stand another touch, your mind breaks, and you become yet another mindless drone drifting along with no hope. It's miserable."

The truth of her words hit him like a rock. He'd felt the hopelessness before. The ebb and flow of time, some weeks more hopeful than others, but never quite able to cast off the cloud of despair looming overhead. The faster you ran from it, the faster the winds blew. Without respite.

"I was not always a threadweaver," her voice grew more solemn, "I was an accident, unlike you. A bout of fate changed me. When I discovered threadlight, the darkness that had taken root in my soul seemed to fade away. I felt real happiness for the first time."

Alverax knew the feeling. Every time he let threadlight pour through him, he felt it. It was as if threadlight rebuffed the darkness.

"That is what I want. I want to give away freely that which has been hoarded by chance. I want every person in this world to have the choice to be a threadweaver."

Heralds save me. She was insane...but was she? Here *he* stood. A week ago, he hadn't been a threadweaver, and now he was. What if it were possible? It *was* possible. If threadweaving were available to everyone, how would that impact the world?

"You're skeptical. I understand," she said. "I'll be the first to admit that the plan is overly ambitious. Sarla and I weren't even sure it was possible, nor did we have the means to make it a reality...until you. You were the missing piece. The key. You have the chance to change the world. To improve lives. We have the opportunity to give the world the gift of joy."

His mind was a blur. He might have tried to run if there weren't guards at the door, but he was glad that wasn't an option. This was important. This was a defining moment, for himself and for the world. This was where he could choose who to be. Not the thief's boy. No, he didn't want to take anymore. He wanted to give. What greater good could he give the world than the gift of threadlight? He wanted it to be true. He wanted to trust her, and as he looked into her Amber eyes, just for a moment, he did.

"What do you need me to do?"

29

Dark clouds gave way to a light rain, falling gently on the valleys below the Everstone Mountains. The wind roared over the peaks, and Laurel smiled. In Zedalum, high above the forest floor, the winds blew with such fury that the walls of homes would hum and shake beneath the storm. Tonight, she stood on a tall peak overlooking Endin Keep, and the winds were with her.

After the debacle at The Black Eye, they'd gone to Luther's home, sneaking past guards placed in the woods. He hadn't been hard to convince.

"*Two threads; one bond,*" he'd said.

Laurel, Willow, and Laz had hiked for several hours up the mountainside, keeping out of sight while they moved toward their destination. The clouds and rain helped obscure their travels, but it also soaked them to the core. Fortunately, a bit of threadlight in the veins was enough to keep Laurel warm.

Now all there was to do was wait. At some point, they'd see a blinking torch in one of the tower windows. According to Chrys, there was a window on the fifth floor that was always left unlocked in case of emergency. Reina would scale the tower exterior until she reached the window, open it, and signal for the others to come. When Willow had asked if Reina could handle it, the white-haired woman had smiled and said, "*They don't call me the Alirian Spider for nothing.*"

Luther was to scout the hallways and meet them at the dungeon. Every entrance to the keep had an added guard detail, and they checked every person going in and out. Luther would be watched, but he wouldn't be denied entrance.

Laurel felt like she could trust Reina and Luther, but something about the stupid grin on Laz's face worried her, especially with how key his role was.

Standing on the high peak in the rain, she watched Laz unpack what they called a skysail. It looked like nothing more than a sprawling piece of black fabric, but as he laid out thick rods down the length, it locked the material into a large triangle shape.

Supposedly, they were going to fly into the keep...

Laurel had her obvious doubts, but Reina seemed to be the least convinced that it would work, especially with the rain—but Reina wasn't the one using it. Willow said they needed the rain to cover their travel, and that it would discourage the guards posted on the eastern wall from looking up. Laz swore that the skysail would work in the rain. Something about Sapphires and their weight.

It did little to reassure Laurel.

A light breeze angled the wind to the south, each bead tapping against Laurel's cheek as she stared toward the tower. A small shadow crawled along the stone walls. The Alirian spider, indeed. The rain must have been oppressing as Reina scaled the stone tower.

Laurel closed her eyes for a moment and let more threadlight pour through her veins. The warmth comforted her. Even in the cold rain, atop a lonely mountain, it felt like home. When she opened her eyes, the rain seemed to blur together. The tower grew further and further away. A distant memory. A forgotten purpose replaced with the rush of threadlight.

Willow slapped Laurel's shoulder. "Cut that out. I don't think I've seen your veins free of threadlight since we met. Save some for later."

Laurel pulled her arm away. Now, of all times, Willow decided to scold her like an over-dramatic mother? She just didn't like being cold in the rain. It wasn't a big deal.

"Look," Laz said, pointing to the tower. A small light blinked in the distant window. Reina had made it to her destination. "Ready?"

Laurel stared forward and nodded, feeling Willow's judgmental eyes bearing down on her from her peripheral.

Laz wrapped his thick arms around the waist of both women and took a deep breath as his eyes darted around at the falling rain. "Is fine."

Before Laurel could process the comment, he took them running toward the edge of the cliff and leapt. Wind caught the wings of the skysail and they glided upward, beads of rain pelting the top of the fabric overhead. She looked down and saw a group of keep guards far below, each of them with hoods pulled up over their heads.

It was actually working.

Just then, a gust of wind launched them up into the air. The right wing dipped low, and she heard Laz curse under his breath. The skysail started to shake as the air pressure shifted. Laz's veins flared blue. He *pushed* against the dipping wing and leaned toward the other. As the wings evened out, he turned the skysail back toward the tower window.

"Are we okay, Laz?" Willow shouted through the wind and rain.

Laz turned and smiled a toothy grin. "Is fine!"

Slowly, the skysail glided down until it reached the open window. It was in that moment that Laurel realized that they had never planned for how the journey would end. The wings snapped off with a crack as they passed through the opening. Laz, Willow, and Laurel tumbled forward, limb crossing limb, hair lodging in unimaginable locations. As they settled, Laurel found herself face-to-face with Laz. He was still smiling that stupid smile of his. She rolled off him as fast as she could.

Reina had taken a seat and was staring at them. "A short ride and a poor ending. Laz always did know how to treat a woman."

Laz laughed as he rose to his feet. "Is better to end with bang, no?"

"Father of All," Willow groaned. "It worked well enough. Laz, get this room cleaned up. Reina, lead the way and make sure we don't run into anyone unexpected. Did you get the bread?"

Reina nodded and tossed her a loaf of bread wrapped in a leather lining.

Laurel and Willow removed their cloaks, handed them to Laz, and exited the room. It was warmer inside than Laurel expected. Oil lamps lined the corridor. In Zedalum, where the moss that grew on the feytrees was even more flammable than the photospores, every open flame was a danger. Here, in a forest of stone, there was no such risk.

Reina led them down a series of pathways, at times narrowly avoiding run-ins with staff or worse. She turned and gestured to them to hide. They ducked into a doorway as three guards rounded a corner, talking about some nobleman named Tyberius who had gotten punch drunk at dinner and made a fool of himself. As they passed the doorway, one of the guards turned to look at the two women. "What have we here?"

Laurel hissed at him. It wasn't a gentle hiss. It was guttural, savage even. The guard startled back, bumping into one of the others, and walked away ashamed as his comrades laughed at his behest. He looked back once for a very short glance that she ended with a predatory stare.

Willow raised a brow. "What are you?"

Threadlight and adrenaline coiled together in Laurel's veins, pulsing a deep blue hue. She wanted to sprint through the hallways, drifting as she *pushed* against her corethread. They'd make better time, surely, but they needed to be discrete.

"You're doing it again."

Laurel frowned. "What?"

"Let go of the threadlight. It's not healthy."

"I'm fine."

Willow scowled at her. "I haven't come this far to have it all thrown away because you wasted yourself on unnecessary threadweaving. You'll get your chance to use it later. Now is not the time."

Laurel surrendered, damming the flow of threadlight. As it faded away, her muscles tightened. Her breath grew heavier, like she was trying to fit an apple down a straw. It took all of her self-control not to let threadlight course back through her veins. She walked beside Willow and wondered if she could be subtle enough that the old woman wouldn't notice if she started threadweaving again. But her arms were uncovered, so even subtle threadweaving would be noticeable.

Reina motioned for them to follow. They followed several staircases down, moved through long hallways, and had no more close encounters with staff or guards. Finally, they came to a nondescript staircase leading down below the surface level.

Willow paused at the top of the stairs. "Reina, you stay here. If Luther doesn't show up soon, play his part. Otherwise, keep watch and make sure he's the only one coming down after us."

Laurel followed Willow down the stairs. They spiraled down, long shadows flickering from staggered sconces. What awaited them below was the biggest unknown. Willow had seen it before, but the guard detail had increased dramatically since her escape. The bottom of the staircase led to a short tunnel with a locked gate. Six guards stood at attention, drawing swords as the two women approached. Laurel hoped that Luther was a punctual man.

One of the guards stepped forward. "No one is allowed down here. Identify yourselves."

Willow pulled out a loaf of bread from the bag at her side. She curtsied and held it up for the guards to see. "My lord sent us down here to feed the prisoner, but we'd be happy if one of you wanted to do it instead."

"The prisoner already ate today."

They needed to stall.

Laurel had to think fast. "You're right, of course. Mum, we shouldn't lie. No one sent us down here. We just...we wanted to see the prisoner. My mum and I heard he had horns and red eyes. A demon priest, or some kind of corespawn. Is it true? Can we see him? Did he really kill a temple worker?"

The guard stared blankly for a few moments. "Get back upstairs. We don't have time for this nonsense. Take your lady-gossip elsewhere."

"Lady-gossip? How dare you," Willow shouted. She'd found her opening and proceeded to unleash her inner nobility. "We are esteemed ladies of this state, and I demand that we be treated with the respect we deserve."

The head guard shifted in his boots. "Apologies, my lady, but the fact remains. You cannot be down here. The prisoner is dangerous."

One of the others elbowed his friend. "Not after how Jurius left him."

Laurel didn't like the sound of that, and she couldn't imagine how it made Willow feel. The woman kept her air of dignity as she stood facing them, but Laurel saw Willow's eye twitch just the slightest.

Footsteps echoed up the pathway behind them. Willow and Laurel turned and walked backward toward the guards while facing the staircase. Luther came jaunting down the stairs three by three and panting like he'd been running for miles.

"Stop those women!" he shouted. "That is Lady Willow Valerian, wanted by the Great Lord on counts of collusion and evading arrest!"

The guards looked around at each other, unsure what to do. The head guard tossed down his weapons and lunged at Willow, who had her back turned still. He grappled and pinned her to the ground. Another guard, following his lead, did the same to Laurel. The two women cried out to let them go, but the men held them hard against the ground.

Luther walked and stood over them. "Jurius will be very pleased. Open the gate and put them in a cell until we can get word to the high general. And cover their eyes! Stones, have you never dealt with a threadweaver before?"

As if for the first time, the guards realized that the women were threadweavers. Several dropped their swords to the ground, realizing the danger any held item posed.

"You, go get shackles and blindfolds," the head guard ordered. "And you two, go get the gate keys from General Henna."

"Wait." Luther held up a hand. "You don't have the keys?"

The head guard looked at him with a brow curled up. "Of course not. That would be a security hazard."

"Smart. You two get the keys from General Henna. We'll keep the prisoners here." Laurel could hear Luther's voice faltering. This was not part of the plan. They'd assumed that the guards would have the keys. If they had to wait, then Laz's timing would be off, and the escape would be ruined.

The three guards with assignments raced off and disappeared up the dark, spiral staircase. Laurel, Luther, and Willow all seemed to have the same thought at the same moment. Luther lunged forward and drove his heel hard into the chest of the guard holding Willow, then dropped and slammed his fist into the neck of the guard holding Laurel. The women jumped up, veins flaring with Sapphire threadlight and swung their fists into the heads of the men who had held them. They both fell unconscious.

The only remaining guard threw his hands up into the air in defeat, knowing full well that he couldn't fight three threadweavers on his own. "Don't, please!" He dropped to his knees with his hands still in the air.

Willow took a step toward him. "Move and you die."

Luther patted down the guards but didn't find what he was looking for. He walked over to the kneeling man, searched him, then looked into his eyes while he spoke. "Not complaining, but if the high general knew you surrendered this easily there would be hell to pay. Is there any other way into the cells without the keys?"

The man shook his head. "No, I swear it."

Luther scowled. "Get on the ground and don't move."

Willow approached the locked gate and examined the keyhole. She grabbed hold of the iron rods and shook it; loud clanking echoed throughout the dungeon. "We need the key, but we don't have time to wait for it. Any ideas?"

"Can we pick it?" Willow asked.

"The locks are too heavy," Luther said, "and we don't have anything to pick it with anyway."

Laurel walked forward and kicked as hard as she could. The gate rattled back and forth but held firm. "Let's break it down."

"The bars are solid iron," Luther sneered. "You can't just kick them down."

Her foot throbbed beneath her. What a stupid idea. Who kicks iron? Even so, something about kicking the gate had felt good. She reimagined the kick, her foot connecting hard with the lock, and the whole gate shaking back and forth.

"We're threadweavers!" she shouted. The others stared at her. "We don't need to kick them down. Willow, you and I *push* on the top bars. Luther, you *pull* on the threads of the bottom."

Willow looked to Luther. "You have a better idea?"

All three of them let threadlight course through them. Hundreds of lines of brilliant light flowed through the dungeon, but Laurel only needed one. Willow's and Laurel's veins lit with brilliant blue as they *pushed* on the threads nearest to the top hinge, and Luther's veins blazed green as he *pulled* on the threads nearest to the bottom hinge. The gate groaned and creaked as the force flowing through the threads affected the physical world.

"Full force on three," Willow counted. "One. Two. Three!"

The gate twisted, metal groaning like thunder, until the hinges snapped off and the gate rotated like a wheel. The center hinge bent itself to accommodate the new position.

"Ha!" Laurel laughed. "I told you!"

"Nice work. Let's get inside, quickly now. You too," Willow said, kicking the guard's back.

Laurel, Willow, Luther, and the guard all crawled under the twisted-up gate and into the dungeon. There were no gates on the individual cells, but each had double shackles built into the walls. Each of the cells was empty, except for his.

When they reached Pandan, he didn't look much better. Open wounds festered on his arms, and bruises lined the entire left side of his face. The other cheek had something seriously wrong with it. Black, burnt skin crusted over the center. In the low light, Laurel could barely make out the lethargic movements of his chest as he breathed.

"Pan!" Willow rushed forward, checking his vitals, and removed the blindfold from his eyes. She worked quickly to release the latch of the chains. His arms dropped to the side, and he started to fall forward. She caught him and sobbed as she squeezed. "You're okay, little brother. We're going to get you home."

For a moment, Laurel imagined Bay chained up instead of Pandan. Tears formed in her eyes and her heart filled with anger and fear. She knew Pandan. He'd been kind to her. He did not deserve this.

Pandan coughed and tried to open his eyes. His brows furled in pain and the pace of his breathing increased. "Willow?"

Willow had never smiled so wide. "It's me."

"I'm so sorry."

"There is nothing to be sorry about. The elders told me everything. We're going to get you out of here."

"I," he groaned. "I had no choice. Please, forgive me."

Willow leaned forward. "Stop talking. You need to relax. It's going to be okay."

In the corner of her eye, Laurel saw Luther's chest rising and falling at an increasing rate. He had murder in his eyes and a quiver in his lip. Laurel didn't understand what was going through his mind, but she could tell he was looking at Pandan. And it didn't look good.

"You lied to me," Luther said, addressing Willow.

She turned from embracing her brother and looked at Luther, confused. "What are you talking about?"

"You lied to me," Luther growled. "You knew it was the priest, and you said nothing."

"He was a spy, not a real priest. Everything I told you was true. He is my brother, and Chrys' uncle. What does it matter?"

"It matters to me!" Luther roared. "He took my son!"

Willow stood up, her lips curling into something feral. Laurel knew the feeling. The anger. The need to protect. Laurel was Willow, and

Pandan was Asher, wounded as the alpha approached. Willow said nothing; her eyes had said enough.

"Move," Luther ordered. His breathing grew sporadic. He was a predator prepared to pounce. "Someone has to pay for what happened to my son."

"It was the Rite of Revelation!" Willow spat. "It was your choice. You knew the law. You played the game, and you lost. If you think to lay the blame on my little brother, I swear on the wind that I will end you."

Every part of Luther's body shook. His jaw clenched with such fury that Laurel was sure his teeth would shatter any moment. Then, he closed his eyes. Laurel thought she saw tears forming. "Someone has to pay," he repeated.

A loud bell echoed down through the spiral staircase and into the dungeon. The Keep alarm. That meant Laz had played his part and created a distraction on the other side of the keep. If Luther was right, guards would also swarm to the Great Lord's chambers to protect him. That should keep him occupied.

"We need to leave," Willow said. "Luther, I need you. Chrys needs you. Can we count on you?"

He nodded meekly.

"Good," she said. "Laurel, place the guard in shackles so he can't follow. Let's get out of here before the others come back."

Laurel led the cowering guard into a cell and locked him up.

Luther stood and watched as Willow attempted to lift Pandan's bloodied arm over her shoulders. Rather than waiting for him to help, Laurel stepped forward and grabbed the other arm. Together, they moved him all the way to the twisted dungeon gate where they had to lay him down and drag him underneath. The old man moaned and cried while they pulled him across the cold stone. The whole time Luther watched on in silence.

They pulled Pandan the rest of the way through and then back up onto his feet as they summited the dungeon stairway. When they reached the top, they were not alone.

Two Alirian women.

One bound.

One wearing the uniform of a high general.

Gale take me.

As soon as High General Henna saw them with Pandan, she pulled a dagger out, spun it in her palm, and smiled. "Willow."

"Henna."

"We need to talk."

"Unfortunately, we have a prior engagement."

Willow exploded forward into the air, screaming as her veins blazed a bright cerulean blue. Behind her, Laurel stood carrying the full weight of Pandan. She had to *push* on her own corethread just to keep from falling under the weight.

There was no grace to Willow's movements. She was a feral animal descending on her prey, claws jabbing with no remorse. But she was no fighter. After the first exchange, it was clear that Henna held the advantage. She blocked each savage swipe with ease, sidestepping as Willow tried to tackle her and tossing the older woman down to the ground panting.

Luther snarled as he rushed forward. This time, Henna didn't wait for the attack. She charged him, prowling low to the ground, and swung forward with her blade. Luther blocked attack after attack until she landed a kick into his stomach. He stumbled back, spit on the floor, and put his hand forward as his veins lit with green threadlight.

Nothing happened.

The General took the opening and swiped out at his hand, the black blade cutting through the skin of his palm. He retreated back, clutching at his hand, then he charged forward. Laurel saw him reach his hand to *pull* the knife in Henna's hand. Again, nothing happened. The high general thrust with the knife and sliced into his left arm. Green blood turned red as it fell to the stone floor.

Luther retreated again, holding the wound on his arm.

Henna lunged forward and threw her fist, but he chopped down and spun to the side, throwing his weight into his elbow. Luther was stronger, but Henna was faster. She ducked below and sent a swift uppercut into his ribs. His torso contracted, and she kicked hard at the back of his knee, but Luther moved his leg just in time. Willow was back up and dove onto Henna's back, clawing at her face as they toppled forward.

The knife fell out of Henna's hand as they hit the ground, crashing out in front of Laurel. She laid Pandan down, then picked it up.

She paused.

Impossible.

It was identical to the knife in her pocket—the one that Chrys had dropped in the Fairenwild. The same obsidian blade. The same flat hilt. This dagger must have been forged by the same smith.

General Henna jabbed behind her with an elbow that caught Willow in the jaw. A loud crack echoed in the hallway. Luther pounced forward and mauled her across the head with a heavy fist. The high general toppled over, unconscious.

Luther ran over to Reina, removed her bindings, then went to check on Willow. She was moaning on the ground holding her jaw. He helped her up and led her back over to Pandan. For a moment, he hesitated, his jaw clenched tightly. "I'll help you carry him."

Laurel slipped the second blade in her pocket and threw Pandan's arm over her shoulder.

Struggling to walk, Willow turned to Reina. "Go check on Laz and make sure he is okay. Luther and Laurel, follow me."

Reina nodded. "Henna sent for more guards. Be careful."

They took slow, steady steps as they made their way through the long corridor. Reina sprinted off toward the adjacent hallway. The bell rang out once again, this time louder. There would be no way of getting out the front entrance, but that wasn't their plan anyway.

As they rounded the corner, Laurel looked behind her. General Henna was on her feet once again, shoulders hunched forward, her entire body heaving with each breath. She saw them, and she took a step.

Laurel quickened her pace. "We need to move faster."

30

It was late by the time they'd reached the edge of the Fairenwild, but Alabella said they were right on schedule. Several hundred people traveled with them. The assembly had started small when they'd left the warehouse, but group after group had joined the mass by the time they'd reached the edge of Alchea.

All around him men and women lit torches and others held onto the broken stalks of strange, radiant plants. Slowly, they stepped into an environment unlike anything Alverax had ever seen. There were few species of trees that thrived in the desert, even near the water's edge at Mercy's Bluff, and none of them looked anything like these. The trunks were the size of homes and the branches only sprouted at heights so far overhead that it felt like a second sky. Even surrounded by so many others, the daunting nature of the Fairenwild gave Alverax the chills.

Alverax studied every plant and creature that crossed him, but nothing was as fascinating as the bulbous lights bobbing on the ends of long reeds. They looked like something that should exist in the ocean. Every few steps he thought he saw creatures lurking behind the trees, and more than once he thought he saw something crawling up one.

It was hard to believe that people lived here. When Lady Alabella had explained that there was a city deep in the Fairenwild, it seemed like a fantasy, but he trusted her, and so did hundreds of others. When howls echoed out in the distance, he was glad their group was as large as it was. Better odds.

As they continued, Alverax became sure that creatures were stalking them, big enough to be seen at a distance, and smart enough to stay hidden. It wasn't that he was scared; it was more that he was filled with a horrific anxiety that urged him to curl up and die. He should have stayed at the factory, but Alabella said that she needed him there with her. It felt good to hear.

They traveled for hours before they arrived at the edge of a clearing. It wasn't the end of the Fairenwild—feytrees surrounded the clearing on all sides—but it was definitely out of the ordinary. Bright flowers and green grass glowed in the radiance of the bulbs, and in the center of the opening lay a massive stone slab. A perfect circle, so thick it reached up to a man's knee. So out of place it must have been put there by the Heralds themselves.

"It's true," Alabella said, smiling to herself. Her eyes drifted upward, past a drove of spindly insects, and into the distant treetops.

Alverax stood next to her. "What is it?"

"When you were a child, did you ever wish the Heralds would visit you?"

"I guess so."

Alabella nodded to herself. "Wishing. Hoping. They are dangerous words. If you hope for something to be true and it is not, that realization can break you. But until then, while that belief runs warm in your blood, it can drive you to do amazing things. This was my moment, Alverax. And what I hoped with all my soul to be true...is."

"Does that mean we're done walking?"

"It does."

Alverax rubbed his eyes, blinking away the fatigue. "And what's next? Where are the people?"

"Patience. We haven't sent our invitation."

LAUREL STAGGERED through the halls of Endin Keep, frustrated with their pace, but they were carrying a half-conscious man. She knew that High General Henna couldn't be far behind, though in the general's current state, she would be moving slowly as well.

They came to the end of a hallway and Willow paused, looking both ways. By the time Luther and Laurel reached her, she still had not moved.

"What is it?" Laurel asked.

Willow turned around with a serious look on her face. "Do you trust me?"

"Not particularly," Luther said.

Laurel almost smiled. She'd thought the same thing, but she was glad he'd been the one to say it. It's one thing to trust a noble mother of a high general, it's another to trust an emotional sister barely out of her battle rage.

"You don't have a choice," Willow responded. "Change of plans."

Behind them, Henna scrambled around a corner and into view. She met Laurel's eyes and, for a brief moment, Laurel thought that she might actually have a chance if they fought, given Henna's current state, but best not to test that theory.

Willow took over for Laurel and helped Luther as they fled with Pandan in tow. Laurel followed closely behind. They raced down another hallway and up a flight of stairs. Pandan's feet dragged along the staircase like a rhythmic drum beating to each step. At the top of the stairs, Laurel looked down. Henna was gaining on them. And fast. She took the stairs two by two, the dazed look in her eyes beginning to fade.

"Faster!" Laurel shouted.

A group of serving women scrambled out of the way as they plowed onto the second floor. Willow stopped at a large painted door with a sigil Laurel didn't recognize. At the same moment, High General Henna reached the top of the stairs. Close enough to strike.

"It's over!" Henna spit blood as she spoke. She screamed at the servants to leave.

Instead of responding, Willow knocked hard on the door in front of her. A man's voice called out, but she did not respond. Instead she knocked even louder.

"What game are you playing?" Henna spat.

"Stones, Willow! Is that—" Luther was cut off as the door opened.

A tall man with a scarred face and high general uniform stared back at them. "What do you—"

Willow punched him in the neck.

ALVERAX WATCHED as Alabella raised her hands toward the crowd, her pale-yellow eyes glowing in the torchlight. "History is not made by coincidence. You are not here by coincidence. History is taken! History is seized upon by those with the gall to bear it. The Heralds have led us here, and tonight, we will take what belongs to us. We will take what belongs to every man and woman on this god-forsaken earth! Power is not meant to be hoarded. Power is the tax of a shit life. The world owes you! It owes you for the pain, for the misery, for the loneliness. For every grave. Tonight, we say to the world, that tax is overdue! Tonight, we harvest a future that has been ripe for far too long. Brothers and sisters, raise your blades! Raise your bows! Fight knowing that, with this victory, the power of the gods can be yours. Change is coming, and we are its Heralds!"

The crowd was captivated by her, each word a savory morsel to their famished souls. Alverax felt his blood rising as he listened. This was the moment she'd promised him. This was their chance. Whatever came next would change everything. He could feel it in his bones.

"There are those who would stop us," Alabella continued, face alight with passion. "They wish to withhold what is rightfully yours. They would keep you in the dark. Me? I want threadlight to pour through your veins like a river of living water."

The crowd responded to her words as if they were infallible. As if she were a Herald come to guide them. To save them. They not only respected her. They revered her. Alverax was beginning to feel the same. When Alabella spoke, it demanded reverence. It was sacred. And when she spoke, it felt as though she spoke to you. As if you were the only thing she cared about in the world. Even standing in a mob of hundreds, it felt as though she were speaking to him.

"It is the day of equality. If they wish to stand in our way while we embrace a better world for all mankind, we will pluck them like the weeds they are."

They cheered, banging swords and chanting unintelligible words into the night. Alverax felt a rush of adrenaline as he looked out over them. These people were not here for a peaceful negotiation. There was fire in their eyes just as much as it was in their hands. What exactly *was* her plan? *Pluck them like weeds?* A core-rotten feeling surfaced in the pit of his stomach.

Alabella quieted them down. "You will have your chance but, before we begin, I need every woman or man holding a torch to step forward."

A group of nearly a hundred stepped forward holding bright flames. Alverax watched as Alabella walked down their line and spoke to each of them individually, thanking them for being there, touching their cheek with a motherly hand, bewitching them with guile. He felt like he was going to vomit. These people were slaves. Willing or not, they looked to her as a deity. Each touch was a divine blessing. Each word a pronouncement of life.

She addressed the assembly one final time. "A smith lays flame to metal in order to form something new. Tonight, we lay the same transformative flames. They will sing out into the night and fill your ears with nightmares. Do not dwell on the horror! Think of the polished blade that comes out the other end of the furnace. And, if that is not enough to silence your fear, think of me. I will not lead you astray. Remember, the greatest good requires the greatest sacrifice.

"Emeralds, light the moss and branches. The rest of you, light the spores."

The mob of torchbearers walked forward and laid their torches at the base of the photospores. Each spore exploded at the first touch, spitting out fire as its bulb erupted. The burning liquid drooled along the base of the feytrees like magma, lighting the bark aflame.

A half dozen Emerald threadweavers ran up the feytrees like workerants, lighting patches of dry moss along the way, until they reached the branches high overhead. Soon, as the flames jumped from branch to branch, the dark roof of the Fairenwild came to light.

Alverax looked around at each of the faces in the crowd and cowered as he saw the myriad forms of evil garnishing their faces.

The flames grew brighter and brighter.

Alverax was unable to blink as he watched the majesty of the feytrees light up in a horrific blaze.

Alabella looked up into the treetops. "Now, my children, we wait."

CHRYS LOOKED out over the eastern horizon, rocking back and forth with his son in his arms, imagining Alchea beneath the Everstone Mountains.

In reality, it was nothing but feytrees and storm clouds as far as the eye could see. Moonlight trickled over his son's cheeks. He was so small. So helpless. So brittle. As if to argue, a small groan emerged from Aydin's lips. Chrys bounced him gently until his eyes were closed once more.

He pulled the wool blanket tight to cover Aydin from the cold chill of the wind from the east. Dark clouds rolled toward them on the horizon. Chrys never liked the rain, but found himself smiling knowing that if rain was the worst of his worries, everything was going to be okay. They were safe.

A loud sound drifted on the wind from just outside of Zedalum. Followed by another, and another. Horns trumpeting. Chrys' mind flashed back to the Wastelands, charging toward the enemy. The wastelanders' beady eyes were void of emotion while the rest of their faces screamed out in a rage. Horns trumpeting. Charge. Horns trumpeting. Clash. Horns trumpeting. Hundreds of dead lay at his feet.

Mmmm. You remember.

Chrys rose to his feet, ignoring the voice.

A handful of Zeda people ran down the wooden paths, shouting frantic words. As they approached, their words became clearer, but they were not welcome words.

"Fire in the Fairenwild! Get to the ground!"

Fire? He'd seen no lightning and heard no thunder. Even the rainfall had yet to find its way to the Fairenwild. Chrys ran into the Elder's lodge holding Aydin tight in his arms. The news had spread throughout the lodge and it was alive with activity. He shoved his way through the hallway and back to his room. Iriel lay so deeply asleep that the growing commotion passed over her like a summer breeze.

He took her hand and rubbed it. "Iriel, wake up."

Nothing.

He shook her arm, and the jolt finally broke her out of her sleep. "Iriel, we have to go. There is a fire in the Fairenwild. Everyone has to get to the ground."

She yawned and stretched. "In the middle of the night?"

He nodded and helped her up.

By the time they left the room, most of the lodge had cleared out. The wide wooden paths outside were filled with Zeda as they all headed toward the ground. Chrys saw a few Sapphire threadweavers *pushing* and leaping between the large wooden poles to the sides of the walkway. The people were panicking, and that concerned Chrys more than anything.

Outside the lodge they ran into Elder Rosemary. She was directing a dozen young women and men toward the market.

"Elder Rosemary!"

She turned to face him. "Chrys, you need to get to the ground."

"What's going on?"

"Fires. It's not the first time, but it seems to be spreading faster than normal. I've sent people to bring tents and food for the evening. Others will use water from the cisterns and dirt from the fields to calm the flames. There should be nothing to worry about."

Chrys looked toward the walkway that led to the entrance platform. "How do the achromats get down?"

"There are many Sapphires amongst our people. They will carry the others. It takes very little effort with the help of the wonderstone, so there is no danger of threadsickness. You should take your family and go. You're a Sapphire, they should let you down without delay. I'll be there shortly. Go."

Chrys followed the crowd and headed toward the entrance platform. To the east, small fires began to rise between the trees. Flames hopped from dry branch to dry branch. Zeda people heaved buckets of dirt and water at the growing flames. If they couldn't stop it before it reached the city, perhaps the rains would.

"Wait your turn! Patience, please!" A Sapphire threadweaver directed families to the platform where other Sapphires helped them drop to the surface. "If there are any other Sapphires willing to help, please come to the front of the line!"

"Iriel, take Aydin. I'll get you both to the ground and see if I can't help some of the others."

She nodded and reached out to take Aydin. They walked past the long line of anxious faces waiting to drop to the ground. Chrys looked at them all. Fear. Anxiety. Irritation. He could tell by the look of some children that they were excited to go to the ground, perhaps for the first time. Born and raised on the treetops.

They reached the platform and Chrys approached the man in charge. "I'm a Sapphire. Let me take my wife and son down to the surface, and I'll help others after that."

The man looked at him and Iriel suspiciously, then nodded and stretched out his hand. "I heard about you. We'll take whatever help we can get. Call me Dogwood."

"Chrys—" he paused. "Chrysanthemum."

Dogwood nodded his approval.

Chrys led Iriel down the steps to the platform. Far below, he could see the massive wonderstone. As he let threadlight wash over him, the wonderstone illuminated with supernatural light. Iriel held fast to the child, and Chrys picked her up in both arms.

"My hero," she said, batting her eyelashes and curling in her shoulder.

"More of a horse, really," he said without missing a beat.

Iriel smirked. "Jump to it stallion."

He did.

Wind rushed over them as he leapt from the platform. Other Sapphire threadweavers passed him on their way back up, narrowly avoiding a collision. Down they fell. Faster. He grabbed hold of his corethread and *pushed* against the force of gravity. They slowed and, at the last moment, he *pushed* hard. His feet hit the wonderstone with a soft thud.

"You both okay?" he asked.

Iriel looked down at Aydin who was squirming in her arms and nodded.

Chrys let her down and looked at the crowd of Zedas standing in the field surrounding the wonderstone. What would happen if their home was consumed? He shook the thought away. The wonderstone called to him to *push*, and he did, launching himself back up toward the entrance platform.

As he looked out at the blazing fire consuming the feytrees to the east, he remembered a conversation with Malachus in the Great Lord's study. They'd spoken of life being like a flame, and what had he asked? *"Do you want to burn the world, Chrys?"*

A mere moment into his flight, he heard a child screaming. Not a whine. Not a plea of hunger, or fatigue. It was pain. Chrys looked down and saw Iriel falling to her knees. Her arms fell toward the surface of the wonderstone as if being gripped by an invisible force. She screamed for help in harmony with their newborn son, forced flat on the surface of the stone.

Chrys stopped *pushing* and let gravity take him back toward the ground. As he fell, he stopped filtering threads from his vision and looked into the bright light of the wonderstone. He saw what he hoped never to see again. Dozens of tendrils of threadlight grasped hold of Iriel and Aydin, latching onto their limbs and sucking them toward the surface of the wonderstone. Tears poured down Iriel's face as she screamed. Her body was crumpling from the force.

There was only one person who had that kind of power.

Alverax and the others hid behind feytrees just outside the clearing. Silently they watched a crowd of people fall from the sky and congregate in the flower-filled opening. Alabella held up a hand for them to wait a little longer, and they did. Alverax watched men run their thirsty fingers down blades. He watched women breathe like feral animals. They watched on as innocent families gathered unknowingly to be slaughtered.

Then he heard screaming. A woman lay flat against the giant stone slab, crying for help, and beside her, barely visible at the distance, was a child. The forest people turned to them, but no one moved to help. He wanted to help them, but feared what Alabella would do if he gave away their location. But he couldn't just sit there. He couldn't do *nothing*. As anger filled his soul, threadlight filled his veins, and what he saw did not comfort him.

Threadlight blazed forth from the stone slab. Tiny tendrils of threadlight wrapped themselves around the woman and child, like snakes constricting their prey. He knew it was her. Alabella was doing it, and he had to stop her.

Just then, Alabella stepped out of the shadows. "Now!"

It was too late. Alabella, like Jelium, was the worst kind of thief: the kind that stole life. Over in that clearing were women and children, families that had done nothing to deserve death. He looked at Alabella, and the motherly figure he'd seen had been replaced by a monster. Whatever part she'd wanted him to play tonight, he would refuse.

He watched the mob of warriors rush the forest people. A volley of arrows rained down toward their unarmed foes, striking many.

Alverax stepped away from Alabella. Her eyes seemed to sink deeper into her skull. Her skin had lost its grace. The light in her eyes had faded from passion to cruelty. He knew it wasn't true—she hadn't really changed—but now he could see it clearly.

And he wanted no part of it.

This could well be the night he died for good, and he would go with a clean conscience. With the child's cries ringing in his ears, he knew that there was at least one good thing he could do.

Laurel stood in shock as the older man dropped to his knees, grabbing hold of his neck as he struggled to breathe. Willow smiled to herself and swung down with a hard fist toward his face, but he raised a quick hand and caught her blow. His eyes fixed to hers as he rose back to his feet.

"Big mistake," he growled.

He swung his other fist like a tornado, crushing down on Willow's face before she could block it. She dropped to the floor.

Henna approached from the top of the stairs. "Jurius, are you okay?"

That name. Laurel recognized it. The high general who was working with the Bloodthieves, who were responsible for kidnapping her. The one who had tried to kill Chrys at the edge of the Fairenwild, then tortured Pandan.

Jurius nodded.

High General Henna stepped forward slowly, eyeing Luther and Laurel. "No one else has to get hurt. It's over."

"Oh, it is most certainly not," Jurius said, reaching down toward Willow.

Luther dropped Pandan and launched himself forward to intercept. He screamed out as he crashed into Jurius. Green veins burned bright in both of their arms as they launched into a flurry of fury-filled blows.

Fists collided. Elbows struck. And knees slammed into thick muscle. Luther dropped low, *pulled* on the wall's thread, and smashed into Jurius with the strength of a storm. They crashed into the stone wall, cracking it with the force of impact.

Laurel saw it in his eyes. Luther had found a new home for his rage. Pandan had been freed, and Jurius would pay the full price. This fight wasn't for Willow, or Pandan, or Chrys; this fight was for the son he'd lost.

Jurius thrust his knee up into Luther's stomach over and over again until he finally released him. Luther struggled to catch his breath when Jurius launched a series of vicious blows, each connecting hard with Luther's face. Right. Left. Right. Left. Blood spewed out of Luther's mouth. Jurius sent a brutal uppercut into Luther's jaw, and he fell away, landing hard on his back.

Jurius laughed. His eyes searched for his next victim and stopped when they found Pandan on the floor. Willow came back to consciousness, and she watched with tears as Jurius approached her brother. Laurel stood still.

Jurius picked up Pandan and looked at Willow. "Is this what you came for? This worthless shit? Did Chrys care for him? Wants him...alive?"

"Jurius," Henna said, addressing the tone in his voice, "we need them alive."

Laurel, done standing by idly as her comrades were pummeled, *pushed* against the wall, and launched herself onto Henna's back. They toppled to the floor. Laurel used her long legs to wrap around Henna's waist then jammed the black knife against her throat. "Kill him and I kill her!"

Jurius hesitated for the slightest moment, then cocked his head to the side, amused. He spit blood and snorted with a cruel grin. "Nice try, but little girls shouldn't play grown up games."

He took his hand across Pandan's face and twisted. The sound of shattering bones echoed throughout the hallway, and Pandan fell to the floor.

"No!" Willow screamed, her hands coming up to cover her mouth.

That did not happen.

It couldn't be.

Pandan wasn't dead.

That's not how this was supposed to go.

Tears poured down Willow's face. She wailed over the death of her little brother. What if it had been Bay? Laurel pictured her own brother, lifeless on the floor.

And it was her fault.

Laurel loosened her grip, falling into her own mind.

It was her fault.

She rolled away from Henna, rose, and made a mad dash toward Jurius. Out of the corner of her eye, she saw Willow do the same. Jurius crouched low, anticipating their arrival. Both of their veins blazed with Sapphire threadlight. Willow arrived first, but she was smart enough to wait for Laurel. Unfortunately, Jurius was not as patient.

He dashed toward Willow, his fist swinging in a wide arc. She slipped under it, but he *pulled* his arm toward the ground and his elbow crashed down at an inhuman speed directly onto her shoulder. Laurel arrived just as his elbow hit. She stabbed forward with the obsidian blade and sliced hard into his shoulder. He spun around, snarling, and reached for her hand that held the blade. She pulled it back and blood sprayed out as the blade cut into his palm.

"I don't know who you are," he said, "but you die next."

He dove at Laurel. She *pushed* her corethread to counteract the weight, but he *pulled* with even more force. In an instant, he'd pinned her arms down and smashed his head into her face. The force nearly knocked her out. Blood came drooling out of her nose as she stared into his face. The face of a Bloodthief.

Laurel spit blood in his eye and rammed her knee into his groin. He released her, instinctively wiping his eye clean, and she seized the moment. She squeezed the obsidian blade with all her strength and thrust it straight through his sternum. She'd expected more resistance, but it slid in with ease.

He gasped. Both of his hands came to the hilt of the blade as he stared down at his chest.

Gale take him.

"Jaymin," he mumbled. With his final moments, he grabbed the hilt, pulled the blade out of his own chest, and slowly turned it around.

He screamed and jammed it into Laurel's heart.

Threadlight exploded from Laurel. A sound, like shattering glass, echoed against the stone walls. Then, as if the world itself grieved the reality, the earth trembled beneath their feet. Walls groaned and wood splintered as decorations came crashing down onto the floor. Laurel tried to steady herself. Inside her, it felt as though her soul were slowly draining from her body.

She knew she was dying, but, at least for a moment, she'd helped.

THE WORLD SEEMED to expand and contract in odd pulses as Chrys looked down at the threadlight grappling onto his wife and son. His feet hit the stone and he ran to them, but there was nothing he could do. If he'd had the obsidian blade, he could have cut them free. But it was gone, the Zeda people had never found it.

He *pushed* on the artificial threads, his veins flaring blue, but it accomplished nothing. His family was going to die, and he was helpless. Powerless. He'd promised to protect them, and he'd failed, again. No matter how hard he tried, no matter how strong he tried to be, it would never be enough. Alone, he wasn't enough.

Mmmm. You are not alone.

Chrys shook his head. *No, I can't.*

Would you have them die for your own pride?

Stop!

Your sacrifice can save them. I can save them. Yield your soul to me.

The sound of swords and screaming lifted his gaze to the east. Hundreds of shadowy figures rushed toward Zeda families. A volley of arrows rained down through the vaulted treetops. Chrys *pushed* on as many arrows as he could, but too many fell. Zeda fell with them.

A dark fury washed over him as he stared out over the oncoming army.

From the corner of his eye, he saw a massive feytree, consumed by fire from trunk to crown, break at its midpoint. The world seemed to slow as the falling giant ripped free of its neighbors, hundreds of branches snapping off the tumultuous weave. A cacophony of sound. The entire Fairenwild seemed to mourn its fall. And as it fell, it fell toward him.

If nothing stopped it, it would smash into the wonderstone, and everyone on it.

Chrys refused to succumb.

He lifted his hands high above his head. It was audacious, impossible. He let the power of the wonderstone rush through his veins. It burned. Channeling more threadlight than he'd ever dreamed possible, he *pushed*. The massive tree groaned from the force, slowing its freefall. But still it fell. He doubled his efforts, *pushing* with every ounce of will and strength he had, his veins expanding with the pressure. A man holding the weight of a mountain. It stopped. The feytree hovered in the air above Chrys and the wonderstone. His entire body trembled beneath him.

Mmmm.

His son screamed beside him, threads still constricting his brittle bones. Zeda families cried out as swords fell on their loved ones. The unknown army laughed as they fought.

He couldn't hold the feytree any longer. He couldn't save them. He wasn't enough. He was never enough.

But then he saw her, jet black hair slicked behind her ears, Amber eyes dancing in the light of the raging fires. Standing in the shadows as everything around her burned to the ground. The woman. She was responsible. Every problem. Every trouble. Every bit of pain. He looked back at his wife and son strapped to the wonderstone by a hundred threads of light. He heard their screams. He felt their suffering, and he would not let them die.

Mmmm.

"You can save them?" he spoke aloud.

Yes.

"Then I am yours."

Threadlight exploded from his body as ice poured through his veins. The commotion of the world blurred for just a moment before a dam inside him burst asunder. His neck moved without request. His lips curled into a smile even as his mind cried out in fear of what he'd done.

"Mmmm."

Chrys felt the Apogee reach out with his mind, tendrils grasping for prey until they finally latched onto the mind of a Zeda man who'd just landed on the wonderstone. He didn't understand how, but he could feel the man's soul. Then another. And another. Three Zeda souls bound to his own in the briefest of moments. Their souls wove together in a blinding tapestry of light. He could feel their threadlight, like wells of power, ready to be siphoned. It was pure power. Borrowed power.

The massive feytree blasted away, splintered wood bursting out over the battlefield. A shiver crawled up his spine, and the air around him seemed to expand. His lungs strained within his chest. He felt the three Zeda men collapse to the ground before he saw them.

The Apogee leapt off the wonderstone. Zedas scattered, terrified. Finally, after years of patient waiting, he was free. And this time he wasn't bound by the mutation.

He walked forward as the fastest of the army approached. He sidestepped the man's sword and gripped his throat. The impact sent the man's legs swinging forward as his momentum came to a sudden halt. "Such frailty," he said before snapping the man's neck and tossing him aside.

A spear came soaring toward him. He snatched it out of the air, turned and launched it forward into another man's eye.

He'd forgotten how feeble men were.

A blade came down from behind. He ducked below, spun, and delivered a blow so hard into the man's chest that his ribs bent inward below the skin.

He grabbed a blade off a dead man and strolled casually through the battlefield. It moved in his hands like a sickle sifting wheat, impaling, severing, striking down Zeda and Bloodthief alike. He never slowed. He never tired. He never stopped.

These men were playthings, not worthy of his effort, but there was one different. An Amber threadweaver. A wonderful twist of fate.

When she saw him approach with blood smeared across his face, a dozen tendrils of light sprang out of the ground and hooked their claws into his body. But he was stronger. He screamed out like an animal, threads bursting apart. In his own mind, Chrys could hear the screams of three Zeda threadweavers.

Fear grew in the woman's eyes. This time, a hundred tendrils of light burst out from beneath him and latched onto his body. He fought them all. They were nothing to him. He could not be stopped. The agony of the Zeda men rang out in the back of his mind.

The Apogee fought the weight with all of his strength, his legs buckling beneath the pressure. He took two steps—the woman's eyes growing wider with each—before he stalled in front of her, howling like a caged animal, blood dripping from his cheeks. Her eyes blazed with yellow threadlight, her yellow-veined arms trembling with the effort.

Her eyes grew wide. "What are you?"

The earth quaked in response.

ALVERAX GAVE a wide berth to the combat as he sprinted toward the woman and child. There was little he could do to stop the fighting, but there were at least two people he could save. If Alabella found out, she would kill him, but he'd already died once. It wasn't so bad.

He approached from the far side and stopped in awe as a man with threadlight coalescing around him *pushed* the entire upper half of a feytree out of the way like it were a single branch. Threadlight coiled around the man as he jumped down off the stone.

Alverax shook away the awe and stepped up onto the stone platform. A strange urge to threadweave poured over his mind. It felt like the stone was calling to him. It reminded him of sailweed cravings, an incessant need to consume.

He looked down at the woman and child, pinned to the stone by the artificial threads latched onto them, screaming in pain and fear. He focused on the threads wrapping the infant and squeezed. The threads resisted with a strength unlike anything he'd experienced before. He *squeezed* harder, screaming at them as his veins burned black.

"Break!" The threads burst apart like grain thrown into the air, including the threads wrapping the woman.

Before he could celebrate, the threads reappeared, small threads at first, but each grew larger and larger. And then he saw it. The child's eyes, wide open as it screamed, were a brilliant pale yellow.

Alverax threw his energy back at the blossoming threads and shattered them once again. The child was doing this to himself, overcome by the cravings of the stone and without the will to deny it.

He looked down at the bright threadlight of the stone. It was the source. He dropped down to his knees and placed both hands on the stone. This was it. A task only he could perform. A family only he could save. With every ounce of his soul, he grabbed onto the stone's threadlight. Its energy ripped through his body, filling him with such intense pressure he was sure his skin would burst. He screamed out in pain, but held fast, squeezing harder against the bright threadlight. The pressure continued to build inside him; the pain rose to a crescendo.

He threw every death, every betrayal, every mistake, and every heartache into the burning threadlight. It was a trade, his life for theirs. The veins in his arms turned blacker than death. It was unbearable. His body shook. His legs convulsed beneath him.

But it wasn't just him that was shaking.

As he fought against the power of the stone, the world shook around him. Cinder and ash fell from burning treetops. Feytrees teetered back and forth, the world itself groaning against the quaking earth. He was afraid, but he'd never felt such purpose.

Thunder cracked in the sky through gaps where branches used to be. He squeezed harder. Another flame-consumed feytree toppled to the ground. His body was on fire from within, and he let it burn.

The stone beneath his feet fractured, a mountain rending in two. The threadlight bathing it burst apart in a cloud of mist.

Alverax fell forward onto his face, smiling as he lost all consciousness.

THE APOGEE FOUGHT the threads that bound him while the earth beneath shifted like ocean waves. A terrible pain surged through his mind with each quake, weakening him. He could feel the man inside him trying to escape. A futile effort. This time he was prepared.

He watched the Amber-eyed woman flee into the darkness. Her threads weakened with each passing moment. She would need to die, and whoever had made her. He turned back toward the wonderstone and saw hundreds of dead lying in the dirt. Bloodthieves and Zeda alike, equal in death. Massive, scorched branches had fallen and crushed a dozen people. Men groaned as they tried to get out from under them. A group of Zeda threadweavers walked through the chaos, ripe for the taking.

The Apogee looked further and saw Iriel seated on the edge of the wonderstone. She held the baby in her arms, crying. If the child grew, it too would be a liability. The Apogee looked on them with fondness. Too long spent in the mind of another.

Iriel's eyes lifted and caught his own.

He nodded to her—a token of respect—then turned and walked away.

All around him, men cried out for their lost.

Women wept for their fallen.

They gathered their families and hurried west.

But the Apogee traveled east.

31

As Jurius hit the floor, the walls of the keep shook. Willow steadied herself on the ground and waited out the earthquake. When it finally stopped, she rushed over to Pandan and grabbed hold of him tightly. He felt heavier than he had just moments before. As much as her heart wanted to deny it, the brother she'd finally found again was gone once more.

She turned to Jurius who lay clutching his chest, gurgling up blood as the life fled from him. She grabbed the black blade lying on the ground between him and Laurel and thrust it back into his chest. Screaming, she thrust it in a second time. And a third. As if quickening his death would bring back her brother.

She wiped the blood on his shirt as she rose. It was then that she realized what she held in her hand. The blade matched the description Chrys had given. Could it be?

"You need to leave."

Willow snapped her head around at the sound, hiding the blade as she turned. Standing straight-backed and strong was High General Henna.

"You need to leave," Henna repeated. "Before anyone else sees you. The window in Jurius' study opens to the north end of the keep. If you drop down from there you should be able to get to the wall."

Willow tilted her head. Henna had just tried to kill them. "I don't understand."

"Chrys warned me," Henna said. "The day we visited him in his home, he slipped me a piece of paper. It was hastily written, but it said *Jurius is a Bloodthief*. I had someone look into it. They came back with a lot of questions. Tonight, it was clear; Chrys was right. I should have trusted him. There will be hell to pay for his death, but you should not be the ones to pay it."

Willow turned and remembered Laurel. The young girl lay on the ground, a small pool of blood across her chest. She ran to her and checked her vitals. "She's still alive!"

Luther moved to join her. "I watched Jurius stab her in the heart. She should be dead. If we can get her to a doctor, maybe she still has a chance."

"I'll take her," Henna said, walking toward them. "If you take her with you, you'll never make it out fast enough. Go. I'll get her to a doctor."

Willow paused, still doubting Henna's sincerity, but she had no other choice. She was right. They'd never make it out if they had to carry Laurel. She turned to her brother, dead on the floor next to Jurius, and ground her teeth. "Can you see that he gets a proper burial?"

Henna nodded. "I will try, but I cannot make that promise."

"Willow," Luther said urgently. "She's right. We need to go, now."

Willow knelt down beside her brother. "May the winds guide you," she whispered, tears swelling in her eyes. She leaned down and kissed his cheek. "And carry you gently home."

With one final nod of appreciation, Willow and Luther entered Jurius' study. It was filled with books, maps, paintings, and a single oil lamp lighting it from within. As they opened the tall window, a cold breeze brushed past the curtains. The rain continued, though it had dulled to a gentle beating. Willow jumped out of the window, *pushing* on her corethread to soften the fall. Luther ran down the wall and rolled as he reached the surface.

Neither spoke a word as they ran toward the outer keep wall.

They had failed.

32

Alverax awoke from a nightmare.

Fire and quake and rain pouring down on a field of death.

He shielded his eyes from the bright sunlight beating down on him. His head pounded and his stomach felt like a ship at sea. A figure stood over him. He tried to blink away the haze. It was his father. His dead father stood over him smiling, and all Alverax could do was laugh. The nightmare wasn't over yet. All his father said as he looked at him was *"thank you."*

Tears welled up in his eyes. His father, the infamous thief of Cynosure, a cheat and a liar, had wormed his way into Alverax's dreams. But the truth was more painful, and no matter how hard he tried to deny it, Alverax missed him. His father's words, even in a dream, were water to a thirsty soul.

The pain in his stomach flared. He leaned over the side of his cot, heaving more than he vomited. Another figure rushed to his side, keeping him from falling over the edge. He coughed until his stomach settled once again. He looked back up to his father, but he was gone. In his place stood a woman. An angular face, dark hair, and green eyes. Alverax panicked and his body trembled. His breathing became more and more sporadic as chills covered him from head to toe.

"Get me some lavender!" a second woman shouted. An older woman by the sound of her voice. She held him down and looked directly into his eyes. "I need you to breathe. Focus on each breath. Long and deep. Keep your eyes closed. You are having a panic attack. It will end."

When the other woman returned, the older woman began rubbing something onto Alverax's chest. It was fragrant and calming. He focused on his breathing and, over time, he relaxed. The shaking subsided. The world ceased its spinning.

He opened his eyes again and found more people standing over him. Two older women with gray hair and a woman holding a child. He recognized them but couldn't place how.

The older woman spoke again. "You need to rest, boy. I've not seen such threadsickness in years and I thought Dogwood was in a sorry state. You are lucky to be alive."

"Where am I?" He tried to sit up but groaned at the pain.

"West of the Fairenwild. The fires your people set destroyed our homes before the rain came. It is no longer safe for us there."

Alverax pictured flames slowly crawling up the enormous trees of the Fairenwild, split wood falling from the sky as the earth shook. Alabella had planned it all along. She had forced them down and slaughtered them. But why? At the very least, he was no longer by her side. Whatever purpose she'd had for him, she would need to find another way. Deep down he'd known who she was, but he'd wanted to trust her, and so he had.

"I'm so sorry," he said. "I had no idea that was going to happen."

The woman holding her child shook her head. Her eyes were red. She must have done her share of crying. "Don't you dare be sorry. You saved my son's life, and mine. Whatever the others did is not on you."

He didn't agree, but it was nice to hear. "Are they gone?"

"From what we could tell," the old woman said with a curious look in her eye, "all your people were killed."

The other elderly woman huffed. "We'd be better off if you were dead too. We know what you are."

"He saved us!" the younger woman interjected.

"At what cost!?" the scowling elderly woman shouted. "The coreseal is broken. We've failed."

"You don't think I understand the cost?" the younger woman said. "My husband is gone. My son may have permanent health issues. I saw the piles of dead with my own eyes. Counted myself among them. And I *would* be among them if not for him. The boy lives."

The old woman's scowl grew deeper. "Obviously, I'm glad you're alive, but the seal is broken, and that is a matter greater than you or I."

"The boy lives," the younger woman repeated. She was cold fire.

"The Bloodthief with Amber eyes. If nothing else, he can help us stop her."

The old woman's lip curled in disgust. "Unless he can get her to help us with the seal, again, there is a more serious matter to attend. Besides, how can we trust that he's not working for her even now?"

"I'm not," Alverax said, shaking his head. "I swear it. I didn't even know what she was going to do."

"You don't need to explain yourself," the younger woman said. "If any harm comes to him, Rowan, I will hold you responsible, and you'll find that my husband isn't the only one handy with a blade."

Alverax was surprised to see the young mother slip into some kind of battle stance, even while holding a child in her left arm. He didn't know much about fighting, but he could tell when someone else did.

The scowling elderly woman walked away, grumbling under her breath. The others followed silently.

Alverax looked around and saw that he was on some kind of homemade, cloth carrier-table. There were hundreds of people around him, maybe thousands, many over by a stream where they gathered water and washed off soot and dirt. Most of the people looked happy despite their loss.

"My name is Iriel," the young mother said, extending her hand.

"Alverax."

She took a seat next to him, looking down at the newborn in her arms. "They're scared of you. People are often afraid of what they don't understand. Be patient. You'll gain their trust over time."

"Unless that old woman kills me before I have the chance."

"Don't you worry about her."

Alverax took a deep breath. "I just wish she would believe me. I really am done with Alabella. I didn't know what she was going to do."

Iriel cocked her head to the side. "Alabella? The woman with the Amber eyes? Why did she do it? What does she want?"

Alverax closed his eyes and Alabella flooded his thoughts. Why *had* she brought him to the Fairenwild? They were supposed to meet up with the people who lived there, which was only partially true. She'd also said that he was the key. But why? The only thing he could do was break threads...which he had.

Heralds save me.

"The stone's threadlight. I think she *wanted* me to break it."

33

Laurel awoke in a strange, stone room wearing clothing that did not belong to her. Somehow, despite being tucked beneath a layer of wool blankets, her body shivered. In a matter of moments, she became painfully aware of every ache and pain in her body, including a sharp pounding in her skull. When she tried to sit up, her chest erupted in pain. Her head slammed back down on her pillow as memories came flooding back to her.

Willow, Luther, Reina, Laz...Pandan...Jurius. She pulled her gown down and looked to the source of pain in her chest. A row of stitches lined up over her heart. The sharp pain was too much to bear, so she let threadlight pour through her veins.

Except it didn't.

She tried again, relaxing her mind despite the pain, and opened herself to threadlight. But again, no warmth flowed through her veins, no threads appeared in view, and there was no comfort from the pain. An immediate, overwhelming sense of fear gripped her from within.

She tried again.

Nothing.

And again.

Nothing but the sharp pain in her chest and a pounding in her skull.

Her entire body shivered. *No, no no.* Tears fell freely from her tired eyes. Her breathing grew frantic. Each breath was a battle unto itself.

"Help," she pled, her voice quivering. "Please, anyone."

She heard footsteps from somewhere outside the room. She wanted to look but, with every movement, it felt like Jurius was stabbing her through the heart once again. Agony. Dread. Panic. Terror. Acceptance.

Pandan.

He was dead because of her. She'd been so stupid, thinking she could stop Jurius. Instead, she'd dangled a slab of meat in front of a hungry chromawolf. If she'd stayed back—if she'd stayed home—Pandan might still be alive. Willow would never forgive her. Laurel would never forgive herself. If anyone deserved to be dead, it was her.

"Good, you are awake," someone said.

The footsteps continued until a woman stood over her with dark hair that lay slicked back behind her ears. She smiled beneath a pair of Felian lightshades.

"Are you a doctor?" Laurel asked.

The woman removed her lightshades, revealing bright yellow irises. "Of a sort."

Laurel's heart beat faster. It was her. The woman Chrys had told them about. She was what Aydin would become.

The woman placed her lightshades on a side table. "You are both the luckiest, and most unfortunate person in the world right now."

She knew about Jurius; Laurel was sure of it. She'd come to finish the job. "Please, just kill me quickly. I know why you're here."

"You do, do you? Well in that case, I suppose I should cut to the point." She reached into her pocket and pulled out a brilliant, obsidian blade. "First, I'd like to know where you got this."

Laurel lay quiet, refusing to respond.

The woman let out a deep sigh, grabbed a chair, and took a seat next to the bed. "We can come back to that. You should know that you were unconscious for many days. To be honest, I wasn't sure if you were going to wake up, but, when I heard what happened, I had a feeling that we may be able to help each other. The pain you are feeling will fade. You will recover, but you will never be the same. Like I said, you are extremely lucky that his blade landed where it did. These last few days, your body has shown signs of a chemical addiction to threadlight, which, ironically, is what saved your life. You must have had a sea of threadlight coursing through your veins.

"Now, there is good news and there is bad news. The bad news is that you are no longer a threadweaver."

The woman had spoken something Laurel was too afraid to put into words. She was no longer a threadweaver. It was gone. Every last trace. Still her mind longed for it, like a lost friend that would surely return.

She could feel the hunger inside her, the craving, the pure desire. All she needed was a bit of threadlight and all her pain would be gone. She'd taken it for granted, and now she wasn't sure that she could live without it.

The woman's eyes grew sad as she looked on Laurel. "It seems that you've already discovered that truth. The good news—and I want you to hear me and understand what I say next—the good news is that if you come with me, in time, I believe I can make you a threadweaver once again."

"You're a liar," Laurel spat. "I know you're here to kill me. Hurry up and get it over with."

"Oh, my dear. I have no plan to do such a thing. I believe I can make you whole again, but not because of me. Because you are unique. You were already a threadweaver. Your body accepted it once. There is so much that has been hidden from you. So many truths that the world has withheld. I swear I will never hide the truth from you. For instance, I know you are a Zeda."

Laurel's heartbeat rose, each beat a resounding drum against her chest. She thought of her grandfather, and her big brother. Tears streamed down her face. "I don't understand. What do you want from me?"

"I want to give you what you deserve, my dear, and no one deserves a life without threadlight." She glanced behind her and pulled out a vial of red liquid. She placed it on the table next to Laurel's bed. "If you'll let me, I can help you. Drink that. It will help with the recovery and the cravings."

Alone and defeated, mentally and physically, Laurel watched the woman walk away. She stared at the vial on the table. She didn't need to ask. She knew what it was. The queen of the Bloodthieves had offered her a boon, and Laurel was going to drink it.

If anyone deserved to be dead, it was her. And yet, somehow, it seemed that death refused to bring her under its wing. But a life without threadlight was no life at all.

Laurel lifted the vial and drank.

EPILOGUE

For years, the swamps near the entrance to Relek's Cave had been quiet—ever since the Builders had killed their god. The An'tara claimed that Relek was alive, that he could not die. Whether it was true or not, none of their people had seen Relek since that dark day in the mountains.

Tonight, that familiar peace was broken as footsteps echoed from deep within the cave.

Skyp poked his twin in the ribs. "Aye, Piksy, you hear that?"

"I hear it," Piksel whispered, stretching her arms. The An'tara would be furious if they discovered that Piksel had slept, but Skyp would never tell. "What do you think it is? Is it Relek?"

"I hope not."

They picked up their spears and stood in front of the entrance. The footsteps grew louder, a single set staggered in cadence. They looked at each other and backed away. They were supposed to make sure that no one went into Relek's Cave, but the An'tara never said anything about something coming out.

Finally, a shadow emerged from the mouth of the cave. The withered husk of a woman limped toward them, sunken eyes, skin gray as the cave itself with swollen veins running across every inch of her skin. She stopped when she saw them, her smile showing a mouth full of rotten gums. Despite the decrepit state of her body, her eyes were bright and alive.

As she approached, she spoke with a voice like gravel. "Where is my brother?"

BOOK 2 OF THREADLIGHT

Stones of Light

BY ZACK ARGYLE

SYL
SYL PUBLISHING LLC

1

It was a curious feeling, being trapped in his own mind. Helpless. Powerless. Looking on as each step rebelled against him. Every breath had become a dark reminder of his own insanity. Of the sacrifice he'd made. Of that singular moment when he'd given up control to save his family. When Chrys had once again become...the Apogee.

A week had passed since the coreseal had shattered. The accompanying quakes had wreaked havoc across Alchea, causing unstable buildings to collapse, stone roads to crack, and avalanches from the mountains to come crashing down with fury. The Apogee seemed to care about none of it. Nor did he care if he was seen. He wanted only to reach his destination. As they ascended the Everstone Mountains, Chrys thought it may have something to do with the thread-dead obsidian that Henna had found.

"Mmmm."

The Apogee reached into his pocket and pulled out a pocket watch. Chrys groaned inside at the reminder of his son who had received the gift from Great Lord Malachus. It was the only physical reminder he had left of his family, and the Apogee, annoyed at its mere existence, tossed it on the ground with disregard. It landed along the well-worn mountain trail, and the last Chrys saw of it was a shimmer in the corner of his eye.

He felt his mind slacken into deep despair. He'd lost so much—his wife most of all. The memory of his own eyes meeting hers in the Fairenwild—so pleading, so hopeful—just before he turned and walked away. She would never forgive him. He was the husband who deserted his wife. The father who abandoned his son. The friend who forsook. The man who slaughtered. Even if he could regain control, there was no returning to how life was before.

His boots trudged through a tangle of weeds as they made their way through a familiar mountain pass. The last time he'd walked this ground was when he'd returned from a massacre. It felt fitting. The first time he'd let the dark part of himself take control was just beyond the peaks of these mountains, and now he returned with the darkness once again in control.

The Apogee continued onward, following a dim set of boot prints toward Ripshire Valley, the site of the slaughter. Beyond that was the unknown. The Wastelands. Home to the small, inhuman people who fought savagely to defend their mountain border.

He wondered where Iriel might be. If their son, Aydin, was safe. He'd left them in the Fairenwild, in the midst of flames and bloodshed, with nowhere to go. He would never forgive himself for that. What is a man if he cannot protect those he loves?

The sun had begun its descent but, at such an altitude, it seemed to drag on for an eternity. Fresh footprints appeared. They passed a soiled patch of dirt. Chrys had a guess at who they may find ahead. For their sake, he hoped that he was wrong, that it was a lone hiker. Or even a small group of climbers. However unlikely, still he hoped, because he knew the grim alternative.

"Mmmm," the Apogee whispered as he inspected the footprints.

His feet trampled forward, following tracks of pressed grass until they rounded a small peak. Alchean soldiers huddled around a fire in the entrance of a large cave. The same cave from which the obsidian had come. High General Henna's soldiers were still exploring its deep tunnels.

One of the soldiers looked over and saw them. There did not seem to be any official lookout on duty, just those nearest the fire. "Hello!" he shouted through the wind.

Chrys felt his hand raise into the air, a spurious white flag. The Apogee smiled in return as they approached the camp. Half of the soldiers were asleep in the cave, safe from the wind and latent rain, tucked beneath piles of wool blankets. Those around the fire stayed seated, unafraid of the stranger approaching. Blankets pulled tight around their shoulders as they shared sips from a warm broth.

"Finally. We've been waiting to hear from the general for a week."

The soldiers all stared at him as he drew near. One gestured next to himself on the log they were using as a bench. "The wind is freezing out there. Come on in."

The Apogee cocked his head to the side. "I think I will."

He opened himself to threadlight, watching as his veins lit a bright, cerulean blue and warmth flooded through him. Hundreds of thin lines of incandescent light illuminated before him, connecting him to the world. His veins, like rivers of glacial water, flowed blue beneath his wind-bitten skin. By the time the soldiers noticed, it was too late.

Chrys felt something stir within him, a cold storm seething in his chest. Then, it moved, reaching out, searching, grasping, inviting, until finally, it delved into the depths of the closest guard's very soul. Energy flowed through the connection, and the guard brought his own blade to his chest. That same man looked down in shock as he slid the sword between his own ribs.

The Apogee moved forward with a cold intensity. He grabbed the soldier's blade from his ribs, pulled it out, and let it drag across the dirt as he entered the cave. Those awake stumbled back. Those asleep awoke to death.

Chrys felt anger swelling within the Apogee as he moved through the camp, and in that anger, he felt the barrier that bound him weaken.

Please, they are innocent, Chrys begged.

The Apogee snarled. *There can be no mercy.*

The remaining soldiers stared at the Apogee from within the cave, knowing well that there was little they could do against a threadweaver. Little did they know, the Apogee was much more than that now.

One brave soldier stepped forward. The others stood cautiously behind him. "General Valerian. You don't have to do this. I was there during the War. I saw the aftermath, and I saw the regret in your eyes. Please, we've done nothing."

Chrys recognized the man. Henry, perhaps? He, along with many others, had descended the mountain to observe the massacre in Ripshire Valley. He knew what the Apogee was capable of.

In that still moment between deaths, Chrys threw all of his will against the barrier in his mind. His hope and anger joined together in a massive wave, crashing against the wall, trying to regain control.

But the wall held firm, and the Apogee clenched his teeth. "You will pay for that."

His mind reached out to Henry; a bridge formed between them. Then, something flowed from Chrys *into* the soldier. Henry screamed, clutching his skull with both hands as he fell to his knees. Somewhere, even deeper in the recesses of his own mind, Chrys felt something odd, the vibration of a plucked string.

"Kill yourself," the Apogee demanded.

Henry brought a blade to his neck and pulled.

Curses erupted throughout the line of soldiers as his body fell to the dirt.

"I need two of you," the Apogee said. He pointed to the only female soldier, a sharp-faced woman with shoulder-length dark hair pulled back in a tail. "You will be one. Come here. Of the rest of you, I will take the strongest. Choose amongst yourselves, or I will choose for you."

He tossed the sword forward at their feet and, for a moment, the soldiers stood in silence, staring.

Chrys needed to help. With every ounce of his bound soul, he wanted to protect them. To save them from himself. From the dark part of his soul that had taken control.

The dark-haired woman ran forward just as a man with red hair turned to his neighbor and rammed a knife through his gut. The others gasped in shock, not knowing what they should do. The same red-haired man attacked another, and, with surprising speed, the soldiers turned on each other. One man tried to grab the sword off the ground but was brought down with a savage strike to his spine. Teeth bit into necks. Fingers jammed into eyes. Blades ripped through cartilage.

Not all fought—some tried to hold onto their honor—but it ended the same, nonetheless.

Chrys felt his hope flutter away.

When the brawl ended, dead men lay in piles on the rocky floor. The red-haired man was the only soldier left standing, despite a cut down his cheek that would surely scar. His build and hair reminded Chrys of Laz but, where Laz was carefree and naive, this man had the look of a feral beast who found himself just where he'd always wanted to be.

"You're not Chrys, are you?"

"Do not use that name," the Apogee growled. He eyed the woman. "We will come to know each other quite intimately. But first, tell me your names."

"I'm Velan." The red-haired man brought a fist to his chest.

The woman held back tears, but Chrys could see the fear in her eyes. Still, bravely, she replied, "Autelle."

"Good. You may call me Relek. You cannot yet understand, but you have been chosen. You will be gods among men." He gestured to the corpses littering the cave. "Burn the bodies. We do not want an army coming over the pass before we are ready for them."

Velan nodded and got to work.

Autelle joined in with tears in her eyes. Together, they stacked the bodies into a pyre, stuffed it with moss and mushrooms, and let it burn.

"Mmmm," the Apogee said, watching. "Let us go. She will be waiting."

2

Laurel's dream of living in the grounder city was not what she'd imagined. All of the wonder and splendor lay overshadowed by a new reality: she was thread-dead. She could still feel the knife piercing her skin, splitting between her ribs and driving deep into her heart. Pain. Surprise. Shock. Pressure building, surging, crescendoing until something broke inside of her. Shattered glass.

She should have been happy that she was alive, but it hardly felt like living. The world had lost its color. The wind had ceased to blow. She was a spec of sand on a gray beach waiting for the waters to rise.

And yet, in the aftermath of the storm that broke her, there was still one sliver of hope.

Alabella.

The Amber-eyed woman who led the Bloodthieves claimed that she could make Laurel a threadweaver again. Laurel knew there had to be a catch—some stipulation within the generosity—but did it matter? Could the cost possibly outweigh the reward?

She wasn't stupid; she knew who she was dealing with. These were the same people who had kidnapped her and tried to have Chrys murdered—the same people who Jurius had worked for. To their defense, they hadn't harmed her, and Chrys' baby *was* strange. If there was anyone that understood what it meant to have Amber eyes, it was Alabella.

The truth was that as soon as she had her threadweaving back, she'd head straight for Zedalum. Her grandfather was probably fighting the elders to let him leave the Fairenwild to search for her. Her biggest hope was that Chrys' mother, Willow, had explained everything to them. They would have to understand.

She missed the Fairenwild, the scents, the hypnotic flight of the skyflies overhead, and Asher. She wanted nothing more than to tackle him and squeeze him with all her might. But those could wait; they weren't going anywhere. When she was fixed, Zedalum and Asher and her family would all be waiting there for her.

Carefully, Laurel lifted herself from the bed. She moved to the large mirror beside the armoire. In its reflection, she inspected the stitches over her left breast. The skin seemed to be healing well but, as she looked up, the heart beneath the wound broke yet again. Staring back at her was the ghost of who she was. Her cheeks seemed more gaunt, her frame more thin, and those eyes... Still the sight of them was enough to drive her mind to madness. So insignificant. So colorless.

In death, she'd lost the blue radiance of a Sapphire. If being thread-dead wasn't punishment enough, achromatic eyes were the final falling autumn leaf.

She glanced to the door; no one was there. No one ever was, but it didn't stop her from checking. Her shaky hand reached out and opened the chest beside her bed. It was temporary—at least that's what she told herself, as she pulled out a small vial of red liquid. Alabella had called it a *transfuser*. Where she came from—a city called Cynosure—it was common for threadweavers to sell their blood. What the people of Alchea called a Bloodthief, the people of Cynosure called an apothecary.

She downed the vial in a single drink. Lukewarm iron slid down her throat, and the magic diffused into her bloodstream. Her veins simmered with Emerald threadlight. She'd have preferred Sapphire, but she didn't have the luxury of being selective.

The transfusers barely tempered the withdrawal and, though she was only supposed to take one with each meal, she found herself sneaking them more and more. What did they expect? She was stuck in a room all day, alone, with nothing but the inescapable craving of threadlight to accompany her. After a week, the part that disgusted her was not the fact that she was doing it, but that she'd grown fond of the taste.

She looked down at the chest and stared at the vials. The threadlight that infused the blood kept it from spoiling, so the blood in front of her would be good as long as it was available. But at the pace she was using it up, she worried it wouldn't last as long as it was supposed to.

The morning sun gleamed through her window, reflecting rays of glaring light through the glass vial. It was too cold outside to keep the window open, and too cold inside to keep the drapes closed. Regardless, the sun's position told her it was time for her physical therapy.

Laurel left her room, taking slow, careful steps down the hall until she arrived at a large room. A woman greeted her, thick with long brown hair and hands the size of dinner plates. "Laurel," she said with an energetic smile.

"Gelda," Laurel mumbled.

She hated therapy, but the tightness in her chest had already begun to fade, despite the stitches holding strong. As she approached the chair to sit, she recalled being chastised for wanting to lie down. Gelda claimed that being in a constant upright position would stimulate blood flow and aid in her recovery. So not only was she sleeping in a cold, stone building, but she was forced to sleep upright.

Gelda unlaced Laurel's shirt and inspected the wound. "Stitches look well. Nothing's torn. Thank you for being careful, I know it's hard with the limited mobility."

The next part was Laurel's least favorite; she'd even tried to convince them to let her do it herself. Gelda's wide hands compressed across Laurel's breast, firm and slow. She then rotated her hands and pushed down again. And again. And again. Each compression was agonizing, but necessary, in order to "promote clearing of internal secretions." She could have lived her whole life without learning the word "secretion."

"Do you have any plans for the day?" Gelda asked.

Laurel winced as Gelda's hands pressed against her chest. "It's not like I'm allowed to go anywhere."

"Oh, don't be so dramatic," the large woman said. "You'll be out and about in no time. You're recovering incredibly well. For an achromat that is."

Thanks for the reminder.

Laurel finished the rest of her physical therapy in silence. They took a walk, climbed some stairs, and did breathing exercises that included an absurd task that Gelda called "guided huffing." Breathe in for three. Huff once. Huff twice. Huff a third time. Carefully, of course. Huffing too hard could tear a stitch.

Gale take her and her stupid exercises.

Laurel turned to the doorway and left, making her way back through the hallways to her room. As she approached, she found a strange looking woman waiting for her. The woman's two-toned hair draped over each of her shoulders, one half a dark maroon, and the other a pitch black. The glasses she wore must have been custom made, because the oversized lenses curved along the edges of her brows. Laurel had never seen the style and wondered if the woman had come from somewhere else entirely.

The woman waved and smiled with bright silver teeth on her canines.

With the smallest sliver of hope, Laurel looked over her shoulder. There was no one there. She looked back at the strange woman and smiled cautiously in return.

The woman approached with remarkable swiftness. "Achromic eyes," the woman said with a clear voice while staring at Laurel. "Disproves my theory of a secondary mineral source."

Laurel raised an eyebrow and took a step back.

"My apologies. I only just arrived and had the most curious conversation with Lady Alabella concerning your recent traumatic event. She believes we could be of use to one another." She gestured to Laurel's door. "May we sit?"

The last thing Laurel wanted right now was to talk to a stranger. Her chest still hurt from Gelda's compressions, and her feet were so cold on the stone floor that all she wanted was to crawl into her bed. Unfortunately, if Alabella sent her, Laurel had no choice. She needed to play along if she was going to get what she wanted.

"Any friend of Alabella is a friend of mine," Laurel said before stepping forward and opening the door. They entered the room, and the woman took a seat in a chair in the corner. Laurel sat on her bed. "So, who are you?"

The woman laughed. "Forthright, I can appreciate that. My name is Sarla. Sarla Maltess. I'm a scientist, a physicist, an engineer, and most recently a surgeon. I am whatever is needed for the question at hand, and you are an exceptionally unusual question."

"There's nothing exceptional about me anymore." Laurel lay back against the wall.

"You were a threadweaver, no?"

"I *was*," Laurel replied.

"According to the debrief, you *were* a threadweaver. Your chest was punctured by a blade which, theoretically, shattered your theolith. The Alirian general carried you to the hospital where you were stabilized by the attending physician, only possible due to the high volume of threadlight in your veins, and, when you awoke, your novel achromacy manifested. Lady Alabella's people heard your story and she had you extracted. Fortunately for you, her transfusers have tempered the withdrawals, but your cardiovascular system maintains dependency on threadlight.

"How much has Lady Alabella explained to you about the process of ventricular mineral grafting?"

What? From deep in her chest, Laurel felt her heartbeat quicken. The stitches over her scars seemed to stretch in harmony with each pulse. She wanted to crawl into her bed and throw the sheets over her head. *Ventricular mineral grafting*? She didn't understand half of what the woman said, which terrified her.

"I'd like to speak candidly with you. The surgery we are going to attempt has resulted in the death of most who have received it. We recently had our first successful procedure, but we've been unable to reproduce the results. I have a theory that some human systems see threadlight as a virus and reject it. Your body has accepted its presence once before, and I believe it will again."

Light from the rising sun reflected off of the lock from her bedside chest. She raised a hand to cover her eyes.

Sarla smiled a curious smile. "It will be a risk, of course. Fortunately, there is time for you to decide. The surgery will depend both on your own recovery and either awaiting shipment of our last theolith or recovering more from the Fairenwild."

Laurel perked up. "What about the Fairenwild?"

"Infused gemstones can only be found below the surface," Sarla said, as if Laurel should understand. "Lady Alabella believes there is a cache in the Fairenwild."

"What? Why would she think that?"

"She has some old texts that speak of a path to the core in the center of the forest. We are hoping that there will be a surplus found therein."

Laurel's mind raced. The elders were right. A path to the core. The coreseal. The wonderstone. What did it mean? The elders believed that it guarded the world from evil. Alabella believed it led to what...a cave? The last thing she wanted was for the Bloodthieves to find her home. Alabella had already admitted that she knew about the Zeda people. But if the Zeda guards spotted them, who knew what they would do.

"I want to come," Laurel said.

"Where?" Sarla startled. "The Fairenwild? I'm not certain that you're well enough for that type of journey at the present."

"When are you going?" Laurel asked. "I'll be ready."

"We're going tomorrow."

Gale take me.

"I can handle it. Anyway," Laurel said, grasping for an excuse, "I can guide you there safely. I know the path. I can spot hugweed and treelurks, and even help if the chromawolves attack."

Sarla frowned. "I'll talk to Alabella. It could be nice to have a native guiding us."

"How many are going?"

"Tomorrow is no more than an exploration," Sarla explained. Her eyes seemed to be searching Laurel's. "We'll be no more than ten. If we find infused gemstones, we will return with a larger party for extraction."

Ten people. If they were careful, it was possible. And if they were lucky, Alder would be sleeping on guard duty. She was curious how they planned to open the coreseal and... "What exactly *is* an *infused gemstone*?"

Sarla opened her mouth to speak, then stopped. She clenched her jaw and looked up for a moment before leaning forward. "Threadweaving is not a blessing from the Heralds like most believe, nor the Lightfather, nor whichever deity it is you worship. The truth is more easily explained. Every threadweaver is born with a small sliver of gemstone in their heart called a *theolith*—a mutation of sorts. This gemstone is the source of threadlight that runs through a threadweaver's circulatory system."

Laurel wanted to laugh at the absurdity, but the doctor seemed so serious. "Wait, so you're saying I have a rock in my heart?"

"Had," Sarla said flatly. "The blade shattered your theolith. It then poured its threadlight through you, which saved your life but removed the source. Thus, you are now achromic. Once we've obtained more of these theoliths, or gemstones infused with threadlight, we will insert a small shard into your left ventricle to serve as your new theolith."

Laurel's mind was a whirlwind, racing this way and that, crashing through memories and tearing apart all that she knew to be true. Was being a threadweaver nothing more than a pebble in your chest? The Zeda people taught that it was a sign of being "chosen" by the Father of All, and that the reason so many Zeda people were threadweavers was because they were a chosen people. Perhaps they were both true?

More importantly, it explained how they planned to fix her. It wasn't safe. It wasn't sure. It was an assumption that her past would allow her to live where others had died. But it was the only trail ahead; there was no other route to take if she wanted to undo what had been done. She couldn't live the rest of her life without threadlight.

"Okay," Laurel began. "Tell me what I need to do."

"Continue your physical therapy. We must wait for your heart to recover. Enough to survive the surgery, but not so long that threadlight becomes viewed as a foreign substance. On that note, it is important that you continue drinking the transfusers. We need your body to think nothing has changed, to decrease the chance of rejection."

Sarla adjusted her glasses and nodded as she stepped out of the room, leaving Laurel once again in silence.

Laurel sat back against the wall. She had a lot to think about, but, more than anything, she needed to prepare. Tomorrow, she was headed to the Fairenwild.

Heralds save me.

Empress Chailani of Felia sat atop a rose-colored throne, flanked by an immaculate collection of white drapes that flowed down from the ceiling like rays of threadlight. White roses filled the outskirts of the room, budding along the walkway, up the carpeted stairway, and amassing beneath each of the colossal throne-room windows. The ceiling towered overhead, each step—though muffled on the velvet floor—a choral prelude to their presence.

Alverax walked behind the Zeda elders, beside the woman he'd saved, Iriel Valerian. His hands shook as he passed a dozen threadweaver guards who stared at him with their chromatic eyes. He tried not to return the gaze, but their dark skin instilled in him an immediate sense of kinship. Of the dozens of Felians in the throne room, only one was not dark skinned, an Alirian man with hair like white marble. Being in Felia felt good, and not just because he'd spent the last weeks trudging through the countryside and smelling like a taractus turd.

As they reached the bottom of the stairs leading to the throne, the Empress rose to her feet. Her hair danced as thick dreads fell gracefully past her cheek. The gold in her crown matched the gold of her dress and the clasps adorning her hair harmonized flawlessly. White sleeves faded to the same shimmering gold along the curves of her waist. Against her umber skin, each golden accent shone like the sun. And her eyes, blue as the sea itself, froze the room with the simplest gaze.

Two others stood beside her.

Before he realized it, Alverax found himself standing while the rest of his retinue knelt before the Empress. He quickly corrected his mistake, cursing under his breath.

A man with a sultry voice raised his hands and spoke. "Introducing the Lady of Light, the Sun Queen, Empress Chailani Vayse. And with her, the Mistress of Mercy, her sister, the Sun Daughter."

"Please, stand," the empress commanded. "It is not every day that a people lost to myth come promenading into my city."

Elder Rosemary smiled. "Privacy is a boon only in its broadest application. Empress Chailani, you honor us with your invitation."

The empress furrowed her brows. "In the City of Sun, we value transparency, so let me be clear. I do not trust you, nor your people. Some believe you to be counterfeits, a guise for mass immigration. Perhaps a constituent of the Bloodthieves to infest our streets. Others do not believe the Bloodthieves would be so forthright. That you are who you claim to be. If the latter are correct, then we will have much to discuss, and perhaps reparations to be made. If they are wrong, then the Heralds will greet every one of your people by the end of the week."

Alverax swallowed hard. What if they were both right? If they found out that Alverax *had been* a member of the Bloodthieves, it would jeopardize the entire safety of the Zeda people. The last thing he needed was to be responsible for mass genocide.

"Then I pray our story finds its way into honest ears." Elder Rosemary gestured to the women standing beside her. "Please, allow me to introduce the Elders of our people. We do not have a singular shepherd. Instead, five women are called to be the ruling council. Our most senior member is Elder Violet here to my left. Beside her is Elder Ashwa and Elder Ivy. To my right is Elder Rowan. And I am Elder Rosemary. As I presume you've heard, our home was destroyed by the very Bloodthieves you fear. We have come seeking sanctuary."

Empress Chailani nodded as she observed each of the women. She turned to the older man at her left and whispered something Alverax could not hear. While he responded, the young woman to Chailani's right spoke up.

"And who are the others?" she asked.

The empress turned to the young woman and scowled. "Excuse my sister. She has forgotten her place. However, the question stands. Who are the others you have brought with you?"

If Alverax had felt uncomfortable before, the feeling blossomed as the Elders turned to look at him and the others. He had not wanted to come in the first place, but the Elders insisted that keeping the presence of an Obsidian threadweaver a secret would endanger their people. The Felians valued truth and transparency; their justice for dishonesty was renowned.

Elder Rosemary continued to be the voice of the Elders. They hoped that her calm demeanor would encourage at least a small measure of sympathy from the Felian royals. She gestured to the only other man in the group. "He is called Dogwood. In Zedalum, he led the training and application of our threadweavers. You should know that the majority of our people are threadweavers, though few are trained to fight. Beside him are Trill and Anise. They are our historians.

"The other two are not of our people. The woman is Iriel Valerian, wife to High General Chrys Valerian of Alchea. The young man is Alverax Blightwood. We have brought them both here in the spirit of transparency, and because we know you would not believe us otherwise." She paused just long enough to regain their full attention. "Alverax is an Obsidian threadweaver, and the child in Iriel's arms is an Amber threadweaver."

The older man standing beside the empress huffed, then whispered something. He had the brilliant green eyes of an Emerald.

The empress began her descent of the velvet-inlaid steps beneath her. "Stories of Obsidian threadweavers have been passed down among our people for centuries. If what you claim is true, then I, for one, am comforted to know of their reality. It is confirmation of our truths. However, Watchlord Osinan has reminded me that there is one particular line of relevance in the Tome of the Heralds: 'purge Amber lest their chains bind you.'"

Alverax turned to Iriel who clutched her child with a little more fervor. Were they implying that they would murder a child? What did he know of their culture and religion? He knew they worshipped the Heralds, whom they called The Timeless Ones. But that was all. He didn't know *how* they worshipped the Heralds. Human sacrifice? Infanticide? Religion—even true religion—has a tendency to twist itself into nothing more than justification for human turpitude.

"Though it is a less obscure doctrine, it is doctrine nonetheless." The empress continued her descent. "It is also our custom to reward candor —of which you have shown much—and for that I make you this promise. I will allow no harm to come to the child. The decision is not, however, invariable. And so, if our scholars discover reasons to revise it, we will do so. Concerning the Obsidian, in our texts, such threadweavers were seen as the closest allies to the Heralds. Their right hand. Tell me, boy, are you dangerous?"

Alverax froze. The Empress of Felia was addressing *him*. "Umm, I don't think so? Elder Rowan does. Iriel doesn't. That's another story. But, in general, I don't think I am. I've never killed anyone. Directly at least. So, I guess on that count I'm not."

Iriel came to his rescue. "Alverax is brave and strong, but he is not dangerous. He saved my life in the Fairenwild, and that of my son. If anything, he is a hero."

From behind Elder Violet's head, Alverax saw the empress' sister leaning over so she could see his face. They caught eyes and her head tilted to the side. She was even more beautiful than her sister. In Cynosure, all of the Felians hid the coarseness of their hair by keeping it slicked or dreaded, but the empress' sister let it explode into a cloud of dark curls, celebrating the texture. Not to mention the smooth skin she flaunted so effortlessly. *Heralds*. He was staring.

"It does not surprise me to hear of heroism coming from a Felian. Although I'd wager only one of your parents was from here. Was it your mother or father?" the empress asked.

"My father," he replied. "I never knew my mother."

She turned from him, as if his presence had run its course, and turned back to Elder Rosemary. "*Your* paternity is far less clear. You claim to be the people of Zedalum, a secret city deep in the Fairenwild. Osinan, share what we have learned about the Zeda people."

The man to her left stood forward. His long hair flowed back behind him in thick braids, and his gray beard moved as he spoke. "There have long been rumors of a people living in the Fairenwild. Some accounts call them ghosts, others call them spawn of the earth's core. One account claims they are separatists from the days of the Timeless. We do not know the truth, my Empress, but it is *possible* that they are who they claim to be.

"However, it is more likely that they have come to infect our city, cattle bearing a plague. The timing is too coincidental to be ignored. The

Bloodthieves arrive, and not a month later a swarm of locusts follow. True or not, their presence is a threat."

Alverax had gotten to know the Elders fairly well over the last week of travel, and he knew that look on Elder Rowan's face. Pure, unadulterated indignation. He honestly wasn't sure how the old woman was still alive. Someone with such a high level of anger must be constantly on the verge of a heart attack. For whatever reason, the bubbling ire creeping out from the corner of her mouth brought Alverax a weird sense of comfort.

Until she spoke.

"Madness!" she shouted. "You threaten our children, you threaten our people, and you threaten our honor. We came in the spirit of honesty, not to be slandered by conjecture and fear-filled guesswork! Come, Rosemary. We will find elsewhere for our people to live."

"Rowan," Elder Rosemary said sternly. "Now is not the time to be unreasonable."

Elder Ashwa spoke for the first time. "We are all on the same side. Our home was destroyed by the Bloodthieves, and we have come to a city under similar threat. Perhaps the Father of All has led us here so that we might help each other."

"As heroic as that may sound to you," Empress Chailani cut in, "we have more than enough strength to protect ourselves. The Bloodthieves are a mosquito. They pose no real threat to us. An army of threadweavers, however. Where you see a chance to help, we see a chance to attack from within."

"If we could prove our pedigree, would you let us stay?" Elder Rosemary asked.

Watchlord Osinan nodded. "Now is not the time to play games. If you have proof, bring it forward."

"We do," Elder Rosemary acknowledged.

"These pagans don't deserve our secrets!" Elder Rowan shouted.

"Guard your tongue!" Osinan's eyes were fire.

The empress' sister jumped to her feet. "Osinan, stand down! I understand your hesitation but, if what these people claim is true, then they deserve our patience. Test your feet in their waters. Uprooted from their homes. Run out by wicked men. Forced to find shelter in a foreign world with foreign customs. They have every right to be tired, and angry, and impatient. Let us be patient. Careful, yes. Thorough, without a doubt. But let patience be our guiding light."

Bright sunlight filtered down through towering windowpanes. Both parties, humbled by the princess' words, bowed their heads in shame. Alverax stood breathless, staring. The corners of his vision seemed to blur as the world focused on her. There was something about her. She was the first ray of light in the dawn. But, to his heart's lament, she was also a damn princess.

"The Sun Daughter is right." Empress Chailani stepped back and took her seat on the throne. "Elder Rosemary, I apologize for our manners. Please come forward and present your case. We will try our best to be honest truth seekers, but do not expect blind acceptance. The world is shifting, and dangers are rising like the tides. We must protect our people, as you must protect yours.

"The rest of you may leave. We will speak with Elder Rosemary alone."

Alverax and the others were led away by the guards. He looked back over his shoulder and saw Elder Rosemary ascending the dais carrying a chest. While looking behind, he saw Elder Rowan smiling to herself and, in that moment, he understood. The old bat had faked it. Somehow, she'd known that the empress' sister would come to their aid.

He slowed down and approached Elder Rowan. "How did you know?"

"Know what, boy?"

"How did you know that the sister would defend you?"

Elder Rowan smiled at him for the first time. "You are more observant than I would have given you credit for. The most important lesson in politics is: assess your assets. We asked around and learned who was likely to be in the room. The empress' sister is known to be empathetic and merciful, a balance to her sister's staunch sovereignty. We knew that they would put on a strong front and, if we could get Jisenna to show us mercy, we would have a better chance at—"

His mind lost track of the Elder's voice, focusing only on a single word she'd spoken. A name. A symbol. Jisenna. Her name was Jisenna.

Focus, he told himself. *Forget about the girl.*

"—It helps that I am old. Both men and women are more sympathetic to the elderly. So, in short, we didn't know. It was a well-informed wager."

A well-informed wager. Alverax had underestimated her. He'd assumed she'd gotten where she was because people were afraid of her, but there was clearly more to it. It made sense. Not just any old lady could become an Elder. He wanted to know more. How did she get where she was? Was she married? His grandfather was—

"There are a dozen rooms in the east wing you may use to rest," one of the guards said, a tall man with a nose ring and a bald head. He led them down an empty corridor. "The empress has asked that you stay in your room until the negotiations have concluded."

Elder Rowan nodded and turned back to Alverax, offering the remnant of a smile. "I'm quite certain that you didn't hear a word I just said. If I may offer one suggestion before we part ways—and I hope you are listening now—don't do anything stupid."

With a tone soaked to the core with sarcasm, he replied, "I'll do my best."

They parted ways and Alverax ended up in a large room with an unbelievable view. Out of his window, the Terecean Sea stretched as far as the eye could see, dotted with a large archipelago that formed the start of the Alirian Islands. Dozens of ships traveled between, carrying valuable trade cargo. Down below, at the piers, thousands of people traveled like ants along the streets and boardwalks. Nearly every building in Felia was white. He'd seen similar designs in Cynosure, inspired by Felian architecture, but these were something else.

If Cynosure was the moon, Felia was the sun, and he basked in its warmth.

HE'D SLEPT LONGER than anticipated, but the mattress was a billowing cloud, and he felt nearly weightless on its surface. He smiled and severed his corethread. Threadlight burst apart beneath him, and his body drifted into true weightlessness. It surprised him how casually he was able to threadweave now. At first, he'd had to open himself to all threadlight and then filter all of the threads he didn't want to see. Now, he could shift just his corethread into view. It was less awe-inspiring, but much more effective.

Just as he embraced his weightless state, a knock came at his door. He scrambled to sit up but, without the force of gravity pulling him down, he went spiraling up into the air. The ceiling greeted him with a thud. He scratched at the wall, scrambling in a chaotic display of clumsiness, then finally pushed off down to the ground. He grabbed onto the bed's corner post, repositioned himself, and pushed off once again, gliding toward the door in time for a second knock.

Unsure how to open it in his current state, he spoke. "Yes? Hello? Who is it?"

A deep voice replied. "The first stage of negotiations is complete. The empress has released the room restriction, but we ask that you do not step outside the palace gates."

Alverax smiled. "Great. Thank you."

Now that he was rested and no longer confined to his room, he was ready to explore.

But first he had to awkwardly float in the air for another minute.

When his corethread finally reappeared, he fell to his feet, with more grace than he deserved, and opened the door, stepping out into the broad hallway where he dodged a stream of busy workers. The decor in the Palace of the Sun was unlike anything Alverax had ever seen. Flowers everywhere, lining stairwells and windows, and tied together into immaculate bouquets everywhere he looked. Against the white stone used for the majority of the palace, the red was a striking juxtaposition.

Within the sprawling main entryway, a massive indoor fountain centered the room. Hundreds of potted plants lined its edge. The greenery, draped with white and red linens, connected each plant with the next. He'd never had the chance to step inside Endin Keep, but he had a feeling it didn't share the same elegance as the Palace of the Sun.

The flowing fountain reminded him of a small waterfall back in Cynosure, deep in a cave east of Mercy's Bluff. He and his friends had spent countless nights soaking in the base of the fall, talking and dreaming. Often, they'd dreamed of leaving Cynosure.

For the next hour, Alverax wandered the palace, silently exploring, admiring, and daydreaming. What he'd most wanted to explore was the colossal hippodrome he'd seen on their way to the palace. It was like an elegant, regal version of the Pit in Cynosure, and he imagined himself seated in the stands, cheering on whatever games they played within.

It felt so good. These were his people. His grandparents were Felian, born and raised, but had left to Cynosure for reasons he'd never cared to ask about. Alabella had as well, but he hated thinking about her. He'd never had a mother, and he knew that deep down there was some weird psychological need he'd let her fill, despite her ill-intent. What worried him more was what she was planning to do now that the coreseal had been broken. Was the rest of her plan a lie? Or did she really want everyone to become a threadweaver?

He turned a corner and felt a surge of warm air billowing out from an open doorway. A small sign marked the room as *The Sun Bath*. He appreciated the pun but was more excited about soaking in the warm waters. Steps inside led down to a vast, open space with two separate pools of water, lit only by a few wall lamps. Steam rose up from the farther pool.

Alverax stripped off his clothes and placed them under a bench as he made his way over to the far side of the room. He stepped down into the water, embracing the warmth. The smell of the steam reminded him of stone after a good rainfall. The water had always been comforting to him and, now that he was an Obsidian threadweaver, it felt even more like home. Weightlessness. He'd never made the connection before. His love for water had, in a way, been a precursor.

He let himself slip below the surface of the pool. Back in Cynosure, he was the undefeated champion of breath-holding. A dozen people had tried to dethrone him in the pools not far from Mercy's Bluff—one kid passed out trying—but he always won. He had a vivid memory of his father glaring down at him in disapproval after one such game. Once a giant taractus turd, always a giant taractus turd, and his father was the largest of them all.

As he meditated below the surface of the pool, he opened his eyes and noticed a large grate on the far wall. He wondered where the water came from. But then, as he was floating and enjoying the surrounding warmth, massive hands reached down, grabbed his shoulders, and wrenched him out of the water like a beached whale. Two fit men in black pinned his naked body to the stone floor.

"Who are you?" the first shouted with a deep voice.

Alverax struggled to respond as his face pressed harder to the floor.

"Answer him!" the other demanded.

"I'm nobody!" Alverax whimpered. "I was just relaxing!"

A woman's voice cut the tension. "Wait. I recognize him." Her bare feet pressed against the floor as she came closer. "Cheth, give him a towel. Innix, release him, but stay close."

His cheek throbbed from the stone and his back still ached from the guard's sharp knee. He wanted to stand up and yell at someone for mistreatment of fine assets, but instead he stayed sprawled out on the floor until Cheth returned with a towel. He wrapped himself and turned around.

Heralds, no.
It can't be.
Princess Jisenna.
The Mistress of Mercy.
The Sun Daughter.
In the Sun Bath.
Don't do anything stupid, Alverax.

After a brief moment, the princess tilted her head to the side.

"Alexander Grant," he said before he could stop himself.

"What?"

"I—" he shut his mouth...finally.

She raised a brow. "Do you know who I am?"

He nodded, afraid to speak.

"If my sister discovered that you were in my bath waiting for me, she would likely consider you an assassin. She could have your entire people imprisoned or executed."

"Well, they're not exactly my people," Alverax blurted out. Without thinking. Again. Because surely thinking would not be helpful given the current situation.

"So, you would be content should they all die?"

"No—" he stumbled. "Of course not. I was just in here relaxing. I swear I didn't know it was your bath. I should go." He shuffled away from the pool toward his clothes beneath the bench.

"Is it true?" she asked.

He turned to her.

"Is it true that you are an Obsidian threadweaver?" Her eyes danced from each of his black eyes, looking for a deeper truth. She stepped closer. "Truth be told, I never believed such a thing was possible."

Alverax let out a laugh. "Neither did I."

"How do you mean?" she said, looking puzzled.

Heralds save me.

The Elders definitely did *not* want him to share his connection to the Bloodthieves. If the empress found out, who knew what they'd do. And as much as he liked to pretend that he was a good liar, he knew it wasn't true. It was the one useful trait he could have inherited from his father. Instead, he got the man's smile.

Jisenna pursed her lips. "It appears I've stumbled upon some secret that perhaps the Zeda elders would not have me know."

Seriously, Heralds. Any time now. "It's not a secret. It's just that I don't even understand it fully."

"Maybe I can help?" Her hair fluttered as she spoke. The closer she came, the more clearly he could see the freckles on her collarbone and the curves of her neck.

He caught himself, quickly shifting his gaze to meet hers once again. "I know it sounds crazy, but I wasn't born a threadweaver. So, unless you know how someone can become a threadweaver, I'm not sure you can help."

Her eyes never left his as she listened. It wasn't until that moment that he realized...her eyes were brown. She was an achromat. But her sister's—Alverax remembered from the throne room—were blue as the sea itself.

"You're serious," she said, brushing her hands over her arms. "I have chills, Alverax. There have been rumors of such things in the past. They say the Heralds gifted powerful threadlight to their most trusted. Those are stories. But you are *real*." She paused, eyes narrowing. "I must ask you—and I will know if you lie to me—are you here to kill me?"

"No," he said defensively.

Her eyes narrowed. "You are not a Bloodthief?"

Heralds. Any question but that. His eyes fell to the surface of the water. His myriad thoughts crashed into each other, a cacophony of waves against a rocky shore. There was no honest way to answer without damning himself and the others. He wasn't, but he had been. Maybe if he just left it at that. Omission.

"I am not," he replied.

Her lips curled into a frown. "But?"

"No *but*. I am not a Bloodthief."

"Then why do your words taste like stale bread?"

He didn't respond.

"Well, if the negotiations continue as they have today, I imagine we will see each other again soon. They will want to study you and dig into the particulars of your conversion. Thank you for the unexpected company. I promise not to disclose of our meeting here. Perhaps someday you will be more forthcoming. For now, I am still in need of a bath. Innix, please show our friend to the exit."

The large man nodded.

"Oh, and Alverax," she said, holding her black and gold shawl with both hands. "Next time we speak, you should tell me about this 'Alexander Grant' character."

She winked and it nearly killed him.

4

A WEEK HAD PASSED since the Apogee—who called himself Relek—had slaughtered the Alchean soldiers in the Everstone Mountains. Chrys' last vestige of hope, a single spark in the chaotic darkness, was the dream of reuniting with his family, and it faded with each step he took.

The red-haired man, Velan, practically worshipped Relek. Autelle, on the other hand, hadn't spoken a single word since they left the campsite in the mountains. Every night, as Chrys lay dormant within the Apogee's mind, he could hear the sniffling sound of Autelle's tears. If he were able to cry himself, Chrys might have joined her.

As they continued their trek, they entered a swampy forest east of the mountains. Thick vines hung between trees, and most of the ground was submerged in varying levels of water. Strange creatures swung from tree to tree on arms that seemed too long for their bodies. Others hung from branches by their tails, making noises that sounded dangerously close to laughter.

The first night in the swamp, Relek killed one of the creatures and cooked it on an open fire. Skinned and roasting on a flame, the animal had the rough appearance of a small child. Velan ate his worth, but Autelle refused. Chrys thought he heard her whisper the word *cannibal* under her breath at least once.

Chrys didn't know what to think of Relek. He'd assumed that it was some broken piece of his own subconscious, but, with each passing day trapped in his mind, Chrys began to doubt. Relek was something more. He had to be. If he wasn't, none of it made sense.

The worst part was that it had now been weeks since he'd left Iriel and Aydin in the Fairenwild. The truth, though he still refused to accept it, was that he would likely never see them again. Even if he regained control, he was lost in the Wastelands.

What hurt the most was knowing that Iriel would forever see him as the man who'd left her when she needed him most. Part of him wondered if Relek was only in control because Chrys allowed him to be. Because he was too weak to fight. Too defeated to contest. A failure. Nothing but an empty voice in another man's head.

They kept pace for another two days, Relek guiding them past hidden traps and unseen dangers. At one point, a hairy gray creature—like the great apes of western Alir—twice the size of a man, with yellow spikes down its back, sat at the base of a tree, peeling a bright red fruit. Thick tusks wrapped around its jaw like a wild boar. When Velan pointed it out, Relek called it an *ataçan* and instructed them not to make eye contact.

Autelle's mind seemed at the verge of collapse. She'd begun whispering to herself, looking over her shoulder, paranoid about each and every crunching leaf or drip of water. The first time she spoke, she ranted about the entire experience being nothing more than a nightmare. She claimed that she was still in the cave, asleep, with a high temperature, and none of it was real.

If only that were true.

The terrain sloped upward, and Relek paused. "Beyond this ridge is Kai'Melend. The people there will not take well to our arrival. Be calm, and do not act."

Velan nodded and Autelle stared at the ground.

They hiked over a mossy ridge and found themselves looking out over a sprawling jungle city. A massive statue of a beast similar to the one they'd seen previously stood on a raised pedestal in the center. Homes built on low stilted foundations fanned out in tight groups just above the swamp water. Ladders. Rope swings. And hundreds, if not thousands, of wastelanders. Young and old, all with small frames, gray skin, and beady, gray eyes.

A memory of the war flashed in Chrys' mind. He remembered the first wastelander he'd ever seen. So close to human, yet so very different. Large canine teeth glinting in the sun as the enemy screamed their attack. Drooping, pointed earlobes waving as they rushed forward. White hair, like the people of Alir. And the tattoos. Every wastelander had strips of black curling over their arms and necks.

The memory faded, and the swamp returned.

Wastelanders shouted and grabbed weapons as they sprinted toward Chrys' group. One of the massive ataçan creatures leapt down from a platform, hitting the ground with a resounding thud and an explosion of water. It moved forward, using its long arms to pull itself on all fours, until a wastelander with impossibly thick arms leapt atop the beast's shoulders.

Relek stepped forward and raised his arms in the air, crossing his wrists, then bringing the tips of his fingers together, palms out.

The wastelanders hissed.

The warrior atop the ataçan leapt off and strode forward, his thick arms swinging low as he eyed the strangers. In a nasally voice, he spat a smattering of foreign syllables and, somehow, Chrys understood. *This sign is not for your kind.*

Relek released the sign and reached out a hand in invitation. Odd sounds formed from his own tongue. *I have returned to the hive.*

The ataçan beat its chest and released a series of deep grunts. The wastelander stepped back, scowling with its wide, thin lips. *If it is true, say it. Speak his name.*

Deep in his mind, Chrys heard the response, clear as though it were spoken in his own tongue. *I am Relek, the Great Anchor, God of the An'tara, King of the Hive.*

Every wastelander who could hear his voice dropped to their knees, crossing their arms and connecting the tips of their fingers in the same way, prostrating themselves before him.

In that moment, Chrys knew with certainty. The Apogee was not a piece of his imagination. It was not a broken shard of his soul. It was a monster. A wastelander spirit of some kind, worshipped by the pagans of the east.

Relek never told them to rise. He let them bow as he led Velan and Autelle toward the village. In the distance, another figure appeared. She wore more clothing than the rest of the wastelanders, covering almost the entirety of her limbs and torso. Neither she nor Relek spoke until they were close.

Brother, the woman said with a gravelly voice.

Lylax, he replied. *You look well.*

She coughed. *Now is not the time for humor. How you managed to live in one of these frail corpses for so long, I will never understand.*

It was no easy feat.

It is crippling.

It is, but do not worry. I anticipated your distaste. Relek smiled. *This woman is human. I brought her for you.*

Lylax raised her brow. *She is not gifted.*

My options were few.

It will do.

It is good to see you, Relek said. *Though I am surprised that after so many years you have not returned with an army in tow. I hope you have not grown soft. There is no room for mercy this time.*

Do not worry, brother. I've given instructions to the smartest of the beasts. They will prepare the way for us.

Like most wastelanders, Lylax was a full head shorter than Chrys. She looked up, inspecting Autelle, then pulled out a knife. Tears streaked down the Alchean woman's cheeks as Lylax drew close. The wastelander woman cut into her own palm, followed by a clean slice into Autelle's, then placed both palms together. As soon as the hands touched, both women screamed out in pain. Their backs arched. Their heads threw back with force. The wastelander body convulsed wildly, her head shaking back and forth in an unnatural blur of speed. Then, finally, she fell to the ground, swamp water splashing beneath her lifeless corpse.

For a brief moment, Chrys felt a sliver of hope that something had gone wrong, and that Lylax had died. But then Autelle smiled, and the curve of her lip was wrong.

She was no longer Autelle.

What Relek had done to Chrys, Lylax had done to Autelle.

Another memory from the war flashed in Chrys' mind. A wastelander, strong, taller than the others, his entire cheek covered with dozens of perfectly circular tattooed dots. There was a certain greed in his smile as he eyed Chrys' Sapphire veins.

That smile.

Relek.

She is stronger than she looks, Autelle said, the words ripping Chrys away from the memory. She waved her hands back and forth, inspecting them.

"My god," Velan said with excitement in his eyes. "I...am I to be a vessel as well?"

Relek turned to face him. "Yes."

"Is there another?" he asked.

"You will be *my* vessel. This man, Chrys, killed many of the wastelanders. I will give him to them as a gift."

Velan's eyes grew wide. He dropped to his knees and tried, poorly, to mimic the sign of worship that the wastelanders had made, but his hands were trembling. "I am ready."

"Come here," Relek commanded. Velan stood and took a step forward, putting out his hand like Autelle had done. Lylax handed Relek the blade and he cut a line down each of their palms.

Chrys could feel the pain of the blade as he stood watching the exchange. He realized that these might be his final moments. The woman's previous vessel, the wastelander, seemed to be dead in the swamp water. If Chrys did nothing...

He would never see his family again.

Chrys threw his will against the barrier in his mind, one last savage attempt at freedom. Weeks of pent-up anger, fear, and hopelessness came surging down against the barrier like an avalanche, crushing against it, demanding release. He felt the barrier weakening in his mind.

Relek gasped.

Chrys did it again. For his wife and for his son, he beat at the barrier with every scrap of strength he had within him.

"You are too late," Relek whispered.

Chrys felt his body convulse. A raw scream came pouring out of his throat as his back arched in pain. He threw his will one last time against the barrier, but it was already gone.

His body toppled into the swamp water.

THERE WAS a much-needed comfort in returning to her training exercises. Iriel Valerian breathed in as she bent her knees, keeping her core tight, and running her fists through the fighting forms she'd practiced so many times before. Performing them again felt like coming home, and the quiet of the Felian courtyard gave her life.

It wasn't that she didn't like being a mother—it was beautiful, and she already felt herself growing in ways she never would have otherwise—but she just wasn't convinced she was good at it. She'd barely been able to keep Aydin alive, and that was the bare minimum for the job.

The worst part was that he knew. Somehow, the little newborn knew that she was failing and refused to latch for his feedings. The truth of it nearly crushed her, settling in her stomach, in her heart, her mind. Anxiety for her child's wellbeing. Anxiety that she wasn't capable. Anxiety that she was failing. And resentment every time Aydin cried when she just needed one minute alone. Then guilt for her own resentment.

Iriel shook her head and cleared her mind of her child—she cleared her mind of Chrys and where he might be—and she embraced the kata.

She brought her foot up into the air and stumbled as her muscles reminded themselves of months-long deprivation. But soon enough, she felt the quivering muscles in her stomach steady themselves, and her stance solidified. She couldn't imagine women giving birth without threadlight to speed up the recovery.

She moved onto the next, and the next. Her hands moved like blades through the air, cutting forward, then pausing while her shoulders and forearms tightened.

Her father had paid for her first lessons when she was young. The confidence that came from being an Emerald threadweaver often came at the expense of injury or harm. While Sapphires could *push* weapons and change the flow of a fight without much thought, an Emerald had to be smarter. Since she was young, she'd trained with palmguards, a technique first developed on the islands of Kulai. A special glove that was worn with metal only on the insides of the hand. When a blade struck toward an Emerald, they could *pull* the weapon to their hand, grasp hold of it with the shielded palm, and disarm or reverse the attack. She missed the feel of the steel against her hand.

Running through the forms gave her the sense of control she needed. Since fleeing Alchea, it felt like she hadn't made a choice for herself. Every decision came down to what Aydin needed. It didn't upset her—frustrated, perhaps—but there was still an overarching sense of pressure that seemed to cloud her. She just needed to be alone, and, stones, no one ever told her how difficult it would be to find alone time as a mother.

She finished up her kata, brow glistening with sweat, and nodded to the Felian guards posted along the wall-walk, a habit she'd picked up from Chrys.

As she walked slowly through the hallway, she thought of her missing husband. She wished Chrys were there with her. Stones, she just wished she knew that he was okay. She'd seen the look in his eyes, the coldness, that foreign gaze, and she feared what it meant for him. Would he ever return? His mother, Willow, had also yet to return, and, though she knew it was stupidly selfish, Iriel wished Willow were there to help with Aydin.

It seemed silly to feel so lonely. She was surrounded by people, and there were many among the Zeda that she'd grown close to. Like Cara, the burly chromawolf trainer who'd been unable to have children of her own, who had offered to help with Aydin whenever Iriel needed a break, or at least whenever Iriel's guilt of unloading her child on another was less than her need for solitude. At times it felt like Cara was mothering Iriel as much as she was Aydin.

Then there was Alverax, the biggest surprise. Throughout their time traveling from the Fairenwild to Felia, she'd become unexpectedly protective of him. Almost like a younger brother. Sure, he'd saved her life and the life of her child, but, even more than the debt she owed him, she saw in him a young man trying to do what was right.

When she finally arrived back at her room, she pushed open the large, oak door and found Cara seated in the rocking chair with Aydin quietly asleep on her shoulder. She gave Cara a silent wave as she entered.

The broad Zeda woman smiled in return. "Never woke up," she said. "He's a hard sleeper, this one. Doesn't seem to have much of a preference for position either."

"I'm glad he slept for you," Iriel said, taking a seat on the bed. "He's had some rough nights since we arrived in the city. I swear he liked it better out on the road."

"A boy after my own heart," Cara said. "All this stone...it's too stuffy. I don't like it. Nothing quite like the smell of tree bark and a chill breeze to give you life."

Looking out the window, Iriel remembered the cold nights she'd spent traveling from the Fairenwild, fearing for the health of her newborn.

"It gets easier," Cara said.

Iriel turned to her.

"How you're feeling," she continued. "It's more common than you'd think."

"What do you mean?"

Cara smiled. "People focus so much on the physical pain of childbirth that they forget the mental burden is often worse, and longer lasting. I saw the smartest woman I know barricade herself in a room for two days, a few weeks after she gave birth. People thought she'd gone mad. When she finally came out, she was perfectly fine, apologized, and now she's the best mother I know. Point is you have to give your roots room to grow and accept that you're bound to run into a few rocks along the way."

"Is it that obvious?" Iriel asked.

Cara didn't need to respond.

Iriel put her head in her hands. "I just feel so restless. My husband is missing, and I'm stuck here. I want to be out there searching for him, fighting for him. Helping. Doing something. Anything. I was worried about it before, but I thought it would just go away. If anything, it's gotten worse. I'm starting to think that maybe I'm just not made for motherhood."

"Iriel," Cara said with a soft voice. "It's like comparing granite to clay. The clay may take shape more easily, but the granite, once you've chiseled it into place, is so much stronger. For some people, motherhood comes more easily. For others, it takes a hammer and chisel. No one is *made* for motherhood. Motherhood is made for *you*. Some of us aren't so lucky."

Her words cut Iriel to the core. She felt so ungrateful. Here she was complaining to someone about something they'd spent decades craving. Given the circumstances, Iriel had plenty to be grateful for. "I'm sorry. I...shouldn't complain."

"You've been through hell," Cara said. "Complaining is healthy. I just don't want you to be so hard on yourself. A few dark clouds don't make a storm. Just give it a bit of time."

Iriel smiled and moved to lift Aydin from Cara's shoulder. "Thank you...for everything."

"You know I love doing this." Cara helped lift the child so he wouldn't wake. "Reminds me a bit of taking care of my little chromawolf pups. But I never had them this young."

Carefully, Iriel laid the child's head back onto her own shoulder. He seemed to fit perfectly in the crook of her neck.

Cara stood and walked to the door. "I'll chat with the elders and see if they have anything you can help out with. It's good to stay busy when you're feeling down. And don't forget, you're not in this alone."

Iriel mouthed the words "thank you" and settled into the rocking chair.

Despite Cara's calming words, a deep restlessness remained.

She only hoped she could rein it in.

STONES OF LIGHT
6

IN THE EARLY MORNING AIR, long before the sun had peaked its grand eye over the horizon, Laurel breathed in the dew and repeated the same lie over and over again.

Everything will be okay.

But she knew better.

The Zeda people would see Alabella's party as they approached the wonderstone and, in no time at all, dozens of armed threadweavers would descend from the trees. They would never let the grounders leave alive, and Laurel would never receive a new theolith. For her own sake—for the sake of the tremble in her left hand that refused to steady itself—she needed to make sure they weren't seen, even if that meant incapacitating the guard stationed on the entrance platform.

Part of her dreaded the idea of returning to Zedalum. She hadn't left things well with her family, and there was a good chance her grandfather would be taken by the next Gale. If she was too late, she would never forgive herself.

While she waited, she felt at the stitches over her breast and was surprised to find very little pain. It still held soreness deep below the surface, but the skin and muscle had recovered well. Sarla had explained to her that drinking the transfusers would accelerate the healing of her chest, but it had its own side-effects. Laurel had to drink extra water to account for the vomiting.

When the others arrived, Laurel was sitting under an apple tree hiding from the moon and a growing mob of storm clouds. Her eyes—heavy with bags and the whites stained red from lack of sleep—opened at the sound of footsteps. Alabella walked along the path accompanied by a thick Alchean man with arms too large for his shirt, carrying a sack over his shoulder.

Up until now, Laurel had only seen Alabella in fanciful dresses, but now she wore a pair of dark trousers and a loose-fitting top. "Laurel," Alabella said. "I heard you were out here waiting."

The man smiled and extended his hand. "Name's Barrick. Nice to meet you."

Laurel rose to her feet and was surprised at how large Barrick's hand was; it seemed to envelope the entirety of her own. "Hello."

"Are you sure you're up for this?" Alabella asked, with the slightest twitch of her brow.

"I'm fine," Laurel quipped. She rubbed at the veins on the back of her left hand while eyeing the bulging Sapphire blue running through Barrick's forearm.

"Just, take it easy," Alabella said. "Every rose begins a bud."

Barrick snorted. "As long as I don't end up with a thorn in my arse."

Alabella ignored him. "The others will be awaiting us at the border. Let's be off."

They traveled many hours before reaching the edge of the Fairenwild. There, dwarfed by the great feytrees, five people sat in shadow with a large wooden pushcart and a few bags of supplies. It felt odd to be approaching the forest with others. All of her messenger runs had been done alone. Now, not only was she not alone, but she was with a dangerous group of Bloodthief grounders.

The closer they came to the rest of the party, the more quickly Laurel was able to note the colorful eyes of each of them. Together with Barrick, that made two Sapphires, four Emeralds, one Amber, and a Laurel, the lone achromat. If chromawolves attacked, they looked well-able to defend themselves. If it was Asher, maybe they wouldn't have to.

She thought of her friend, and she would have felt more guilty for leaving him if he didn't have his new pack. He was happy with his new family, which gave her just enough peace of mind to offset the sadness at losing him. And as much as she liked to believe that their bond was special, she was replaceable. At least with Alabella, she wasn't. Where else was Sarla going to find a living person who'd shattered their theolith? They needed her as much as she needed them.

One of the new companions, a man with unnaturally bronzed skin characteristic of the people of Kulai, rose and greeted them. "You must be the Zeda girl."

Alabella stepped forward before Laurel had a chance to respond. "She is from Zedalum but has not been to the Fairenwild in some time now. Her goal today is the same as ours: to see what lies beneath the coreseal. There is much to do and little time to do it if we wish to be out of the Fairenwild before dark."

It was the first time Laurel had heard Alabella call it the *coreseal*, and she wondered how the grounder woman knew that name.

They traveled quickly, following the path of the yellow roses. Surprisingly, Laurel didn't have to guide them. It was as if they walked a familiar path. The ominous feeling inside her resonated with greater boldness. Barrick carried his large sack, and the rest ripped out photospore reeds and held them high overhead to light their way. Laurel looked up into the canopy and was confused that she had yet to see a drove of skyflies. They were usually everywhere, fluttering near the entangled feytree branches.

As they continued on, she was able to spot three treelurks and a few patches of hugweed before the others stumbled into them. Barrick was particularly grateful when he nearly stepped into a stretch of writhing vines. Laurel pulled him out of the way just before he took the final step.

Hours had passed, and Laurel knew that they would soon approach the entrance to Zedalum. In the distance, where the wonderstone would be, it looked as if they were about to come out the other end of the Fairenwild. Daylight poured through the darkness.

"That's not right," she whispered.

Alabella turned to her. "What was that?"

"That light ahead," Laurel said. "It shouldn't be there."

"Rumors in Alchea said that there was a great fire in the Fairenwild the night you were hurt. Perhaps it is related. A little extra light could be useful to us if that is our destination."

Barrick, who had been eavesdropping, stepped closer. "Heard the same thing. Your people live anywhere near here?"

Oh, no.

Laurel sprinted forward without answering. If there was a fire near the wonderstone, it could have wreaked havoc on Zedalum. The moss on the feytrees was flammable, and the photospores were quite nearly explosive.

She ran and she ran until the field came into view. What greeted her sent a shiver up her spine.

Carnage.

Destruction.

Fallen trees and bloodied bodies left for dead. Many among the corpses were Zeda people, but not all, and some were not whole.

She looked up, but in her heart she already knew. Whatever fire had raged here had spread to the north quickly, devouring trees and roads and homes. She saw only the edge of the city through the burnt treetops, but it was enough. She didn't need to see it all to know that the devastation had overcome the treetop metropolis.

She dropped to her knees, buried her face, and let tears pour down her pale cheeks. The dark of her mind filled with images of shredded corpses lying in a field of colorful roses. The tranquil memory of a quiet wonderstone was shattered and replaced by the raw noise of death and destruction.

It hurt—all of it. The truth most of all. That she should have been there.

What happened? Where had they gone? Surely, not everyone was dead. Something, or someone, had driven them away...

Alabella.

She knew about the coreseal. She knew about the yellow flowers. She already knew how long it would take for them to reach the wonderstone. She had been there before. And—gale take her—she had done this to Laurel's people.

Just then, a soft hand reached out and found rest on her tense shoulder. Her body jerked awake from its furious dream. The hand, so gentle, so caring, pressed on her with the weight of a thousand deaths. Her heart pounded. The stitches ached. Her addict hands trembled with rage. She wanted to turn around and throw herself at Alabella. Run cold steel through her heart until *her* theolith cracked. She would make Alabella suffer. She would make her taste the pains of an entire people.

But not yet.

She needed to be smart. If Alabella was responsible, this could be a test, and Laurel wasn't strong enough to fight back. She couldn't let

Alabella know that she knew. She had to play along like the young, ignorant, sheltered girl they believed her to be.

Lie.

She had to lie. And if there is anything Laurel knew how to do, it was that.

The rage and fury coursing through her thread-dead veins bubbled up until her eyes filled with tears. It didn't all have to be a lie.

Laurel turned to face her demon. "They're gone," she cried.

Alabella's eyes were ice as she brushed the back of her hand against Laurel's cheek, wiping away the tears. "Laurel, these are your people? What darkness has fallen upon this place?"

It took all of Laurel's self-restraint not to charge the lying old hag.

Alabella continued, "I bet it was Great Lord Malachus. Retribution for the priest, and your friends invading his home. It is terrible, Laurel. I am so sorry you had to see this. If I'd known…"

Laurel's jaw clenched, and she spoke through grinding teeth. "My brother and my grandfather were there."

"Take that anger," Alabella said, her voice growing stronger. "Do not forget it. Anger is the great fuel of life. Take it and let it burn inside your veins until we can replace it with threadlight once again. These Alcheans believe they can kill without consequence. They think they are more righteous than you. Stronger than you. But we will heal you, Laurel. And then we will make them pay."

Laurel's heart was a skyfly's wings, fluttering with terrible speed. What ripped deepest into her heart was the ease with which Alabella weaved her lies. Her reality was malleable. Her truth was clothing donned for the occasion. She was a treelurk, shifting its hues to snare its prey, and Laurel was the passerby.

When she didn't respond, Alabella removed her hand. "Take your time. We will be at the coreseal when you are ready."

A minute later, after Alabella's footsteps faded to silence, Laurel took in a deep breath. The scent of roses laced with death danced in the swirling breeze, but none of that mattered. On top of it all, the wonderstone had broken in two, and the Emerald threadweavers were pulling the pieces apart. How had she not seen it? The wonderstone *was* the coreseal.

The warnings of the elders echoed in Laurel's mind. Something was down there. Something dangerous enough to compel an entire people for hundreds of years to protect it. Laurel's feet moved with quiet apprehension, curiosity overcoming the voice that urged her to run. What if there was nothing? What if her people had damned themselves to protect a bunch of infused gemstones? Surely, they wouldn't have considered *that* to be dangerous.

"Toss down some of those spores," Barrick directed. One of the men stepped over and threw a dozen photospores into the darkness below the broken wonderstone.

"You seeing that?" one of the others asked.

Whispers of "damn" and "Heralds" and "gods" rode the wind. Laurel reached the wonderstone and looked down. "Gale take me," she added.

"This is good news," Alabella said, nodding her head as if to convince herself.

Below them were the partial remains of people long dead. Bits of cloth, and jewelry, and bone lay strewn throughout the cavern, with teeth littered across the floor like pebbles. "These must be the heretics. Barrick, would you like to do the honors? Keep an eye out and threadlight in your veins at all times."

The large man nodded and stepped forward. He held his broad shoulders high, and his bearded chin even higher. Blue veins came to life just before he jumped, and Laurel found herself suddenly longing for her old power again. His feet landed without a sound. He picked up one of the photospores and looked around. To the east, he disappeared down some kind of corridor, just for a moment, before reappearing.

He shouted from below, "There's a path down here, but it's caved in."

"Probably the earthquakes," one of the others said.

One by one, they each dropped into the cavern—Barrick *pushed* himself back up and offered to help Laurel descend safely. When she landed, she waved away a cloud of dust drifting in the air. It was so quiet that every step, every breath, and every shuffle of clothing clung to the air like a screaming child.

She drew up close to the pile of rubble blocking the pathway and paused. "Do you hear that?" she asked.

Barrick, who'd stayed close beside her, leaned closer to the rocks. "I don't hear anything."

"I thought I heard something," Laurel said.

He shrugged his shoulders.

Alabella rose from inspecting a bracelet on the ground and smiled. "We're close. Let's *pull* these stones out of the way. Everyone, keep threadlight in your veins. Who knows what lies on the other side."

A pale, Alchean man with short brown hair and eyes the color of spring leaves stepped forward. Laurel and the others moved out of the way. He dug his boots into the ground, veins coming to life with Emerald threadlight, and *pulled*. Stones and rocks and pebbles exploded away from the path. The pile tumbled down as higher rocks replaced lower rocks. He repeated the process in a series of quick *pulls* until, finally, the gap in the path was wide enough for a person to pass.

Part of Laurel expected a moment of awe and wonder, as if a golden chest or mountain of bright gemstones would shine its glory through the opening. But there was nothing to greet them but silence.

"Stay vigilant," Alabella said.

The group filtered through the opening deeper into the cavern. Laurel stayed at the back with Barrick. She cringed as they passed a pile of teeth. Photospores held high overhead continued to light their path forward. As they rounded a bend, Laurel felt the hairs on her arms stand. There was an energy there. Something that pulsed with power. Even as an achromat she could feel it.

Not far away, the tunnel opened up to a large cavern, but the photospore light was too dim to see beyond the opening.

"Do you smell that?" Barrick asked.

The others all paused, lifting their noses high and taking in deep breaths.

"The hell?" one of the others responded. "Smells like a rose garden."

He was right. It *did* smell like roses, but that didn't make any sense.

Suddenly, a soft patting sound echoed from the end of the tunnel. They all looked at each other until Barrick, eyes shining with Sapphire threadlight, shouted. "Good gods."

Laurel followed his gaze but saw nothing, until she noticed the slight compression of dirt ahead of them. Footsteps, but no feet.

"Threadlight!" Barrick shouted.

Those who had ignored Alabella's instructions let threadlight pour through their veins. They cursed as it flooded into their vision. Laurel knew they could see something she could not, something invisible to weak, useless achromats like herself.

Then, as if to answer the many questions budding in her mind, the creature screeched and attacked. The pale Emerald man fell first, grabbing at his ankle and hacking down with a dagger. Three of the others surrounded him, attacking a creature Laurel could only imagine. But their efforts failed, and one by one they cried out in agony as the creature ripped them apart.

"Run!" Barrick screamed, grabbing Laurel's arm and pulling her up the tunnel.

Chaos erupted with the remaining group as they cursed and scrambled and fought their way back toward the entrance. Laurel's heart raced as she ran.

Another scream.

Then another.

Alabella, Barrick, and Laurel made it to the cavern beneath the wonderstone. Barrick prepared to *push* off the ground toward the surface, his arm wrapped around Alabella. Laurel met the woman's eyes. Not the Amber eyes of an altruistic leader, but the cruel, piss-colored eyes of a woman who would sacrifice Laurel with no remorse. The two Bloodthieves stood in the pillar of light descending from the opening, and just before Barrick kicked off the ground, Alabella's veins blazed to life.

"Wait!" Alabella shouted at Barrick while she stared into the tunnel. "I got you."

Her eyes were twin suns glowing in the shadows.

"Are you alone?" Alabella asked the invisible creature.

"Quick, Laurel, come with me!" Barrick shouted.

"Laurel," Alabella commanded. "I assume you brought a transfuser?"

She had, even though the transfusers were never supposed to leave her room. She reached into her pocket, removed the lid on the vial, and drank threadweaver blood. It took only a moment. She closed her eyes and the thick fluid drained down her throat, energy diffusing through her body.

When she opened her eyes, threadlight burst into view all around her, brilliant hues of pulsing light connecting her to the world. And there in front of her, thrashing against dozens of brilliant Amber threads, stood the creature. It stood on four limbs that cut out like blades into the ground. Every inch of its body, where skin or fur should have been, swirled with radiant threadlight, both captivating and terrifying as she stared. Its mouth, open wide as it screeched its defiance, was nothing more than a black hole in the center of a blazing fire.

Alabella walked forward, withdrawing the obsidian dagger that once belonged to Chrys Valerian, and stabbed the blade through the creature's skull. As soon as the blade struck, the creature exploded in a violent surge of threadlight. Then it faded away as though it had never existed.

"Stones," Barrick cursed, his blue eyes nervously watching the tunnel. "What *was* that?"

"We should leave," Alabella responded. "It'll be dark soon, and your mother may have warned you about being out at night when the corespawn are near."

7

THE IDEA of a woman summoning Alverax to her room had always seemed exciting but, when the woman turned out to be a staunch-faced Zeda elder, his excitement shriveled like an old grape.

He had an ominous feeling about the request; Elder Rowan wasn't the friendliest of callers. His mind assumed the worst—that the Felians had discovered his connection to the Bloodthieves, or that Princess Jisenna had told her sister about the Sun Bath.

It was altogether possible that he was overreacting. Perhaps the negotiations had concluded, and they were free to live in Felia peacefully.

He'd rather bet on Jelium being an herbivore.

Slipping into a pair of dark trousers, Alverax glanced at the map in his room. He'd never spent much time looking at maps, but seeing all of Felia laid out so carefully held a sense of peace and clarity that he deeply needed.

He shoved the door open and there, standing in front of him, hand raised ready to knock, was an unquestionably beautiful Felian princess. Her curls moved like the fronds of a fern as she smiled. Against the brilliant white of her summer dress, Jisenna's skin burned a radiant shade of dark walnut.

"Alverax," she said with a smile. "What propitious timing."

"Jisenna, what brings you here?" He coughed, realizing for the first time that she was flanked by two familiar, well-built guards in black.

"I had a curious dream last night," she whispered with a sparkle in her eye. "In it, I had the most delightful conversation with a handsome young man who had a rather distinct scar on his back. As you can imagine, I've spent all morning going door to door throughout all of Felia asking men to disrobe in hopes that I might find him, but, alas, he eludes me yet. I hoped that, perhaps, with your *vast* connections in these lands, you might know where I could find such a man."

"Such a man," Alverax repeated, holding back a laugh, "would be wise to stay far away from a woman such as yourself."

Her brows rose in surprise. "A woman such as myself?"

"A woman such as yourself," he taunted.

"And what precisely would you know of a woman such as myself?"

"Don't you know?" he teased. "The smart younger sibling of the powerful monarch always ends up being the evil villain."

She sighed and laughed. "Is that so?"

"Oh, yes," he grinned. "After spending her life in the shadow of her sister, the once beloved princess turns from the light and embraces a dark path."

"Let me guess. Only one man has the power to stop her?"

"No, no, no." Alverax waved his hands. "She cannot be stopped! She is a storm. She is the sun itself. A force of unbridled power. However, the day she is to unleash pure darkness upon the world, damning it to utter oblivion, a yellow-bellied starling perched itself on a nearby tree branch. In a tiny voice, the bird asked, 'Are you certain?'"

Her eyebrows rose.

"Then the bird turned into a handsome prince and they kissed and did other less wholesome recreations and, before they knew it, the day had passed, and the world was saved."

Jisenna gave a light clap of her hands, fingers to palm. "A strong beginning. A gripping climax. And a devastatingly awful conclusion."

"A villain *would* hate the happy ending."

"It's the bird," she explained. "If an evil villain were about to destroy the world, no sane person would flutter over to them and ask, 'Are you certain?'"

Alverax lifted his palms. "Who said anything about sane?"

"You are a curious boy, Alverax Blightwood."

"More than you know," he smiled. "You really shouldn't be seen with someone like *me*."

"I suppose that's true," she agreed. "After all, you are the last of the Obsidian threadweavers. Heir to the Watchlords. Blessed of the Heralds.

The boy with the black soul. We wouldn't want people thinking you've corrupted me."

Alverax smirked. "To be fair, my irises are black, not my soul."

"Eyes are the windows to the soul, are they not?"

"Not mine. My lips are my windows." He winced at the insinuation, stealing an awkward glance at the guards standing watch. "That is because of...food! What I meant to say is that I am very hungry, and my little starling stomach could really use some of that fresh Felian fish I keep hearing about."

"Ah, so you *are* the starling in the story," she laughed. "Down at the pier, one of the vendors sells a zesty tuna bowl that'll make your lips sizzle. If you're not busy, I could take you."

Alverax couldn't suppress his smile. "I assume you're paying? I'm a little short on shines."

Princess Jisenna rolled her eyes as she covered her head with a shawl and started down the hall. "Come on, little birdie."

Alverax moved awkwardly past the black-clad guards trailing behind her.

As they made their way to the pier, they spoke of many things, finding great surprise at how much they had in common. Jisenna's mother too had passed not long after she'd been born, and both had a special relationship with their grandfathers. They spoke of the ocean, the calm of the crashing waves against the shore, the prickle of cold as you step into the water that sends shivers of excitement up the rest of your body, and the peaceful feeling of weightlessness below the surface.

She told him about her father, glancing up to the sky and explaining which star she'd chosen for him. He noted the reverence she carried when she spoke of him, and wished he held the same for his own father.

When the Terecean sea came into view, Alverax felt once again like he'd seen threadlight for the first time. A delicate warmth swelled in his breast. Countless rows of ships drifted back and forth with the waves, anchored along a labyrinth of wooden docks. Sailors hauled crates, farmers sold their fares, children scuttled along the boardwalks like grasshoppers, and street performers entertained crowds of cheerful onlookers. The energy poured through his soul. And the water called to him.

"Heralds," he muttered to himself.

The warmth in Jisenna's eyes as she looked out over the pier said more than any words she could have spoken.

"I don't think I could ever tire of this view," Alverax said.

"My first tutor—" Jisenna smiled, remembering. "I would make him read the same book to me over and over again, a short story about a bee with no wings. Every day he would ask me if I wanted to read something new, and every day I told him to read *The Song of the Flightless*. After we finished, he would tell me, 'Every wave is wont to break'."

She brushed a curly strand of hair from her eyes. "I never liked him. In fact, him saying that fueled my stubbornness. I asked for that book every day for months until he finally quit. Point is that I disagree with him. Not all waves are wont to break. Some waves, like the awe that fills me when I look out over the Terecean sea, those waves forever remain at their crest."

Alverax nodded, a serious look in his eyes. "Hmm, yes. Much like my hunger."

She rolled her eyes and led him down a long staircase toward the lower pier. The shop owner, a short woman with a dozen thick braids, bowed to the princess and offered her their bowls for free. Jisenna kissed her fingertips and placed them on the woman's forehead. They sat at the base of a grassy hill and ate while they watched street performers. Alverax took a large bite filled with rice, tuna, and a savory green fruit, all topped with the slightest drizzle of a zesty cream that sizzled on his tongue. After finishing every last grain of rice, he laid back and enjoyed the performances.

He was surprised to find that nearly all of the performers were threadweavers. Their acrobatics seemed an unconventional use of threadlight, but it made for the most amazing stunts. Flips that soared high into the air. Levitating human pyramids. Sapphires juggling with no hands. Emeralds juggling upside down.

One of the threadweavers asked for a volunteer, and Alverax quickly raised his hand. The performers applauded him as he approached. "What's your name, friend?" the lead asked.

One of the threadweaver acrobats, a small woman with dreadlocks and a pierced nose, spoke something indiscernible as she dropped to a knee.

Within moments, the crowd was whispering, and dozens more were pointing and dropping to a knee. There were many who looked genuinely confused at what was happening, but some followed their peers' response. Alverax looked behind him, searching for Jisenna. But as he turned, he found himself face to face with an empty green hill. Behind him, he finally heard the words being whispered.

Heralds.

Watchlord.

Obsidian.

Fear became panic, and panic became paralysis as Alverax faced the reverent throng of Felians. Jisenna stood quietly near the wide stairs with her head still wrapped in her shawl. She watched on, waiting to see how Alverax would handle the situation.

An elderly woman, with cracked skin and hair down to her hips, stepped forward. As she approached, she lifted her hand forward and pressed it to Alverax's cheek. "Heralds, save me. It is true." A single tear rolled down her cheek and fell across her lips.

"I'm sorry," Alverax whispered. "I'm not who you think I am."

"My cousin told me there was an Obsidian in the palace!" another shouted.

"Impossible!"

"A sign of the Restoration!"

"The Heralds are returning!" cheered another.

Alverax stood in awe as nearly a hundred fisherman, farmers, sailors, and others gathered around him. They spoke in hushed tones, questioning, debating, some giving looks of disapproval and scorn. Part of him wanted to stand tall and spin a beautiful lie and become what they believed him to be, but that was something his father would have done. He had to be better. He had to be honest. He had to be good.

A hand touched his arm. He turned in time to see Jisenna pulling the shawl off to reveal her face to the crowd. Those who were not already prostrate fell to their knees. The older woman's soft eyes smiled as she bowed her head. "Blessed Sun Daughter."

"All of you, please rise," she commanded. Her shoulders seemed to pull back. Her chin rose a little higher. "Since we were children, we were taught of the great prosperity during the time of the Heralds, and the Watchlords have since taught that one day the Heralds would return. The first Watchlord was the man closest to the Heralds, their chosen, blessed to become an Obsidian threadweaver. The man beside me is Alverax Blightwood. It is true that he is an Obsidian threadweaver, but there has been no sign that the Heralds have returned. If his arrival *is* a sign, if the Heralds *are* to return, the best way we can prepare is to humble ourselves and to work hard so that, should they come, we can welcome them with great abundance.

"The two of us are needed back at the palace. Please, friends, return to your work, and may the Heralds bless you all." She leaned in to Alverax and whispered. "Time to go."

Alverax followed Princess Jisenna back up the long staircase, stealing glances back toward the pier. While most of the crowd had dispersed, returning to their work, there was still a small crowd, huddled together, watching Alverax climb the steps toward the Palace of the Sun. He wasn't sure how he was supposed to react to what had happened. Was it a good thing? Or would they think he was trying to amass some kind of cult following? The Elders would probably hate that he'd drawn any attention to himself.

Heralds...the Elders. He was supposed to meet Rowan ages ago.

"Jisenna," he called to her. She paused on the stairs and looked down at him. "I'm so sorry. I didn't know that would happen."

She cocked her head to the side and stared at him for a moment. "Were it not my idea to go to the pier in the first place, I might have thought you staged the whole event."

"I swear that's not the case."

"I believe you," she replied. "Unfortunately, apologies do not absolve the impact. Word of your arrival will spread. Stories will emerge. My sister needs to know about this so that we can control the spread."

He ran a hand through his short hair. "I have to go meet with one of the elders, but...thank you. The food was amazing, and the company was tolerable."

She sighed and shook her head with a smile. "Take care of yourself, little birdie. And you might want to avoid the pier for a while."

He nodded and she took off in another direction with the two guards following closely behind. His feet moved with surprising speed in hopes of keeping his mind occupied. He reentered the palace, then wandered through a series of corridors looking for Elder Rowan's room. He'd gained a decent mental map of the palace, but the rooms themselves all looked the same.

What he couldn't decide was whether or not he should tell Elder Rowan what had happened. On the one hand, she'd be furious if he told her and, on the other hand, she'd be furious if she found out he hadn't.

Eventually, he found the room and gave a knock.

As the thick door slid open, Elder Rowan offered him the only look she knew how to give. In the diffused morning light, her green eyes seemed even more bothered. Many of the Zeda people had slowly begun to adopt the fashion of the region, abandoning their monotone outerwear for the more colorful and revealing picks of the season. Unsurprisingly, Elder Rowan clung to her Zeda browns. "You've taken your time."

Alverax stepped into the room. It was smaller than his—there was something oddly satisfying about that. He took a seat on a wooden chair that was less comfortable than it looked, which seemed to match many of the Felian styles. Beauty over utility. Even some of the dresses were so tight and awkwardly cut that the women had a hard time walking. Not that he was complaining.

"We've important business to discuss," she said curtly. "It appears there are fundamental differences between our histories and those of the Felian people. Their texts claim that Amber threadweavers are the enemies of the Heralds. Our people are descendants of Amber threadweavers. You see the predicament?" Elder Rowan remained standing as she spoke, her arms now crossed over her chest.

Alverax let out a sigh of relief. "That doesn't sound good."

"How astute," she said. "Additionally, our texts speak of the dangers of Obsidian threadweavers, while their texts celebrate Obsidian threadweavers as the Herald's greatest allies. Apparently, the first Watchlord was an Obsidian threadweaver."

Alverax paled. That would have been nice to know before he'd gone to the pier. "But that's a good thing, right?"

"Perhaps. Perhaps not." She took a seat across from him. "I know that I have been harsh in my judgments of you, and I hope that you understand my reasons were not insubstantial. However, it is time for me to put aside my bias. The livelihood of the entire Zeda people is at risk, and you may be the key to it all. Rosemary has kept the empress away from you during the negotiations, to protect you, but also to protect us.

"It is time for that to change. We need you to immerse yourself in their society. You already look like them. We'd like you to become one of them. A neighbor. A friend. Because of your powers, the empress will trust you. If you can convince her that we are allies worth investing in, then perhaps we can still save our community."

A weight poured over him, dragging him down into the stone beneath his feet. His heart beat faster as her request sank in.

Alverax, can you please fix all our problems?

Alverax, turns out we're all going to die unless you can make friends with people that will kill you if they find out that you were a Bloodthief.

Alverax, don't do anything stupid.

Too late.

He didn't understand their culture. He didn't understand their politics or their religion. They were smarter, stronger, richer. Who was he to become one of them? He was nothing. The failed son of a thief who refused to die when he ought to. The last good thing he did may have doomed the world.

"Trust me, boy, I would prefer not to bet my coffin on you either. We will continue to work the angle of cultural histories and current events, but it would be foolish of us not to use every tool available."

"I'm not a tool," Alverax mumbled.

"You are today," she said flatly.

"And what happens when they find out I was a Bloodthief?" he nearly shouted. "It's not like we've been *transparent*. My eyes aren't going to save me."

"And what is the alternative? You wish to sit back and smell the roses while our people are smeared and slandered? You wish to lay by the sea and taste the salt while my people are killed for your people's actions? That is unacceptable. Iriel thinks you are a good man, but I've seen plenty of good men turn sour when the sun sets. Tell me, Alverax Blightwood, what manner of man will you be?"

Ah! She was infuriating. Obviously, he didn't want to sit back and watch them be killed. Frankly, he'd be killed with them, so the point was moot. But the question. That damned question burned inside him. What kind of man *was* he? He'd spent his whole life answering the opposite question. He knew he didn't want to be like his father, but that was an evasion of the more important question. Who *did* he hope to be?

He thought of his grandfather. Strong. Resolute. Merciful. Good to the core. That's what he wanted to be. A light. A giver. He wanted to be who Iriel saw—a man willing to sacrifice himself to save people in danger. The Zeda were fighting an ever-growing onslaught of dangers. Like Iriel and Aydin on the coreseal, more and more dangers were enveloping the Zeda each day, and they too needed him.

"I don't know," he said softly. "I want to bring hope to people."

"Hmm," she huffed. "If nothing else, this day, in this city, you have the chance to do just that."

He sat up a little taller, the weight beginning to dissipate as his resolve grew stronger. "Okay then. What do you need me to do?"

The old woman stood up and walked over to an enormous armoire. She opened the double doors half-way and paused. "Tell me, boy. Do you know how to dance?"

STONES OF LIGHT

8

Much to his surprise, Chrys Valerian awoke on a bed of leaves, feeling much like the death he thought he had embraced. But he *was* alive, despite the throbbing in his skull and the pain in his...

Pain.

He could *feel*, which meant...he was in control.

Chrys pushed himself to a sitting position and waited for his burning eyes to adjust to the sunlight. He rubbed his neck and smiled at how good it felt for his hands to do what he asked. When Relek was in control, it had felt like he was paralyzed, but worse, because he could watch as his body obeyed another.

When he looked around, he found himself in a small hut. He stood, carefully, and took the few steps required to reach the opening. It was clear that he was still in the Wastelands, which made what he saw even more curious.

Humans.

Four of them.

Beside them, a thriving population of purple and yellow flowers sprouted from long stems growing out of the swamp water. Thousands of red and white bees darted back and forth between the flowers and a collection of buzzing hives in the trees. Surrounding the scene was a wall built of tall spikes bound together with green ropes. In the trees above the wall, Chrys counted eight wastelander guards perched on platforms, their inhuman faces keeping careful watch.

He was in a prison.

Chrys let threadlight pour through his veins—at least, he tried. When he did, he felt his chest expand as though he were taking a breath, but no threadlight came through. Instead, a sharp pain surged from his heart. He clutched at his breast and groaned, fighting off his instincts to release more of the healing threadlight.

One of the humans spotted Chrys, a woman with ratty blonde hair and a hooked nose. "Aye, Roshaw. Bad news, buddy."

"What?" The dark-skinned man, Roshaw, turned and saw Chrys sitting up, and frowned beneath a shaggy beard.

"Did we settle on five shifts, or six?"

"Everyone gets lucky," Roshaw said. "And you know it was three." He turned to the other female prisoner. "I swear if I get stung on one of Esme's shifts, I'm gonna throw her down the Well."

Esme burst into laughter.

The other woman, thin as a reed with a jagged cut to her auburn hair, rose to her feet and looked to Chrys. "Ignore them. Just a friendly wager. We thought you were dead."

Chrys raised a brow. "You wagered on whether or not I was alive?"

"As long as you're not an ass, it was a win-win," Roshaw said. "Either you wake up and we have a new member of the crew, or you don't, and I get to skip out on harvesting for a few weeks."

"Harvesting what?" Chrys asked.

"We'll get to that," the thin woman said. "I'm Agatha. That's Roshaw and Esme. And the last one is Seven." The latter waved and Chrys caught a glimpse of his hand. It was clear where he'd acquired the name.

"Real question is who are you?" Roshaw said.

Esme rose to her knees. "And what the hell was a threadweaver doing east of Everstone?"

"Stones," Seven whispered, rising to his feet as the others turned to him. "Lightfather be damned. Chrys?"

Chrys looked again at Seven. Past his thick beard and gnarled hair, there was something familiar about the man. Something in his eyes. Not the achromic brown, but the shape and intelligence. *Stones.* Chrys recognized him. He'd been one of his soldiers during the War of the Wastelands.

"Pieter," Chrys whispered.

"Aye," he replied. "But Seven has grown on me. It's good to see you, sir."

"Wait a minute," Esme said, waving her arms. "You two know each other?"

Seven nodded. "That's Chrys Valerian. He led my battalion. Damn fine soldier."

"How did you end up here?" Chrys asked.

"Captured during the war."

"No," Chrys said in disbelief.

"Everyone but him," Esme added, pointing to Roshaw. "He doesn't get to be an official member of the crew until he hits five years."

Five years.

Captured during the war and caged like cattle ever since. The reality of it loomed over Chrys like a storm cloud, threatening a deluge, and darkening the moment of lightheartedness. The fact that these people had not escaped, or died, or killed themselves, seemed impossible, but no one was laughing.

When Chrys failed to respond, Agatha sighed. "It's not all bad here. They feed us well, and it's generally safe. The company is good—"

"Debatable," Esme said.

"—what I'm saying, is that it could be worse."

"Sure," Esme said. "When we first arrived, they would beat us and such, but they mostly ignore us now."

Chrys looked at each of the people now standing in front of him. Four prisoners left alone for five years in the middle of the Wasteland swamps. "I don't understand. You've been here for five years? Why keep you alive for so long?"

Agatha's face grew somber. "There were sixteen of us when we first arrived. Two died shortly after from infection. Three have died over the years from the et'hovon—the bees. A few escape attempts killed five others. And there were two friends who couldn't take it anymore and threw themselves into the Well. We're the only ones left. We've all picked up a bit of their language—Roshaw more than most. From what we can tell, they kept us around as a gift for their god. But he never showed up, so they started using us to harvest the honeycrystals."

"That's—" Chrys started.

"Horrible?" Esme cut in. "Depressing? Hell yeah, it is. But at least we're alive. And we have each other...for now."

"We've tried everything," Seven said. "We made weapons and tried to fight our way out. We dug a tunnel under the hut. Someone tried playing dead once, and they stabbed him in the heart to make sure he wasn't faking it."

"This is our life now," Agatha said quietly.

Roshaw rubbed his palms and a small grin carved its way onto his lips. "There is one difference—"

The others turned to him.

"Now we have a threadweaver."

9

STONES OF LIGHT

A SINGULAR SCREAM drifted through the dreary streets of Alchea, weaving its way through the stormy night air, and climbing through Laurel's window. She sat up, cold and sweaty, with an army of goosebumps covering her arms beneath a wool blanket. They'd barely just returned from the Fairenwild, and her mind still raced with fears and questions. She'd tried to sleep, but every flicker of a shadow had threatened her peace.

Beside her bed, the chest that held her transfusers beckoned her.

Sounds from the midnight streets. Voices. Laurel wasn't sure if they were even real. Losing her threadlight was affecting her mind, and that scared her even more.

Once again, screams echoed in from her window.

She rushed over, scratching her arm as she investigated the noise.

A light rain misted over the moon-lit city, puddles forming in haphazard pockets across the cobblestone. A pair of elderly women clutched large bags and sprinted as fast as their brittle bones would take them. A unit of Alchean guards stomped through in the other direction, each carrying a steel blade.

A tree branch rustled in the wind and its shadows wavered.

Then the empty street came alive. Small puddles at first, splashing in chaotic bursts. Rain falling in impossible ways. A subtle stirring of the ground beneath her. Then it grew. More puddles displaced. More rain struck nothing, then dripped down the same nothingness. It took her only a moment, memories of the dark beneath the coreseal fresh in her mind.

Gale take me.

Laurel reached into the chest beside her bed and pulled out a transfuser, swallowing the contents with haste. Blood ran down her throat like sugar water, threadlight seeping its way into her veins. It filled her with a vile warmth that pressed her goosebumps back into their homes.

When she looked back out the window, her heart skipped a beat. Hundreds of creatures of various shapes and sizes trampled through the street, spectral monsters born of brilliant, prismatic light. Some as small as a skittering rat, others like alien horses trampling hard against the stone. It was a disturbing beauty, celestial and captivating.

Slamming her curtains shut, Laurel moved to the hallway. If there was one thing she knew about the corespawn, it was that Alabella could kill them. The safest place she could be right then was with her.

Luther Mandrin, friend to the missing High General, Chrys Valerian, had just finished a drink at the Black Eye when a guard came through shouting about an attack on the city. Luther tossed some shines on the table near Laz and was out the door before the guard could finish his words.

After losing his youngest son to the Order of Alchaeus, and watching a false priest die at the hands of a traitor, Luther had taken to drinking more than he knew he ought to. He stayed out later and later and spoke harsher and harsher to those he loved, but it was all he could do to ignore the building pressure that threatened to consume him.

None of that mattered now. If there was danger, he had to get to his family.

Screams in the distance passed through his ears with disregard. He had one purpose, and nothing would distract him.

He turned a corner with beads of rain dripping down his bald head and entered Beryl Boulevard. He nearly tripped as he came to an abrupt halt. In the center of the thoroughfare, half a dozen caravans lay toppled over, their contents spread throughout the street like blood splatter. Men and women lay dead in the street, bleeding, bite marks and scratches painted across their corpses. But one woman was alive, crawling along the road. For a moment, Luther thought of rushing to her to help, but, instead, he chose his family.

Just then, as if the world was mocking his decision, the woman's torso was torn in half, one side vanishing into nothingness, while the other sprayed blood in a horrific display of death.

"Stones," Luther cursed aloud.

He let threadlight pour through his veins. The dark stage surrounding him dropped its curtains. Multicolored threadlight danced through the streets like actors in a demonic play. Where once there had been nothing, creatures hewn of pure threadlight prowled the streets. Small beasts nibbled on corpses. Massive creatures on two legs circled the caravans, searching for prey.

One of the smaller creatures jerked its head away from its meal and lifted itself to all fours, following Luther's movement across the road. It screeched, and Luther watched a dozen more of similar size turn their heads in unison.

He set his jaw and ran as fast as he could, threadlight and adrenaline coalescing in his veins like rivers of oil-filled water. His heart raced in his chest. Drops of rain slapped across his face. He finished crossing the street and turned to find a small battalion of beasts gaining on him.

As he turned the corner, he crashed into a younger man, knocking him to the ground. Luther didn't hesitate, he *pulled* himself against the closest building and scaled the side of the wall as if the world had turned on its side. He reached the top and looked down just in time to see the creatures overwhelm the young man.

Luther took off across the rooftop and *pulled* himself toward the next building, extending his arc, then landed hard against the rooftop. He scanned the streets below for the invisible creatures, but found none, so he dropped to the ground and continued toward his home.

By the time he arrived at his house, his lungs felt ready to burst and his heart was a beating war drum. He rushed inside and found his wife, Emory, sitting with their younger daughter on her lap, the other child clutching her arm with a feral grip.

"We heard the screams," she whispered. "What is it?"

Luther slammed the door shut behind him and pushed their dinner table in front of it. He stepped to the kitchen window and shut the drapes, peeking through a gap in the middle. "Shhhhh."

"What is it?"

His lip snarled as he stared out the window. "Hide the kids and stay quiet. They're coming."

LAUREL RAN down the hallway and into the warehouse where clothing and equipment lay sprawled out across long tables. From the front wall, screams rose in terrific harmony. Laurel rushed over and slammed open the door to find Alabella and Sarla surrounded by a dozen corespawn, different in shape than the one they'd found beneath the coreseal—these were wider, with tall ears that stood erect—but still seemingly shaped by threadlight itself.

Threads stretched forth from the ground, grasping the corespawn and binding them in place. They thrashed back and forth while Alabella groaned, spreading her mind thin as she bound them all.

Sarla cried, clutching a fresh wound on her left arm. In her hand, she held the obsidian blade.

"Hurry!" Alabella roared. "I can't hold them forever!"

"They're invisible!" Sarla shouted angrily.

"Give it to me!" Laurel shouted over the pouring rain.

When Sarla saw who it was, she tossed the blade clumsily through the air. Laurel reached forward and snatched it, then lunged ahead, driving the blade hard into the nearest creature. She could feel the blade connect, its edge connecting with light-wrought flesh, but, as soon as it pierced through, the creature's body exploded like a pin to a bubble, thousands of beads of threadlight erupting in a cloud of radiant color.

Laurel flipped the blade in her hand and smiled.

The next closest corespawn was only a few paces away, its radiant light seemingly dimmer than the previous. She ran to it and slammed the blade through its neck. Again, the creature burst apart in an explosion of threadlight.

"Is it working?" Sarla shouted over the sound of the growing rainfall.

Laurel ignored her and continued her rampage, water pouring down her blonde hair as, one by one, she drove the obsidian blade through each of the beasts. Every time one of the corespawn burst apart, there was a certain feeling of catharsis that accompanied it, a similar pride she'd felt flicking spiders off of their webs in the Fairenwild.

Suddenly, all signs of threadlight vanished.

She swept her eyes in a full circle, searching for the remaining corespawn, but, in her rage, she thought that, perhaps, she'd already killed them.

Alabella looked troubled as she glanced to the other side of Sarla. "What are you doing, Laurel? Finish them off. I don't know how much longer I can hold this."

Laurel looked again and saw nothing, then realized the truth: the blood from the transfuser had worn off. She cursed under her breath and moved to where Alabella was looking. She urged threadlight to pour through her veins as she had done so many times before, but none came. Only the cold emptiness she'd learned to live with.

As she approached the location, she swung the blade wildly out in front of her like a machete sifting through undergrowth. She breathed in deep, glancing toward Sarla who watched her with curious eyes. Then, quite suddenly, the dagger struck true and she felt the familiar feeling of connection and release as a corespawn burst apart beneath the blade.

"Point me to the last one," she said. But when she turned, she saw Alabella collapsing to the rain-soaked stone.

Gale take me, Laurel cursed.

There was still one corespawn left, she had no more threadlight, and it was no longer bound.

LUTHER'S FAMILY huddled into a closet in their younger daughter's room while Luther kept a lookout in the kitchen. A creature the size of a large horse circled the building, walking on two legs as it sniffed at the doors and scratched at the walls. Luther hoped the beast would become bored or disheartened and leave their home alone, but it seemed content to wait out its quarry.

As it disappeared around the back side of the house once again, Luther rushed into his room and lifted a long bundle out from beneath a floorboard. Swords were uncommon among threadweavers in Alchea, seeing as how dangerous they were to use against another threadweaver. But many in Felia maintained the warrior art, including Luther's grandfather who had gifted him this sword when he was young.

Luther slid the long blade out of its sheath. It was heavier than he remembered, but with such a large creature outside his home, he needed a heavier weapon.

A roar, like the rumble of a quaking mountain, filled their home, and Luther heard his children cry from the other room. He ran out of his room and was nearly blasted off of his feet as the front door shot from its hinges in an explosion of splintered wood. Luther dove out of the way of the table he'd propped up behind the door as it came hurtling through the air like a stick.

Threadlight poured through the doorway as the creature stepped in.

Luther snarled and set his feet, gripping the blade as he'd been taught. Like holding a woman's hand. Tight enough for conviction; loose enough for trust.

It launched toward him, but Luther rolled out of the way before its long arm struck. The creature was fast for its size, but Luther *pulled* against the wall behind it, doubling his speed, and came crashing down atop its head with fury. He drove the blade down into its skull. It was an odd feeling as it entered, as if the blade were digging through molasses. He yanked it out, leaving a gaping crevice where the blade had pierced it, then dropped back to the floor.

He moved himself out of the way as the creature teetered, then watched as threadlight pooled around the wound like blood, coagulating, then resealing. In moments, it was as if his blade had never struck its skull.

The creature turned to him, leaned forward, and let out a roar that caused the walls to shake in terror.

Luther cursed. If that didn't kill it, he didn't know what would. He needed to get his family to safety or distract the beast long enough for them to get away. He had to do something, because it was only a matter of time before the building and everyone inside would be crushed by its fury.

As his mind raced, calculating his next move, Luther saw movement in the shattered doorway. Just outside, eyes and veins blazing brightly with threadlight, stood Lazarus Barlow and the Alirian Spider, Reina Talfar.

"Is too much light," Laz said, smiling his toothy grin. "Time to put out."

Laurel turned in a panicked circle, searching for the final corespawn. With Alabella unconscious, there was no one to stop it from attacking. In the shadow of a moment, she'd gone from predator to prey.

From the corner of her vision, she saw invisible footsteps in the puddles between the cobblestone, and they came right for her. She set her feet and waited for her moment. As the footsteps approached, Laurel dove out of the way, slashing the dagger down as she moved. But she missed, and the creature bit down on her forearm.

Laurel screamed out in pain, dropping the obsidian blade. The weight of the invisible foe came over her, knocking her to her back. She closed her eyes and felt the air shift. Her arms extended and caught the corespawn around the neck as it thrashed back and forth near her face. She kept her eyes closed, knowing that sight would only confuse her senses. Her arms burned as they struggled to keep the creature at bay long enough to—to what?

She needed the obsidian blade.

In that moment, the smell of roses overwhelmed her senses. It brought her back to the Fairenwild, home to the various varieties, each unique in their own way. But now, smelling the scent so powerfully, in the midst of stone and death, the joy it should have brought to smell such a lovely creation was ripped away from her, replaced with a new truth: death smelled of roses.

Laurel let out a guttural cry as she curled her legs in beneath her and kicked with every bit of strength within her. She felt the skin of her forearm scrape away as the corespawn was flung from atop her. She opened her eyes in time to see a puddle, not far from her head, splash where the corespawn hit the ground.

With her own battle cry, Sarla rushed the puddle and drove the obsidian blade down where the invisible creature must be. Then she backed up, swinging the dagger back and forth, watching the puddles in the street for movement. Laurel lifted herself to her feet and fixed her eyes on a single point in the cobblestone, letting her peripherals scan for movement.

After a minute of peace, she relaxed.

Sarla rushed to Alabella, checking her pulse and lifting her eyelids. "Excessive use of threadlight, but she should recover."

Laurel clutched at the gash in her arm. "She'd better."

Laz looked down at Luther's sword and raised a brow. "Nice pointy stick."

"Not now, Laz."

The creature stalked toward them. Its entire body was nothing but a writhing mass of undulating threadlight. It had to have a weakness, but Luther didn't have time to figure it out.

"We need to get it out back," Luther said.

Reina nodded. "Easy."

She picked up a chunk of splintered wood and hurled it at the creature. It struck true and the creature roared in return.

"Come get me, ya big *hole!*" she shouted.

Laz gave her a nod of approval.

Luther clenched his teeth and the beast launched forward with terrifying speed. Luther, Laz, and Reina sprinted out of the house with threadlight burning in their veins and cut back around the side toward the backyard. As they turned the corner, a stable and a large shed came into view, along with a well-maintained garden of flowers.

"Laz, there's rope in the shed," Luther said, gesturing for him to go. "Still know how to lasso a bull?"

As he ran toward the shed, Laz understood the request. "Ha! I can do this thing!"

Luther and Reina had to distract the creature long enough for Laz to get into position. If they could tie it down and bind it, they could figure out how to kill it later.

"Be careful," Luther said to Reina.

"Worry about yourself," she said with a smirk. "Your bald head reflects more light than the moon. That thing's coming for you first."

She was right.

As it rounded the corner of the house, the creature doubled its pace and rushed directly at Luther. He held the longsword in both hands, preparing for the next attack, but the beast had learned, pausing as it approached. It lunged in, testing the boundary, and Luther swung in a wide arc, narrowly missing the creature's face. It lunged again, but retracted when he swung, and, when the blade had passed, it swiped furiously with both hands in quick succession. Luther heaved the hilt of the blade toward the creature's head, but it was too fast. Its head cracked into his ribs and knocked him over.

"Hey, big boy!" Reina yelled to distract it. "Over here!"

It gave no heed to her and, instead, leapt toward Luther on the ground. But as it soared through the air toward him, its entire body was yanked back. Luther lifted himself up and saw Laz's rope wrapped around its neck. The hulking Emerald reeled it in like a fisherman, then leapt atop its back, wrestling it to the ground as he gathered three of its legs. He looped the remaining rope around the legs and tied it off faster than Luther could have imagined possible.

"Ha!" Laz bellowed as he jumped away from the writhing creature. "Is easy!"

"Will it hold?" Luther asked.

"Yes, probably. Most likely."

Reina stepped forward. "What do we do with it?"

Luther swung the blade around in his hand. "Now we figure out how to kill it."

10

ALVERAX FELT SIMULTANEOUSLY a great king and a greater fool. He wore a single-breasted black tuxedo with a dozen golden buttons down each lapel and chains that ran from the back of each button up to the shoulder. It was slightly altered from the current Felian fashion to emphasize his shoulders by pulling the seams under his arm up higher. It made it very difficult to move his arms but, according to the seamstress, his shoulders were "delectable" and she had "no choice but to make the alteration." He'd have nightmares about that conversation for years.

The more interesting piece of his attire was the mask. Once a month, the nobility held a masquerade ball to "diverge from their transparent culture." The mask would be removed upon entrance to ensure only the invited guests would attend but, once inside, the mask was reapplied, and all were considered "equal." It wasn't exactly true, most people were still recognizable, and some tried little to hide themselves, but, in spirit, they were equal. Elder Rowan claimed it would be a good time to immerse himself in their culture and customs. Alverax thought it was a terrible idea.

Fortunately, he wasn't alone; Iriel Valerian walked beside him.

It was, perhaps, the first time Alverax had ever seen her without Aydin. The fit of her dress accentuated her toned arms and slender waist. It seemed like every day since they'd met, she'd grown more fit. When they'd traveled through the countryside west of the Fairenwild, she'd told him stories about her martial training in Alchea. And now, the veins in her forearms served a suitable testament.

"How are you feeling?" she asked as they approached the ballroom.

"Honestly?" He grimaced as he adjusted the feathers on his mask. "If

I lift my arms, I lose feeling. And if I turn my head just right, it feels like a feather duster is giving my nose a very thorough cleaning."

He could see her smile beneath her mask. "Oh, mine is dreadful. I'm pretty sure they glued it to my forehead. But it's honestly a welcome distraction."

It was easy to forget that she'd lost her husband, literally. No one knew where he was, or if he was alive. And her son was a short step from being labeled a demon by the Felian aristocracy. The mask over her face hid much, but it failed to hide the hint of loneliness in her eyes.

"I think we could all use a little distraction," he said, though he knew she could use it more than most. "Any news of your mother-in-law?"

"If she'd come west, she would have arrived days ago," Iriel said with a sigh. "No one's heard anything."

"Well," Alverax said, lifting his head high. "Tonight, you and I are going to forget it all! I will be Alexander Grant, purveyor of fine wines from a vineyard just north of the Malachite Mountains. And you will be Jacquelyn Joy, heiress to the largest collection of goats east of the Fairenwild."

Iriel let out a clipped laugh. "And here I thought the purpose of us going was to make a *good* impression."

"You drive a hard bargain," Alverax said with a straight face. "I'll drop the name, but I'm keeping the vineyard."

She shook her head.

Finally, they entered the ballroom. Alverax was astounded by the grandiosity. Hundreds of windows covered the circular, vaulted ceiling. Starlight trickled in alongside a full moon, combining with a host of sconces lit with tiny flames along the periphery of the room. Theatrical costumes. Elegant live music. And the flowers. If the palace entryway was a bed of flowers, the ballroom was a field. Roses—white, red, and violet—filled every inch of the space not meant for socializing. The scent filled his soul.

They walked the room, filled with attendees, and found their way across the dance floor to a collection of long tables filled with food and drink. Alverax took a sip of wine, then picked up a small, triangular pastry and took a bite. A burst of apple with a pinch of honey exploded in his mouth. His eyes opened wide as he ate the rest in a single bite.

With his mouth still full, he turned to Iriel. "I heard the secret ingredient is goat milk from the Jacquelyn Joy estate."

She rolled her eyes and led him away, but not before he grabbed one more and shoved it in his mouth. As they moved, his eyes drifted to the corner of the room where something curious caught his eye. It was as though a small section of the wall, from waist high and below, blurred in his vision. But as soon as it appeared, it was gone. The wine in Felia was clearly stronger than what he was used to.

A man and woman linking arms approached them. The man wore a white suit with a sharp red mask with the antlers of a deer. The cut of the woman's dress crept up her leg to just below her hip, with a neckline to give any man pause. Her taupe mask shot up on one side and curved into the shape of a crescent moon. She wore a dark violet lipstick.

The woman spoke as they neared. "Merikai, is that you?"

"No, no, no," the man said. "The hair is too short, and that is certainly not Zoelle."

Alverax removed his mask. It was uncommon—or so he had been told—but it was also the elders' instruction. *Let them see your face and make them like you.* The first part was easy. He smiled wide and extended his hand. "Alverax Blightwood. It's a pleasure to meet you. Unless, of course, this Merikai character is horribly unattractive, then a Herald's curse to you both."

"Ha!" the man laughed, shaking Alverax's hand. "Always an unexpected treat to meet the new couple."

"Oh, no," Iriel nearly shouted. "I'm married. Alverax is a friend. I am called Iriel."

The woman gave a small curtsy. "Santara Farrow. And this is my eternal partner, Rastalin Farrow, first in line to the post of Watchlord."

"It is a pleasure to meet you both." Alverax placed his mask back on. A bit of feather came off and fell to the floor. "I'm embarrassed I have to ask, but can you explain to me what exactly a Watchlord is? We're both new to Felia."

Santara gave a knowing smile. "It is not often that those new to our city are invited to occasions such as these. But men like you are an occasion until yourself."

Rastalin laughed. "A warning, my young friend. The women of Felia are teases. Trust what they say, but beware what they do not. The

Watchlord is, as you asked, the guardian of truth, and the chosen of the Heralds. It is his duty, first and foremost, to prepare the people for the Heraldic Restoration. In the meantime, they serve as head of the Felian army and counselor to Empress Chailani."

Alverax's grandfather had never taught him much of his religion, but he knew the basics. Once upon a time, the Heralds walked the earth. After establishing peace, they disappeared to never be seen again. Someday, they would return and heal the hearts of men.

"And you are first in line? Meaning if the current Watchlord—Osinan, was it?—was to fall ill and pass away, you would take his place?" Alverax pursed his lips. "That is a terrifying amount of responsibility."

Rastalin's smile was egregious. "Faith conquers fear, my young friend."

Just then, the music stopped.

All heads turned to the entrance.

A woman stepped forward, her pure white dress so large, the train so long, that several attendants had to carry it as she moved. Somehow, the dressmaker had woven in dozens of white roses into the dress itself. Then he saw her. Just beyond the empress, another woman entered. Her mask did little to hide her identity. Alverax would recognize that flowing black silhouette anywhere.

The Farrows took the distraction as an opportunity to leave, and Iriel leaned in to whisper. "If all of the Felian nobility are that arrogant, I swear I'll jump out one of those windows before this night is over."

"They're not *all* that arrogant," Alverax replied.

They talked to a dozen other people, including a young man wearing a horned mask that he claimed gave him supernatural strength. Alverax was quite sure the young man was mad. Finally, no longer able to resist, he left Iriel and approached Princess Jisenna. She was surrounded by a dozen women, laughing and trying their best to impress. She looked genuinely happy, despite the social politicking.

She looked up and, when their eyes met, his heart pounded. He steeled his nerves and advanced.

Princess Jisenna stared at him as he approached, the dozen women surrounding her turned and did the same. He immediately regretted his decision. What did he expect? That they would all leave so he could talk with her?

A woman with a reddish tint to her long dark hair spoke first. "Who do we have here?"

"I don't recognize him."

"Is he new?"

"What is your name, my lord?"

"He has a very strong jaw."

"Dark eyes. Must be rich."

"Are you from out of town?"

"That tuxedo is a quite fetching fit."

"It is certainly a flattering cut."

"Ladies," Jisenna said, coming to his defense. "Please, do not scare him away. He is one of our special guests this evening. This is Alverax Blightwood, the last Obsidian threadweaver."

Alverax smiled awkwardly as the introduction settled. Two of the women gasped aloud. Several whispered to each other, and Alverax was certain he saw one squeeze the hand of another.

A woman with a thick strand of white in her long black hair took a step toward him just as a new song began. "An honor, my lord. Please pardon our manners. These masquerades are so often filled with the same people that a little novelty is quite exciting, especially when the novelty is—if I may be so bold—a singularly handsome man."

"It was just a bit of fun. No harm done," Alverax replied, trying to hide his discomfort.

"If you're not spoken for," the woman continued, "I would be honored if you would join me for the next dance."

Heralds, save me.

"Actually," Princess Jisenna cut in, "Alverax promised me the first dance of the evening."

He turned to her.

She gave not the slightest hint of deception.

"It would be a shame to break a promise," he said with a smirk. "Perhaps another time?"

He held out his hand and Jisenna took it. Together they left the group behind and walked to the dance floor. He looked at the dozens of others already dancing and was relieved to find them moving in a style similar to what he'd practiced. He stretched out his hands, palms up, and she placed hers with the palms up atop his own. Couples who had promised themselves would dance with their palms together and, even though theirs were not, the brush of the back of her hand on his lit a flame inside of him.

For the briefest moment, despite all rationale, he let himself believe that she liked him more than she surely did. The Princess and the Obsidian. The Sun Daughter and…the Bloodthief. Who was he fooling? They would find out sooner or later.

"Is something wrong?" she asked as their feet carried them in a circle. "You've the face of a man who's made a mistake. I'd hate to think that was on my behalf."

Alverax gave her his most convincing smile. "No, no. It's just…I'm not used to all of this. Especially the attention."

"You will get used to it. In truth, you will likely tire of it." She laughed to herself. "That is assuming, of course, that you plan to stay."

"I don't think there would be a warm welcome for me where I'm from. Although, I would love to see my grandfather again before he passes away."

"Is he ill?" she asked.

"Oh, no," Alverax said. "Us Blightwoods don't die easy. He's just old. Though being old is really just being sick of life. So, I suppose he is a bit ill."

"If being sick of life is a symptom of old age, I must be ancient," Jisenna said with a wide smile.

"Well, you look amazing for your age."

Elder Rowan's words echoed in his mind. *Don't do anything stupid.*

"I…" he said, quite awkwardly. "I forgot that Iriel needed me for something. Thank you for the dance! And thank you for saving me earlier!"

He left without giving her a chance to respond and cringed when he saw the confused look in her eyes. Elder Rowan had been quite clear about what he needed to accomplish during the masquerade, and a poor attempt at flirting with the princess was *not* one of them. He still needed to talk to Empress Chailani and the Watchlord.

Near the food tables, he saw Iriel engaged in what seemed to be an enjoyable conversation, so he looked for the empress. She stood near the front of the ballroom, flanked by two guards and a serving woman who held the train of her dress. The man she was conversing with gave a bow and started to leave. Alverax let a bit of threadlight run through his veins to steady his nerves.

Perfect, he thought.

Hoping to step in before another had the chance, Alverax moved toward the empress. But just as he arrived, a blurry shift in the air flickered in his vision. For a moment, he thought it a mirage—no one else seemed to see it. He opened his eyes to threadlight, and a swirling maze of radiance blazed to life. It stood on two legs, like a person, but a thin tail arced up over its head. The end of the tail, spiked like a scorpion's stinger, stretched back to strike.

No.

Alverax dove forward to stop it, but it was too fast. Its stinger pierced into the empress' chest. Its arms threw Alverax atop Chailani's body as she gasped in pain. The prismatic light swirling across the creature's body called to him and, so, Alverax reached out to it with his mind and *broke* it. In a split second, the creature exploded into a million beads of light and vanished.

Screams erupted in the ballroom. The music stopped. Heads turned. The guards were on top of Alverax before he could breathe, blades ready to bear down.

It all happened so quickly.

"No!" Princess Jisenna shouted. She ran across the room, ripping off her mask, and fell at her sister's side. "Heralds, please, no!"

The world blurred in front of him. Time, like a wave against the bluff, crashed to a halt. The white roses from the empress' train seemed to fill the entirety of the room; red specks of blood stained them like drops of rain down a wet canvas.

And Jisenna, hands clutching her sister tight, tears flowing down her perfect cheeks, turned to Alverax with rage in her eyes. "What have you done?"

11

Those four words, Jisenna's words, broke him.

What have you done?

Alverax may be many things—a fool, a poor judge of character, a fraud—but he was no killer. Unfortunately, the people of Felia didn't know that.

"Something attacked her," he shouted into the marble floor. "It wasn't me!"

Jisenna screamed in pain as she clutched her sister's corpse. The entire ballroom seemed to pause in time. The dancing ceased. The blaring shock faded to a silent fright, leaving only the sound of Jisenna. She was a meteor falling to the ground, and the people stood, bewildered, watching as the devastation unfolded.

The empress was dead.

"I swear it wasn't me!" Alverax shouted. "The creature! There was a creature! Someone had to have seen it!"

"Save your lies!" Watchlord Osinan shouted, appearing from the crowd.

The guards shoved Alverax's face down into the floor. Their knees dug into his back, forcing the air out of his lungs. A young guard with Emerald threadlight glowing in the veins of his neck stood nervously at the edge of the crowd. For a moment, Alverax thought the guard would come to his rescue, verify that there had been a creature. But instead, he closed his mouth and said nothing, and Alverax felt his hope slipping.

Watchlord Osinan looked to Alverax, bound by thick guards, his face smashed against the floor. "We never should have trusted you. Your people lied. I want every last one of the Zeda imprisoned. They will pay for what they've done."

"You know me!" Alverax shouted to Jisenna. "I would never do this!"

She said nothing, but, when her eyes met his, he could feel her response more strongly than any spoken word could have conveyed. The quiver in her lip. The twitch of her eye. All of it said, *I don't believe you.*

The guards lifted Alverax to his feet and tied his wrists behind his back. But then, just as they were about to take him away, he saw her in the corner of his eye. Iriel Valerian stalked through the crowd like a viper, slithering between masked onlookers, fists clenched ready to strike. With deadly speed, she leapt forward, *pulling* against the far wall and ripping her way through the air toward the guards. She crashed into both, knocking them over, then grabbed Alverax's shoulders.

"Break your corethread!" she shouted, shoving him toward the window. "Now!"

His corethread *broke* with urgency, and he felt gravity dissipate. In the same moment, Iriel *pulled* again on the wall and, together, they shot through the air toward the window. The glass shattered as metal ripped out of the sill, shards drifting through the air like beads of rain, cutting at his cheeks and hands.

And then...freedom.

He *broke* Iriel's corethread as they burst out of the window into the night sky. High above the palace grounds, drifting horizontally like carefree gulls toward the Terecean Sea, he looked back behind them and nearly screamed as a spear shot passed his head. Several guards stood at the shattered window, shouting words that Alverax couldn't hear—he wasn't sure he needed to.

"We shouldn't have run," he said to himself. "Heralds, we shouldn't have run!"

"There was no other choice," Iriel said confidently. "Someone set you up."

"No one *set me up*. There was some kind of invisible creature!"

Iriel scowled but said nothing.

"The Zeda," Alverax remembered. "The Zeda! We have to do something! We have to warn them!"

"We need to get Aydin," Iriel said. "Stones, we need to get *down*."

As soon as their corethreads reappeared, they began to fall back toward the ground and, as soon as they did, Alverax *broke* their corethreads once more, sending them down at a comfortable speed for landing. Fortunately, they were far enough from the palace that there was no way the guards could follow them. That meant that they had a little time before the Felian armies would surround the Zeda encampment. On the other hand, the elders staying in the palace were trapped already.

Their feet hit the ground on a field of jade, thin grass swaying in the coastal breeze. Neither said a word as they took off running as fast as they could toward the Zeda encampment near the southern wall. In no time at all, they left the field and entered the cobblestone streets of Felia. Tents and pavilions and small stone shops lined the labyrinth. With the sun set low beyond the western sea, they tried their best to keep course.

When they arrived, a battalion of Felian soldiers surrounded the tents. The encampment, nestled against the high city wall, was an agitated beehive. Scared Zeda ran around, gathering their children and shouting at guards. A swarm of raging women roared at a man surrounded by a dozen guards.

"Stones," Iriel whispered under her breath. "We're too late."

Alverax stood quietly, catching his breath. This was his fault. If he hadn't left Cynosure, he wouldn't have been caught by Alabella. And if she didn't have him, she wouldn't have attacked Zedalum. They would still be safe and content living alone in the Fairenwild. Now, they were being rounded up like fish in a net.

He had to do something.

He had to help.

He turned to Iriel. "I have an idea, but you're not going to like it."

ALVERAX APPROACHED as close to the Felian guards as he dared, hiding behind a half-full wagon, and waited for Iriel to get into position. From his new vantage point, he watched one of the guards reach out and slap a sobbing Zeda woman. The blow knocked her to her knees.

Iriel arrived in position and gave him a nod. He wasn't sure if it was going to work, but he knew he had to try. The thought reminded him of his grandfather as they sat along the steep cliff at Mercy's Bluff overlooking the Altapecean Sea. His grandfather had looked down at the water far below and asked, "Do you think there are any sharks down there?" Alverax had shaken his head in doubt. His grandfather smiled and said, "Perhaps not. But we can't know for certain up here. The only sure way to know what's below the waves is to take the dive."

He took a deep breath and let threadlight pour through his veins. Thousands of strands of brilliant luminescence burst into his vision, pulsing in chaotic harmony. Before he could doubt himself, he took the dive. One by one, with a focus like never before, he *broke* the corethread of every soldier within sight. Pressure built in his veins, pressing against his skin. Still, he continued, systematically hacking his way through corethreads like a farmer sifting wheat. But, before he could finish, a sharp pain erupted in his chest and he dropped to his hands and knees. His heart burned within him. Throbbing. Squeezing. Stabbing. He struggled to breathe.

He clenched his jaw and opened his eyes to survey the effects of his work. Dozens of soldiers screamed, and Alverax gasped. The entire squad of soldiers floated away on the westerly wind like the seeds of a dandelion to a child's breath. Watchlord Osinan was one of them, tumbling head over heel and flailing with terror stricken across his face.

The remaining soldiers struggled to hold back the fleeing Zeda people as they scattered in every direction. Other soldiers fled and tried to help their drifting comrades. But one soldier, a short man with a wide frame, shoved down a young Zeda girl. Alverax recognized her. The soldier walked forward and kicked her in the stomach, shouting for her to stay put.

Alverax lifted himself up, breathed like a raging beast, and rushed the man. With every ounce of his remaining strength, he leapt, both feet forward, and just before his feet struck, he *broke* the soldier's corethread. The collision sent the soldier blasting into the air and over the tents.

"Poppy?" Alverax asked the girl, grunting as he rose to his knees. "Are you okay?"

The girl looked up and noticed the man was gone. Her mid-length hair fell in just the right way that it looked like the droopy ears of a Felian bloodhound. "I'll be alright," she managed.

"You have to run. The soldiers will be back any minute."

She nodded and ran.

Just then, another wave of soldiers arrived, bolstered by their allies who had returned to the surface. They swarmed forward through cobblestone streets like millions of desert scarabs.

As he stared, paralyzed with fear and exhaustion, a hand grabbed his shoulder. He startled, then turned to see Iriel holding Aydin.

"Let's go!" she shouted, pulling him away from the incoming soldiers.

Alverax nodded and stumbled after her toward the wall on the other side of the Zeda tents. When they reached it, Alverax steeled his gut, and *broke* his corethread one last time while kicking off the ground. His chest seized as he floated up over the wall. No matter how hard he tried to breathe, the air refused to comply. An odd sensation blossomed near the top of his spine, like a wound breaking open. He grabbed hold of a stone crevice along the peak of the wall and flipped over flat on his stomach.

Iriel screamed.

He looked down with blurry eyes and saw Iriel halfway up the wall with an arrow jutting out of her calf. Aydin was in her arms, screeching, and she—Heralds, save the woman—was falling to the ground.

Alverax, knowing his body couldn't handle it, opened himself to threadlight one final time and *broke* her corethread. He couldn't stop her fall, but he could lessen the impact.

Soldiers swarmed her and the child as soon as they hit the ground.

Time slowed to a crawl. Below him on one side of the wall was chaos, and on the other side, the intoxicating lull of peace, a calm river that ran parallel to the wall. He knew he should run—only then would he have any semblance of hope in helping the others—but a potent instinct grabbed hold of him from the inside. For all Iriel had believed in him, for the trust she'd offered him, he owed her more than a lonely prison cell.

With blurry eyes and a mind on the edge of blackness, he was in no state to save her, but he couldn't let her go alone.

As his mind faded to darkness, he tried to lean toward her, to go with her. But instead of falling toward his friend, his mind blurred and he slipped. His body drifted off the far edge of the wall. The world moved slowly, trees drifting in the wind, rays of light bouncing off the water. It all seemed to slow more and more the further he fell, and then, just before he hit the surface of the river, his vision grew black.

STONES OF LIGHT

12

CHRYS FELT a wave of fear as he approached the multi-layered hive of the wasteland bees. Thousands of red and white insects, each nearly as large as a man's thumb, buzzed around the central trees of the prison enclosure, moving in and out of a conglomerate of nests. Tunnels, like man-made corridors, linked each nest together into a catacomb of terrifying proportions.

Every instinct told Chrys to open himself to threadlight, but, same as they had every day, the wastelanders had fed him a drink that blocked his source. For now, he would have to go without.

Roshaw led him forward, carefully watching each step so as not to accidentally step on one of the insects. The buzzing sound intensified as they approached the center, and dozens of bees brushed up against their bare arms. One sting, the crew said, was enough to kill a man, though it would also kill the bee. The crew claimed that no one had been stung without previously disturbing the bees—like stepping on one of their family.

"Almost there," Roshaw whispered, careful to keep his mouth mostly closed.

Then Chrys saw it. In the center of the closest nest, protruding from the bottom like a dripping stalactite, was the solidified purple material they called honeycrystal—Esme called it "bee snot." Once a week, one of them would enter the hive and extract however many honeycrystals had grown. The result was then brought to the chief of the ataçan.

Roshaw reached his hand up toward the crystallized material. Bees landed on his slow-moving hand and darted away when they decided he was no threat. Chrys watched in awe, terrified that at any moment one of the bees would fly into his eye or sting his hand. He wanted to fight back.

If he was going to die, it wouldn't be while he was standing still in a tornado of wasteland bees.

Finally, Roshaw's hand reached the base of the honeycrystal and grabbed hold. He twisted and the shard broke free of the nest. Slowly, he pulled down. A hundred bees, like bats exiting a cave, rushed out of the newly formed hole at the base of the nest. Roshaw stood frozen while bees swarmed around him, prodding, testing, measuring the danger. Chrys hated watching and feeling so helpless. The memory of Iriel and Aydin on the wonderstone flashed in his mind as they were overwhelmed by dozens of tentacles of threadlight. In that moment, he'd been completely powerless.

Roshaw's hand began to lower, still holding the honeycrystal. "Back up."

Chrys obliged, and, after an eternity of slow movements, they were finally free from the spread of the hive. A great relief washed over him.

"Not so bad, right?" Roshaw said with a triumphant grin.

"Stones," Chrys cursed. "If the bees don't kill me, the stress will."

"The stress is more likely to kill you than the bees. Apparently, they don't care about humans. Now, if you were a wastelander, the whole hive would come down on you. Agatha is convinced it's their smell."

"Their smell?" Chrys repeated.

"The wastelanders have a very distinct smell. Somewhere between the sweet smell of magnolia and a man's sweaty ass." Roshaw smiled at his own joke. "You can wait here or go join the others. I need to go check for more honeycrystals."

Chrys eyed the hive with reservation.

"I'll be fine," Roshaw said, pulling on his earlobes. "One-hundred percent human."

With a nod, Chrys joined the others sitting in a bunch at the doorway to the hut. Seven was massaging Esme's feet while they watched Roshaw perform his duty. They had seen the honeycrystal extraction hundreds of times over the five years they'd spent trapped. They no longer saw danger in the act. Only duty. That, Chrys could understand.

"Well?" Esme said, her mouth open while Seven rubbed her feet. "Pretty crazy, right?"

"I would be happy to never experience that again."

"You'll get used to it," Seven said. He patted Esme's foot and stood up. "If you step on one, you'll get stung. But otherwise, you'll be fine."

"I don't plan on getting used to it," Chrys said. "I plan on showing the savages what happens when you imprison Chrys Valerian."

Agatha rose to her feet, a hint of excitement in her eyes. "The wastelanders are *not* savages. In fact, they are quite fascinating."

"Oh, no," Esme said. "You've activated the professor."

"Hush, hush," Agatha said, swatting the other woman in the shoulder. "Though they are inhuman, their culture is still quite rich. One of the more interesting aspects is their reverence for both the et'hovon—the bees—and the ataçan—the gorillas. They see the relationship between the two the same way they see their own relationship with their gods. The wastelanders are a hive. Each individual is willing to sacrifice themself to protect the greater whole. In fact, their leaders are often selected from those who have willingly sacrificed themselves yet survived. The other great purpose of the hive is to provide food for the ataçan with the honeycrystals. For the wastelanders, this means giving themselves in service to their gods."

"*Dead* gods," Esme corrected.

"Possibly," Agatha said. "From what we can gather, something happened just before we arrived. Their god, whom they call *Relek*, vanished."

Stones, Chrys thought. *He is their god. And now he's returned.*

What would that mean to the wastelanders? Would they gather forces and finally head over the mountains? It would explain why they'd been so passive in their defense during the war. They'd never pushed a victory. Never come further than the valley. His mind raced. The wastelanders knew of Relek's ability to inhabit other bodies. That was the real reason they'd kept the prisoners alive. A gift for their god when he returned. Honeycrystal for their ataçan.

He wasn't sure what it all meant. Were they in danger? Did the wastelanders no longer need them?

Before he could respond, Roshaw returned holding a third honeycrystal, each shard a varying shade of violet, but all shaped like a thick icicle. "Aye, you ready to make a delivery?"

Chrys had so many questions for Agatha and the others, but there would be time for that. He was just as interested in the next step of the harvest, when they would deliver the honeycrystals to the chief of the ataçan, whom they called Xuçan.

The two of them left the others and walked to the large gate. Roshaw showed Chrys how to present himself so that four wastelander guards could bind their wrists together with a rope at the end that they held like a leash.

The guards accompanied them out of the enclosure, and they began their journey to the Endless Well. When he'd asked about the location, the crew had all laughed and said that he just had to see if for himself.

Chrys hated that he couldn't understand the wastelanders as they spoke to each other, especially given all of the smirking and laughing they did on Chrys and Roshaw's behalf. It felt very much like they were being led to a trap, and the guards couldn't help but revel in the inevitability. But Roshaw knew the path, and made no comment, so Chrys disregarded his instinct.

On their way, he spotted the edge of the village, which appeared much larger than Chrys had originally thought. Small wooden buildings hung suspended between trees with shaky wooden bridges between them, ladders dangling haphazardly amongst the chaos. Young wastelanders leapt from one platform to another while others swung from vines between buildings. What surprised him most was the mass of wastelanders lying on their backs in the swamp water, seemingly asleep.

They continued on and the edge of Kai'Melend faded behind mossy trees. They passed a small body of water where dozens of wastelanders knelt quietly. The still water shimmered a pale golden color as if reflecting a hidden sunset. The wastelanders approached one by one and drank from it reverently.

"What is that?" Chrys asked.

"They call it *oka'thal*, which means *life water*." Roshaw rubbed at his beard. "It's sacred. From what I understand, every wastelander comes here each week and drinks from it."

"So, they worship the bees, the apes, *and* the water?"

"Yeah, and our people revere shiny rocks," Roshaw said with a laugh. "You have to get out of that mindset. Their world is different; that doesn't make ours better. In some ways, they're more evolved than we are. Did you know their eyes see better in the dark? Or that they're partially amphibious?"

"I—" Chrys started.

Roshaw cut in. "I'm not trying to make you feel guilty. I'm just saying that there is good among them. And we're not all that different. As for the ataçan, the wastelanders don't worship Xuçan. They fear him."

Chrys turned and looked at the four guards, and felt a new sense of respect for them. They were soldiers just as much as he was, serving their commander to the best of their ability. Could he fault them for taking prisoners? Alchea had done the same. The only difference was that Alchean prisoners never would have survived for five years.

Eventually, they crested a small hill, following a well-worn path through thick vines. When they stepped out of the jungle, Chrys' heart skipped a beat. Before him lay a sprawling panorama lit by a cloudless sky, a large lake feeding a collection of majestic waterfalls that sent their waters cascading down into the Endless Well.

Chrys had expected it to be small—how large could a "well" be? But the opening in the earth was so wide that an entire battalion could step off the ledge at once without breaking rank. To his left, atop a sheer cliff overlooking the lake, a troop of ataçan stretched out over the rocks. Sitting on the highest boulder, like an emperor overlooking his kingdom, sat an ataçan nearly twice the size of the others with four thick arms. Even at such a distance, Chrys felt the power and pride of the chief of the ataçan.

"I assume you don't need me to tell you which one is Xuçan?" Roshaw slapped Chrys on the back and smiled. "The trick to the next part is to not make eye contact."

"Has he killed anyone?"

"None of the crew, but a few years back he ripped a wastelander in half who tried to bond him."

Chrys paused, not at the brutality, but at the penultimate word. "Tried to *bond* him?"

"Ah," Roshaw said. "The bond is fascinating. Some few of the ataçan choose a companion amongst the wastelanders, and a bond is formed. Honestly, I don't know much about it, except that the wastelander becomes a little more like the ataçan, and the ataçan a little more like the wastelander. There are only a handful of wastelanders bonded, and it is an instant elevation in status. Kind of like if your kid became a threadweaver suddenly. Good for the kid, but also good for the family."

The wartime reality of having an ataçan on your side was terrifying. As far as Chrys knew, no ataçan had shown up in the battles in the mountains. But if the Alcheans ever came further east, thinking the wastelanders would be easy to conquer, a single ataçan would kill dozens, if not more.

Roshaw continued. "Lots of young wastelanders attempt the bond. Even if they fail, it's a well-regarded sacrifice for their family. Generally, the ataçan kill them. Since I've been here, only one wastelander has formed a bond, and it was a young one. Xuçan exiled the ataçan who formed the bond. Supposedly, he's hundreds of years old and has never accepted one himself."

"Not even from their god, Relek?"

"Hmm," Roshaw said thoughtfully. "I guess not."

They both grew quiet as the terrain grew steeper. Their guards slowed, slackening the leash and giving more space between them. The urge to run, to escape, to fight now that they had the advantage of the high ground and a little space to work with, wiggled its way into Chrys' mind, but he pushed it away. Maybe if he had access to threadlight.

The time would come, and it wouldn't be when they were sandwiched between warriors and ataçan.

As they grew closer, Chrys got a better look at the beasts, and at their leader, Xuçan. He'd seen sketches of the apes of western Alir, tucked away in the jungles of a secluded island, but those were roughly the size of a man. The ataçan were twice that size, mostly gray with varying shades of blue. Short yellow spikes ran down the length of their spine, and tusks cut out from their jaws, curling upward. Their arms were so thick that Chrys had no doubt about the stories of ripping a wastelander in half.

If the ataçan were a beating rain, Xuçan was a thunderstorm. Larger than the rest, he was the only ataçan with four arms, each as thick as the last. One of his tusks was broken mid-way, with the jagged edges even more threatening than the whole. He sat upon a flat boulder with brows set so deep his eyes were bathed in shadow.

Xuçan and the others noted their arrival and fixed their gaze upon Chrys and Roshaw. The wastelander guards dropped the leash and stayed behind, keeping their eyes fixed to the ground. As they approached, Roshaw lifted the lavender-colored honeycrystals, following the example of the guards and keeping his eyes down. When he was close enough, he dropped down to a knee.

Never in his life would Chrys have expected to see a man bowing before a beast, bringing him a gift as though he were the true emperor of the land.

The closest of the ataçan, a large beast with a blue streak across its face, beat at its chest with massive fists, each hit resounding like a war drum. Chrys clenched his teeth and met its gaze. It let out a series of deep-throated grunts and slammed its fists against the ground.

Then Xuçan roared. The sound seemed to come from every direction, bellowing in Chrys' ears, threatening to break his mind. Chrys turned his gaze to the ataçan chief.

A voice like thunder echoed in Chrys' mind. *You disrespect us.*

A cold shiver traveled up his spine. The beat of his heart quickened. Somehow, the words echoing in his mind belonged to Xuçan. A sense of preservation urged Chrys to fall to his knees like Roshaw beside him, to express his respect to the ataçan, but he refused. He would not bow to Relek. He would not bow to Alabella. And he would never bow to an oversized wasteland gorilla.

The great chief stepped down from his perch, passing the other ataçan as he knuckle-walked down the sloping cliffside. Chrys watched in silence, never averting his gaze from the powerful, deep-set eyes of the chief.

"Heralds, save us," Roshaw said under his breath. His eyes bore into the ground, his arms shaking as he held up the honeycrystals.

Xuçan stopped in front of Chrys, his face impassive save for the constant downward curl of his lips. *Tell me, he-who-does-not-cower, who are you?*

The words, simple as they were, seeped into Chrys' soul. A creature like Xuçan was not asking for his name, nor his history. He was asking who he was at his core. What truths laid his foundation? Chrys was a husband, a father, a threadweaver, a warrior, but in each of these things he had fallen short. He was a failure, and his legacy was a trail of broken glass. He was a man who had given everything and received nothing in return.

Speak! the great Xuçan roared in Chrys' mind.

"I am he-who-sacrifices-all," Chrys said aloud, adopting the ataçan's style of speech.

Xuçan placed all four fists down on the ground surrounding Chrys, leaning in and letting his breath mist over Chrys' cheeks. *You are like him, but different. Do you serve he-who-perverts-the-bond?*

"I—" Chrys started. "I don't know who that is."

He-who-steals-life, Xuçan said. *The creature of many faces.*

Chrys furrowed his brow, then relaxed as understanding washed over him. "Relek."

Xuçan rose high onto his broad legs and roared a guttural cry that filled the entire world around them. *DO NOT SPEAK THAT NAME HERE!*

"Heralds," Roshaw said, quivering. He peeked to the side, still prostrated, but confused at the one-sided conversation. "You're gonna get us killed!"

Chrys ignored him. "He-who-steals-life has taken everything from me."

Xuçan settled down, his breath still heavy. *That name is forbidden here. He-who-perverts-the-bond is forbidden here. You will leave now.*

Chrys nodded and gave a small bow. "Thank you."

He grabbed Roshaw's arm and instructed him to drop the honeycrystals at Xuçan's feet before dragging him to safety.

"What the hell just happened?" Roshaw asked, glancing back over his shoulder toward the massive ataçan chief.

"I'm not sure," Chrys said. "But it gave me an idea."

13

Each morning when Chrys arose, the wastelander guards forced him to drink a murky liquid that suppressed his threadlight. After a few days, he'd realized that it was an inherent flaw in their stewardship. Any plan of escape was far from complete but being able to identify an area of weakness would give them a leg up when the day arrived.

Several days passed, and Chrys was surprised that the wastelanders did, in fact, leave them alone almost entirely. He was also surprised that the crew had built a functioning game board for a traditional Alchean game called Scion, a triangular board with a series of holes. Each player had ten pegs that they used to capture those of the other players. The last remaining player won.

They used the time around the board to badger him with questions, and Chrys told them everything. If they were going to escape, he needed them to trust him. So, he held nothing back. Agatha, who was so enraptured by his story that she refused to take a turn playing, asked the most questions, and gasped when he told her what happened when they'd arrived in Kai'Melend. Chrys shared that Xuçan referred to Relek as the "creature of many faces," and it seemed to haunt them all. They wondered if the fear the wastelanders held toward the ataçan was related to the apes' disdain for their god.

The wastelanders had been wary of Chrys ever since the encounter with Xuçan. None of the other members of the crew had ever spoken to the ataçan, and the occurrence seemed to affect them as much as it did the wastelanders who'd seen it from a distance. When the guards looked at him, instead of looking on with disregard as they had before, they now showed him open hostility. One slammed his spear into Chrys' stomach when he had failed to swallow the murky drink fast enough, which ended with them having to leave and come back with more.

But beyond all of the questions and answers, one vital conversation occurred: how to escape.

The crew had come together and created a plan for how they could all escape the enclosure, and, more importantly, get back over the mountains. Rather than traveling west, as they'd done before and as the wastelanders would expect, their plan took them south. Roshaw knew of a path around the southern border of the Everstone Mountains that would take them safely to the west.

But their plan hinged on two key, unresolved contributions. First, they would need Xuçan to let them pass over the ridge without allowing the ataçan to murder them all. Chrys felt confident that with one more conversation, he could arrange that. The other piece required a test.

Chrys fell to his knees and clutched his stomach, doubling over and groaning in pain.

"Aye!" Esme shouted much too loudly. "Are you okay?"

He groaned dramatically, falling to his back and writhing against the muddy ground. All four members of the crew ran to him, surrounding him in a circle.

"Help!" Seven shouted, turning to the wastelander guards. "He needs help!"

Roshaw called out for help in the wastelander tongue, but the guards watched on impassively. They were happy to let Chrys die—especially given the conversation with Xuçan—which was exactly what they were counting on.

Chrys rolled over onto his stomach and reached his finger down his throat, shoving it as far as he could before the heaving began. His stomach seized up, and his throat tightened. Again, he inserted his fingers, triggering a series of painful heaves until, finally, he vomited into the swamp water. He smiled and did it again, unloading all of his food and water onto the floor of the enclosure. Then, he rolled over and let the others lift him up, carrying him to the hut in the center, and laying him down.

They waited for the wastelanders to realize what they'd done, but the guards stayed put in their perches above the wall and happily remained wrapped in the warmth of their apathy.

After a few minutes of quiet, Chrys signaled for the others to surround him. Chrys relaxed his mind and let threadlight pour through his veins. His body braced itself for pain, knowing that the murky liquid they fed him could very well still be in his system. Instead, the warmth of threadlight flowed from his chest down to the ends of his toes, sizzling beneath his skin. The heat engrossed him like the warm embrace of an old friend, squeezing, and promising that, no matter what, he would always be there.

The others looked at his glowing veins and tried not to smile, but Roshaw's smile was wider than them all. "This is really gonna work. I'm gonna see my kid again."

"He probably doesn't even love you anymore," Esme said.

Roshaw's smile faded.

"Psh." Esme rolled her eyes. "Don't be a baby."

Seven stared at the radiant, Sapphire hue running along Chrys' arms. "Either this is going to work, or we're all going to die."

Chrys flicked a rock through the air, giving it an extra *push*. "This is going to work."

14 · STONES OF LIGHT

THERE WAS a certain biting chill to the morning wind that blew throughout the streets of Alchea, a fitting complement to the destruction left in the wake of the corespawn. Laurel, like many others, had spent the remainder of the night bunkered down, listening to the dissonant melodies of devastation that filled the night air.

Runners from Endin Keep had announced throughout the city that the attacks had ended with the rising sun, and Great Lord Malachus called for all citizens to assemble in the sprawling courtyards outside the keep. Laurel had traveled with a company of the Bloodthieves that included Alabella, Sarla, and Barrick, the large man who'd accompanied them to the Fairenwild. They said little as they traveled to the keep, none daring to speak the truth. In the Fairenwild, beneath the coreseal, it was *them* who had released the corespawn.

When Alabella removed her Felian lightshades to wipe off the lens, Laurel caught a glimpse of her eyes. The woman had always seemed so confident, so strong. But something had changed. A shadow of fear. What they had done cracked the façade, and now, a pinch of doubt spread its roots within the woman.

When they arrived at the gates of Endin Keep, Laurel winced at the reunion. She'd only been there once, and the result had been devastating. She feared what conclusion this day would bring.

Already, thousands began to gather in the courtyard of the keep, huddled below a raised platform on the far side of the great central fountain. Laurel looked at the faces of the grounders who surrounded her. Eyes sunken with fatigue. Shoulders slumped. Heads bowed. In a single night, these people had been broken. And for those who were not threadweavers, who could not even see the enemy, how could they not be?

Laurel and the others approached the platform. Hundreds of soldiers lined the periphery, creating a wall of protection between the people and the dais from which the Great Lord would address them. Atop the platform, dozens of threadweavers, men and women, stood at attention, their eyes and veins still tinted from the extended use of threadlight. Laurel had a transfuser in the inside breast pocket of her jacket, but she hated herself for needing it. She clasped her shaking hands and tried to calm her fluttering heart with steady breaths.

A trumpet rang out, announcing the commencement of the assemblage. The threadweavers on the platform stood at attention and, from a ramp on the far side, a familiar woman stepped forward. High General Henna wiped the white hair from her eyes, then stood with her hands interlocked behind her back. She scanned the crowd for danger.

Behind her, the Great Lord himself arose. There were no cheers, no chants of admiration, the city stood on edge to hear how their leader would respond to the tragedy that had decimated their world. He approached the front of the platform, head held high, and the last remaining whispers of the crowd gave way to an eerie silence.

"We are under attack," Great Lord Malachus exclaimed. "I will not insult your intelligence by claiming it to be anything less than what it is. You have seen the devastation. You have walked the broken streets. You have mourned your fallen friends and family. It is the obligation of a responsible leader to acknowledge such reality. Only then can we move forward.

"A leader must—above all else—see to the safety of their stewardship. Today, we assemble because a new danger has arisen, something the likes of which this world has not seen in centuries. But we are Alchea! We are stone! We will stand united! We will fight! The streets of Alchea belong to *us*! Tonight, we will be prepared. And when the enemy comes, Alchea will prevail!"

The crowd let out a boisterous applause, a choir of cheers bellowing out over the sprawling courtyard. Laurel could feel their enthusiasm. She saw it in their eyes and in the curves of their lips. Great Lord Malachus wasn't just a ruler, he was *their* ruler. The powerful, bichromic Great Lord.

"To prepare for the return of the beasts, we will hereby institute the following measures effective immediately. Listen close, as these three measures will affect all of us.

"First, a mandatory curfew from sundown to sunset. Just before the sun rose over the Everstone Mountains, the creatures fled to the west. To the cover of the Fairenwild. We believe a second attack is most likely to happen under cover of darkness. Luther Mandrin, one of our most decorated soldiers, was able to catch one of the creatures. Our people are studying it as we speak. With the limited knowledge we have, a quarantine is the most effective strategy to ensure the safety of our people.

"Second, all windows are to be boarded up, in both homes and stores. The majority of the creatures are small enough that they cannot break down your walls, and those that are we hope will ignore homes that are dark and quiet. Tyberius and Mirimar Di'Fier have offered to provide all of the lumber necessary, which you will find available at their mill in the upper west side. If you are unable to board up your home before the sun sets tonight, find a neighbor who has and join them for the evening.

"Lastly, as the head of the Stone Council and the Order of Alchaeus, it is my solemn duty to protect those who have dedicated their lives to the Lightfather. Until the threat is gone, the Temple of Alchaeus will be closed and all its occupants moved into Endin Keep. There is nothing I hold with more gravity than the safety of this people. Be vigilant. Be responsible. And, above all else, be strong. Together, we *will* prevail."

Again, the crowd broke out in raucous applause. But this time, to Laurel's surprise, pockets of men and women cursed their ruler. A young man standing not far from Laurel shouted up at the Great Lord. "We want to fight, not hide!"

"Aye!" the group surrounding him exclaimed.

"Give us swords!"

"Let us fight!"

"Cowards!"

The crowd turned course like a shifting wind. One by one their enthusiasm and doubt began to spread like a plague, until Malachus pointed to the young man who started it all and gestured for him to join him on the platform.

"Tell me," Malachus said to the young man with a booming voice, "have you seen one of these beasts?"

The young man shook his head.

"Have you?!" Malachus shouted, pointing to an angry man in the crowd. "You? Or you?" He continued to single out individuals closest to the platform. "You may have heard the rumor, but I tell you now that it is true. These creatures cannot be seen by achromats. If I handed you a blade, you would die to an enemy that you could not even see.

"We have a plan, but you must trust us. Stay in your homes. Board up your doors and windows. Keep your lanterns dark. And under no circumstance should you attempt to fight these creatures. Bravery and stupidity are ever at odds, and, in this case, to fight is to prove your own ignorance.

"Now, gather your supplies and go home. Tonight, stay safe. The time to fight will come."

A somber chill covered the crowd as they cowered beneath their chastisement. Laurel watched as parents clutched their children a little more tightly. Slowly, the courtyard emptied and the guards atop the platform guided the Great Lord toward his keep.

Laurel turned to Alabella and found the woman staring off into the distance. She nearly asked what was on her mind, but she knew. Their trip to the Fairenwild. The shattered coreseal. Opening the tunnel. Alabella had caused this with her reckless goals and ambitions. She'd wanted equality for all, and she'd found it. All are equal in death.

Alabella turned to Laurel and the others. "I have an idea. Come with me. We need to have a conversation with the Great Lord."

A GROUP of Alchean guards ushered them to the Great Lord's study high in the keep tower. Laurel felt a tightness in her chest as she walked the halls, the painful echo of a memory. She felt at her breast pocket to make sure her transfuser was still there. Her nerves urged her to take it and drink, but she refused. Sarla had only given her enough for one in the morning and one in the evening. She needed to save it.

Finally, the door opened, and the guards led them inside. Alabella, Sarla, and Laurel were led in gracefully, and Barrick was searched before they allowed him to enter. Inside the room, Great Lord Malachus Endin stood behind a large table, flanked by a wide window that overlooked the city. Surrounding the table were a host of other men and women, two of whom Laurel recognized: High General Henna and Luther. When they saw her, they gave each other a confused look.

"Great Lord," one of the guards said. "This is the woman I told you about."

Malachus took a deep breath and looked up from the city map sprawled across his table. "I was told you have a means of making the creatures visible. You have two minutes to explain."

Alabella placed two fingers to the rim of her Felian lightshades. "I only need one."

When she took off her lightshades, Amber threadlight blazed from her irises. One of the older generals gasped, but they all seemed to distance themselves at the revelation. But Luther knew—Laurel could see it in the fire of his eyes. He'd known of the Amber-eyed leader of the Bloodthieves, and now he saw her. His teeth crushed together as he fought to maintain his composure.

Alabella did not smile or taunt—she gave no undue provocation. Instead, she stood tall and eyed the Great Lord with confidence. "I will be honest, if you will be patient. In this time of unexpected darkness, we must all be willing to ally ourselves with unexpected associates."

Malachus eyed her warily. "I've heard of you, and now that I see you, I do believe we've met before."

"To the future," she replied, pretending to lift a glass.

"Ah, yes. I believe we toasted to those words." Malachus lifted his hands to address the others in the room. "Friends, allow me to introduce the leader of the Bloodthieves."

Every eye bore down on her, as though she were a snake, waiting to strike. But that was not why she'd come. As much as Laurel loathed the woman, she respected her decision to offer aid to the Alchean people.

"Sheath your egos," Alabella said, calmly. "We are all here to save lives, and I come to offer a donation. Your men do not stand a chance against the corespawn, because they cannot see them. I have a supply of threadweaver blood that will give your men the ability to see threadlight, and thus see the enemy. I understand that you see the consumption of threadweaver blood as immoral. However, in desperate times, men must choose between morality and victory. You must ask yourselves if your conscience is worth more than the lives of your people."

"This is absurd!" A man in his late forties with Emerald eyes and an ill-placed scar on his lower, spoke with a gruff voice. "We can't—"

"Rynan," Malachus cut in. "I know for a fact that you would kill a thousand men to save one of your own. Would you not take one drug to save a nation?"

"It's not a drug!" Rynan said. "It's a blasphemy! You would be feeding *blood* to our soldiers. Blood that once ran in the body of another man."

Malachus hardened his gaze. "The smallest speck of dust can change the fate of a duel. You know this. We are not talking about a speck of dust in the eye; we are talking about an entire battle without sight."

High General Henna stood with her chin high. "The Order of Alchaeus would never support this. The Stone Council—"

"I *am* the Stone Council," Malachus cut in.

"Respectfully, sir, you are the Great Lord," Henna said. "They may call you the head of the Stone Council, but, in reality, you know that is not true."

"Whether they believe it or not, it is what it is. The Order of Alchaeus is living under my roof at this very moment. I control their future. They are in no position to question my decisions."

"What do you want, Malachus? Do you want our opinion?" Rynan asked. "Or do you want us to sit down like good little boys and do what we're told?"

"You go too far, Rynan," Malachus said, eying the man. "We've been discussing ideas for hours and we have no plan. We would be fools not to entertain an idea that could offer an advantage. I am not agreeing to it outright, but I am not foolish enough to discard the idea on the basis of some variable definition of morality. Remind me your name," Malachus added.

"Alabella Rune."

The Great Lord met her gaze, her Amber connecting with his Emerald and Sapphire. "Lady Alabella, bring your blood to the keep. We need to be prepared to use it should we find no other alternative."

Alabella nodded. "To the future."

15

When he came to, Alverax was lying on the rocky floor of a river, completely submerged. His body groaned as he ripped himself out of the water and drank in the air above. The skin over his upper spine stung as if he'd gashed it on a rock.

He took off his tuxedo jacket, which had rips along the seams of both armpits, and tattered edges along the chest. He tossed it aside and unbuttoned his shirt. When he examined the white dress shirt, he found only the slightest remnants of blood along the back, so he figured he would be okay.

The sun rose over the eastern horizon, illuminating the white walls of Felia across the river.

He must have been unconscious for hours.

Heralds.

Iriel and Aydin had been captured. The Elders were prisoners. If they were lucky, some few of the Zeda had managed to escape. But the more he remembered the swarm of incoming soldiers, the less likely that seemed. They were all apprehended. And they were going to be executed.

For what? A crime he didn't even commit. What *was* that creature? Was it even real? Was he losing his sanity? He felt okay, but perhaps madness only felt like madness to those not fully mad. No, he was fairly certain he was sane. He'd seen the creature. He'd watched it kill the empress. Then he'd watched it explode.

What worried him more than anything was wondering if there were more of them.

He picked himself up, took a step toward Felia, and paused. If he went back, they would kill him. He could head east and find a nice quiet town. Or maybe join a caravan headed south, jump on a boat, and spend the rest of his life on the beaches of Kulai. That didn't sound half bad. But that damned question—the question posed by Elder Rowan simply to torment his brittle mind—had taken a firm grip on his soul. He could hear her voice. *What manner of man will you be?*

I don't know. I want to bring hope to people.

With the great walls of Felia looming in the distance, Alverax knew what he had to do.

He made his way to the main road and met a small group of traders who let him join their caravan. One kindly old man offered him clothing to wear in exchange for his wet clothing, a deal that Alverax was certain would benefit the old man in the long run.

It didn't take long to reach the main gates of Felia. An army of soldiers crowded the entrance, but they were more focused on people attempting to leave, and the leader of the caravan knew one of the guards who let them in. After they'd passed through the gates, Alverax thanked his companions and headed north toward the palace.

He traveled down quiet paths, away from the main thoroughfare, and several times he nearly walked into patrolling guards. With the numbers he'd seen, he assumed that they hadn't been able to round up all of the Zeda, and still searched them out. Their pale skin set them apart, and the tattoos on their backs were an easy identifier. Their people were not prepared for assimilation, especially in Felia.

As he grew closer to the palace, he grew more and more worried about his plan. It was audacious and required a little more bravado than he'd normally presume, but if he could pull it off, he might just be able to do something truly good. There were plenty of ways it could go wrong, but, at the end of the day, Jisenna was the Mistress of Mercy, and he hoped that would be enough.

By the time he reached the palace, he was as cold as he was tired. The pain along his spine had faded only the slightest, even when he let a bit of threadlight into his veins. He looked out over the palace grounds and found even more guards than he'd expected. They were like weeds, infesting every inch of the walls, with large groups covering every entrance. He followed the wall from a distance, looking for any area that might have fewer eyes watching—maybe he'd be able to float over without being seen—but the guards were efficient in their duty. By the end, he stood near the large canal that fed the palace with fresh water from the river upstream.

Which gave him an idea.

He dove into the water, letting himself sink far below the surface, and followed the current toward the palace. Soon, the canal ended with a series of large pipes, each closed off with a grate. He tried pulling on one, but it wouldn't budge. He spent a full minute underwater thrashing against the grate before he realized that there was a latch. After he released it, the grate opened with ease.

He carefully ascended for a gulp of air, then paused to prepare himself. If he went through the pipe, he'd end up somewhere in the palace. He wasn't sure where, or if he could hold his breath long enough, or even if he could find an exit large enough to fit through. But it was the best chance he had to get inside, and if anyone could hold their breath long enough, it was the breath-holding champion of Cynosure.

He filled his lungs with air and dove down, filled with renewed purpose. The tunnel grew pitch black, and he worried for a moment that he would lose his sense of direction. His hand trailed along the edge of the tunnel as he kicked his legs behind him.

After several minutes in darkness, taking twists and forks that he hoped would keep him centered, he stopped to feel the surroundings. He hadn't seen even a glimpse of light, and it was quite possible that he had missed whatever path he should have taken. He'd known it was a foolish plan, but it wasn't until that moment, surrounded in darkness and entombed by frigid water, that he realized just how foolish he had been. He'd only wanted to help, to force their hand somehow, but now he was going to die somewhere where no one would ever find him.

It was too late to turn around. He knew he wouldn't be able to hold his breath long enough to return back the way he'd come, not to mention he'd be swimming against the gentle current. So, instead, he continued on. Swimming for his life. Swimming for the lives of his friends. Swimming because he was the only hope the Zeda people had, and he'd be damned if he'd let them die without giving everything he had to save them.

And, fortunately for him, Blightwoods don't die easy.

With renewed hope, Alverax pressed on. His hand brushed along the side of the tunnel, and he steadily kicked his feet back and forth. He *would* find an exit. He had to. But the further he went, he still found nothing. He let the last of his air out, releasing pressure from his lungs, and knew he only had one more minute to find air.

He swam as fast as his legs could propel him, but the faster he swam the more he needed to breathe. His lungs screamed in silent protest, begging for just the smallest bit of food to fill their emptiness. A rhythmic beating echoed in his skull, and he knew that consciousness was only moments away from fading.

He'd tried. It was the most he could do. He knew he was close; he could sense a shift in the water. Warmer, perhaps? But it was too late. His feet refused to kick. His body floated down to the bottom of the tunnel, scraping against the rounded walls and tearing at the wound on his back. As his mind wrestled with consciousness, he thought he saw a light in the distance. If he could only make it.

Just as he opened his mouth to breathe in his defeat, air seemed to pour into his lungs, rejuvenating him just enough to push off the ground toward the light. His body moved through the water like he was a creature of the sea itself. The light grew along with his hope. Before he knew it, he was crashing face-first into another grate. He opened the latch, pushed it open, and shot out into the open air above.

His lungs took it in like a father returning from war and squeezing his children with all his might. Never again would he depreciate the value of a single breath. Never again would he be dumb enough to swim into an endless tunnel of water without knowing what was on the other end...

He looked around and found dim lamplight illuminating a large room filled with two pools and shameful memories. Of all the places, it seemed the Heralds were playing a cruel joke.

He was in the Sun Bath.

Alverax lifted himself out of the pool and remembered his first encounter with Jisenna just days before. A mountain of curls piled atop her head. The way she'd winked at him as he left. He could wait for her there, but he needed something a little more dramatic. A little more nefarious.

Unfortunately, his clothes were soaked and there was no spare clothing in the Sun Bath. He took off his shirt and trousers, wrung them until they no longer dripped, and put them back on, pressing down with his palms to straighten the wrinkles. It would have to do.

He wasted no time, briskly hiking through the grand hallways. Servants scuttled past him, eyeing his wet clothes, but ignoring him in favor of their own tasks. As he drew closer to his destination, Alverax slowed his pace and stole a man's jacket hanging from the bottom of a sconce. He put it on and made his way forward with the fine gait of noble arrogance.

A pair of sturdy guards flanked a pair of sturdy doors chiseled to depict the two Heralds and their blessing. They eyed Alverax as he approached.

"My apologies, gentleman," Alverax said with a clipped tone.

Both guards moved in unison to intercept him but found themselves unexpectedly freed from the confines of gravity. They each tumbled forward with eyes as large as the fish their movements resembled.

Alverax strode forward and heaved both doors open, Obsidian threadlight now coursing through his veins. The heavy oak slammed against the walls and he strode into the room. His eyes moved to a large throne, occupied by a woman who seemed both too little and too great for the seat.

A dozen fastidious guards, all threadweavers, shifted in their boots. When they realized who it was, they rushed him as one, their training so well-instilled that their very footsteps fell in unison. In a wave of threadlight, Alverax *broke* their corethreads, sending the entire group tumbling through the air, screaming for others to come. His veins burned, and his chest flared like a smith's forge, but the scale was nothing compared to what he'd done at the Zeda encampment.

One of the guards hurled a spear, but it went wide, and the man tumbled backward in the air.

Empress Jisenna rose from her throne, white fabric falling from her like feathers. The elder man, Watchlord Osinan, stood beside her with fire in his eyes.

"How dare you," Watchlord Osinan said, his lips trembling as he spoke.

"I'm here to make a deal," Alverax said calmly.

"We will not make a deal with a murderer!"

"I AM THE HERALD'S CHOSEN!" Alverax screamed. He needed

them to fear him. He needed them to believe that he was dangerous, even if it tore away at the part of his soul that cared for Jisenna. "Look around you. Your people are nothing to me."

Watchlord Osinan took a step forward, clutching the hilt of the sword at his side.

"I don't think so." Alverax *broke* the older man's corethread and he rose into the air. "I will not repeat myself, and there will be no negotiations. Your people honor the truth, so if you agree and go back on your word, I swear that the Heralds themselves will smite you down."

Jisenna stood alone, tears welling up in her dark eyes as she watched all those around her tumble through the air like specs of dust in the wind. "I...don't understand. What do you want?"

"I want all of the Zeda people released. They will not be harmed, and they will never return."

"Absolutely not!" Osinan shouted, still hovering in the air.

"In return," Alverax strode forward, ignoring the Watchlord and looking at Jisenna, "I will take their place. They are not to blame, however much you'd like to lay it at their feet. You have my word that I will make no attempt to escape. I will pay the price of your sister's death."

Jisenna's chest rose up and down and her bottom lip quivered, but his words had gripped her. He knew that they were grieving—Jisenna most of all. They were angry and confused. And if the Mistress of Mercy could save the lives of innocent people while still finding justice for the one responsible, he hoped she would take it.

Alverax stood in silence, waiting for her to respond. His own emotions welled up within him. He still cared for Jisenna and hated that he was deceiving her. But it was for the best. *A man would be wise to stay far away from a woman such as yourself,* he'd said to her. Oh, how right he'd been.

Jisenna glanced up at the guards still tumbling through the air and over to Osinan floating beside her. Her jaw clenched so hard Alverax was sure she would shatter a tooth, but at last her muscles relaxed and she closed her eyes. "I accept your offer."

"I want everyone in this room to hear you say it."

She opened her eyes and gazed into his own. "In exchange for

Alverax Blightwood, the Zeda people will be released and banished from Felia."

"And none will be harmed," he added.

"And none will be harmed."

Alverax dropped to his knees as the guards returned to the ground. "Heralds, save me."

16

Once again, Alverax found himself in shackles; it was what the son of a thief deserved. He sat on cold stone with his eyes covered, thinking about his journey. Life had taught him brutal lessons, but one lesson most of all. Hope is a sham. A trick of the mind. Hope is opening your eyes at dusk and believing it is dawn. His life—he'd decided—was a setting sun.

There was a phrase his grandfather used to use in prayers: my life for yours. In the days of the Heralds, the people would speak the words when pledging themselves to a lifetime of service. His grandfather would speak them in prayer offering his own form of commitment. Alverax felt the words deep in his core, and he knew that, despite the impending reality, he was giving his life for a righteous cause.

The hardest truth was knowing just how much his death would simplify the world for everyone. The Zeda would be released. Jisenna would feel justice for the death of her sister. The Bloodthieves would have one less loose end. And Jelium would have one less fly to swat.

Watchlord Osinan had arranged his execution for the following day. The Zeda people remained in captivity awaiting the execution before they would be released. They allowed no visitors—there was no one who would have visited anyway—so, instead, he stared at the stone, imagining the ocean, knowing that a great wave would soon take him away.

He *had* had one good idea while sitting there. If they cut off his head, he could use his last moment of consciousness to *break* the head's corethread, making it float in a horrifically creepy display. He probably couldn't *actually* do it, but the thought was stupid enough to bring him some semblance of joy.

He had to give it to the Felians; they had treated him well despite his imprisonment. No one had beaten him. No one had spat at him. Most curiously, no one had even talked to him. They had simply thrown him in a prison cell and left him. The only food they'd brought was a single apple. He laughed out loud to himself about that one. He'd always wanted to try an apple. He never expected it to taste like execution.

That night, as he lay hungry and sore, guards approached his cell, a few by the sound of it. They stopped outside the door. It should have been intimidating, but Alverax didn't care. He was an exotic animal, and they had come to study him. Part of him wanted to growl at them but, in the end, he stayed quiet.

If he looked down just right, he could catch glimpses from beneath his blindfold. There was a small crack on the ground that looked like a scar. Apparently, Felia had also felt the earthquakes. He wondered if the crack had already been there, or if it had surfaced the night the coreseal was broken. Maybe the whole prison would just collapse on him and save him the embarrassment of a public execution.

"Aye, rip," one of the guards spat. "On your feet."

Alverax dismissed the command. What were they going to do? Kill him?

"I said, on your feet."

A wave of freezing cold water poured over him. The cold was bad, but the worst part was knowing that his clothes would stay wet for some time, and the cold would continue. But then he remembered that he was an idiot, and he let threadlight run through his veins. He couldn't threadweave anything unless he could see it, but he could still let threadlight warm his veins.

"Hands behind your back," the same guard demanded. "I see your veins. Threadweave, and you'll regret it."

They turned him around, bound his hands behind his back, and adjusted the blindfold over his eyes. Once his hands were tied, they sat him on his cot and tied him to the frame. The thoroughness gave Alverax a pinch of pride knowing that they truly believed he was dangerous. Apparently, he was a better liar than he'd thought.

He sat quietly as their footsteps left him alone once again. It was better this way—being alone. Would anyone even miss him when he was dead? His grandfather would, but not any more than he already did. None of the Zeda would. None of the Felians would. None of the Bloodthieves would. Was there any point in living if no one cared if he was alive?

He heard the slightest stirring near the entrance to his cell and looked up as if he could see through his blindfold. The cold of his wet clothes was beginning to awaken again, so he let a little more threadlight into his veins.

A woman's voice broke the silence. "Why did you not kill me in the Sun Bath?"

He knew that soft, delicate voice, though it was now stained with a pinch of malice.

Princess Jisenna.

No, Empress Jisenna.

"You were obviously waiting for me. And you could have incapacitated my guards easily enough. So, what was it? Were you waiting for my sister? Was I simply the wrong visitor?"

She wanted something from him. Another confession?

"She never trusted you," she said, her voice quivering. "She sent me to keep an eye on you. Did you know that?"

"I just want to be left alone," he said.

She never replied.

As much as he was already hurting, her words wounded him. He thought, even now, that their friendship had been real, something genuine in the field of lies.

He felt a slight breeze near his face and flinched. He hadn't even heard her move. She lifted the blindfold off his eyes, and then he saw her. Dark eyes filled with tears. Black smears dripping down her cheeks. She looked so angry. So tired. So desperate.

Guilt flooded over him.

"I'm sorry," he said without thinking. She had just lost her sister. All she wanted was closure.

She slapped him. "Stop it! Don't you dare be kind to me! Don't you dare! I liked you, Alverax, and you ripped out a piece of my soul. My sister was my everything. She was a light shining on the reefs not just for me but for this entire nation. Is that what you wanted? Ships crashing in shallow waters? You want this nation to fall? I will not let that happen. Her death will *not* be in vain."

She stopped.

His heart beat faster. He wanted to shout. He wanted to defend himself, to tell her the truth. He wanted to comfort her. His mind was a blur of emotions and it took all of his willpower to hold himself back.

He looked down.

One. Two. Three. Four. Heralds calm a troubled core.

When he looked back up, Empress Jisenna was staring at him with confusion in her eyes. "I don't understand you. Yesterday I was so frightened by you, but today you seem so...different. Something is wrong with you. You are broken. I see now that the world will be truly safer without you in it."

He wanted to scream out his innocence, to explain that one of those men wasn't real. But it wouldn't matter. They'd preconceived his guilt, and their justice would either be his singular death or the death of the entire Zeda people. He had to be strong...for them. For Iriel. For Aydin. For once in his Heralds-forsaken life.

Empress Jisenna stood, gave him one last look, and walked away without a word. The guards came in, covered his eyes, and removed his bindings. Once again, he was alone in his cell, lying down on a cot staring at the darkness of a blindfold. For a moment, he wondered if his father could have escaped the cell. He pushed the thought aside. He wasn't like him. He wouldn't run from his promises. He would do what was right simply because it was right.

17

The grassy fields within the walls of Endin Keep were filled with soldiers. The only clouds in the sky had retreated earlier in the day, leaving a lasting warmth even as the sun fell below the western horizon. Laurel stood beside the doctor, Sarla, handing out small vials quarter-filled with blood. She stole three vials and, though she hated herself for doing it, the constant tremble in her hands left her no other choice.

Sarla was certain the small dosage would grant the recipient at least a short access to threadlight, but the minuscule amount compared to what Laurel had been taking seemed fit only for the smallest child. Malachus had directed the soldiers to stagger their consumption, so as not to leave their unit vulnerable. It was as good a plan as any and, still, Laurel felt a rotten feeling in the pit of her stomach.

Once the last of the transfusers was distributed, Henna confirmed her plans with the lieutenants and commanded them to take their units and assume their positions. Boots stomped in unison over the wide fields until each unit disappeared past the walls of the keep.

Alabella arrived shortly after with dark bags peeking out from beneath her eyes. "Sarla," she called out. "How did we do?"

The odd woman cracked each of her knuckles one by one as she spoke. "Given the circumstances, we were able to ration the blood quite effectively. Some units will have a little more than others, and some soldiers will never taste it, but there should be enough to last through the night."

"Good."

"I should note that the Great Lord had me double the quantity for the units with the most direct path from the Fairenwild."

"A wise move."

"He also wanted to make sure that the soldiers were unaware of the order."

Alabella smirked. "He needs them all to feel equally prepared if they are to fight with the kind of loyalty he needs."

Sarla, with an eager look in her eyes, leaned forward. "Were you able to procure a few moments for me to study the captive corespawn?"

"Unfortunately, no," Alabella said. "They were eventually able to kill it. I was told its threadlight expired."

"Fascinating," Sarla whispered. "If it expires then there must be a way for its threadlight to be renewed. An energy source, like food."

"A mystery for another day," Alabella said, turning to Laurel. "What do you think? Do we have a chance?"

Laurel shrugged her shoulders. "If the rest die as easily as the ones I killed, I think we'll be fine."

"We can hope. That reminds me," Alabella said. She pulled out the obsidian dagger and handed it to Laurel. "I believe this belonged to you. I want you to have it. A token of my trust. You've saved me with it once before; I pray you won't have to again."

Laurel took the dagger in her hands and, as she looked down its shaft, she remembered Chrys. But she also remembered that, in the keep the night she'd killed Jurius, there had been two identical blades. Something about that seemed significant.

"Thank you," she managed.

Alabella gestured to one of the towers. "It's time."

HIGH OVER THE ANXIOUS CITY, clouds obscured the only light the moon intended to provide. Quiet ruled the Alchean streets like a tyrannical scourge, infecting the hearts of the people, and instilling a profound dread in the minds of those who gathered to protect them. The wind itself seemed afraid to show itself.

The entire Alchean army was spread out along the western border, spanning from the north to the south, covering as much of the land between Alchea and the Fairenwild as possible without stretching their numbers.

Laurel sat along the windowsill in one of the tower rooms overlooking the motionless city far below. A map lay sprawled out on the wide table, dozens of markers scattered in a wide arc around the Alchean border designating key locations of troops. Soldiers at each position would light a bonfire as soon as they were in position, and, if the corespawn arrived, they would toss in a bag of borax salt to turn the flames green.

No flames had yet to shift their hue.

"So," Alabella said without shifting her gaze, "when do you plan to do it?"

"Do what?" Laurel asked.

The woman turned to face Laurel and met her eyes. "When we first met, I promised you that I would never lie to you. We could debate the technicalities, but the truth is: I deceived you, Laurel. I know that you know what happened in the Fairenwild."

Laurel's heart skipped a beat. Her hand had been tracing the outline of the vials in her pocket but shifted to the blade now hooked to her belt.

"If you want to kill me, you would be justified. I've even given you the perfect weapon for the job." Alabella glanced down at the obsidian blade. "This path we walk is not toward an unworthy destination. When we restore your threadlight, you will be living proof of the world we could have. A world without achromacy. A world without inequality. No fortune of birth. Imagine it, every single person able to experience the joy of threadlight. That is the future we're fighting for."

Laurel ground her teeth. Angry. Frustrated. Bothered by the fact that she agreed with Alabella. Why did some deserve threadlight over others? That which Laurel loved more than anything, why did she deserve it more than her brother? And still, unjust or not, how many deserved to die to bring that dream to life?

"I do want to kill you," Laurel said, unable to make eye contact. "For my family. For my people. And for myself. Did you know that your people kidnapped me? If not for a bit of luck, it would be my blood out there in the soldiers' hands."

A weary sadness played itself in Alabella's eyes. "I've been so overcome with the destination that I've forgotten that there are many ways to arrive. I see that now, and I want to find a better way."

Laurel raised the obsidian blade. "Do you want me to kill you? Is that why you gave this to me? You think dying will make up for all the shit you've caused?"

"I gave it to you, because I need you—"

Time dragged to a halt. Every beat of Laurel's heart was a raucous pounding that shook her to the core. The obsidian blade reflected a bit of lamplight, glistening, taunting. Memory overlaid atop reality. Jurius' blood dripped from the edge of the blade. Revenge, like the sweet nuzzle of a chromawolf, brushed against her mind. It would take only the simplest of movements to slide the dagger forward into Alabella's chest. A single choice to change everything.

"—and you need me."

"I don't need you," Laurel snapped. "But these people do. At least for now."

Alabella nodded grimly and turned to look back over the city. "The night is young. Let's pray the Heralds are with us."

THE NIGHT PASSED in eerie silence, and the enemy never arrived.

STONES OF LIGHT
18

EACH MORNING, Chrys awoke with a growing hollowness within himself. It wasn't about being a prisoner; it was about his family. Even if he and his friends were able to escape, he was afraid of what life would be like when he returned. It had been his own choice—made with clarity—that had given control to Relek and sent him trekking to the wastelands, abandoning his wife and son. The battle in the Fairenwild wasn't over when they'd left. If anything had happened to Iriel and Aydin while he was away, he would never forgive himself. And even if they were okay, he feared that they would never be able to forgive him.

More than anything, he longed to hear Iriel's sweet voice tell him that she understood, that it was the right decision, like she had the night Aydin was born. If there was anyone capable of forgiving him, it was her. Yet still he feared.

While Roshaw was paying his debt to Esme and harvesting that week's growth of honeycrystals, Chrys would be the one to deliver them to Xuçan. Their plan hinged on that conversation. If the great ataçan refused to aid them, they would be forced to take a more dangerous path through the jungle, where the wastelanders would have the advantage. But Chrys hoped that their disdain for the "creature of many faces" would be enough to make them agree.

After they ate the fruit and meat

that the guards provided them for the day, and after Chrys consumed the murky threadlight-blocking substance, Roshaw steeled himself to enter the et'hovon hive. But before he did, the entrance to the enclosure swung open, revealing an entire host of wastelanders; Chrys counted more than twenty. Agatha rose swiftly to her feet and the others followed suit.

"What's going on?" Chrys asked.

Roshaw, who still stood beside him, looked to the wastelanders with reservation. "No idea."

The mob of guards split, and the god siblings stepped forward. Relek, the "creature of many faces," and his sister, Lylax, had transformed from the Alchean guards Chrys had last seen. True, they still wore the skin of Velan and Autelle, but their hair and clothing had adopted an entirely new look. Lylax wore a long, flowing gown that dragged carelessly behind her in the swamp water. Her hair was done up with pins, and Chrys was surprised with how regal the once-guard had become.

And their eyes. No longer were their eyes the brown of an achromat. Instead, they sparkled with the entire spectrum of colors, like prisms refracting the sun's rays. Chrys had never seen anything like it.

Relek smiled with cleanly shaven cheeks and strode forward with his sister. "Chrys Valerian…the Apogee…it is good to see you, friend."

Chrys clenched his jaw and said nothing. Somehow, Relek's voice still sounded the same as it had in his mind, and each word sent a shiver of bad memories crawling up his spine.

"I want to thank you," Relek continued, his prismatic eyes bearing down on Chrys. "Not only did you give me freedom, but your actions freed my sister as well. When we've risen to our former glory, it will be because of you."

Chrys spat at their feet. "Go to hell."

Relek frowned and turned to his sister. The goddess, Lylax, spoke in the wastelander tongue, and the host of guards gathered and surrounded Chrys, Roshaw, Esme, Seven, and Agatha. They were pushed, shoved, and shepherded forward like cattle through the swamp.

They needed to escape…now.

They could no longer wait for the end of a guard shift during the night. Nor could they wait to speak with Xuçan. Whatever they were going to do, they needed to figure it out fast. Chrys' eyes darted back and forth through the swamp, looking for anything that would give him an idea.

The procession stopped at the edge of the jungle, where the crew was ushered forward to a ledge that led down to a sunken, muddy pit, wide as a field. The far side of the pit ended at one edge of the Endless Well.

The wastelanders shoved the crew over the ledge and down into the pit. Chrys and Seven landed on their feet, but the other three stumbled forward and crashed into the mud on their hands and knees. Chrys helped Agatha to stand. When he turned, he saw an army of wastelanders—young and old—surrounding the edge of the pit with fire in their eyes.

Relek approached the ledge above them. "The people of Kai'Melend believe in the power of sacrifice," he said. "Today, your choice is *how*. There are those among these people who would be leaders in the coming war. You will fight them, and they will prove to me their valor. Those of you who wish to die fighting, you will step forward. For those who will not fight, the Well awaits you."

"What the hell is he talking about?" Esme whispered to the others.

Roshaw clenched his jaw and spoke through his teeth. "He's saying we can let the wastelanders kill us, or we can kill ourselves."

Suicide. The word crawled out from a dark cave beneath Chrys' skin. He'd always been so focused on the next step, the next goal, that he'd never considered what he would do when there were no more steps to take. Looking out over the mass of wastelanders, it was clear that there would be no escape.

In a way, death would be such a relief. To forget about his failures. To forget about that look in Iriel's eyes as he walked away. To forget the child he'd abandoned. To them he was already nothing more than a rotten ghost. A bad dream better left forgotten. The only person he had was his mother, but he would never see her again. And if he did, she would see no more than the disappointment he'd become.

He walked forward and stared into the latter option. The Endless Well extended into infinite darkness. One simple step and he could fall into nothingness. One simple step and he could end the guilt. He could end the suffering. One step...

Chrys looked down into the pit, into the void that welcomed him.

There was a certain serenity deep in the abyss. A calm in the shadow. It beckoned to him, calling out, *come and be still.*

Serenity.

Tranquility.

An end to the pain.

An end.

The end.

"No," he said forcefully, shaking his head.

That was not how he would end his life.

I am He-who-does-not-cower.

If all the enemies in the world—be they wastelander or ataçan or worse—came to claim him, he would stand and fight. He would resist with every last breath within him, and, when he was at the edge of death, he would spit fire with his final breath. If they wanted a fight, he would make them pay.

For Iriel.

For Aydin.

For the men and women who died at the hands of the Apogee.

Chrys dropped to his knees and leaned over the edge, staring down into the infinite void of darkness. He reached his hand into his mouth, shoved his fingers down his throat, and vomited into the abyss.

19

A STREAM of liquid came flooding out of Chrys' stomach, a waterfall crashing down into the infinite darkness below. He gripped the edge of the Well, breathed in the putrid stench of swamp water, and vomited again. His throat burned, and his stomach riled, but, if he was going to fight the wastelanders, he had to get the fluid out of his system. He needed threadlight.

The other members of the crew stared as he turned to face them. His eyes burned with purpose. When he looked at them, he felt a strong yearning to protect them. These people were in no state to fight. Even Seven, who had once been a strong soldier, was little more than skin and bone. If they fought, they would last no longer than a few seconds.

Chrys turned around, trudged back toward the wall of the pit, and looked up at the throng of wastelanders. He stepped as near as he dared and met Relek's gaze. "If you want to prove your champions, then give them a challenge! Killing these prisoners will prove nothing. If you really want to test them, let them fight me. Alone."

Relek grumbled, weighing the challenge. "You think I would extend mercy to these people?"

"To hell with mercy," Chrys said, choosing his words carefully. "I want your warriors all to myself."

"Mmmm."

"When I fall, you have your champion. But until then, for every one of your warriors that I kill, you will release one of the prisoners."

The tall god looked down on him, seeing the remains of vomit in Chrys' beard. He turned his eyes to the rest of the human prisoners. "You are a fool, Chrys Valerian. Have you forgotten that I spent years inside your mind? I know you better than you know yourself. You think you can win, but you *will* die. And I will watch with glee as each wastelander warrior cuts away at your life until you are nothing but a rotten stump of flesh." He paused, leaving enough of a break for a bead of sweat to slide down Chrys' forehead. "It is agreed."

Chrys nodded and turned to the others. "Find my wife," he said. "And tell her that I did everything I could."

The four of them, with shock and sorrow twisted over their dirty faces, gathered together and moved away from Chrys. Roshaw gave him a nod of gratitude.

Lylax spoke in the wastelander tongue and the crowd consumed her every word, cheering with each throaty syllable. A thick, fierce-looking wastelander stepped forward. He stood taller than the others—though still shorter than Chrys—with the noon sun shadowing the curves of his arms and bare chest. He'd pierced his pointed lobes, and his face was covered with white paint and dark lines to mimic an empty skull. Blue and red feathers fanned out at his hairline down to his neck. When he jumped down, Chrys saw that the warrior wore gloves with sharpened bones for nails.

Chrys took one final look at those he would be fighting for, then set his jaw and widened his stance.

The wastelander champion stepped forward, and the horde of onlookers rose up, screaming and shouting into the open air.

In a burst of speed, the champion dove toward Chrys. His bone claws lashed out, swiping again and again as Chrys barely managed to dodge each attack. He stepped into the champion's reach and drove a fist into his ribs. The wastelander groaned and retreated, screeching something foul in his otherworldly tongue.

Again, the wastelander attacked, this time in horrific harmony with his bone claws. Each jab grew in ferocity, each growl rising in a barbaric crescendo. The warrior let loose a flurry of kicks to throw Chrys off balance.

But Chrys was the Apogee, even without a god in his mind.

He leaned into the wastelander, grasping his wrist and driving an elbow up into his neck. Sharp pain burst in his side as bone claws cut into him. But it didn't matter. Up close, the bone claws were mosquitos nipping at his skin. Chrys' fists were lead hammers slamming into the wastelander's ribs.

Planting his forearm into the warrior's neck, Chrys tripped him and sent them both toppling over onto the murky floor. With rage fueling his every movement, Chrys pummeled the wastelander's face. Brittle bones shattered beneath his fists while claws scratched at his back. Finally, Chrys ripped out a handful of feathers from the champion's headdress and drove the sharp shafts deep into the wastelander's neck. The bundle of feathers snapped in half, still embedded in the skin. Blood pulsed out of the hollow shafts, dripping into the water.

Chrys rolled the body over face-first in the mud, then pulled off the bone claws and lifted himself to his feet. He took in heavy breaths and watched a strange crevice along the wastelander's spine open and close before its lungs ceased their rhythm.

The crowd of wastelanders grew quiet.

Chrys placed the bone claws over his own hands and looked up to the crowd. "Who's next?" he shouted.

The crew, as stunned as the wastelanders, deliberated, and sent Agatha up the steps of the ledge. The wastelanders accepted her above but did not let her pass. She turned, and Chrys saw the worry and fear in her eyes. She was frail, and surrounded by the enemy, with no belief that they would truly let her go.

Relek raised his head up high. "Ah, yes. The *power of appearance*. I remember how important you believed that to be. But I know you. I see you growing tired already. How much longer can you last, old friend?"

Lylax shouted more words Chrys couldn't understand and pointed at the crowd. She stepped forward, her voice rising and falling with vigor. While the language seemed a fitting companion to Velan's harshness, it seemed unnatural coming from Autelle's body. Chrys knew that somewhere, locked away in her mind, there was a scared woman still alive.

Two wastelanders jumped down off the ledge into the pit. They matched in nearly every way. Long, white hair, pale gray skin, each holding a weapon that looked like a bone-colored meat cleaver. The crowd burst out in raucous applause, screaming at the top of their lungs, their voices ringing out like wild beasts.

Stones. The only deal they'd made was one kill for one release, they'd made no deal about the number of combatants at any given time. But he still had a trick up his sleeve: the threadlight running in his veins.

Chrys sprinted forward with speckled blood trailing from his open wounds. He focused on the slightly smaller of the two and dove in fast to get out of range of the cleaver. Up close, he would have the advantage.

The other wastelander chopped down hard with their cleaver and nearly cut Chrys' hand off, but he *pushed*, his eyes blazing to life with radiant Sapphire energy, and the cleaver swung wide, slicing off the ends of several of the bone claws. Chrys jabbed forward with his other hand and claws pierced through the wastelander's shoulder. Both of his opponents backed away, muttering incomprehensible words to each other.

Chrys stepped back, panting. The layer of swamp water on the floor made it more difficult to move, and he found himself fatiguing faster than he'd hoped. He let more threadlight into his veins.

Both leapt forward in unison, combining hard overhead swipes of their cleavers with short punches from their offhand. Chrys *pushed* hard against both cleavers, sending one tumbling through the air far away. The other cleaver was tossed to the ground by the warrior to avoid giving Chrys any more advantage.

With both hands free, the warriors grew more ferocious, quicker, and more daring. When one kicked low, Chrys *pushed* off the ground, and soared over them both, putting them between him and the Endless Well. He needed to do something. They were fast, and well-trained. If he did nothing, it would only be a matter of time before they overcame him.

They rushed him once more, and Chrys kicked swamp water up into the air. It wasn't much, but it was enough. Chrys used the distraction to launch his own offense. He let loose a series of swipes with the bone claws and connected with one of the warriors' chests. Chrys smiled just in time for the other wastelander to lift the cleaver from the floor and swing it upward at Chrys' outstretched hand. It connected with terrible momentum, slashing through three of Chrys' fingers.

Chrys' eyes bulged.

Pain blossomed at the end of his hand.

But there was no time. Chrys tripped the first and pounced atop the second. His bone claws tore into the wounded wastelander's chest like a swarm of bees, stinging and stinging again and again until the wastelander could no longer breathe, and he fell back, limp. Chrys rolled to the side, narrowly dodging another strike from the other. He *pushed* on the cleaver and it flew from the wastelander's grip, launching into the Endless Well.

Lifting himself up, Chrys set his footing and eyed his final opponent. There was fear in the wastelander's eyes, hidden behind a façade of rage.

"Give up," Chrys spat.

The wastelander, unable to understand, rushed him. Chrys brushed aside his blow, stabbing bone claws into the pit of his arm, and spinning. His elbow cracked the side of the wastelander's head. While his opponent was dazed, Chrys stepped forward, spun, and kicked the wastelander in the middle of his chest. The force lifted his small frame off the ground and sent him crashing over the edge of the chasm, screaming into the endless darkness.

Chrys looked down at his hands. The right hand was missing three fingers, and blood was drooling from the frayed edges of each appendage. With his other hand, he walked over and retrieved the fallen cleaver. When he looked up to the crowd and saw Relek snarling, he thought that, just for a moment, his plan might actually work.

"Two more!" he spat.

Roshaw gestured to Esme and Seven. They gave him a sad look but took the offering and ascended the stairs to join Agatha. Chrys felt the thrill of victory. If he could only kill one more, then he could die knowing that he'd protected those who could not protect themselves.

Relek and Lylax stepped to the ledge of the pit. The beating sun seemed to distort the air around them. Then, as if the world had decided to play a sadistic joke, a floral scent drifted in the wind. Chrys' eyes darted about, searching for the source, but he found nothing. The wastelander goddess spoke and the mass of spectators gasped at her words.

The crowd split in two and a distortion in the air darted through them. Chrys opened his eyes to threadlight and beheld a lithe creature, born of light itself, leaping from the ledge and into the pit, landing with a splash. It stood on two legs, with long arms that ended in sword-like points. The wastelanders whispered amongst themselves as Lylax's full lips curled into a perverse grin.

A memory, long forgotten, swept over him in a wave.

※

"T ELL ME A STORY, MOTHER," *little Chrys asked.*

Willow shook her head and smiled. "It is late. Perhaps a short one."

"Do the scary one!"

"Only because you are so brave, little flower." She tucked him in and began the story. "There was once a girl who was not loved by her family. She was the only one in the whole town who could see threadlight, and none of the others believed her."

"That's silly," little Chrys cut in.

"Perhaps, but it is hard to believe what you cannot see. Still, she was happy, finding her joy in other pastimes. One day, an older boy from her village was killed by an invisible creature, a corespawn from the dark parts beneath the earth. When a group of men went to kill the beast, they never returned. The village elder brought everyone together behind the walls of her home. After two days, the little girl missed her family's garden, and so, when she smelled roses on the wind, she snuck outside and made her way home."

Little Chrys squeezed his mother's hand. "She shouldn't do that."

"No," Willow said, smiling. "As she walked, she opened her eyes to threadlight, and saw the corespawn circling the walls of the elder's home. She stood still as an oak tree, raised her bow, and let loose her arrow. It struck true, and the creature died. No one believed her until the creature never returned, and then they celebrated her as a great hero. You see, Chrys. Sometimes our greatest gifts are those that others do not understand."

He settled down onto his pillow and asked, "Are the corespawn real?"

"Of course not, little flower."

But Willow was wrong.

Standing before him, with flesh born of pure threadlight, was a creature of myth. The light-shrouded silhouette of overgrown fangs jutted out from its maw. It prowled forward and snarled.

Chrys, who had already accepted his end, snarled back.

It dashed toward him in a blur. Chrys set his feet and sprinted forward in response. The beast leapt and Chrys dropped a shoulder, covering it with the flat end of the cleaver. They collided in an explosion of power. Chrys was knocked to his back, the beast atop him, and it clamped down on his shoulder with its overgrown fangs. He screamed, hacking into the creature's torso with the cleaver until it rolled away from him.

But, as he scrambled again to his feet, Chrys watched a swirling mist of light coagulate over the wounds in the creature's side. In moments, the corespawn was healed completely.

His mother had forgotten to mention that part...

Chrys cringed as he watched the creature's wounds heal. His own had not. Chrys' shoulder was torn apart, fingers left behind like fallen soldiers, and his lungs were near ready to collapse. Threadlight crawled beneath his skin, but it was a salve not meant for serious injury.

As the creature dashed toward him once again, Chrys raised the cleaver high overhead and extended his right arm. He had one more idea, and it took the bait, clamping down its massive fangs on his left forearm. Pain shot up through his tendons, up through his shoulders, and blossomed in painful agony. With his other hand, he brought the cleaver down with every ounce of his strength, fueled by rage and the promise of redemption, and cut halfway through the corespawn's neck. He yanked it out and brought it back down again. And again. And again. Until, finally, the cleaver passed through the brilliant, sinewy flesh of the corespawn.

Its jaws released his shredded arm as the severed head fell to the murky floor with a splash. Alone, it looked like a massive photospore, glowing haphazardly in the mud. Chrys kicked the headless body away from himself and fell to his knees, clutching at his shoulder and hand. Despite the pain echoing throughout every inch of his bloody body, he grinned.

One more freed, he thought to himself. He'd done it.

Then, as though time itself were playing back, the creature's head turned to ooze and slid across the water like oil until it reattached itself to the fallen body. The ooze reformed itself, slowly, into the same fanged maw of the creature he'd thought dead. Its newly formed head shivered back and forth, then settled, returning its radiant gaze to Chrys.

Stones.

He was going to die.

At least he'd saved three of them. *Sorry, Roshaw.*

His eyes locked with the corespawn. It stood still, watching his movement, waiting for some unspoken command to finish him off. Pain crept into his vision. He shook his head, clearing his sight.

He should stand. He should fight. He was the Apogee! But his mind was growing hazy. The adrenaline was fading, and pain was slithering through his veins.

Chrys turned and saw Roshaw standing alone, trembling as his only chance at survival faded away.

Screams echoed out in the open air.

Chrys looked to the west as a dozen spears slammed forward in unison, cutting down Agatha, Esme, and Seven. Time slowed as he watched his friends accept their fate with terror-stricken faces. Slowly, with spears still embedded in their flesh, they sagged to the floor.

"NO!" he screamed, reaching out with his mutilated hand. He sprinted toward them, knowing well that there was nothing he could do.

He heard the splash of footsteps behind him and turned just in time to *push* off the ground and avoid the leaping corespawn. It slid along the wet floor and spun back toward him as he fell back to the earth.

He'd failed. He never should have trusted Relek, and their lives were the payment for his stupidity. Like every other person in his life, he had failed to protect them. As he stared back at the corespawn before him, he knew that he couldn't even protect himself. These were creatures and beings far beyond his own power. Gods and mythical creatures? Who was he to pretend that he could fight back?

In that moment, he wondered if he should have leapt into the Endless Well.

But then he heard it.

A voice.

A familiar pitch.

A timbre that sent a shiver down his spine and awakened a powerful force within him. When he looked to the sound, he saw a woman soaring through the air, eyes and veins blazing with Sapphire threadlight, wielding a blade as black as Relek's soul.

An indomitable hero. A fearless protector. A herald of hope.

It was his mother.

Willow's feet hit the ground in an explosion, water erupting in a spray of droplets.

"My son is mine!"

All of the fear, the hate, the sorrow, and the pain came bursting out of Chrys' lungs in a single breath, replaced by the only emotion capable of displacing such feelings.

From his earliest memories, Chrys thought he knew how much his mother loved him. She'd provided for him, mentored him, supported him. But it wasn't until his own son was born that he'd realized the true power of a parent's love. Chrys had given up everything to protect Aydin. He would do it all again. And now, standing in front of him with ratty hair and clothes painted with dirt, Willow Valerian had done the same.

Chrys smiled so wide it nearly broke his jaw.

The corespawn leapt at Willow and she threw herself forward into it. Chrys, overwhelmed by her arrival, became suddenly aware of the danger she was in. But as the creature opened its arms in a deathly embrace, launching toward Willow, she roared and slammed her dagger up into its gut.

As soon as the blade pierced its hide, a hideous screech cut through the dull of the enraptured crowd. The corespawn burst apart in an explosion of threadlight, thousands of specs of multi-colored sand erupting in a thunderous blast.

Willow turned to Chrys and his eyes drifted to the dagger in her hand. He knew it well; it was once his. The thread-dead obsidian blade.

He had so many questions, but there was no time. The corespawn was dead, and it was clear the wastelanders would not let them live. They had to move.

Chrys scanned the throng of wastelanders lining the wall of the pit. The entire crescent was filled. There was only one other way to go.

"Roshaw!" Chrys yelled. "To the Well!"

The lone man reacted decisively, sprinting at full speed toward the Endless Well, while Chrys and Willow did the same.

A hoard of wastelanders leapt into the pit, sloshing through the puddled ground, and rolled toward them like an avalanche. With each second, the sound roared louder. Screaming. Howling. Chrys peeked back and saw one of the wastelanders riding a bonded ataçan, its massive limbs thumping against the earth with each step.

As they approached the edge of the chasm, Chrys came to a halt. He turned just as Willow reached him. "I can't believe you came for me," he said.

"There is nothing in this world that could have stopped me," she said with a smile.

Stones, but he'd missed that woman. He looked down into the void, grabbing hold of her hand with his good one. "If this kills us, I'm glad I saw you one last time."

She smiled with a twinkle in her eye. "If this kills us, it would still be worth it."

"Heralds, save me," Roshaw whispered as he arrived.

Chrys smiled, and, together, all three leapt into the infinite darkness.

Stones of Light
20

THE REMAINDER of the Alchean night passed in a timeless blur, waiting, fearing, then rejoicing when the sun rose. Every man and woman in the city had dark eyes and hearts that sagged in their chests, but when not a single corespawn arrived, it was as though a fog had lifted.

"Laurel, grab your things. We need to leave, now."

Laurel shot up in the chair where she'd nearly fallen asleep. She rubbed at her eye and gazed out of the large window that looked over the city. Alabella moved throughout the room, gathering papers and shoving things into a bag.

"What is it?"

Alabella listened at the door. "Our safety is predicated on the presence of the corespawn. If they do not return—even if the people believe they will not—then you and I are no longer safe. If they don't need us, then we will be imprisoned or killed. If we leave quickly, we can be gone before they come for us. A caravan can take us somewhere safe."

"What? No," Laurel said. "We can't leave."

"You have to understand. Every moment they allow us to stand beside them is a moment of disrespect. It doesn't matter that we were trying to do the right thing. We are their ally only when there is a greater enemy and, if that enemy is gone, then their eyes again turn to us."

"Even if the corespawn never came, your transfusers prevented a widespread panic. They had no plan to protect their people."

"No single action can scrub clean a mountain," Alabella said, as she continued to gather her belongings.

Laurel's hand rubbed at the transfusers in her pocket. It was a new day—she'd waited long enough—so, she kept one eye on Alabella to make sure her back was still turned and pulled one out. She brought the vial to her lips with trembling hands. Iron slid down her throat, and warmth suffused her body. The quaking of her hands faded away.

Still, that didn't fix the larger problem. They had to leave Alchea. Maybe... "If they're going to pursue us, we should go west. There's nothing to the north, and it's too flat to the south. It would be too easy to track us. Plenty of hills to the west and, if we can make it all the way to Felia, they won't be able to follow."

Alabella thought it over for a moment. "I'd prefer we go south, but you are right about the visibility. It would be dangerous. If we keep the group small, we could ride horseback to Feldspar, then pick up a carriage to continue west through the night. We'll need to move quickly, and we'll need Sarla."

Laurel nodded.

They moved to the door and Alabella knocked. In a few moments, the door opened, and a group of uniformed guards glared at them. One, a shorter man with a mustache, put a hand on the door. "What is it?"

Alabella's veins blazed to life with Amber threadlight. "I *am* sorry." Her eyes glowed a brilliant yellow just before the guards all clutched at their legs and sank to the ground, overcome by a tangle of invisible threads. In seconds, they were sprawled out across the floor in a writhing mass of blue and white uniform. The door drifted open.

When Laurel stepped out, a single guard remained standing, just beyond the others. He looked ready to soil himself and, when Alabella met his eyes, he dropped to the floor. But Laurel was quite sure that it was of his own accord, rather than Alabella's threads.

It was just before dawn and the night sky still flooded the hallways of the keep with an eerie darkness. They ran down the hallway with their shadows wavering in front of them like spirits, beckoning them to follow. They moved swiftly, but cautiously, taking care to not rouse suspicion from the servants who worked quietly.

They turned a corner near a staircase and came face-to-face with three people Laurel would never have expected to see.

Luther, holding a small crate, paused beside Laz and Reina. When they saw her, Laz's cheeks flushed, and she knew that the three of them were doing something they ought not to. Alabella's veins began to glow, and Laurel put a hand on her arm.

"What are you *doing* here?" Laurel asked.

"We could ask you the same," Luther replied, eyes narrow as he clutched the box. Laurel thought she heard the sounds of movement coming from within the box.

"We *could*," Reina added with a nudge. "Or we could all pretend like no one saw anything, and continue on about our business..."

Despite how badly Laurel wanted to know what was in the package, she knew that she and Alabella also needed to move quickly. "If you didn't see us, then we didn't see you."

"Is good," Laz said with a thumbs up.

When Laurel and Alabella moved to descend the staircase, so did Luther, Laz, and Reina. They looked at each other uncomfortably for a moment before continuing down. Each step of the spiraling stairs echoed loudly as they made their way to the bottom floor.

As soon as the stairs ended, Laz gave her a final nod. A small cooing sound came from the box just as they moved to go. Luther looked to Laurel. His cheekbones cut tightly against his skin as he clenched his teeth. Before she could ask, he nodded and took off. Laz and Reina followed closely behind.

Alabella had a curious look in her eyes but let them go. They each tossed their hoods on and walked quietly past the guards posted outside the keep. Laurel spotted a tint of Emerald in the veins of one of the guards. His tired eyes scanned the courtyard while the others stood still. With the threat of a corespawn invasion, their priority was making sure nothing came in.

Once outside of the keep walls, Alabella cut south and they made their way to the warehouse where they'd been staying. Laurel still had a hard time keeping the direction, but she thought she was finally starting to recognize some of the grounder streets and landmarks.

However, it all felt different now. Windows were boarded up. Doors barricaded. Carts and stalls were left abandoned in the streets. Holed up inside each home were children sleeping and parents with red eyes who stressed over the future of their families. Laurel hadn't thought about it, but, in a way, she was glad that the Zeda people had been forced west. Perhaps, the world was safer away from Alchea and the corespawn.

They reached the warehouse and, after knocking and waiting for the barricade to be shoved aside, they entered. Laurel was surprised with how many people were there. There must have been hundreds, young and old, spread out across the warehouse floor like cocoons. She recognized some as the seamstresses and tailors that worked the floor for Alabella's legitimate business.

Alabella smiled as they entered.

"What is this?" Laurel asked.

"Many of our workers have homes on the outer rim of the city, or out in the countryside. I asked Sarla to offer them a safer home for now."

Laurel stared at the woman. She couldn't understand her. In some ways, she would sacrifice everything to move toward her grand vision of the world. But then this? An outpouring of empathy.

Alabella continued through the quiet warehouse, waving at a few of those who remained awake. When they entered Sarla's quarters, they found the strange woman sleeping on her back, cradling a stack of parchment with her odd glasses placed atop. Alabella strode forward and woke up Sarla with a gentle hand to the shoulder.

When her eyes opened and she saw who it was, Sarla shot upright and shoved her glasses on. "I am quite certain that I did not fall asleep. There is far too much to do, and too little time to do it all."

"Pack your things," Alabella said. "Whatever you can carry on a horse. We need to leave the city."

"Humans or corespawn?" Sarla asked.

Alabella smirked. "Humans. The corespawn never came."

"An unlikely outcome," the odd woman said, jumping to her feet. "Then the Alcheans will have no further need of our product or our alliance. I'll gather my things." She paused. "There is something you should know."

Alabella cocked her head to the side.

"Jelium knows about the boy."

"Heralds be damned," she cursed. "It was only a matter of time. We'll need to get our shipment out before he finds it. I've no idea what he'd do with it, but he would destroy it for nothing more than to molest us. Send one of our people back. I want it out of Cynosure and out to Felia as soon as possible."

They found Barrick awake in his room and asked him to fetch some horses. While they waited, Alabella gave instructions to a short, blonde woman on how to continue running the warehouse. When Barrick returned, the four of them saddled up and never looked back.

21 — STONES OF LIGHT

When the hood lifted and his eyes adjusted to the bright sunlight, Alverax nearly peed himself. Tens of thousands of Felians solemnly assembled throughout the colossal hippodrome, staring with broken hearts at a broken young man while a choir of circling birds sang his death march. They gathered to witness the death of the last Obsidian threadweaver, and to watch their hopes of a Heraldic return die with him.

The strength he'd shown while trading his life for the Zeda people had all but vanished. Now, he stood upon frail bones and hunched with the posture of a man resigned to his fate. He turned his eyes from the people; it was more than he could bear. He could weather the storm raging in his own mind—a story of failure and ill-fate wrought by his father's curse—but each time he locked eyes with one of the Felian people and saw the tragedy in their gaze, it broke another piece of him.

He felt more alone than any man should in a sea of souls.

Somewhere, the Zeda were still imprisoned, forced to wait until after his execution before they were exiled. He wished he could have seen even one of them again, a single nod of approval for the only selfless choice he'd ever made.

As he stared at the circular stone floor beneath him in the center of the hippodrome, he was taken aback by the familiarity of the runes carved upon its surface. It reminded him of what the Zeda called "the coreseal." This platform was much larger, but its shape and style were certainly comparable. His eyes followed the chain wrapped around his ankles that ended at a point fixed to the ground.

"It is typically our custom," Watchlord Osinan said quietly, his chin raised high as he inspected the chains, "to allow the condemned an opportunity to address the people. However, we have decided that you are not deserving of such a platform. So, you will be given no such opportunity."

The slightest commotion broke through the crowd, like leaves rustling in the wind. Alverax turned his head to see Empress Jisenna summiting the platform, dressed in a flowing black dress with dozens of thin, golden tassels draping from her sleeves. In another life, the bright sun and the singing birds would have been a fitting accompaniment to her arrival, but, today, Alverax looked away and cursed the birds to silence.

As the empress approached the center of the platform, she kissed her fingertips and placed them in the air in front of her.

"Today, we grieve the loss of our beloved empress." She spoke with power, letting her voice travel through the acoustics of the hippodrome. "While her ship may now sail the infinite sea, her spirit and her ideals remain with us. The truth is that we have been deceived. A ship, flying a false flag, entered our harbors and stole a piece of our soul."

Stole.

The word seared itself into Alverax's mind. Was that how he would be remembered? The man who stole a life? For years, he'd fought to distance himself from the tainted heritage his father had left, and now, history would etch his name beside the very man. The thought broke what was left of his brittle pride. Tears swelled up in his Obsidian eyes. His lungs quaked within his chest. His lips quivered. He'd sworn to never be like his father, and, whether he was or not, the world believed he was.

The world spun around him in a blurry mass of prismatic color. He closed his eyes and tried to hold back the tears from streaming down his cheeks, but the cracks in his heart were too wide, and his mind was too feeble.

"I have been called the Mistress of Mercy," Jisenna continued. "But there can be no mercy without justice. It is true that this man is an Obsidian threadweaver. We welcomed him in the name of the Heralds, and now we enact justice in their name. My sister's death will not be in vain if its redress serves to protect the world from further pain."

Watchlord Osinan stepped beside the empress. "It is our custom to allow the accused a chance to provide evidence of their innocence. There are times, however, when we must break custom. This man has pleaded guilty, and both Empress Jisenna and I have agreed that he will not be given a final address. We will not let his tear-filled fabrications sully this moment of restitution."

Alverax had been holding out hope that Jisenna still believed in him, but her words shattered that hope. It was inevitable now, and yet, he felt a strange sense of relief. As odd as it was, he felt at peace knowing that he was sacrificing himself for others. He'd been worried that, given a platform to defend himself, he would break down and plead his own innocence. Now, with no platform to speak, he could continue in silence, following through with his decision with the smallest semblance of grace.

Two dark men in bright white garb lifted the massive wooden beam and walked it over to Alverax. In the center of the beam, a space had been carved out for a man's neck and, at the ends, metal rods arched upward like twin scythes. Together, the men heaved it high and placed it over Alverax's shoulders, then clasped both sides together around his neck.

The weight of the wood alone was staggering. No one had explained the process to him in the prison cell, but the metaphor seemed obvious to him now; he would bear the weight of their grief.

A familiar face from the masquerade, the prideful man, Rastalin Farrow, approached the platform first. "Two stones for the people of Felia."

The men in white grabbed two circular slabs of stone with holes in their center, lifted them high, and placed them over the metal rods on the end of Alverax's cross. The wood near the base of his neck dug hard into his skin, the weight of the stones compounding with the weight of the beam.

As Rastalin returned to his position, Watchlord Osinan approached the front. "Two stones for the Heralds, who look down with disgrace."

Again, the men lifted two slabs of stone and placed them over the metal rods. The pain seemed to multiply exponentially. His legs could barely carry the weight, but, if he collapsed, the beam would crush him. He groaned in agony as he fought to remain standing. Then, he realized that he could, at any moment, break the threads of the stones and lighten his load. The pain would stop. The suffering would cease, but he would taint his own sacrifice.

Empress Jisenna returned to the front of the stands and paused, raw eyes lifting to meet Alverax's own. On her cheeks, he saw the remnants of a morning filled with tears and sorrow. The next stones would crush him—he could feel that truth in the grinding of his vertebrae—and, though she may be the Mistress of Mercy, she had accepted his fate as much as her own. "Two stones for the Lady of Light, the Sun Queen, the Empress of Felia, my sister and my dearest friend."

The circling birds chirped louder, taunting him as he awaited the placement of the final stones. He wanted to scream, to fight, to survive, but this moment would define him.

The men approached with the final circular stone slabs, larger than the rest. They lifted the stones with concerted effort.

"My life for yours!" a desperate voice screamed from the crowd.

Alverax lifted his eyes, barely able to keep his knees from buckling, and looked to the source of the voice.

An old woman with green eyes and a scowl shouted from the crowd. Alverax knew her. Elder Rowan, red-faced and filled with passion, screamed once more. "My life for yours!"

Alverax choked on his breath. Beside the elder, he saw a group of the other Zeda people, piled together and bound in chains, forced to watch the death of their companion.

The Felians would execute her for what she'd just done.

He wanted to scream at her to run, to take his sacrifice and go, but he could do nothing with the stones weighing him down.

"Enough!" Osinan screamed, "There will be no surrogacy!"

A second voice, a man's voice with a certain gruffness to it, repeated the phrase. "My life for yours!"

Alverax looked and saw Dogwood standing tall in the crowd, raising a fist high overhead.

Before Osinan could respond, yet another voice shouted, "My life for yours!"

Elder Rosemary.

The rest of the Zeda elders, speckled throughout the crowd, joined in the chorus, repeating the same words.

Then, a child's voice called out, "My life for yours!"

When he looked, he saw the young girl, Poppy, whom he'd protected from the Felian soldier.

Something about the little girl's offering snapped the last remaining cord in his mind. He fell to his knees, the weight of the stone slabs bearing down on his body while the words of his friends bore down on his soul. Tears flowed down his cheeks, and he heard one final voice.

Iriel Valerian, her child nowhere to be seen, stood firm in a storm of uncertainty, and said the one phrase that Alverax would never wish her to speak. "My life for yours!"

"Enough!" Osinan shouted. His eyes alternated between Alverax and the increasingly agitated crowd.

Alverax glanced at Jisenna and thought he saw a shimmer of doubt in her eyes, but then she turned to the men in white. "Two stones for my sister!"

Just then, one of the circling birds fluttered down to the platform and landed near Alverax's head on the wooden beam. It stayed for only a brief moment, then took off into the sky.

The world faded around him, and Alverax fell into a story, a memory of his own construction. He saw Jisenna standing atop a green hill overlooking an endless sea. An evil princess set to destroy the world. A small, yellow-bellied starling rested on her shoulder. As she looked out over the tumultuous waves, the little bird spoke to her and said, *"Are you certain?"*

When the words were spoken, the vision fled, and Alverax returned to a painful reality. The weight of four stone slabs tore into his shoulders, blood trailed down his torso where the wood cut into his skin. The entire crowd of men and women stared, awaiting his death. And the empress, the woman who'd once shown him such wonderful kindness, stood in silence, a single tear drifting down her cheek.

Only a few moments passed before the little bird flew away, but, sometimes, a few moments change everything. Her eyes softened. Her shoulders fell. The quiver in her lips faded away as they parted. "Wait," she whispered through the commotion.

The white-garbed men lifted the stone slabs and placed them over the metal rods of Alverax's cross.

"Stop!" the empress screamed as the weight of the final slabs settled.

The addition of the final two slabs would have crushed Alverax had he not heard Jisenna's plea. He opened himself to threadlight and *broke* the threads of all six of the stone slabs. The overwhelming weight of the beam and stones lifted from his shoulders, and he rose once again to his feet.

"Do not touch him!" Jisenna said as the men in white reached for the swords at their waist.

Watchlord Osinan stepped forward, fire in his eyes. "Sun Daughter! What is the meaning of this?"

"Sun *Queen*," Empress Jisenna corrected with a powerful resolve in her gaze. "This man did not kill my sister."

STONES OF LIGHT 22

Falling to his death, Chrys had never felt so alive. The light from above was fading fast, and he was beginning to fear that the Endless Well would live up to its name. In the split moment he'd made the decision to jump, based on the assumption that there *would* be a bottom, he'd not taken into account the real possibility that by the time they reached the bottom, there would be no light. If they couldn't see, they couldn't threadweave. And if they couldn't threadweave, their landing would be much less graceful than he'd hoped.

He looked to his mother, and his eyes swelled with pride. The dirt in her hair, the scum caked on her clothing, she was a mess...for him. The damn woman had crossed mountains. She'd trekked through uncharted jungles. And she'd found him. She was to him, what he hoped to be to his family. Come what may, he *would* find them again.

So long as he didn't die at the bottom of the Endless Well.

They fell for what seemed an eternity with no end in sight, until, quite suddenly, hundreds of orbs of dim light faded into view below them, spread out in tightly coupled bunches. The orbs illuminated a lake of clear water with an island of barren stone at its center. Water, fed from the waterfall on the other side of the Endless Well, crashed in foamy bouts into the lake.

"NOW!" Chrys shouted over the rush of the wind.

Willow understood, and both of their veins blazed to life with Sapphire threadlight. Chrys grabbed hold of Roshaw and *pushed* against the ground. Their descent came to an abrupt halt as their feet landed hard atop mossy rock.

Roshaw collapsed to his back, hands atop his head, and caught his breath. Despite the massive width of the opening, the light coming down from high overhead was nothing but a spec in the darkness, like a single star in the night sky. Chrys spun in a circle and dozens of patches of photospores shined their bioluminescence in the sprawling cavern. Below one patch, the broken body of a wastelander floated face up in the water. He saw other bones scattered throughout the cave, with bits of broken spear and shredded clothing.

"Well," Willow said, rubbing at her chest. "I love what you've done with the place. A little dark, and the size is a bit pretentious. But you know me, I've always liked cozy cottages more than subterranean chateaus."

Chrys let out a clipped laugh.

"On the other hand," she continued, "I'm sure there was a discount for the gaping hole in the roof."

Chrys shook his head. "Would you believe they charged me extra for it? The corpse cost me eighty shines."

"Unbelievable," Willow said, laughing. Then, without another word, she lunged forward and embraced him, squeezing him with a ferocity that only a mother could know, and held it until her arms were shaking. Chrys shuddered at the pain in his shoulder where the corespawn had left its mark.

Despite his myriad wounds, Chrys' heart filled with joy. "I thought I would never see you again. How did you find me?"

"When I saw what happened in the Fairenwild, I turned around. Luther let me hide out at their home for a few days until a raving soldier from the mountains claimed that the Apogee had slaughtered his camp. No one believed him, but it was all I had to go on. Then...I found this." She reached into a pocket and pulled out a pocket watch. The same one that Relek had discarded in the mountains. She handed it to him, and he held it carefully, surprised to hear the ticking sound still played.

Chrys couldn't help but smile. "Let's hope it wasn't for nothing."

"I found you," she said. "That's enough for me. Now let's get you back to *your* son."

Roshaw had lifted himself to his feet with tears in his eyes. In the days Chrys had known him, Roshaw had always been so lighthearted, the first to gamble and the first to laugh. But now, at the bottom of the Endless Well, his eyes burned with fury. And Chrys understood him. The wastelanders had lied. Relek had lied. They'd promised freedom, but instead they offered death. Chrys could still see the spears piercing their skin. Agatha, so frail and delicate, crying out in agony, while Seven, eyes filled with betrayal, looked to the ever-smiling Esme. Five years they'd searched for freedom, patiently biding their time, only to die to the whims of a god.

Roshaw's lip twitched. "He killed them."

"Don't focus on that right now," Chrys said. "Focus on getting out of here."

"It should have been me." Roshaw looked back up to the spec of light high above. "They were good people. If anyone deserved to die, it should have been me."

Chrys nodded to Willow as he left her to stand beside Roshaw. "You don't deserve to die."

"Neither did they!" he shouted, his words echoing in the vast cavern. "Agatha, Esme, Seven, they were good people. Better than me. I'm a piece of shit."

"You know," Chrys said. "My mentor once told me, after a battle where the wastelanders wiped out half of my men, that the only difference between the living and the dead is that the dead are done changing. The moment you die, your life and your legacy are fixed in stone. He told me that the best way to grieve the dead is by using the gift of life to make yourself a better man.

"I don't care if you're a piece of shit or a piece of gold. Someone or something is out there waiting for you. If you want to grieve Agatha, if you want to grieve Esme and Seven, then let's get the hell out of this cave and make ourselves into something better."

Roshaw was silent for a moment, clenching his jaw as he thought. The man's age seemed more pronounced amid the flickering lights of the photospores. There was a certain weariness in the expression of his eyes. When he finally spoke, he nodded and met Chrys' gaze. "I don't know. It's a nice thought, but it's just not that simple. The people I hurt will never forgive me for what I did."

"Who cares?" Chrys said. "Whether or not someone forgives you doesn't change anything. This is about you, and me, and my mother. We received a gift today that, as sickening as the truth is, not everyone around us received. Now, I don't know about you, but I'm not going to waste it. I'm getting out of here. I'm going to find my wife and son. And

I'm going to squeeze them so tight their eyes bulge out of their damn heads. And I'm going to do that with or without you, but I would much rather have you by my side."

Roshaw met him eye to eye in a battle of resolve. Chrys watched the older man's jaw flexing beneath his gaunt cheeks, his chest rising and falling beneath his tunic. "I just...I wish they could have made it out too."

"Me too," Chrys said.

"When we get out of here, I'm going to name a star for each of them. And if I can, I'd like to find their families and share their story."

"I think that would be very nice."

"Yeah," Roshaw said mostly to himself. His eyes wandered along with his mind, drifting off into the surrounding darkness of the cavern.

Chrys turned to Willow and she gave him a warm smile. He gestured for her to follow. They stepped carefully over wet stones, wading through knee-deep water, and made their way toward the periphery of the cavern. The small lake in the middle of the Well gave way to slick, slime-covered stone that Roshaw stumbled on, but managed to keep his footing. Eventually they found their way to the outer edge of the cavern, each pulling off a few photospores to illuminate their path. Little shadows danced along the walls and over the rocks as they searched for a path.

Willow was the first to see the tunnel, but Roshaw, filled with a new sense of determination, was the first to enter. The walls were smooth, as if the stone had been pounded flat. The smallest drips of water leaked from overhead along the edges, and stalactites grew from the ceiling. The silence was broken only by the occasional skittering of tiny footsteps in the puddles.

As Chrys walked on, he squeezed at his palm, eager for the bleeding from his missing fingers to subside. There was a sick form of irony in the fact that, after losing three fingers, he'd taken upon himself Seven's title. It would take some getting used to, but if it was the price required for freedom and a reunion with his mother, he'd pay it a thousand times. Either way, he needed some fresh water so he could clean out his wounds. Otherwise, infection would soon take hold, and he didn't have access to any of the salves he knew of for dealing with such an affliction.

From further down in the tunnel, a subtle voice echoed across the smooth stone.

Willow had the obsidian blade out before Roshaw had even stopped walking. Chrys whispered for them to leave their photospores behind and follow him. They approached with soft steps, and soon found light emanating from further ahead. When they rounded the final bend, they saw the most curious sight.

A man wearing a wide-brimmed hat sat at a table hewn of a single rose-colored stone. Haphazardly placed around the table, an array of wood chairs were filled with oddities: a translucent snake wrapped around petrified wood, a glowing fish swimming around a large crystal bowl, and a half-finished statue of a monster with the tail of a scorpion.

But odder than the rest was the man seated at the table. Beneath his hat, his eyes were closed tight, and long, dark hair fell to his naval.

"Sister?" the old man called out. When he turned his head, keeping his eyes closed, the sight reminded Chrys of the blind priests of the Order of Alchaeus.

Chrys clenched his jaw and gestured for the others to remain still. The likelihood that a blind man was alone in the caves far below Kai'Melend was nearly zero. So, they waited patiently, hoping he would think their steps were something else.

"You know I haven't bathed in years," the man said with a laugh.

When no one responded, the odd man took to his feet. He was old and wiry, and his loose-fit tunic opened up at the chest, exposing a wildly undernourished body. The man took a few steps toward them, leaning in with his ears toward their direction.

"Lylax?"

Chrys and Roshaw swiftly backed around the corner at the word, and Willow followed.

"He definitely said *Lylax*, right?" Roshaw said.

Chrys nodded and turned to his mother. "Quick debrief. The voice I was hearing in my head turned out to be a wastelander god who can inhabit other people. His name is Relek. He's taken a new body, and he has a sister named Lylax who can do the same. If that man out there knows Lylax, then we can't let him know we're here. If they know we're alive, we're in danger."

Willow, after a momentary blank stare, closed her eyes and shook her head. "I...Iriel told me about the voice. A wastelander god?"

"Turns out I wasn't losing my mind, only sharing it."

"Stones," she cursed.

Roshaw cut in. "What do we do? Find another tunnel back at the Well?"

"No," Chrys said. "We need food and supplies, or we'll die down here. If that man is here, then he has to have something we can use."

"He's an old man," Willow said. "We can't kill him."

Chrys held his finger up to quiet her. "We're not going to kill anyone. We're going to steal from him." He thought he saw a smirk on Roshaw's lips at the suggestion. "But we also can't leave him here. So, we're going to tie him up and bring him with us. If we're lucky, he can help guide us out."

"He's blind..." Roshaw said.

Chrys rubbed his beard. "I have enough experience with blind people not to underestimate—"

"Hello," a voice said from behind them.

The three of them startled back, and Willow's blade swung forward, slicing Roshaw's forearm on the way up. Chrys pushed the others back and took a fighting stance between them and the bare-footed old man, then let a bit of threadlight course through his veins, lightening his stance.

"Oh, my," the odd man said, his eyes still shut tight. "I'm so sorry! I thought you were someone else. You see, I don't get many visitors. I've forgotten my manners. Please, please. Do come in and take a seat. You've a fine story, I'm certain of it. And I mean to hear every last word! If you promise me no harm, I will happily return the gesture."

The old man gestured for them to follow him, but Chrys stood in complete astonishment. Now that he was closer, something tickled at the edge of Chrys' mind. Maybe the old man *was* a priest and he'd seen him before. But why was he down there? Either way, Chrys knew there was information to be learned.

"Thank you," Chrys said. "Perhaps you could help us."

"Ah!" the old man choked on his word. He was quiet for a moment, then touched a finger under his closed eyes, wiping away a tear that fell down his cheek. "I...cannot explain how lovely it is to hear your voice. I'm so sorry. It feels almost like a dream. How many of you are there? I thought I heard others."

"There are three of us," Willow said.

"Three!" he laughed. "Three companions explore the caves far beneath the surface. I'm afraid I know the ending of such a story. Three is a cursed number, I'm certain of it. Better if there were only two of you. It is a safer number. Please, please. Do come in."

He shuffled away and a little creature darted out from beneath the table. It looked like...Chrys let go of threadlight and the little creature vanished. He let threadlight flow through his veins, and the little creature reappeared.

"Stones. Is that—"

"He's called Chitt," the old man said. "He's quite harmless."

Chrys stared at the creature, curious about its connection to the corespawn he'd fought in the wasteland pit. "You're sure it's not dangerous?"

"Quite certain. His is one of the few friendly breeds. Though—don't tell him—not one of the most intelligent."

As they followed, the little corespawn scuttled up the old man's leg and came to rest atop his shoulder. Chrys turned his gaze to survey the rest of the cavern. Light filled every corner of the sprawling space from dozens of photospores that grew in perfectly lined bunches along the outer edges. A dozen different tunnels led in every direction, and, on the far side, a massive pool of golden water emanated a faint glow of its own. A small waterfall fed the pool, leaving an ever-present glimmer as the water rippled at the surface.

There were no other corespawn creatures.

Out of the corner of his eye, Chrys could see Willow squeezing the obsidian blade in her hand. Everything about this felt wrong. The place. The company. The glowing fish that Chrys was certain was watching him. It almost felt like a dream, like he'd been drugged by the wastelanders and now slept while his mind delved into a deep psychosis. He looked down at his hand, and hoped that were true, but the pain he felt was real. Which made it all the stranger.

Down one of the corridors, a collection of instruments and gadgets was strewn about haphazardly across the floor and against the wall. Chrys noted the room, assuming that it was where he'd find any useful supplies for their exit.

"If I had known you were coming, I would have taken a bath," the man said. "My sister told me to jump in when she left, but...ha! I must sound mad! Of course, none of this would make sense to you. I'm so sorry! It's been so long."

"No apology needed," Willow said with a soft voice. "We are grateful for your hospitality. Though we are certainly curious what it is you are doing down here."

"Ah! Another collector of stories! And this is the grandest of them all." He paused, scratching at his overgrown beard as he pondered his response. "I suppose the summary is that we often do silly things for family."

Willow raised a brow. "Your family sent you here?"

"No, no, no. We discovered it, together," he said. "You know, I have often dreamed of sharing our story—the whole story. But my sister thinks it would be unwise."

"Your sister?" Chrys asked. "Is she here?"

The blind man turned to face Chrys and, though his eyes were closed, he seemed to take in Chrys' expression. "She should return any moment. However, I think it would be better if you were gone before she returns."

Interesting. The tone assumed that Lylax was dangerous, but Chrys had the sneaking suspicion that the old man was more than he appeared. Either way, if Lylax would return, they needed to get answers quickly, and get out even more so. "We know your sister and your brother, Relek. They slaughtered our friends."

The air in the cavern chilled as footsteps echoed down one of the tunnels. The old man froze in his seat, his hands resting on the table. With his eyes shut, it was as though he had become a statue. But the little corespawn on his shoulder reached its neck out toward the sound and made a chirping noise.

The old man spoke in a hushed tone. "Do they know you are here?"

Chrys, Willow, and Roshaw all rose to their feet.

"Come, quick," the old man said. "You must hide!"

23

Luther held his wife quietly in a farmhouse outside of Alchea. Their life would never be the same, but sometimes you have to make changes to make room for what's important.

"Try to get some sleep," he whispered to Emory, pressing his lips against her forehead.

She nodded but said nothing. She hadn't said much since they'd left, but he knew she would come around. It was the right decision, especially with the inevitable return of the corespawn. Even still, he should have warned her beforehand—he knew that—but he knew her deeply held beliefs would have clouded her judgment.

He rose from the bed and stepped to the door, pushing it open as quietly as he could. It made the slightest creak as he closed it behind him.

What he needed more than anything was a drink. It had been such a long day, and emotional, and horribly stressful. If not for threadlight to send a bit of liquid comfort throughout his body, he wasn't sure he could have made it through.

Fortunately, when he rounded the corner to the main room, Laz stood with a mug of ale in each hand, waiting for him. "Is time for drink."

"Please tell me that's not all there is," Luther said as he accepted the mug.

"Is whole barn full!" Laz said with a toothy grin. "Cousin is wild man."

Luther chugged half of the mug in one go, cringing at the taste. It was foul—much worse than city ale—but he knew he wouldn't sleep that night if he didn't drink more. It had been that way ever since the priests had taken his son. If he didn't drink, his mind would spin for hours while he lay awake, or he'd wake up to nightmares and fits of stress.

"You good?" Laz asked.

"I'll be okay." Luther sipped again on the ale. "It'll take some time. Our whole life was in Alchea. Family. Friends. But what the hell was I supposed to do?"

"You did right thing."

"I hope so," Luther said. "I think so. Stones, but I wish Chrys were here. He always knew what to do."

"Chrys would say, 'To be boss, must know how to count. Now, you have right count!'" Laz laughed at his own terrible impression.

The right count. It was a strangely wise way to look at it, coming from Laz especially, but he was right. Luther had been feeling incomplete, like an arch without its cornerstone, and alcohol only filled the gap with mud.

"Thanks, Laz. For everything."

"Is no problem," the thick red-headed man said as he sipped his own mug.

"I'm not drunk yet," Luther said. "So, I hope you believe me. But I'm really going to miss you, Laz. These past months have been hell, and you've been there beside me every damn day, sipping your nasty milk stout and helping me keep my demons at bay. You're a damn good friend, and I owe you more than I could ever repay."

He paused, waiting for Laz to make a joke, but, instead, the big man wrapped him in a bear hug, his massive hands squeezing against Luther's back. Laz was the only man Luther knew whose heart perfectly matched their frame. He found himself feeling unexpectedly emotional as he embraced his friend for what could be the last time.

When they pulled away, Laz had tears swelling in his eyes. "Don't tell Reina I cry. She would make more fun of me."

"Your secret is safe," Luther said.

Laz lifted a bag off the floor and tossed it over his shoulder. "Time for me to go back now. Take care of yourself, you hole."

No matter how many times he used the insult, Laz had still yet to explain what it meant. But, somehow, that felt perfectly fitting for the man.

"I still think you should stay. It might not be safe for you back there."

"Is fine," Laz said, brushing it off. "Reina will lie for me."

Luther nodded. "Okay, then this is it. Lazarus Barlow, it has been a pleasure being your teammate, your friend, and the one who can always outdrink you."

"I share secret," Laz said, smiling his dopey grin. "I always can outdrink. I let you win. Ha! Goodbye, friend."

With that, the big man pushed open the door and stepped out into the starry night. Luther turned back to the hallway and stepped toward the room. Laz's cousin's farmhouse had an extra room that they weren't using, which was all they could ask for. With everything going on, Luther wanted his kids in his room with him at night. It felt safer, even though it was unlikely anyone would find them there. Still, old habits die hard, and paranoia was a healthy habit for a soldier.

When he entered the room, Luther stepped over to the bed and smiled. Two children lay quietly asleep beside Emory, unaware of the growing dangers in the world. He wished he could be like them.

He looked to the foot of the bed where a small white bassinet lay. Inside, slept a small child.

His third.

Luther reached down and rubbed the little boy's cheek, filled with an overwhelming joy that he was once again theirs, sad only that the boy would forever be blind. Every other piece of his soul felt like a missing gear had been replaced, and finally his life would run again.

To hell with the Order of Alchaeus.

No one would take his son from him ever again.

Stones of Light
24

THE OLD MAN in the caves beneath Kai'Melend led Chrys, Willow, and Roshaw to a curved, dead-end tunnel. His little corespawn, Chitt, skittered toward the far end and disappeared into the darkness where the light from the golden pool faded away.

Roshaw entered first, scrambling to follow the little creature. They passed crates filled with cloth, mounds of colorful gemstones, and a variety of carefully organized tools and items. In the far corner of the tunnel, a collection of nearly one hundred man-sized alabaster statues stood in a carefully aligned collection.

As they approached and their eyes adjusted, Chrys could see Chitt popping in and out from beyond the shadows. The statues, like stone sentinels, were carved with precision, each one depicting a different breed of terrifying beast. Some stood on two legs, others prowled on four. Spikes protruded from the shoulders of some, while others had horns or barbed tails. But each creature bore two clear quartz gems fastened to the place where the eyes would be.

They moved among them, brushing up against cold stone, hardly able to see their own movements. Willow grabbed Chrys' good hand, and a dark feeling grew in the pit of his stomach. There was something off about the statues. Something darker than the lack of light.

They settled between them and let go of the threadlight in their veins. The Sapphire radiance faded away, and their bodies succumbed to the shadows.

Muffled voices echoed from beyond the bend. Though he could not hear the words, the tone he would never forget.

Relek.

They stood in silence, living statues among the dead, hoping that the old man would keep their secret.

"Agh," Chrys groaned. He shook his hand and brought it upright near his chest. Without threadlight in his veins, he couldn't be certain, but he had a feeling the little corespawn had licked the dried blood on his missing fingers. Chrys looked down the tunnel, and flickering shadows grew along the wall.

Relek's voice resounded along the stone. "I heard about your stonemasonry. Lylax says your collection of corespawn is quite impressive."

"It's not exactly a collection," the old man replied. "More of a taxonomy really."

With a look that said, "I don't care", Relek continued his approach. His eyes were alive with color, a turbulent swirl of spectral light. He leaned in and touched the face of one of the statues, a large creature the size of a bear, with two massive fangs that cut out to its jawline. "I must admit, I don't much like seeing these creatures without threadlight."

Relek's eyes moved over the collection of statues. Chrys, Willow, and Roshaw hid themselves behind the alabaster figures, breathing through their mouths only when they could no longer hold their breath. Relek moved to investigate further, but then the old man crouched and made a clicking noise with his tongue. Skittering feet, starting from within the collection of statues, scratched against the floor until the old man rose back to his feet, cradling an empty hand. "Like I said, brother. It was only Chitt. Don't be so paranoid. You are immortal after all."

"It's not the ones who escaped that I am afraid of. There are at least two Creators west of the mountains. A woman—powerful, but limited in her knowledge—and a child."

"You are frightened of a child?"

"Don't be a fool. It is simply that I refuse to be trapped again."

"I know a little about being trapped," the old man said, turning from the tunnel and stepping toward the larger cavern.

Relek followed. "But you could explore the endless caverns of the core. The wastelanders die if they do not drink the elixir regularly. What matters is that I will take whatever measures are necessary to never be trapped again. This time, there can be no mercy." His voice trailed off as they rounded the bend into the cavern.

Chrys, Willow, and Roshaw remained still for what seemed an eternity, not daring to assume that Relek had left.

Without threadlight in his veins, Chrys began to feel the effects of his fighting. His shoulder throbbed, and his hand pulsed with every beat of his heart. He closed his eyes, wincing at the pain. When he opened them, the quartz eyes of the corespawn statues all seemed to turn and look at him. The bruised flesh over his ribs tightened and his breathing increased.

When Willow squeezed his good hand, he startled, nearly knocking over a statue in front of him.

"Your hand is shaking," she whispered. "Are you okay?"

"No." His voice came out strained.

"You need to lie down. You've lost a lot of blood."

"I'll be fine."

Willow let go of his hand and he saw her make her way out of the collection of statues. The closer she drew to the bend, the more her silhouette grew in the rippling gold light. She stood at the edge of the tunnel, pressed up against the stone wall, and waited. Chrys found himself praying in the back of his mind, hoping that Relek would not find her. Failing to fight off his blurring vision, he grabbed hold of a large spike protruding from the back of a statue nearby, and its feet began to wobble against the stone floor.

Roshaw reached over and steadied the statue before it made more noise. "Grab my arm," he whispered.

Chrys took hold of Roshaw's upper arm with his good hand and tried to breathe, but the air amongst the statues was stale and cold, with hints of chalky dust that swirled in his lungs. He stifled a cough, but the pressure in his chest was worse. The little light remaining in the far recess of the tunnel warped into shifting shadows and blobs of taunting darkness that coalesced and split in nightmarish waves. Time passed, and Chrys felt his entire world dissolving into a chaotic dream, filled with pain and confusion. And just as he closed his eyes to flee from it all, his legs collapsed beneath him.

Willow felt a wave of relief as the wastelander god, Relek, cupped the back of his brother's head, bringing their foreheads together, then left. As his footsteps faded away down a far tunnel, the blind old man waited patiently at his table, running his hand along the back of his invisible pet. They continued for another minute, Willow spying and the old man waiting, until finally he rose from his seat.

"Psss," Willow said. "Are we safe?"

The old man nodded. "They will not return for quite some time now."

Just as Willow felt a sense of relief, the sound of shattering stone exploded through the cavern. She whipped her head around and raced through the small tunnel to find the dim outline of Roshaw holding Chrys. Beneath them, one of the corespawn figures was strewn across the floor in a hundred broken pieces.

"Chrys!" Willow rushed to her son. She hadn't come this far to let him die in a cave. As much as she wanted him alive for her own self, she knew more importantly that his wife and son needed him. No matter the cost, she would reunite them. Her grandson deserved to know how good a man his father was.

She helped Roshaw lift him out of the assembly of corespawn statues, feeling at Chrys' forehead and panicking at the burning temperature. The old man was close now, and she turned to address him. "Please, my son is dying. Do you have any herbs or medicines? A bed at the least where we can lay him until his fever breaks?"

"I—" The wrinkles of his forehead creased and his lips puckered. "He will die, you say?"

"He's lost a lot of blood," she said.

"He collapsed out here," Roshaw added. "Looked really dizzy before he did."

The old man frowned and nodded. "Life is more valuable than secrets," he said to himself. "Come, come. There is a way. Your son will live."

Willow *pushed* against her corethread, offsetting Chrys' weight, and carried him chest-to-chest with his arms wrapped around her neck. Despite his size, the position reminded her of the many years she'd spent carrying him this same way. Her little boy. She'd been so lonely during those years, refusing to grow too close to anyone lest they discover her secret. The intimacy she craved, she could not have, because the tattoo on her back would give too much away. And as much as she wanted her new life, she would not have it at the expense of revealing the Zeda people. So, instead, she'd only had Chrys. Her son. Her little flower. The firm root in the storm.

She'd needed him, and now he needed her.

They entered into the large cavern space, and the old man walked carefully toward the sprawling golden pool. Chiseled steps led up to the surface of the water where small ripples refracted the gold light emanating from within.

"If you want him to heal," the old man said, "place him in the pool."

Willow looked into the shimmering pool. Stalactites high overhead reflected from its surface and a strange energy seemed to draw her toward it, beckoning her to enter. For a moment, she lost herself in the beauty of the water, transfixed by each singular ripple as it extended from edge to edge. But she shook the feeling away and focused instead on Chrys.

"In the water?" she repeated. "How deep?"

"All the way," the old man said.

"He'll drown."

"You may keep his head above the water if it comforts you, but it is not necessary."

She placed Chrys along the edge of the pool. His feet slid in first—it seemed to be only as deep as a man's waist—and then she slid in the rest of his body, keeping a hand beneath his head. Once he was fully submerged, she let go of the threadlight in her veins, and slumped against the steps.

"Are their salts or herbs that we need in the water?" Willow asked. "Roshaw can fetch them for you."

"No, no," the old man said. "The truth is that this is *not* water. It is the first great secret of my family. We call it *elixir*. When we discovered it, we soon found that it contained within it a certain healing property. Your son will come out stronger and healthier than ever before."

"The wound in his shoulder?" she asked.

"Healed."

"His missing fingers?" Roshaw asked incredulously.

"Restored," the old man said with confidence. "It will reset his body to its ideal state. If he were old, it would even *heal* him of his old age."

It all seemed so...impossible. An old man in a cave claiming there was a pool that would heal any wound? Even old age? If something like that existed, it would change everything. If you could heal old age, people would be—"Immortal," she said aloud.

"The first great secret," the old man repeated.

Roshaw shook his head. "No. Come on, now. If that were true, why are you so old? Jump in the pool and soak for a few minutes and you'd be young again. It doesn't add up."

"Ah," the blind man said. "A keen observation, and a question I've discussed with my sister many a time. To me, age is not a curse, but a core part of the human experience. Choosing to ignore such a central part of humanity would be to become less and less human. I do believe my brother and sister are examples of this divergence. Where I hope to maintain my humanity across the centuries, they seek to disavow it. It is not easy to grow old, or to lose your sight, especially knowing that you could at any moment change your situation. But to me, it is better to see truth than light. It is better to hold on to the crux of the human experience."

Roshaw looked stunned. "Well, there it is. The old man is completely mad."

But Willow wasn't so sure.

If Relek and Lylax were immortal—which they had reason to believe—then their brother would be as well. And the old man *had* protected them from Relek, so Willow had no reason to disbelieve him. "Will Chrys be immortal now?" she asked.

"No, no," he said. "It does not prevent death. However, if he were to journey here every twenty years for the rest of his life, then yes. He would never die of old age."

"So Relek can die?" Roshaw asked, suddenly interested once again. "And if he doesn't come back here, he would grow older and eventually die?"

The old man clenched his teeth. "My siblings have long moved on from needing the elixir. It is the reason we parted ways so long ago. But I conceded eventually, not because I agree with them, but because they need me at their side. It is important to keep ties with those who do not believe what you do. If your beliefs are never questioned, they become sour."

"You said they've moved on," Willow pressed. "What do you mean by that?"

The old man grew quiet, taking steady breaths while he debated within himself. Willow knew there was something here. Something important. She needed him to tell them.

"Do you know that they are amassing an army?" she asked.

He pursed his lips.

"Our friends were only the beginning," she continued. "They will kill many more. If you know anything that can help us stop them, countless lives are at risk."

"They promised me!" the old man shouted. "They swore that they would not seek revenge."

"We can stop them, if you'll help us," Willow prodded.

The old man dropped his head. "I am no fool. I knew they were lying when they told me. I just...hoped that it would be different. That somehow time had changed them for the better."

Willow wanted to press him again but held back. She could see in the way his shoulders fell forward, his hands fidgeting, that he was close to breaking. Whatever secret he held back, was standing on the precipice, ready to leap.

"It *will* be different this time." Slowly, the old man lifted his head and opened his eyes. Two prismatic irises, slightly muted by a cloudy film, swirled with every color in the spectrum. It took only a split second to realize...they were the same eyes that Relek and Lylax now had.

Willow's free hand fell to the obsidian blade at her side.

The old man turned his gaze to Willow and held his head high. "It is time for my siblings to die."

STONES OF LIGHT
25

THE SUN QUEEN, Empress Jisenna of Felia, stood quietly in the doorway. Both hands rested on her hips, separating her billowy white harem pants and an off-the-shoulder white top trimmed with gold.

Alverax tried to hide the last hint of red in his eyes and the salty tears that had dried over his cheeks, but, as soon as their eyes met—something about the way she looked at him—his façade was torn asunder, and the tears he'd hoped to hide came pouring out of his sunken eyes. He didn't want her to see him like that, but tears have a mind of their own, and no man can impede their arrival once they've chosen to surface.

Jisenna approached him and sat, gesturing for her guards to stay outside the door. But she didn't speak. She simply sat, her shoulder brushing his own, and stared at the floor. They sat in silence for a time. Her presence brought with it a feeling of peace despite everything they'd been through. Finally, after longer than he'd wished, his tears stopped, and his breathing calmed.

"Jisenna" was all he managed, but it was enough.

"I was so *angry*," she said quietly. "And you were right there. Such a convenient enemy. I knew—Heralds save me, but I knew—it was never you. But I was in shock at what had happened, and then you ran. Heralds, Alverax. If you didn't run...I don't know. I'd like to think that we would have believed you."

"I shouldn't have run," he said sheepishly. "I know that, but you should have seen how the people were looking at me. Your sister already didn't trust us. Osinan had blood in his eyes the moment it happened. And when *you* blamed me...I don't know. I was terrified."

She closed her eyes. "I wish you would have come to me, even after you ran."

"Well, technically I did," he said with a fake smile. "I hope you don't blame yourself. Heralds, if I didn't look guilty enough at the masquerade, I admitted to doing it in front of a room full of your guards."

Jisenna looked deep into his eyes. "But you *didn't* do it, and deep down I knew that. And you...you knew that confessing would end in your death, and still you gave yourself to save them."

"You make it sound so heroic, but it was just guilt. I deserved it more than they did."

She eyed him carefully. "You think you deserved it?"

"More than they did."

"Why?" she asked.

Alverax ran his fingertips over his eyes. "I don't know."

"Come now," she prodded. "Why do you think that you deserved to die?"

"I said I don't know."

She scowled. "I cannot understand you. In one moment, you're full of wit and charm, and, in the next, you believe yourself deserving of death. So, which is it? Who are you? And don't you dare say you don't know."

He felt his pulse quicken, a rising tide of frustration and anger billowing beneath his skin. "You want to know the truth?" he asked, nearly shouting. "I am nothing. I'm the son of a thief. I hurt people. I break promises. I make stupid choices. I'm not a hero. I'm just a dumb kid who thought that maybe, just once, he could finally do something good with his life."

She moved to speak but paused. Her eyes pierced deep into his soul. "I don't know what you've done in the past, but I do know this. The choices we make when no one is watching bear more weight than the choices that are forced upon us. You alone made the choice to give up your life to save another. I wish I saw it sooner. But when I saw you fall to your knees, on the verge of death, I finally understood what you'd done. And it had nothing to do with my sister."

"I'm not who you think I am," he said, looking down at the floor.

"Then tell me."

Her quick words stunned him. He wanted to tell her everything. He wanted to unload the burden of his secrets. But he knew he couldn't. It was hard to remember that she was the empress of all of Felia now, here she was speaking with him like they were friends. The truth was that one wrong word and he'd go right back to prison.

"It's about the Bloodthieves, isn't it?" Jisenna turned her shoulders to face him more fully. "Alverax, I swear to you as Empress of Felia, with my heart uncovered for the Heralds to see, that anything you tell me now will bring no judgment upon you. We all make mistakes. Your past only defines a single trodden path, but who you are here, and now, in this very moment, is another path filled with infinite possibility. I don't want to know who you were so that I can judge you. I want to know who you were so I can understand you."

He wanted to...he wanted to so badly.

Her lips parted, and her eyes softened. "Alverax."

The persistence that should have been infuriating was a warm invitation. "I've trusted the wrong people too many times, and I just—"

"There's nothing to be—"

"I know. I know. I'm in my own head," he said. "You're honestly one of the kindest, most good-hearted people I've ever known. When I look at you, it feels like threadlight is burning through my veins. I know that I should trust you, but Jisenna, you're the *empress*. That terrifies me."

She lifted the crown off her head and placed it beside her. "Today, I'm not the empress. Today, I'm just a girl hoping that a boy will trust her as much as she trusts him."

Her voice, calm yet absolute, felt like springtime to his wintered mind. This was the real her. Free of her crown. Free of her duties. One on one, overflowing with empathy for those she cared about. She may now be the Sun Queen, but she was still the Mistress of Mercy.

They locked eyes and he spoke. "I do trust you."

"Then let's start from the beginning," she suggested.

Alverax nodded to himself and took a deep, steadying breath. "I guess the first thing you should know is that I've never met my mother. Back then, my father used to leave home for months at a time and come back with stories that no one fully believed. But he always brought trinkets and treasures that lent some bit of credibility. Once, he left for a whole year, and, when he returned, he returned with me. Met a woman in a small village, fell in love, and a short time later I was born. But she died in childbirth, and he brought me home."

"That's horrible," she said.

"There have been times when I wish I'd known her. My grandfather helped raise me while my father continued on his trips. That's when he started working for Jelium."

"Who is Jelium?"

Alverax pursed his lips. "He's the ruler of Cynosure."

"Hold on," she said, waving her hands. "You are from *Cynosure*?"

He nodded.

"Watchlord Osinan will want to know all about that!" she said with excitement. "Our spies have told us all about the little commune of criminals."

"Little?" Alverax cut in. "I wouldn't call twenty thousand *little*."

Jisenna's brows perked. "Twenty thousand? We were told two thousand at most. They said it was 'nothing to worry about.'"

"Twenty thousand, at least. You might want to check the back pocket of your *spies*."

She paused, thoughtfully. "I'm sorry I diverted us. You were saying... about your father?"

"He started working for Jelium, one of the Amber threadweavers who rules Cynosure."

"An Amber threadweaver?" she said with a pinch of fear in her tone. "Is he dangerous?"

"Only if you're a slab of meat," he said with a smirk. "The man's a human sandhog. Mean, tough, and fat."

She paused, opened her mouth as if to respond, then furrowed her brow. "You're better than that."

"What?"

"Mocking others' appearance is the lowest form of humor. If a man is cruel, speak of his cruelty. If a man is vain, speak of his vanity. Physicality plays no part in the morality of men."

"Oh, come on," he replied. "He is a horrible person. Heralds, he killed my father! I'm not allowed to mock him?"

"I've seen your wit, Alverax Blightwood. If you're going to mock him, pay full price. You debase yourself with such discounted humor."

"Where I come from people think it's funny."

"I don't doubt that," she said flatly. "But you and I walk a different path than most, and it will require us to change in uncomfortable ways."

Her words stung, because they were true. If he wanted to make a difference in the world, he had to become something more than what he was in Cynosure. Something more than what he was in that very moment. And with Jisenna there next to him, he thought that he just might be able to do it.

"You're right," he replied.

"What was that?" she said with a smile. "I'm not certain I heard you."

"Let me try again," he said, rolling his eyes. "O great Lady of Light, your words are brilliant rays, illuminating the shadowed recesses of my soul. And now I, a humble sinner, humbly come before you to shower your feet with humble tears. The humblest of tears. So humble. Humbleness of the like this world has never seen. Such humility that the ocean of my tears will cause your toes to wrinkle in their humble tide. A humility of such grandeur that—"

"Okay, okay," she said laughing.

Before he could continue, a knock came at the door followed by the entry of one of her black-clothed guards. "Empress," he said with urgency.

She rose to her feet. "What is it?"

"Smoke signals are rising from the watchtowers," he said, glancing at Alverax. "Empress, we are under attack."

Stones of Light

26

Alverax followed Jisenna to a balcony overlooking the whole of Felia. The sweeping landscape nearly filled the view from horizon to horizon, the high walls of the city proper looming over the tiny homes along the perimeter. To the east, smoke plumed up in billowy clouds from a signal fire in the guard tower.

"What is happening?" Jisenna asked.

Watchlord Osinan, hand on the hilt of his sword, scowled when he saw Alverax. "There is an enemy at our walls."

Jisenna lifted her chin. "Are we prepared for something like this? Surely, they can't get past our defenses."

"The walls are sturdy, Empress," Osinan said, "but they are not impenetrable. Our nation has not seen war for many years, and time is an erosive substance. For now, we must wait for messengers to bring us word. I've sent the generals to lead on the front lines."

As they looked out over the city, two more towers lit their warning fires.

The doors pushed open and the first messenger arrived, panting and sweaty from his journey. "Watchlord," the messenger said gruffly. "Empress."

"Quickly, now," Osinan said. "What is happening?"

"We're not sure, sir."

"What the hell does that mean? You came all the way here to tell us that you're not sure?" Osinan's eyes were bright as the warning flames.

"Sir, the enemy is invisible."

"What?"

"If I had not been there myself, I would not believe it. An entire army of invisible beasts. Well, not entirely invisible, sir. Our threadweavers can see them in threadlight. And some are as large as a house."

Osinan's lip quivered. "Heralds, save us. It cannot be."

Jisenna stepped forward. "What is it, Osinan?"

"If it is true..."

"Osinan," Jisenna commanded. "Tell us what you know."

The elderly Watchlord looked worried. His thumb rubbed at the hilt of his blade. "Within the Hallowed Library, the Anathema contains our oldest texts. Many are deemed heretical, but it is a duty of the Watchlords to know even the darkest parts of our religion. These texts speak of times long past, when the Heralds still walked the earth.

"There are records from this time of a scourge covering the land, beasts that destroyed everything in their wake. But the Heralds protected the people, casting the creatures back to their dark home. These beasts could only be seen in threadlight, and some could not be killed by mortal blade. Were it not for the Heralds, the creatures would have ended mankind.

"They were called corespawn, and, if the creatures at our walls are the same creatures from the texts, then we are in grave danger."

The words bounced around in Alverax's skull like razors, cutting away at his memories and butchering his understanding. Invisible creatures only able to be seen in threadlight. It had to be...

Jisenna shook her head. "How have I never heard of these corespawn?"

"They are heretical texts, locked away in our vaults," Osinan replied. "Most of them have little or no evidence to their truthfulness, or they contain information that we know to be false, but we keep them for the preservation of our people."

"Jisenna," Alverax cut in. "Your sister...I think it was a corespawn."

She turned to Osinan, her eyes growing wide. "Didn't one of your guards say they saw an anomaly of threadlight?"

"It is possible," Osinan said, his eyes growing thin. "But none of the other threadweavers saw the creature."

Alverax recalled the moment. Graceful dancers spun in unison through his mind, sweeping over the marble floor. Empress Chailani conversed with a group of Felian nobles, and Alverax watched as he approached. He'd been nervous to speak to her, but knew he needed to if he wanted to help the Zeda people settle into Felia. He'd let threadlight enter his veins to calm him. And that's when he'd seen the creature. A spindly monster of pure light, blazing in a dark room, reaching toward the empress, and thrusting its tail into her chest. Alverax had run toward her—how could no one else see it? He reached out with his threadlight toward the creature to *break* its corethread, anything to protect her. But as soon as he'd reached it, and pressed against it with his Obsidian power, the creature had burst apart.

"I killed it," Alverax said in realization. "I tried to *break* it like a thread, and it exploded. I...I thought it vanished somehow—or maybe I was crazy and it was never there—but I remember. I reached out to it like any other thread, and it *broke*."

Watchlord Osinan eyed him suspiciously, his hand still resting on his blade. "It is possible. It would explain why the Heralds valued the Obsidians so highly."

"The Heralds are with us," Jisenna said. She turned to Alverax. "Can't you see it? The only Obsidian in the world shows up in our city just before an enemy arrives that only he can defeat. The Heralds might as well be walking our streets for how closely they are watching over us."

Osinan pulled his sword out of its sheath, the moon reflecting across the all-black blade. "This sword is called the Midnight Watcher," he said. "It has been passed down from Watchlord to Watchlord for centuries, ever since the departure of the Heralds. It is no ordinary blade. From cross-guard to point, it is hewn of a unique obsidian material that can pierce through threads. It was once used to slay corespawn alongside the Heralds. Alverax, I still do not trust you completely, but even I cannot deny that the people of Felia need you. If the corespawn are here, it is my duty—and your heritage—to end their assault." He reached out a hand. "Will you join me?"

Alverax stared for a moment, incredulous. This was it. The Heralds had saved him that day when he'd awoken in the pit of bones. They'd saved him from the death that every other failed experiment had suffered. For this. So that he could protect the people of Felia. He had never been a religious person, but, in that moment, he was certain that the Heralds had played their hand.

"I will," Alverax replied, grasping the Watchlord's hand.

Osinan sheathed the Midnight Watcher and untangled one of the golden tassels dangling near his shoulder before allowing a hint of a smile to cross his lips. "Then we fight."

As they exited the Sun Palace, a retinue of guards and horses awaited them. They rode for what seemed an eternity as the distant smoke signals continued to rise into the night sky. The closer they came, the louder the commotion at the walls. Screaming and shouting intermixed with the foul cries of their invisible enemy. Alverax felt his heart quicken and his hands tremble knowing the danger that awaited them, but, if he could save even a few, all the fear in the world would have been worth it.

They rounded the edge of a large building with a geodesic dome roof and came into view of the carnage. A Felian guard crawled along the dirt, half of his leg missing, the other half tattered and bloody. They rode past him without hesitation. High above on the wall-walk, men and women flailed their blades in chaotic strokes, swatting at an enemy they could not see.

Alverax jumped down from his horse and let threadlight pour through his veins. A warm tingle flowed from his chest out through his arms and legs, filling his body with warmth and energy, but his eyes filled with dread. As threadlight blossomed in his vision, hundreds of creatures came into view, each a different shape and size, but all formed of a brilliant, pulsing light. His eyes grew in horror as he looked up and saw more and more of the corespawn lifting themselves over the top of the wall, overwhelming what was left of the guards.

His fear faded to anger, and his anger swelled, until his black eyes saw nothing but red. But he was too focused on the wall and didn't see the corespawn dashing at him until it was mid-flight, pouncing toward him. He pulled back, flinching at the sudden movement in his vision. Just before it reached him, the corespawn exploded into a cloud of threadlight as the Midnight Watcher cut through its spindly body.

"Careful, boy," Osinan warned, his eyes blazing with Emerald threadlight. "If you can truly kill them, it is time for you to go to work."

Alverax nodded, planted his feet firm into the dirt, and searched out the closest corespawn. A small, skittering creature darted back and forth across the field of grass, frantically searching out its next victim. Alverax focused on it, gathered his energy, and directed it toward the creature just as he would to *break* its corethread. He felt a mild resistance, like a knife cutting through bread, and then gasped as the creature screeched and burst apart, as though it had exploded from within.

Watchlord Osinan stopped in his tracks, whipping his head toward the explosion of light. He turned back to Alverax. "Was that you?"

Alverax nodded, incredulously.

"If we survive this, I owe you an apology." The elder Watchlord swung his blade in a circle. "You take the north; I'll take the south."

With that, they split paths and Alverax ran forward, filling himself with wild amounts of threadlight. One by one, he *broke* the creatures, and each time they burst asunder. One corespawn, larger than the others, with long arms that it used to stand upright as it walked, leapt down from the high wall, hitting the ground with a rumble. Alverax grabbed hold of it with his mind and squeezed. The pressure built—he could feel it intensifying—like gripping an orange and knowing that if he just squeezed hard enough the entire fruit would burst. He shouted into the battlefield, every muscle in his body tensing with the effort, until finally the corespawn exploded into misty beads of light.

Alverax dropped his hands to his knees, panting at the exertion. He knew it wasn't wise to threadweave too much—he'd made that mistake in the Fairenwild and nearly killed himself—but he also knew that he was one of the only people who could fight them. He had to. He was willing to give up his life for the Zeda people. Why would he not do the same for the people of Felia?

Suddenly, the ground trembled...then stopped. Alverax looked up just in time to watch the entire outer wall quiver as again the ground quaked. And again. And again. Men and women steadied themselves. Guards fell from the wall-walk, tumbling to their death far below, until finally, with a deafening groan, the outer wall shattered and collapsed. Stone crumbled in upon itself, tumbling down like an avalanche.

Then, between the dust and smoke and debris, Alverax saw a nightmare made manifest. A corespawn twice the height of a home, blazing like the sun itself. It stepped toward the shattered wall and threw its fist once again. Stone blasted through the night sky. A massive tail, like a scorpion's stinger, dragged over rocks and shrubbery.

Heralds save us.

Coming from the southern wall-walk, Watchlord Osinan dashed toward the monstrosity. He leapt up onto one of the crenellations and launched himself in a deathly arc toward the creature with the Midnight Watcher held high overhead.

The creature swung its massive head toward Osinan.

Alverax reached forward with all his strength and lashed out against the creature. Trying to *break* it felt like trying to move a mountain, but he had to try. If not, Osinan would die. The corespawn roared in pain, thrashing its head back and forth as it fought the stranglehold of his Obsidian threadlight. Alverax's body felt ready to burst, his veins swelling and his heart pounding against his ribs.

Watchlord Osinan fell atop the monstrosity's head and slammed the Midnight Watcher through its light-wrought skull. Its tail whipped out with terrible speed, impaling Osinan in the blink of an eye. The old man screamed in pain as the corespawn let out its own deafening roar. Its body succumbed to the combined power of the obsidian blade and Alverax's threadweaving, bursting apart and sending Osinan falling to the ground.

"NO!" Alverax screamed, sprinting forward. He was too slow; there was no way he would make it in time to catch him.

But he didn't have to.

Alverax reached out as he ran, grabbing hold of Osinan's corethread. Then, he *broke* it. Gravity let go of the man, but still his momentum carried him down until he crashed into the ground. Alverax reached him shortly after and held him down until gravity took back hold.

He was still breathing, but blood drooled out from his side where the corespawn's stinger had pierced him.

"They're running away!" someone shouted behind him.

"Heralds be praised!"

Threadweavers cheered while achromats cowered in disbelief, unable to trust what they could not see for themselves.

Alverax looked up from Osinan, and surveyed the battlefield, taking in the destruction to the wall and the hundreds dead along its perimeter. They were right...the enemy was retreating. Alverax assumed it was because they'd killed the largest of the corespawn, or perhaps they retreated to regather their numbers. But, either way, he had a feeling they would be back.

27

The sun, barely over the Everstone Mountains, cast long shadows as Laurel traveled west. After sneaking out of Endin Keep, they'd rode in silence for the entirety of the day, looking over their shoulders, worried about who may be pursuing them. When they reached the small town of Feldspar, the only trouble they'd had was Laurel's ass burning like a bonfire. She decided, quite handily, that horses were less fun to ride than she'd been made to believe.

In Feldspar, they purchased two carriages to take them on the journey west. The sun had long fallen, and they sat in silence, heads bobbing as the carriage raced away from the grounder capital. Part of Laurel wanted to stay, to fight, but what could she do? And she hoped that their final destination was where her family would be.

The second carriage was occupied by Sarla and Barrick, whose snoring could be heard from the moon. Across from Laurel in their own, Alabella sat upright, her elbow leaning against a small armrest. She scratched at her forearm as she stared out of the open window. The lush Alchean countryside, filled with sprawling viridian plains and fruit trees in all their variety, seemed to roll by more slowly than it should have.

Pity, though try as she might to deny it, crept its pearly tendrils into Laurel's heart. In no way was Alabella an innocent woman—her crimes were as plentiful as the stars in the sky—but the weight of it burdened her. When she looked closely, she thought she saw a hint of Amber in the veins on the back of Alabella's hand. Laurel imagined the soothing effects of threadlight and yearned for it herself. But they'd given all their supply to the Alcheans—except for a single remaining vial that Laurel kept hidden in her pocket.

Alabella closed the window, then turned her head slowly until she was fully facing Laurel. "All I ever wanted was to make the world better," she said, mostly to herself. "And we were so close. Just a few more days and we could have returned to the coreseal. We'd have an endless supply of infused gemstones. We could have offered threadlight to everyone." She paused. "Did I ever tell you about how I became a threadweaver?"

Laurel shook her head, and, though she had hoped to keep quiet, she *was* curious.

"I was born in Felia. My mother had too many men to name a father, so we lived alone. She beat me from the time I was very young. Four, maybe? She said our misfortune was my fault. If I had been born a threadweaver, we wouldn't have to suffer like we did. If I had been born a threadweaver, the empress would provide for us. If only I had been a threadweaver...When I was twelve, she died of an infection, and I was all alone. I fell in with some people who saw the value of an unexceptional girl, one who no one would give a second glance to.

"Our little group thrived. Once we even conned the Farrows—a powerful Felian family—out of ten thousand shines. Our leader, a boy called Pai, found out about a section of the Hallowed Library called the Anathema, filled with treasures. We planned it all out—Pai and I would be the ones to break in—but the place was much different than what we'd been told.

"It wasn't filled with treasure, but old books. Not a single shine in sight. I opened a few of the books—we thought they might be worth something—and since Pai couldn't read, it was up to me to decide which books we should take. One of them had an image of a man lying on a table with one of the Heralds standing over him, placing a stone near his heart. A girl walked in the room, blonde like yourself. After her shock at seeing us there, she pushed Pai aside and stabbed me in the chest.

"I woke up in a prison cell, surprised to be alive, and even more surprised to find threadlight in my veins. Somehow, I'd become an Amber threadweaver. It wasn't hard to break out from there. But I couldn't stop thinking about that image, especially with what happened to me. So eventually, I made my way back to the Anathema and stole a few of the books. That's where I learned about theoliths and the coreseal. And that's when I made it my mission to bring threadlight to everyone."

Laurel was completely entranced by the woman's words. "How did you end up in Cynosure?"

Alabella laughed. "My friends...well, that's a story for another time. The point is...my dream is dying, and watching a dream die is the cruelest form of torture."

The carriage slammed to a halt, nearly knocking them out of their seats. Laurel grabbed onto the windowsill for balance. Once they'd settled, Alabella opened the door but it slammed back shut.

"Stay inside and keep quiet," the driver whispered with urgency. "Stones, but I thought they'd be gone by now. They killed a whole caravan just the other day."

"We are in a hurry," Alabella said as she kicked the door open. "Come, Laurel. Let's teach these thugs a lesson in civility."

Laurel nodded and followed her out of the carriage. The bright sun warmed her skin as she surveyed her surroundings, but there were no bandits in sight. To the south, fields of endless grass. To the west, open road as far as the eye could see. And to the north, nothing but a field of pear trees. She thought, if she caught the right angle between trees, she could see the edge of the Fairenwild in the distant northern horizon.

"I don't see anything," she said.

"You shouldn't be out here," the driver said.

Alabella ignored him. "Where are they?"

The carriage driver pointed toward the pear trees. "I seen 'em hiding behind the trees up ahead. No idea how many. Blend into the grass, they do."

Laurel rubbed at her arm with a shaky hand. She felt jittery, like a child who refused to stay still. It didn't help that there was a slight wind that chilled her arms. She looked back down the road from where they'd come, expecting an army to appear at any moment. They needed to keep moving, and if some thugs thought they could slow them down, then the Gale could take them all.

Alabella and the driver turned to her just as she pulled out the obsidian blade and took off at a sprint toward the field of trees. Behind her, the driver shouted something, but she ignored it. When she reached the orchard, she hid behind the closest pear tree, which was plenty wide to hide her thin frame. Adrenaline pumped through her veins, a weak substitute for threadlight.

Laurel crept forward, tree by tree, staying low in the overgrown grass. A light breeze danced between the leaves, causing branches to quiver and dandelions to take flight. She peeked around the thick trunk of a pear tree and thought she saw movement up ahead, hidden within the grass. She'd expected to find the bandits partially obscured behind the trees, but they were smarter, hiding on their stomachs in the underbrush.

She mimicked their stealth and dropped to her hands and knees. Dirt slid beneath her fingernails. Long strands of green grass swept across her pale skin. She held the obsidian blade as she bear-crawled through the brush, the tips of her toes pressing deep into the soil.

There was a rustling up ahead.

Something deep inside her flared to life, and she rolled to the side just before a massive body came barreling through the grass, pouncing where she had just been. Her heart pounded and adrenaline raged. As she rolled back to a steady position, she turned to see a massive creature. Green fur blurred into the surrounding grass, white strands blew in the breeze, and, far behind it, two tails danced back and forth with fervor.

Fear began to sink its teeth into her racing mind as the chromawolf turned to bare its yellow fangs. Step by step, she moved back, keeping her eye on the chromawolf's movement. Her offhand reached up toward the transfuser in her breast pocket. She was going to die, and she knew the drug wouldn't help.

Behind the chromawolf, green-furred heads rose through the grass as the rest of the pack joined their brother. Laurel's heart pounded against her ribs. There were so many, a dozen at least. She needed Alabella.

From the back, a final head rose through the grass. Green fur with a strand of white running near its left ear. Twin tails danced up over its head. As it saw her, its eyes lit up like two crescent moons grown full.

"Asher!" Laurel said with a smile as wide as a feytree.

Asher stepped forward, barking and howling as he passed the others, then launched himself toward her in a burst of joyous energy. They tumbled over dirt and grass, wrestling like children, growling at each other and swiping with playful paws. When they finally came to rest, Laurel on her back with Asher standing over her, the tone shifted. Asher whipped his head to the side and snarled.

"Laurel," Alabella's calm voice spoke, dragging out each syllable.

"There is at least a dozen more behind you. Roll to the side, I can *yolk* it, then you run. On my count."

Laurel lifted her head to see Alabella standing a short distance away with her palms outstretched.

"One—"

Asher snarled.

"Two—"

"No!" Laurel shouted. "Asher's my friend!"

Alabella stood with a wide stance, brows furrowed in confusion.

Laurel lifted herself up and rubbed Asher's fur. The other chromawolves lay spread across the orchard, some still crouched beneath the tall grass, and others standing tall, ready to defend their leader. "Asher's my friend. He won't hurt us. Will you?"

Asher nuzzled her shoulder. She was certain he'd grown even in the short time they'd been apart.

"And the others?" Alabella asked warily.

"He won't let them hurt us." Laurel reached forward and hugged the chromawolf's neck. "I've missed you, big guy." A happy growl rumbled from its chest. "I saw what happened at the Fairenwild. Then the corespawn. We both lost our home. Asher, I'm so sorry." She looked into his eyes and rubbed the top of his head. "I wish we'd never parted ways. From here on out, it's you and me, no matter what."

Asher pulled back and looked into her eyes, unblinking, knowing. He lowered himself and brought his forehead to hers. She could feel his warmth as they pressed their minds together. And then she felt something curious. A single spark burning inside her. Growing. Roaring to life until it raged like a bonfire. Asher howled and his eyes glowed white with hints of green reflecting from his fur. The pain struck, and Laurel howled too. She felt flames inside her escaping through her skin. Heat beyond reason.

The world seemed to shift around her. Distance shortened. Colors shifted. She could hear the leaves shuffling beneath Alabella's feet. She could taste the musk of the chromawolves upwind. She felt her veins expanding.

"Laurel," Alabella said, still wary of the other chromawolves. "Are you okay? What's happening?"

Her mind swirled like a whirlwind, blurring and twirling in chaotic disarray. Her eyes burned like never before until a single spot of darkness began to spread like oil over her heightened vision. The world grew darker. Trees faded away. Chromawolves vanished. And finally, as new energy charged through her body, the darkness filled the final vacancy in her mind, and she collapsed to the earth.

Stones of Light

28

WHEN CHRYS AWOKE, he felt...different.

Where once a fog clouded his mind, now there was nothing but clarity. He felt more alert than he had in years. It was as though a veil had lifted, and the storm clouds had given way to a flawless sky.

He put a hand down to push himself to a sitting position and gasped as the realization hit him. It couldn't be. It was impossible. He was dreaming. Even still, tears formed. Where once there were only seven, again there were ten. He looked down at his hand to confirm and swelled with emotion while his newly regrown fingers wriggled back and forth.

"Chrys?"

He turned and found his mother rising from the rose-colored table where the old man and Roshaw sat. She gestured for him to join them. "I'm sure you have questions," she said with a knowing smile.

"I—" he paused, lifting his hand and inspecting it. "This is a dream, right?"

"It's not," she said, smiling and nodding to the old man. "He healed you. The golden water has kept him alive for hundreds of years, and today it kept you alive...and some."

Chrys turned his eyes to the pool, golden light shimmering across the surface and emanating into the cavern. It called to him, *drawing him in*, beckoning him to bathe in its warmth. When Chrys turned his eyes back to the table, he saw the old man...or the man who *had* been old. His eyes swirled with colors, and his face, though still pale and wrinkled, seemed to have shaved off a dozen years.

"Why don't you have a seat, Chrysanthemum," the old man said with a grin. "Willow, would you and Roshaw go see if you can find a box in the storage room containing a collection of talismans? Each should have an engraving of four circles knotted together within a gemstone. We'll need three of them."

Willow nodded and led Roshaw away.

He turned back to Chrys. "While you were recovering, your mother shared with me your story. It is a tragedy, I must admit, but the ending is yet to be written. And that is where we must focus. Relek and Lylax have caused you to sacrifice so much already, and I worry that what comes next will bring even more. Though I tried to dissuade him, my siblings *will* take power once again. Chrys, if you are to stop them, you must understand the dark power they possess. What do you know of the source of your power as a threadweaver?"

Chrys tried to breathe steadily, but every time the old man spoke of his siblings, Chrys' heart raced within his chest. "They say it is a gift from the Lightfather."

"Perhaps, if there is a god, he does play a part in the selection, but the source is different. Chrys, embedded within your chest, in the center of your heart, is a sliver of a gemstone. This stone absorbs energy from the realm of threadlight, and, when you release it, that energy flows through your veins and gives you power. We call this gemstone a theolith, and it is the only thing that makes you a threadweaver. Without it, your eyes would fade to brown and you would be powerless.

"Over time, my siblings and I discovered this truth, and, with the aid of the healing elixir, we embedded within our hearts each of the four gemstones, giving us the power of all of them. Open yourself to threadlight and see for yourself."

Chrys let threadlight pour through his veins, feeling the warmth in his chest, and wondering at the truth of the words. The old man lifted his hand and *pushed* a cup across the table. It slid, scraping over the rose-colored stone and, just before it reached the edge, he *pulled,* and it slid back to his hand. Then, he picked it up and held it in the air. In the blink of an eye, the cup's thread *broke*, shattering into a hundred beads of light. He let go, and the cup floated gracefully in the air. He *created* four threads that latched onto the cup and sent it tumbling back to the table.

"Such a display is silly, surely. But I'm certain you can understand the implications." The old man tipped the cup over and let the water spill across the rosy surface. "What happened next, we did not expect. Once all four gemstones enter a heart, they fuse together into a singular structure, and a subtle change occurs. Not only could we see and manipulate threadlight, but we could suddenly see something else. A flickering spark of red energy in the center of a man's heart. At first, we thought it was a theolith, but we realized it was something else entirely. And so, we called it *lifelight*."

Seeing Chrys' confusion, the old man continued. "My brother was the first to discover that we could both see *and* manipulate lifelight, though I refuse to participate in the latter. You see, my siblings and I held the secret of the pool to ourselves, but our immortality was bound to it. Relek discovered that he could create a connection between his own lifelight and the lifelight of another. His own mortality became tied to theirs. From then on, their life drained into him. He no longer aged. When he would be killed, one of the others would die in his place. And then, he discovered that he could transfer his own lifelight into the body of another, which is what you experienced. And so, his own immortality was no longer tied to the pool.

"I tried to stop them, but they would not listen. They left the cavern for good and became gods among men, with thousands of souls bound to each. They discovered that binding a threadweaver allowed them to siphon their powers, and so their threadweaving became unparalleled. They used the elixir from the pool to create more and more threadweavers, binding their lifelight and expanding their own strength. There was no end to their greed, until their own followers saw the darkness.

"A group of Amber threadweavers banded together, tricking Relek and Lylax to return to this very place. They combined their powers, using knowledge my siblings had mercifully given them, and sacrificed their own lives to create a web of threads that sealed the core of the earth from the surface world. But Relek was not beneath the surface at the time as they'd thought. He was with the wastelanders, wearing one of their own's skin so that they would bind their lifelight to him. But when the seal was created, he was stuck in the wastelander body with no way to return here.

"What you must understand is that the wastelanders have a crippling mutation. They cannot survive without the elixir. A pool above ground contains trace amounts of it and allows the wastelanders to survive, so long as they drink from it often. If they do not, they die. And so, both of my siblings were trapped. One with me. The other, with a people who cannot leave their home.

"And that, my young friend, is the crux of our story. All building to the conclusion that you cannot kill my siblings."

"We can't kill them," Chrys repeated.

"Unfortunately, no. And they came down not long ago, so their human bodies are once again hybrid threadweavers, able to manipulate lifelight."

Chrys leaned forward cross the table. "I refuse to accept that they cannot die."

"Accept it or not," the old man replied. "Truth is not dependent on your acceptance of it. But that does not mean that there is nothing we can do. The group of Amber threadweavers bound my sister once before; we could do it again. Willow says there are two Amber threadweavers. A woman and your son. You must bring them to me. With their power we can bind my siblings beneath the earth again. Perhaps not permanently, but long enough. When a generation has passed, and the lives of all those bound to them have ended—"

The old man trailed off for a moment, his prismatic eyes drifting to the stalactites high overhead. Chrys thought he saw, hidden in the bags under the old man's eyes, a tear forming.

"—I will kill them," the old man said faintly. "Chrys, your child is the key. You must protect it. My siblings are wise, and they will not be so easily tricked a second time. If they find your child, they will not allow it to live."

A storm raged within Chrys. A storm swirling with rage and purpose. A storm that called him to action. Lightning crackled in his veins. Thunder pounded in his chest. If the immortal gods of the wastelands conspired to take away his son, then he would be there waiting, life or death.

"That is not the only way," Chrys said. "If every person bound to them were to die, then they would be vulnerable."

"My siblings have bound every living wastelander. Would you slaughter an entire race?"

"For my family, I would consider anything."

The old man hesitated. "If that is true, then you are no better than they are."

"I said I would *consider* it," Chrys said with a fire in his eyes. "Obviously, we will move forward with your plan. Bring the Amber threadweavers and use their power to bind Relek and Lylax beneath the earth. Then you kill them."

The old man eyed Chrys warily. "Your mother and Roshaw are already in agreement, which means that we are ready for the first step in the plan."

"What is that?"

The old man held up two slivers of gemstone, one green, one black. "It is time for one to become three."

29

Alverax stood in a cramped room, watching as physicians and nurses attended to Watchlord Osinan. They'd stitched the wound, but the stinger had poisoned his blood. One of the physicians believed that the introduction of foreign threadlight from the corespawn had attacked the threadlight already in his veins, causing them to bulge beneath his dark skin.

There was nothing they could do...Osinan was dying.

Empress Jisenna sat on a stool beside the bed, holding the older man's hand. The two of them had a long history together, and, by the way she leaned into him, Alverax knew just how much she cared for the man. He wasn't family, but he was the closest thing she had left.

Outside the room, Alverax spotted Rastalin Farrow, whom he'd met at the masquerade. The man leaned against the wall with a self-satisfied look that made Alverax want to punch him in the face, but Rastalin was first in line to become the new Watchlord when Osinan passed, and Alverax knew not to slap a happy hog.

"Clear the room," Osinan said, coughing and wincing at the pain. "Clear the room, please."

Jisenna turned and nodded to the others. Alverax followed the physicians and nurses toward the exit.

"No," Osinan said with a growl. "Alverax, stay."

At the sound of his name, Alverax turned and raised his brows. Osinan nodded and Jisenna gestured for him to pull a stool beside her. He did.

Osinan pushed himself to a sitting position, wheezing and moaning as his stitches pulled at his side. Jisenna moved to help and he brushed her away. "The only thing that frightens me about death is that I'll no longer be able to help those in need."

"Don't say that, Osinan," Jisenna said. "We'll find a way to heal you."

"Sun Daughter," he said, smiling at her like a father smiles at his child. "It's not weakness to embrace the inevitable. What matters most is what you do next. In this case, there is little more I can do. Alverax, would you please bring me my blade?"

Alverax lifted the sheathed sword off of the ground beneath the bed and laid it across Osinan's lap. The Watchlord placed his hands atop the sheath and moved his hand down its length. The image reminded Alverax of stories he'd heard as a child of mighty warriors being buried with their blades. Seeing Osinan's reverence toward the weapon brought those stories to life just a little more.

"Do you know how long I have been Watchlord?" Osinan asked. "Twenty-eight years, before either of you were born. The previous Watchlord passed away unexpectedly, leaving me a long letter detailing the true duties of the office. I wrote a similar letter many years ago. Publicly, we preach that a Watchlord is to prepare for the return of the Heralds, guiding the people so that they might make of themselves a righteous offering to our gods. The truth is that the Heralds are not going to return. We say they left to prepare the afterlife for the righteous, but we don't truly know why they left. One day they were simply gone, and never returned."

Jisenna grew pale, her eyes wide as she shook her head back and forth. "Don't say such things, Osinan."

"Just by speaking them I feel a weight lifted." He closed his eyes for a moment and breathed. "The priests would have me slain if I spoke the truth in their presence. They only know what the Watchlords of the past have told them, which is what the people needed. Hope, Jisenna. The world needs hope, and the truth is often at odds. So, for the greater good, we lie, and we say that the world is one way when it is in fact another. But when it brings them hope and gives them reason to live a good life, we pat ourselves on the shoulder. Perhaps, over time, we even begin to believe the lies ourselves, because hope is sweet, and the truth can be quite bitter."

"Why?" Jisenna whimpered. "Why are you saying this?"

Alverax shifted on his stool, staring at the ground as he listened to the dying man. He recalled the many years sitting together with his grandfather, while his guardian taught him about the Heralds, that one day they would return and, if Alverax was a good boy, the Heralds would take him into their fold. He hadn't questioned the words until after his father was killed, something about the loss had cracked the façade. He'd spoken their name out of habit—*Heralds, save us*—but never in true prayer.

"Everyone!" Osinan shouted, a firm resolution in his voice. "Please, come back in! I have an announcement I would like to make!" He smiled and slumped back against the wall.

"Please," Jisenna said. "You cannot say these things to them. It would break our nation."

Osinan turned to her. "Felia needs hope now more than ever. Do not worry, Sun Daughter."

The physicians and nurses entered first, followed by a drove of men and women in noble regalia, including the ever-stately Santara and Rastalin Farrow. They filed in reverently, awaiting the words of the man whom they exalted above all others, their proxy for the Heralds themselves. Only Alverax and Jisenna knew the truth, that his celestial calling was drafted of men.

As they settled in, Alverax faded away to the side of the room so that he would not block the others' view. The black and gold of the Watchlord's deific robes flickered in the lamplight. The sword remained draped across his lap as he began his final sermon.

"At a young age, we speak the sacrificial oath: my life for yours. I have done my best to offer my life in service to the Heralds, in preparation for their inevitable return." His eyes moved confidently from one attendee to the next. "Our world is changing. The corespawn have returned, but the Heralds have not left us defenseless. It is no coincidence that an Obsidian threadweaver has found his way to our city in our time of need. It is a sign that the Heralds are pleased with us. It is a sign that their return draws near.

"It is with this knowledge that I share an announcement, born from the very heritage I symbolize. The first Watchlord was an Obsidian, and so shall it be again."

Eyes, like the sharpest of blades, turned on startled hinges toward Alverax. His heart raced in his chest, and his hands trembled at his side.

"Alverax Blightwood, son of Felia, I solemnly bestow upon you all of the rights and honors associated with the office of Watchlord, and declare you now the Highest Servant, He-Who-Watches-The-Sky, the Surrogate of the Heralds themselves."

His chest burned inside of him, constricting and coiling like a snake stuck in a furnace. It was a dream. It was a mistake. Alverax was the son of a thief, not the Surrogate of the Heralds.

Osinan gestured to the sword on his lap. "Take it, son. The Midnight Watcher is yours. The protection of these people rests in your hands now. You have been preserved and you have been prepared. One day you will see this."

Santara Farrow, filled with indignation, huffed at the words. "This is absurd. Tradition is clear, the office must pass to the next in line, chosen by the council."

"It *is* rather unusual," another man said.

Rastalin, unable to contain himself any longer, spat as he shouted. "The boy was nearly executed days ago and now he is to be Watchlord? It reeks of conspiracy, and the people will see that. Such an accusation, true or not, would endanger our peace in a very delicate time."

"It *does* seem rather odd," another said.

Rastalin continued, gaining confidence with each word he spoke. "I suggest we delay the transference of power until after we have dealt with the invasion."

"For the safety of the people," his wife added.

Osinan scowled and tried to push himself to a fully upright position, but he failed, groaning and gripping at his side. "The people will trust my judgment."

"The people will see a dying man," Rastalin replied. "A man whose mind is warped by a seditious poison from our enemy. How could they trust the judgment of one under the influence of our adversary?"

"Under the influence..." Osinan began, his voice rising.

"Enough!" Jisenna said. "Rastalin, you have made your point. Could you, in good conscience, tell everyone in this room that Osinan is 'under the influence of our adversary'?"

Rastalin's eyes darted back and forth across the room, teeth grinding between pursed lips.

"Then as your empress, I expect you to relay your confidence and endorsement to any people who may express doubt of the decision made this day."

His eyes burned with fury, and Jisenna met his gaze with her own.

"Good," Jisenna concluded. "Alverax, I believe your sword awaits you."

Alverax moved forward, hesitation guiding his steps. Every eye watched his movement, judging him, weighing his worthiness, and he knew he could never live up to their expectations. But even as he doubted, he reached the edge of the bed and stared down at the sheathed blade.

Osinan spoke quietly, lifting it toward him. "People will see the clothing, they will see the sword, and then they will see your eyes. They *will* accept you, if you will accept yourself."

The room grew silent.

Alverax reached his hand forward and grasped the hilt of the Midnight Watcher.

THAT EVENING, former Watchlord Osinan passed away in his sleep, smiling while the Empress of Felia slept beside him.

30 · Stones of Light

"Ahhhh!" Roshaw screamed as the old man stabbed him in the heart for a third time. He writhed in pain until Chrys poured a pitcher of the healing water over the wound. As soon as it touched the broken flesh, new skin grew over and the wound closed. Roshaw dropped his head back onto a dense pillow.

Since crossing the mountains into the wastelands, there was one word that had evaded Chrys completely: hope. Even their plan to escape had held a feeling of unlikelihood that he'd merely brushed aside. But now, everything was different.

He let threadlight pour through his veins and marveled at the change. Where once his veins had lit with a piercing blue, like the hottest flame of a smith's fire, now they swirled with blue, green, and black. Three of the four theolith variants. Unfortunately, Lylax had purged all of the Amber theoliths they'd discovered over the years, though the old man knew she kept a few somewhere; he just didn't know where.

Another sleeveless arm came up beside his own, veins matching in their chaotic dance of multi-colored threadlight. "Hard to believe it's real," Willow said.

Chrys nodded, but his mind wandered to his son and the Amber in his veins. Somewhere, he was with Iriel. He wondered where they were, and what they were doing. Willow claimed that Zedalum had been destroyed, which meant that, if Iriel and Aydin were alive, they would have headed west toward Felia. It was on the other side of the continent. Weeks journey even were they above ground. But the old man claimed to have a way to expedite the journey. If it meant finding his wife and son sooner, he was open to anything.

Chrys turned to the old man, who inspected Roshaw lying on the ground. "Any concerns?"

"No, no," the man replied. "Without the elixir, he would have died. The two of you would likely have survived, since your theolith provides a measure of healing in and of itself. With three theoliths, the healing effects should be magnified now, as with the rest of your abilities."

"How has no one discovered this before?" Willow asked. "Surely, someone would have thought it odd when they saw a rock in someone's heart."

"Ah," the old man said with a smirk. "A theolith is no ordinary rock. When it enters a person's heart, it is bound to the lifelight of that person. If you detach it, or if the person dies, the connection is broken and the theolith crumbles to dust."

"So, you cannot remove a theolith from one person and use it in another?"

"Fortunately, no," said the old man. "If that were possible, I can't imagine the dark things men would do."

Willow shook her head as she stared at the old man. "All these years, we believed threadlight the gift of some unknowable god, when it was simply a stone in the heart."

"It could be both," the old man said.

"*You* believe in a god?"

He shrugged his shoulders. "There is much that it would explain, and many other questions that it would create. What I do know is that we know so very little. We are nine parts ignorance and one part enlightenment, but we grab hold of that little knowledge we have and pretend that it is greater than it is. The man who is ignorant of his own ignorance holds most tightly to his perception of the truth. Unfortunately, I have lived long enough to know just how little I truly know. And, so, I do not claim to know whether there is or is not a god, only that it is certainly possible."

If the past weeks had taught Chrys nothing else, they had taught him just how little he knew of the world, its inhabitants, and its machinations. He'd once thought the wastelanders nothing more than savages, but now he knew more of their story, like their willingness to sacrifice for the greater good. There was a beauty in knowledge—a danger in ignorance—and he hated knowing just how little he knew.

Whether *he* believed in the Lightfather or not, he wasn't sure. He remembered the Zeda elders speaking of *divine providence*, and he wanted to believe it true. But he feared that, even if there was a god, he couldn't trust a being willing to let creatures like Relek and Lylax walk the earth.

Roshaw awoke with a gasp, clutching at his chest and springing to an upright position. "I'm done!" he shouted. "That was three, right? No more? Heralds, please, let that be the last one."

"Heralds—" the old man mumbled.

"I feel," Roshaw continued, "incredible! Willow, Chrys, did you both feel this *light* after? It's almost like..." He looked down and, with multi-colored veins spiraling beneath his skin, he floated in the air just inches above the ground. "I'm flying! Ha! My father—my son—they would never believe this!"

"Careful," Willow said. "If you threadweave too much, you'll get sick."

The old man's eyes lit up. "Actually, you'll find that with three theoliths you are able to threadweave for a longer period, and with a greater intensity."

"Stones," Chrys cursed.

"Indeed," the old man laughed. "Three of them."

WHEN THEY WERE ready to leave the cavern, the old man took them to the supply room and provided them with packs and wide-brimmed hats that he'd made himself. Chrys stared at the hat he held in his hands. The color and the shape held something familiar, a memory of another life, a moment buried in his mind, scratching at the surface. Then it vanished, like a silk handkerchief slipping through his hands.

He stared at it for a moment longer, but the feeling was gone. He placed it on his head and followed the old man as they departed the cavern.

Together, they traveled through a dimly lit tunnel filled with stale air. Water dripped from the ceiling, running off of stalactites and staining the wall with dark streaks. Chrys steeled himself for a long journey, knowing that their destination would be well worth the time. The small tunnels soon grew into massive corridors that seemed more fit for giants than men.

As they progressed, the vast tunnel split into multiple paths. The old man had warned them that corespawn often roamed the same tunnels, but they saw none. Still, Chrys kept threadlight in his veins.

They followed dark paths for hours, reiterating their plan to trap Relek and Lylax below the earth, but spending most of the time in silence. Chrys, Willow, and Roshaw tested their new abilities as they walked, *breaking* threads, *pushing* and *pulling* on rocks. It was disorienting, after so many years, with such an intimate familiarity of the Sapphire ability, to suddenly be able to manipulate threads in new ways. As he practiced *pulling* against the wall and walking along it like a spider, he thought of Reina and his old crew. He wondered if Luther was still drinking away the loss of his son, or if he'd found a more sustainable way to move forward. A part of him yearned for his friends, but not in the same way that he yearned for Iriel and Aydin. His friends were a warm blanket, but his wife was the raging fire. And he was shivering.

"We are almost there," the old man said as they passed over a small bridge spanning a large crevice in the ground.

Roshaw looked down the crevice as he passed over. "Did you make this?"

The old man nodded. "I've explored every corner of this underground world. If we had time, I would show you a lake of molten lava, or gemstones so large a man could live inside if they were hollowed out. There are countless wonders here, but around this bend is one that surpasses them all."

Roshaw jogged ahead, excitedly.

As Chrys rounded the bend himself, he saw Roshaw standing perfectly still, his wide eyes radiant with multi-colored threadlight, gazing out into a sweeping cavern. Chrys stepped forward and a vast dome of prismatic light burst into view, swirling and spinning as bolts of energy broke out across its surface.

"We see the world as a collection of threads, each connecting one small piece to another." The old man settled into position beside Chrys and the others, who all stood in awe, their eyes radiant with threadlight as they took in the spectacular view. "The space between one location and another is a thread of sorts, representing the distance between them.

But, like your corethread when you *push* against it, it is possible to manipulate that connection. This place," he gestured to the dome of energy, "allows you to manipulate space itself."

"Manipulate space?" Roshaw repeated.

The old man smiled, and the wrinkles of his eyes deepened. From his pocket, he pulled out a string and pinched both ends. "Pretend that this string is a road between here and your home. You could walk from here to there." He pulled his finger along the string from one end to the other. "Or you could travel from there to here." He repeated the gesture in the other direction. "But there is another option." Pinching both ends, he slowly brought them together. "Same string. Same connection. Shortened path between the two. Think of this concentration of threadlight in front of you as one end of the string."

Chrys ran a hand through his scruffy beard. "And where is the other end?"

"Ah!" the old man said, waving a finger. "That is the question indeed. It may be hard to distinguish because you are not yet acclimated to your new powers, but did you feel the change in energy as we approached? Can you feel your own threadlight being magnified? From what you have shared with me, I don't believe it is the first time you have been near a place like this. A *convergence*."

The realization shot through Chrys like a surge of lightning. He *had* felt a similar feeling to this. A place where his own threadlight had been magnified, allowing him to reach greater heights than he ever had before. The place where he'd left his wife and son.

"The coreseal," he whispered.

"Indeed."

Chrys stepped forward, connecting pieces of the puzzle. "There is a *convergence* beneath the wonderstone. The Amber threadweavers used the magnified power to create the coreseal and bind you and your sister below the earth."

"That is right," the old man said.

"Stones," Chrys cursed.

Roshaw approached the dome, and the others followed. There was something intoxicating about the warbling mass of threadlight, an invitation, a strange beckoning to enter, to stay and take root. Chrys remembered the feeling when he'd first stepped on the wonderstone—the overwhelming desire to threadweave.

"Thank you," Willow said as she gave the old man a slight bow, "for everything. You could have turned us over to your brother, but instead you chose to help. It is a hard thing to go against your own family."

The old man's eyes seemed to grow more tired. "Yes, it is. But it's a harder thing to betray your own sense of morality."

"Do you think it will work?" she asked.

"If the Ambers can gather at a *convergence*, they should be able to combine their power to create a new binding. Just be sure Relek and Lylax are below the earth before the seal is formed."

All three nodded in unison, an unspoken acceptance of their path. Chrys was filled with purpose. It permeated every piece of his soul. He had a destination. He had a goal. He had a plan. Slowly, he was regaining control of his life and his destiny.

Chrys lunged forward and wrapped the old man in an embrace. "Your sacrifice is going to save countless people. When this is over, the world will know your name."

Roshaw turned to face the old man, a slight blush reddening his cheeks. "I don't actually know what your name *is*."

Chrys opened his mouth to answer but realized that he too did not know the man's name. They both turned to Willow and she shrugged.

"I'm sorry," the old man said. "My manners once again elude me. I am called Alchaeus."

"Alchaeus?" Chrys repeated, emphasizing the word. "As in the Order of Alchaeus?"

"I'm certain I don't know what you mean."

"The Order of Alchaeus! Stones, you even quoted scripture before. Better to see truth than light?"

The old man scratched his head. "I...you must be mistaken. I've not left this place in many centuries."

Willow placed a hand on Chrys' shoulder. "He's not the only man ever to be named Alchaeus. It was common enough before Alchea was established."

"And the quote?" Chrys said.

"A coincidence?"

The only coincidence, Chrys thought, *was the brother of the eastern gods having the same name as the god of the west.*

"Perhaps," Alchaeus said thoughtfully. "Perhaps it is yet...no." He looked down at the string, still pinched at both ends hanging like a bridge between his hands. "You should go. You'll have a head start before my siblings head west. Find the Amber woman. Find your son. Bring them to me. When their powers are amplified by the *convergence*, they should be able to create a seal that will endure."

They offered him a final goodbye and stepped toward the *convergence*. Its influence grew stronger with each step, a drink taunting an addict. His mother took his left hand, squeezing with maternal ferocity.

Together, they stepped into the light.

31

After an evening of being pampered and worshipped and taught the extent of his new duties, Alverax was certain he'd never been more tired in his life. He picked at one of the tassels dangling beneath his arm that had become tangled with the others and walked toward a tent erected not far from the breached wall. He urged the priests following him to remain outside and stepped through the opening. A group of veteran generals examined him as he entered.

A younger general with a well-trimmed goatee stood. "Watchlord," he greeted with a nod of approval.

"Generals," Alverax said, cautiously.

Before the Divine Council could whisk him away, Alverax had spoken with Jisenna. She'd told him what to expect and described dozens of people he would meet—if only he could remember them now. More than anything, she'd explained how respected Osinan had been. The office of Watchlord is first and foremost a religious appointment, but he was also the head of the Felian army. Each Watchlord down the line had balanced the two responsibilities in their own way, and Osinan was renowned for his contributions to both. Alverax would be happy if he lived through the night.

"Please, continue," Alverax added. "I'd like to learn about the plans to protect the city."

"Maybe he can help answer the question we're debating," the same younger man added.

An older man, hunched over in his chair with a scowl, let out a loud harumph.

Alverax nodded. "I'd love to help however I can."

"General Thallin, and these," the younger man said, gesturing to the older generals, "are Generals Nevik, and Hish. I'll speak for all of us when I say congratulations, and we are eager to learn more about you." Each of them was a threadweaver with eyes as hard as they were bright.

Alverax wasn't sure if he should step forward and greet them but, based on their looks, he decided to stay put. "It is nice to meet you."

"The debate," Thallin continued, taking a seat, "is about the effectiveness of using tar to cover the corespawn. We're limited by the number of threadweavers we have, but if we can drench them in some kind of dark substance, they'll be visible to our achromat soldiers as well. General Nevik and I agree that it will work, but General Hish is not convinced that their invisibility is based on the laws of nature. You fought beside Osinan. You've seen them first-hand. What say you?"

All three generals shifted in their seats, curious to hear his response.

"It's a wonderful idea," Alverax said. "Their greatest advantage is their stealth. If we can take that away, then we have the numbers. The problem is that General Hish is right. It won't work."

General Hish perked up.

Alverax continued. "I saw hundreds of corespawn last night of every shape and size, and do you know what I did not see? Dirty feet. If nothing else, their feet would have been covered with dirt and mud. Not to mention the blood. I saw a corespawn bite into a man's chest, and not a drop of blood was in the air where its face would be. If dirt and blood don't stick, I wouldn't bet on tar either."

"Hmm," General Nevik said, pursing his lips. "I will admit that his logic is difficult to dispute."

General Hish nodded. "The evidence is light, but we have no reason to believe otherwise. Besides, even without spending time planning out a way to mark them, we have more preparations than time."

"What else do you have planned?" Alverax asked.

General Nevik stood. "We plan to make them pay. With fire and with alchemy and with our most valuable weapon."

"That sounds promising," Alverax said with interest. "And what is that?"

General Thallin smirked. "You."

As the sun fell, Alverax rose high to the top of a quickly constructed tower near the eastern wall. It overlooked the portion of the wall that had been breached, though they'd hastily rebuilt it as well as they could in a single day. The generals were expecting the corespawn to re-enter from the same route and had built up a series of ambushes for the creatures, the last of which was their very own Obsidian threadweaver.

The young General Thallin accompanied Alverax at the top of the tower as the armies below fell into position. With the sun falling, they expected the assault would come at any moment. They only hoped their preparations would be enough to fend them off while they learned more about the enemy.

A westerly breeze was the only sound as soldiers stood their ground, wielding swords and preparing for what came next. Lines of Sapphire archers stood atop the remaining wall-walk, overlooking the surrounding countryside.

Alverax had always hated silence, but never more so than in that moment. It pricked at his skin like a mosquito, sucking away at his confidence. He knew they'd set him upon the tower as nothing more than an emblem for the soldiers and, no matter how hard he tried to explain that as an Obsidian he could kill the creatures, they still wanted him away from the frontline. A beacon of hope amidst the eerie silence.

"Do you see something?" Thallin asked.

"Huh?" Alverax looked down and noticed that he'd begun to threadweave, his veins pulsing with a dark radiance. "Oh, no. Just keeping warm."

"I'll have the men bring you a blanket."

"No, no. It's really okay."

Thallin stared back at him. "I'm surprised you haven't soiled yourself yet."

"What?"

The young general smiled with one side of his lips. "I said that I'm surprised you haven't pee-peed down your fancy Watchlord pants yet."

Alverax started to laugh but was so taken aback that instead he simply stood with his mouth wide open.

"Come now," Thallin said. "I remember the first day I became a general a few years ago. The weight of the responsibility, the fear of not being enough, and the damn looks everyone gave me. There were a dozen others who wanted the position. I lost a lot of friends that day. I remember a sinking feeling in the pit of my stomach just certain that at any moment someone would realize I was a fraud."

Alverax nodded. "Is it that obvious?"

"Of course, but that's not a bad thing."

"What did *you* do to get over it?"

"Ah," the young general said, shaking a finger. "I dueled."

"You...dueled?"

General Thallin unsheathed his sword and brandished it in a wide arc. "It's the reason I was selected in the first place. I'm the best swordsman in all of Felia. So, when doubt started to creep in, I focused on my strength instead of my weakness. Instead of being intimidated by the other generals, or anyone else, I'd look at them and think just how easy it would be to destroy them in a duel. And that was it."

"Heralds know I could use a lesson or two on how to swing this thing." Alverax patted the hilt of the Midnight Watcher.

Thallin shoved his sword back in its sheath. "I'd be more than happy to show you sometime, but that was not the point of the story. Dueling is not your strength."

Alverax let out a small laugh. "No, it is not."

"However, it's pretty clear what is." Thallin pointed to Alverax's Obsidian eyes. "The first Obsidian threadweaver in generations! I'm honestly surprised by how humble you are. If I had eyes like yours, I'd be pride incarnate."

"Trust me, it's not humility," Alverax grumbled. "It feels like I'm swirling in a cyclone and everyone but me is holding a steel bar. I'm standing atop a tower in the middle of a war with fabled creatures as the bloody figurehead of the nation's hope. I have no idea how I ended up here, and Herald's know I don't belong."

Thallin let the words simmer as he pondered them. "Why do you think Osinan chose you?"

"He was dying. I don't know. Guilt? I don't think he liked Rastalin much either."

"Oh, come now. No one likes Rastalin, but that's not the reason. And we both know he didn't break generational tradition because he felt guilty about being mean to you."

"I don't know."

"Do you even know what people have been saying about you?"

Alverax stared out over the wall, saying nothing.

"There are rumors that you cannot die."

"Well, that's—"

"The night the Empress was killed, an entire army tried to capture you, but you escaped. Then you sacrificed yourself, and again you were saved from death. And last night, with mythical beasts rampaging our city, you fought a corespawn as tall as a building, and you came out unscathed. Where our Watchlord fell, you stood. The unkillable Surrogate of the Heralds."

"Well, that's ridiculous," Alverax said.

Thallin stepped forward and leaned over the edge of the tower. "We become what the world believes we are."

Unkillable. Technically, his grandfather had been saying it for years: *Us Blightwoods don't die easy.* But this was different. This was a child embracing a wolf, expecting it to protect him from the night. Hope standing on a tightrope while the winds surge all around. The people needed hope, and so they grasped hold of the anomaly, and eased their fear with lies.

But what is truth if not a lie that has yet to be revealed?

"I don't know if I want that," Alverax said, leaning over the edge next to him.

"It's a heavy burden to bear," Thallin said, still gazing into the night. "But you have a gift, and with it you can literally ease the burdens of those around you, including yourself."

"It's not the same."

"Perhaps not, but I've seen you give hope to an entire people without a drop of threadlight. I don't think it's the Obsidian in your eyes that is the gift. And that, Alverax, is why Osinan chose you. He saw it, and one day I expect you will too."

A spark flickered to life within him, not much, just the smallest of flames, but even a small flame can warm an empty heart.

His mind warped the world around him, and a memory swirled in the darkness. He was young, and he walked with his father along the steep path from Mercy's Bluff to the shore. They sat on the rocks they'd named the Lost Sisters with their feet swimming beneath the surface of the ocean. Cool waves splashed at their knees, and the noonday sun beat overhead. The smell of the ocean filled his lungs. His father told him he was leaving.

"Can I come with you?" little Alverax asked.

"Not this time. Someday, I'll take you with me. I'll show you the mountains, the forests, the orchards. I'll even show you where I met your mother. But it's not safe for a boy your age."

"But I'm a Blightwood!"

"You are," his father said laughing. "But you're much more than just a Blightwood, son. One day you will see that."

He tried to shake the memory away, but his eyes filled with emotion. That wasn't his father. His father was a thief. He was all of the parts of Alverax that he refused to be. He would not lie. He would not steal. And most of all, he would not abandon his responsibilities to another.

They spent the rest of the evening in silence, only broken on occasion when guards came to relay information to Thallin and Alverax. Throughout the night, Alverax forced himself to remain standing at the edge of the tower where the soldiers could see him. His legs shook and his eyes hung like a crescent moon, but he remained steadfast.

A beacon of hope that was never needed, because the corespawn never returned.

32

WHEN CHRYS STEPPED into the *convergence*, a surge of energy washed over him. Pockets of colorful energy danced around like skyflies in the night, hovering for a moment, suspended, weightless, then streaking through the air back into the greater whole. His heart expanded in his chest, absorbing the raw power that radiated all around.

Chrys could feel his mother's hand in his own, but where she should have stood, there was only light. He held tight and searched through the chaos, looking for an exit, but the world around the *convergence* had faded away, replaced by a void of blackness. There in the distance, he thought he saw a face. And he knew those eyes—the brilliant Amber eyes of his son, Aydin. But as soon as he saw it, an overwhelming surge, like a great wave, poured over him, pushing him away. He stood his ground, reaching out to his son, screaming out into the void for him. One after another, waves of energy washed over him, filling him with such immense pressure that his veins felt ready to burst, urging him to turn back.

An odd ticking sound accelerated beneath him.

He felt his mother's grip tighten.

Finally, as the dancing colors shifted their hues once more, he succumbed and felt his body swept away in a torrent. Lights blurred around him in all directions. He tumbled head over heel, losing his mother's grip, and falling into nothingness. He tried to right himself, to stabilize, but his body simply spun in a cage of light as the world pulsed with brilliant energy.

He spun and spun in an endless cycle, until, like a bird emerging from a cloud, his body burst through the edge of the *convergence*, crashing into the hard stone. Another thud sounded beside him, and he saw his mother. Finally, Roshaw came tumbling through, landing further away. They all slowly rose to their feet, checking themselves for injury and eyeing the seemingly undisturbed dome of energy.

"Everyone okay?" Chrys asked.

"I'd be happy to never do that again," Willow said.

Roshaw nodded. "I'd be happy to never *see* that thing again."

"We'll have to see it one more time if our plan works," Chrys said.

They made their way through a dark tunnel, feeling their way along the walls and floors, stumbling at times, and cursing at others. Eventually, they found their way through the silent darkness to a large cavern with a gaping hole high overhead. A dim light shone through the hole. Chrys had never felt such relief. Part of him wanted to fall to the ground and rest, soaking in the smallest of victories. But their journey had only begun. They needed to get to Felia, find his family, and find the queen of the Bloodthieves. Only once the coreseal had been reformed would they be able to rest.

With the added strength of the *convergence* magnifying their Sapphire abilities, they each *pushed* off the ground and soared up through the opening, landing atop the broken remains of the wonderstone. Where once the feytrees had eclipsed the canopy of the Fairenwild, now the moonlight shone through an open sky. Stars sprinkled across the heavens, twinkling as a light breeze ruffled the feytree leaves. Across the fields surrounding the wonderstone, flowers lay flat across the ground, fallen beneath a stampede of footprints, or crushed by fallen feytrees. The dark intensity that had once permeated throughout the Fairenwild was gone, replaced by the quiet reverence of a ruined civilization.

Roshaw stared up at the sky. "There, beside the Broken Wheel."

"What?" Chrys said as he looked up at the stars.

"There are three stars right there at the southern edge of the Broken Wheel. It's perfect for Agatha, Esme, and Seven." He shook his head, the slightest smile on his lips. "They deserve to be remembered."

Chrys squinted and thought he saw the small cluster in the sky.

"That small one up there, beside the Siblings," Roshaw pointed to the western sky where two bright stars shone. "That's my mother's star."

Willow joined them, looking up into the heavens. "I've heard a little of that tradition from a Felian family I once knew. We don't have it in Alchea. How does it work?"

Roshaw took a breath and laughed to himself. "When my father explained it to me, he said that when people die their spirits drift up into the heavens. When you choose a star for them, it gives their spirit a home. Then, whenever you miss them, you can look up into the sky and know they're looking down on you from that very place."

"That's beautiful," she said.

"I used to think it was bollocks," Roshaw said, looking down at the swirl of colors running through his veins. "But, Heralds, if we can travel half the continent in an instant, and immortal gods are real, who's to say what is or isn't possible?"

"I'd like to name a star for my brother, if that's okay?"

Roshaw nodded with a smile.

"Something near the Siblings would be fitting," Willow said, as her wide eyes took in the sky. She closed her eyes for a brief moment, her face still directed to the heavens, then opened them with a soft smile. After a moment of quiet, she sighed. "I think he'll like it there."

They all grew quiet and gazed at the stars for a time. Looking out into the infinite expanse, Chrys felt a sense of peace wash over him. Everything was coming together.

For many hours, the three companions walked through the ominously quiet darkness of the Fairenwild. At first, Chrys had led them cautiously, wary of chromawolves or treelurks, or any number of the native dangers, but the forest was empty, not even the sounds of birds from high overhead. So, with photospores in hand, they quickened their pace, watching the ground for hugweed, and made quick progress through the forest.

Each time they came across a body of water, they rested, taking the opportunity to drink and to find whatever berries and vegetation were available. It seemed an endless hike through the darkness. At times they thought themselves lost or circling back, and each time Roshaw would run up a feytree to get a look at the sun above the woven canopy.

Finally, after days of roaming through the forest, they stepped out of the Fairenwild.

Chrys looked out over the horizon to the southwest, toward Felia, and hoped with all his soul that Iriel and Aydin were there. That they were safe. And that he could find them in time.

"Any change?" Alabella asked, looking down over Laurel's unconscious body. The girl looked more at peace than she had the entire time Alabella had known her.

"Not yet," Sarla said.

Their carriage had continued its journey west, despite what had happened to the young Zeda girl. There was too much to do, and too many dangers if they were to pause their trip. The army of corespawn, and the subsequent disappearance of the same, had thwarted all of Alabella's original plans. Alchea was closer to the coreseal, and would have been a better central location, but Felia would still work. And there was a certain poetic justice in returning to her birthplace after so many years.

"When the supplies arrive," Alabella said, "I want her graft done immediately."

"Of course," the doctor replied. "If she survives the surgery, then we can proceed with a more typical achromat candidate. If transfusers are enough to predispose their heart to threadlight, then this could be the breakthrough we've been waiting for. But if it doesn't work on the girl, then it certainly won't work for others."

Alabella nodded. She could feel it in her bones. They were so close. Her life mission so near to a reality. "Have you had time to think about Alverax? I'm still convinced that there is something we're missing. If transfusers are the key, why did he survive?"

"The boy is an anomaly," Sarla replied. "I'd like to believe there is a reason behind his success—it would greatly simplify my work—but even in science there are deviations. I'm not convinced he's anything but lucky."

"Perhaps," Alabella said thoughtfully.

"Do you think he'll be there?"

Alabella looked out the window at the passing countryside. "If any of the Zeda survived, they would have gone west. If the boy's alive, he'll be with them."

"And what if the corespawn are in Felia as well?"

"Enough about the corespawn! Heralds, I've already had to listen to you drone on and on about their metaphysical properties for days."

Sarla pursed her lips and adjusted her glasses. "You are the closest thing I have to a friend, Alabella. Which perhaps isn't saying much for either of us, but it is true, nevertheless. If you want to talk about it, I am here for you."

"About what?" Alabella said.

"It's our fault the corespawn are free," Sarla said, bluntly. "It's our fault they attacked Alchea. It's our fault that hundreds are now dead. Even I can see the weight you bear because of it."

"I am fine."

"Are you?"

The doctor had her use, but she was insufferable. Alabella had long ago learned to bind up all of the suffering she held and bury it deep within herself. As a little girl, she'd learned that feelings would get you killed. It was better to be strong. Smart. No one can hurt you if you can't feel.

"I am fine," she repeated more forcefully.

"Because there is no reason to feel guilty," Sarla continued. "There is no way you could have known this would happen."

"You want to know the truth?" Alabella asked. Since the beginning, she'd held onto one secret above all else, because she knew what it would mean if others knew. "I knew the corespawn were there. I knew when we broke the seal that they would come. I knew when we traveled to find the infused gemstones that they were most likely trapped behind the collapsed tunnel. But they were a necessary part of the plan. When we show the world that we can create threadweavers, just imagine how much more willing they will be to accept our cause. An enemy that only threadweavers can fight? It is the simple economic law of demand.

"The only thing I feel guilty about is underestimating their numbers.

There will always be casualties in the path that leads to greatness—I know this. I only hoped that there would be less."

Sarla's eyes darted back and forth across the floor as she digested Alabella's confession.

It was a relief, finally sharing the truth with someone. Sarla would understand, in her own way, but she would also never look at Alabella quite the same. That was fine. Sarla was in too deep to back out when they were so close. Still, Alabella would have to kill her eventually, but not until they'd perfected the ventricular mineral graft. At that point, when they were creating hundreds of new threadweavers every day, the doctor would only be a liability.

Then, the world would place Alabella's name amongst the Heralds themselves. She would give threadlight to the entire world.

And no one would sully that for her.

34

THEY WERE a day away from Felia, according to a local farmer, when Chrys felt the earth begin to shake. It started small, a distant note he couldn't quite hear, but then it grew in intensity. Soon, the entire grove shook, leaves from the orange trees quaking like fearful children in the night.

"What is happening?" Roshaw groaned.

With the sound of the bellowing earth, and oranges falling from trembling trees, Chrys' mind returned to the war. The first battle in Ripshire Valley. He saw soldiers, scattered along the grass, bleeding out as their comrades ignored them to save their own lives. Thousands of wastelanders fought with bloody abandon, falling by the dozens from Alchean arrows, screaming out in the rage of battle. He saw their leader—he'd forgotten that face, those beady eyes flanked by tattoos that wrapped up from the edge of his brow to his chin like tusks. Chrys had seen the man cut down Alchean soldiers with ease. But when Chrys had attacked, the wastelander had thrown himself at Chrys with a smile. A swirling cloud of darkness. Hundreds of dead around him. And a voice that roared in his mind.

Sweat beaded down Chrys' forehead as he remembered the moment the Apogee was born.

"Stones," Willow whispered, her multi-colored eyes growing wide as she looked back the way they'd come.

Chrys shook off the memory and opened himself to threadlight. An army of glowing corespawn stampeded through the orange grove, small ones darting back and forth between the trees, large ones charging straight through, and massive corespawn, like towers of light, toppling trees beneath their feet.

He'd only seen two living corespawn before that moment, and neither prepared him for the vision before him.

"RUN!" Chrys shouted.

Their veins lit with threadlight as they *pushed* off the ground, lessening their weight just the slightest as they ran for their lives. From tree to tree, Chrys, Willow, and Roshaw sprinted over fallen leaves.

Thud, thud.

The corespawn grew closer. Chrys heard Roshaw curse as he twisted his ankle on one of the fallen fruits. But he kept going, hobbling along at a breakneck speed.

Thud, thud.

Chrys turned and saw the horde of corespawn closing on them. The massive monstrosities crushed trees like blades of wheatgrass.

Thud, thud.

The edge of the grove was close; they were almost there. If they could make it out before the corespawn caught up...then what? Chrys realized their mistake, but it was too late. They could never outrun the corespawn. The creatures were too fast, and there were too many.

If they...wait, where were the others?

Chrys turned and saw Willow hunched over Roshaw behind a tree, trying to lift him up. He ran to them, but he knew in an instant that he wouldn't reach them before the corespawn. Still, he didn't care. His mother had risked everything to protect him; he would do the same.

He ran with reckless abandon, *pushing* off trees behind him, *pulling* on trees in front, accelerating with all the speed of a rushing wind. But it wasn't enough. Corespawn rushed past them on both sides of the tree, ignoring them, or not seeing them, for now. Roshaw rose to his knees, clutching at his ankle, and Willow looked up to see Chrys. As soon as their eyes met, Chrys spotted a massive foot, wrought of pure threadlight, descending atop the tree behind which they hid.

"NO!" Chrys screamed.

The monstrosity trampled the tree, snapping it like a twig, colossal force falling down upon Willow and Roshaw. His mother screamed out, her hands lifted high overhead, her veins a raging torrent of multicolored threadlight. Energy engulfed her like a dome, a barrier that seemed to pulse with life. When the monstrosity's foot connected with the dome, it roared out in pain as sparks of threadlight exploded at the point of collision. The monstrosity stumbled back, then continued forward, stepping on a safer section of the orchard.

Chrys fell to his side, sliding across the leaves as his momentum took him the rest of the way to his mother and Roshaw. "Your corethreads!" he yelled to them. "Break them now!"

They both looked to him and the dome of energy disappeared as their corethreads burst asunder beneath them. Then, grabbing them both by the arm, and with a surge of threadlight, Chrys *pushed* off of the ground and they shot up into the sky with such tremendous force that Chrys nearly lost his grip.

In moments, they were in the sky, looking down on the stampeding horde of corespawn. From such a height, they took in the full panoramic view of the Felian countryside. To the southwest, in the path of the corespawn army, the grand city of Felia gleamed white behind its high walls.

"Heralds, save us," Roshaw said as they floated amongst the clouds.

The stampede of corespawn looked like an army of ants that trailed for miles. There were tens of thousands of the creatures, all on their way to the city where he hoped his wife and son would be.

35

"She's waking up," a man's voice said.

Laurel opened her eyes and felt her entire body shiver. A deep sweat glistened over her pale skin, and her muscles ached as though she'd been crushed by a tree. She lifted herself to an upright position and stabilized herself with both hands as blood rushed to her head. A sharp pain in her stomach greeted her along with a pair of familiar faces.

She tried to remember what had happened, but the only thing she could think of was the last remaining transfuser in her pocket. "Where's my coat?" she said, scrambling around the bed. "WHERE IS MY COAT?" she shouted.

"Laurel," Sarla said, grabbing her shoulder. "It's okay. You're okay."

"I NEED MY COAT!" Laurel yelled again, swatting away the woman's shoulder.

"I can get you a blanket."

Something in Laurel broke. She burst into tears—she wasn't even sure why—and buried her face in her shaking hands. Another shiver skittered up her spine. "Please," she whimpered. "I need my coat."

Sarla fiddled with her glasses in silence, before finally understanding. She moved across the room and grabbed the last remaining transfuser out of a drawer in the desk. "Is this what you wanted?"

Laurel didn't *want* it. She *needed* it. And while she poured the blood down her throat, she hated herself all the more. But it helped. In moments, warmth rushed through her veins, and she felt the bitter fog inside her burn away to clarity. That's when she finally looked around the room. She certainly wasn't in a carriage anymore, and the style of the décor seemed odd.

Sarla turned to Barrick on the other side of the room. "It appears I am correct once again."

"You said she would be better a week ago," Barrick replied. "I don't think that counts."

"No one is counting anything. Merely observing the realization of a hypothesis."

"Whatever you say."

After first flicking her hand out as if to shoo away Barrick's words, Sarla reached toward Laurel's face.

"What are you doing?" Laurel asked with a flinch.

"I wanted to get a good look at your eyes. With the other physical changes, I was curious if your iris would have been affected as well, but it seems that is not the case. Although, your pupil does seem slightly dilated."

Laurel pushed herself to the other side of her bed, distancing herself from Sarla. "What are you talking about? What happened?"

"You fell in the field, next to the chromawolf," Sarla explained. "You appeared to have some kind of episode. Do you have a history of blood issues? Any neurological problems run in your family? It could have been stress-induced. However, I am unfamiliar with any such conditions that would cause the change in your hair."

Laurel reached up, feeling her hair, and grabbed a lock to inspect it. It was ratty, and could use a good wash, but otherwise seemed normal. "What's wrong with my hair?"

Sarla leaned forward. "May I?" When Laurel nodded, Sarla grabbed a chunk of hair toward the back of Laurel's head and brought it forward.

It was...green.

"Gale take me," Laurel cursed.

"At first, I believed it was stained from the grass, or perhaps an odd moss. But I gave it a thorough cleansing when we first arrived in Felia. The color is permanent, Laurel. It happened when you fell. Most curious symptom I've ever seen. If I can make it to the Hallowed Library, I'll see if I can find any information. It's possible your fainting spell was singular, but it is also possible that it is a symptom of an ongoing illness, in which case it would be wise for you to take it easy."

Laurel rejected the comment and rose to her feet. "Honestly, I feel better. Absolutely starving but, other than that, I feel okay."

"Hunger is expected. I had Barrick fetch an assortment of breads and fish for you. They are in the other room. Eat slowly. Your stomach will have shrunk considerably."

The comment awoke a reality within her. "How long have I been asleep? You said we're in Felia already?"

"You've been passed out for a week," Barrick said flatly. "Sarla's been feeding you like a baby."

"It is not healthy to go so long without food," Sarla said, defending herself. "I only gave you a bit of grape juice. A little energy to keep your body going. And you should know that we expect your new theolith to arrive any day now along with the supplies I need to perform the ventricular mineral graft."

"Thank you," Laurel said abruptly. A flicker in her mind brought her back to the orchard. "Asher! Where is Asher?"

"Asher?" Sarla repeated.

"The chromawolf."

"Ah," Sarla said with a laugh. "The entire pack followed us until we arrived at the walls of Felia. A singularly strange experience at first, until we realized they weren't a threat. For a moment, I thought they might try and enter the gates with us."

"Are they still out there?" Laurel asked.

"I don't know, but the alpha—I assume that's the one you call Asher—seemed particularly keen on staying near you. I expect they are still out there somewhere."

Laurel turned to Barrick.

"Don't look at me," the large man responded. "I need to run a few errands for Alabella, but just so you both know, she's in a sour mood. So, I'd suggest you steer clear."

"Why?" Laurel asked.

"So you don't get killed."

"No, why is she in a bad mood?"

"It seems an old friend of hers isn't so easy to kill." Barrick smirked. "Sarla, you'll be interested in this as well. Apparently, Alverax Blightwood is now a special advisor to the empress. He arrived with a group of Zeda. They're camped out near the eastern wall."

Laurel's chest nearly burst apart with happiness at the words. The Zeda. They were alive! And they were there. She tried to restrain her hope, in fear of what the truth may hold. She had no idea who had survived the attack in the Fairenwild. If her brother, Bay, or her grandfather, Corian, were hurt, she wasn't sure what she would do.

As Barrick stepped out of the room, Sarla looked as if her mind were racing in a hundred different directions all at once. Her eyes darted back and forth across the room and she whispered to herself before she left without a farewell.

Laurel smiled and tried to steady her racing heart with deep breaths, but she could neither calm the storm nor wish it departed.

She'd found her people.

36

THREE NIGHTS HAD PASSED since the corespawn breached the eastern wall of Felia, and they had yet to return. Empress Jisenna and the generals found themselves suppressing their hope, fearful that the creatures would return as soon as they let their guard down. So, instead, the army maintained a healthy detail along the walls, preparing smoke signals for the day the corespawn would return.

Alverax, like many of those in Felia, had begun sleeping during the day and staying awake at night, as if the enemy would only attack when the sun had set. The Divine Council lectured him daily on theology and letters, claiming that a Watchlord required a certain level of education, regardless of the present danger. All the while, Osinan's final words resonated in his mind.

While the other generals had begun to tolerate his presence, General Thallin had become a true friend. They spent a bit of every evening together while Thallin taught Alverax Felian military history, tactics of famous Felian victories, and...Felian swordsmanship.

"Good!" Thallin shouted with a smile. A light sweat shimmered across his bare chest. "Again."

Alverax lifted his practice blade. "Can I please take these off?" He still wore his Watchlord robes, despite the sweat dripping from his forehead.

"If you're expected to wear the robes at all times, then you'll be wearing them when you need to fight. Better to train your body to be used to it. Now, again!"

Alverax groaned, then set his feet and attacked. Dull steel clashed against dull steel. Alverax swung to the side, and Thallin parried it with an inverted blade. Again, and again, Alverax attacked, faster and harder each time, until Thallin sidestepped a wild lunge and slapped Alverax across the shoulder.

"Be patient, and never lunge without the proper footing for a hasty retreat. Lunging is a dangerous commitment. Better to move in circles as you swing. I heard you once danced with the Empress. Think of it like that! I am Jisenna, and you are the eligible bachelor dancing in circles around her."

"Mmhmm?"

Alverax and Thallin both turned in unison.

In the doorway of the practice room, Empress Jisenna stood smirking. She wore a long, black dress under a gold-patterned shawl, her tight curls pulled back into a braid. Her guards stood looming behind her.

"Empress," General Thallin said, dropping to a knee with his practice sword held behind his back. He looked down at his bare chest and reddened. "My apologies. I was not aware you would be coming."

"Nothing to apologize for, General. I came because I had a feeling that our new Watchlord may have forgotten about his responsibilities this evening at the Sanctuary, and it appears I was correct."

Responsibilities? Alverax thought. *Heralds, save me.* He'd forgotten that it was the day of prayer, and he was to preside. At least Brother Henthum would be giving the sermon, and Alverax had only to attend. "Thallin, we're going to have to finish this tomorrow. Thank you again."

Thallin nodded and Alverax walked over to Jisenna. She smiled as he approached, and he couldn't help but return the offering.

"Watchlord."

"Empress."

She gestured for him to follow, and they left the practice room. "It's nice to see you getting along so well with one of the generals."

"Honestly, he's the closest thing I've had to a friend in a while. If you can—I don't know—give him some more land or something, he totally deserves it."

"More land? For being friendly?" Jisenna laughed. "I suppose it would set a pleasant precedent, but, as my advisors would say, friendship itself *is* the reward."

Alverax shook his head. "Not in my experience. Friendship is just the appetizer before the burnt meal."

"The more I learn of it, the more Cynosure seems like an altogether unpleasant place."

"The views are nice," he said, shrugging his shoulders. "But what can you expect from a city where all of the people are runaways, outcasts, or criminals."

"Not all of them," she corrected with a wink. "A few of them are kind and selfless and trying their best to do what is right, even if they have oddly shaped scars inside and out."

Alverax stopped walking and stared at the Empress.

She stopped beside him.

As he looked in her eyes, it was if all that was good in the world had coalesced and taken root between the various shades of brown. She'd read his story and, rather than toss them aside, she held the pages against her breast as if they were the most precious thing in the world. She held the promise of who he could become, and it made him want to be better.

The words she used to describe him—kind, selfless—these were her words to claim more than any other, but he could see it in the way she looked at him how much she believed they were his.

"Is everything okay?" she asked.

"I—" he began, fumbling his own thoughts. "Just thank you."

"Come on, we don't want you to be late to prayer."

<hr />

AFTER TRAVELING FOR SOME TIME, passing maids and servants and fawning nobility, they arrived in the vestry attached to the backside of the Heraldic Sanctuary. The priests had previously explained his limited role in the services, but, as they walked, Jisenna had educated him on the history of the Sanctuary itself, where the Heralds held their annual covenant ritual, or so the Divine Council taught. The Heraldic Sanctuary was a tall structure with white stone that had become overgrown with all manner of budding greenery. The building overflowed its capacity with those who'd come to see their new Watchlord preside.

Inside, they greeted Brother Henthum of the Divine Council, who was scheduled to give the sermon. He gave Alverax a firm embrace, which made him altogether uncomfortable, but he still wasn't sure what he should, or could, refuse. Eventually, they led him through a doorway where he found himself looking out over a packed room with hundreds of attendees who all perked up when they saw him enter. Alverax kept his head high and took his seat on the dais.

"Today," Brother Henthum announced to the audience, "is a most extraordinary day. Behind me, we are presided over by Watchlord Alverax Blightwood, the first Obsidian threadweaver in all of Arasin for generations. Please, join me in welcoming him with the Sign of the Giver." Smiling faces lifted both palms to their foreheads, covering their eyes, then extended their outstretched hands to Alverax. He'd seen the gesture before and did his best to mimic the same.

While Brother Henthum continued with the sermon, Alverax found himself preoccupied with the weight of his new world. The title. The expectations. Not to mention the impending army of mythical corespawn. It had only been three days since he became Watchlord, but it felt like an eternity.

Brother Henthum concluded his sermon and, afterward, seats began to empty. Alverax could see in the way they stepped, in the way they held themselves, that they'd received an added portion of hope to accompany them. It was then that he truly understood Osinan. Despite knowing that the Heralds would never return, Osinan had dedicated his life to giving people a worthy reason to be good. He'd filled the void, and, false though it may have been, it had made the world a better place.

A small child, no more than four years old, ran through the Sanctuary, between the chairs and up the stairs of the dais until he stood smiling from ear to ear in front of Alverax. Despite having little experience with children, he'd always enjoyed their company.

Alverax crouched down and smiled. "Well, hello friend. What's your name?"

"Kyan."

"And how can I help you, Kyan?"

"Can you ask the Heralds to take care of my daddy?" The boy shuffled his feet. "The monsters killed him. But my mommy says you can protect us from them."

Alverax clenched his jaw. He knew that many had died the night of the attack, but he'd never thought about children losing parents, or men and women losing a spouse. Death was a landslide that muddied the earth for miles. "Don't worry about the monsters. I'll take care of them. Have you found your dad a star yet?"

Kyan shook his head.

"You know, my father died too. How would you like to come outside with me so we can name a star for your father?"

The little boy's eyes grew twice the size of the moon. "Really?"

"If your mother will allow it, of course."

Kyan's mother stood beneath the dais, mortified at her son's actions, but filled with pride in their conversation. She nodded her head, her eyes glistening in the flickering light.

"Follow me," Alverax said.

He took the boy by the hand and gestured for the mother to follow. They exited the Sanctuary through a side door and stepped out into the night. Out of habit, Alverax looked to the east, wondering when plumes of smoke would once again signify the return of the corespawn. But that night, only moonlight and stars filled the dark expanse.

He crouched down beside the boy. "Do you know any of the constellations?"

Kyan looked confused.

"Some of the stars look like shapes," Alverax explained, "and we give them names to help us describe where they are. Look over there." He pointed high overhead to the north. "See how some of those stars are brighter than the others? And the bright ones make a circle? We call that circle of stars the Broken Wheel."

"Broken?"

Alverax laughed. "I remember asking my grandfather the same thing. Wheels are meant to spin, and that one doesn't, so they say it's broken. Look at that one over there, the brightest star in the whole sky. They say that one is the Moon's Little Sister. The Empress told me that the small star right next to it is the one she chose for *her* father when he passed away. Maybe your father's star could be close to that one, so he can be friends with the emperor."

Kyan's grin widened. "Yeah! Daddy would like that!"

"Well then, it's settled. Now look at the star, think of your father's name, and his spirit will fly to it. And every time you miss him, or you're feeling scared or worried, you can look up into the sky, find the Moon's Little Sister, and see your dad's star watching over you."

When Alverax looked up from Kyan to his mother, he found her cheeks stained with tears. She mouthed the words *thank you* to him before ushering her son away.

He watched them walk away, then looked up into the sky. He'd avoided the tradition for so long, never feeling that his father deserved a named star. As he gazed into the infinite expanse, thousands of stars glittering in the darkness, he closed his eyes. Some day he would forgive his father for leaving them. Someday he would name a star for him. But he wasn't ready for that just yet.

When he opened his eyes, plumes of smoke from the signal fires billowed up from the eastern wall.

37

ALL OF FELIA buzzed to life as men and women prepared for the attack. The sun had just fallen below the western horizon when Alverax arrived at the war tents. He leapt off the horse and entered to find the four generals hard at work, giving orders to their lieutenants, receiving scouting reports, and puzzling over the map.

"Watchlord," General Thallin said. The other generals gave him a nod of acknowledgment, which was more than Alverax had expected.

"I saw the smoke and came as fast as I could," Alverax said as he approached the table. "Are the corespawn attacking the same part of the wall? Where can I help?"

"Take a seat." General Nevik looked to him with a grim countenance. "The corespawn have yet to attack."

"They are gathering outside the wall," General Hish added, the veins in his thick neck radiated Sapphire threadlight.

"Gathering?" Alverax repeated. "That's—"

"Terrifying," Thallin finished for him. "Bloody terrifying, because it means they are smarter than we thought. Not to mention the numbers."

"At least ten thousand," General Hish said, "and more gathering every minute. The monstrosity that broke through our wall wasn't the last of its kind either. Our lookouts have seen at least ten of them in the gathering."

"Heralds, save us," Alverax whispered.

General Nevik lifted his chin. "I wouldn't count on the Heralds showing up for this one, Watchlord. We have the tools, and our traps are in place; the fight is ours. However, General Thallin had an idea on how to improve our odds even more, and we think you could help."

"Anything, what is it?"

Thallin cocked his head to the side. "The Zeda are nearly all threadweavers. Most of them aren't soldiers, but we need eyes more than swords. If you could convince them to help, we could use their threadweavers."

Alverax looked to the three generals, each of them eyeing him warily. They were right that only a select few of the Zeda were warriors, but, if they could help coordinate the use of weapons and traps, there was a chance their help could change the tide. "I'll see what I can do."

With that, Alverax left the tent and stepped back into the brisk open air.

If they were going to use the Zeda, he needed to get to them quickly.

LAUREL WANDERED the streets of Felia, using the fallen sun as her guide. Where she'd thought Alchea a rushing river of people, Felia was an ocean, filled with such diversity and movement that it was hard for her to keep focus. Still, nothing could distract her from finding her family. She only hoped it wasn't too late.

People rushed around the streets in a hurry, some with smiles, some with looks of terror. She heard people yelling, but she brushed them aside. She stopped a young boy who stood against a white building and asked him if he knew where the Zeda were, and he gave her directions. From there, it didn't take long to find the encampment.

In what looked like a series of large fields, a sprawling metropolis of quickly constructed tents dotted the landscape. She recognized the clothing immediately, and the hair, and the manner in which the Zeda carried themselves. Familiar faces walked the grassy paths between tents. Laurel ignored their expressions as they greeted her. There were only two people she needed to see, and she found herself hoping with all her soul for their safety. If they'd been taken from her, she wasn't sure her thread-dead heart could handle it.

She stepped forward, like a widow wandering a graveyard, each tent a headstone marking her fallen family. The tremble in her hands crept up her arms and covered her with ghostly shivers. Her hand rubbed at her empty breast pocket.

Then she saw Bay. Her sweet, sickly, do-gooder brother stepped slowly out of a tent holding a book, and Laurel felt a weight lift from her shoulders. When he saw her, he stopped in his tracks, leaned toward her, and blinked his eyes.

"Caterpillar!" Laurel shouted as she sprinted toward him.

As soon as he heard the word, his lips opened into a wide grin and he tossed his book back in through the open tent door. He braced himself for impact, and Laurel leapt up onto him, wrapping him in a tight embrace.

"Little wolf," he whimpered. "You're quite heavy."

She released him and dropped to the ground. He panted and shook his head back and forth with a smile.

"I saw what happened in the Fairenwild. I thought you were dead. I swore if anything had happened to you—"

"Me?" he asked, incredulously. "When you and the others never returned, the elders were certain that *you* were dead, or at least that we would never see you again. How did you find us?"

"It's a long story," she said. "Where's grandfather?"

Bay's face grew grim. "In the tent, but he's sick, Laurel. The physicians think he'll pass in the next few days. He'll be glad he was able to see you one last time."

Laurel's heart sunk in her chest. He was old—she knew he only had so much time left—but still the thought of him passing away squeezed at her insides. She looked to the tent, the scent of sickness wafting out from the opening.

Her pulse beat faster than a hummingbird's wings as she stepped inside. She couldn't even see her grandfather yet, and already tears were forming in her eyes. As she approached, she saw him lying on a cot in the corner, bundled up beneath a pile of wool blankets, his chest rising and falling with each breath. Laurel walked to him and stopped beside his bed. His skin seemed paler, and his hair thinner. Looking down at his frailty, tears flowed down her cheek. She wiped them away and sniffled away her running nose.

The sleeping man stirred, taking in a deep breath as his eyes began to open. Laurel tried to contain her joy as he awoke, but it came out as a curtailed giggle. He turned his head and saw her for the first time. Their eyes met and his lips quivered.

"Laurel," he whispered.

Hearing her name from his lips broke her. She collapsed into his arms, squeezing him harder than she knew she ought to, but she loved this man so dearly that no logic could prevent her from expressing it. "I thought I would never see you again."

With her head on his chest, she could hear his lips part into a smile.

"I'm so sorry," she continued. "For everything. I was reckless and stupid. I don't know what got into me. I should have stayed with you and Bay. I never should have gone with the grounders."

"No," he said with a deep weariness to his voice. It seemed scratchier and deeper than she remembered. "You know, you remind me so much of your mother—how I've missed you both."

"I missed you too."

He let out a series of coughs, each worse than the previous.

She took his hand and squeezed it gently. "Do you remember the night my parents died?"

He nodded. "How could I forget?"

"Do you remember what you told me?"

He shook his head.

Laurel sat on the edge of his cot. "You held Bay and I, one in each arm, and squeezed us like the wind would take us away as well. I still remember staining your shirt with my tears. And you just held us in silence. After a time, you let go and it felt like I could finally breathe again, but I didn't want to. You sat us on the kitchen chairs and knelt in front of us. You took our hands, and you finally spoke. 'When the dead look down on us, they don't want us to mourn. They want us to live.'"

She watched as a single tear traced down his cheek. "Your mother would be so proud of you."

Would she? If she knew the truth—that Laurel was working with the Bloodthieves, that she'd killed a man, and was addicted to drinking threadweaver blood—there would be little to be proud of. But there was still time. She could still make them proud, somehow.

Curiously, the slightest scent of citrus entered the tent.

"A fallen leaf ne'er travels far from the tree."

Laurel startled at the voice, turning to see a pair of elderly women standing in the doorway of the tent, each a stark contrast to the other. Elder Rosemary's lips curled up, and Elder Rowan's curled down, but their eyes both held a similar sense of relief. Laurel wasn't sure how to respond to the old adage.

"A thorn in the hand will tomorrow be a thorn in the foot," Elder Rowan added.

"Oh, come now, Rowan," Elder Rosemary said, slapping at the older woman's shoulder. "Laurel, we are both so delighted to see you. I can't imagine your journey has been altogether pleasant."

"I...I want to apologize," Laurel replied.

Elder Rosemary rose a brow. "Whatever for?"

"For everything. You were right to take away my position as a messenger. I see that now. And I understand if you're still frustrated with me—you've every right to be. But I'm going to be better. I want to make sure my brother and my grandfather are safe. That's more important than whatever it was I was trying to prove to myself."

Elder Rowan eyed her grandfather. "She sounds more and more like Tarra every day."

"Looks like her too," Elder Rosemary added. "Except...is that a streak of green in your hair? And your eyes..." She paused. "A story for another time. Laurel, we came here for the purpose of apologizing to *you* and welcoming you home. These are dangerous times, and our people need to be more united than ever before. Darkness has come to this city, and it will come again."

Laurel perked up. "The corespawn."

The elders turned to each other in surprise. Elder Rowan spoke first. "An army of them attacked the city. They killed many and destroyed a portion of the outer wall."

"They attacked Alchea too."

"Father of All, help us," Elder Rosemary said. "I assume you know that Zedalum was attacked?"

She nodded again, biting the inside of her cheek.

"Laurel, we failed," Elder Rosemary said sternly. "The coreseal was shattered, releasing the corespawn."

A voice echoed behind them from among the tents, but Elder Rowan ignored it. "We need to find a way to fix it. We don't know how our ancestors created the seal, but we know that they were Amber threadweavers. It is no coincidence that the Father of All has brought an Amber threadweaver to Felia to help us—"

Laurel shifted in her boots. How did they know she'd come with Alabella? The woman had destroyed their home and orchestrated the shattering of the seal. Surely, they didn't believe she would help them fix it.

"—We just need to survive long enough for him to grow into his powers."

Gale take me, she thought. *They mean Aydin.*

Laurel's mind flashed with an image of Iriel carrying Aydin while Asher carried Chrys through the dark of the Fairenwild. It seemed an eternity ago. She was a different person then; she was still a threadweaver.

"Chrys and Iriel are here?" Laurel asked.

A dark pain settled over their faces. Elder Rosemary clenched her jaw before she spoke. "Iriel and the baby are here, and they are safe. We've not seen Chrys since the night we left the Fairenwild."

Suddenly, a figure appeared in the doorway behind the elders. A boy, not much older than Laurel, standing tall in clothing that seemed fit for both fighting and priestly duties.

"Elders," he said, addressing the older women.

"Alverax?" Elder Rowan said with a hint of bitterness in her tone.

His eyes slimmed. "The corespawn are here. We need your help."

STONES OF LIGHT
39

LAUREL STARED at the boy standing in the doorway of the tent. His eyes were black as the Fairenwild at midnight, and his veins pulsed with darkness. And that name...*Alverax*. It took only a moment to make the connection. He was the Obsidian threadweaver Alabella had created. He was the proof that she wasn't lying. That Laurel *could* have her threadlight back.

But there was no time for that now. If he was right, they were all in danger.

Laurel had hoped to never hear the word corespawn again, but it was like a fly that followed her from room to room, buzzing in her ear wherever she went. She felt at her side and the presence of the obsidian dagger gave her a sense of relief. With it, she could protect her family. She could protect her people after failing to be there for them before.

"The corespawn have returned?" Elder Rosemary asked with a grimace.

"Gathering outside the walls," Alverax said. "They're not attacking, but they are amassing an army ten times larger than before. But I'm not here just to warn you. We need the Zeda people. Most of the Felian soldiers are achromats. They can't even see the corespawn. We've done everything we can to prepare, but we need more threadweavers so that soldiers know when to spring traps and when to cast arrows. If any Zeda will fight, Heralds know we could use them. But if they're not, we need lookouts even more. I know the Felians don't deserve your help, and I have no right to ask for it, but this city will fall if we do nothing."

Elder Rosemary lifted her chin and looked to him. "If anyone has a right to ask for our help, it is the man who saved us all from captivity and death. Alverax, I do not care for your new title nor your new associations, but I know you. And you would not put our people in danger if it were not necessary."

"In a way, you are to blame for the return of the corespawn," Elder Rosemary added with a flat tone. "It is fitting that you be the one to lead the charge to destroy them."

Laurel saw the boy redden. He was a curiosity. On the one hand, he wore immaculate robes and stood tall and strong, speaking with confidence. But on the other hand, he seemed so young.

"I'm trying," he said. "I know it's my fault. Heralds, I can hardly sleep some nights. But what's done is done. I can blame myself every day for the rest of my life, but it wouldn't make a difference. Fighting will. You both know I'm not a warrior. But if it means I can save some lives, then I'm damn well going to fight with everything I have."

"I'll fight," Laurel said.

Corian coughed from his bed and tried to rise. "Laurel."

"I fought the corespawn in Alchea. Killed a handful myself." She pulled out the obsidian dagger. "If the corespawn are coming, then sitting behind a wall won't keep us safe. It's time the Zeda did their part. I'm going to do mine."

The two elders looked to each other in silence for just a moment before they nodded. Elder Rosemary turned to Alverax. "Our people were tasked with protecting the coreseal, so that the corespawn could not return. We failed that duty. I will speak with Dogwood, and we'll gather the threadweavers. Some of us are old, but we yet have threadlight in our veins. Where would you have us?"

THE EASTERN WALL of Felia loomed high overhead with a wide crack splitting the finely joined stone. The gaping hole had been filled with wood and rocks and all manner of material, but it was haphazard and would not stand long against an attack. The scent of death still rode the wind, but no one save Laurel seemed to care. Even her brother, Bay, who stood uncomfortably close to her as they traveled through the wide dirt field, seemed unaffected by the horrible stench.

Hundreds of Zeda trailed behind, silent in their commitment to aid the grounders. Laurel felt an overwhelming pride for her people, though she understood their choices were limited. Dogwood, one of the true warriors of the Zeda, led a large group up the long staircase leading to the wall-walk. They spread out across the entire eastern wall, providing added coverage of the surrounding terrain.

With Zeda support, the amassed army of corespawn would have no way to sneak up on the city. And when they came, the archers would loose their arrows, fire would rain down from trebuchets, and a hidden layer of spikes at the base of the wall would be lifted. Lastly, in preparation for the enormous monstrosities, dozens of ballistae were in position to launch a volley of burning steel.

Laurel found herself beginning to believe that with all of the grounder preparations, they just might be able to win.

But then the earth shook.

Over and over, like fists pounding against the earth, ripples of energy quaking along the surface. Chaos erupted throughout the city, with lookouts shouting for everyone to stay calm. The corespawn weren't moving, but that didn't stop the people from panicking.

Bay grabbed Laurel's shoulder for support. "What is happening?"

"I don't know," she said. "I need to find Alverax. Go somewhere safe."

As Laurel rushed through the pandemonium, she lifted her head and sniffed the air. Her mind filled with faces and odd assumptions about the world around her, but one in particular stood out. She turned toward a tent not far away and ran as fast as her legs would take her. She never knew how much she loved the wind in her hair until she was dashing through the dirt with danger all around. Her heart pounded and her eyes pierced through the darkness. She felt so free.

She rounded the other end of the tent and saw Alverax standing in the doorway, talking to a man with a sharp jaw. "Alverax!" she shouted, coming to a stop. "What's happening?"

The other man turned to her with a look of confusion. "Who are you?"

"She's one of the Zeda," Alverax responded. "She helped me convince the elders. Laurel, was it? This is General Thallin."

She nodded just as another resounding thud shook the ground. "Did this happen the last time the corespawn attacked?"

"No," Alverax said.

Again, the earth shook.

He turned to the general. "Should we send out scouts to see what they're doing?"

"They're too far away from the wall," Thallin replied. "There's nothing they can do from that distance, and I wouldn't want to send one of our threadweavers on a suicide scouting mission."

Alverax turned to Laurel. "I need you to work with Dogwood and make sure the Zeda are in position and ready. The last thing we need is for whatever this is to frighten people and ruin our preparation."

Laurel nodded. In that moment, she realized that Alverax had no idea that Alabella and Sarla were in the city. When Sarla had told her all about the Obsidian threadweaver they'd created, she told her that the boy had abandoned them and was likely dead. Whatever his reason, Alverax would certainly want to know that they were here. But not now. They had bigger problems.

The quaking of the earth grew stronger.

Screaming.

Laurel, Alverax, and Thallin turned their gaze to the screams coming from the south, where a large creature dashed through the streets at terrifying speed. Somehow, she knew, even before she saw his green fur blending in with the moonlit grass.

Asher.

The chromawolf sprinted toward her and she took a step in his direction. Thallin unsheathed his blade, and Alverax followed suit.

"No!" she shouted, pushing them aside and rushing forward. The wind bit at her cheeks as she picked up speed. She had to get to him before the grounders hurt him. They were right to be afraid, but wrong in the most important way.

As they approached, she slid on her side, reaching out for threadlight to *drift* across the dirt, but finding none. She came to a halt and watched as an arrow cut through the night and smashed into Asher's shoulder. The chromawolf crashed to its side and Laurel howled out into the night. Pain ripped through her arm, gripping at nerves and tendons. She stumbled to her feet and lifted her other arm high into the air, waving it in the direction from which the arrow had flown.

When she looked to her own shoulder, there was no wound. Whatever pain she'd felt wasn't real. But Asher's was. She knelt beside the chromawolf, his fur now marred by blood and dirt. His breath was heavy, his chest heaving up and down as his head writhed back and forth in pain. She touched his chest with an outstretched palm, and he turned his eyes to her.

And in the middle of the chaos, with armored boots stomping over rubble and soldiers and civilians shouting hymns of terror, Laurel heard a voice in her mind.

Danger, Asher growled. *Tunnel.*

Stones of Light 40

Laurel continued to press her hand against the chromawolf's chest. Somehow—impossibly—he had spoken to her. But they weren't words, they were ideas, passed into her mind and translated to words with a voice that sounded just like Asher's growl.

"Danger?" Laurel asked.

Asher shook his head. *Digging. Far.*

She couldn't believe that it was really his voice. Had he always been able to communicate with her? Could other chromawolves do the same? But wait...

Digging.

"Alverax!" Laurel screamed, looking back over her shoulder. "Alverax, come fast!"

She turned her attention back to Asher and looked at the arrow in his shoulder. She grabbed it by the shaft, and, as she gripped it, she felt a dull throb in her own arm. Gritting her teeth and taking a deep breath, she pulled the arrow out of Asher as fast as she could. Her own arm throbbed as she felt the shadow of an arrow pull free.

Alverax approached, his black blade returned to its sheath. "Laurel, are you okay? Did that thing hurt you?"

"I'm fine," she said. "Asher would never hurt me."

"Asher?"

Laurel sat up, one hand gripping her shoulder, though the pain had all but vanished. "Asher is with me. If anyone so much as touches him, there will be hell to pay."

Alverax looked down at the wound in Asher's shoulder. "Is it going to be okay?"

"*He* will be fine. Alverax, the corespawn are digging a tunnel. They're going *under* the wall."

His eyes grew. "Under? All our traps would be useless. Wait, is that even possible? Thallin!" he shouted. "Ahh, never mind. Come on. Can it walk? I wouldn't leave it here or someone will do something."

In response, Asher rose to his feet, though he favored the injured one as he hobbled beside Laurel. On every side, soldiers and civilians gawked at the massive chromawolf sauntering through their homeland beside a Zeda girl and their Watchlord. Something about it made Laurel feel powerful, as if her bond with Asher was some great expression of strength.

"Thallin!" Alverax shouted as they moved. "The corespawn are digging a tunnel under the wall! I don't know how far they've gotten, but we need to get ready in case they emerge from the ground on this side."

General Thallin furrowed his brows and stared at Asher with his head held slightly back, then shifted his gaze to Alverax. "Slow down. What are you talking about?"

"The corespawn!" Alverax repeated. "The quaking is *digging*. They're making a tunnel that will go right under the outer wall."

"Heralds," Thallin cursed. "Where is the messenger? I want to know every detail."

Alverax turned to Laurel who turned to Asher. "Laurel, where's the note?"

Laurel paused. "What note?"

"The message that the wolf brought you. You said it brought you the warning."

"No, I didn't," she said. In that moment, she realized how insane it would look if she tried to explain the truth. No one would believe that Asher could speak to her. And even if they did, how could they believe information from a chromawolf? "Ohhhhh," she said, backtracking. "Sorry, yeah. The note was from a Zeda scout."

"Can I see it?" Thallin asked.

"I..." Laurel patted at her pockets. "It must have fallen out. The paper doesn't matter as much as the message. You have to turn your attention inward and rearrange the traps, you can still catch them by surprise."

Thallin stared at her with doubt in his eyes. "If we turn our attention inward and you're wrong, then the corespawn army can simply march forward and destroy our wall again, uncontested. I need more than a missing note to change all of our preparations."

Laurel clenched her jaw and turned to Alverax. "I swear it on the wind. They are digging a tunnel and, if you do nothing, people *will* die."

The ground rumbled beneath them, intensifying with each passing minute.

Alverax looked to the ground, thoughtfully, and Laurel thought that he just might believe her. But then he turned to the general. "I trust your judgment. Is there any way we can watch both?"

General Thallin shook his head. "Not without sacrificing one or the other. One option is to turn the ballistae inward, and if we see the corespawn approaching from the outside, we can swivel them back around. But the people and the traps are too connected to the wall. Moving them could be catastrophic if we're wrong."

"Do that," Alverax said. "If they tunnel in, I can help with the smaller corespawn. The ballistae can hold off the larger ones."

"I'll have them position the ballistae immediately." With that, Thallin rushed off to the tent where a group of messengers awaited orders.

A few minutes passed while Laurel watched messengers deliver their orders to the soldiers on the wall-walk. Several large ballistae shifted their aim, rotating the huge bow-like machines inward. It wasn't much, but it was something.

As they stood side by side, Laurel looked at Alverax. If they survived this, she wanted to know his story. Especially the part where he betrayed Alabella.

Just then, she caught an odd scent on the wind.

It smelled like...roses.

The earth just inside the wall spewed forth dirt and rubble. Soldiers shouted, scrambling about. Dirt blasted out of the ground. Laurel searched for threadlight, but found her mind grasping into an empty void. For a moment, she thought she felt something, a prickle of power, but then it was gone.

She cursed and took out the obsidian dagger.

Alverax unsheathed his blade, and it gleamed in the moonlight. Laurel looked back to her own and was surprised to see the similarity.

"Nice sword," she said.

He looked at her dagger. "Nice knife."

"Mine's better," she said.

Alverax let out a clipped laugh and looked to the tunnel.

Laurel knew it would be difficult to fight the corespawn if she couldn't see them. But it wouldn't be impossible. If only she still had a transfuser, something to give her access to threadlight, then she could make the beasts pay.

Eyes, Asher's voice growled in her mind.

Yes, Laurel thought. *I can't see the corespawn.*

No, his voice echoed. *Eyes.*

Laurel looked at her friend, confused. "I don't understand," she said aloud.

Share. Mine. Eyes.

The scent of roses saturated the night air, and that simple fact gave Laurel pause. Ever since the incident in the orchard, something had been changing with her. The smells. The speed. The pain. The...hair. It was as if she was becoming more and more like a chromawolf. And now, she could feel Asher's pain. She could speak with him. Somehow, their souls had bonded. *Share. Mine. Eyes.*

What if...

Laurel closed her eyes and reached back into the empty space where threadlight had once lived within her. She searched for a single leaf in the howling wind...and she found it. There, like the smallest seed, a spec of threadlight that echoed with Asher's soul. She reached out to it and felt power surge through her. She could hear the crunch of fallen leaves underfoot on the other side of the field. She could hear the breath of the guards atop the wall-walk. An entire world of information came pouring into her.

And then she opened her eyes.

Threadlight burst into her vision. Tens of thousands of multi-colored threads pulsing and dancing in the moonlit air. And in the midst of the field, in the center of thousands of Felian soldiers, a horde of corespawn came crawling out of a gaping hole in the ground.

Alverax gripped the hilt of the Midnight Watcher with white knuckles as he watched a swarm of skittering corespawn digging their way out of the growing hole. With each corespawn, the opening grew, until a massive hand plunged its way out, slapping against the ground and pulling itself out of the tunnel. It was one of the same monstrosities that had broken through the wall before, twice the height of a house and a barbed tail dragging behind it. Threadlight swirled across its massive body.

Every ballista that had been turned inward fired off a thick bolt at the monstrosity. Steel blasted into the creature, embedding deep in its glowing body. But no sooner had they hit then the beast grabbed hold and ripped the bolts back out, tossing them aside as threadlight pooled in the wounds.

The wounds healed, and the monstrosity roared.

Next to him, Laurel smiled, and Alverax was quite certain the girl was mad. But despite the fact that she seemed quite feral, she'd been right, for all the good it did them. He should have listened to her.

He was surprised to see her lips curl into a snarl as she flipped her dagger in her hand and whispered something to the chromawolf. Then, she took off toward the corespawn with Asher stumbling after her.

"Heralds, save us all," Alverax mumbled.

Then, he too rushed toward the tunnel.

Even at a dead sprint, he could pick off the smaller corespawn nearest to him. He would latch onto their threadlight with his mind and *break* it, instantly bursting the creatures apart in a cloud of misty magic. But Laurel and Asher were so fast that they arrived long before him. He watched as she slashed at the corespawn with reckless abandon, dashing in, swiping, spinning, and slamming down her dagger into the neck of the next. She seemed to move with inhuman speed, the corespawn falling apart at the touch of her obsidian blade.

The chromawolf seemed interested only in protecting Laurel as she continued in her mad rage. Each time one of the corespawn, whether small or large, tried to attack her from the flank, the chromawolf would lunge forward, striking the creatures down and fending them off until Laurel could turn around and finish them.

Alverax finally caught up. "Watch my back and I'll watch yours!" he shouted.

Laurel barely managed a nod before diving back in to explode the next corespawn. Alverax held his sword in a battle stance he'd learned from Thallin but focused on using his threadweaving. While Laurel thrashed out at the creatures, cutting them down like a child popping bubbles, Alverax picked them apart from a distance. One along the wall-walk about to attack an archer. *Pop.* Another climbing the wall to kill one of the Zeda lookouts. *Pop.*

He searched through the chaos, looking for where he could best help the people, all the while threadlight burned beneath his skin, sizzling from his chest to the ends of his fingertips. By the dozens, corespawn swarmed out of the massive hole like lava, oozing out over the land, devouring everything in their wake. Alverax wasn't fast enough. There were too many.

Another monstrosity ripped itself out of the hole. It swung its arms out over the field and flung soldiers through the air, crashing against tents and towers and the stone wall. Screams filled the battlefield, and it took all of Alverax's willpower not to add his own to the chorus.

All around him, chaos reigned. Soldiers toppled from the wall-walk. Others were flattened beneath the feet of the monstrosities. And yet others lay strewn out across the grass, their corpses torn open from the smaller, feasting creatures. He spun in a circle, and, everywhere he looked, he saw death. Their defenses were broken.

Rage boiled beneath his skin. The Heralds had saved him for a reason. He couldn't just stand there and watch the corespawn destroy the entire city. He had to do something.

The largest of the monstrosities broke away from the field and marched toward the palace. Flaming arrows and balls of acid exploded across its body, and it continued as if they were nothing more than rainfall.

Alverax ran. He ran faster than he'd ever run, gripping the Midnight Watcher as if it might try to turn back. Step by step, he gained on the slow-moving monstrosity; he had to stop it before it arrived at the palace. Jisenna was inside.

He cursed his heavy robes and charged forward. With threadlight burning through his veins and his heart pounding with fury, Alverax reached out to the monstrosity and attempted to *break* it. The threadlight forming its body vibrated like a magnet repelling its twin, pushing back against Alverax's efforts. Inside, it felt as though his veins were expanding under the pressure, but Alverax ignored it and raced forward.

The corespawn monstrosity swung about face, crushing a building with its tail. When its head faced Alverax, it leaned forward and roared.

Alverax *broke* his corethread and launched himself, weightless, through the cool night air in a straight line toward the beast. He lifted the Midnight Watcher high above him and, as he crashed into the monstrosity's head, he slammed the obsidian blade into the mass of pulsing threadlight. The sword connected. Energy shocked through his arms and throughout his body, sizzling and burning beneath his skin. The monstrosity burst apart like a mountain exploding into millions of shards of rock and dust.

The force sent Alverax crashing toward the ground, his corethread reappearing just before he struck earth. The sword tumbled away from him. His breathing came in bursts while his heart beat in chaotic pulses.

The moon's little sister winked at him.

No.

He refused to give up. He pushed himself to his feet and rubbed at his chest. But when he stood, the battlefield had changed...for the worse.

The remaining monstrosities had broken through the wall while the smaller corespawn were attacking soldiers and lookouts from within. Now, they prepared to march through the city, devastating everything in their path. Alverax knew he had to fight, but he couldn't kill all of the monstrosities by himself, even with the Midnight Watcher. Still, if he didn't try, what would that mean for the people of Felia?

"Alverax!" Laurel's voice shouted in the chaos. The wild Zeda girl, bloody and clutching at her arm, ran up to him, followed by her chroma-wolf companion. "We can't stop those things. What do we do?"

But he didn't know. Heralds, save him. He didn't know.

General Thallin was nowhere to be seen; the other generals had been in the tent that was torn apart by one of the monstrosities. There was nothing left for them to do.

They were going to lose the city.

They'd failed.

Suddenly, two pairs of boots crashed into the ground, landing in a crouch not far from Alverax and Laurel. A regal man who seemed to glow in the sky, and a woman with a flowing dress that drifted in the wind. Their eyes, like perfect prisms, radiated the full spectrum of colors. There was something about them, a confidence, a power.

The man looked to Alverax and smiled. "Do not worry, child. The Heralds have returned."

41
STONES OF LIGHT

THE TWO BEINGS who called themselves Heralds leapt into action toward the stampeding monstrosities. In moments, they were hovering above the corespawn army, speaking to the beasts. Their words caused the creatures to howl and thrash about as they backed away. The woman flew forward and struck at the closest of the massive beasts. To Laurel, it looked like a bird crashing into a feytree, but in reality, as soon as the monstrosity was struck, it was launched backward, tumbling over dozens of the smaller corespawn prowling in the field.

The rest of the monstrosities roared in unison, then fled toward their tunnel. One by one they dropped into the gaping hole and disappeared. Thousands of smaller corespawn scuttled in after them. However impossible it seemed, the streets and wall were soon free of the enemy, populated only by the wounded Felians and Zeda who'd stood their ground and fought.

Laurel stared at the Heralds who hovered in the air overhead.

Danger, Asher growled in her mind.

"Alverax," she said. "Who are they?"

The young Watchlord was frozen in place, eyes plastered to the godlike beings who'd saved them. "Osinan was wrong."

"What?"

"The Heralds *did* come back," he said. "The bloody HERALDS!" A smile broke out across his face. He rubbed his dirty hands through his hair, his feet dancing back and forth. "Do you know what this means!?"

Laurel looked back up to find the Heralds slowly descending back to the earth, hands outstretched to the congregating soldiers and civilians. They were everything she would expect of a god, graceful and benevolent, saviors to a fallen people. But something tickled at the back of her mind.

"People of Felia!" the male Herald announced. His voice carried far in the silent aftermath of the battle. "Your Heralds have returned. Come to us and be healed."

Men and women flocked to the gods. Laurel followed Alverax as they joined the amassing throng. Asher kept his distance.

As they grew closer, Alverax led them through the crowd. When the people saw his robes, they parted. Soon, they came into view of the Heralds once again, and Laurel watched in awe as a dying man was placed in front of the gods. A bite had opened the dying man's stomach, blood pooling across his naval and down his sides. The male Herald poured a few drops of water into the open wound, then pressed his hand down gently atop the bleeding, whispering words of power. The dying man inhaled until his lungs were filled to bursting. Then, his head fell to the earth.

The crowd gasped, and the Herald lifted a hand to calm them. As he raised his other hand, he revealed the gaping wound from the man's stomach. It had been completely healed. "This man will live but must now rest."

"Come all who are wounded, and we will care for you," the female Herald said.

They continued their healings until General Thallin appeared. Laurel saw Alverax take a step forward but hesitated as his friend approached the gods. They finished healing a woman who'd had a series of scratches across her face but left without blemish. Part of Laurel wanted to offer herself to them, to have them heal her bruises, but she knew others had greater need...like her grandfather.

As soon as the thought entered her mind, she moved to go fetch him, but paused when Thallin spoke.

"Divine Heralds!" he said. "I am Thallin Haichess, swordmaster and general to the Sun Queen, Empress Jisenna Vayse. We have long awaited your return to this world."

The male Herald stepped forward. "As have we, Thallin Haichess. Tell me, where is the empress now?"

"She is in the palace, my god."

"Go. Tell her to prepare for our arrival."

Thallin nodded. "It will be done."

As the general departed, hundreds of Felians crowded the field. Laurel pushed herself through the growing crowd until she finally escaped its clutches. She ran, and Asher joined beside her. Together, they headed to the Zeda encampment. People gawked as she ran opposite the crowds, some in fear and some in awe at her enormous chroma-wolf companion. But she ignored them all. This was the miracle she needed to save her grandfather.

If she hadn't seen it with her own eyes, watching them hover in the air and banish the corespawn with nothing more than words, she'd think the grounders had lost their minds. But she *had* seen it. She'd watched the monsters fleeing through their dark tunnel like frightened insects, and she'd seen the gods descending from the skies, taking wounded and healing them.

If the Heralds were real, and they *had* returned, what did that mean of her own beliefs? The elders taught of the Father of All, a singular entity who created the world and all of the beauty upon it. And then, when the world was rich with life, he offered drops of his own soul to inhabit the world. People. Divinely born children of a heavenly being. And when a person died, the Father's essence would ride the winds back to the greater whole to continue in a cycle of rebirth. The elders claimed their beliefs predated the beliefs of the pagan grounders, but the age of a belief doesn't make it any more true.

If the Heralds were real, and they *had* returned, was none of it real? Was there no Father of All? Was the divinity of man a lie? What of the Gale? If there was no rebirth, and no essence to return to the Father of All, why would they sacrifice the elderly to make room for the young?

Anger swelled within her, but she pushed it away. It didn't matter, not right now at least. What mattered was that there was a way for her to help her grandfather.

She reached the Zeda encampment and was surprised to find it as empty as the rest of the city. Her people, who didn't believe in the Heralds, had gone to witness the pagan gods in person. She wandered the tents, trying to remember which one was her grandfather's. So far from the battlefield, silence seemed to linger in the air like a thick fog.

She kept her bond with Asher, illuminating the threadlight around her. If there were any corespawn still around, she wanted to know. She lifted her nose to the wind and followed the putrid trail of illness.

When she found the tent, she pushed the flap back and stepped inside. Her grandfather slept on his bed and she hoped with all her heart that the Heralds could heal him. He was a good man, and good men deserve good things. But the world had a tendency to step over good men and leave them with nothing but muddy prints to lie in.

She approached Corian and took his hand in her own. "Grandfather, I found someone who is going to heal you."

She rubbed the back of his hand with her other.

"You wouldn't believe it, but I saw them heal a grounder missing half of his stomach."

She moved her hand to his shoulder and pressed.

"I'm sure your cough will be nothing."

Her grandfather continued to sleep. He was so calm, a firm root in the soil, basking in the lamplight. She imagined herself after *bonding* with Asher, quietly sleeping for days while she recovered, her chest rising and falling as her mind sailed through the storm.

But her grandfather's chest did not rise, nor did it fall.

His body rested in the perfect measure of stillness. It was a painting, so vivid she could see the wrinkles in his cheeks and smell the odor of his skin. So lifelike that she could feel the coarseness of his fingertips. It had to be a painting—it couldn't be real—because, if it was, that would mean...

Her grandfather was dead.

No.

Please, no.

Not him.

Not now.

Father of All, I just need one more hour.

Please.

She reached up to feel for his pulse but stopped. She couldn't. She wouldn't. In her heart, she already knew, but she could not let herself truly *know*. She could feel it in the stiffness of his palm. She could see it in the tint of his lips. But she refused to accept the truth. He wasn't gone.

Not him. His essence was a bird migrating for the winter, and, at any moment, it would return, and he would resume his life once again.

Tears swelled within her, a cracked dam in a raging river, but it was her brother's voice that broke her. "Laurel."

That single word slammed an axe through the wood, and she broke in two. She could no longer hold back the pain. She could no longer lie to herself. Asher nuzzled her, whimpering as he tried to comfort her.

She turned as Bay limped toward her. He ignored Asher—he ignored their grandfather—and he wrapped her up in his long arms more fiercely than a mother clutching her sickly child.

They held each other as they embraced the cold darkness swirling in the tent. Laurel felt a strange sense of deja vu as she remembered mourning the death of their parents. But, where once her grandfather had lived to comfort them, now they were alone to comfort themselves. It wasn't fair. After all they had gone through. Laurel felt a stirring inside her, a harsh pressure squeezing against her mind, burning away the pain and leaving nothing but the charred remains of anger. It wasn't *fair*.

She pulled away from Bay, an idea beginning to bud. "They can still heal him."

Lifting herself to her feet, she looked at the cot her grandfather was on.

Bay's eyes were like two red sunsets set against a pale sky. "Laurel, what are you—"

"Asher," Laurel said, stroking the chromawolf's face. "I know you don't like doing it, but I need you to carry my grandfather for me."

Asher nodded, and his gravelly voice resonated in her mind. *Carry. Good.*

"Bay, help me lift him onto Asher," Laurel said. "It's not over yet."

"Laurel!" her brother shouted. "What are you talking about!?"

"The grounder gods are here. They're at the battlefield healing the wounded. They can save grandfather."

He furrowed his brows. "Laurel, I want him back as much as you do, but he's gone."

"No, he's not."

"Laurel..."

"He's not gone yet!" she shouted. "Help me get him on Asher. I can still save him."

Bay hesitated but complied. Together, they lifted Corian face-down onto Asher's thick green fur, draped over like an old rug.

It was going to work.

It had to.

Otherwise, she didn't know what she'd do.

42

Alverax stared in awe as the event for which he was sworn to prepare came to pass. He wanted to believe—hell, they'd saved the city and healed nearly a hundred people—but, even with such astounding evidence, he found himself doubting. If only Osinan could have seen it, he could have died knowing that the words he'd preached for so many years weren't just hollow hope; they were true.

The Heralds had literally saved them!

His grandfather had told him that the Heralds watched men from their divine realm, only transcending to ours in the world's hour of greatest need. Which, in a way, meant that the Felian resistance had failed. The corespawn would have destroyed them all. But, in a more important way, it meant that they were safe now.

"Watchlord!" a voice called out. A young woman with hair pulled back in tight braids against her scalp pointed at Alverax in the midst of the crowd.

He hesitated as the people around him suddenly became aware of his presence. They backed away, eyeing his robes.

Both Heralds turned to him.

His heart raced in his chest, threadlight beckoning him for release. Their prismatic eyes bore into his soul, weighing him, judging his worth and questioning his loyalty. He wanted to run, and keep running, until he was back in Cynosure where he could hide in the shed out back behind his grandfather's home. Somewhere far away from responsibility and expectation.

"Who is this?" the female Herald asked, approaching him as she finished healing a minor scrape.

The male Herald eyed the sword still dangling from Alverax's limp wrist. "It cannot be." He approached Alverax and stretched out his hand. "May I?"

"Of course," Alverax said, handing the Midnight Watcher to the Herald.

A pale hand caressed the length of the blade as the Herald smiled at the sword. In that moment, Alverax realized that both of the Heralds looked more Alchean than Felian. He'd always imagined them with darker skin, similar to his own.

"Where did you get this?" the male Herald asked.

Alverax tried—and failed—to keep the gaze of the Herald, but the prismatic eyes were too much. Instead, he alternated his gaze between the ground and the Herald's eyes. "It was given to me when I became Watchlord. They told me that it's been handed down from generation to generation. A gift from you to the first Watchlord."

"Mmmm," the Herald said. "Tell me, what is a Watchlord? I do not..." He trailed off and smiled. "You are a Destroyer."

"I—what?" Alverax said, his heart quickening.

"Ah, yes. You would call them Obsidian threadweavers. I can see it in your eyes. You have the power to destroy, do you not?"

Alverax nodded.

"And what of the Amber threadweavers? Are there any here?"

The question caught him off guard and, at first, it angered him. He thought of Alabella. He imagined her becoming the right hand of the Heralds, and the idea boiled his blood. But then he thought of Aydin, the little Valerian child, he was an Amber threadweaver too. Maybe, he—

"All Amber threadweavers," the Herald announced, opening himself to the rest of the crowd, "are to be brought to us at once. We will need them for the days to come. Anyone with information about the whereabouts of such people will be rewarded."

"I know where to find one!" a familiar voice called out. The crowd parted in chaotic fashion as Laurel and her chromawolf stepped through the throng. A man was draped over the back of the massive chromawolf. As she approached, her voice grew quieter. "If you heal my grandfather, I can bring one of the Amber threadweavers to you."

"You..." the male Herald said, pausing to contemplate the request. "You are bold to make such a demand. But I am feeling generous. Bring him to me."

Asher growled, and Laurel reprimanded him. Alverax thought he saw her whisper something to the chromawolf as if it could understand her. The animal strode forward and rolled its shoulder so that the Herald could lift the man off its back. Alverax was close enough to see that it was the same old man that had been lying on a cot in the Zeda tent. His skin was pale and stiff.

The Herald turned his head to Laurel. "This man is dead."

"You're a god," Laurel said flatly. "Bring him back."

"Death can be prevented, but it cannot be undone."

Laurel stood tall, staring into the Herald's prismatic eyes, a slight quiver in her lip.

"Mmmm," the male Herald said, tilting his head slightly. "You say you know the location of one of the Amber threadweavers? Bring them to me, and I will help this man."

"You can bring him back?"

"Yes," the Herald said. "If you bring the Amber threadweaver to me."

A deep growl emanated from the massive chromawolf beside Laurel. She snapped her head to him and furrowed her brows. She shook her head, then whispered something.

"I'll be back," Laurel said. She turned to Alverax and her eyes released their tension. "Can you help me lift him?"

He nodded, and they lifted her grandfather, setting him atop the chromawolf.

Surprisingly, Laurel leaned in for an embrace. Alverax softly returned the gesture as Laurel whispered so only he could hear. "Don't trust them. Meet me at the clocktower in two hours. Alabella is here."

Laurel let go of the embrace and led Asher back the way they'd come.

43

Chrys gestured for Willow and Roshaw to follow as he crouched behind a large rock formation. Not far beyond, the army of corespawn had amassed, but, instead of battering against the massive Felian wall, they'd dug a hole. A gaping hole wide as a large house, that extended deep into the earth. The massive corespawn monstrosities slid their hands through the ground like dough, kneading and discarding it in colossal chunks.

"If we head further south, we can sneak around them," Chrys said to the others. "We need to find a way in."

"Are you being serious, Chrys?" Roshaw asked. "There are corespawn around the *entire* city. We're not going to sneak around them."

Chrys clenched his jaw. "So, what? We go through the tunnel? You want to fight your way through thousands of corespawn in the dark?"

Roshaw raised his brows. "Chrys, I love you, but you're an idiot."

Chrys scowled.

"We're basically the most powerful people in the world now." Roshaw raised his hands, showing off his multi-colored veins. "We don't have to go through...or under. We can just go over."

"Stones," Chrys said. He'd spent his entire life becoming the pinnacle of a Sapphire threadweaver, but he was so much more now. "Let's stick together, make sure we don't drift apart, and try to stay low. We should still wrap around to the south where there are less gathered, ideally where there are none of the big ones. I don't want anyone getting swiped out of the sky, or any boulders flying our way."

"Sounds good to me." Roshaw nodded. "But first, I want to know how Willow stopped that thing's foot from coming down."

Willow, lifting her chin with a bit of pride, gave him the smallest smirk. "Sapphires can *surge* their threadlight, *pushing* out with an unfocused burst, but it does little good. There's not enough energy to stop the incoming force of any projectiles. Unless you surge both Sapphire and Obsidian at the same time. The Obsidian *breaks* the projectile's acceleration, and the Sapphire *pushes* it away. "

"Heralds, but that's clever."

"I always knew my overwhelming wit would one day save lives," she said with a grin.

Chrys looked out over the field. "We should go. It's only a matter of time before—"

Chaos and clamor bellowed out from beyond the Felian wall.

"Stones," Chrys cursed. "Their tunnel must have breached the city already. We need to go, now!"

The three companions snuck around to the south, finding a section surrounded by relatively few of the corespawn horde, and none of the giants. They *broke* their corethreads and *pushed* off toward the top of the city wall, drifting in an unnaturally straight line. A howling wind blew them slightly off course, but they linked arms and stayed together. As they drifted over the top, they *pulled* on threads connecting them to the wall, and landed back on solid footing.

A pair of guards and a young boy stood paralyzed a short distance away. The guards held swords, but their stance told Chrys enough about their experience.

"It's okay," Chrys said, his own eyes glowing with multi-colored threadlight. "We're here to help."

The young boy, Emerald eyes aglow, took a step back.

Chrys raised his hands to calm their fear. "We're going to continue on. Keep an eye out for the corespawn. Do not let them over this wall."

The guards seemed to accept that, relaxing their guard, but still eyeing the three with caution. Chrys waved for the others to follow him and they leapt from atop the wall-walk, *pushing* off the ground for a graceful landing on the dirt far below.

They moved eastward, toward the site of the breached tunnel. Surprisingly, the sound of warfare had ceased. There was no screaming. No battering of metal and wood. No trembling of movement across the ground. Only eerie stillness, sweeping through empty streets.

The cobblestone felt good beneath his feet, a familiar feeling he'd never have expected to miss, and, as they searched the streets for people —for his wife and son—the sense of familiarity soothed the rising tension in his shoulders.

As they walked, Chrys caught Roshaw filling his pocket with a handful of nuts from an abandoned stall.

Suddenly, a green blur came barreling through a side street, accompanied by a young blonde girl. It took Chrys only a moment to recognize *the one that got away*.

"Laurel?"

He took off after her and the others followed.

44

As Laurel walked through the Zeda camp, the stillness took on the calm serenity of a haunted field, people wandering like unsettled ghosts. Bay helped Laurel place Corian back in his cot, and she took off to the north to find Alabella.

Each Felian city-street brought with it a life of its own. As Laurel wandered through them, trying to find her way back to Alabella's safehouse, she saw some streets bustling with festivities, and other streets so still and quiet that they might have been nothing but a mirage.

She reflected on her experience with the Heralds. The man had told her exactly what she'd wanted to hear, but only after she'd promised them Alabella. Something about that bothered Asher as much as it did her. Either way, her grandfather was now back in the Zeda camp with Bay.

Asher's words, as she'd spoken with the Heralds, chipped away at her hope, but she ignored him. What else could she do? If she didn't try to save her grandfather, she would never forgive herself.

They passed a cart filled with smashed elletberries, a delicious striped yellow and red fruit that turned the color of dung when mashed together and had a very distinct scent.

Disgust, Asher said beside her.

She picked one from the abandoned cart and ate it—they'd been a favorite of hers growing up—but now, as the flavor touched her tongue, she spit it out. Somehow, it tasted the same but also disgusting at the same time.

"Disgust is right," she said to Asher, wiping her fingers on her pants.

"They're better in jam," a man's voice said.

Laurel turned to see a large man with his massive hand outstretched in greeting.

"Barrick!" she shouted with excitement.

"Heard a girl and a chromawolf were wandering the streets."

"I'm lost," Laurel said. "I'm glad to see you. I need to find Alabella."

"Of course, of course. The house is just around the corner," he said, gesturing for her to follow.

She did and in no time they were entering the small safehouse. Barrick gestured for Asher to stay outside, but the chromawolf refused, and Laurel assured Barrick it would be fine. The large man seemed to doubt her, but also seemed uninterested in fighting them on the matter. The door swung open with a loud, creaky groan. And when they entered, she found Alabella and Sarla sitting beside a small table in the corner of the kitchen.

"Laurel!" Sarla said with excitement. She'd changed her clothes, now wearing a bright red dress that matched the color of her two-toned hair. "We have news!"

Alabella waved her over. "Come, come. It's not safe out there, and there is much to discuss. Like why Asher is with you, and why you smell so terrible." She paused. "Wait, you were there, weren't you?"

"Where?" Laurel asked as she approached the table.

"The battle," Alabella said. "Barrick heard rumors on the streets, people saying the Heralds have returned. Do you know anything about this?"

"It's true," she said. "I saw them with my own eyes."

"Heralds—" Alabella began, but she caught herself and laughed. "Guess I'll need a new curse."

Sarla's eyes grew wide beneath her odd glasses. "I *must* speak with them. Think of all the knowledge they must possess! The questions that we can answer! Infinite possibilities. Imagine the inventions, the progress! Everything could change."

"We did this," Alabella said. "They are here because of the corespawn. I knew there was a connection! We brought back the bloody Heralds!"

"At what cost?" Laurel said.

"Cost be damned!" Alabella said with a laugh. "The loss of a few forgettable lives in exchange for the return of the Heralds? It makes it all worth it. Everything we've done."

"They can tell us why the previous grafts have failed," Sarla said. "They can show us the proper way. Laurel, you can receive a theolith from the Heralds themselves!"

"Speaking of," Alabella said, pushing her chair into place beneath the table and looking to Laurel. "The ship arrived with your new theolith."

Laurel's eyes grew wide, her breath catching in her chest. Threadlight. The gift she longed for more than anything else. The gift she still reached for out of habit, though its influence had long left her behind. If they had a theolith, the warmth of threadlight could once again run from her chest out through her veins, heating her from within, and healing her. A slight tremble returned to her hand, or perhaps it had always been there, and she only now remembered it.

"There is nothing more for us to do but take a trip to the docks." Alabella continued. "I had not expected it so soon, but it is time. Laurel, you are going to be a threadweaver again."

"I..." Laurel trailed off.

What had once seemed impossible was now within her reach. One trip to the docks and she could be a threadweaver again. Then she'd be done with...

Alabella.

The woman the Heralds wanted.

But the Heralds were not what they seemed. As soon as the man had told her he could save her grandfather, Asher had growled into her mind: *lies, evil, run.* No matter how much she wanted to believe the Herald, he'd said it himself. Death cannot be undone.

Laurel wandered in her mind, grasping at truths that shifted like shadows in the night. But still Alabella's words echoed throughout her.

"Laurel?" Alabella said, tilting her head to the side, still waiting for her answer.

But Laurel didn't respond, instead she stood in silence with a single word sizzling on her tongue: why? Why did she want to be a threadweaver? Because it made her feel powerful? The part of her that craved threadlight was a crutch. Her weakness was not that she wasn't a threadweaver, but that she needed it to feel whole.

The truth fueled her, burning energy within her. She didn't need threadlight to be whole. Look at her! Without threadweaving, she'd stood in a sea of mythical creatures and slaughtered them like livestock. She was already strong.

She was already enough.

So, she made a decision.

In the blink of an eye, Laurel slipped out the obsidian dagger and thrust it into Alabella's chest. The woman's eyes and veins blazed with Amber threadlight, but it was too late, and the thread-dead blade could not be stopped.

Sarla gasped, her hands springing up to cover her mouth.

"No!" Barrick shouted. He rushed forward with fire in his eyes, but Asher leapt between him and Laurel. The large man attacked the chromawolf, fighting to get through to Alabella, kicking and attempting to wrestle the massive wolf. But Asher was strong and smart. And though he tried not to kill him, Barrick wouldn't stop. He landed a massive fist across Asher's face, and the chromawolf responded with teeth bearing down on the flesh of his neck. Barrick slumped to the floor.

Laurel leaned into Alabella and used the leverage of the knife to shove her up against the wall. Blood drooled from the dying woman's mouth. Laurel stared into her Amber eyes, twisting the knife into her chest. "May the winds guide you."

The door of the safehouse creaked behind her and a familiar—but unexpected—voice screamed, "NO!"

45

Chrys rushed forward and, when Asher growled and tried to stop him, he *broke* the chromawolf's corethread, leaving him to float helplessly. He rushed to Alabella, shoving Laurel out of the way and ripping the knife out of her chest. He pressed against the open wound with his palm. Blood streamed from the gash, running over his hands like an overflowing kettle. She coughed blood onto his face.

He couldn't let her die. Their plan would fail without her. Aydin was the only other Amber threadweaver, and they couldn't put the fate of the world in the hands of a child.

"Come on! Breathe!" he shouted.

He pushed harder against the wound, but it made no difference. The woman's eyes went cold, and her body sagged to the floor. He watched as the life faded from her Amber eyes.

She was dead.

Chrys turned to Laurel, his lips quivering with rage. "What have you done?"

Laurel took a step back, her brows furrowed, and her cheeks flushed. "She destroyed Zedalum. She killed my people. She...she tried to kill your family!"

"Child," Willow said from the doorway, standing beside Roshaw. "You have no idea what you've done."

"I'm not a child," Laurel snarled.

"No," Chrys spat. "You're the little woman who damned us all."

"What is your problem?" Laurel said angrily. "We all wanted her dead. You. Me. All of the Zeda wanted revenge. Even the Felians want the Bloodthieves dead! You should be thanking me!"

"I should rip your damn heart out!" Chrys shouted.

"Chrys Valerian!" Willow said sharply. "Laurel had no way of knowing. She did what she thought was right with the information she had. Calm yourself."

Ahhh! Chrys wanted to throw his fists against the wall. Bash them until they were bloody pulps. This was their chance! She was the crux of the plan. Not Aydin. He wasn't strong enough, and they couldn't wait however many years it took. He strangled the hilt of the obsidian blade, barely holding himself back from hurling it across the room.

"No way of knowing what?" Laurel said.

Willow stepped into the room, eyeing the dead man on the floor and the odd woman who stood quietly in the corner. "The corespawn are only the beginning. There is something much worse coming."

"Worse than the corespawn?" Laurel asked.

Willow nodded. "We came from the Wastelands. Their gods are planning a slaughter. We came to stop them, but we needed her." She gestured to the dead woman.

Laurel clenched her jaw and pursed her lips, looking to Asher for a brief moment. "Why does it have to be Alabella?"

Willow sighed. "We need Amber threadweavers."

"So, take her theolith and put it in someone else," Laurel said. "It doesn't have to be her."

Chrys paused.

"It doesn't work like that," he said.

Laurel kept his gaze, challenging him. "You still have Aydin."

"You know where he is?"

"They're both here," she said. "In the palace."

Tension flowed out of Chrys like a smith's bellows releasing its air. They were alive! He felt the winds of rage within him shift their course, homing in on a greater purpose. He needed to find his family, and he needed to get them to safety.

A light seemed to flicker in Laurel's eyes. "Wait," she said. "We don't need an Amber threadweaver! We have something better."

All eyes in the room turned to her.

"The Heralds!"

"What are you talking about?" Willow asked with a sense of reservation.

"The Heralds have returned! I was there. They fought off the corespawn and won the battle. They've been healing the wounded ever since."

"The Heralds," Chrys said, wincing as he tried to make sense of it all.

"Stones," Willow cursed.

Chrys looked to her. "What?"

"No, no, no, no," Willow repeated, running her hands through her hair. "We were so wrong."

"What?" Roshaw repeated.

Willow looked to Laurel. "Those are not the Heralds."

46

THE HERALDS HAD SPOKEN LITTLE on the journey from the battlefield to the palace, but there was something about the look on their faces that disturbed Alverax. A certain sense of displeasure or disdain that seemed uncharacteristic of a god. But still, he'd seen the miracles, and witnessed their victory over the corespawn. He never would have expected such an event possible had he not seen it with his own eyes.

When they entered the throne room, he felt a chill in the air, the shadow of a fear not yet realized. Jisenna stood beside the throne, not daring to claim such nobility in the face of gods. Even her clothing seemed less extravagant. Where she normally wore white and gold, she'd changed to wear black and silver. He found himself smiling when he saw her, the face of peace in a turbulent time.

She dropped to a knee and bowed. "My Heralds," she said. "There are not words to express our joy at your arrival. Not only because of the war at our walls, but because of our long-held belief that you would one day return to reclaim your people."

The male Herald strode forward, head held high. He looked around the room at the swarm of guards lining each side of the dais. "We will speak to the empress alone," he said.

The guards, hesitating despite the order from their god, bowed and filed out. Alverax moved to join them, but the Herald gestured for him to stay.

"It is my understanding that the two of you are representatives of the people, and, in a small way, you are also meant to represent the two of us." He and the female Herald approached the dais, eyeing Jisenna's clothing that draped along the floor where she knelt. "In the coming days, your loyalty will be tested. We will protect Felia. We will protect its people. But the corespawn are not the only enemy. Other nations are plotting your destruction. With our aid, you will bring all other nations to heel, and Felia will be the greatest empire this world has ever seen."

Jisenna, biting her lip, lifted her head to meet the Heralds' eyes. "We are at peace with the other countries. If you help us stop the corespawn army, surely there is no need for further bloodshed."

"You think you know more than your gods?" the female Herald asked with a hint of spite. "You are a pebble advising the mountain on how to stand firm. Do not question our words."

Jisenna bowed her head. "Of course, my gods."

A knock sounded at the door, and the female Herald moved to open it. A guard spoke to her then retreated into the hallway.

She turned to the male Herald and smiled. "They found the child."

"Good," he said. "Take care of it."

She nodded and exited the throne room, leaving only Alverax, Jisenna, and the male Herald.

"You," he said, turning and gesturing to Alverax. "Do you also question us?"

Alverax bowed his head, suddenly feeling that being in the presence of gods was more dangerous than he'd expected. "No, my Herald. And I don't think that Jisenna would ever question you either. There is a reason the people call her the Mistress of Mercy. She will serve you well."

Jisenna peeked up from her kneeling position and gave him the slightest smile. It was then, with that smallest of gestures, that Alverax realized how much he cared for her. Jisenna was all that was good in the world. She'd made him a better man. She'd made the world a better place with her words and deeds.

The Herald scowled. "What did you say?"

"She will serve you well," Alverax repeated, feeling a sudden tightness in his chest.

"No," the Herald said. "What did you call her?"

Alverax felt a sense of relief. "The Mistress of Mercy. She's built a reputation for being kind and merciful to the people of Felia."

"Mercy," the Herald said, lifting his chin and eyeing Jisenna from narrow eyes. "There can be no mercy."

He raised the Midnight Watcher and the world slowed.

Alverax's chest swelled.

Every bit of breath vanished from his lungs.

A fire raged in his soul.

And he froze as the obsidian blade struck down Jisenna.

A cloud of darkness swirled in his vision, dizzying, burning, pulling at the warmth he felt for her. But it was too late. Still kneeling, the blade struck her neck. It lay embedded in her like she was just another log for the fire.

The Herald yanked it out of her bloody corpse, and she collapsed to the floor with her brown eyes wide open.

He turned to Alverax with a face free of all emotion. "The empress gave her life to strengthen the Heralds. It was a heroic offering, and she is to be remembered for her sacrifice. You understand?"

Alverax nodded, but he barely grasped the words.

She was gone.

Jisenna, the woman who'd saved him.

The woman who'd changed him for the better.

Dead.

"Good," the Herald said, wiping the blade and handing the hilt of the Midnight Watcher to Alverax. "The sword is yours, Destroyer. I have no need of it. So long as you are loyal, I will make you a god among men. Now, go. Tell the people of their empress' sacrifice. They will love her for it."

47

Chrys felt a shiver crawl up his spine. As soon as the words left her mouth, he knew Willow was right. Two Heralds, showing up to save the city from the corespawn? It had to be Relek and Lylax.

"What do you mean they're *not* the Heralds?" Laurel asked.

Willow's gaze intensified. "Let me guess. One of the Heralds is a tall, light-skinned man, mid-thirties, red hair. The other is a woman, maybe forty, dark hair? They both have eyes that shine like prisms?"

"I don't..." A light turned on in Laurel's eyes. "Gale take me. They're the wastelander gods."

"It doesn't make sense," Roshaw said. "They were coming to destroy the city, not become their gods. Why would they...oh, shit."

"What?" Chrys said.

Roshaw massaged his temples. "What if they *are* the Heralds? The stories say the Heralds just disappeared one day at the height of their power."

"The coreseal," Willow said.

"Exactly," Roshaw said, pointing his finger at her. "The Amber threadweavers bound them far away from here, and now they're back for revenge."

Chrys took in every word, feeling the weight of it pulling on him like a thousand Amber threads. Relek and Lylax were not just the gods of the east, they were the gods of the west as well. But Alchaeus claimed they were coming to exact revenge for their centuries of imprisonment. Why would they become the Heralds again?

There was too much at stake to let the details go undiscovered.

Laurel paled. "They said they needed the Amber threadweavers for their plans, but really they wanted them out of their way."

"Only the Amber threadweavers can create the binding to stop them," Chrys said.

"Gale take me," Laurel whispered to herself. "I did exactly what they wanted."

"You had no way of knowing," Willow said. "We'll find another way."

"We need to find Iriel and Aydin," Chrys added.

"There..." Roshaw hesitated. "There is another option. In Cynosure, there is another Amber threadweaver. A man called Jelium. I would have mentioned it before, but we didn't need him. And I doubt he would be willing to help us."

Chrys scowled. "The lives of hundreds of thousands of people are at stake. If there is someone who *can* help us, I will not take no for an answer."

"You really don't know Jelium," Roshaw said.

"No," Chrys said with fire in his eyes. "And he doesn't know me. If he's the last chance we have at protecting the world, then that's too damn bad. When the world is at stake, you don't get to be a selfish asshole."

"The ship!" Laurel chimed in. "There is a ship at the docks that came from Cynosure. The crew will know how to get back."

"Good," Chrys said with a nod. "Laurel, take the others and prepare the ship."

"Gale take me!" she nearly shouted. "I'm supposed to meet someone at the clocktower. He's *from* Cynosure. If I can convince him to come, he can guide us when we're there!"

"Fine," Chrys said, tossing her the obsidian blade. "But be at the docks as soon as you can. Roshaw, see if you can figure out which ship it is." He turned to the odd woman in the corner. "What do we do with her?"

Laurel responded as she walked toward the door. "She's harmless."

"Okay." Chrys nodded, looking to the woman. "You are free to leave."

She did, quietly.

Chrys turned back to Roshaw. "At the docks, don't hide that you're a hybrid threadweaver. The crew may need a little convincing. My mother and I will go find Iriel and Aydin in the palace. I want the ship ready to depart as soon as we arrive. There's a chance we'll have an army, or worse, chasing after us."

Laurel rushed out the door with Asher, followed by Roshaw.

Willow looked to Chrys and smiled. "Let's get your family back."

Entering the palace was surprisingly easy, as most of the guards were posted around the outer wall, and those still guarding the palace held no fear of human enemy. Willow asked a servant shuffling down one of the hallways where they could find the Zeda guests, and they quickly made their way up two flights of stairs and down a series of winding pathways.

Anxiety prickled away at Chrys' mind. From the proximity to Relek and Lylax, to the search for his wife and son, to the scent of roses filling the palace that now reminded him of the deadly corespawn. Ominous feelings surrounded him like a midnight mist.

As they walked through a particularly wide corridor, Chrys heard a voice, and it set his heart aflame. He ran to the end of the hallway, and, when he glanced around the corner, he saw Iriel, holding Aydin, encircled by a squad of Felian soldiers in black.

He left behind all sense of caution, and ran at them head on, letting a river of threadlight pour through his veins. One by one, he grabbed hold of the corethread of every guard and *broke* it, then, with as much force as he could muster, he *pushed* off the wall behind him, launching forward like a ballista bolt. He crashed into one side of the guards, and his momentum transferred to their weightless bodies, sending them flying down the hallway, crashing off the walls and each other.

Chrys rushed in close to the remaining guards, using a mixture of hand-to-hand combat techniques. With their corethreads *broken*, every blow—even those that were blocked—knocked the guards off balance, tumbling in awkward, weightless flips. He brought his foot up and kicked the final guard, launching him down the hallway in an impossibly straight line.

When he turned and saw her, his heart burst into flame

Iriel.

His heart and soul.

His purpose.

His uncut diamond.

He tried to smile, but his quivering lips refused to form the arch. It seemed a dream to see her again, a trick of the eye. Her eyes swelled with tears, and, when she said his name—no more than a breath slipping from her lips—Chrys shattered. He rushed to her, and she to him, and they embraced with such ferocity that he thought their souls would meld together.

He looked down and saw Aydin, eyes open, cooing in her arms. Such innocence caught up in such chaos. But his father was there now. He would protect him. And someday soon, Aydin would aid in protecting the entire world.

"I knew you would come back," Iriel said.

Chrys smiled, remembering his mother's words. "There is nothing in this world that could have stopped me."

Willow, only a few paces away, smiled. "Chrys, we need to go."

He nodded and took Iriel's hand. "We're getting far away from here. I'll explain everything later."

She lifted his hand, kissed it, and let go.

They took off down the hallway, threadlight in their veins, but just as they rounded the first bend, they stopped in their tracks. In the center of the walkway, accompanied by an older man with a sword, stood Lylax, goddess of the Wastelands, immortal Herald of the west.

And she was smiling.

48

"You," the goddess said with a smirk. "I thought you were dead."

Chrys' lip twitched. "Iriel, get Aydin to safety. Mother, you know where to go."

As soon as he said the words, he felt a wrenching in his gut. He'd traveled hundreds of miles, through the wastelands, through the core of the earth itself, to reunite with his family, and now he sent them away. But he had no other choice. They couldn't kill Lylax—she was immortal. More people only meant more danger for everyone, especially Aydin.

No, this was Chrys' fight.

He-who-does-not-cower.

The Apogee.

"Chrys," Iriel said. "I can help."

"Not this time," he said, fighting off the pain of their shortened reunion. "I'll be right behind you."

Willow hesitated, then nodded. He knew it would tear her apart to leave him behind after giving so much to get him there, but she understood, and he loved her for it all the more. She tossed the obsidian dagger to Chrys, and they headed down a different hallway, Iriel leading the way.

Chrys spun the dagger in his hand and looked to Lylax. "I heard you can't die. We'll see about that."

The guard standing beside Lylax stepped away, carrying his sword with trepidation.

Chrys rushed her, and her lips curled into a sadistic grin.

Lylax's veins swirled with prismatic color, and threads, like ghostly hands, stretched forth from the ground, grasping at Chrys' legs. His own Obsidian threadlight surged and the artificial threads burst apart beneath him. He continued forward, his voice growing to a crescendo with each step. She tried once more to bind him with threads, and once again he *broke* them without breaking stride.

Finally, she snarled, set her feet, and took off toward him. As they collided, Chrys found an opening and slid the obsidian blade up through her sternum. With both hands free, and one of his still clutching the hilt of the dagger, she set to work pounding into his skull and scraping her raw nails against his skin. He rolled to the side, kicking her away and yanking the dagger back.

He looked to the place where he'd struck with the blade and saw less blood than he would have expected. Instead, threadlight pooled in the wound, swirling as if a gust of wind were drawn into her body. Somewhere far in the east, a wastelander was collapsing into the swamp water as their lifelight was drained by the goddess.

He couldn't kill her—he already knew that—but it had still felt damn good to run her through with the blade. The truth was that he didn't need to win; he just needed to keep her occupied long enough for his wife and mother to escape.

The man who'd accompanied her was standing off to the side, closer to Chrys now than Lylax. He stood quietly marveling at the immortality of one of the Heralds—this fight would cement her godhood in his eyes. But that didn't matter...Chrys had an idea.

He took off toward the man, *pushing* off the wall behind him and *pulling* on the wall in front, blasting through the air faster than he'd ever moved. He crashed with such force that he was sure the man was dead on impact. Chrys felt a pain surge up through his legs as he hit, but threadlight coursed through his veins in record amounts, providing strength and a small trace of immediate healing like never before.

When he looked up, Lylax was walking toward him, frowning with Autelle's lips and scowling with her eyes. Chrys reached down and lifted the man's longsword off the ground. It had a good length, though it was lighter than he'd have preferred. He had to be careful. As a prismatic threadweaver, Lylax could *push* and *pull* the blade just as easily as he could. It would make the fight more dangerous. He hoped that her inability to do the same to the obsidian dagger would be enough to confuse her attention.

Suddenly, he felt a sense of vertigo wash over him, and the walls seemed to close around him. Something reached into his soul, grasping at his lifelight. It was her. She was trying to do what Relek had done in the mountains to the soldiers. Chrys threw his will against it, just as he had done to Relek in his own mind, and he felt the attack retreat.

"You're out of practice," Chrys said, feeling a sense of relief.

She glanced at the sword in his hand. "Perhaps, but you are only delaying the inevitable. You cannot kill me, and you will make a mistake soon enough."

"You lost once. You can lose again."

At the final word, Chrys pounced at her, slashing down hard with the longsword. She *pushed* on the blade, sending it wide, so he thrust in with the obsidian dagger in his offhand. She *pushed* again, but the blade continued forward, cutting at her side. Her dress slit and the skin cut open for a moment before resealing.

Chrys reached out to her corethread and *broke* it. She responded with the same, while simultaneously creating a new corethread for herself from artificial threads. Chrys *broke* those as well, and soon they both hovered in the air, weightless. This was the moment his idea would succeed or fail, and, if it failed, he would have no choice but to run.

He pointed the longsword at her, letting threadlight build up within him until his veins were ready to burst, then released it all in a surge of energy, *pushing* the longsword in a straight line. He then reached out to the blade with his mind, and—thanks to Willow—created a dome of energy around it. The sword shot forward in a blur of light and, when Lylax tried to *push* it out of the way, the dome rejected her. The longsword shot through her chest, impaling her, and sending her weightless body blasting backward into the nearest wall. The force of the momentum embedded the blade in the wall through Lylax's stomach to the hilt. The goddess choked, hanging on the wall like a tortured painting.

As soon as his corethread reappeared, Chrys walked over to Lylax. Her own gravity had also returned, and her body sagged against the longsword, coughing and choking, though no blood came out.

"You will pay for this!" she spat.

Chrys calmly cut off a piece of his tunic and tied it over her eyes. "This isn't over."

Then, he ran.

49

Alverax ran outside, gasping for air, and dropped the sword as he collapsed to the ground. His heart throbbed in his chest, pounding with such fervor it threatened to burst. He tried to breathe, but each breath was a war that he wasn't sure he wanted to win. Nothing mattered anymore. He didn't *care* anymore. Jisenna, the woman who'd cut her way into the deepest part of his soul, was gone.

He looked up into the night sky. The sea of stars blurred and shimmered, distorted by the layer of tears that poured from his eyes.

It wasn't fair. Not her. Anyone but her. She was too *good* to deserve such an end.

The Moon's Little Sister sparkled in the darkness. Beside it, the star that Jisenna had chosen for her sister. He scoured the sky for the brightest star he could find, it was what Jisenna deserved, but none shone as bright as the Moon's Little Sister. And in that moment he realized, that *was* Jisenna's star. It had been all along. Her father was the sun, Chailani was the moon, and she was the little sister that outshone them all.

A small spec shimmered beside the cluster, and Alverax recognized it as the star that little Kyan had chosen for his father. A simple gesture, meaningless in the grand scheme of life, but significant for the little boy to move on—something Alverax had yet to do. In that moment, he decided it was time. Not for his father. For himself, and because he knew that it was what Jisenna would have wanted. She had once said that their path would require them to change in uncomfortable ways. And as uncomfortable as it felt, he knew it was time.

The endless sky of stars grew in clarity as his resolve overcame his sadness. He searched for a star for his father. Something small, discreet, perhaps easy to forget. The thought gave him pause, and he realized that he didn't want to forget his father. He may not have been around much, but, when he was, he'd been good to him. There were no bad memories of his presence, only sad memories of his absence.

There, to the east of the Broken Wheel, three stars clustered together. He chose the smaller of the three and committed it to memory. That would be his father's star. Each time he looked into the sky in the dead of night, no matter where he was, his father would be with him now. He felt an odd comfort in the statement, but also found himself missing the man more than he would have ever expected.

Alverax picked up the Midnight Watcher, though it sickened him to do so, and promised himself that, come what may, he would avenge Jisenna. Gods or not, the Heralds would pay for what they'd done.

He ran from the palace, remembering Laurel's words. He couldn't avenge Jisenna alone—he knew that. A dark hollowness permeated through him as he traveled through the streets of Felia. To his mind, there were no shops. There were no people. There was only the cobblestone beneath his feet that carried him forward.

Soon enough, he arrived at the clocktower. The wide plaza was empty, though bits of food and fabric dotted the stone from where tents had sold their goods earlier in the day. He stared at the slow turning of the long arm of the clocktower, wishing that he had the power to turn it back. But instead, as if taunting him, it spun forward with disregard—a cruel reminder that some deeds cannot be undone.

By the time Laurel arrived, side-by-side with her chromawolf companion, Alverax wasn't sure how long he'd been staring at the clocktower. A chilling numbness prickled at his skin, and, where he should have felt some measure of curiosity, or danger, or even hope, he felt only emptiness.

"Alverax!" Laurel shouted, running the rest of the way. She came up beside him, but he didn't move. He simply stood, continuing to stare at the large, ticking hands overlooking the empty plaza. "You okay? You don't look so good."

"I'm fine," he said.

Laurel looked up at the clocktower to see what he was staring at. "I need you to listen, and I know it might sound crazy, but the Heralds...they aren't what you think they are."

His mind seized at the mention. He turned his eyes to her, feeling a bit of heat return to his chest.

"Gods or not, they are evil. Chrys knows more, but whatever good they're doing here, it's a lie. Something bad is going to happen, unless we stop them." She paused, letting the words sink in. "Alverax, we need your help."

Alverax nodded to her, accepting the offer, despite not knowing the details. He knew her words were true before she spoke them. There was something *wrong* about the Heralds. They weren't deities come to save the people like the Felians believed, and Alverax no longer cared about his duty or his responsibilities. He glanced down at the Midnight Watcher at his side and wanted only revenge. "What do you need me to do?"

A gleam flickered in her eye. "How would you feel about taking a trip to Cynosure?"

50

When Chrys arrived at the docks, it didn't take long to find their ship. He went directly to Iriel and embraced her again, this time kissing her with the enthusiasm of a man half his age.

He caught up with Roshaw and met the crew, who seemed at awe of their multi-colored eyes. They spent their time waiting for Laurel and finishing last-minute preparations of the ship. The captain and crew were six others. When one refused to work for Roshaw, he'd *broken* the man's corethread and kicked him off the ship, flying out into the ocean. From that point forward, the crew seemed eager to serve.

More importantly, Chrys learned about Jelium, the Amber threadweaver they would recruit to their cause. Although Cynosure had no formal government, Chrys could tell from Roshaw's words that Jelium was the closest the city had to a king. How a single man could have one hundred brides, Chrys could not understand, but it did tell something of the man's disposition.

Roshaw went below deck, but not before Chrys saw him sneaking a glance to the heavens and smiling at the stars he'd named for Agatha, Esme, and Seven.

Finally, as the moon hit its highest point, Chrys spotted two figures and a chromawolf striding forward from beyond a distant building. As they approached, he noticed the fine clothing of Laurel's new companion, a young Felian man with a sheathed sword at his side. Laurel had a pension for rash choices, and Chrys hoped that her new companion was not one such decision.

Willow joined Chrys at the starboard railing.

As Iriel did the same, her eyes lit up as she saw the two approaching.

"Alverax!" she said excitedly. "Chrys, that's the young man who saved Aydin and I in the Fairenwild."

Surprised, Chrys took another glance at the young man. He was tall, handsome in a morose sort of way, with strong shoulders. "Then I owe him everything," Chrys said quietly.

The captain and crew, even having been warned, backed away from Asher as the final three travelers boarded the ship called the Pale Urchin. The crew began to settle, and the ship groaned as it pushed away from the Felian harbor. The sun was beginning to rise in the east, and the winds were strong for sailing. Chrys felt a sense of accomplishment as the ship departed. They had a goal, and they had a plan. It was all coming together.

When Roshaw surfaced from below deck, he was smiling and waving his hands. "Finally got the damn thing to fit. Didn't expect—"

He stopped himself mid-sentence and his face paled.

The young man, Alverax, leaned forward. "Dad?"

EPILOGUE

FAR BELOW THE SURFACE, in a dark cave lit only by a few haphazardly placed photospores, an old man stared into a dome of threadlight. There were so many truths Alchaeus had learned over the centuries, truths few could have learned without immortality to guide them. But the *convergence* was still a mystery. A congealed mound of threadlight that sparked with the light of the world. Had it always been there? Or had it grown over time? Were the convergences the source of the world's threadlight? Or was there yet another source?

He'd traveled through the portal countless times over the years during his many explorations, but as Chrys and the others stepped through, a new question beckoned him. A question born from Chrys' words. A question far beyond his own understanding. But it was close. A brilliant fruit ripe to be plucked if he could only reach it.

The string in his hand dangled from his fingertips, taunting him. Teasing him. His own words mocked his understanding. It was possible. It had to be. But there would be consequences. There always were. He took the string between his thumb and index finger on each hand and held it up. His eyes traced it from end to end.

It would explain the answer to another riddle. He replayed his trips through the *convergence*, visualizing each step, each feeling. There was something there.

Alchaeus took a deep breath, feeling the youthfulness of his younger body. If he was right, perhaps he could stop his siblings. If not, then he would need to enter the waters. He would need to be stronger for the coming events, both physically and mentally. An air of sorrow washed over him at the thought of what he would have to do.

He stepped toward the *convergence*, taking in the massive, warbling mass of threadlight. It beckoned to him, pulsing with otherworldly energy, calling him to bathe in its transcendence.

He put the string in his pocket and stepped in.

BOOK 3 OF THREADLIGHT

Bonds of Chaos

BY ZACK ARGYLE

SYL
SYL PUBLISHING LLC

BONDS OF CHAOS

1

GENERAL THALLIN CLUTCHED the hilt of his blade, torn between faith and honor, between the very gods he worshiped and the moral weight of his own soul.

He looked at the five women kneeling before him—the elders of the Zeda—then out over the imprisoned crowd behind them. The sun was high, and a light breeze blew through the Felian courtyard from the west. Thallin hated what he had to do. But even more so, he hated himself for doubting the Heralds. So, he pushed aside the unrest, the fear and doubt, and breathed in his lifelong beliefs, letting them fill the cracks that ran through his soul.

The youngest of the elders, a woman in her early forties, looked up at him with tears streaming down her cheeks as he approached. "Please, I have a daughter."

Thallin clenched his jaw and ignored her words, refusing to let them shake him. Not now. Not in the midst of the first true trial of his faith.

"Please," she said again.

He drew his blade, and the familiar weight in his palm brought him comfort, reminding him of old doubts he'd fought through before. Doubts that he had overcome. Today, he would do the same.

This was his path.

The blade was his instrument, and he was ready to play its godly song.

In a blur, he lunged forward with perfect form and pierced the young elder through her heart. He retracted his blade, blood dripping from its edge, and watched as she toppled to the dirt.

"Gale take me," one of the other women cried under her breath.

Somewhere farther back, amid the throng of Zeda, each of them bound and awaiting their fate, screams called out into the mid-afternoon sky.

He knew he should turn away, move on and forget. Instead, he stared at the elder's body until it stopped quivering. Her eyes were open, her brown tunic stained red. Helpless. He closed his eyes to pray for strength, and the irony of it broke his heart.

The next closest elder was a larger woman with a certain kindness in the wrinkles of her face. Though her lips quivered, she kept her head high. "You don't have to do this," she said.

Thallin took a step closer. "I will do whatever my gods ask of me."

He lunged again and felt a swelling of emotion in his chest as he watched the second woman fall to the grass.

Three older women still knelt before him. One with wrinkles deeper than the ocean floor. Another with fury brewing in her Emerald eyes. And the last looked to her fallen friends with a sadness that permeated every line of her posture and expression.

He approached the closest—the oldest of the five—and she opened her eyes at the sound of his footsteps. They were blue as the sea, and beneath their careful gaze, her lips curled into a smile. "I commend your faith," she said, taking a breath and offering a slight nod. "I am ready."

Thallin squeezed the hilt, letting all of his guilt seep into the polished steel. The old woman knelt reverently before him, a paragon of peace.

Faith is not meant to be easy, Thallin's mother had once said.

With a swift strike, he cut down the elderly woman.

Faith is meant to try you.

His stomach churned, and a dark cloud swirled in his mind.

He kept his eyes down, focused on his blade as he wiped blood on his pant leg.

"Violet," the next elder said with a growl.

Thallin did not look away from the sharp edge of his sword.

"Ivy and Ashwa," she continued. "Those women had names!"

He ignored her and set his feet.

"Violet, Ivy, and Ashwa!" she screamed.

"QUIET!" Thallin roared, finally bringing himself to look at her. The fire in his eyes clashed with hers. "You will die today, and you will be forgotten."

"And you will be damned," she spat.

He swung his blade and watched her corpse collapse face-first to the dirt.

Adrenaline flowed through his veins, burning him from the inside. He clenched his teeth with such ferocity that his jaw felt like splintered wood.

One more.

One more and his test was over.

The Heralds would see his faith.

The final elder was a kind looking woman with soft blue eyes. She looked at him with a profound sadness, like a mother who'd lost a child and blamed herself. The last death seemed to have hit her the hardest.

He took a few steps, and, as he set himself in front of her, she dropped her gaze to the ground. There was nothing about her that looked dangerous, no sign of evil or darkness. He didn't *want* to hurt her. An enemy in battle was one matter, but an old, grieving woman? It choked him from within. He'd always imagined exercising his faith would fill him with joy, but all he felt was a thick darkness deep in his core.

Tears dripped down the woman's cheeks, but she said nothing. She simply stared, shoulders slumped with age and grief.

The sword in his hand seemed to grow heavier with each moment. He feared that if he delayed, the weight would overwhelm him.

He lunged forward, fighting himself more than any enemy, and met her eyes as the steel cut flesh.

Wide-eyed, her lips moved.

I forgive you.

His heart swelled as the sword drove into her chest. She stared at him, choking, blood dripping from her chin. And, somehow, even through the pain and the sorrow, she looked peaceful. Content, despite the cold steel between her ribs. As she finally collapsed to the earth, her lips curled into a smile.

Thallin dropped to his knees. A flood of tears pressed against his skull like a dam ready to burst. He fought their release with every measure of strength he contained.

He hated himself for being so weak.

He hated himself for having such feeble faith.

He hated himself...

He would be better. He had to be.

"Stand up, Thallin Haichess," Relek said, draped in black robes. The second Herald, Lylax, stood beside him. A pale yellow crystal hung from a silver necklace that swung over her white robes.

Thallin lifted himself to his feet, with the tip of the blade dragging against the ground, and turned to the Heralds. "My gods, I have done as you asked."

"You have done well," Relek said, voice deep, prismatic eyes gleaming in the sunlight. He turned away from Thallin, toward the newly instated Watchlord, Rastalin Farrow, whose face brimmed with haughty pride as he stood in his black and gold garb. "Has he not done well, Watchlord?"

Rastalin lifted his chin. "He has done sufficiently well, my god."

"It is rare to find such devotion," the Herald added. "In the days ahead, we will need a man like Thallin by our side. A man whose actions speak louder than his clothing."

The Watchlord shifted in his boots.

"Thallin," Relek said, turning away from the Watchlord, "I am afraid this day may grow longer. I have two further requests."

"Of course," Thallin said, bowing his head with his blade ankle deep in the dirt. "Anything."

Relek's face grew still, his eyes void of emotion. "The Watchlord is meant to be the right hand of the Heralds, but this man," he said, gesturing toward Rastalin, "is unworthy. Take his life, and take his place."

Thallin turned to Watchlord Rastalin. The look of arrogance was gone. The fire in his eyes had gone cold. There was only fear. Rastalin reached for the sword at his side and pulled it from its sheath. Thallin took a step forward.

Something about the movement of the sword as it lifted in defense relieved Thallin. This man was not innocent. He was not valiant. This man was a coward. A nobleman who'd never had to sacrifice anything. Not for Felia. Not for the Heralds. Thallin hated this man. He hated how Rastalin spoke and how he walked. He hated that Rastalin wore the Watchlord clothes that once belonged to Alverax.

While each death of the Zeda elders had been a trial, this death would be the reward.

Thallin parried the Watchlord's blade with such force that the decorative replica of the Midnight Watcher shattered into a thousand shards of obsidian. Rastalin was left with nothing but a hilt and his broken pride.

One second later, steel was in his chest.

Ten seconds later, blood ran like the Tourmaline River.

Sixty seconds later, the former Watchlord lay still on the wet grass.

When Thallin turned back to the Heralds, he felt proud. All his life, he had fought for himself, for his own pride and accomplishment. Now, he would fight for his gods. He would be their most devoted disciple.

He would be their Watchlord.

And he would be their blade.

THE PALE URCHIN drifted over the Terecean Sea, rising and falling with each crest of the frigid waves. Chrys Valerian stood at the bow, holding his son and breathing in the salty air. His wife, Iriel, stood beside him, resting her head on his shoulder, and together they watched a flame-tailed halken soar high overhead, wings outstretched, twin tails flared in a wide arc. Against the backdrop of the setting sun, it almost let them forget about the rising darkness.

A woman's voice called out from behind them.

Chrys turned to see his mother, Willow, approaching from the middle of the ship, climbing up from below deck. Her clothes were a mess, though not as dirty as they'd been in the Wastelands. Every speck of dirt was a reminder of all she'd done for him. The sacrifices she'd made. He would never forget the look in her eyes as she'd dropped into the pit to stand between him and the corespawn.

"You look much too excited," Chrys said. "I'm a little scared."

"Come now," Willow said, brushing his comment aside as she looked up into the sky. "Oh, wow. Look at that. I would *love* to have a halken for a pet. They are so majestic."

Chrys raised a brow. "You hate pets."

"No one *hates* pets," she said with confidence. "I just haven't found the right one yet."

"If you haven't found it in fifty years," Chrys said, "I'm not sure there is one."

Iriel turned to Willow. "I never took you as a bird person. Always figured you'd be happier with a low-maintenance lizard or something."

Willow's eyes lit up. "Like Chitt! Oh my, I could definitely do that. But, ah! No more distractions. I came with something much more exciting. First, a question: how do the Heralds fly?"

Chrys looked back up into the sky. "I haven't really thought about it. I guess I assumed it was a power that came with having all four theoliths bonded together. Maybe related to lifelight?"

"A good guess, but no!" Willow shook a finger. "Think about what we *do* know. With Obsidian, you can cut your corethread and float."

"Sure, but that's not the same as flying."

Willow gave him a look. "Patience, little flower. Mommy's not done talking."

Iriel stifled a laugh.

"Without a corethread tethering you to the ground," Willow continued, "any movement would send you floating off. At first, I thought maybe we could create wings and use those to fly. But that wouldn't work, and the Heralds don't need them anyway. There had to be another way. So, again, what do we know? Do you remember the orange grove with the corespawn stampede?"

Chrys nodded. "I remember you made that force barrier by releasing a concentrated burst of Sapphire and Emerald."

"Exactly! Now watch what happens when you combine it all."

Multi-colored threadlight swirled through Willow's veins, running down her arms, through her hands and neck, pulsing brightly in her eyes.

Chrys opened himself to threadlight, too.

In an instant, Willow's corethread was broken, and her feet drifted from the ground. Her lips curled into a smile just before she let out a surge of threadweaving. In front of her, she released a wave of Emerald. Behind her, a burst of Sapphire. Her body reacted, launching itself through the air like a hummingbird in flight. Quickly, she did it again in the other direction, counteracting the forces and bringing her floating form to a halt. She grabbed hold of the mast to keep herself from drifting off.

"Stones," Chrys cursed under his breath.

Iriel stared in awe but still managed to slap Chrys' shoulder. "Not in front of Aydin."

"He's a baby..." Chrys mumbled as Iriel took the child away from him, slipping the boy into the wrap on her chest.

At the far end of the ship, a group of sailors pointed, gawking and muttering to each other.

"It's a little dangerous to practice while on a ship," Willow said, steadying herself against the wooden beam. "But once we're on land, I'll be in the air every chance I get. Having an Amber theolith would make landing a lot simpler."

"And with three theoliths, we're the only ones besides the Heralds who can do it." Chrys paused. He pictured the frail image of his mother when they'd landed at the bottom of the Endless Well. The quiver in her hand. The tightness in her chest. Surging required a lot of threadlight. "Just be careful. It's a lot of threadweaving."

Roshaw came bounding out from below deck a changed man. His long shaggy hair from years in the Wastelands had been cut short, and his beard trimmed just enough to show the smirk on his face. "Sometimes I wonder which one of you is the parent." He winked at Willow. "She just showed you how to fly, Chrys. Give her the damn victory!"

"It's just—" Chrys began.

"Chrys," his mother interrupted, "our bodies are stronger than they've ever been. The elixir healed us, and our extra theoliths have given us even more strength. There's nothing to worry about."

Iriel chuckled to herself. "Asking Chrys not to worry is like asking the rain to stop being wet."

"I'm not that bad," Chrys said.

Iriel, Willow, and Roshaw all raised a brow.

"I'm not!"

They stared back silently.

"Whatever this is," Chrys said, gesturing to the three of them, "I don't like it. I'm going to check on the others."

He heard their faint laughter behind him as he walked around to the stern and descended a flight of stairs. At the end of a narrow hallway, he knocked twice and opened a door. Inside, he found Alverax lying on a long cot, with Laurel and her chromawolf companion, Asher, seated along the far wall beside several fixed crates of week-old Felian fruit.

Upon discovering his father was alive, Alverax had holed up in the cabin and refused to speak to anyone. After the first day, Laurel and Asher had joined him, silently sitting, not saying a word. Chrys had asked her once why she was doing it, and she'd simply replied, "It's not good to be alone."

She was right.

As Chrys sat down next to Laurel, he let out a long breath. "Captain says we're almost to Cynosure."

Laurel slumped further against the wall. "Too late. We've already died."

Asher mimicked her, collapsing across her lap.

Since the moment they'd first departed Felia on the *Pale Urchin*, the chromawolf had taken poorly to life at sea. From such a powerful creature, the delicate whimpers seemed to reach in and grab at the hearts of the crew. No matter how many times Chrys told Laurel that fresh air would help, they still stayed in the cabin with Alverax.

Chrys shook his head. "Everyone on this ship is so dramatic."

Laurel pushed herself back up and smiled, rubbing a hand down Asher's green-furred shoulder all the way to his paw. "Our kind is meant for land."

Our kind. The physical changes alone were enough to believe it—her hair had taken on more and more green throughout their journey—but, somehow, the curious bond between Laurel and Asher was changing them both.

"How's Alverax?" Chrys asked quietly.

Laurel looked over to the cot. "He's okay. Getting better, I think."

Chrys massaged his temples, then rubbed at his eyes. "I wish I knew what we could do to fix him."

Laurel lifted her chin and looked to Chrys with a certain intensity in her eyes. "You can't *fix* people." She paused, and Asher let out a low growl of agreement. "That's not how it works. People are like...trees."

"Trees?" Chrys repeated.

"Yeah," Laurel said thoughtfully. She turned her gaze toward the far wall, as if she were seeing another place in the distance. "You don't *fix* a tree. You can take care of it, sure, but it's the tree that has to heal itself."

Chrys thought for a moment, considering the wisdom in her words. Alverax was broken and hurting, overwhelmed on top of it all. But if he refused to speak, there wasn't much anyone could do to help him. Maybe she was right, and all they could do was wait for him to heal himself. Alverax was a person, not some chipped blade that needed repair.

A month ago, Chrys wouldn't have labeled Laurel as *wise*, but she wasn't the same brash girl he'd met in the Bloodthief warehouse. She'd made mistakes—everyone does—but she was learning to move forward with a new focus.

He stood and offered Laurel a smile. "You know, you're smarter than you look."

She pursed her lips. "And you're nicer than you smell."

"Rude." Chrys smirked.

"I could smell you from across the hallway."

"Oh, come on," Chrys said.

"Asher's pack could probably track your scent all the way from the Fairenwild."

"It's not that bad, is it?"

Her only response was a flat stare before she laid her head back against the wall. The chromawolf nestled its head into her.

Chrys gestured toward Alverax. "Okay if I have a few words with him?"

Laurel gave a slight nod and closed her eyes.

As he stepped over to the cot, he found Alverax with his eyes closed, but Chrys wasn't convinced that the young man was asleep. A hint of black threadlight pulsed through Alverax's veins, even more pronounced due to the weight he'd lost while aboard the ship. The darkness surrounding his eyes extended across his face, shadows rolling over the gaunt edges.

"Hello again," Chrys said.

Iriel had visited Alverax every day of the journey, never speaking more than a few words, but often bringing him meals that she would lay on the side table. Chrys had visited a few times, but mostly to check on Laurel. Still, Chrys understood that he owed the young man so much, not the least of which was Iriel and Aydin's life. And if there was anyone who understood what it was like being trapped in your own mind, it was Chrys.

He took a seat on a crate and rested his head against the wall, feeling the sway of the ocean through the wood. "I know you don't want to talk. Which is great, because I really just need someone to listen. I guess I just need to say it out loud." Chrys took a deep breath and steadied himself, feeling the pulse in his chest begin to quicken. "I...am a failure. I'm trying—Lightfather knows it—but it just doesn't seem to matter. Nothing I do is ever enough. Or maybe it's just not *good* enough. It feels like I'm stuck in a rip tide, and no matter how hard I swim, the shore gets farther and farther away. And worse, everyone around me is drowning. The truth is...friends are *dead* because I wasn't enough."

An image flashed in his mind: Esme and Seven shuffling pieces over the makeshift Scion gameboard with Agatha laughing beside them. He'd brought them hope, promised them freedom. Then, he'd watched them die. Chrys closed his eyes and felt his heart seize in his chest. Tears welled, and he shut his eyes, as if closing them would dam the pain. But it was still there, beating away at him from the inside. So he opened them and looked to Alverax, whose chest seemed to be heaving as much as Chrys'.

"I don't know all that you've been through, Alverax, but I do know that empty hole in your chest that feels like it'll never fill again. More than anything, I just want you to know that you don't have to suffer alone. I made that mistake once." He turned and caught a glimpse of Laurel, eyes shut in the far corner. "A friend once told me that people are like trees. The way I see it, it doesn't matter how many broken branches you have, or how many leaves you've lost. If a tree is standing, it's no less whole than the trees beside it.

"I watched my friends die because I wasn't enough to save them, and I can still feel the pain where those branches split. But new branches grow where old ones break. No matter what it might feel like right now, how dark or empty you feel, it gets better."

<hr>

A surge of emotion coursed through Alverax's body as Chrys stepped away from the room.

I watched my friends die, because I wasn't enough to save them.
Jisenna.

He could still see her face the moment she'd realized what the Herald was about to do. The seconds before the sword struck her down. The cold minutes after. Alverax opened his eyes and saw the Midnight Watcher staring at him from across the room, propped against the wall, shimmering in what little lamplight made its way to the corner.

Jisenna was dead, and it was his fault.

He'd told the Herald her title.

She'd saved his life, and now she was dead because of it.

And if that wasn't enough, the father whose death he'd finally come to terms with was still alive. Something about the revelation had broken him, as if the star he'd named had come spiraling through the night and crashed into his soul, shattering him into a thousand pieces, each reflecting a memory of his broken life.

Was he even alive anymore?

Perhaps this was the afterlife: an endless journey with nothing but painful memories for company.

AFTER AN ETERNITY OF QUIET, words echoed through the hallway from above.

"Cynosure, straight ahead!"

3

The *Pale Urchin* was nearly silent as a swarm of men stepped aboard, heavy boots knocking against the creaky wooden deck. Chrys watched them carefully, noting the cutlasses dangling at their sides and thick arms that knew how to use them. Their leader, a burly man who looked like he came from the farmlands outside of Alchea, stood nearly a head taller than the others, with a hooked nose and long hair. His hand rested on the hilt of his blade.

"Problem is," the man said, accentuating each syllable. "Ain't no ship ought to be dockin' tonight. Next ain't coming for three days. You folk didn't leave with the *Urchin*. Now you *with* the *Urchin*. So, question is...what the hell you doin' at my dock?"

Iriel stepped forward with Aydin tucked away in the wrap on her chest. "This is my family," she said. "I'm Iriel. There are...dark things happening in Felia. We just want to take our son somewhere far from there."

"Ship came in speakin' stories of gods and monsters," the man said, side-eyeing the others in the group. "Well...Iriel...what of the rest? Ain't no chance you all family." He turned and gestured to Alverax and Laurel. "You two lovers?"

Alverax stared at the man, but his face gave no hint that he'd even heard.

Laurel, on the other hand... Chrys held his breath, fearing how the erratic young woman might respond.

"Friends," she said with a strange sense of cool. "He's from here, spent some time working for Alabella, but she's dead now."

The man nearly choked. "What the hell you just say?"

"Alabella Rune, the Amber-eyed Queen of the Bloodthieves, is dead."

He clenched his jaw, nostrils flaring. "You sure?"

"Oh, I'm sure," Laurel said.

He pointed a finger at the others. "I don't care what the hell the rest of you do." He lunged forward, grabbing hold of Laurel's arm and pulling. "You're coming with me."

In a split second, Asher leapt out from behind a crate, dashed forward, and tackled the man, teeth bared mere inches from his face, slobber dripping down his snarling maw. The other guards reached for their blades, but Alverax—black veins ablaze—broke their corethreads without moving an inch. In a split second, the swarm of men were floating in the air, panic stricken across their moonlit faces.

Laurel said nothing when Asher looked at her, and Chrys swore the massive chromawolf nodded before releasing the man and taking a step back.

Chrys stepped forward, looking down at the man who suddenly seemed much less confident. As his eyes met Chrys', his brow furrowed and his jaw slackened. Chrys leaned lower and whispered. "We have no trouble with you or your friends. Tell us where we can find Jelium, and we'll be on our way."

The man, both confused and relieved, pushed himself to his knees, keeping an eye on the chromawolf. His gaze slid from person to person, finally seeming to realize their peculiarities. Alverax, blank-faced and black-veined. Laurel, green strands of hair matching the chromawolf at her side. Chrys, Willow, and Roshaw, eyes swirling with multi-colored threadlight. And Iriel, standing with the grace of a warrior, a child strapped to her chest.

"Who the hell are you?"

Chrys looked at his friends and back to the man. "Just a few friends looking to kill a few gods."

AFTER DISEMBARKING THE *PALE URCHIN*, they walked over to an enormous staircase carved into the face of the bluff. Thick rods jutted out from the face of the rock every few strides, attached at the ends to form a guardrail on the opposite end of the stairway. A complex pulley system ran from the peaks of the cliffside all the way down to the docks. Chrys, having lived his entire life with the safety of Sapphire threadlight, had never been afraid of heights, but he saw a hint of nerves in some of the others. He even caught Willow and Roshaw, who now knew they could fly, taking an occasional peek over the edge with a glimmer of doubt in their eyes.

As they climbed, the *Pale Urchin* became nothing more than a shine in the gravel. Chrys could still see the dock workers and sailors below, like tiny smudges on a midnight canvas.

When his head peeked over the top of the bluff, Chrys saw Cynosure for the first time. It was no Felia, yet, even still, the size of the separatist city was staggering. A giant sandstone protrusion loomed over half of the city, sheltering it from the elements and blocking even the light falling from the moon. Tents in various shades of brown, white, and black dotted the sandy world like weeds, with tall towers of stone built at seemingly random intervals throughout the city, burning red flames to light the night.

What surprised him more than anything was the amount of activity. In Alchea, when the sun dipped below the horizon, the city settled into a peaceful calm. Of course, there were areas, like the lower west side, that remained active, but even they kept their voices and activities hidden behind closed doors. Here, it seemed the entire world had yet to notice that the sun had set. People moved through the city like it was mid-morning, trading, joking, kissing, fighting.

Roshaw, having noticed Chrys' reaction, laughed and grabbed his shoulder. "You'll find that this city is late to rise and later to bed."

Chrys nodded. "I can see why you were so certain that Jelium would be available."

"I didn't just know he would be available," Roshaw said. "I told you exactly where he would be. The man is a creature of habit, and he has a habit of stealing from people and calling it a game."

Chrys licked his teeth beneath his upper lip. "The more I hear about Jelium, the more I'm afraid I might just try to kill him myself."

"Don't even joke about that," Willow said from his other side. "We need an Amber threadweaver to make the new coreseal, and he's the only option."

"Honestly," Roshaw added. "I wouldn't mind sticking a blade in him myself."

"It's not worth it," Laurel said from behind.

They all turned to the young Zeda girl.

"It doesn't make you feel better," she said.

Chrys raised his brows, looking hard at Laurel. The young woman looking back at him wasn't the same girl he'd met in the Bloodthief warehouse, not the girl from the Fairenwild. He felt an odd sense of pride watching her grow.

"She's right," Chrys said. "Besides, killing Jelium helps no one."

"I can think of at least twenty people it would help," Roshaw said with a shrug. "But you're right. We can't kill him. But we don't have to let *him* know that."

They traveled for a long while, down well-lit paths, past tents and stalls and flat-roofed homes built with clay and sandstone, finally passing through a large cave corridor into what Roshaw referred to as the Pit. Noise echoed from every inch of the enormous cavern. Alirian men puffed on long stems of sailweed as they wormed their way through circles of drunken Felians. Small wagers were taken as men squared off to fight, shirtless, exposing bodies of tattoo and brawn. Prowling whores leaned against the walls, heads high, lips puckered. Loud men shouted about their goods, gesturing to sprawling displays in open cases.

A woman bumped into Chrys, a giantess of a woman. Her thick arms tightened, and her heavy brows furrowed as she made eye contact with him, taking in the swirl of colors in his irises. Then she noticed the chromawolf standing beside Laurel and took a step back, vanishing with surprising speed.

"Let's keep moving," Chrys said, mostly to himself.

As they passed through the crowd, a shrill voice lifted above the chaos. Chrys looked and found a thin man with ghostly skin, smiling wide as he lifted a handful of shines into the air, shouting at the top of his lungs, calling for bets. As they moved, Chrys caught more and more of the crowd looking their way, some pointing, others scowling. A significant number of drunken men cursed and hobbled away at the sight of the chromawolf.

They continued their way forward, moving toward the stadium-like depression in the cavern leading to a sprawling racetrack. Even from the top of the Pit, Chrys could see the writhing necrolytes beating against their cages. When Roshaw had first told them about the races, no one had believed him; no one was doubting him now.

Without warning, the crowd began to settle.

A deep, booming voice broke through the quiet. "GATES READY!"

Chrys looked down and saw a tree-stump of a man standing with his arms raised at the front of the racetrack. Six men sat atop the caged necrolytes, hooked onto leather saddles that fit snugly between hand-wide spikes jutting from the creatures' backs.

Even before they were released, Chrys could imagine their movement. His mind drifted to the War of the Wastelands. He imagined men riding necrolytes into battle. Even if they couldn't fully control the creatures, fear and panic would roll through the enemy like a tidal wave. No sane man would stand up to such a creature. If they lived through this, Chrys was done with war.

"THREE!" the man yelled from far below.

"TWO!" Every Alchean, Felian, Kulaian, and Alirian, every man and woman in between, joined the chorus.

"ONE!"

The gates slammed open, and all six necrolytes burst forth.

Roshaw pulled on his arm. "Come on. Let's get down there while the crowd is distracted."

They descended a set of stairs with Roshaw in the lead, Chrys and the others trailing behind. While they walked, they watched the necrolytes race across the sandy track, crashing into each other with blunted tusks jutting out from their jaws like the wild boars of Kulai. Even before Roshaw pointed him out, Chrys found Jelium in the crowd, seated atop a makeshift throne near the front of the track, surrounded by women Chrys guessed must be part of his Hundred Brides.

Mixed throughout the retinue were guards in black, faces covered, eyes scanning the crowd. Rage boiled under Chrys' skin as a memory blossomed in his mind. The night he'd first failed as a father—the night Aydin was born—masked men had come through the trees. Iriel's birthing cries echoing from the house. The moon glaring down from overhead. The voice of the Apogee. He let a bit of threadlight into his veins to settle his mind.

"Alverax," Roshaw said with an air of warning.

Chrys turned and saw the young man with his black blade half pulled from its sheath, staring down at Jelium with fire in his eyes. It was more emotion than Chrys had seen from the young man since they'd stepped onto the ship. It was a look he'd seen before, from Luther. The look of a man who had lost something dear. The look of a man who wanted revenge.

Alverax's chest heaved up and down, but he slipped the blade back into its sheath.

They continued down and finally arrived at the edge of Jelium's roped off quarters. The race had finished and the excitement of the crowd had again been replaced by the buzz of activity. As they approached, a half dozen of the Masked Guard came to meet them.

Roshaw wasted no time. "We're here to speak with Jelium."

"You'll have to wait until after the races," one of the guards replied.

"Tell him Roshaw Blightwood is here."

"I don't care who you are," the guard said, his voice growing louder. "Walk away."

"Too late," Roshaw said. His eyes blazed to life with threadlight. In the shadow of a moment, he broke the corethread of all six guards and let a surge of Sapphire threadlight pulse from his body, like Willow had done when she was flying. The closest guard was rocketed through the sky, and the others stumbled back, tumbling through the air like autumn leaves.

"I guess we're doing this," Chrys mumbled as threadlight poured through his veins.

LAUREL'S EYES darted back and forth as men in black appeared from every direction, eyes alive with threadlight. Some held blades, others wore what Iriel had referred to as palmguards—the molded metal hand shield used by many Emeralds—but all crouched like wolves ready to defend their territory. In a way, Laurel felt bad for them. They had no idea what they were up against.

She pulled out the obsidian dagger and crouched.

The closest guard leapt forward, feet first, *pulling* himself toward her with unnatural speed. The world seemed to warp around her, warmth flowing through her limbs, and the masked guard's approach slowed. She stepped aside with ease and drove her elbow down into his stomach as he passed. She turned her head and took in the movements of the others. The entire world seemed to have slowed just the slightest.

Beside her, she saw Alverax parrying a blade with his own, backing up and tripping on the stairway. The guard attacking him made to drive his dagger down, but Laurel moved like the wings of a hummingbird, blurring through the air and closing the distance. Her boot crushed into the guard's shoulder, launching him back, tumbling down the stairs.

The warmth faded from her, and a frigid wind settled over the tunnels of her veins. She shivered and breathed, a similar feeling echoing in the back of her mind. Asher, only a few strides away, shivered beneath his dark green coat. The wolf nodded to her, and somehow she understood. He'd leant her his speed.

She reached down and helped Alverax to his feet. "I think you need a smaller sword."

"Not until the Heralds are dead."

Simple words, and yet they took her aback. They were the first words she'd heard him speak since they'd left Felia.

CHRYS LEAPT over the ropes surrounding Jelium's quarters. Masked guards appeared from the crowd, leaping down between him and their leader. Chrys, Roshaw, and Willow all released a wave of Obsidian threadlight, bursting apart the guards' corethreads. One of them attempted to throw a spear, which Willow flicked aside with an effortless *push*. Another threw a dagger. Both guards tumbled backward head over heel through the air. Chrys and the others strode forward with confidence as the remaining guards drifted into the sky.

"Well, I'll be damned," Jelium said, rising to his feet. His skin was bronzed, his hair dark and thick, and he smiled with the confidence of an emperor. Robes of black and gold flowed from a high neck down to his toes. Beneath the wrinkles and sagging skin, Chrys saw a spark of the man's true nature in the reflection of his eyes. "Roshaw Blightwood. I was ninety percent certain you were dead, and ninety-nine percent sure you would never again show your face in Cynosure."

Jelium brought his fingers to his lips and let out a shrieking whistle. The chaotic sounds of combat and fear cut off into an eerie silence.

"There is no need for violence," he said with a booming voice. "Let us leave the Pit and have a civilized conversation in a more private setting." He paused, taking in the group, a flicker of a smile twinging his lips. "And you brought your son. You are full of surprises."

"More than you know," Roshaw said flatly.

Chrys surveyed the stadium, noting more Masked Guard arriving. Throughout the Pit, people stared, muttering amongst themselves, pointing, wondering what Jelium would do. Chrys could see their fear mixed with curiosity.

Jelium smiled. "Why don't we go to my home and have a conversation?" He turned an eye to Asher. "You'll understand, of course, that the dog will have to stay outside."

Chrys turned to Laurel, noting the snarl on her lips. "Laurel, why don't you and Alverax head out. We can handle the conversation. And if possible, keep an eye out for Felian ships. Last thing we need is unexpected visitors."

Laurel and Alverax gave each other a nod and walked off toward the stairs with Asher.

Chrys turned to Jelium. "Let's talk."

4

JELIUM'S COMPLEX was a maze of corridors, each seemingly identical to the last. Chrys was so convinced that they were being led in a circle that, at one point, he scuffed the sandstone wall with his boot and kept a look out for the mark. Shortly after, they were led to a wide room with a high, Felian-inspired domed ceiling. Jelium took a seat in a wide leather chair in front of a hexagon-shaped table with a game of Theo arranged atop it. As he had with many of his studies, Chrys had spent years mastering the complex dynamics of the game, even studying under the Alchean masters.

Chrys and the others remained standing, despite being encouraged to sit. The room was opulent, filled with the art of foreign peoples and wondrous places, both sculptures and paintings. Thick rugs lined the floor, and gold-threaded tapestries covered the walls. A trough of indented brass followed along the length of the walls with a stream of oil running through it, flames eating away at the source and feeding the room both light and warmth.

"Welcome to my home," Jelium said with a grin as the edge of the room filled with a retinue of Masked Guard. "Let us speak openly. Several of you have Obsidian in your veins. How? Alabella, perhaps? Doesn't matter. My power cancels yours, and yours mine. We are on even ground. And you, Roshaw, old friend, you deserve an apology. I have long regretted our falling out."

"Our *falling out*?" Roshaw spat. "You tried to have me killed. And then you tried to have my son killed!"

"I never tried to kill your boy," Jelium said with a cool calm. "I gave him to Alabella—which was a success, I might add. After that, I simply wanted him on my side. I never had any plan to kill him."

Roshaw scowled. "They left him for dead in the desert."

Jelium smiled. "They did, true. But *I* did not."

"Enough!" Roshaw growled. The Masked Guard along the periphery of the room tensed. "What's done is done. There are more important matters." He gestured to the others. "This is High General Chrys Valerian of Alchea and his family, Willow, Iriel, and Aydin. The child is an Amber threadweaver."

Jelium leaned forward, intrigued.

"But we're here for something even more important." Roshaw pointed back out the door. "The Heralds have returned to Felia."

"Ah, so the reports are true," Jelium said, leaning his chin against his palm.

"Or some dark form of them," Roshaw corrected. "They're planning something. Revenge. War. We don't know. But a lot of people are going to die unless we stop them."

"You want to stop the gods, and you need...me." Jelium's lips curled into a sly smile. "I assume it's not because of my warmth and kindness. So you must need an Amber threadweaver." He looked down at the baby. "One with more experience. And...hmm. It was only a matter of time before Alabella got herself killed. Was it the Heralds?"

Chrys ground his teeth as Roshaw's lip twitched. This was not how they wanted the conversation to go. Jelium already knew he had leverage. He knew they needed him for whatever they were planning. And now he knew that he was the only person in the world who could help.

Jelium reached down and grabbed a Sentry from the game of Theo in front of him, spinning the black circle in his fingers. "She was much more altruistic than I am. The greater good, at the expense of the few. Silly, if you ask me. That line of thinking has a tendency to get people killed."

Chrys took a step forward, glancing down at the gameboard. "We are not here to lie to you. Alabella is dead. And we do need you to help us stop the Heralds. This is not a problem you can ignore. Sooner or later, this war will come to Cynosure. And when the Heralds come, they will slaughter your people like hogs. And if you think you can fight them, I drove a sword through one's chest, and it did nothing more than annoy her. This is not about altruism, Jelium. It's about survival."

Jelium let out a roaring fit of laughter. His voice took on an air of mockery. *"This is not about altruism, Jelium. It's about survival. Ha!"* He settled back and wiped away a tear. "I don't know you, Chrys Valerian, but even I have heard of the Apogee, the so-called Butcher of the Valley. Why would I trust you? And why would I trust Roshaw who lied to me for so many years? From what we've heard, the Heralds saved Felia from an army of invisible monsters. That doesn't sound so malevolent to me. So, either you're all mad, or you're all fools who think they stand a chance against gods. Either way, I've no reason to help you."

Chrys started to move forward, but Iriel caught his arm. What he wanted to do was knock Jelium out, *break* his corethread, then carry him away like a bag of sand. But there were too many guards and too many good people who might get hurt in a skirmish. He needed to play to Jelium's weakness.

"You're a gambling man, no?" Chrys asked, hatching an idea.

Jelium tipped his head, raising a brow. "Perhaps."

"And, I assume, you play Theo?"

The large man leaned back in his chair and smiled. "I dabble."

"Let's make a little wager then," Chrys said. "We play a game. And if I win, you come with us to stop the Heralds."

Jelium stared at him, his eyes only half open as he weighed the proposal. "And what is it exactly you want me to do?"

Chrys lifted his hands. "We want you to use your Amber to create a sort of prison."

"Intriguing." Jelium's head nodded up and down as he thought through the proposal. "So, to paraphrase, you want me to leave the comfort of my home, risking my life and all I've built in order to fight a pair of supposedly immortal gods. In short, you win, I risk my life for your goals. Which begs the question: what happens if I win?"

"If you win," Chrys said, reaching to the sheath at his side, "I give you a one-of-a-kind, thread-dead obsidian dagger."

Chrys pulled out the knife and handed it to Jelium. The older man ran his hand over the blade, Amber threadlight shimmering in his eyes. He looked at the pommel, the grip, the cross-guard, then scratched a nail near the point.

"This is not obsidian," Jelium muttered to himself. "A true obsidian blade would shatter the first time it was struck. This is something different, though it does look quite similar. I would very much like to know where you found it. It would certainly be a worthy prize."

Chrys let out a breath, feeling a weight in his shoulders relax. "Then it's settled."

Jelium smirked. "I said it *would* be. Unfortunately, it is not enough."

"Jelium," Roshaw said with fire in his eyes. "Be reasonable."

"Be reasonable?" Jelium repeated. "You come to my home, spouting madness, demanding that I join you to imprison evil gods, then accuse *me* of being unreasonable? If I am gambling my own life for your plan, why should you not gamble a life for mine?"

A flurry of thoughts tumbled through Chrys' mind, one after the other, crashing, colliding, exploding into a million more ideas. He wanted to reach across the table and thrust the obsidian dagger into Jelium's chest. They could find another way to deal with the Heralds.

But he knew that wasn't true. They'd discussed it a hundred times on the ship from Felia. They couldn't kill the Heralds. They couldn't run from the Heralds. The only option was to trap them. And that left Jelium, and the game.

Fortunately, there were only a handful of people in all of Alchea who could beat Chrys in a game of Theo. Tucked away in a desert city of scum and lowlifes, how good could Jelium be?

"I'll do it," Chrys said confidently. "If I win, you come with us. If you win—"

"A life for a life," Jelium finished.

"Chrys," Iriel said sternly. "You can't...you... This is not your decision to make!"

He moved in close, grabbing her shoulders and lowering his voice. "Iriel, I know this isn't the first time I've asked, but you have to trust me."

"I do, but I don't trust him," she said, nodding toward Jelium.

"I'm going to win," Chrys said.

Her jaw clenched. "And what if you don't?"

Chrys hesitated longer than he wished. "I will."

Jelium, sitting quite pompously in his chair, reached out a hand. "Then we have a deal. If you win, a life is yours. If I win, a life is mine."

Chrys nodded and shook his hand.

Jelium placed his Sentry back on the board. "Well, Chrys. I do hope you're up-to-date on the latest theory, I'd hate to win without a good fight."

Chrys took his place at the other end of the table, straightening his nine Sentries and each pair of Emeralds, Sapphires, and...Heralds.

5

LAUREL AND ASHER rushed through the Pit with black-veined Alverax at their side, crowds scattering as men and women backed away from the oddly placed chromawolf. She felt a sense of relief wash over her once the crowds were behind them and they were back into the quieter part of Cynosure, though the streets still held varying degrees of activity. At least in the heart of the city there were no more watching eyes. No more feeling that someone would leap out and attack at any moment. Just the dimming hum of a city marching toward rest.

Neither Laurel nor Alverax spoke a word as he guided their path. They passed a woman packing up a cart of elletberries, the acrid smell wafting its way into Laurel's mouth. She looked to the south and Mercy's Bluff where, even at such a distance, all they could see was ocean all the way to the horizon. She didn't miss being aboard the *Pale Urchin*, with its constant rocking and cramped quarters, but she did miss the smell of the untouched air, and the solitude. She wasn't sure she would ever again want to live somewhere with so many people.

If they even survived the coming storm.

Eventually, they strode up to a small home with a shed out back and a wild pilliwick trying to nibble at a garden through a wooden lattice. She'd read about the creatures, with their unnaturally long tongues and penchant for kleptomania.

She watched as Alverax walked up to the front door and paused. For a moment, she thought of saying something—she knew he was still struggling—but instead, she waited, because that's what she would have wanted. Sometimes, people just need a moment, and, if that was the only thing she had to sacrifice to help him, she'd give up a thousand more.

Finally, Alverax pushed the door open, an inch at a time, the creak of it ringing out into the quiet neighborhood. It was dark inside. Quiet too. And as they stepped inside, Laurel felt an odd sense of nostalgia for her own home in the Fairenwild. But that home was gone. Alverax may have lost much, but at least he had a home.

He turned and looked at Laurel.

She nodded knowingly, then turned to leave.

CHRYS AND JELIUM sat across from each other, each staring down at the fifteen game pieces they controlled. Nine black Sentries. Two Sapphires. Two Emeralds. And two glass Heralds. Each piece had a black or white border; Chrys was playing black.

The most common opening was to advance one of the Sentries between the Sapphire and Emerald, opening the board and providing the more powerful pieces space to create threats. It was safe and led to a number of interesting variations, each with their own exploits and pitfalls.

Jelium, instead, slid forward a Herald's Sentry.

It weakened his position, unless you were going for...

Chrys advanced his left Sapphire, leaping over the Sentry in front of it.

"Good," Jelium said with a smirk. "You are familiar with the Agatos opening."

He pushed another Sentry forward.

"Made popular by Mennik Thorn," Chrys added, as he advanced one of his own. He had never been so grateful for the year he'd spent absorbed by the game. The Agatos opening had several nasty traps that worked well against many young players.

Jelium examined the board carefully. "And you wish to punish my opening with the Grievar Advance."

Chrys smiled. There was no immediate counter to his opening, which meant that they would enter the middle game with Chrys having more space and a stronger center.

Jelium clearly knew what he was doing...but so did Chrys.

As Laurel and Asher walked down dark, sandy pathways, she couldn't help but miss her own grandfather. Beginning with the death of her parents, it seemed that all life had to offer was loss, a slow biting tax for merely existing. Her parents, home, grandfather. Her threadlight. One by one, they had all been taken from her. And yet, despite it all, she was not alone.

Together, Asher whispered to her mind, feeling what she was feeling. And they were.

Laurel and Asher raced through the outer edge of Cynosure. Despite the sand, it was hard to believe that on the other side of the massive sandstone wall lay a sprawling desert. There was an ethereal beauty to the scale of the cavern that housed the city, like the Father of All had scooped out a section of rock from a mountain and placed a city in its crevice. It felt so foreign, so strange. Hardly a tree in sight, and the ones that did grow were prickly or stunted.

As they ran, they passed a fenced enclosure with a dozen odd creatures. To Laurel, they seemed somewhere between a cow and a horse, but green and with spines covering their bodies. The creatures moved slowly, and, based on the abandoned carts beside the pen, she assumed they must be used as pack animals.

They continued, and Asher spotted a small, lizard-like creature. In moments, he'd pounced upon it, shattered the creature's shell, and bitten into its flesh. Watching Asher feast on his prey gave Laurel the odd desire to do the same. If only there were a duskdeer or a small rabbit. Her grandfather had the best herbs for cooking rabbit.

Finally, they reached Mercy's Bluff, where they collapsed on the sandy overlook. Asher crawled closer and rested his head on her lap. She brushed the green fur along his back, feeling each movement of his ragged breath beneath the thick coat.

They sat in silence for some time, looking out over the Altapecean Sea, an endless horizon of various shades of blue. A few weeks ago, the color would have given her pause, a reminder of her lost threadlight. But she was content now. Instead, the color faded away, and all she felt was the motion of the waves, like the rustle of leaves in the wind, and the explosive spray as those same waves crashed against the rocky shore.

"It's beautiful," Laurel said.

Asher's voice whispered in her mind. *It is.*

"I wish we could enjoy it."

Laurel leaned back with one arm posted behind her and watched the waves. Whether today or tomorrow or the day after, a ship would come hunting for them. Whatever measure of peace and confidence they felt now was just as likely to turn with the tide.

MOVE AFTER MOVE, Chrys and Jelium advanced their pieces, adding pressure, opening lines. The game was close, despite Chrys' strong opening. He'd played too defensively, worried about losing what little advantage he had. He needed to be more aggressive. This game was too important.

He had a clever idea and used his Emerald to *pull* one of the enemy Sentries forward.

Jelium laughed. "The Bessarion Gambit! Now, I haven't seen that one in years. Shawn Paul would be proud. It is, of course, a dangerous move were I to accept. The immediate advantage would require me to play nearly perfectly to account for the positional disadvantage. Which is tempting, to be clear. Tell me...Apogee, are you familiar with the Sarilla Countergambit?"

Chrys raised a brow as Jelium made his move. He could see the immediate threat, the potential fork after an Emerald *pull*, but it all seemed manageable. Chrys ignored the taunt, accepting the countergambit with his Sapphire.

"There is a funny line," Jelium said, swaying his head back and forth and reaching for a Sapphire. "Made popular by Nelson of Brun, though it first appeared in Eidyn, played by Khraen himself. A natural extension of our current positions. Are you familiar with the Volund?"

Chrys ignored Jelium to think, but the pressure was beginning to rise inside of him. He racked his brain trying to remember the line to which Jelium referred. He knew Khraen, of course. One of the most influential players in history. And Nelson of Brun had become a champion during his stay in the Alirian islands. But Chrys had no recollection of the game.

"It appears not," Jelium said, smiling as he moved one of his Heralds. "This should be interesting..."

With every move, Chrys felt the pressure intensify in his skull, a rhythmic beating that began with a simple tap, now ringing out like two mallets against a war drum. He didn't need books on Theo theory to tell him that his position was dangerous, but, even still, he held out hope. His Heralds were safe. And if he could keep the position defended long enough, he could find a way to get back on the attack.

"I must say," Jelium said, with his chalky voice, "that you have played impressively. You've warded off traps that would have fooled some of the most skilled players in Cynosure. However, as a man who has been in real war, you must see that the game is lost."

Chrys rubbed at his temples, staring intensely at the board. Jelium was taunting him. There were no immediate threats. "Your mind games won't work. My Heralds are safe. The game is far from over."

Jelium smiled, a single twitch of his upper lip. "Are you so certain?"

Adrenaline poured through Chrys like an old whiskey, burning him from the inside. He'd missed something. No. His Heralds were safe behind a wall of Sentries. There was no way for Jelium's pieces to get to them. Not unless...

Stones.

TOGETHER, Laurel and Asher stared out at the breaking waves in silence and solemn happiness, enjoying the calm before the storm, knowing that these days may be the last before the clouds of evil returned. Somewhere across the ocean, the Zeda people lay sleeping. Laurel wondered what was happening in Felia. She'd spent so much time away from the Zeda that she was beginning to feel a distance growing in her heart. In an odd way, Chrys and the others felt more like family than Bay now, and Zedalum felt less like home than the world at large.

She watched as, high above the ocean, a flame-tailed halken twisted in the air, diving toward the water, then pulling up and drifting as if floating. Two more halkens appeared, flying in a straight line from the northwest. Whereas the first seemed to be playfully tumbling through the air, these two seemed focused. They had a purpose, a destination. Laurel could appreciate that.

As she watched, the birds grew in size. They were massive flying creatures, lit only by a half-hidden moon. Suddenly, they paused in the air, as if all of their momentum had been taken away in an instant. It was then that Laurel realized: they were not birds.

"Gale take me," she cursed.

Danger, Asher added, his bright eyes fixed on the creatures in the sky.

They were both on their feet in an instant, eyes on the heavens, neither wanting to speak aloud the dark truth.

The Heralds had arrived.

No, no, no. There was always a move—that's what Malachus had taught him. Theo was like war; until the final move was played, there was always a way to turn the tide. And if anyone could find it, it was the Apogee.

Chrys scoured the game board, calculating exchanges, looking for the flaw in Jelium's position. More than once, he thought he'd found something, a way to at least even the match, but every line ended with his defeat.

Chrys moved a Sapphire, knowing full well that it would not stop the inevitable, unless Jelium made a mistake.

"Heralds have always been the heart of Theo," Jelium said, watching Chrys' eyes as they darted back and forth across the board. "Despite them being the most powerful piece on the board, most players prefer to keep them locked up behind a wall of Sentries. The fear of loss is greater than the eye for victory." His eyes dimmed, and he tilted his head to the side. "How fitting that a sacrifice will be what brings about your own."

Jelium moved one of his Heralds forward, capturing Chrys' Emerald with a sacrifice that would begin a forced sequence that would march Chrys toward defeat.

Willow brought a hand to her mouth. "Lightfather, no."

"What?" Iriel said quickly.

Roshaw took a step toward the board. "What is it?"

"The game is over," Willow said, her eyes wide with disbelief. "Chrys lost."

BONDS OF CHAOS
6

ALVERAX BREATHED as he entered his childhood home.

Silence.

Dark as it was, he felt a ghostly sway in his legs, as if he were back in the creaking cabin on the *Pale Urchin*. So many days lost in the memories that swirled in his vision like a noxious fog, infecting his mind, polluting his thoughts. He wanted to move on, to forget what happened to...her. But want and reality were at odds, and, no matter how hard he tried, he couldn't hide from the look in her eyes as she sank to the floor in the throne room.

There was a certain aroma that lingered in the air of his home. While living there, he'd never really noticed it, as though a hint of saffron had stained the walls from all of his grandfather's cooking. But now, returning after so many months, it filled him with warmth.

A few pebbles crunched beneath his foot as he took another step forward.

"Is someone there?" a voice called out in the darkness.

"Grandfather?" Alverax stepped toward the light.

A hunched man made his way out of a room on the far end of the house, a small candle illuminating his frailty. The old man rushed forward, slamming the candle's base down on the side table and wrapping Alverax in the warmest embrace he'd ever received. His grandfather's hands gripped tight against Alverax's back, squeezing, digging in with what little strength the old man had left. For a moment, Alverax forgot about the pain.

But only for a moment.

"My boy," his grandfather whispered, emotions adding an even greater quaver to his voice. "I knew you would come back."

"I..." Alverax didn't know what to say. He didn't want to talk about Jisenna, but he did. He needed to tell him about his father, but he couldn't. Instead, all of the pain and anguish, all of the fear and doubt and sadness, every bit of sorrow that had bottled itself in his broken soul came pouring out of him in a stream of tears.

Once, in a moment of stupidity, he'd told Elder Rowan that he wanted to bring hope to people. But now he understood that a shooting star was the sign of hope because it leaves as quickly as it comes.

His grandfather's calloused hands moved to the back of Alverax's head, and he pulled him in even tighter. "No matter what you've done, no matter how bad things are, I will always be here. You are a good man, Alverax...You are a good man."

He dug his head into his grandfather's shoulder and sobbed.

A few minutes later, Alverax collapsed into the soft fabric of a chair in front of the fireplace. His grandfather took a seat opposite him.

When Alverax finally felt ready, he spoke. "He's alive. Dad... Your son is alive."

His grandfather's eyes grew wide, the wrinkles along his forehead becoming deep chasms. "How?" His voice wavered. "How is it possible? Did you see him? Where is he now?"

"He's meeting with Jelium. We traveled here together—well, there was a group of us—but he and I still haven't spoken."

For a moment, his grandfather watched him, reading his story in the pain of his eyes and the weight of his shoulders. "You haven't forgiven him for leaving." His words were not a question but a statement of truth.

"How could I?" Alverax said, his voice growing with anger. "What kind of man abandons his family and never returns? And do you know where he was? In the Wastelands! What the hell kind of a father abandons his family for the Wastelands?"

"I'm sure he had his reasons."

Alverax shook his head. "You're defending him? He abandoned us. He abandoned you!"

Again, his grandfather gave a pause before responding. "When I was young, I carried deliveries all over the streets of Felia. Crates of fruit. Books. Flowers. It paid well enough. One of our clients needed a box of paper delivered to a small bookshop every other week, and I took the job. On the way there, I ran into a friend. When she found out where I was going, she asked if I could take a flower pot with me that belonged to the same bookshop owner. I agreed and set the flower pot on top of the crate of paper. But as soon as I lifted it, I knew it was a mistake. The pot was too heavy. But I was stubborn. So, I took it anyway. I was walking up the final hill when my arms finally gave out. The pot came crashing down. It shattered into so many pieces it was hardly recognizable. The crate, too, had broken.

"The point, Alverax, is that some burdens are handed to us, but others we pick up for ourselves. Our job is not to wallow in the gravity of it, nor to simply push forward and accept it. Our job is to ask ourselves which burdens are worth the weight and which are not. My boy, don't wait until you're falling over to lighten your load. This grudge you have for what your father did, you have to set it down."

Alverax took a breath. "I don't think I can do that. He doesn't deserve to be forgiven."

"Of course not—most people we forgive are undeserving—but the only person a grudge hurts is the one who carries it. If you want to live a life hunched over in pain, go ahead. But if you want to stand as tall as the world deserves to see you stand, then you need to shed your burden."

The words reminded him of *her*. She'd once told him that he would have to grow in uncomfortable ways, and he had! It felt like around every corner the world required him to change even more, and he wasn't sure he could handle it. Even if he didn't believe in himself, she did. But she was gone.

Alverax cried into his hands. "I can't."

"Not alone," his grandfather said quietly. "But you don't have to be. Alverax, I would take your burdens from your shoulders if I could. But I cannot. What I can do is share the weight, if you will let me."

So, he did.

While his grandfather stoked a small fire, Alverax told him everything. And when he spoke of Jisenna, his grandfather cried with him.

As they sat in tired silence, an aggressive knock pounded on the door. Alverax stood quickly and pulled out the Midnight Watcher, gesturing for his grandfather to stand back. As he walked toward the door, it burst open, wood splintering where the lock had failed to keep it closed. On the other side, Laurel and Asher stood panting in the doorway.

"Laurel," Alverax said, startled. "What's going on? What's happening?"

"The Heralds are here!" she blurted out. "There's no time. We need to warn the others, and I need you to show me where they went!"

Alverax turned to his grandfather, jaw clenched, eyes filled with regret. "I'm sorry. I have to go."

"It's okay," the old man responded. "You have always been destined for more than this city. Seeing you again has brought me more joy than you will ever know. And to know that my son is alive...Tonight, Alverax, you have brought me hope."

Alverax gave his grandfather one final, ferocious embrace. "I love you, old man."

"The depths of the ocean could not see you as highly as I do." His grandfather pulled away and looked him in the eye. "Take care of yourself. And take care of your father for me. I would very much like to see him again."

Alverax smiled one last time. "I promise."

With that, they stepped away from the house and raced toward Jelium's complex.

Bonds of Chaos 7

CHRYS' vision warped as he stared at the gameboard, pieces slowly drifting away, breaking through the cracks of reality. He replayed each move in his mind, desperately searching for where he'd failed. But no matter how much he wanted to blame Jelium for cheating—Lightfather knows he would—Chrys couldn't hide from the truth.

Jelium leaned back, throwing his hands behind his head. "It was a good game, I will admit. One of the best I've played. You surprised me with the Bessarion. Despite the loss, you should be proud. You've clearly studied the game. But as it goes, the better man won."

"You knew," Chrys said with a snarl. "Spinning that piece around between your fingers. You wanted one of us to propose a game. You were probably going to suggest it yourself. You played us!"

"Be reasonable," Jelium said, failing to suppress a hint of amusement in his tone. "You came to me. I had no way of knowing that you even played the game. I am a man of my word, though. If I had lost, I would have willingly gone with you on your foolish adventure. But, alas, it seems that the game has played out differently. Perhaps, we can play again some other day."

"THIS IS NOT A GAME!" Chrys shouted, swiping his hands across the table, launching the Theo board toward the wall, sending pieces flying in every chaotic direction. The Masked Guard all drew their weapons. "People's lives are at stake!"

Jelium calmly rose to his feet, meeting Chrys' prismatic eyes with confidence. "People's lives are always at stake. How is that my problem?"

"Chrys," Willow said from behind him, shaking her head cautiously.

"Jelium," Roshaw cut in, raising his hands in an attempt to calm the rising conflict. "How long have we known each other?"

Jelium cocked his head to the side, scowling at Roshaw. "You. You're lucky I haven't gutted you. You think after a few years that you can return home and pretend like you didn't lie to me for more than ten? You will never be welcome in this city until you hand over whatever prized possession you brought back from the Wastelands. For the rest of you, the game is done. I won. You lost. The child is mine."

A shocked silence warped the room.

Chrys' head jerked to face Jelium. "What did you say?"

"I won," Jelium said with cold eyes. "And I want the Amber-eyed child."

"Over my dead body," Iriel said with a snarl.

"That was *not* the deal," Chrys growled.

Roshaw's eyes burned into Jelium. "You sick bastard. Don't you have enough children?"

Jelium's lip twitched. "For thirty years, I have tried to bear an Amber-eyed child. Not one of my wives could give me what I wanted. I have an entire army of children, and they're useless. Thread-dead, the whole lot of them. But your son...mmm. If he were with me, no one would even question it. He would be celebrated throughout Cynosure. He would be a king. Everything I have would be his."

Chrys gripped the hilt of his dagger. "It's not happening. The deal was my life for yours."

"That's simply not true." Jelium lifted a hand into the air, fingers extended wide. "If I win, a life is mine. That was the deal you shook on. A life for a life. And if you won't honor your promises, they will be honored for you."

Jelium closed his hand, the Masked Guards shifted, and the room went dark.

Fear crawled its spindly legs through Chrys' mind. Their biggest advantage was their threadlight. But if they couldn't see, the advantage was lost. And Jelium knew that. Chrys pulled his dagger out of its sheath, waiting for his eyes to adjust, but the door was closed, and the room had been cast into an inky void of blackness.

As he tried to orient himself, a body rammed into him, sending them both tumbling over and crashing into the wall. His eyes bulged as a knife bit into his thigh. Quickly, he threw his hips up and over the attacker, unable to see, but fully aware of his attacker's position. Once he was on top, he rammed his own dagger through the man's chest. Once. Twice. Three times. Squeezing his hips until the man went limp.

"The child is mine, Chrys," Jelium called out into the void. "Give him to me, and I will treat him as if he were my own flesh and blood."

"Go to hell," Chrys shouted back, before realizing that words would give away his position.

Jelium let out a roaring laugh. "Look around you. We're already there!"

Iriel's voice called out from the dark, a wordless scream of rage.

Before Chrys could move, a man's voice grunted out in pain from the same direction. A loud pop rang throughout the domed room, followed by the same voice calling out in agony.

"Who's next!" Iriel shouted. "I'll kill every last one of you!"

Chrys pulled himself toward her voice and whispered. "Iriel, you have Aydin?"

"I gave him to Willow," she said. "She's hiding in the corner."

"Chrys," Jelium's voice taunted. The room was quiet, save for the sound of feet shuffling. They were surrounded and without threadlight. There was no way out. "In a few minutes, there will be more than fifty of my Masked Guard surrounding this room. Give me the child, and I will let you leave the city alive."

"The Heralds will come for you!" Roshaw said. "And they will kill you first. They're hunting Amber threadweavers, and you and the baby are the last. It's only a matter of time before they find you!"

Jelium let out a grunt. "Lies. You were a coward then, and you're a coward now. Now, GIVE ME THE CHILD!"

Just as he screamed the words, the door burst open, letting in a flood of flickering light from the hallway, illuminating three silhouettes. The first, a tall man with dark skin and a sword that dragged along the ground. The second, a woman with hair stained green and fire in her eyes. And the last, a beast nearly as tall as the woman, twin tails dancing in the firelight, crimson blood dripping from its maw.

Threads, like hungry eels, slithered out of the ground, latching onto the newcomers. But as soon as the threads were born, Alverax's veins pulsed with Obsidian threadlight, storm clouds swirling beneath his skin, and the Amber threads shattered.

"JELIUM!" Alverax shouted, stepping forward. Again, threadlight surged through him as he broke the corethread of every barely-visible guard in the room. Those who moved lost their connection to the earth and began to float toward the domed ceiling. "This ends now!"

He ran forward, lifting the Midnight Watcher. Jelium's eyes glowed a brilliant gold as he tried to bind the blade, but it would not be touched. It could not be touched. This was its purpose. It was born to hunt Amber.

Chrys pushed himself to his feet, but he couldn't get there in time.

From the other side of the table, Jelium seemed frozen.

Alverax screamed out as he pulled the blade down over his head.

But he stopped, the shimmering thread-dead obsidian mere inches from Jelium's skull. He let it hover for a minute before speaking. "Let me be clear, Jelium. You are used to being the most powerful man in the room, but those days are over. If we want you dead, you are dead. If the Heralds want you dead, you are dead. You will help us, or we will find another way to stop them."

Jelium's lip quivered.

"Chrys!" Laurel shouted from the doorway. "There's no time. The Heralds are here!"

"Stones," Chrys swore. "In the city? Or on their way?"

"Here. Now."

Chrys turned to Jelium, a look of resolve in his eyes. "This is the first place they will look, and if they find you, you won't live through another sunset. Come with us if you want to live. Or stay and die."

The room grew quiet.

Jelium remained frozen beneath the Midnight Watcher, chest heaving up and down as he contemplated his position. His eyes darted back and forth between Chrys and Alverax and his Masked Guard, clearly unconvinced of the Heralds' arrival but keenly aware of his waning control of the situation. The man didn't have to say the words for Chrys to know his response.

"Alverax," Chrys said. "Lower the blade. Jelium is coming with us."

Everyone looked to Jelium, and he nodded.

Alverax sheathed the sword. "There are only three exits. The bluff. A tunnel to the northwest that spits you out into the desert. And another to the northeast that leads to the canyons."

"If we're heading to the Wastelands," Roshaw added, "we should take the northeast tunnel."

"Can we get there without being seen?" Iriel asked.

Laurel shook her head. "The city's too open. If the Heralds are in the air, they'll see us any path we take."

"Then we're going to need a distraction," Chrys said.

Alverax opened his mouth, then closed it with a wince. "I have an idea."

"What is it?" Chrys asked.

Alverax cocked his head to the side. "We're going to need a lot of rope."

BONDS OF CHAOS
8

AFTER THE MOON passed beyond the sandstone overhang, darkness spread over Cynosure. Chrys and the others peeked out of a window, catching short glimpses of the Heralds as they circled the city like bloodthirsty bats in a cave. Laurel was always first to spot them, marking their appearance with a growl.

It was time.

Chrys nodded to the others, then headed toward Jelium's underground passage with Willow and Alverax. It was a cramped, narrow passage, darker than night, lit only by the finely crafted bronze lamp Chrys carried. Below ground, he wasn't sure which was more unnerving, knowing where the Heralds were, or not.

When they finally exited the tunnel, they found themselves in a familiar setting from a new perspective. The underground stadium known as the Pit was lit by a single torch tower casting dwindling light from cooling embers. The track and stands crawled with unnerving shadows. In one corner, hidden away behind thick iron bars, nearly a dozen necrolytes slept coiled up in their cages.

Willow motioned to Chrys and they fell behind, whispering to him as they approached. "I really don't think this is a good idea."

"It's not," Chrys said, admitting the truth. "But we don't need good ideas right now. We need a distraction. And if nothing else, this will be a spectacular distraction."

ON THE EASTERN edge of Jelium's complex, waiting for their signal, Laurel, Iriel, and Roshaw crouched in a small room with Asher and

Aydin, staring out of a window. Behind them, a host of Masked Guard stood in the hallway with Jelium in their midst. Beyond her typical distrust, it took only a single moment in his presence for Laurel to decide that she hated the man. It wasn't his appearance, or even his demeanor, but a scent. A dank, putrid aroma. If darkness had a smell, it would be his.

High in the sky, the Heralds still roamed, gods surveying their kingdom while the people lay asleep in soft beds. Three times, Laurel had seen the two separate then come back together, hovering in the air like skyflies. For now, all their party could do was wait.

Laurel rubbed at her shoulder, then her chest and thigh. Her hands refused to settle. This moment—and her role—was too important. If Jelium decided to do something stupid, like try to take Aydin, Laurel and Asher had to stop him. Roshaw's Obsidian would counteract Jelium's Amber, and Laurel was certain that she and Asher could do the rest. Still, deep inside her, like a woodpecker tapping away at her ribs, the urge to act remained. But she was done listening to that voice. Laurel was willing to sacrifice for her pack, even if the sacrifice was time.

Suddenly, from the distant tunnel leading to the Pit, she saw the first of them.

CHRYS STEPPED FORWARD to the first necrolyte with a rope outstretched. He studied the spikes along the massive reptile's twisted torso, looking for two that were jutting out in opposite directions that could be used to lasso the beast. "There," he said, finding the perfect spikes. "Those should work."

"Careful," Willow said.

"Don't wake it up," Alverax added.

Without responding, Chrys used a y-shaped stick and lifted the end of the lasso toward the spikes. With the care of a surgeon, he looped the rope around the closer of the two spikes, letting the hemp fall toward the base without touching the necrolyte's scales. Then, taking the other end of the loop, he stretched it out as far as it could reach, but the lasso had tightened, and it wasn't wide enough. Carefully, he added pressure to the other end of the lasso, waiting for the loop to enlarge. The pressure pressed against the first spike, stirring the necrolyte from its rest.

He paused.

After shifting its position, the necrolyte returned to its sleep, the lasso still hooked around the first spike. Fortunately, its movement had loosened the loop, and Chrys was able to quickly wrap it around the second spike. He used the stick to tighten the lasso, then pulled it out of the cage.

Weight seemed to fall from his shoulders. He felt like he had when he'd pulled his first honeycrystal from the et'hovon hive.

"Easy," he whispered with a smile.

Willow shook her head. "This is such a stupid idea."

"It'll work," Alverax said.

"Oh, I know that," she replied. "Doesn't make it any less stupid."

One by one, they looped lassos around the caged necrolytes, ensuring the rope ends would be free when the cages were opened. Then, once all of the ropes were set, Chrys, Willow, and Alverax tied the free end of the ropes together, creating a bouquet of thorned necrolytes.

Chrys and Willow stood at the gates.

Alverax wrapped the rope around his wrists.

Obsidian threadlight poured through their veins.

One by one, they *broke* the corethread of each necrolyte, a million tiny suns bursting through the air like billowing sand.

They opened the gates, and Alverax ran.

Chrys watched as Alverax pulled the weightless necrolytes along. Despite their broken corethreads, the massive creatures still had considerable mass, and it took a slow effort to get them moving. Chrys and Willow followed, being careful to keep their distance.

Alverax ran up the stairs and flailed for a moment as his feet lifted off the ground from the momentum of the necrolytes at the top of the stadium stairs. He recovered and took off down the entrance tunnel.

Necrolytes thrashed in the air behind him.

Crashing into each other.

Ropes groaning.

As they stepped out of the entrance and into the sprawling cavern housing the sleeping city, Alverax unknotted the ropes, spun, and hurled the necrolytes upward with every ounce of strength in his slender frame.

"Gale take me," Laurel cursed.

A writhing mass of necrolytes floated into the air, screeching, flailing...flying. Ropes fell from them like shedding skin. Slowly, they drifted apart, spreading out over the city like dragons in the night.

"Stones," Iriel cursed beside her.

The first scream broke through the dark sky as the people of Cynosure awoke to the sounds of the necrolytes.

Laurel turned to Jelium. "We leave at the next—"

Before she could finish her sentence, a choir of voices screamed out from the four corners of Cynosure. More and more people awoke. Fear flooded the night. Men, women, children. Lamps flickering through open doors, torch towers blazing to life. Shattered peace.

"We leave now," Laurel finished. "And leave your pack behind; they'll give us away."

"My pack?" Jelium raised a brow. "I'm not bringing—ah, no. They're coming with us."

"They stay!" Laurel shouted, her voice lined with a wolf's growl. "The Heralds will see a large group. If they come, we all die. You're in no danger from us. We need you alive."

"Damn it," Jelium grumbled and turned to the Masked Guard. "Stay here. Stay hidden. Don't let whatever those things are find you. I'll be back as soon as I deal with this."

Laurel pushed open the door and peeked around the corner into the night sky. There was no sign of the Heralds, though the necrolytes continued to spread out over the canopy like vultures. She waved for the others to follow, and they did.

Street by street, Roshaw led Laurel, Asher, Iriel, and Jelium toward the northeastern tunnel. As they moved, they passed frightened men and crying children, women wielding blades and others nocking arrows. Laurel felt the urge to comfort them, but the truth was that they had every right to be worried. Evil gods and monstrous beasts roamed the sky.

That was when the first necrolyte fell toward the earth.

CHRYS GRABBED Alverax and pulled him to a rocky corner where they hid, watching as the city sprang to life. Chrys wanted to shout at the people to stay in their homes, to bar their doors and windows. To stay safe. The chaos was only beginning, and when the necrolytes fell to the ground, some of them would survive, and people were going to get hurt. Chrys looked toward the northeastern tunnel passage. But they couldn't move until there was enough chaos in the city to keep the Heralds distracted.

As the pandemonium developed, Chrys leaned closer to Alverax and Willow. "I think we should go. The corethreads could reappear any minute."

"Ready when you are," Willow said in agreement.

"It's happening," Alverax said, looking toward the sky.

Chrys whipped his head around. "What?"

But then he saw it. One of the necrolytes was diving tusk-first through the air toward the ground, mouth wide open, teeth bared.

"Go, go, go!" Chrys shouted, taking off at a sprint along the eastern wall.

"I NEED TO STOP," Jelium groaned behind them, leaning against a sandstone wall, his chest heaving up and down.

Laurel growled. They didn't have time to stop. They needed to get to the tunnel as soon as possible. "Roshaw!" she shouted, an idea blossoming in her mind. "*Break* his corethread."

The older man looked at her, puzzled. "Jelium's?"

She nodded vigorously. "*Break* his corethread, and we can drag him along so he doesn't have to run."

Roshaw's eyes grew wide. "Brilliant." He let Obsidian threadlight pour through him and *broke* Jelium's corethread. In moments, the man was weightless and angry, but she also saw a flicker of understanding in his eyes.

"Asher," Laurel whispered, turning to her companion. "Don't make it gentle."

The chromawolf nodded, biting the sleeve of the big, Kulaian man's robes, and took off. Jelium bounced up and down against the sand, wincing while they continued their path.

Every few paces, Laurel would turn her eyes skyward to look for the Heralds and the necrolytes. The gods were nowhere to be seen, and most of the snakes were either writhing on the ground or falling through the air. One necrolyte was fumbling about against the edge of the eastern wall, throwing its tusks against large stone stalactites.

When they reached the tunnel entrance, Roshaw pulled Jelium down, and they hid behind a large boulder, waiting for the others.

CHRYS' heart throbbed in his chest as they ran, adrenaline and theadlight coalescing in an oily mixture that burned like lightning in his veins, surging through him and pushing him forward. He and Willow were *drifting*, lightening their weight and increasing their speed, leaving Alverax barreling after them, long legs striding over sand and rock.

Chrys' eyes fixed on their destination, where he could see the others crouched behind a boulder, waiting.

He smiled.

This was actually going to work.

Just then, a necrolyte fell from the sky, crashing into the ground not twenty feet away, between them and the cave entrance. The ground shook as it hit, and its body grew still.

Chrys and Willow slammed to a halt, staring, speechless.

Was it...?

The necrolyte stirred.

Stones.

If only he had Amber threadlight, he could bind the creature and run around it. Instead, the only way was through. "Alverax," he said without turning to the young man who had finally caught up. "How good are you with that sword?"

"I was trained by the best swordsman in all of Felia."

"Good," Chrys said.

"But only for, like, one week..."

Chrys turned to him. "Could have led with that."

Alverax shrugged. "I got pretty good in that week."

"Better than nothing." Chrys unsheathed his dagger. "We attack from both sides."

"Chrys Valerian," his mother said from behind them with a stern tone.

Both men turned around.

She shook her head. "Men are such idiots sometimes."

Chin held high, she strode toward the writhing necrolyte, massive spikes jutting out from its body, curled tusks cutting from its jaw, rows of teeth glittering in the moonlight. It saw her and coiled its body like a spring, preparing to pounce. The veins in her arms glowed with the ghostly mist of Obsidian threadlight, then she *broke* the necrolyte's corethread. It lashed out at her, but the absence of gravity caused it to flip over itself, bounce off the ground, and float back into the air.

She never broke stride, walking under it as it hissed from above.

"Damn," Alverax muttered.

Chrys shook his head and smiled. "That's my mother."

They took off after her, and in no time at all, they were reunited with the rest of their party. Chrys pulled in Iriel and Aydin for an embrace, kissing her forehead as he squeezed them close. He caught Laurel's eye, and she gave him a nod.

As he let go of his own family, he watched Alverax approach Roshaw. "I haven't forgiven you," the young man said. "But I'm ready to move in that direction."

"I'm sorry," Roshaw said, tears swelling in his eyes.

"I know," Alverax replied.

Laurel, unaware of their conversation, pointed to the sky. "Is that...?"

Chrys looked up.

The Heralds.

"RUN!" he screamed.

Everyone, including Jelium with a newly formed corethread, sprinted down the corridor.

A loud slam quaked through the ground from behind them.

"CHRYS VALERIAN!" Relek called out, his voice reverberating through the tunnel.

Everyone stopped and turned.

Relek and Lylax, the Heralds of Felia, the gods of the Wastelands, they-who-pervert-the-bond, stood in the mouth of the tunnel, looking down their noses.

"You cannot run from us," Lylax said, her gravelly voice biting through the air.

"Give us the child," Relek demanded.

Chrys took out his dagger and spun it in his hand. "Hey Lylax, how's your stomach?"

Iriel touched his arm.

Lylax took a step forward. "The mountain cares not for the fallen tree."

"Chrys," Iriel said.

He turned.

"I have an idea," she whispered, turning to the others and speaking quickly. "Four of us have Emerald threadlight. We're going to cave in the tunnel."

Roshaw nodded. "Hell yeah, we are."

"If we are," Chrys said, turning back toward Relek and Lylax. "We need to do it now."

"On three," Iriel said.

Relek took another step forward. "I must say that I was surprised to find that you had taken to the sea."

"One," Iriel whispered.

"I should have known," Relek continued with a sadistic grin. "You always run. At the Temple. In the Fairenwild. The Endless Well. Only now, there is nowhere to run."

"Two," Iriel continued.

They opened themselves to threadlight, and Emerald energy swam through their veins.

"It has been...fun," Relek said with a smile.

"Three!" Iriel shouted.

Their eyes blazed with viridian threadlight. The roof of the tunnel rumbled, shaking with the force of a hundred hammers beating against the stone. Rubble fell from overhead, then rocks the size of fists. Then, breaking apart from the surge of power that *pulled* it down, the tunnel shattered like a pane of glass, raining death from above.

Through the stone storm, Chrys saw Relek.

He wasn't angry.

He wasn't annoyed.

He was...amused.

And that scared Chrys even more.

BONDS OF CHAOS

9

Rixi stepped into Relek's Cave, followed by a group of three other wastelanders. After having guarded the entrance for so many years, there was something unnatural about finally stepping inside. But the stone felt like any other stone, and the damp air felt like any other cave. Still, he knew there was something inside. Something the false gods didn't want them to see.

He lifted a photospore overhead, the light glancing off the shiny skin of a half-healed gash on his forearm, and continued forward.

A small—but growing—division of the An'tara no longer believed in their gods. Not that they didn't believe they existed, but after Lylax had gone through body after An'tara body, discarding them like soiled clothing when they withered under her control, a faction began to wonder if the gods were worthy of their devotion. Some had already given themselves in defiance. It was not an easy path to walk—the An'tara were a hive, one mind united—but even the et'hovon must at times abandon their rose.

Together, the band of An'tara plunged deeper into the cave, through a winding tunnel system, farther and farther. It seemed empty, save for the occasional dripping of water from the ends of broken stalactites and the glimmering puff of photospore mist.

More than once, Rixi caught the others glancing back up the tunnel from where they came. Yearning, perhaps, to return to their home. Doubting, almost certainly, the path of disobedience they trod.

It would be worth it—he assured them.

There was something down here.

Something the gods wanted to keep for themselves.

They traveled deeper, down and down until, finally, a light gleamed ahead. They slowed their pace, careful to silence their steps. This was it; Rixi could feel it.

He turned the corner and entered a sprawling cavern, high and wide, lit by dozens of photospores and a strange light emanating from a pool of golden water at the far end. They stopped, mesmerized, afraid yet excited. There were signs of people living here, a table, chairs, bedding. Was this where Lylax had lived before she came out of the cave? Whatever the case, it seemed abandoned now.

No matter how hard he tried, Rixi could not stop his eyes from looking at the light emanating from the golden water. It called to him, singing. It was warmth, and his soul was freezing in the darkness.

He stepped toward it, and the others followed.

When he reached the edge, he kneeled, staring into the hypnotic light. He saw his face in the reflection, gray skin, tattoos down his nose. His brow was broader than it ought to be, the only physical change he'd experienced from his bond with the young ataçan, Koi'Ma. In a way, the pool reminded him of oka'thal, the water that kept their people alive, but its brilliance was ten-fold that of the life water. If oka'thal could sustain them, he wondered what this would do.

Rixi placed his hands in the water, cupping the glowing liquid in his palms, and brought it to his lips. It slid down his throat, cold but warm as it flowed through him.

Nothing happened.

As he stared down into the light, tears welled in his eyes, and his heart broke. This was it; he was certain. There was an answer here, somewhere. Some path forward for the An'tara without the gods. But maybe he was wrong. Maybe their only path was to submit themselves and move forward, content in knowing that they were nothing more than vessels.

Then, his heart burned. Small at first, like a hand held over a fire, but then the flames grew, a field of dry grass blazing. He gripped at his chest, crying out in pain, struggling to steady himself. His whole body burned. He was the dry grass, and his skin was the bonfire.

Suddenly, the pain was gone, replaced by a steady stream of warmth coursing through his limbs. He felt alive—more alive than he'd ever felt —like electricity danced in his blood.

When he stood, he caught a glance of his arm and smiled. Fresh gray skin had stitched itself together, leaving no sign of the painful gash. He had been healed.

And as he breathed in the stale, cavern air, he understood that, even more than the healing of his arm, something within him had changed.

One by one, the other An'tara drank from the golden waters, marveling at the transformation, wondering at the possibilities.

But a resounding voice broke their hope. "You should not be here."

Invisible threads latched onto the others, dragging their bodies to the floor before they could even scream. In seconds, the pressure collapsed their bones, and their bodies crumpled to the floor, blood pooling out from the mangled heap of sinew and organs.

And all Rixi could do was watch.

"I understand why you are here," Relek said, striding forward with his chin held high. "It is a hard thing we have asked of your people, but it is necessary. Tell me, Rixi." He emphasized the name. "Were you there when the Builders killed so many of your people?"

Rixi nodded. Only five years had passed since the Builders had come over the mountain, threatening to invade their land. And in so doing, they had killed thousands of the An'tara.

"With this," Relek said, gesturing to the glowing pool, "we can avenge those who fell. We can heal the An'tara and remove their dependence on oka'thal. We can lead them over the mountain. With the bond you hold with your ataçan, the An'tara look up to you. Together, we can unite the Hive. We can seek revenge on the Builders, if you will join me."

Rixi was no fool. He understood that, though there was a question presented, there was only one correct answer. But was it so bad? If he stood with the gods, perhaps he could protect his people. Perhaps, he could steer their path through safe roads. If there was no way to stop the gods, he would do everything in his power to limit their devastation.

Dropping to a knee, Rixi crossed his hands at the wrist, bending the fingers back to touch at the tips. "My god, we will unite the Hive."

BONDS OF CHAOS
10

A LIGHT BREEZE fluttered its wings through the canyons east of Silkar. A peck of pilliwicks darted across the hard ground, scuttling up and over the sandy walls. Chrys and the others were just as skittish as the wildlife, eyes constantly watching the sky, flinching at every shadow. Despite that, after a full day of wandering, the Heralds had yet to be seen.

Chrys had Aydin strapped to his chest, trailing behind Roshaw and Alverax, Iriel and Willow at his side. The canyons seemed to be an endless crevice wrapping back and forth, but Roshaw assured them that they were headed in the right direction. Still, Jelium complained with nearly every step. But if he ever stopped walking, Laurel and Asher were there, snarling to push him forward.

When the sun finally dipped below the western horizon on their first night out of Cynosure, they took shelter against a canyon wall with enough of an overhang to hide them from the open sky. The evening brought with it a desert chill, but rather than build a small fire and risk being seen by the Heralds, they pulled their clothes tight over their shoulders and dealt with it.

As they settled, Aydin began to stir, so Chrys passed the child over to his wife, who sat with her back against the sandy wall. She lifted her shirt and offered a breast to their son, who latched with ease. Chrys thought he saw the sliver of a smile on her lips as she watched him nurse.

As far as children go, they were lucky. Like most threadweaver infants, the healing power in his veins made Aydin a healthy child who slept well and only cried when he was hungry. Still, Chrys felt guilty for the life he'd forced upon his son. Hopefully, if all went well, they'd be back in their cottage one day where Aydin could learn to crawl and walk and talk with a sense of safety and security.

Chrys sat back and laid his head against the wall beside Iriel's. His feet were tired, and his eyes begged him to rest. Instead, he watched the two people he loved most dearly in the world. "Remember how we talked about having another child?"

Iriel turned to him, brows raised.

Chrys held back a smile. "Seems like a pretty terrible idea right about now."

Iriel quivered as she held back her laughter, Aydin bouncing on her chest. "For a moment, I thought you were implying we should...here. I was about to make you sleep on the other side of the canyon."

"No, no," Chrys said, looking past the ledge into the star-filled night. "It's just that the entire world is growing darker, and if we can't stop the Heralds, who knows what will be left. I want to be able to think about the future, but part of me is scared that there may not be one."

"So don't," Iriel said flatly. "Why do we always have to think about the future? Look to the future. Plan for the future. Prepare for the future. Let's keep it simple. I have you. You have me. We have a beautiful, healthy boy. So forget about it. Forget about the Heralds. Forget about everything. Enjoy the peace we have right here, right now. Who knows when we'll have another chance."

She was right, of course.

"Iriel," he said softly, "I know I don't say it enough—I'm not sure I ever could—but I want you to know that if everything we've gone through, from the day we first saw Aydin's Amber eyes until now...if that was the cost of being here with you, I would pay it every day for the rest of my life."

She leaned into him and placed her delicate lips against his own. Warmth washed over him. Iriel was a warm blanket, and his soul had spent a season in the rain. Her kiss sent fire coursing through his veins, weaving its way through his blood like a flood of threadlight, warming him from the inside.

"I love you," he whispered as the last bit of their lips parted.

"I love *you*," she said with a smile, their noses still touching.

Chrys pulled himself closer and wrapped his arm around Iriel and the baby. "When I was in the Wastelands, I wasn't sure that I would ever get to say that again."

"I can't imagine what you went through."

"There were some really dark days, especially when Relek was in control. Part of me wanted to give up. It just...it felt like it was already over. Like I'd already lost. But I just couldn't stop thinking about you. I couldn't stop thinking that the last memory you had of me was," he faltered, his voice taking on the slightest tremble, "when I abandoned you."

She tilted her chin to look at him. "Chrys Valerian, don't you dare. There wasn't a single moment that I believed you had abandoned us. I know you: the man who would do anything to protect his family; the man who would miss his son's birth if it meant keeping us safe. When I saw your eyes from across the field before you walked away, I knew it wasn't you. *You* didn't abandon us."

"I don't deserve you," he whispered.

She smiled. "Probably not."

Chrys reached down and pulled out the pocket watch that Malachus had gifted to them. When he opened it, all three of the small hands continued their graceful rotations, each at their own pace. "When my mother found this in the mountains, she said it was a sign that I was alive. I think it's a sign, too, but for me it represents us. Our family. When she gave it back to me, it was like the Lightfather was telling me that we'd be together again. That we'd have a little more time." He squeezed the pocket watch shut and held it up to his ear. "As long as I hear that steady tick, I know that everything is going to be okay."

"Everything *is* going to be okay," Iriel said. "Now put that away and stop talking. I need you to be my blanket for the night."

Chrys smiled and gave her a gentle squeeze, laying his head atop hers. No matter what the coming days would bring, it would all be worth it if it kept his family safe.

ALVERAX SETTLED down on the edge of the camp, rubbing his hands together for warmth. He offered to take first watch, and the others took the opportunity to catch whatever sleep their minds would allow. He knew he wouldn't find much.

His father sat silently beside him while the others dozed off.

The stars overhead seemed brighter in the shadow of the canyons. The Moon's Little Sister shone down at him, and instead of feeling overwhelmed with thoughts of Jisenna, he found an odd sense of peace. There was still pain—profound pain cannot fade so quickly—but the hurt seemed wrapped in a quilt of tranquility. Someday, he would join her in the stars.

"You can sleep if you want," Alverax said quietly to his father. "I'm not tired."

Roshaw's lips curled into a smile. "Couldn't sleep if I tried."

Alverax watched the man he'd admired for so many years. The man who had raised him, taught him, then abandoned him. When he was a child, his father was perfect in his eyes. Strong. Able. A provider. But as Alverax grew older, flaws seeped through the façade, and the shock of it made those flaws seem more than what they were. The promise of perfection had been broken, and all his angry eyes could see were the cracks. But now, Alverax could see more clearly, as if a fog had lifted from his younger lens. And it was enough to see that, despite the imperfections, his father was a good man.

"I have been debating with myself," Roshaw said. His eyes seemed pained.

Alverax took the opportunity to let out the words he'd been holding in, speaking before his father could finish. "We don't have to do this right now."

"I know, but," Roshaw said, rubbing at his temples, "it's just...there's so much I haven't... Sorry, I'm not very good at this."

"It's fine. We don't have to." Alverax felt an odd sense of dread. He was just starting to make peace with his life, and whatever it was that his father wanted to tell him, he wasn't certain he wanted to hear it. "Whatever it is, I'm sure it can wait."

Roshaw closed his eyes, relieved at the offer but still filled with the pain of withholding. For a moment, he said nothing. Alverax could feel the tension, the heavy decision his father was weighing. Some truths are painful to hold, and others are painful to share. Whatever truth Roshaw held, it hurt like hell. As Roshaw's chest rose up and down with each breath, Alverax was certain that this was the latter.

Finally, his father let out a breath. "Have you named a star for her yet?"

Alverax startled, looking to his father.

"I heard what happened," Roshaw continued. "Those bastards killed people I cared about, too. Three of them." He looked up into the dark sky. "The southern edge of the Broken Wheel. See those three stars? Those are theirs."

Alverax looked and saw the dim, little cluster beside the brighter circle. There was another cluster just to the east of the Wheel. One of those was his father's star. He pushed the thought aside, feeling an old grudge clawing away at his insides. "As soon as I looked in the sky, I knew what star would be Jisenna's."

"The Moon's Little Sister," Roshaw whispered as he stared up into the vast expanse.

Alverax nodded. "It was the only one bright enough."

"I think she'd like that." Roshaw's head bobbed up and down as he breathed in the night air. Quietly, almost as if to himself, Roshaw said, "It's the same star I chose for your mother."

A chill ran through Alverax. His father's life had not been easy. He'd suffered and lost, tried and failed. Alverax may not have forgiven him fully—not just yet—but he certainly felt like he understood the man more deeply than he ever had before.

And that was a start.

BONDS OF CHAOS
11

THE NEXT MORNING, before the sun was up, Laurel and Asher took off to hunt for water and a sandhog, both of which Roshaw claimed were in the area. Just one of the creatures would be enough to feed the whole group for several days. If it was large, maybe a week. Either way, it was refreshing for the two of them to get away from the pack for a while. If they could find food before everyone woke up, she might not have to listen to Jelium complain so much. Then again, a full belly wouldn't stop him from complaining about his smelly clothes, tired feet, or the dirt in his hair.

Together, they stalked through the desert. It was nothing like the Fairenwild. No shade. No grass. No trees. The only plants and shrubs seemed skeletal in comparison. Tall cacti. Brown clumps of balled up tumbleweed. Knee-high grass that was deader than a beetle in a treelurk web. There were hints of green, enough to give the illusion of life, but even the colors seemed muted and dulled by the heat.

Laurel wasn't convinced they'd find anything but the occasional leafling, and the small lizards were barely a snack. They wouldn't keep anyone sustained for the long journey ahead. Fortunately, after an hour of searching, they came across a herd of sandhogs grazing on what was certainly the brownest grass she'd ever seen. The patch sat at the base of a hill with a large rock formation beside it.

She felt Asher's excitement as they stalked forward in lock-step. Slowly, carefully, they inched forward, feet sinking into the sand with each step. They needed to get close enough so the sandhogs—with their wide feet that barely sunk in the sand—couldn't outrun them. When they were in position, they would decide on a single sandhog. Focused. A wolf that becomes too distracted by the bounty loses it all.

Without a word, they chose the closest sandhog, the fattest of the herd, with black freckles along its back and jowls that hung nearly to the floor. In perfect harmony, they pounced, feet dancing across the sand. They were one mind. Hunters in pursuit. Eyes fixed on their prey.

By the time the sandhogs noticed them, throaty squeals piercing the morning air, it was too late. The animals all scrambled in different directions, some running up the hill, others dashing toward the rock formation, and others, confused, running directly at Laurel and Asher, including the fattest of the herd. They leapt atop the sandhog, claws gouging its ribs, dagger tearing into its neck. The cleaner the kill the better, so they struck fast and hard, claws and dagger pulling in and out in quick succession. The creature took its last breath and flopped its wide head against the sand.

Overhead a flock of vultures grunted as they departed to the west.

Something about it gave Laurel pause. Wouldn't the vultures stay close so they could swoop in and steal the carcass?

Laurel turned her head to the south.

Two figures flew in the distance.

"Hide!" she shouted, scrambling on all fours toward the rock formation.

Laurel and Asher clawed their way to the stone and leapt into the shadows of two overlapping boulders, nestling in as deeply as they could. Twenty feet away, the dead sandhog lay on the ground, bleeding out over the dead grass. Moments later, the two figures flew overhead, seemingly unaware of Laurel and Asher below. By the path of their flight, Laurel was fairly certain the Heralds had not flown over the canyon where the others hid. She stayed hidden beneath the rocks for several minutes before stepping away.

If the Heralds had seen them... This time, there was truly nowhere to run.

They needed to be more careful.

Laurel and Asher walked over to the dead sandhog, kicking away a red and black striped snake that had come to claim the prize. Asher bit down on the leg of the carcass and began dragging it in the direction of their camp.

The whole way back, Laurel watched the sky.

Bonds of Chaos

12

AFTER SEVERAL GRUELING days of travel surrounded by the constant threat of the Heralds flying overhead, Laurel and the others exited the desert canyons and entered sprawling plains. After another day of gentle flatland, they stepped into a thick, mossy forest. Asher was filled with excitement but lost his enthusiasm when the ground became soggy and wet. Soon enough, they were treading through Wasteland swamps with an inch of water ever present beneath their feet.

The paranoid joviality they'd shared over the previous days faded with the openness of the desert, replaced by the feeling of constant attention from their surroundings. Frogs calling from overgrown leaves. Birds chirping in the canopy. Snakes twisting around branches. And the odd, long-armed creatures that leapt from tree to tree, watching. Always watching.

Despite it all—despite the nagging feeling that told her she shouldn't —Laurel was beginning to feel hopeful. They were so close. A few more days and they'd be at the place the others had called Relek's Cave, preparing to trap the gods once more. But it wasn't over yet, and there were still a million things that could go wrong, so Laurel pushed aside her hope and clung to resolve.

The farther north they traveled, the more long-armed creatures they spotted. At first, Laurel had thought that *they* were the wastelanders, but Roshaw and Chrys assured her that they were not. In fact, the wastelanders hunted and ate the creatures, which made Laurel wonder what the meat would taste like.

Perhaps the biggest surprise was Jelium's change in mood. He'd given up complaining—perhaps because Willow carried a stick she used to prod him with—and had instead taken on an air of curiosity. Every few steps, he had a question about a fern, or a mushroom, or some little bug crawling on his arm. After a while, Laurel wished he would stop talking and go back to the occasional complaint.

After four more days, Laurel and Asher had taken to hunting a variety of smaller creatures in the swamps. The sandhog meat they'd carried with them had not lasted as long as they'd hoped, but Laurel and Asher had become quite adept at hunting together. The most difficult part was finding places to sleep. The swamp was wet, everywhere. On rare occasions, they would find a patch of dry ground and take a rest, but the patches were small and rare. During their breaks, Willow had taken to weaving hammocks—they now had three—that they shared in rotation for those not on watch at night.

The next day, when the sun was high overhead and their feet moved thoughtlessly forward, Asher noticed something. A creature, with two arms and two legs, kneeling on the ground, motionless, partially obscured by the surrounding shrubbery. To be more precise, Asher smelled the creature—an oddly sweet smell laced with a familiar foulness. It wasn't human, and it wasn't one of the swinging creatures. This was something different.

They advanced carefully, poised to pounce in case the creature was hostile. As they grew closer, Laurel saw that there were two others beside the first, each kneeling in the same position, grouped up in a tight cluster. It soon became clear that the creatures were dead. They looked mostly human, though their skin was a charcoal gray. Their eyes were small and beady, and their earlobes were pointed, like downward facing triangles.

"Roshaw," Chrys said quietly. "Have you seen anything like this before?"

The older man nodded as he approached the closest. "Once, a long time ago. Maybe a month after I was first imprisoned."

Willow leaned closer, examining each of the three with curiosity. Finally, she touched one, and her brows lifted. "They're...hard. How is that possible?"

"*Pintalla mox*," Roshaw said. "At least, that's what I heard it called. Translates to *surrendered spirit*. The guards weren't exactly eager to explain the details, but I think it was some kind of wastelander disease. They separate themselves so the rest of the hive doesn't get sick."

"It sure smells like a disease," Laurel agreed.

"Certainly looks like one," Willow added. "But how would a disease kill all three at the same time in the same place?"

"Who said they all died at the same time?" Iriel kept her distance with Aydin in her arms.

Chrys gave a thoughtful nod. "If they were all sick, they probably came out as a group and let the plague run its course."

Jelium eyed the bodies warily. "The more important question that no one seems to be asking is: if the wastelanders are dying of a plague, why the hell aren't we turning around and getting as far away as we can?"

Laurel snarled at him. "Because not all of us are selfish pricks who would rather let the world burn than catch a cold."

Jelium stared at her with more than a hint of anger. "I would watch my mouth if I were you. It would be a pity if I were suddenly unwilling to make your little coreseal."

Laurel ground her teeth together. As much as she hated Alabella, at least she understood the woman. She'd had a purpose, a goal. Jelium was nothing but a cancer, infecting the world around him with greed and pride. Didn't help that he smelled like sour sweat and piss.

"Three dead doesn't make a plague," Willow said, cutting the tension.

"Agreed," Roshaw added. "If it was a plague, it would have killed a lot more than the one wastelander I saw a few years ago."

Chrys stepped back from the three statue-like wastelanders. "Plague or not, our course is set. We're the only ones who can stop the Heralds. And the only way that's going to happen is if we can get them below ground and seal them in. If we get sick, we get sick. Either way, all roads lead to Kai'Melend."

"Great," Jelium said. "Not only are the Heralds waiting for us, but a plague is too."

Chrys smirked. "Let's not keep them waiting."

BONDS OF CHAOS
13

W͟HEN C͟HRYS A͟WOKE, the sun remained hidden below the eastern horizon. Iriel slept above him, hanging serenely in a large hammock with Aydin strapped to her chest, the pair wrapped in a warm blanket. Chrys and the others lay on a patch of raised grass above the murky water. Despite being several feet above the swamp itself, small beads of morning dew had still crept their way up the hill to settle on their sleeping bodies.

He stood and stretched, looking around the quiet swampland. The first thing he noticed was a grape-sized frog staring at him with big red eyes from atop a wide leaf. Chrys leaned forward and leveled his gaze, mesmerized by the beautiful array of green and yellow across its belly. He wondered if it was one of the poisonous varieties.

Soon, the others awoke, and they set out to the north.

Two days passed before they came to the outer edges of Kai'Melend. Keeping hidden, they watched the city, early afternoon sun filtering through the breaks in the trees. Where once there had been a small village, now there was a hive. Thousands upon thousands of wastelanders swarmed Kai'Melend, traveling the rope walkways, swimming the shallow waters.

Roshaw whispered to the others, "This is more wastelanders than I've ever seen. It looks like all of the nearby tribes have gathered to see the gods."

"No, this isn't just a gathering," Chrys said with confidence. "This is an army. Even the children have weapons. They're preparing for something."

Iriel looked to him. "Alchea?"

"Can't be," Chrys said. "They can't be away from the oka'thal waters for that long."

"Maybe the Heralds just don't care," Iriel said grimly.

Chrys scowled. "Either way, Alchaeus might know what's going on. Just another reason to get down there fast."

They left their perch and headed to the rocky overhang marking the entrance to Relek's Cave. By the time they reached the trees south of the cave, Chrys and the others were tired and wet, and what they found made matters even worse. The entrance to the cave was guarded by fifty wastelanders. With four Obsidian threadweavers, getting rid of that many guards wouldn't be a problem, but they needed to be discreet. They didn't want Relek and Lylax following them down until they were ready to create the coreseal. There had to be a way inside without being seen.

"We need a distraction," Chrys whispered to the others.

Everyone looked to Alverax.

"Don't look at me," the young man said. "I got enough grief for my last idea."

Laurel crouched beside Chrys, crawling forward on her hands and knees to get a better view. Her eyes were wide, her brows furrowed. Asher, beside her, bent low, as if ready to pounce.

"I could get their attention," Roshaw said. "Make them chase me, then once they're far enough away, I could launch myself into the sky. Circle back to the cave before they return."

Willow shook her head. "They wouldn't *all* chase you. Most would probably stay at the cave entrance."

Jelium, sitting with his back against a tree and his ass in the mud, shook his head. "You're all making this more difficult than it needs to be."

Chrys looked to the older man and scowled. "Please, enlighten us."

"Just kill the savages," Jelium said. "It would be so simple. I *yolk* them, and the chromawolf tears them apart. It'll look like some wild beast did it."

Alverax offered an unamused expression. "What kind of wild beast would attack fifty wastelanders...and win?"

"Ridiculous—" Roshaw began.

"Corespawn?" Willow said, thoughtfully. "We could make it look like the corespawn did it."

Jelium had a self-satisfied look in his eyes.

"That wouldn't work," Chrys said. "The Heralds control the corespawn. And it doesn't matter if it would work or not. If we kill them, we're no better than the Heralds. There has to be another way. During shift changes, or when they're eating maybe."

"We don't have time for that," Roshaw said. "If there were just one or two of us, maybe. But we're too many. If we spend another day out here, someone is going to see us, if they haven't already."

Jelium pushed himself to his feet, glaring at Chrys and the others. "I'll handle it myself."

"Stop!" Laurel hissed, jumping toward Jelium and shoving him back to the ground.

"Get off me, you little shit!" Jelium spat.

Asher darted in close, baring his fangs mere inches from Jelium's face. The Amber-eyed man snarled back but knew his place. Laurel glared at him with her hand on the hilt of her obsidian dagger. "You're not in Cynosure anymore. No more gambling with lives."

Jelium clenched his jaw and settled back against the tree. "I vote we kill them and be done with it."

"There has to be another way," Chrys repeated.

"Literally," Willow said, her eyes lighting up. "There *is* another way. The Endless Well. There's no way they can guard all of it, and it leads to the same place."

Chrys looked to his mother. "You're a genius."

"I am what I am," she said with a modest shrug.

Alverax leaned closed. "That's the big hole, right?"

Chrys nodded.

"And we're going...*down*...the big hole?" Alverax said. "Didn't that almost kill you last time?"

"It did," Willow said flatly. "But the second time is always easier."

Roshaw stifled a laugh. "Plus, we can fly now."

"I like it," Chrys said. "Unless someone has a better idea... Roshaw, do you know the way?"

Roshaw nodded and, with only the smallest measure of grumbling, they were back traveling through the swamps toward the place they'd almost died once before.

. . .

THE WALK through the swamps went as smoothly as it could have for a party of seven plus a baby and a chromawolf. Roshaw had done well keeping them distanced from the wastelander city, and Iriel had done well keeping Aydin quiet. The only eyes that watched their path belonged to the colorful birds perched in the trees. Though Chrys had grown accustomed to the putrid smells of the swamp, he was eager to take a big breath of the stale cavern air below ground.

Before they reached the clearing that led to the Endless Well, Chrys' mind drifted back to the day he'd last been there. The day that Agatha, Esme, and Seven had been killed. The day he'd failed to save them. But he couldn't think about that now. He may not have been able to save them all, but he *had* saved Roshaw and reunited him with his son. It was just as important to remember the good as it was to remember the bad.

As they approached their destination, Chrys pushed aside a veil of vines, blue skies bursting into view. But as the fields became visible, a wave of fear washed over him. Not because of the Endless Well, sitting like a lake of inky blackness in the center of the field. Not because of the jutting rock formations and wild waterfalls. It was the stench of two hundred dead wastelanders, blackened from the *pintalla mox*, kneeling motionless in the dirt like a field of statues.

There was no cursing, no jokes or mirth. The scene was too surreal. Too morbid. Macabre. A slight breeze rustled the leaves as Chrys and the others looked upon a field of the dead, a shrine of the surrendered.

The Endless Well stared from across the field like the Lightfather's all-seeing eye, beckoning them through a corpse-filled maze.

Finally, Jelium broke the silence. "What were you saying about it not being a plague?"

They all ignored him, and Chrys turned to the others, dropping the vines and concealing them once more. "Willow, Roshaw, and I should be able to fly everyone over."

"What if we're already infected?" Iriel asked, keeping the swaddle over little Aydin's face.

"Wouldn't change the plan," Chrys said flatly. "In fact, if we get infected, it would just be another reason for us to get below ground so we can drink the elixir. Roshaw, you take Alverax. Willow, you can bring Laurel. I'll bring Iriel and Aydin."

"What the hell?" Jelium said. "You're just going to leave me here?"

Chrys nodded. "Unless you want to walk through a field of dead wastelanders, we'll come back for you and Asher."

"Take Asher first." Laurel set her hand atop the chromawolf's back. "There's something not right. A foul taste in the air."

"You're in a swamp," Jelium grumbled. "What is wrong with you all? Just go already. It feels like I'm the only damn person who wants to move forward."

Willow pursed her lips and winced. "While I don't agree with the tone, I'm with Jelium on this one. Looks clear to me, and I'm keen to move quickly."

Chrys looked to Laurel and Asher. "You two have the best eyes. Did you see anything?"

"Nothing," Laurel said, furrowing her brows. "But that's the problem. Where did all the frogs go? Snakes. Insects. They were everywhere, and now there's not so much as a bird call. I don't know what it is, but something doesn't feel right."

"IT'S A FIELD OF DEAD PEOPLE!" Jelium said. "Why the hell would frogs be hanging out in a grave? Look around. There's not a single savage in sight. You're acting like a bunch of frightened children. Here, you want proof?"

The large Kulaian man pushed his way out of the mass of ferns and onto the grassy field. This time, no one was fast enough to stop him.

Chrys panicked. His eyes darted back and forth across the tree line, up into the sky, and over toward the rocky cliffs. Jelium was the largest of their party. If anyone was going to be spotted, it was him. Chrys looked to the others and noted the same angry fear on each face.

A moment passed, and the wind glided quietly over Jelium, tossing his dark hair across his face. The bronze-skinned man smiled wide, lifting his hands, palms up. "You're welcome. Now, let's get on with it. I'm eager to meet the brother of the gods."

Just as the words left his lips, a thin, feathered shaft darted through the air and embedded itself in his shoulder. He looked down and pulled it out. Black ooze drooled off of the long needle-like tip. "What the hell?"

The trees just north of them rustled slightly, and a dozen more darts lanced through the air, whistling in the wind, piercing through clothing and sinking into Jelium's flesh.

"No!" Chrys shouted.

Alverax leapt forward to grab Jelium, but Laurel tackled the young man to the ground just as a series of darts flew over their heads. They rolled over, and she plucked one of the thin needles from where it had embedded in her shoulder, grimacing as it left her skin stained with the same black ooze.

"Laurel!" Willow shouted. "Are you okay?"

The young girl nodded as she and Alverax crawled back to the safety of the overgrowth.

It took all of Chrys' will power not to run forward to help. But if he ran out of their cover, they'd both be dead. Even now, Jelium was face-down in the dirt, spasming. Chrys grabbed Willow and Iriel beside him and forced them to the ground.

Chrys turned to the others. "We have to get Jelium to the Endless Well." They needed him. Their plan wouldn't work without an Amber.

"How?" Willow asked. "We can't fly with all those darts."

"We run," Chrys said. "You and Roshaw can create threadlight barriers to deflect the darts. Iriel, Laurel, and Asher will stay close and keep Aydin safe. If we can get to the dead wastelanders, we can use their bodies for cover. Alverax, help me carry Jelium; we can cut his corethread first, and I'll create a barrier for us. Our only hope is to get Jelium to the elixir."

Everyone nodded, including Asher.

"Good," Chrys said, looking back to Jelium and the Endless Well.

Jelium's chest heaved, his arms trembling along the grassy floor.

"No time," Chrys said quickly. "Go now!"

Chrys stood up and let threadlight flood his veins. As soon as they left the cover of the swamp, darts soared through the air. Willow and Roshaw's veins lit up with multi-colored threadlight, and a surge of energy pulsed around them. The darts struck the barrier, some stopping completely as they hit the wall, others passing partly through as if they'd been shot into a bubble of water.

Everyone moved in chaotic unison.

Alverax *broke* Jelium's corethread and lifted the big man over his shoulder like a bale of hay.

Chrys created a barrier for them.

The others took off toward the dead wastelanders faster than he'd ever seen them run.

The barrier Chrys held required too much threadlight to sustain, and he felt a sharp pain blossom in his chest. He let go just as they reached the statue-like dead, hoping the cover would protect them from the darts.

He glanced back, and his attention shifted to the sky as a flicker of movement fluttered above the trees. There, hovering in the skyline, he saw the last thing he ever hoped to see. Relek and Lylax stood in the air like the gods they were, smiling down at the chaos.

"FASTER!" Chrys screamed.

He watched as the others, staying low, dodged back and forth between the maze of dead wastelanders. Two steps forward. One step to the side. Twisting, leaping, sprinting, all while darts pelted through the open air. Plague or not, they needed to get to the Endless Well before the Heralds caught up. Chrys and Alverax trailed the others, Jelium's floating form knocking into dead bodies behind them.

The others slipped past the last of the dead wastelanders and reached the edge of the Endless Well, finally turning and seeing what Chrys had seen. Flying in their direction, the Heralds moved through the air like falcons on the hunt.

"Chrys!" Iriel shouted. She clutched Aydin with both hands, legs bent, ready to jump into the void. Even at a distance, Chrys could feel the fear in her eyes. It was the same look she'd had when she was bound by Amber threads on the wonderstone. Helpless terror.

He looked over his shoulder just as the Heralds swooped down from above. His veins sizzled with heat, and threadlight burned from his theoliths into his bloodstream. Despite the pain, he created another barrier, and the Heralds crashed into it, *pushed* back by the unseen shield. But the force knocked Chrys over, sending him tumbling into a pair of dead wastelanders, their hard skin cracking as they crumbled into the dirt.

Alverax continued to run with Jelium dragging behind him.

They were so close.

Chrys looked up and saw the others still standing at the edge of the well, waiting, feet set as they prepared to leap. He turned around just as the Heralds roared and shot forward. Chrys reached inside himself to create one last barrier, but his heart seized in his chest, refusing to provide any additional threadlight. His jaw clenched and fire burned beneath his ribs.

Without a barrier, Relek crashed into Chrys, slamming into him with so much force that Chrys felt his bones rattle. He rocketed through the air, sharp pain surging through his arm, and collided with a dead wastelander that shattered on impact. Chrys' vision blurred, but he pushed himself to his feet as the hazy shape of Relek approached at a steady pace.

Chrys threw a tight fist, but Relek caught it and smirked. Knocking the god's wrist away, he bent down and dove into him, but Emerald threadlight *pulled* Relek toward the earth, increasing his weight ten-fold. Chrys crashed into him like a brick wall. The Herald reached down and grabbed Chrys' neck, lifting him up like a sack of wheat. Relek looked deep into Chrys' eyes with the deformed smile of a mad god.

"Stop fighting," Relek commanded.

The words lashed out at Chrys' soul like a viper, squeezing its jaws against his will. Their intent seemed to echo in his skull, bouncing around, pounding away at the walls of his mind, a hammer on stone. But Chrys knew what would happen if he let Relek in. He threw his will against the command, refusing to succumb to the god's control.

"STOP FIGHTING!" Relek screamed, spittle raining down on Chrys' face.

But Relek was not the Apogee any more.

Chrys was.

"I...AM...IN...CONTROL!"

A blur of green leapt over him, barreling into the Herald. Chrys inhaled sharply, then turned to see Asher tackling Relek to the ground, ripping into his flesh.

Lylax took the opportunity to lunge at Chrys. She moved with terrible speed, closing the distance nearly as fast as Chrys was able to lift his hands in defense. Her white robes blurred in the afternoon heat, and a pale yellow shard on a silver chain swung from her neck as she moved. He blocked her savage hands with practiced movements, barely able to keep on his feet as he stumbled on the foot of a dead wastelander. She pressed again, and he stepped under a wild hook. Using the mistake, Chrys landed a quick boot to her shoulder that sent her stumbling away.

Beside them, Relek roared in pain. Asher's teeth cut through skin and cartilage, disconnecting his left hand from his arm. The torn limb sprayed crimson over dead wastelanders, dripping over the Herald's black robes. Relek reached down with his other hand and gripped the chromawolf's neck, lifting it into the air and staring into its bright eyes, both snarling. Challenging. The mad god screamed out as he snapped Asher's neck, the crack reverberating through the field. He pulled his arm back and hurled the chromawolf through the air, over the open space, and down into the Endless Well.

Chrys watched in shock as the limp body of the massive chromawolf toppled over the ledge.

Laurel grabbed her throat as though Relek's hands were around her own neck. She stumbled back, choking, eyes wide with shock and fear. Her foot slipped on the edge, but she caught herself, still struggling to breathe. Her eyes rolled back, and she finally collapsed, falling from the edge and following Asher into the darkness.

Willow and Alverax dove in after her.

"Chrys," Relek said with a frown, watching as threadlight pooled along the edges of his stump hand. Slowly, as if watching a flower bloom outside of time, his hand reformed, tendon by tendon, until the stub became a hand once again. "You cannot stop us."

Lylax spat on one of the dead wastelanders. "You are a fool if you think you can fight gods."

Iriel's voice called out to Chrys from the edge of the Endless Well, but he kept his eyes on the Heralds. There was no fear in their eyes, no worry or doubt. To these immortal creatures, Chrys and the others were no more than mosquitos.

"If that were true," Chrys said, meeting their gaze, "then you wouldn't be here."

Snarling, Relek and Lylax stared back at him with dead eyes.

"No," Chrys continued. Keeping a hand behind his back, he signed a countdown to Iriel and Roshaw.

Five. Four.

"You're here because you're scared. Because we know your secrets. The elixir. Theoliths. Lifelight. It's only a matter of time. Whether it's us or another, there will always be people who see you for what you truly are."

"You always did believe you were smarter than your enemies," Relek said, lifting his chin. "Unfortunately for you, Chrysanthemum, men cannot outwit gods."

Three. Two.

Chrys lifted his chin in response, opening himself to threadlight, feeling the same sharp pain in his chest. "We'll see."

One.

Chrys turned and surged Sapphire, hurling himself toward the Endless Well. Threadlight burned in his chest as he *pushed* harder, blasting toward Iriel and Roshaw as they leapt into the well with Jelium in tow. Glancing over his shoulder, Chrys saw the Heralds flying forward.

He dove head first into the Endless Well, twisting in mid-air, keeping his eyes fixed on the ledge, waiting for the Heralds to appear.

Moments later, they did, flying into the center of the gaping hole but stopping as Relek held back his seething sister. For a few seconds, they simply watched, floating in the air side by side until threadlight began to blaze from their bodies with such otherworldly radiance that Chrys had to shield his eyes.

Threads. A hundred. A thousand. Ten thousand, pulsing and swirling in patterns of pure chaos. The mass continued to expand, larger and larger, until it surged and contracted, folding in on itself, compressing into a single point of limitless energy.

Relek and Lylax threw out their hands and the mass of energy hurled down the Endless Well. To Chrys, as he continued his descent into the darkness below, it was as though the sun were falling from the sky directly toward him. Toward his family. Toward his friends. He crossed his arms in front of his body, as if his feeble strength could stop such a power. But before the energy consumed him, it exploded.

Blinding light.

A burning in his veins.

But there was no wave. No burst of destructive force. Instead, the mass of threadlight spread its tendrils out like a sheet of pure power, rippling out from the epicenter, stretching across the Endless Well from edge to edge, extending its web through the stone and beyond.

As Chrys fell through the darkness, staring up at the pulsing threadlight above him, the truth struck him harder than if the sun had truly fallen.

Stones, no.

14

"Laurel!" Willow cried out. "Laurel, wake up!"

The older woman crouched over the Zeda girl surrounded by dark waters at the bottom of the Endless Well. Alverax knelt beside her, photospore bulbs puffing their luminescence into the darkness, casting long shadows over the girl and her animal companion. Occasional drips of water sprayed over them from where the cascading waterfalls struck the underground lake.

A brilliant flash of threadlight erupted above her, filling the cavern. Willow shielded her eyes, waited a few moments, and then looked back up. Chrys floated down gracefully through the air beneath what looked like a net hewn of pure threadlight that covered the entirety of the well above them.

Iriel and Roshaw—now carrying Jelium—landed on their feet only a few paces away.

A moment later, Chrys struck the ground beside them.

"Chrys!" Willow called out. "Laurel and Asher are still breathing, but I don't think they're going to last long."

Roshaw leapt from stone to stone as he approached Willow. "We need to get them to the elixir."

"I'll take Laurel," Alverax said, already leaning down to lift her.

"I'll take Asher," Willow added.

"Let's be quick about it," Roshaw said. "The Heralds could be right behind us."

They all gathered themselves and made their way to the outer rim of the cavern, toward the tunnels leading to the elixir pool. Willow's veins turned black as she *broke* Asher's corethread; Roshaw did the same to

Jelium. With Alverax carrying Laurel and Iriel holding Aydin, they all carried their burdens. All except for...

Willow turned and saw Chrys standing motionless in the center of the cavern, surrounded by jagged rocks and clear water, staring up at the threadlight-wrought enclosure high above.

"Chrys!" she shouted, her voice echoing in the wide-open space. "We need to go!"

He dropped his head for a moment, then silently followed.

The group arrived at the mouth of the tunnel together, taking one last glance up the Endless Well, ensuring that the Heralds had indeed not followed them down. As Asher's corethread reappeared, Willow let Obsidian threadlight pour through her, shifting the chromawolf once again into weightlessness.

Memories flooded through her as she recalled their first time walking through the tunnel. It seemed a lifetime ago. Back then, every shadow seemed to jump out at them, and every drop of water falling from the stalactites felt like a hand grabbing at her shoulder. She'd barely had a moment to enjoy being reunited with her son, and every step was filled with the fear of losing him again.

More than anything, what had changed was how long it took them to get from the Endless Well to Alchaeus' cavern. This time, there was no caution, no quiet steps. Instead, they trudged through the tunnel like a herd of corespawn, footfalls echoing through the wide corridor, announcing them in every direction.

When the familiar golden light of the elixir pool appeared ahead, they all seemed to find renewed energy, sprinting forward with even greater speed. The vaulted cavern was quiet—the pale, pink table still surrounded by the third god's oddities. From the far side of the space, Willow could see part of the collection of corespawn statues peeking out from behind the corner. The air was moist and warmer than she remembered. Beside the pool, she thought she saw the remnants of a bloody trail.

And was that...roses?

"Stones," Chrys cursed beside her.

Willow's veins blazed to life as she looked around for the source of the scent. There were no corespawn in the tunnel they'd come from and none in the far tunnel. She looked for Chitt, but even the small, lizard-like corespawn was nowhere to be found.

A scraping sound overhead was the only noise she heard before a corespawn with eight legs dropped from the ceiling. She tried to move, but Asher was still in her arms, and the chromawolf was too large to maneuver. She braced herself for impact—but before it crashed into her, the creature burst apart into a thousand beads of light, dissipating out into the open cavern air, then slowly drifting toward the pool of elixir.

When she turned, she saw Chrys with a scowl on his face and Obsidian threadlight in his veins. "I'll keep watch," he mumbled, walking toward the tunnel entrance.

Willow nodded, then approached the pool, sliding Asher into the golden waters. Alverax carefully set Laurel beside him. Roshaw placed Jelium on the ledge and pulled out the darts before lowering him into the water. They all watched as pockets of red misted out from each of the wounds. Jelium's body drifted away from the others, but Laurel and Asher seemed drawn together. Soon, as their corethreads reappeared, each of them sank deeper into the depths.

The room grew quiet.

Chrys' footsteps echoed as he stepped farther down the tunnel.

In the silence, they watched their companions, praying, hoping that the healing power of the elixir would be enough. Willow reached down and cupped a bit of elixir into her mouth. While it healed her physical wounds, her mind and spirit still ached.

Guilt swept through her as she realized that Laurel's death was her fault. She should have never let the young girl come with her to Alchea to rescue Pandan. Laurel should be with her brother and her people. If Willow had stopped her then, Laurel wouldn't be dying now. She was too young to die. Too young to pay the price of another's mistake. If anyone was going to die, Willow had lived a good life—longer than most threadweavers—and if it came to it, she would sacrifice herself for any of these people. Her son. Her daughter-in-law. A man she'd come to respect. His son. Laurel and Asher.

"How do we know if it's working?" Alverax asked with a look of worry in his eyes.

Roshaw leaned over the edge. "We should at least know soon whether or not they'll live."

"They will live," Willow said through clenched teeth.

Alverax stared into the pool. "I hope so."

"They will live!" Willow shouted, frustration and failure bubbling to the surface. The fire in her eyes faded as soon as it came, giving way to the same guilt that pervaded her mind. They couldn't be dead. She refused to accept that reality. "They will live," she repeated quietly.

Roshaw comforted her, wrapping an arm around her shoulder. "You're right. If the elixir can keep Alchaeus alive for hundreds of years, it can heal the girl. They're going to live."

Willow's chest heaved up and down as she fought back her fear. With her head nestled into Roshaw's shoulder, she watched the three bodies floating in the water. The golden energy of the elixir seemed to gather along the edges of their skin, flickering like a candle in a distant window. She looked at Laurel, floating beside her chromawolf companion. She remembered the crack of its neck, and Laurel collapsing into the well. Whatever bond they shared had caused Asher's pain to extend to Laurel. Now, Willow wasn't certain that either would survive.

No, she thought. *They will live.*

As if the young Zeda girl could hear her thoughts, Laurel's body heaved in the pool, spasming up and down. Asher's body followed suit, thrashing back and forth as the golden light glimmered across its green fur.

"They're choking on the water!" Alverax yelled.

"They can't drown," Willow said, taking a step toward the pool. "Not in the elixir."

Asher's eyes opened.

Roshaw and Alverax took it as a signal and jumped into the water, sinking to their chests before their feet hit the ground. They grabbed hold of Laurel and Asher, heaving them up and over the lip of the pool. The two bodies limped over the ledge and rolled onto the stone as Roshaw and Alverax pulled themselves up and over. Roshaw went to work checking Asher.

Alverax leaned down, fear and worry rippling across his face, and moved his mouth toward Laurel's. But then her eyes opened.

He met her gaze, and she threw up a gushing river of elixir water all over his neck.

Alverax pulled back and looked down at his soaking shirt, wiping it off with his already wet hands.

Willow's chest was a torrent of emotions, laughter cut off by tears of joy, guilt crashing into hope. But when she looked over and saw Laurel and Asher embracing, all of it faded away, and all she felt was...gratitude. They were alive.

"Are you okay?" Willow asked, standing over the young girl's soaking body.

Laurel nodded. "We're okay."

"Good," Willow said with a curt voice. "Because if you ever die like that again, I swear I'll kill you a third time."

Asher lifted his head, and Laurel gave a strained smile.

"What about Jelium?" Alverax asked. "How much longer until he's healed?"

Roshaw leaned over the edge of the pool to get a closer look; Alverax and Willow followed. As she looked at the large, Kulaian man, she noticed that the dart wounds no longer leaked streams of red into the golden waters, but still he drifted aimlessly, his thick arms spread wide. As his body rotated, his bronze face reflected the golden light, and Willow felt a rush of sorrow. She knew that look—she'd seen it before.

Jelium's soul had fled from his mortal frame to travel the winds.

"Is he...?" Alverax asked, not daring to finish.

Roshaw stepped into the pool, waist deep in liquid magic, and moved Jelium toward the edge. Lifting his shoulders—and Alverax the legs—they pulled him out of the elixir and laid him on the wet stone. His cunning eyes were wide, staring at nothing, and his bronzed skin had taken on the color of pale sand. Roshaw placed a hand over Jelium's face and closed his eyes. Silence filled the air like a cloud waiting to storm—even Laurel and Asher had turned to watch. Roshaw opened his eyes and shook his head. "We were too late."

The words pricked the expanding bubble, and Willow felt every last ounce of hope fade away into the dark cavern. They'd come all this way, and for what? Without Jelium, there would be no way to create the core-seal. There would be no way to stop the gods.

They had failed.

"Dammit!" Roshaw cursed, kicking Jelium's dead body. "Wake up, you piece of shit!"

"Roshaw," Willow said, placing a hand on his shoulder.

He looked up at her with bloodshot eyes.

"It doesn't matter," Chrys said.

Willow hadn't noticed her son's return. He looked like how she felt. Instead of the passion he'd had while standing against two gods at the top of the Endless Well, Chrys seemed nothing more than a shell, as though his spirit had been ripped from his body.

"What do you mean?" Willow asked.

"We've already lost."

"Chrys," Iriel said, bouncing a squirming child in her arms. "What are you talking about?"

"No one's lost anything," Willow added. A rising bile in her throat proved that not even she believed her own words.

"Did no one else see it?" Chrys said, his voice rising. "They knew. The damn Heralds knew. And they were waiting for us. They wanted us at the Endless Well, and all it took was a small group of dangerous-looking wastelanders to shepherd us there. They knew what we were planning to do, and they beat us to it."

"What do you—" But Willow understood now. The events of the Endless Well replayed in her mind. The Heralds floating in the center of the shaft, threadlight shining like the sun, the explosion. The pattern forming. "Stones," she cursed. "The threadlight in the well. They created a coreseal..."

Alverax's eyes grew wide. "But we're—"

"—trapped," Roshaw finished.

"It doesn't matter," Chrys repeated one final time, an emptiness in his eyes. "They won. Jelium won't make a difference. Aydin won't make a difference. Even if we find Alchaeus, it won't make a difference. It's over. We lost."

"To hell with that!" Roshaw cursed, throwing his hands up in the air. "Alverax broke the coreseal once before. We can do it again. Hell, we have four Obsidians."

"With the power of the Convergence, maybe," Willow said, thoughtfully. "But if Alchaeus and Lylax couldn't break the coreseal when they were trapped down here, I have a feeling it won't be so easy for us either."

Roshaw rubbed a hand through his short hair. "So, what do we do?"

Willow looked to her son, feeling the defeat in his eyes. "First we rest," she said, eyes drifting toward the distant tunnel. "Then we find Alchaeus."

BONDS OF CHAOS — 15

HIGH GENERAL HENNA stepped up to the study and pushed open the thick, mahogany door. When she entered, she found Great Lord Malachus seated alone at his desk, the curtains open wide to let in great beams of light that refracted from the tall windows behind him. He gave her a curt nod but continued to read from a thick, leatherbound tome. Henna walked up to the chair near the table but did not sit. She simply stood, the bag at her side weighing as heavily on her mind as it did her shoulder.

A minute later, Lady Eleandra entered, offering Henna a smile and a nod as she took her place beside Malachus. She whispered in his ear, and he pressed a piece of parchment into the center of his book, closed it, and set it aside, finally acknowledging Henna's presence. "Did you find her?"

Henna shook her head.

"Any news from Felia?" Eleandra asked.

Henna shook her head. "Still none."

After Alabella escaped, Henna had been tasked with finding her. The Queen of the Bloodthieves had moved quickly, making her way out of Alchea to the west. They had spies in Felia looking for her, but they'd had no news from Felia in weeks. The last they'd heard, the city had been saved by the Heralds—an utterly absurd claim—when the corespawn had attacked.

"What the hell is going on over there?" Malachus leaned back in his chair and ran both hands through his graying hair. He still had yet to name new high generals to replace Chrys and Jurius, so he'd taken their workload on himself. The few months of additional stress had aged him physically but had also given him a renewed sense of ambition. "And what of our preparations?"

"We have guard pits set throughout the north and west. Threadweaver lookouts rotate every two days with supplies to last three and flares to signal incoming corespawn. The only thing they've found was a herd of elk in the north. But I'm not here to give a report, sir."

He tilted his head.

Henna reached down and lifted the bag off her shoulder, dropping it on his desk with a jarring thud.

Malachus placed his forearms on the table and leaned forward. "You have my attention."

"Do you remember the thread-dead obsidian we found a few months ago? From the mine in the Everstones?"

Eleandra raised her brows. "Have you found another?"

"More than that," Henna said as she turned over the bag, unloading a pile of several dozen thread-dead obsidian shards.

"Stones!" Malachus cursed, a smile beaming across his face. "That's enough to make a full spear. Can you imagine? How much does it weigh? Is the material strong enough? Or would it break against iron? Hell, imagine a thread-dead shield! Or both. I can have my smith—"

"Malachus," Henna said, cutting him off. He scowled but stopped. "There's more."

Malachus failed to hide his disdain for being quieted. "More news or more thread-dead obsidian?"

"Both." Henna glanced back at the door, then leaned in closer. "The recent quakes must have opened up sealed paths in the cave, because our people found crates—hundreds of years old by the look of it—filled with thread-dead obsidian. Malachus, we have a hundred times this amount."

"Lightfather be damned," he whispered. "We need to get it to the keep immediately. That cache is more valuable than all the shines in Alchea."

Henna nodded. "Already on it. I have a team of three loading it on carts and a team of thirty to bring the carts back. Only the loaders know what it is, and they're men I trust who have been sworn to secrecy. The transporters are all achromats, so even if they look, it won't mean anything to them. It will be safely within the keep's walls by the end of tomorrow."

Malachus reached forward and grabbed a shard, inspecting it with Emerald and Sapphire threadlight swirling in his veins. "This could be it..."

"Could be what?"

"My legacy," he said with a serious look in his eyes. "A man of my age often thinks of what he will leave behind. What he will be remembered for. The power you wield, the influence you amass, none of it matters unless it is attached to a creation of significance. Something the world can look at in awe. In one hundred years, no one will speak about my rise to power, nor this time of peace. Alchea was, and Alchea continued to be. Malachus the Dash."

Henna furrowed her brow. "I'm not sure I understand."

"There is a year attached to the creation of something and a year attached to its destruction. Those are the true moments of significance. Everything else is just a dash." He reached forward, grabbed a second obsidian shard, and held them both up. "But with these, this will be an unforgettable year. With these, we will create a legacy."

"What are you going to do with the obsidian?" she asked.

"Fight," Malachus said with a smile.

Eleandra looked to her husband. "War is the laziest way to build a legacy, and certainly the most brittle. If you want to be remembered for centuries, use that brilliant mind of yours and be creative. You have the chance to do something truly spectacular here. A new material with endless applications."

Malachus considered her words, then turned to Henna. "I want a spear and a handful of daggers. Have our smiths turn the rest into arrowheads. If we come up with a better idea, we can have them reshaped. Otherwise, we prepare for war. If the corespawn come, we will be ready. And if Felia has fallen, the Endin Empire has a nice ring to it."

"It will be done," Henna said with a nod.

As she left, she saw a glimmer of sorrow in Eleandra's eyes.

BONDS OF CHAOS
16

WILLOW STARED up at the coreseal with magic coursing through her veins. Like threadlight itself, she understood the *what*, but she still didn't understand the *how*. The Amber-wrought threads created a lasting mesh, a web of power that not only stretched across the width of the Endless Well, but through stone and dirt and roots. Given that the previous coreseal had stretched from beneath the wonderstone all the way to the Endless Well, she could safely assume that the opposite would be true. But did it stretch beyond? How far? Across the entire world? And how did it endure when other Amber threads faded? Was the Convergence feeding it power?

"It's pretty," a deep voice called out behind her. "In an eerie sort of way."

She turned to see Roshaw approaching. His eyes shifted between watching the coreseal and glancing at the ground as he navigated past rubble and puddles, finally coming to a stop a few feet away from her.

"Less pretty when you remember it's a prison," Willow said.

There was a profound sense of sadness in Roshaw's eyes. "We'll find a way out. And then it'll be them trapped down here staring up. Not us."

"I wish it were that easy." Willow sighed. "If I've learned anything from this, it's that it's not so easy to outsmart people who have been alive for hundreds of years."

"I don't know," Roshaw mumbled. "I'm nearly fifty, and I don't feel like my age has made me any smarter."

Willow let out a clipped laugh. "Just wait a few years. When you hit fifty, the world will gift you an added measure of intellect."

"Can I request two measures?" Roshaw raised his brows.

"You can request it, but that doesn't mean you'll get it." Willow winked.

"Gah!" Roshaw said, throwing up his arms. "How are we so old? In my head, I'm still young and energetic, but damn if my body disagrees. I feel like a wheel that got left outside for too long. There's dirt in my axles. And you're over here, stomping through deserts and swamps and caves without complaining at all, while I've been secretly whining to Chrys every day since we left Cynosure."

"Once you've given birth," Willow said calmly, "you can handle anything."

Roshaw nodded. "Especially if you give birth to a baby with as thick a skull as Chrys has."

"Hey!" Willow said, slapping his arm. "He got that skull from me."

"I mean—" Roshaw grinned. "You said it, not me."

Willow let threadlight flood her veins and looked back up at the coreseal. There had to be a way to get past it. Some way to sever a few of the threads wide enough for them to squeeze through. Obsidian seemed the clear answer, but Lylax and Alchaeus had Obsidian all those years and never managed. She was beginning to doubt that the third god would know what to do either.

"How's *your* son doing?" Willow finally said.

"I don't know," Roshaw said. "Seems healthy."

Willow gave him a sardonic grin. "Seems...healthy?"

Roshaw shrugged, though a hint of sadness broke through the guise. "I'll put it this way: he is better than he has any right to be, especially after what I put him through."

"Have you talked to him about it?"

Roshaw paused for a moment, then shook his head. "I tried. But he's just finally talking to me at all—which is more than I deserve, honestly —and I don't want to ruin it. I just feel like, I don't want to rock the boat too soon after the storm, you know?"

Willow nodded along. "Seems reasonable."

"But at the same time," Roshaw continued, "he's a man now. And it's stupid because he's taller than me—probably stronger too, if I'm being honest—but I still just see him as a kid. Like he's still the wild toddler, running toward Mercy's Bluff until I scoop him up. Whenever I look at him, there's this burning desire to protect him, even from the truth. But I also know he deserves to know everything. So, I don't know what to do."

"Good parents protect their children," Willow said softly, "but not from themselves. You'll never have the relationship you want until you're honest."

"I know," he whispered. "I know, but I'm just not ready. Who knows, maybe we'll all die tomorrow, and I'll never have to tell him."

Willow glared at him. "If we're going to die tomorrow, all the more reason to tell him now."

Roshaw took a deep breath through his nose and exhaled through his mouth, rubbing a hand at his brow. "I'll tell him as soon as we get out of here."

The way he said it, she believed him. Whatever it was that he was holding back, it weighed on him. The truth was that Roshaw had been through as much hell as Alverax. They both deserved to shed their burdens and move on.

All the more reason to find Alchaeus.

"In that case," Willow said, grabbing his arm, "let's go get the others. We have a man with at least six measures of intellect to find."

17

Drip. Drip.

Hours passed. Chrys and the others watched their steps as they trudged through the dark caverns leading to the Convergence. Shadows danced from the subtle sway of photospores, feeding light to shimmering trails of water that fell from cracks in the ceiling and ran over the stone walls like tears.

They had no way of knowing if Alchaeus would be at the Convergence, but none of them were keen to sit and wait in the empty cavern, especially knowing that corespawn could arrive at any moment. If he wasn't there, they could always head back. After the first hour, they took Jelium's body and deposited it down an offshoot tunnel. None of them grieved.

Drip. Drip.

Another few hours and Chrys and the party grew quiet. The only sounds were the chaotic pounding of feet on stone and the rhythmic falling of droplets from gnarled stalactites. They were tired. They were hungry. But most of all, they were nervous. They no longer had a clear plan to work with. Now, all they had was the dim hope that Alchaeus might have answers. But that hope was a wet matchstick, and their souls craved a raging fire.

Chrys reached into his pack for his waterskin, knowing well that it was empty. Still, he brought it to his lips and tilted it up.

Drip. Drip.

A sliver of anger slipped its tendrils through his cold veins.

"There's some left in my pack," Willow said beside him. In her arms, she held Aydin, who was awake and staring up at the vaulted cave ceiling.

Iriel, who now carried Willow's pack, slipped it off and opened it. The waterskin was running low as well. She handed it to Chrys, who took a small drink, then she placed it back in her pack. As he looked at his wife, he felt guilt sweep over him. There was a deep fatigue in the curves below her eyes that he couldn't help but feel responsible for. No new mother should have to spend the months after birth hiking through swamps, chased by gods, all while continuing to breastfeed and care for her newborn. It was unfair, and he hoped that—if this ever ended—she wouldn't hold it against him. But she'd forgiven him for worse, and that gave him hope.

As he cinched up his pack, Willow stepped over to hand him Aydin. He tied the drawstring and threw it over his shoulder before taking his son. "Thanks for giving Iriel a break."

Willow shook out her arm, massaging it with her other hand. "He's already getting heavier. I should have borrowed her wrap."

As the party prepared to continue their journey, Roshaw let out a clipped laugh, shaking his head and stifling a slight smile. "Sorry. It's just...I know it's important to hold onto hope and all, but isn't all of this just a little bit absurd? I mean, you all are great, and if I had to choose a group of people to die with while trapped underground like a cockroach, I can't think of anyone better. But...I don't know. I feel like if I don't laugh about this, I'm going to remember how likely it is that we're all going to die down here." Roshaw glanced over to Alverax. "And I just don't think I'm ready for that."

Chrys felt a sharp pain in his chest as he saw the same uncertainty run through the others. Alverax, staring back at his father with doubt in both their eyes. Laurel, looking with sorrow at Asher. Willow, watching them all. When Chrys' eyes met Iriel's, they shared a moment of love and sorrow and pain.

"This isn't about us," Laurel said, breaking the silence. Her voice was filled with a certain sense of self-confidence. "It's about them." She pointed up. "We all have a reason we're here. Something we're fighting for. I'm doing this for my people. If there's any chance that this stupid plan works, I'm sure as hell going to try. For the Zeda."

Chrys nodded. "For Alchea."

Alverax stared at Laurel for a moment, then shook his head while his lips curled into a smile. "For my grandfather. And for the people of Felia."

A moment of silence passed before Willow placed a hand on Roshaw's shoulder. "Being the hero is never easy. But we don't have to do it alone. All of us here, we're in this together. Life or death. I don't know about you, but no matter the outcome, there's no one I'd rather try with."

Roshaw gave her the slightest smile. "I'm in if you're in."

"Then we try," she said.

"We try," Chrys repeated.

"Gale take that," Laurel cursed. "I'm not coming this far just to try. And I'm not dying unless I can take the Heralds with me."

The entire group smiled, and Chrys felt a sense of pride. The Heralds may have won the fight, but they were damn well going to regret it.

Bonds of Chaos

CHRYS WASN'T sure if the feeling in his stomach was worry or excitement. As he rounded the final bend leading to the Convergence, Roshaw pressed a hand against his chest, keeping him from turning the corner. Without thinking, Chrys' stance widened, and his hand reached down to pull out his thread-dead dagger.

"You seeing this?" Roshaw whispered, eyes ablaze with multicolored threadlight.

Chrys followed suit and glanced around the corner. There, surrounding the massive dome of warbling energy, was an army of corespawn, still as Alchaeus' statues. From the massive monstrosities to the tiny scavengers, thousands of the creatures filled the sprawling cavern, some sitting, others standing. Only the smallest of the creatures made any movement at all, like skittering rats amid a field of scarecrows.

"What are they doing?" Chrys wondered aloud.

Roshaw shook his head. "I have no idea. Kind of looks like the *pintalla mox*, but how would a wastelander plague affect corespawn?"

"I don't think so," Chrys said. "At least some of them are alive. It looks more like they're waiting for something."

"Us," Laurel said, crouching low and peeking out from below them.

Chrys gestured for the others to pull back. "There's no way we're getting past that horde."

"I know a way," Alverax said, pulling the Midnight Watcher out of its sheath on his back. "Those things slaughtered the people of Felia. It's time to make them pay."

Roshaw shook his head. "There's too many."

"We've fought more with less," Laurel replied.

Chrys wasn't certain, but he thought he saw Asher's lips pull back into a toothy grin.

"Four Obsidian threadweavers," Iriel said, thoughtfully.

"Plus two obsidian daggers," Chrys added.

"And one obsidian longsword," Alverax finished.

"Against two thousand corespawn." Roshaw looked around the corner.

Laurel gave a wolfish grin. "Easy."

Chrys couldn't help but smile. He knew how they were feeling. The fear and worry were there, certainly, but all overshadowed by the incessant need to act. To do *something*. Anything that might get them closer to freedom. But they still needed to be smart about it.

"Let's take it easy," Chrys said. "Alchaeus isn't even here. There's no point in risking our lives for no reason. Besides, there's a good chance that Relek and Lylax specifically put that army there to stop us from getting to the Convergence. And if we die, we're not getting out of here."

"Ah," Roshaw said. "The Apogee's great wisdom."

Willow laughed. "He's right though. We shouldn't put ourselves in danger for no reason."

Suddenly, threadlight surged in the cavern like a pulsing star. Chrys ran around the corner and saw beads of threadlight floating through the air and into the Convergence. "Something's happening, but it's too far to see. Laurel?"

The young woman and her chromawolf leaned forward, focusing their gaze on the chaos. After a moment, her eyes went wide. "One of the corespawn just burst. I think they're fighting each other. Over food? No, there's something else. I can barely see it through the corespawn. They're moving too much. I think...it's a person!"

Without another word, Laurel and Asher were sprinting forward at full speed toward the army of corespawn.

"Good enough reason for me," Alverax muttered as he took off after her. "For Felia!"

"For the whole damn world, honestly," Roshaw said to himself.

Roshaw and Willow took off after them.

Fire coursed through Chrys' blood, but just as he moved to follow the others, he turned and saw Iriel holding Aydin.

"I..." Iriel said, bouncing with Aydin asleep against her chest. Chrys saw a longing in her eyes as she looked toward the enemy army, but then her eyes rested on her son. "Never mind. Just be careful."

Chrys nodded as he let Obsidian threadlight course through his veins. "Your time will come. Keep an eye on the tunnels."

It took only a moment for the first corespawn to notice them, one of the smaller species, skittering along the floor on all fours as it screeched into the vaulted room. A ripple of enlightenment washed over the horde. They awoke from their pseudo-slumber, and their collective roar shook the cavern.

Veins raged to life with threadlight. Blades brandished. And the battle commenced.

Chrys watched as Obsidian threadlight lashed out at the oncoming horde. The fastest of the corespawn burst apart like bubbles to a pin, showering the room in otherworldly light. He reached out for the second wave, feeling the distance weakening his power. But he had three theoliths surging in his chest, and he could not be stopped.

One of the corespawn, a creature twice the size of a man with horn-shaped threadlight protruding from its light-wrought skull, roared as it trampled over smaller corespawn. Chrys reached out to it, feeling the pulse of threadlight running through its body, and *squeezed*. He felt the resistance, like a magnet refusing its counter, and pressed harder. The beast felt the pressure and roared in response, picking up speed. But, as it grew closer, Chrys' threadweaving grew stronger. With one final clench of his mind, the beast exploded in a wave of threadlight.

As he looked for his next target, focusing on the larger creatures and leaving the smaller ones to the others, he saw Alverax swinging the Midnight Watcher in hectic twirls, cleaving apart several corespawn with each swipe, then reaching out and *breaking* others with his threadlight. Laurel and Asher were close beside him, pouncing on the smaller creatures with unnatural speed, Laurel slamming the obsidian dagger down to finish the creatures off. Willow and Roshaw stood side by side, speaking words that Chrys couldn't hear, but having far more fun than anyone ought to have in the middle of a battle.

Still, the fight had only begun.

A dozen of the same monstrosities that had toppled the walls of Felia came trudging through the cavern, sending quakes through the stone with each step and causing the smaller corespawn to dive out of the way. Chrys took a deep breath and readied himself.

His body rose into the air as he cut his corethread and sent a small surge of Emerald threadlight toward the ceiling. He rose, slowly, until he was thirty feet in the air, surrounded by thousands of beads of threadlight from the felled corespawn that glimmered in the air like fireflies. He sent a surge of Sapphire to steady himself. Floating, hovering above an army of corespawn, he could feel the power of his theoliths coursing through him.

Willow and Roshaw joined him in the sky, leaving Laurel and Alverax to the waves of smaller corespawn.

A few steps away from the Convergence, Chrys could see a man with a wide-brimmed hat amidst the chaos, Obsidian burning through his veins as he fought off nearby corespawn, struggling to deal with the sheer number. Looking at the monstrosities then back to Alchaeus, Chrys made a decision.

"Roshaw!" Chrys shouted to the closer of the two in flight beside him. "You two take the big ones. I'm going for Alchaeus!"

The older man nodded and turned to relay the information to Willow.

Chrys wasted no more time, surging Sapphire and Emerald in opposite directions, launching himself through the air toward Alchaeus far below. His feet slammed into the ground beside the third god with a burst of Sapphire to soften the landing.

Alchaeus looked to him, surprised. "You're back."

As several corespawn descended upon them, Chrys had an idea. Just like he did with Sapphire and Emerald during flight, he reached into his core and tapped into his Obsidian theolith. Then, in an unfocused surge, he unleashed a wave of threadlight that crashed into all of the surrounding corespawn in front of him, bursting them apart into thousands of beads of otherworldly luminescence.

There was a fire raging in Chrys' chest, and it felt good. "Are you okay?"

"I'm fine," Alchaeus said. "A bit confused."

Chrys noticed for the first time the items that Alchaeus held. In one hand, an oddly familiar leather bag, and in the other, an obsidian dagger. "Where did you get that?"

Alchaeus raised a brow. "Perhaps I should be asking if *you* are okay?"

A screeching corespawn the size of a man leapt forward, cutting him off, but Chrys' Obsidian was faster, and the creature burst apart just before it struck.

"We need to get out of here," Chrys said as more corespawn approached. "Can you fly?"

Alchaeus nodded with a look that said he'd forgotten he could, and they each *broke* their corethreads, *pushing* off into the air and leaving a group of hungry corespawn nipping at their heels.

Willow and Roshaw hovered in the air with two of the monstrosities charging toward them. A torrent of threadweaving burst forward, latching onto the corespawns' threadlight core, surging, squeezing. Roshaw screamed out a guttural cry as he fed more Obsidian into the beasts. Willow grit her teeth. Both monstrosities exploded into billowing clouds of threadlight, specks floating in the vaulted cavern heights.

Chrys flew up to hover beside Roshaw. "Everything okay up here?"

Roshaw's eyes lit up. "You see that shit? Woo!"

Willow let out a laugh, though Chrys caught her pressing at the skin above her heart.

"Mother, you okay?"

She nodded.

"Who's next?" Roshaw shouted at the corespawn army.

A dozen more monstrosities were headed toward them, roaring at the destruction of their companions. Their rage overcame their care as they crushed the smaller corespawn beneath them. Each step killed five, then ten. In their wake, they left a flattened throng of corespawn, though the creatures all eventually rose again, their threadlight cores healing their bodies.

Chrys shouted over the frantic sounds of war. "Roshaw, you take the four on the left. Willow, the four on the right. Wait until they're closer, your threadweaving will be stronger the closer they come."

As Alchaeus flew up to join them, a massive tail whipped forward and crashed into his back. His leather bag opened, spilling a handful of golden slivers through the air that fell all the way to the cavern floor. The third god's eyes grew wide. "Save the shards!" he screamed.

Alverax felt all of his pent-up rage release into each swing of the Midnight Watcher. It was safer to *break* the corespawn with threadweaving, but—going through the forms that Thallin had taught him, cleaving through the beasts like they were strands of wheat in a field—revenge felt good.

A larger corespawn came trampling toward him, waving a barbed tail high overhead. A single glance reminded him of the masquerade, of the moment Empress Chailani was killed. A black fire lit within him, anger for her death, for the pain it had caused Jisenna, for the pain it had unleashed on all of Felia, and for the sequence of events it had set in motion, all leading to the deceptive return of the Heralds.

Adrenaline pumped through his veins, swirling in a greasy mixture of Obsidian threadlight. He launched forward, swinging the Midnight Watcher overhead, but the creature's tail whipped out and knocked it from his hands. Without hesitation, he reached his left hand forward, fingers spread wide, and squeezed. Threadlight flowed from him, latching onto the corespawn. Energy fought energy. Power defied power. Chailani flashed in his mind. Crying out. Falling to the marble floor. The creature's tail loomed over him, striking down. Alverax screamed and the corespawn shattered into a thousand pieces.

But it was different this time. Instead of dissipating, the shattered threadlight hovered in the air like fireflies, joining a sky already filled with threadlight essence.

A horde of smaller corespawn shrieked beside it, skittering along the stone floor toward him, but Laurel slid across the ground in front of them, dragging her black blade through their bodies. One by one, the creatures popped out of existence. She spun around and, in harmony with Asher, howled into the open air.

Alverax was glad she was on his side.

"Save the shards!"

Alverax looked up and saw an old man screaming as golden light refracted from something falling through the air. He ran over and picked up the closest one after it clattered to the ground. A pale, yellow light reflected from the transparent gemstone. It was thin, like a hiltless dagger, and something about it called to him.

Laurel nodded to Alverax then swiveled to face more of the corespawn. As she did, her vision split in two.

From her own eyes, Laurel saw the corespawn approaching like ripples of water, light-wrought limbs wavering, slapping against the stone, shrieks of chaos echoing from their void mouths.

From Asher's eyes, she saw red.

Together, they shared their strength, feeling each other's power.

The stench of roses filled the cavern, extending their rancid tendrils through her nostrils, infecting her mind. Her thoughts flickered to the caves beneath the coreseal. Then to the streets of Alchea. That smell, once so inviting, a reminder of the beauty of Zedalum and the floral guides of the Fairenwild. Now, a rotting stench that fueled her rage.

Side by side with her companion, her friend, her second soul, she met the onslaught of smaller corespawn with more energy than she'd ever had before. She was a flaming wall. She was the hand of death. She was the alpha.

Laurel dove forward and buried her thread-dead blade into the next corespawn just as a thin, golden shard struck the ground beside her, flickering in the light of the photospores. She placed the dagger in its sheath and picked up the shard.

Hiding behind the cavern wall, Iriel watched her husband and friends face down a thousand legendary creatures. It was absurd—she knew that—but she couldn't help but feel forgotten, as if they had purposefully excluded her. The truth was that, despite her years of martial training, she was nothing compared to them. Chrys, Willow, and Roshaw all had access to Sapphire, Emerald, and Obsidian. Alverax had Obsidian and the Midnight Watcher. And Laurel's bond with Asher made her faster and stronger than any woman her size ought to be.

Iriel's Emerald was nothing in comparison.

No, that wasn't true. She looked down at Aydin and felt a tear roll down her cheek. She may not be as powerful as the others—she may not be able to fight the corespawn as effectively—but she had the most important role of all. She was a mother. And if all else failed, they still had Aydin, the last mortal Amber.

Chrys sucked in a breath, gasping as his chest sizzled like a volcano's core. Even with three theoliths, the threadweaving required to kill the monstrosities was too much, and there were still more coming.

He reached out to the next, extending his mind to the monstrosity's threadlight frame, and *squeezed* with all his might. Again, he felt the same resistance, power refusing to be broken, a bubble refusing to burst. His mind swirled. His vision blurred, but he blinked it away. He knew that he was on the verge of overextending his new powers. Shaking his head, he regained his vision, and the monstrosity's massive fist crashed into him from above.

Chrys tumbled through the air from the force of the strike. The wind instantly vanished from his lungs, and the world seemed to warp around him. He launched through the air and, just before he struck the hard stone, he surged Sapphire, counteracting the momentum provided by the attack.

Threadlight burned in his chest. Through hazy eyes, he watched as a massive fist flew through the air, smacking Roshaw out of the sky. The man tumbled through the air toward the entrance where Iriel remained hidden.

Chrys squeezed his eyes shut, fighting the clouds swirling in his mind. When he reopened them, a huge corespawn was there, swinging a wide fist through the air where he hovered.

"Stop!" a voice shouted from only a few paces away.

The monstrosity stopped in its tracks, a hundred Amber threads sprouting from the ground like hungry eels, latching to its body. Striding through the chaos with prismatic light swirling in his veins, a black dagger in hand, Alchaeus crossed his arms above his head and roared. The monstrosity reeled back, pain tearing through its light-wrought flesh. A moment later, the massive creature burst apart into ten thousand grains of light that filled the cavern like stars in the night.

Chrys looked to the third god, in awe at the brilliance shining from the man's veins. His eyes, lit like twin suns, seemed ready to burst. The colorful radiance coursing through Alchaeus changed, shifting from a prismatic swirl to an inky blackness. His shoulders pulled back as he screamed out. A wave of Obsidian burst from his body, like a flower blossoming petals of death and destruction.

Dozens of corespawn shattered into thousands of pieces, threadlight rising into the open air like a kettle's steam, joining with the incandescent light that already speckled the cavern's canopy. The entire room seemed to shudder as the Obsidian wave ripped outward.

The sounds of fighting stopped.

Silence permeated the cold air.

The remaining corespawn paused in their tracks, fear rippling through their numbers.

Gravity faded, and pebbles rose into the air from the cavern floor. Across the battlefield, Chrys watched as Alverax and Laurel drifted off the ground.

When gravity returned, everything came crashing back to the earth.

The fearful army of corespawn cried out with shrill echoing voices, turning and running into the Convergence, one by one disappearing into the warbling dome of threadlight.

Overhead, millions of beads of transcendent energy drifted through the air, slowly at first, almost imperceptibly, but then, as the moments led on, the energy moved faster and faster, sucked toward the dome like flecks of iron to a magnet, spilling into the Convergence, feeding it.

Chrys' skin tingled as a ticking noise called out from his pocket, each tick quicker than the last.

The Convergence grew, its dome expanding, spreading across the cavern like an avalanche. Chrys and the others tried to run, but threadlight surged through the room. A wave of power washed over Alverax first, then Laurel, then Willow, and Alchaeus.

Chrys felt a warmth wash over him and a brilliant, white light.

Tick.

19

Laurel opened her eyes, blinking and cringing at the thick smell of leather that surrounded her.

She was no longer in the cave.

And where was...Asher.

She looked around with frantic urgency, lifting her nose, searching for her companion. All around her, thick books lay stacked atop dark shelves. The air was frigid and stale, as though the pages had died and left nothing but ghostly memories floating in the dust. Laurel turned around and saw a heavy door looming over her, carved with intricate filigree and winding layers of brass inlay.

She reached out and felt the door, rubbing her hand along the patterns. It felt so...real.

It's just a dream.

On the far end of the room, a single source of light flickered from around the corner.

Voices.

A young man from the sound of it, and a young woman.

Laurel's hand clenched, and she realized she was still holding the thin golden shard. She ran a thumb down its side as she shifted to the balls of her feet, each step a silent advance along the stone floor. The voices grew louder, and the adrenaline in her veins pulsed to life.

"What the hell is that?" the young man's voice called out.

The young woman responded. "Looks like some kind of ritual, but the words don't make any sense. What is *ventricular*?"

"There's gotta be something down here besides books, something worth some shines."

Laurel stepped forward until she reached the corner. As she snuck a glance, she saw the backs of a boy and a girl—not much younger than herself—anxiously looking through each of the dusty shelves. The boy's gaunt jaw clenched as he flipped through a stack of pages. The thin, Felian girl placed a book back on the shelf and looked for another, tracing the edges of the dark wood with a finger, glancing at a few loose pages and leather spines. She lifted her finger and blew off the dust before reaching for another book.

"This one could be interesting."

The young woman turned around to show the boy, and Laurel saw her clearly for the first time, candlelight shining across flawless ebony skin. There was something about her that looked familiar.

The shape of her eyes. Full lips. The curves of her jaw.

The truth crashed into Laurel like a windstorm.

Gale take me.

ALVERAX LIFTED a hand and turned away from the blinding light.

He was no longer in the cave—that was obvious from the sand inching up the side of his boots—and for a moment he thought he was back in the desert outside Cynosure. But even before his eyes adjusted, he realized it was different. Ocean waves crashed over each other as they fought to gain ground. Salty air drifted on a warm breeze. The sound of distant gulls. It almost felt like he was seated atop Mercy's Bluff, gazing across an endless horizon of blue.

For a moment, he reveled in the beauty. But the urgency of reality pulled it away.

Am I dead...again?

He took a step, expecting the sand to pull him under, as if the warmth of the beach was a veil with a nightmare crawling below the surface. Some dark tiding waiting to reach up its tendrils and consume him.

He spun around, taking in the rest of the landscape. Behind him, a copse of tall trees lined the edge of the beach, wide leaves spreading out from the top, circular brown fruit hanging from their stems. Along the ground, ferns grew in plenty, and lush veridian grass lined the floor like a rich rug.

Farther down the beach, a young kid—no older than twelve—walked toward him holding a fishing spear. Alverax wasn't sure if he should be excited or fearful. Whether it was a dream or something else, he wasn't keen on being surprised, especially by a boy with a spear. Watching, he let threadlight pour through his veins, but...

No threadlight came. No warmth. No euphoric energy.

He rubbed at his eyes, praying to see threads stretching across the world, but there were none.

His heartbeat quickened, and his hand reached for the Midnight Watcher, but even before he touched the empty scabbard, he remembered the skirmish at the Convergence and pictured the black blade lying along the floor of the cavern. His other hand—he remembered—held the pale yellow shard he'd picked up off the floor just before the Convergence consumed them.

The stranger continued his path forward, and as he approached, his free hand lifted in greeting.

Alverax lifted his own hand as well, praying for a peaceful encounter.

But as the boy came closer, bright sunlight reflecting from the ocean waves, illuminating the shadowed bronze skin of a handsome youth, Alverax's heart dropped.

No, no, no, no.

ALCHAEUS STOOD BESIDE A BEAUTIFUL CARRIAGE, the sun beating down from high overhead. He turned away, reaching a hand up to shield himself from the brilliance. To the east, a towering mountain range loomed over a sprawling city, larger than any he'd seen before. To the south, a slow-moving river wove its way through a lush valley.

As he stepped toward the edge of the carriage, Alchaeus looked down at his hands and frowned. Every drop of threadlight had vanished from his veins, Emerald, Sapphire, Obsidian and Amber. Where once chromatic energy had surged through his veins, deep wrinkles lined his hands and arms, sagging skin and sunspots. He reached up and felt the same profound grooves along his cheeks and forehead. He worried that—this time—it would be more than his body could handle.

"GEOFFREY!" a voice shouted from the other side of the carriage. "Get inside and find a doctor!"

There was something familiar about the voice.

The grizzly pitch.

The fiery passion.

Alchaeus took a single, slow step around the corner of the carriage.

A man and woman sat on wide steps leading up to an enormous building with two floral-robed statues standing atop a domed roof. The man on the stairs was crouched beside the woman, staring at the ground and grinding his knuckles into the stone. The woman, partially obscured by the man, was in pain, sprawled on her back across a series of steps.

The man closed his eyes and shook his head with a clenched jaw.

Alchaeus saw him for who he was, and the slightest grin crept along his lips.

He was right.

Alchaeus placed the obsidian dagger into his bag and rummaged until he found what he hoped would be there. One left. The others lay scattered along the cavern floor. But he only needed one. Pulling down on his wide-brimmed hat, he stepped confidently around the corner.

He knew what he needed to do.

Chrys Valerian needed help.

Iriel needed a doctor.

And little Aydin needed an Amber theolith.

LAUREL CLENCHED the golden shard so tightly she thought it might break in two.

This is a dream.

But she knew it wasn't.

Somehow, impossibly, she stood on the other side of the continent, in the center of Felia, deep in the halls of the Hallowed Library, the restricted section, the Anathema.

And in front of her was a young Alabella.

Alverax's eyes grew wide as he stared at the approaching young man. Shirtless, thin but strong, with tattoos running over a bronze chest. Shadows kissed the curves of his arms and the lines of his jaw. In so many ways, he looked like another man.

He was younger...much younger.

Alverax squeezed the shard, and it bit into the palm of his hand. He wanted to convince himself otherwise—maybe he was wrong. Maybe it wasn't him.

But when the young man smiled, there was no question that a young Jelium stood before him.

Alchaeus hurried forward, trying to remember all that Chrys had told him during their time together. The names. The phrases. Everything. If he made the wrong move or said the wrong words, the Lightfather only knew what consequences would follow.

"Chrys Valerian?" he said as he approached. "I am a doctor and, if you want Iriel to live, you must trust me."

He stepped in close and began feeling for the child's head.

"What are you doing?" Chrys shouted. "Get away from her!"

Alchaeus turned to his friend, and a wave of deja vu passed over him. It was Chrys, but it was a different version of him. This man seemed years younger, his beard carefully manicured, his uniform well-pressed and orderly. Yet he still had the same fiery passion in his eyes. For a moment, a wave of sorrow poured over Alchaeus knowing what this Chrys would go through. But it had already happened.

Alchaeus caught Chrys' wrist as the desperate man tried to push him away. "I am the only one who can perform such a surgery. Step aside and let me save her."

Chrys looked at him and furrowed his brow, drinking in thirsty gasps of air. Alchaeus could feel the struggle inside him, the pain of placing his beloved's fate in the hands of another. A stranger, no less. But after a moment, his shoulders relaxed, and Alchaeus saw Chrys' resignation.

"Good. Help me lift her into the carriage. Quickly now!"

Together, they lifted the pregnant woman up the steps and into the carriage, careful to give her space to lie down. Despite what he knew,

Alchaeus still worried that he wouldn't be able to perform the surgery fast enough, that the Convergence would call him home before he finished his work. But if Chrys was right, then he'd already succeeded. There would be time, so long as he stayed focused.

Alchaeus inserted himself into the carriage doorway between Chrys and Iriel. "Give me space to work, and I promise you she will live. There's more at stake here than you know."

Lightfather, I've said too much.

Chrys, angry but resigned, stepped down from the carriage step.

Alchaeus closed the door behind him, opened his bag, and pulled out the two items he would need: a flask filled with elixir and a thin shard of Amber.

He was aging quickly now; he could feel it in the quiver of his hands.

The recoil would happen any minute.

There was no time to waste.

Laurel stepped into the flickering lamplight of the Anathema, understanding her purpose. The Father of All had given her an opportunity to fix everything. A chance to make it all better. If she killed Alabella while she was young, none of it would happen. There would be no Bloodthieves. There would be no fires in the Fairenwild. Her people would be alive. The coreseal would never have shattered. The Heralds would never have returned.

And all she had to do was kill Alabella...again.

She stepped forward.

Alabella and the boy turned to see her.

Laurel looked down at the golden shard in her hand. It was thin, but it would do.

One jab, straight to the heart, and time would be rewritten.

She could save them all.

Laurel lunged.

Rage simmered in Alverax's thread-dead veins. In a way, it was a relief. His Obsidian threadlight was the reason for all their troubles. If he'd never become an Obsidian, Alabella would not have attacked the Zeda. The coreseal would not have shattered. The Heralds would never have returned. Jisenna would still be alive...

And it all began with Jelium. Every bad thing that had happened to Alverax—to the entire damned world—had started with Jelium. The world would have been better off if the man had never been born.

Realization dawned on him, a flash of light in a moonless night.

If this was real...

If this was not a dream...

Alverax set his jaw, squeezed with a fire in his veins, and thrust.

In the carriage, pressed for time, Alchaeus broke off the tip of the shard. Beside him, sprawled out on her back, Iriel cried out in agony, both for herself and for the child she knew was in danger. Alchaeus took the tiny theolith and held it between his trembling fingers, purpose overcoming his doubts. He took a deep breath, reached into the slit in Iriel's stomach, past blood and muscle and warm tissue, through the mother's sac protecting the unborn child—ignoring the agonizing screams—and placed the shard into the baby's heart.

Laurel rammed the shard into Alabella's chest.

Alverax shoved the shard into Jelium.

Alchaeus leaned back, tears forming in his thread-dead eyes, and placed the empty bottle of elixir back in his bag. It would heal her. He had done all he could. He'd played his part in the Lightfather's grand scheme. He only hoped it would be enough.

With a profound weariness, he pushed open the carriage door and stepped to the ground. His body was so weak. The Convergence was leeching all of the magic that sustained his immortal life.

Young Chrys rose to his feet, his face a mess of emotion. Alchaeus wanted to tell him everything, but there was no knowing what dark consequences would follow. He did know, however, that he had already told Chrys something.

"They will be okay," Alchaeus said. This was his last chance to prepare his friend for what was coming. "The recoil will happen any moment. Chrys, you must listen to me. Your child is the key." He thought of Relek and Lylax. "They will come for it. You cannot let them have it. Whatever it takes, you must protect the child."

Chrys' brow furrowed. "What the hell are you talking about?"

"You will need this," Alchaeus said. He reached into the bag, pulled out the obsidian dagger, and tossed it to Chrys. "Use it to break the threads that bind you."

This was it.

He had set in motion everything that led to where they were now.

And even though it would be for the best, it was still the beginning of what would lead to his siblings' deaths. There was no hope for his sister —he could see that now. Perhaps, his brother...his younger brother. The brother who had once been his best friend before the elixir changed their lives. Before they had been separated for so long. For him, Alchaeus still held out hope.

"Relek, forgive me."

20: Bonds of Chaos

Silence.

A cold chill as shadows flickered in the darkness.

Chrys ran hands down his arms and looked at his surroundings. Patches of photospores grew like weeds between wet stone along the edges. Long stalactites hung from the vaulted ceiling. He was alone, standing in the center of a cavern as large as the courtyards of Endin Keep. Something about it made him feel so small.

His eyes followed the walls, past jagged edges and smooth granite, until they found a wide tunnel leading away from the cavern.

He knew that tunnel; he knew this cavern.

Chrys spun around in search of the Convergence. As he opened himself to threadlight, he found nothing but a hollow space inside of him. There was nothing there. No warmth. No power.

The cold chill shivered across his arms.

It was a nightmare.

That was the only explanation.

He remembered the wave of energy spilling out of the Convergence, washing over the cavern and consuming him. Consuming his friends.

Were they dead?

Was he dead?

Only a moment ago, the cavern had been filled with corespawn, filled with his family and friends, filled with drifting beads of light. Where were they? Where was any of it? And why did the silence feel so stifling?

Chrys walked toward where the Convergence had been. Only now, where once a warbling dome of multicolored threadlight had pulsed and shifted, there was nothing but stale air, wet rocks, and that damn chill biting at his skin.

Minutes passed as he stared into the empty cavern, waiting for the dream to fade, waiting for the silence to break. Nightmares were nothing new to Chrys. For years after the war, his dreams had been plagued by flashes of battle. Death, pain, tears, and suffering. But each memory had been filled with blaring trumpets, riotous battle cries, and the sounds of weapons clashing. Never had his nightmares been so very quiet. Never had they been so empty.

He couldn't remember the last time he was alone. Before the Wastelands. Before Cynosure and Felia. Before the Fairenwild. But even in Alchea, he had not truly been alone. Not since the war. Even in moments of quiet, the Apogee had been there, listening. Now, for the first time in five years, he was truly alone. And he did not like it.

Chrys wanted his family back.

He wanted to know they were safe. He wanted to hold them, protect them from the rising darkness. They needed to get out of this freezing cave. There was too much to do. Too much at stake. He didn't have time for this damn nightmare.

A man suddenly appeared in the middle of the cavern, standing where the Convergence had once been with a wide-brimmed hat and a hand over his eyes like he'd been looking into the sun. Chrys recognized him immediately.

"Alchaeus?"

The third god, who'd grown noticeably older since Chrys had last seen him, leaned forward as his eyes adjusted. "Chrys Valerian?"

"It's me," he said, glancing at a leather bag in Alchaeus' hand.

The old man shook his head. "I just had the strangest experience."

"Alchaeus," Chrys said, "you need to tell us how to break the coreseal."

"Coreseal?" Alchaeus raised a brow. "What are you talking about? The coreseal was destroyed." He gave Chrys a dubious look. "If you're here, where are the others? Why are you alone?"

Chrys turned and glanced back down the tunnel, a part of him still hoping he would see his wife hiding around the bend. He turned back to Alchaeus and a realization dawned on him. The hat. His skin, unblemished, yet sickly. Old, yet young. The leather bag. Alchaeus *was* the man who'd saved Iriel.

"It was you!" he said, unable to hold back his frustration. "You lied. You said it wasn't you, but it was!"

Alchaeus furrowed his brow. "I don't know what you—"

"You saved Iriel when she almost lost the baby," Chrys said, pointing a finger and stepping toward the old man. "Why did you lie to me?"

"I..." Alchaeus raised his hands. "I promise, if I—"

Chrys pulled out his thread-dead dagger and held it up. "After you saved Iriel and Aydin, you gave this to me. You said, 'Use it to break the threads that bind you.' Tell me how you got past the coreseal. And no more lies!"

"I didn't get past the coreseal," Alchaeus said. "And where is your threadlight?"

Chrys stepped up to Alchaeus and pressed a finger against the old man's chest. "I don't care if this is a damn nightmare. You're going to tell me the truth. How did you get past the coreseal?"

"A nightmare?" Alchaeus' eyes grew serious. "Chrys, you need to calm down."

"Not until you tell me the truth," Chrys said, shoving the old man with his free hand.

Alchaeus unleashed an unfocused surge of Sapphire, punching into Chrys' chest and throwing him back. The thread-dead dagger dropped from his hand as he fell through the air, landing a few paces away on the hard stone. The old man reached down and picked up the dagger. "There is no time for foolishness. I made a discovery, here at the Convergence. Something that could change everything."

Just as he said the words, a skittering sound echoed over the stone floor. Then another a dozen feet away. Then more and more. Alchaeus' head swiveled back and forth, eyes wide as he took in their surroundings. Chrys saw nothing, but he did smell the sweet scent of a summer rose.

Alchaeus turned to Chrys. "Don't move."

Suddenly, a bright light appeared along the edges of his vision, expanding like a fire toward the center, filling his sight until there was nothing but light in his eyes. It was too bright, but he needed answers. He needed Alchaeus to tell him what to do.

He held up a hand to shield from the brilliance.

Then closed his eyes.

Bonds of Chaos

21

THE CONVERGENCE SIZZLED WITH ENERGY.

Chrys stood in the middle of the same cavern, warm and wondering what the hell had just happened. Was it a dream? Was the Convergence playing with his mind? It had all felt so real. Where was Alchaeus?

His eyes grew wide as bolts of energy suddenly crackled across the Convergence, branching out, warring with dozens of expanding bubbles along the dome, like a kettle boiling over. He turned and saw the others standing all around, dazed, backing away as the erratic energy grew.

Rocks danced along the ground from tremors pulsing through the cavern. Small at first, barely noticeable through his thick boots, but in moments they'd grown until quakes ran up through his legs, vibrating his bones. The cavern groaned, and stalactites rained down like stone daggers.

Then the Convergence exploded.

A cascading tidal wave of raw energy surged through the cavern. Chrys was thrown back, head over heels, tumbling through the air like a pebble in a windstorm, his mind swirling alongside his body. In a stroke of clarity, he embraced the threadlight pulsing through his veins, grateful that it had returned. Hot energy hissed beneath his skin. With a surge of Sapphire and Emerald, he stopped himself from spinning, then *pushed* against the jagged cavern wall just before he crashed. He dropped to his feet, shaking his head to clear the nausea.

Three loud thuds echoed throughout the vaulted cavern, then silence.

Chrys turned and saw Alverax lying still, crumpled along the rocky wall. Roshaw sprinted from the dark cavern entrance over to his son, thick boots stomping over fallen rubble, then knelt beside him, frantically checking wounds while shadows flickered over them from the light of the photospores.

Chrys was so disoriented that, despite his desire to do something, anything, he simply stood, staring at the aftermath of the explosion.

"Check on Alchaeus!" Willow shouted as she ran toward him, her face pale, veins alive with multi-colored threadlight. "I'll get Laurel."

Chrys was still furious with Alchaeus. They were friends. How could he look him in the eye and claim he wasn't the one who'd saved Iriel. There was something the old man wasn't telling them, and Chrys needed answers.

"Dammit, Chrys!" she screamed, spittle flying from her lips. "I didn't raise you to stand by. Not while the ones you love are hurt."

Chrys shook his head. She was right. Liar or not, they needed him. "On my way."

With renewed focus, Chrys spotted Alchaeus and ran to him. The third god lay against the jagged wall at an unnatural angle. His skin was wrinkled and gray, like he'd soaked in a warm bath for hours. Like he'd aged another twenty years since they'd spoken. Blood and water dripped down his face onto the wet stone floor, and his chest lay in such a way that Chrys was certain there were broken ribs. He knelt down and pressed a hand over Alchaeus' heart.

Nothing.

He leaned down and pressed an ear.

There. It was faint, but it was there.

"Alchaeus," Chrys whispered. "Alchaeus, wake up."

The old man's eyes fluttered open, like a newborn desperate to see a world that their mind couldn't comprehend. "C...Chrys?"

"It's me," he said. "I need to get you to the elixir."

"...did it," Alchaeus mumbled, coughing up a sizable chunk of red blood. He tried to lift his hand, but it fell back to the ground. "I was wrong."

"Come on," Chrys said, rising to a crouch and reaching his arm under Alchaeus' shoulder. "We need to get you up."

"It was me." Tears streaked his elderly cheeks. He rolled over and looked Chrys in the eyes. The old man's irises had faded, a layer of gray clouding the colors. "I didn't know..."

Chrys stared down at Alchaeus and felt his chest tighten.

Alchaeus' lip quivered as he reached for Chrys' hand. "Don't leave me."

"I'm not going to leave you," Chrys whispered.

"I don't want to be alone anymore."

Chrys felt tears in his eyes, swelling against his cheeks, pressure building as he watched an old man's desperate plea. If there was anything Chrys understood, it was the fear of being alone. "I won't leave you, Alchaeus."

The old man smiled and leaned his head back, his lips and cheeks twitching through a range of emotions. His hand grew heavy as his eyes moved to the empty cavern heights. A few quiet moments passed, a sense of peace in the pain, then Alchaeus' body grew still, his lips still parted with the slightest hint of a smile touching the corners.

Chrys closed his eyes and squeezed the old man's hand.

So much death.

And he couldn't stop any of it.

Not in the Wastelands. Not in Felia. Not now.

Would there be no end to their loss?

"Chrys?" Iriel's voice rose through the cavern like an angel's song.

He turned and saw her walking toward him, carrying their child through the silent aftermath of death and destruction. "Iriel."

"Is he?"

Chrys nodded.

"I'm sorry." She paused, Emerald threadlight running through her veins as she looked around the cavern. "What happened? I ran to check on Roshaw, and then the Convergence just...exploded. Is it gone for good?"

Chrys turned to where the warbling dome of threadlight had once been and found nothing but staggered puddles of fallen water and debris. Where once the energy had been, now there was nothing. No signs. No crater. Gone. Just like in his nightmare.

"I don't know," Chrys said. "But we should go."

Iriel nodded toward the body. "Are we going to leave him?"

"No," Chrys quickly replied. "I'll carry him. We should bury him at his home."

"I think that would be nice."

A minute later, Roshaw hobbled over with Alverax. The young man looked beat up but okay. Scratches along his cheek, blood seeping out from wounds in his shoulder, but he was alive, and he could walk. He would be okay.

When Laurel, Asher, and Willow joined them, the young woman seemed unfazed by the bone jutting out from her elbow. Chrys was going to ask, but could tell by Laurel's scowl that she didn't want to discuss it.

"Glad you're all okay," Chrys said as they gathered around Alchaeus. "I'd like to bring his body back to the elixir and bury him somewhere nearby."

"I'll help," Roshaw added.

Willow put a hand on Roshaw's shoulder. "We can all help."

Chrys gave them an appreciative nod. "I think we could all use a bit of that elixir as well."

After *breaking* Alchaeus' corethread, Chrys lifted the old man over his shoulders and began the melancholy trek through the winding tunnels to bury yet another fallen friend.

It was a long, grueling return through the caverns, following the white markings on the walls that Alchaeus used to signal the return route. At first, Chrys thought the party's silence had come because of the death of Alchaeus. But as they continued on, he realized that it was more than that. For months they had each been surrounded by death in its various forms, and their hands were just as dirty as any. This was not the silence of a death being mourned. This was the silence of secrets.

No one wanted to discuss what had happened in the Convergence. If any of the others had experienced a nightmare like he had, he understood why. Scared or scarred, they walked on in silence.

The cavern had shifted from the quakes caused by the destruction of the Convergence. In several places, massive stones had detached from the walls, blocking large portions of the way but never enough to fully impede their path.

By the time they reached the final tunnel, the light of the elixir shimmering beyond the bend, they were all tired and sore. Those who were able—Chrys among them—used Sapphire to decrease their weight for the journey, and still he felt a deep weariness. Laurel took the worst of it. Every step seemed to jostle her broken arm and, though she grimaced and growled, not once did she complain. And Iriel—Lightfather bless her—throughout it all, she endured with Aydin strapped to her chest, ever-thankful for the breaks that Willow provided.

Chrys took the final steps into the cave and breathed in the familiar sight. Golden light illuminated the vast cavern, though it too had changed. The rose-colored table had been split in two, rubble and debris scattered along the sides where a boulder had fallen from the ceiling, cracking the table down its center. Dozens of corespawn statues lay shattered along the far corner. And a massive crevice had opened along the wall above the elixir pool, deep and dark where the glowing light failed to reach.

"Damn," Roshaw said behind him.

Laurel and Asher stepped past Chrys, then moved to the elixir. In unison, they both bent down and lapped up a few sips of the golden water before Laurel reached over and placed her broken arm inside. In moments, her tense shoulders relaxed, and she flopped onto her belly along the edge of the pool, letting her arm drift in the water.

Chrys turned to the others. "Why don't you all take a little rest, and I'll start working on a burial mound for Alchaeus."

"I'll help," Roshaw said.

"No, it's okay." Chrys offered a solemn smile. "You go rest. If I use Obsidian, the work will go quickly."

The others understood his need to be alone, to work off the pain of loss, and so they left him for the elixir. Chrys lifted Alchaeus' body one final time and carried him to the far end of the cavern, near a large pile of fallen rubble. One by one, Chrys lifted the stones, deciding not to use threadlight to ease the burden, embracing the physical labor of the work, and set them each down on top of his friend's body. Slowly, the mound grew, first along Alchaeus' feet and legs, rising to consume his chest and arms. Finally, Chrys built a wall of rocks around the man's head, setting aside a single flat stone which he would use to cover the face. The final puzzle piece to commemorate the life of a fallen god.

He stepped away from the burial mound, joining the quiet group still seated along the edge of the elixir pool. Already, they seemed healthier. The cuts on Alverax's cheeks had faded. Roshaw's bloody shoulder was clean. Laurel's arm, though still soaking in the elixir, was regaining its natural form. Iriel's pale face was now more full of life. And Willow...

"Mom," Chrys said, his brow furrowed tight.

"Yes, I did," she said with a laugh, not waiting for him to ask. "I rubbed some of it on my face, because it would be a pity to have this anti-aging juice available and not use just a little..."

Roshaw shrugged beside her. "I hadn't even realized there were wrinkles to begin with."

Chrys ignored them and turned to Laurel. "Are you able to take a quick break? I'm going to place the final stone."

The young woman nodded, pulling her arm from the elixir and bending it back and forth slowly. As she rose, they all followed Chrys over to the burial mound, gathering in a half-circle around Alchaeus' exposed face. They stood in silence for a few moments, staring down at their fallen friend. His skin had already gone nearly white. Thick wrinkles ran over the curves of his face, and the same delicate smile crept along the edge of his lips. Despite everything that had happened, he looked...content.

"What can we say about someone like Alchaeus?" Chrys started, unsure what he would say next. "You embraced us to your own danger, and you helped us when you did not have to. Never once, despite living in darkness for centuries, did you let it blacken your soul. I'm not sure any of us could have done the same. You were a good man, and a good friend. We owe you our lives."

The others remained quiet as Chrys reached down and lifted the flat stone. He paused, taking in the dead man's smile one last time, then placed the stone over his face. "The world may not remember you, but we will."

"May the winds guide you," Laurel whispered.

Willow nodded to the words.

"When we get out of here," Roshaw said, looking tired, "I'm going to find him a star in the east. He deserves at least that."

After a minute of solemn silence, the others stepped away, leaving the third god to rest beneath his stone shrine. Willow and Roshaw walked quietly over to the broken table. Alverax sat on the ledge of the elixir pool. And Laurel wandered over to the corespawn statues. Only Chrys remained, staring down at the man who'd risked his own immortality for them.

Just like that, hundreds of years of knowledge and memories were gone. Their best chance of destroying the coreseal. He didn't know how, but Chrys would finish Alchaeus' work. He would stop Relek and Lylax before they broke the world.

Chrys patted his side, looking for a memento to leave on the shrine. After touching his empty sheath, he realized that his thread-dead dagger was missing. He must have dropped it in the cavern. At some point, he would need to go retrieve it. But they had nothing but time.

He touched his pocket and felt the familiar, circular shape of the pocket watch he'd been gifted by Malachus. He pulled it out, thinking that it might make a worthy memento to leave behind. But when he opened it, a crack ran along the length of the glass, and the hands stood still. His own words to Iriel echoed in his mind.

As long as I hear that steady tick, I know that everything is going to be okay.

An ominous feeling crept along his spine.

Was everything going to be okay?

He looked at the pocket watch again and had a sudden realization.

The ticking sound.

Alchaeus' final words.

A string, held at each end, brought together.

If space was a string that could be folded by the Convergence, what about time?

Chrys needed to think.

22

BONDS OF CHAOS

Alverax stood at the edge of the elixir pool, staring down into the golden light. It called to him—not for healing, not the magic—the water itself. After his experience beneath the Felian palace, nearly drowning in a sea of darkness, he thought he'd never want to be in the water ever again. But he'd always felt some unseen bond with it. A reassurance. A connection that he only ever felt when he lay weightless and entombed.

His eyes drifted up to the massive fracture splitting the wall above the elixir. The earthquake caused by the destruction of the Convergence had done damage across the underground world, but this felt different. It, too, called to him, like a doorway opening to a new world.

Slowly, he stepped around the edge of the pool until he reached the wall. There was no ledge, so he stepped into the water, letting its golden glow crawl up his clothing. He felt a shiver of healing magic crawl across his spine, but his eyes never stopped staring at the fracture. The waters reached his chest as he made his way to the center of the pool's wall. He stared up at the gap, then jumped, grabbing hold of the edge and pulling himself up, lifting until his stomach lay flat along the base of the gap. He placed his hands down and pushed himself to his feet. The gap in the fracture was just wide enough for a man and ran deep enough that none of the golden light reached the end.

He looked back and saw the others. Laurel had moved to the tunnel entrance to keep watch. Roshaw and Willow sat at the broken table quietly talking. And Chrys stared down at Alchaeus' shrine, brow furrowed as he lost himself in his own thoughts. Iriel fed Aydin in the corner.

Alverax stepped farther into the fracture, into the beckoning darkness where jagged rocks flanked either side of him. He moved sideways through it until he reached the end and felt a pang of disappointment. His hand ran along the length of the wall, as if there would be some magical lever he could pull to open it. Unfortunately, there was nothing but stone.

But then he saw it, a speck of light flickering as he moved. A tiny hole at chest level, the size of a pebble. He crouched and looked through it. He had to squint at just the right angle, but he finally saw the other side. His eyes went wide as he took in a sprawling lake of elixir with hundreds of thick stalagmites piercing up through the water like stone swords. And there, in the center of the lake, an island. Even through the small hole, the island glowed like a threadlight sun.

Alverax stumbled back through the fracture, scraping his shoulders and shimmying his way through the jagged walls. Finally, he leapt down into the elixir and waded his way to the end of the pool. When he lifted himself up, his father was staring at him with a raised brow.

"Everything okay over there?"

Alverax stood and ran toward the alcove housing Alchaeus' corespawn statues, while pointing back toward the fracture. "There's something on the other side of that wall."

He stepped over one of the shattered statues—stone arms and legs broken from the torso though a short tail still stood firm—and found what he was looking for. He left the chisel and picked up the hammer, then grinned as he leapt over rubble back toward the elixir pool.

His father was now standing, joined by Chrys, Iriel, and Willow, all staring at him as he ran. Alverax ignored them, jumping down into the pool and making his way back to the fracture. He tossed the hammer up into the gap, then jumped and pulled himself up.

"Alverax!"

He turned to see his father standing at the edge of the pool, hands raised, palms up. Alverax raised a finger. "One second!"

After retrieving the hammer, he squeezed himself forward to the end of the fracture, then bent down to find the hole. He slammed the end of the hammer into the hole, blasting a chunk of stone off into the cavern on the other side. He bent down and took another look. The cavern was even larger than he'd seen the first time, the golden lake extending as far as the eye could see.

Again, he slammed the hammer at the edge of the hole. Then again, and again. With each strike, the hole grew slightly larger, revealing more and more of the sprawling cavern beyond. Once there was a hole the size of a man's head, Alverax stepped back, smiled, and made his way back to the other end of the fracture.

"You're all going to want to see this," he said with a grin.

Roshaw's veins lit with multi-colored threadlight just before he began to float into the air. With a surge of energy, he accelerated toward the fracture. Watching his father fly was still a surreal experience. He'd seen the three hybrids—Chrys, Willow, and Roshaw—practice flying during their journey through the southern Wastelands, but it never ceased to send a shiver of awe up Alverax's spine. He remembered falling from the sky in Cynosure like an awkward fish and felt a small measure of jealousy.

Before Roshaw made it all the way, Alverax leapt down into the elixir to clear the path. While he watched his father disappear into the crevice, he backed away, then pulled himself up over the ledge of the pool. He stood beside Iriel in silence while they waited for Roshaw to reappear.

After a few moments, Iriel turned to him. "What's in there?"

"I don't want to spoil it," Alverax said. "You're going to want to see this one for yourself."

As if to prove his point, Roshaw came bouncing out of the fracture with wide eyes and a wider smile. "Holy hell! You have to see this!"

Willow went in next, bringing Iriel up with her. They squeezed through the fracture one at a time while Alverax stood by his father, feeling quite proud of his accomplishment. By the time they came back down, Willow was in a fit of excitement. "It makes so much sense! The elixir pool is so small. It had to come from somewhere."

"Exactly!" Roshaw said. "I wonder if the lake feeds the oka'thal waters of Kai'Melend."

"Probably with some kind of diluted solution," Willow added.

"Did you look in threadlight?" Alverax asked.

Willow nodded. "Brighter than anything I've ever seen."

"Thought I'd gone blind for a minute," Roshaw joked.

Willow gasped. "It could be another Convergence! But if it is, where does it lead? It could be anywhere!"

Alverax glanced up at the opening. "Do you think it could be our way out?"

From the far end of the cave, Chrys came walking through the tunnel. He'd left without a word, looking quite thoughtful, but now there was a new sense of purpose in his stride.

"Chrys!" Iriel called out. "We might have found another Convergence!"

His eyes grew wide. "Really?"

"On the other side of the wall," she said. "Alverax found it."

"If that's true," Chrys said, eyes dancing between the members of their party. "Then we need to talk about what happened with the last one."

The buzz of excitement faded away as quickly as it had come. Alverax remembered the last image of his vision, a young Jelium falling to the sand with blood dripping down his bronze chest. If that was what Chrys was asking about, then Alverax didn't want to talk about it.

Chrys glanced back at Alchaeus' shrine. "If I'm right, then my mother, Laurel, and Alverax experienced something in there. It's probably why you were so quiet on the way back. I experienced something too, but I didn't understand it. I thought it was a magic-fueled hallucination, some kind of nightmare. But Alchaeus changed my mind. This changed my mind." He held up the pocket watch. "I might be crazy, but I think the Convergence took each of us back in time."

Alverax felt his pulse quicken. He'd considered it, hoped for it even. But it wasn't true. If he'd really gone back in time and killed Jelium, something would have changed. What happened in the Convergence was something else.

"It was just a vision," Alverax said. "If it was anything more, we wouldn't be here right now."

Willow's eyes darted about the floor as she pieced together the puzzle. But as soon as Alverax spoke, her gaze shifted to him. "What do you mean we wouldn't be here?"

Everyone turned to him, and he immediately regretted having said anything at all. "What? No one wants to share their experience, but you all want to hear mine?"

Chrys took a step forward into the center of the circle, turning to meet eyes with everyone in the group as he spoke. "If there is another Convergence, no more secrets. There could be consequences. There could be information that helps us understand how it happened, maybe even recreate it. It could be what helps us break the coreseal and get out of here. Might even give us a clue about how to stop the Heralds. But if we don't talk about it, we'll never know."

"I'm with Alverax," Laurel said. "I think it was just some kind of a dream."

"What makes you say that?" Chrys asked. "Where did it take you?"

"The Hallowed Library in Felia."

Chrys raised a brow, taken aback. "And what happened?"

Laurel looked down at Asher, as if she were asking for permission, then looked back to Chrys. "I killed Alabella."

Alverax felt his mind beginning to spiral. Could her dream have been so similar to his own? Maybe the power of the Convergence just latched on to powerful feelings and placed you in a scene with those you hate. Did every vision end in death? That would explain why no one wanted to talk about their experience.

"You killed Alabella?" Chrys repeated.

Laurel's eye twitched. "This time, she was maybe fourteen years old?"

"So you did go back in time!" Willow said excitedly.

"But if she killed Alabella," Roshaw jumped in, "then we wouldn't be here, right?"

Alverax nodded. "Exactly."

Laurel placed a hand on top of Asher's back. "Like I said. It was just a dream."

"Mine was the same," Alverax added, remembering the beach and the hot sun. "I was in Kulai, and a young Jelium approached me. I figured if I killed him, then none of this would have happened. So I stabbed him with one of those yellow shards that Alchaeus dropped during the fight."

"That's what I used as well," Laurel added.

"Yellow shards?" Willow placed a fist on her forehead and closed her eyes. "Can you show me?"

Alverax shook his head. "It disappeared when the Convergence burst."

"Something's not adding up," Willow said thoughtfully. "I'm actually with Chrys on this. It would explain my experience perfectly. But if you two killed Alabella and Jelium, then why wouldn't...wait. Can you describe the shards you picked up?"

Alverax pictured it in his mind. "Handspan long, half a finger wide. Pale yellow. A bit like citrine."

"And you got it from Alchaeus?" Willow's eyes grew wide. "Stones, you didn't kill Alabella and Jelium. You stuck a shard of Amber in their hearts."

Alverax's heart dropped. He looked over and saw a fire in Laurel's eye and a dangerous twitch in her lip. He pictured the shard in his hand, dripping with Jelium's blood. The tip—such a subtle detail—had been chipped. Then when the Convergence exploded, the rest of the shard had been destroyed by the energy, crumbling to dust in his hand.

Willow continued. "Think about it. Alchaeus told us that no human has ever been born an Amber or Obsidian threadweaver. The only reason none of us have all four theoliths is because Lylax had hidden all of the Amber. Alchaeus must have finally found it. Then he went back and made Aydin an Amber threadweaver. Laurel placed a shard of Amber in Alabella's heart. And Alverax placed one in Jelium."

"Holy hell," Roshaw mumbled.

Iriel looked down at her son, asleep on a pile of wool blankets.

"No," Laurel said with a whimper. "I...I killed her! There's no way she survived that! I didn't. It can't be. I..." She stopped, tears welling up in her eyes as she looked to Alverax for help, but he had no solace to give. Every word, every pause, was a reflection of his own doubts and fears. He felt his chest tighten and tears creep out from his own tired eyes.

I created Jelium.

The truth of it was too much. All of the deaths caused by the Heralds —all of the pain they'd inflicted—was because of him. He'd had the choice. He'd made his decision. Somehow, deep down, he'd known that the shard was Amber. Of course it was. And he'd let his anger and bitterness win. What kind of a man tries to kill a kid? Without hesitation. Without regret. Every dark event that had eclipsed the good parts of his life was *his* fault.

"Laurel," Willow said, moving to place a hand on the girl's shoulder. "You were just trying to help."

"STOP IT!" Laurel screamed, swatting away Willow's hand and taking a step back while she wiped away tears. "I don't want to hear it. *Laurel, it's okay. Laurel, you couldn't have known. Laurel, you tried.* I'm sick of it! First Zedalum. Then Alabella. Now Alabella again. We're all going to die in these caves, and all I wanted was to do one good thing!"

With that, she stormed off with Asher at her side. The others all watched in silence as she disappeared into the tunnel leading toward the bottom of the Endless Well, but Alverax chased after her. She needed him, but he also needed her. They were the only two in the world who could understand what each other was going through. His grandfather had taught him the importance of sharing burdens. Now, he would share hers. And, hopefully, she would share his.

He ran toward the tunnel, wet boots squashing against the hard stone, dodging piles of loose rubble. It didn't take long to find her. Laurel was just around the corner, seated against the jagged wall with her head buried in Asher's fur. Her chest heaved up and down as she let out her tears. Asher rubbed his snout along her shoulder in comforting strokes.

Alverax approached slowly, remembering his weeks on the *Pale Urchin*, locked away in the cabin not wanting to speak with anyone. So, rather than trying to give an uplifting speech, rather than spinning some lie about how it would be okay, he sat down on the other side of Asher, his head resting next to Laurel's. Sometimes, the simple act of being there is enough.

They lay in silence for what felt an eternity. All the while, Alverax replayed the scene from the Convergence back in his mind. The handsome young Kulaian boy. The golden shard. And the moment he chose to kill. It felt like another man—Alverax was not a killer. But it was different with Jelium. Years of hate, years of anger and pain, had all combined to make the act so effortless. So deserved. Even after he'd done it and seen the fear in the young boy's eyes, Alverax had felt no regret. Maybe he was a killer after all.

"How do we make it better?" Laurel's voice cracked.

When Alverax sat up, Laurel's swollen eyes stared back at him, pleading, begging for him to offer a solution.

"Sometimes, there's nothing you can do," Alverax said, shaking his head.

"You don't believe that," Laurel replied.

Alverax looked at the ground. "Not every mistake can be fixed."

"That's not what I asked."

When he looked back up, he saw the intensity with which she looked at him. She was a woman of action—he could see it in her eyes—an arrow begging to be loosed.

"I know we can't fix it," Laurel added. "But I refuse to believe that there is nothing we can do to make it better."

Alverax furrowed his brow. "Make what better?"

"This?" Laurel said, gesturing to the cavern. "Our situation. The Heralds. The coreseal. I don't know, but we have to do something. This is just as much our fault as anyone's, and I'm going to do my part to make it better if it's the last thing I do."

His heart ached thinking of how much Jisenna would have liked Laurel. She was honest, brave, and willing to do what it took to protect the people she loved. Alverax liked to think that he was the same, but when it came down to it, he wasn't so sure.

"Come on." Laurel stood and offered him a hand. "I'm done feeling sorry for myself. People are like trees, remember? The least we can do is stand."

Alverax forced a smile, took her hand, and stood.

Bonds of Chaos

23

It took hours of hammering—even with the aid of threadlight—to break open a hole large enough for a woman to fit through. After considerable effort, sweat, and cursing, Iriel finally managed it. The hard work felt good, like she was finally accomplishing something rather than waiting around for the others. She looked through the opening at the shimmering lake of elixir, ripples spreading across the surface like a siren's song, and breathed in her success.

There was something haunting in knowing that no one had set foot in this cavern, at least as far as Iriel knew. After what had happened at the Convergence, they were all a little wary of what this new phenomenon would hold. In some ways, it seemed so similar—brilliant rays of threadlight buzzing through the air—but in others, it was different. Like comparing the moon and the sun. She looked to the island, a beacon of power, the center of the threadlight.

It still seemed impossible that the others had traveled through time, everyone except her and Roshaw. It wasn't true—none of it was under their control—but it still felt like somehow they'd been excluded purposefully. Not this time. Whatever this new phenomenon held, she would be front and center to find out.

Squeezing her way through, Iriel entered the vast cavern, overlooking the lake of elixir. Golden light emanated from the waters, illuminating the entirety of the cavern which stretched nearly as far as the eye could see. Even at a distance, she could feel the raw power buzzing through the lake, like static crawling over the hairs of her arm.

"Iriel?" her mother-in-law called out from behind. "You better not be exploring without me!" A moment later, Willow slipped through the crevice and stood beside her, staring down at the lake.

"Any chance I could have a lift to the island?" Iriel asked.

Willow smiled. "Just a warning, I still overcorrect sometimes. Might not be the smoothest ride."

Iriel glanced over the ledge. "Better than the alternative."

They wasted no time, flying forward roughly ten feet above the elixir, Iriel clutching Willow like a toddler clutching their mother. In the distance, ripples fluttered across the surface of the lake. The first were far away—nearly imperceptible as they flew—but then the ripples grew closer. Iriel kept an eye on them, but then the ripples stopped. Still, she watched, but no others came. Willow tried to convince her that they were just pockets of air trapped in the earth below the lake, stirring as the bubbles surfaced. Iriel wasn't so certain.

They continued their journey toward the island, which seemed to grow in size as they approached. Soon, their corethreads reappeared, and they touched down on the ground. Now that they were closer, standing atop the surface, Iriel could see that the island's surface had a shine to it, as if it had been polished or hewn out of a single, monstrous slab of onyx. And it was barren, nothing but wet stone and rubble with the occasional remains of fallen stalactites.

Iriel turned to Willow as they walked. "Think it's safe to look in threadlight?"

"Absolutely not," she said. "It was bright enough at a distance. I don't know if threadblindness is a thing, but I'd rather not risk it. What I'm really hoping for is some kind of an anchor in the physical world, a source. We never found one at the Convergence, but it doesn't mean there wasn't one. And I'm still not convinced this is a Convergence."

Iriel furrowed her brow. "I don't know. All I see is regular rocks, wet rocks, and broken rocks."

Willow stopped walking and looked at her with a blank face. "I think Chrys' sense of humor is rubbing off on you."

"Rude," Iriel said with a smirk.

They continued moving forward, and Willow pointed ahead to what appeared to be a stalagmite growing out of the ground. As they approached, Iriel saw it more clearly. Four transparent shafts jutting out of the ground, clear as diamond, twisting in a perfect helix and ending at twice the height of a man.

They walked closer, and the air seemed to hum. Sweat ran down

Iriel's back, and her chest tightened. Their pace slowed—there was something about the diamond structure. With each step, Iriel's heart beat faster, a growing fire coming alive within her chest. Warmth flooded her veins. Comfort. Ecstasy. Power.

Her mind filled with the growing buzz emanating from the diamond. Transfixed, mesmerized by the helix, her mind drank in the energy with each step. Power crackled from the ends of her fingers.

It was so close.

She took a step.

It was beautiful. Distant elixir light refracted from the diamond, splitting into a rainbow of color.

A voice called out to her, but it was nothing more than a passing wind.

Another step.

Raw power expanded through her sizzling veins. Pressure building. Energy swelling. Power unending. With this, she could do anything. She could fight the Heralds themselves and win.

She reached out her hand to touch the helix. Tiny bolts of lightning crackled between the diamond structures and her fingers. A stabbing pain pulsed through her arm. But she didn't care. The pain was nothing compared to the deific power consuming her.

As soon as her skin touched the diamond structure, it cracked with a boom.

A wave of energy burst from the helix, launching Iriel away and snapping her back to reality. She tried to right herself as she tumbled through the air, but her veins were colorless, achromic, thread-dead. Panic consumed her. She was already weaker than the others. Anything but her threadlight.

The world around her shuddered. She closed her eyes and embraced the darkness, waiting for her body to crash into the marble stone. But she kept flying back, farther and farther, until she crashed down into the lake. The air forced itself out of her lungs as she fell below the surface. She struggled up, throwing her head above the water and gasping for air.

Iriel tried to remember what had happened, but the memory seemed to blur in her mind. She'd been approaching the helix. The power...she remembered the power. Had she reached it? The memory flickered in her mind, her fingers reaching out, bolts of electricity crackling between. The break.

Willow surfaced from beneath the water, gasping, and Iriel swam to her. Together, they made their way back toward the island, crawling up, then pushing themselves onto the slick surface.

A familiar glow flickered to life in her veins.

Iriel quickly opened herself to threadlight and felt the magic-filled warmth fight off the wet cold. Relief washed over her.

"What did you do?" Willow asked with an air of accusation. "I was screaming your name, and you just kept walking forward. What happened?"

"I don't know," Iriel said. "I couldn't control myself. That *thing* was filling me with more threadlight than I've ever felt. It was like a magnet, until the threadlight was ripped away from me."

"I lost mine as well." Willow looked down at her multi-colored veins. "Thank the Father of All that it's back. Whatever you did somehow disrupted our theoliths. But the elixir was unaffected. How curious."

"How is that possible?"

Willow shrugged, turning to look at the diamond helix in the distance. "I don't know. I need to think more about it, unless..."

"What?" Iriel pressed.

"No," Willow said quickly. "Even if it were true, the outcome is the same."

"Willow," Iriel said with a glare. "What is it?"

The older woman clenched her jaw and glanced toward the helix. "Some believe threadlight comes from their god, the Lightfather or the Father of All. That the gods either create threadlight and offer it to the world, or that threadlight is their essence emanating out from their bodies. But there are others who believe that there is a different source. A Provenance."

Together, they stared in silence, contemplating the possibility.

"*The* Provenance?" Iriel repeated, knowingly. "You think that helix is the source of all threadlight? What if you're right?"

Willow backed away. "Then this is a very dangerous place to be."

CHRYS WATCHED as Iriel squeezed herself through the gap in the wall, side stepping through the fracture and *pulling* herself as she ran along the wall. Honestly, he was just glad she was alive. After the temporary loss of threadlight, he had feared the worst.

"What happened in there?" he asked. "We were resting when a gust of air came bursting from the fracture. Roshaw and I lost our threadlight for a moment."

"He's being way too nice about this," Roshaw said. "What he means to say is that we were both scared out of our damn minds. What the hell did you two do in there?"

Before Iriel could respond, Willow arrived, leaping from the fracture in the wall and landing beside them. Her clothes were as drenched as Iriel's, and her hair was a mess, but the serious look on her face was enough to quell any comments.

"We need to seal off that fracture," Willow said firmly. "Stuff it with rocks, cave it in, doesn't matter. We have to make sure no one else can get in."

"As much as I love to repeat myself," Roshaw said with a rasp to his voice. "What the hell did you two do in there?"

Iriel wiped away some water from her cheek. "We found something. And we're not certain, but we think it might be—Lightfather, but it sounds absurd when you say it aloud—we think we found the source of threadlight."

"The source..." Chrys repeated. Before he finished, his eyes lit up. "*The* source. You found the Provenance?"

Footsteps echoed from the tunnel leading to the Endless Well. Chrys and the others turned, hands instinctively reaching for their blades.

Moments later, Laurel and Asher came barreling through the photospore-lit cave. "The coreseal!" she shouted. "It's gone!"

"Slow down," Chrys said, holding up his hands. "What do you mean it's gone?"

Laurel glanced back at the tunnel just before Chrys heard another set of footsteps. "I don't know. We were in the Endless Well getting some water, and something happened. Alverax lost his threadlight, and I lost my Asher-vision. When it came back, the coreseal was gone."

"Damn," Roshaw said, running both hands over his face. "If that's true, let's get the hell out of here before it returns."

With that, Roshaw and Willow shared a look and raced off toward the tunnel. They passed Alverax halfway there, but the young man stopped and waved them on, bending down and taking in deep breaths.

Asher growled, and Laurel turned back to Chrys. "He's right. We don't know how long the coreseal will be gone. We should get out while we can. There's nothing we can do for the world while we're down here."

Chrys took one more glance back at the fracture above the elixir pool. If they had a chance to get out, they should take it. But what if they truly had found the Provenance. That kind of energy. Could they use the power? What if they could use it to travel back in time again? What if they could fix things?

Finally, Chrys nodded. "This might be our only chance to get free."

Laurel and Asher nodded in unison and took off.

He turned to Iriel. "You need to be more careful. You could have died in there."

"And you could have died fighting a horde of corespawn," she replied.

"That was different."

Iriel stepped over and picked up Aydin from a pile of blankets on the ground. "It was different because it was you. You're allowed to do dangerous things. All I'm allowed to do is carry the baby."

Chrys shook his head. "That's not true."

She didn't even look at him. "We need to go."

Chrys followed Iriel through the cave toward the Endless Well with a hollow sense of hope in his core. With all that they had been through, he'd begun to see that hope could not be trusted. Hope was a drifter, waving with one hand and stabbing with the other. This time, picturing the bright coreseal stretching across the expanse of the Well, Chrys tried not to let his hopes rise too high.

24

Alverax stood beside Laurel and stared up into the Endless Well. To his side, he could feel Asher's fur brushing up against his forearm. Maybe it was simply because they were close in age, but he'd grown fond of Laurel. She was strange, but in a good way. While on the *Pale Urchin*, she'd hardly said a word to him, but her companionship had meant everything to him. He would never forget those quiet days.

"They're taking a long time," Laurel said.

The subsequent silence grated on Alverax. His father and Willow had gone up to the surface to make sure there was no trap waiting for them. The only problem with their plan was if the Heralds were there waiting, Roshaw and Willow would be dead before they could share their findings. Every second that passed pecked at the raw fear in Alverax's heart. He'd lost his father once; he wasn't going to let it happen again. Not without a fight.

A moment later, Roshaw and Willow came flying down from the heights of the Endless Well—perfectly healthy and alive—and landed with a thud on the rocks beside the water.

Alverax took a step toward them. "Is it safe?"

"It's bright," Roshaw said, blinking and opening his eyes wide as he waited for them to adjust to the darkness.

Willow ignored Roshaw and gave a nod to Laurel. "Coreseal is gone, and there's no army up there waiting for us...yet. As soon as Chrys and Iriel get here, we should go."

"Chrys can get up by himself," Roshaw said. "We should go now."

Willow scowled. "If the coreseal reappears and they're stuck down here without us, they'll die. We stick together. All in or all out."

Asher gave a growl of agreement.

"I agree with Willow," Laurel said. "The pack stays together."

Alverax nodded. "What she said."

Roshaw shrugged, looking up toward the speck of light overhead. "Obviously I don't want them to die alone down here. I just wish they would walk a little faster."

The five companions stood in silence, staring up, praying for the coreseal not to reappear.

Alverax rubbed a hand over his shoulder, not quite able to scratch the itch on his spine where the large scar stretched below his neck. It had been bugging him since they got back from the Convergence. He remembered the first time Jisenna had come to his door, claiming that she'd come looking for a mysterious boy with a scar on his back. Later, she'd told him that he was scarred inside and out. Now, far away from Felia, deep beneath the ground where not even the Moon's Little Sister could see, the biggest scar of all was the one left by her death.

Footsteps broke the silence, and everyone turned to see Chrys and Iriel jogging down the tunnel, Aydin in arm. Willow waved them over, and Iriel offered Alverax a smile as they finished their approach.

"How's it look up there?" Chrys asked with threadlight swirling beneath his skin. "I don't see the coreseal."

Willow nodded. "It's still gone."

"Clear up top as well," Roshaw added. "At least when we checked."

Chrys clenched his jaw, looking up through the vast shaft of the Endless Well. "Then let's be quick, before that changes."

"All together," Willow said.

"I'll carry Iriel," Chrys said in agreement. "Roshaw, you bring Alverax. And mom, you have Laurel and Asher."

As they gathered close together, Alverax felt a rush of nerves flow through him. An hour ago, they thought they would never leave the caverns. Now, they were moments away from sunlight, fresh air, and freedom.

With a pinch of Obsidian, they were all soon floating in the air. Roshaw, Chrys, and Willow each surged a wave of Sapphire and Emerald, and soon the three clusters were blasting up through darkness, watching a single speck of light grow into open skies. Air rushed over Alverax's hopeful smile as they flew. As they approached the top, the blindingly bright skies glared down upon them. Alverax lifted a palm to cover his eyes, squinting as they left the darkness of the cave. The warmth of the sun kissed his skin. He hadn't realized how much he'd missed it.

And damn, the air smelled wonderful.

Willow landed first, dropping Laurel and Asher onto the patchy grass as their corethreads reappeared. Then Chrys and Iriel, landing softly beside them, both immediately surveying the surrounding jungle and cliffside. Alverax and Roshaw were the last to touch ground.

The first thing Alverax noticed was that the wastelanders who had died to the *pintalla mox* were still there, though he felt a hint of guilt at those whose bodies had shattered during the fight with the Heralds. Maybe it was just the angle, but it seemed like there were more of them now, each kneeling in clusters like stone statues.

"We should get out of the clearing," Chrys said, gesturing toward the jungle. "We can head west, avoid the dead. Laurel, do you see anything?"

She shook her head. "Nothing. Smells different, though."

"Not sure how to take that," Chrys said. "Either way, we should move. Conserve your threadlight. Laurel, you and Asher are by me. Keep your eyes open. Everyone else, stay close."

Alverax followed, feeling more stressed out than he'd ever felt in his life. Something about a quiet jungle sent a chill up his spine. The trees had always felt so alive, creatures scuttling over mossy limbs, insects darting back and forth across the swampy pools. Now, the only sound was boots stomping on ferns and splashing in puddles. The only movement was their own. Barely a breeze to tickle the leaves.

They tramped through the jungle, making their way west toward some goal that Alverax realized he wasn't quite sure of. But the mountains were west, and that meant Alchea. He hoped that was their destination.

Suddenly, Laurel stopped and Chrys raised a hand, gesturing for the others to lower themselves. Chrys whispered something to Laurel, and she snuck off with Asher while the others stayed hidden amongst the jungle foliage.

A minute later, Laurel returned, standing tall as she strode through the vines. "It's empty."

"No one?" Chrys asked.

"Not a single wastelander in the whole city. And their scent has already started to fade. They've been gone for maybe two days."

Roshaw stood up and looked through the trees toward Kai'Melend. "Where the hell did they go?"

"Tracks go west," Laurel said, gesturing with a nod of her head.

Willow stepped toward the wastelander city, a puzzled look on her face. "I thought they couldn't leave because of the mutation? What changed?"

"They can leave," Chrys said. "They just can't leave for long. I still don't like it. What if they found a way to sustain themselves? They could take an entire army over the mountain."

"Shit." All eyes turned to Roshaw. "The ataçan weren't at the waterfalls. They must be with the army."

"Gods and monsters," Willow said quietly. "Alchea wouldn't stand a chance."

"Unless someone warns them," Laurel added.

When they'd first escaped out of the Endless Well, the bright sun and fluttering breeze had instilled a sense of victory. A relief. It was so easy to relish in the small win that Alverax had forgotten about the greater danger. The Heralds didn't care about a few threadweavers. They wanted chaos. They wanted bloodshed. They wanted mankind to pay for their imprisonment. In a way, it was like Felia all over again. As soon as Alverax was free of his cell, a war was standing by waiting to be fought.

"Oh no," Alverax whispered, realizing a dark truth.

Roshaw turned to his son. "What is it?"

"The corespawn," Alverax said. "The army of corespawn fled through the Convergence. They're in the Fairenwild with no coreseal to keep them contained. Alchea could get hit from both sides."

"Dammit," Chrys said, gritting his teeth with a fire in his eyes. "There's no way we can beat the Heralds there. They can fly farther and faster than we can. But the wastelanders can't fly. And if this city is empty, then they have all of their young with them. They'll be slow. If we move quickly, we may be able to sneak past and warn Malachus before the full army arrives."

The group grew quiet, letting the plan sink in. Alverax watched them each digest the words. Roshaw, scowling but nodding his head. Willow, calculating their odds. Laurel, feet ready to take off at a run as soon as they said the word. Iriel, holding her child with a pained expression in her eyes.

She was the first to break the silence. "Then what?"

Chrys looked to his wife.

"After we warn them," Iriel clarified, "then what? We couldn't even beat the corespawn, let alone a wastelander army flanking from the other side. What's the point of going there if we can't win? Even if we destroy all of the corespawn, then kill the entire population of wastelanders, including the ataçan—which I'm sure is not so easily done—then what? The Heralds can't die. They'll kill us all eventually. The only Amber threadweaver we have is Aydin, and we have years before he can create any kind of coreseal by himself, if we even figure out how to do that. What's the goal?"

"We have to try," Laurel said angrily.

"No," Chrys said. "She has a point. We need a plan. There has to be another way to stop the Heralds."

Willow perked up. "I think Iriel already said it. The Heralds. Their immortality comes from their lifelight bonds to the wastelanders. If we killed all of the wastelanders, they'd be vulnerable."

"Hold on," Roshaw said. "We're not killing all of the wastelanders."

"Do you have a better idea?" Willow asked.

Roshaw threw up his hands. "We *just* started thinking of plans! Holy hell. The first plan is hardly ever the best, especially when it's genocide! We have time. If we head toward the Everstone Mountains, we can figure out a better plan along the way."

Alverax knew that his father had a soft spot for the wastelanders, despite his imprisonment. And it did seem unfair to sentence them to death because of a path they did not choose for themselves. But what was the alternative? Was the choice really who would die? The humans or the wastelanders? As long as the Heralds' immortality was tied to the lives of the wastelanders, could there be another way?

"I understand your hesitation," Chrys said. "This is no one's first choice. But it may be the only one we have."

"We're not—"

"Roshaw," Willow said, cutting him off with a hand on his shoulder. "We'll figure out the best option as we move. Like you said, we have time. And Chrys, just because we have one option doesn't mean that we stop searching for others. Too many lives are at stake. We cannot settle for anything less than the best path."

Chrys nodded, though Alverax could see a hint of annoyance in his lips. "Thank you, and I agree. Let's scavenge what we can from Kai'Melend. Food, water, weapons, anything you can carry. We leave in an hour."

The group advanced into the wastelander city, eyes darting back and forth as they searched for any sign of life, but the only movement came from the long-armed creatures swinging back and forth on vines in the canopy and the occasional bird in flight. Alverax meandered over to one of the lower huts while Roshaw and Willow flew up to homes built higher in the trees.

He pushed open a door—more like a curtain—made of two dozen braided vines that hung from the roof, then stepped into the small hut. There was only one room, with no furniture or decor. When he looked up, he saw a drawstring hanging from the center of a hammock that was tied up on the roof. He pulled it, and the hammock dropped down, secured on each end from one corner of the room to the other. While lowered, it filled up most of the hut. Alverax pushed open the dangling vines in the doorway, looked to see if anyone was watching, then set down the Midnight Watcher and jumped up onto the hammock. Despite the stature of the wastelanders, the hammock was plenty large for his height. Then he realized that there was only one hammock in the hut, which meant it was probably a shared bed for multiple wastelanders.

After a few minutes, guilt poked its head out from beneath the fatigue, and Alverax jumped down from the hammock. He grabbed his sword and moved on to the next hut, which was more of a rectangular shape with a solid—though thin—wooden door. Inside, he found a much larger space, with two hammocks tied off on the roof, several wooden boxes, and a bead curtain dividing the room at its center. He stepped in, pushed aside the beads, and moved to the largest of the boxes on the far side of the hut. Inside, he found a mortar and pestle and two crude daggers tucked beneath a pile of skimpy wastelander clothing. He placed the weapons into his pack and continued on. The other boxes in the room were empty.

Alverax walked out of the hut and back into the center of the wastelander city where a large statue of an ataçan stood on a raised pedestal.

Not far away, Laurel and Asher were standing at the edge of the city, scanning the surrounding jungle with suspicion in their eyes. Chrys dropped down from a rope bridge a few strides away and joined them.

As Alverax approached, he saw that the head of the statue had been knocked off, crudely, with jagged edges jutting from the neck where the stone had shattered. A few paces away, the head lay in pieces, half-submerged in a murky puddle. Alverax stepped over and bent down, running a hand along the stone tusks. It was far from high quality craftsmanship but, in a place like Kai'Melend, he was surprised to see any kind of art at all. Maybe his father was right about the wastelanders.

Suddenly, Asher and Laurel growled behind him, and Alverax turned quickly, hand reaching over his shoulder. Before he touched the hilt of the Midnight Watcher, the earth shook, and an ataçan four times the size of a man with a broken tusk and four thick arms landed with an explosion of water. The earth shook a second time as the beast released a guttural roar, throwing all four fists high overhead and slamming down toward Laurel.

Bonds of Chaos
25

THREADLIGHT BURNED IN CHRYS' chest, streaming from his heart through his arms and legs as he threw up a threadlight barrier. Xuçan's massive hands struck the invisible shield, creating a ripple of force that shook the ground, sending shivers through Chrys' bones. He glanced over to check on Laurel, but, instead of finding a scared girl clutching the chromawolf, he saw she was already back on her feet, knife in hand, the tips of her boots digging into the dirt.

Asher attacked first, dashing forward and biting at Xuçan's thick leg. Laurel joined him, running and jumping, stabbing out at the ataçan's thigh. But then Xuçan's fist swung in a wide arc, backhanding Laurel and sending her tumbling through the air. Asher howled as Xuçan reached down and ripped the attacker off his leg, blood falling from the wound, and tossed the chromawolf aside.

Chrys stood alone in front of the massive ataçan and looked at the muscle rippling from every part of Xuçan's body. The extra pair of broad arms. The half-broken tusk. The spikes running down from his neck to his back. There was no wonder the wastelanders worshiped him as much as they did Relek and Lylax. Chrys reached for his dagger, until he remembered that it was gone. He'd found a blowgun in one of the huts and stashed it in his pack, but he didn't have any darts. Weapon or not, if they fought, Chrys was certain he would lose.

He remembered their previous meeting, bowing down and presenting the et'hovon honeycrystals. He remembered their words. Their shared disdain. The respect.

Chrys stood a little taller, raising his voice, and hoped that the chief of the ataçan would remember too. "Xuçan!"

Thick nostrils flared as the ataçan froze, looking down at him, a low growl reverberating from his throat. Xuçan's voice rumbled in Chrys' mind. *I know you, human.*

Chrys spoke slowly, carefully. "I am he-who-does-not-cower."

Xuçan leaned forward, bringing his face level, hot steam pouring over Chrys' cheeks with each of the ataçan's breaths. *No, you are not.*

The hairs on Chrys' arms stood at attention as if paying respect to the great chief of the ataçan.

You are he-who-sacrifices-all, Xuçan continued.

Chrys felt a wave of relief, knowing that he remembered their conversation, too.

Xuçan pulled back and looked to the side where Iriel, Willow, and Roshaw stood beside Alverax, watching in fear. On the other side, Laurel groaned as she pushed herself back to her feet, stumbling over to Asher who lay defeated in a puddle, chest heaving up and down. Xuçan pointed at them with a thick finger. *Those have perverted the bond. They are not welcome here.*

For the first time, Chrys made the connection. Whatever bond Laurel and Asher had formed was the same bond the wastelanders made with the ataçan. He remembered Xuçan's words the first time they met, when he referred to Relek as "he-who-perverts-the-bond." But Relek's bond was different; he used lifelight to bind his soul to others. Unless it *was* the same.

Chrys looked up at Xuçan and remembered that the chief had never bonded with a wastelander, despite having lived for hundreds of years. "They have not perverted the bond," Chrys said, an idea forming. "The bond that Laurel and Asher share is pure, mutually accepted. They are not like Relek."

DO NOT SPEAK HIS NAME! Xuçan's voice thundered in Chrys' mind as the chief beat at his chest with clenched fists. *They-who-pervert-the-bond have taken everything.*

Chrys recalled the empty rocks beside the waterfall at the Endless Well, where the ataçan had once been. "They took the others. They took your family."

Xuçan let out a single, pained whimper. *I could not save them. The collars. They-who-pervert-the-bond have grown too strong.*

"We are on our way to stop them," Chrys said, putting on an air of confidence.

They cannot be stopped.

Chrys tipped his head. "There is always a way." An idea blossomed in his mind. "Come with us, Xuçan. We can stop them together."

A series of raspy grunts came from deep in Xuçan's chest. *I will not bond a human.*

"That's not—"

For three hundred years, I have waited for the true King of the Hive. He-who-perverts-the-bond is not he. You are not he. No human can be.

"I am not asking to bond with you," Chrys said, though now that the idea had been spoken, a part of him wondered if there was something there. "They have taken everything from you. There is nothing left here. Come with us, and we will find your family. Together, we can stop they-who-pervert-the-bond."

Xuçan huffed and glanced over to the others.

Laurel and Asher had recovered, though both had taken a bit of a beating, and the others stood together in a cluster with Roshaw in front, holding them back. Chrys noted that Iriel had already managed to equip her palmguards.

"It's not too late," Chrys said as he turned back to Xuçan. "You can still save them."

As the words left his mouth, he wasn't sure whether they were for Xuçan or for himself. The people of Alchea—his people—were in danger. They needed every advantage they could get if they were going to stop the Heralds.

Xuçan slammed his fists on the ground, then leaned in close one more time. *He-who-sacrifices-all,* his voice boomed. *It is a good name. This is the hour of sacrifice.* He pointed a finger out toward the cluster of people. *I would speak to that one, alone.*

Chrys raised a brow, unsure which of the four he was referring to. He thought it might be Roshaw, since he was the only other that Xuçan had met before, but decided that it was better to verify. "Which one?"

The young male.

Alverax? A darkness grew in the pit of Chrys' stomach. Why would the chief of the ataçan want to speak with Alverax? He was an Obsidian threadweaver, but so were Chrys, Willow, and Roshaw. Maybe it was the Midnight Watcher. Could Xuçan have some need for the obsidian blade?

Chrys took a few steps toward the others, raising his voice. "Alverax, Xuçan wants to speak with you."

"With me?" Alverax said, pointing a finger at his chest.

Roshaw stepped forward. "No way in hell I'm letting that happen. He'll tear him apart."

"I don't think he means him harm," Chrys said, understanding Roshaw's protective thoughts. "It should be safe as long as Alverax doesn't do anything stupid."

"It's okay," Alverax said, stepping out from behind his father and approaching Chrys. "Did he say what he wants to talk to me about?"

Chrys shook his head as he stepped toward Alverax. As they crossed paths, he leaned in close and lowered his voice. "I invited him to fight the Heralds with us. Don't say their names. He calls them *they-who-pervert-the-bond*. They took his family. He hasn't answered whether he will join us yet. Try to convince him. Having Xuçan on our side could change the tide."

Alverax looked up at the massive ataçan. "No promises."

Chrys took a deep breath. "Good luck."

ALVERAX TOOK a few more steps toward Xuçan and felt his heart racing in his chest. The massive ataçan reminded him of the corespawn monstrosities, just a little more...solid.

He had no idea what to expect. Why did the ataçan want to speak to him? Laurel seemed the more obvious choice, since her animal bond seemed similar to what Roshaw had taught him about the ataçan bond. Why not his father, who had lived in the Wastelands and understood the culture and language?

What was special about Alverax?

You are not like them, a voice thundered in his skull, bouncing off the walls of his mind with a deep bass.

Alverax looked up and saw a pair of deep-set ataçan eyes, shrouded by the cliff of his brow, staring down at him. Somehow, when Roshaw had explained that Xuçan could speak telepathically, the voice he had imagined had seemed more primitive. But the voice he heard was clear and confident.

Xuçan leaned forward, knuckles flanking either side of Alverax as he examined his body. *What are you?*

The question startled him, both the voice and the words. "I'm, um, Alverax. My name is Alverax Blightwood."

No, the voice rumbled, sending a chill up Alverax's spine. ***What are you?***

Alverax swallowed and glanced back at Chrys, remembering his words. It wasn't the first time someone had told him not to do anything stupid. "I'm not sure I understand. I'm an Obsidian threadweaver?"

Xuçan let out a huff of air, then gestured toward Chrys and the others. *You are like them, but not. You are different. Tell me, he-who-does-not-understand,* ***what*** *are you?*

Still, Alverax had no idea what Xuçan was talking about. How was he any different than the others? If his father wasn't there, it might have been because he was Felian. If not for Chrys, Willow, and his father, it might have been his Obsidian threadlight. He was the tallest of the group, but surely that's not what the chief of the ataçan was referring to.

"I'm sorry," he said, bowing his head. How could he answer a question he didn't understand? "I am no different than the others."

LIES! Xuçan roared, standing up on his feet and beating his chest. As he came back down, all four fists slammed into the dirt, sending tremors through the ground and ripples through the swamp water. *You are not like them! They are human. You are not!*

Alverax startled back, hands trembling. "I don't... I *am* human." He pointed a finger over his shoulder. "My father is right there."

Hmmm, the voice boomed in his mind. *Perhaps. But you are not* ***all*** *human.*

His head whipped around to look at his father. His eyes wide. His mouth hung open. This wasn't happening. It wasn't possible. His mother had... She was from a small farm outside of Alchea. She wasn't...what? Inhuman? Was that even possible? No. Xuçan was an animal. Intelligent, powerful, but still just an animal. And he was trying to get into Alverax's head.

Roshaw took a few steps toward him. "Is everything okay?"

"I...I think he's trying to mess with my head." Alverax glanced over his shoulder, hoping Xuçan hadn't heard that. "I don't know what the hell is going on. He says I'm not human. Wants to know what I am."

And there it was, the compression in Roshaw's chest, the flicker of fear in his eyes, the pursing of his lips. Even before he said a word, Alverax knew something was wrong.

"I...I tried to tell you," Roshaw whispered, tears welling up in his eyes. "I wanted to, but I didn't know how."

Alverax took a step toward him, a hint of anger boiling beneath his skin. "Tried to tell me what?"

He remembered the night around the fire in the desert chasms north of Cynosure. His father had wanted to tell him something. But neither of them was ready. Neither of them was strong enough to open whatever chest the truth had been stuffed inside. Now, Alverax knew. In a wave of understanding, the truth was clear as day. And yet, he still needed to hear his father say it.

Roshaw glanced back toward the others with a look of shame in his eyes, then sighed as he turned back to Alverax. "Your mother was a wastelander."

The swamp spun around Alverax, a twisting vortex of overwhelming reality. His knees quivered. His chest tightened. And his stomach filled with rotten truth. A truth that hovered in the air like a noxious cloud.

He was half wastelander.

"I should have told you ten years ago," Roshaw said, stepping toward him. "But you were such a happy kid. I didn't want to take that away from you."

Alverax took a step back, not caring that he was moving toward the massive chief of the ataçan. The world seemed to cloud over, a dark film blurring his vision so all he had were the words ringing in his ears.

Roshaw continued. "Before you were born—when I worked for Jelium—he would send me out scouting, exploring the world outside of Cynosure. The deserts, the mountains, the chasms. Looking for trade routes or treasures. I loved it, being in the wilderness, seeing places no one else had seen. But then I met your mother.

"On the outskirts of a small wastelander village. She found me as interesting as I found her. We spent the better part of a year together in secret, learning, teaching each other our languages. I never planned...didn't even think it was possible for her to get pregnant. I wish it hadn't been. I didn't lie when I told you she died giving birth. I just didn't tell you why." Roshaw rubbed his hands through his hair, his eyes a mix of desperation and sorrow. "Please, say something."

What *could* he say?

He was half wastelander.

He wasn't human.

The anger boiling inside him crescendoed, flaring in his chest. What the hell did it matter anyway? He'd already thought he was half Felian, half Alchean. Did it make any difference that he wasn't? Did it change who he was? He was still the idiot who broke the coreseal, fell in love with an empress, killed a thousand corespawn, and watched everyone around him die. Who a man is at his core has nothing to do with those who came before him. It may change where you are and who you know, but the true crux of a man is defined by him alone.

And yet...

He turned back to Xuçan and lifted his chin. "My father is human. My mother was a wastelander."

Xuçan's lips snarled into an eerie semblance of a smile. His voice thundered in Alverax's mind. *I have long waited for the true King of the Hive, one who would gather the tribes. He-who-perverts-the-bond claims to be this, but herding is not the same as gathering. Perhaps I have been wrong all along. Perhaps I was not meant to find the King of the Hive. Perhaps I am meant to make him.*

The chief of the ataçan knuckle-walked, stopping with his lower fists placed on either side of Alverax. Their eyes met, unblinking, then Xuçan placed one of his enormous hands atop Alverax's head, wrapping thick fingers around his skull. But rather than fear, Alverax felt a warmth spark in his chest.

It grew, and as it grew, the world grew darker. The jungle faded away, trees reduced to shadow, vines turning to strips of blackness. The ground vanished. He and Xuçan alone existed, hovering like two gods in the dark of the sky beyond. The strength of a dozen men flooded through his body. His veins expanded. His muscles tightened. Darkness slid through Xuçan's veins, and shadows enveloped them both until Alverax found himself alone.

Abandoned in a sea of black.

As the darkness filled his vision, he heard Xuçan's final words.

We are one.

Bonds of Chaos — 26

When Alverax awoke, the world was shrouded in night, and a sky filled with twinkling stars stared down at him. Before he could stop himself, his eyes drifted toward the Moon's Little Sister. It seemed smaller with the sprawling mountains on the horizon beneath it.

He shifted his weight and found that he was curled up in some kind of padded, furry blanket. But when he lifted himself, he realized it was actually Xuçan's thick arm.

The bond.

There, deep inside his core, Alverax could feel it. He reached out with his mind, touching the source of the bond.

Good, Xuçan's voice sounded in his head. *You are awake.*

Alverax sat up and looked around. They were camped in a valley at the base of the mountain near a small stream just outside of the Wasteland swamps. Tall grass whistled in the wind, lit by the light of a full moon. Small embers still burned from a long-dead fire, and a small fish with a flat face lay on a pile of nearby rocks. His father and the others were asleep.

As he pushed himself to his feet, he realized how hungry he was. "How long was I out?"

Three days, Xuçan said. *The humans left you food in case you awoke. The fish was cooked by the others.*

Alverax walked over to the embers and put his hands close to feel the small amount of warmth that remained. On the grass beside the rocks, there was a small wastelander knife that Alverax picked up and used to cut into the fish, removing the head and bones. As he bit into the flesh, he was careful to remove any thin bones that remained, then devoured every last bite, despite it being cold and in dire need of a bit of his grandfather's seasoning.

Once he was finished, he stepped back over to Xuçan. "So, we're bonded now?"

We are.

"And what exactly does that mean?"

The massive ataçan shifted his weight, using his lower arms to support himself. *Our lives are tied together. Your strength is my strength. My strength is yours. If one of us dies, the other dies with them.*

Alverax pursed his lips. "That sounds like a bad deal for you."

Yes, Xuçan said flatly. *There is a reason I have never taken the bond.*

"So why did you?" Alverax asked. "I mean, I know it's too late, but Chrys really would have been a better choice."

He is human.

Alverax wanted to clarify, but there was something about the way Xuçan said it that seemed final, so he left it alone. "So the reason you chose me is because I'm half-wastelander?"

Xuçan let out a series of animalistic grunts. *The wastelanders believe they are a hive, like the et'hovon. When we find them and show them our bond, they will name you the King of the Hive. They will obey you, and they will release my family.*

It all made sense now. Just like in Felia, where the generals used Alverax as nothing more than a figurehead, Xuçan wanted the same. A tool to win a war. The only problem was that being a figurehead always demanded more responsibilities than just standing there.

"How did they take the other ataçan?" Alverax asked. "If your family is anything like you, I can't imagine they went without a fight."

Mmm, Xuçan grunted. *It is true that my family refused to go with them. Those-who-pervert-the-bond used threadlight to bind and collars to control.*

"Collars?" Alverax repeated, wondering what kind of collar could control an ataçan. "They put collars on your family? If we can get them off, would your family be free?"

Yes, Xuçan said with a single nod.

Alverax cocked his head to the side and raised his brows. "That seems doable. We just have to find them." He looked over and saw that his father was stirring.

I can feel them, Xuçan said. *But they are still too far. I cannot speak with them.*

"I'm sorry." Alverax knew what it was like to lose family. "We're going to find them, and then we're going to free them. I promise." The great ataçan nodded as he looked to the west. "Hey, Xuçan, if the wastelanders name me King of the Hive, what does that mean to them?"

You will be their new god. Xuçan said it with such casualness that Alverax nearly missed the enormity of the statement.

"What about Relek and Lylax? Aren't they currently their gods?"

Yes, Xuçan said. *The Hive will be yours, and they will expect their new god to destroy the old gods.*

"That's all?" Alverax said.

It will not be easy.

"I know," Alverax said with a laugh. "I was being sarcastic."

We do not have sarcastic in the Wastelands. This must come from your human side.

"I guess so."

Alverax looked over and saw his father pushing himself up. The old man looked over and saw Alverax awake, and his eyes lit up.

Based on the rising light, Alverax guessed it would be morning soon. The others would wake up, and they would be off. But truth be told, he didn't want to talk to his father. Roshaw had a hundred chances to tell Alverax the truth, even after that night in the canyons. The only reason he admitted it now was because the issue had been forced. Did he think Alverax was too immature to handle the truth? Or maybe Roshaw was embarrassed. He should be, after nearly two decades of lies.

Lies. The word hit Alverax like a slap in the face. After the canyon, Iriel had told him what happened at Jelium's complex. Supposedly, Jelium had mentioned some kind of *prized possession* that Roshaw had brought from the Wastelands when he used to work for him. Something he'd withheld for himself. What if that was...Alverax?

Roshaw came and sat beside him. "You're awake."

"I'm awake," Alverax said halfheartedly.

"Look," Roshaw said, his shoulders heavy with sorrow. "I should have told you about your mother a long time ago. There's no excuse. I had plenty of chances. I just didn't know how. Or I was scared. I don't know. For a long time, I told myself that you weren't old enough, not strong enough, not ready, or that maybe you never needed to know. But the truth is that I was the one who wasn't strong enough. I didn't know how you would react. And we didn't want you to feel like an outsider."

"Wait," Alverax said, grasping at his father's words. "We? Grandfather knew?"

Roshaw nodded. "I had to tell him. I didn't know what to do with your back."

Alverax paused. "What about my back? You mean the scar?"

"It wasn't a scar," Roshaw said. "You inherited it from your mother, Alverax. They're wastelander gills."

A lead weight dropped in his chest.

"Of course, we didn't tell anyone else," Roshaw continued. "Your grandfather helped me sew it shut, and then we told everyone that a surgeon had to fix a birth defect. They believed, because why wouldn't they. No one knew anything about the wastelanders anyway. Only your grandfather and I knew the truth. But you were safe, and that's all that mattered."

Alverax felt like such an idiot. How had he gone his whole life without understanding such an important part of himself, of his own body? Something he'd always carried with him.

It took only a moment to see the truth of it. He'd always been able to hold his breath longer than anyone. And in the waterways below Felia, he'd taken a breath. In the moment, he'd brushed it aside, grateful only that he'd survived, but it was true. He had breathed underwater. It was also how he'd survived in the river, unconscious, with his face submerged.

He also understood why his father had made the choice he did. If anyone had discovered the truth, they would have studied Alverax for the rest of his life. Alabella would have studied him, experimented on him. What if—it was all coming together—the reason he'd been the only one to survive the ventricular mineral graft was because he was a wastelander?

"Say something?"

"I'm..." Alverax began. "I should be mad. I deserve to be mad. You lied to me my whole life and were too much of a coward to finally tell me when you had the chance." He paused and his eyes softened. "But I'm not. You may not have been a perfect father, but you made a huge sacrifice to protect me. And it even worked. So, yeah, I wish you'd told me a week ago. But I also think it was the right decision not to tell me when I was younger. I was a stupid kid. I would have told everyone. And if I didn't, I would have told Truffles, and he would have."

Roshaw's eyes were swollen, but he choked out a laugh. "Truffles was actually a big part of why I didn't tell you. Never liked him much."

Alverax raised his brows. "You know he slept with Jayla?"

"No!" Roshaw gasped. "While you were together?"

"Well, that's where it gets a bit complicated." Alverax laughed. "I was technically dead at the time. But, it doesn't matter. We're done with Cynosure, and we're done with secrets."

Roshaw's lip quivered. "Thank you. I know I don't deserve to be forgiven."

"Most people we forgive don't deserve it," Alverax said, remembering his grandfather's words. "But some people do."

Roshaw threw his arms around his son and fought back tears. "Thank you."

Alverax felt a warmth flow through him. It felt good to let go. As symbolic as it was, he could feel the burden lifted from his shoulders. It might not matter—they could be dead in a week—but at least he'd walk those days with a lighter load.

"Just so you know," Alverax said, still wrapped in his father's thick arms. "If you ever leave again, I will find you, and I will kill you."

Roshaw let go of their embrace and looked him dead in the eyes. "I am where you are, from now until I die."

Bonds of Chaos

27

When the sun rose and the party awoke, Laurel walked over to greet Alverax. Now that he shared a bond with Xuçan, she felt an even closer connection to him, even if Asher wasn't interested in a friendship with the ataçan.

Laurel and Asher led the way after they all packed up their bags. There was something intoxicating about the fresh mountain air, brisk with hints of lavender riding the breeze. After so long in the Wasteland swamps, Laurel's nose thanked her for the change of venue. It also helped that there were no longer puddles of unknown depth at every turn, no vines hooking at their legs, and no strange creatures laughing at them from the canopy. The mountains felt free, open, and alive. The best part was that she could take off her boots. There was nothing better than the feel of wild grass between your toes.

They followed a valley between two peaks, hoping to avoid the ups and downs as long as they could. Eventually, after stopping at a shimmering lake with fresh deer tracks, they made their way up the mountain. They were getting hungry, and Laurel wanted to hunt, but Chrys convinced them all to stay together and continue on their path. So, they collected berries and kept an eye out for wildlife.

The truth was that Laurel and Asher could have made the entire trip much faster. They were twice as fast as the others—maybe more—and possessed higher endurance. But she knew that it was safer to keep the pack together.

Asher growled, and Laurel turned.

Movement, his voice whispered in her mind.

She crouched low and stalked forward, senses honed in on where the creature had hidden. There was a tall patch of wheat grass beside a small alder tree. She listened, focused. Asher stilled beside her, and they set their feet. Without a word, they leapt forward together just as a small rabbit darted out from behind the wheat grass. Asher bit down, but Laurel's hand was faster. She snatched the rabbit by the back of its neck and lifted it up into the air, celebrating with a howl.

Chrys and the others gave her odd looks but smiled happily when they saw what she'd caught. It wasn't much, not for seven mouths, but it was better than nothing. They took a short break, struck up a fire, and feasted. As soon as the rabbit was cooked, Chrys threw dirt on the embers and watched to make sure it didn't cause too much smoke. They were getting close to where the wastelanders were likely to be. And while the wastelanders weren't likely to be watching their flank, even a passive eye might spot plumes of smoke.

As they continued their hike, they reached the start of the lowest pass. Chrys and Willow claimed to recognize the area, but, more importantly, they found tracks. Not the nearly imperceptible tracks that some game might leave as they sauntered by. These were the tracks of an army. Trampled muddy patches. Stamped dirt from thousands of small feet. And on the outskirts, the unmistakable prints of ataçan.

"They're only a day ahead by the looks of it," Laurel said as Chrys and the others approached.

Chrys nodded, crouching down by the prints. "They do look fresh. Might have passed by as recently as this morning. Laurel, can you and Asher scout ahead?"

"On it."

"Just make sure you're not seen," Chrys added. "And be careful. Better to not find them than to have them find us."

Laurel gave him a nod and crouched down beside Asher. "What do you think? Stay on the trail? Or skirt around the outside?"

Outside, his voice echoed in her mind. *Safer.*

"I agree."

With that, they took off at full speed up a small hill on the left side of the pass about fifty paces from the main path the army had taken. It was mostly grass with wildflowers blooming at sporadic intervals.

Laurel knew that the bond had increased her speed, but as they ran and she kept pace with Asher—even at his fastest—she impressed herself. She couldn't imagine going back to a world without the bond. In a way, she'd become just as dependent on her connection with Asher as she had been with threadlight, replacing one addiction for another. She paused at the thought. No, that wasn't right. Her addiction to threadlight was based on fulfilling her own needs. It was selfish and destructive. Her relationship with Asher was based on fulfilling their needs collectively.

Either way, she loved him. At times, he felt like the only family she had left, even if she knew that her brother was out there somewhere. Probably still in Felia with his nose in a book. Maybe he'd found a pretty girl to settle down with. Maybe he was happy. Or maybe the Heralds had already killed him.

She pushed harder, keeping her focus ahead as she scouted for any sign of the wastelander army. She and Asher both paused beside a sprawling pine tree, taking in its scent. But there was another taste on the wind, something foul that stained the woody aroma like oil dripped on a painting. Laurel shook her head, trying to get the scent out of her nose, but it lingered in the air.

The wind stopped, and the scent faded. Laurel looked to Asher, and they both nodded. They knew that scent.

Continuing their path, they traveled even farther away from the army's muddy tracks and slowed their pace. The wind swirled from the other direction, and they hoped the wastelanders wouldn't smell their approach. Crouching, they stalked through the grass, keeping low and moving from tree to tree.

Finally as they summited a small hill, they saw the source of the scent. A dozen wastelanders knelt in a cluster just off the main road, skin blackened and hard. The *pintalla mox* had claimed them. As they stepped closer, Laurel's heart dropped. Two children knelt in the mix, their hands held together. They were no older than three. So young. So innocent. Statues, undeserving of such an end.

The fact that the plague still continued to claim lives, even this far from Kai'Melend, worried her. But none of the others had shown any sign of sickness yet. Maybe humans were immune? What about Alverax?

Laurel and Asher left the statue-like dead and continued on until they reached a hill overlooking a sprawling valley. At the base, there were thousands upon thousands of wastelanders, short and thin, armed with spears, knives, and blow darts, dwarfed by two dozen ataçan with golden collars around their necks. Laurel and Asher crawled forward, careful not to be seen.

What surprised her the most was seeing the wastelanders living so carelessly. They cooked and laughed, played and slept. Rather than an army, it looked like they'd simply relocated the entirety of their people. Though, with only a few dozen tents erected, it was clear this was not meant to be a permanent home.

Laurel had seen enough. She needed to warn the others. But just as she moved, Asher growled, and she turned around to see the two Heralds flying in from the west. They passed the mountain peak and descended into the center of the camp, where a swarm of wastelanders crowded around them, some bowing, others crossing their arms over their heads. Laurel didn't understand it all, but when the Heralds waved their arms, the swarm of wastelanders parted, and the two gods disappeared into one of the tents.

She committed it to memory and left to gather the others.

BONDS OF CHAOS
28

WATCHLORD THALLIN HAICHESS sat in a carriage, surrounded by books. But they were not just any books. They were private writings, handed down from watchlord to watchlord, preserving the truths that ought not be spoken aloud. Some entries inspired, and others enlightened, words of holy men whose thoughts had shaped the lives of Felians for centuries.

He looked down at his notes where he'd written down a series of quotes that resonated with him.

> Faith is to swing the blade before the enemy moves.
> — Watchlord Eleander

> It is easy to trust the captain when the sea is still.
> — Watchlord Chedai II

> Faith is a new world that cannot be reached by the ship of reason.
> — Watchlord Delathor

The truth that most resounded within him was that these men, whose names had been etched into the very fabric of Felia, were simply that...men. Their journals took Thallin behind the veil of poise to reveal lives filled with trials and victories, inspiration and doubt. On the one hand, it gave him strength knowing that they were able to perform their duties despite their struggles. On the other hand, he now knew that the very foundation of the Heraldic Ancestry was built on cracked stone.

In that moment, seated in a carriage on his way to war, Thallin's mind latched onto a short passage, ironically preached by a man he had known personally and respected above any other. A man who had passed away defending Felia from the corespawn.

> *The Heralds may never return, but this does not mean we cease to preach their coming. Men crave faith. They hunger for purpose and thirst for meaning. If we do not offer a path, they will search for one themselves. But those who wander are likely to find nothing, and there lies darkness. It is our duty to keep our people in the light. To offer a proven path of purpose. I find solace in knowing that we inspire goodness, whether or not our gods ever return. And if our words inspire goodness, are they not good in themselves?*
> —Watchlord Osinan

If only Osinan could have lived a few more days, he would have seen the Heralds for himself. Thallin wondered what the man would have thought. Would he have welcomed them with open arms and a ready blade? Or would he have followed Alverax in abandoning the gods? If he had lived, perhaps Thallin would not have had to kill so many in their name.

Perhaps the Heralds would have made him kill Osinan, too.

The carriage came to a slow and steady stop, the sound of footfall quieting beside them. When Thallin opened the door and exited, he saw the borders of Alchea, cottages and small homes, farmland and fields. Decades of peace cast in the firepit, ready to burn.

Two men strode up beside Thallin, hands clasped behind them as they, too, stared out over what would soon become a battlefield. Generals Nevik and Hish knew Thallin well. They had fought beside him against the corespawn, and they knew his interminable faith in the Heralds. So, despite their initial protests, they were resigned to leading the people of Felia to battle against the people of Alchea.

"The Alcheans are unprepared," General Hish said. "It would be wise to press an advance as soon as possible."

General Nevik nodded. "We could sweep through the city by tomorrow eve. Those who do not surrender would be forced to hide behind the walls of Endin Keep."

"No," Thallin said without offering them a look. "The Heralds have been clear in their command. We pitch our tents and wait for their return. I want a defensive perimeter established for the unlikely event of an Alchean offensive."

"You understand," General Hish said, "that if we establish camp now, we are giving Alchea a huge advantage. Our losses will multiply with every hour we delay. Many of our people will die if their army has a chance to properly assemble."

Finally, Thallin turned to the older man. "Do you not trust the Heralds? Do you think your wisdom greater than the gods? If they told us to bury our weapons, I would issue the command and drop my blade, knowing that the gods will provide a way to victory."

General Nevik bowed his head. "Of course, Watchlord. We will prepare for their return."

As the two generals departed, Thallin thought back to Osinan's words. In the coming days, the men and women of Felia would look upon the death and suffering of war, and they would question the gods. They would look to their Watchlord for answers, for purpose and meaning, and he would look to the Heralds. But Thallin knew he would find no answers there. The gods were opaque in their reasoning.

The only thing Thallin had left was his faith, and he hoped it would be enough.

29 · BONDS OF CHAOS

Chrys and the others followed Laurel to the hilltop overlooking the wastelander camp with a setting sun and cool mountain air to guide them. Clouds wandered through the sky like lost children, the light of the waning moon barely visible through the shadowed veil. Ten thousand wastelanders sat in huddled groups without fires while others patrolled the edges of the site. They were hidden away in a valley between two mountains, and Chrys was fairly certain that Alchea was just over the next ridge. Which made him wonder...what happened to the Alchean patrols?

Since the war, Malachus had always kept a watch on the mountains, despite the fact that the wastelanders had never taken the offensive. Still, the Great Lord had been prudent. Which meant that either Malachus had stopped watching the mountains for threats, or the patrols had been killed. Chrys hoped for the former.

"That's a lot of wastelanders," Roshaw said, lying on his stomach beside Chrys, gazing down over the sprawling army. "What do we do now?"

Chrys motioned for them all to retreat down the ridge a ways so that they could stand without being seen. "We're lucky," he said, addressing the entire group. "They haven't attacked yet, which means there's still time for us to make a difference. What ideas do we have?"

"Aren't you supposed to be the idea guy?" Alverax asked.

"I have some thoughts," Chrys said. "But I want to hear your ideas first."

Laurel turned to Alverax. "I don't think he has any ideas."

"Definitely not," Alverax said with a straight face.

"Not the time." Chrys gave them both a serious look. "People's lives are at stake. If you don't have any ideas, then listen. Let the rest of us figure out how the hell we're going to stop an army from slaughtering our people. We don't know how much time we have before they mobilize. We don't know if they have scouts patrolling out this way. We could be walking into another trap for all we know. If you'd ever been in a real war, you wouldn't be making jokes."

"Chrys," Iriel said softly. "Take it easy. They're kids."

"No, they're not." Chrys tried to breathe, but anger raged within him. "We're all the world has left. No one knows what we know. No one has the power or experience we do. The choices we make in the coming days will determine whether we live or die. Whether nations live or die. The time for growing up has passed."

Chrys looked to each of them individually, a general challenging his soldiers. Alverax and Laurel both stared at the ground. Roshaw and Willow gave each other a side-long glance. But Iriel met Chrys' gaze. A few seconds passed, then ten, then twenty. Even with Aydin in her arms, she was the only one of them who looked ready for war, which sent a shiver of pride through his chest, followed by a pang of guilt.

Maybe she was right, and he was being too harsh. None of them were soldiers. But if ever there was a time to understand the seriousness of the situation, the time was now. So as long as they looked to him as a leader, he would do what had to be done.

"Now," Chrys said. His anger had settled, but he kept the severity in his tone. "Does anyone have ideas on what we can do to stop that army?"

Willow spoke first. "I don't know how to stop the army, but we should also figure out a way to warn Malachus. One of us who can fly could go."

"Absolutely," Chrys said. "In the case that we can't stop the army, the next best thing is to have the Alcheans ready for an attack on their flank."

Roshaw gestured to the ridge. "No army is going to be ready to fight gods and ataçan."

Chrys nodded. "Which is why our first priority is to figure out how to stop the army in the first place."

"We can start by freeing the ataçan," Alverax said, lifting his chastised gaze from the grass. "Without them in the battle, Alchea could probably handle the wastelanders."

Laurel nodded. "Maybe Xuçan could convince the ataçan to fight for us."

Alverax shook his head. "The ataçan won't fight the wastelanders. This isn't their war. And Xuçan says that the wastelanders are just as much captives to Relek and Lylax as the ataçan. So, unless they're provoked, the ataçan will leave the wastelanders alone."

"Unless they're provoked?" Laurel said with her brows raised.

"We're not going to provoke them," Chrys said quickly. "Besides, Xuçan is right. The wastelanders are just as much captives as the ataçan."

"What about the collars?" Willow said. "If the Heralds are controlling the ataçan with some kind of collar, we're going to have to remove them if we want to free the ataçan. Maybe we can use the collars against the Heralds somehow. If they can control the ataçan, maybe they can control a god. Does Xuçan know anything about how they work?"

Alverax shook his head. "They lured him away, bound him with Amber, then collared his family. He watched it happen, and there was nothing he could do."

"That's terrible," Willow said. "We'll figure out how to rescue them. First, we need to get down there and examine the collars ourselves."

Chrys had the distinct feeling that his mother's interest was going to get her killed, and enough people he cared about had already died. As long as he was standing, he wasn't going to let it happen to another. "I'll go tonight while they're sleeping."

"No offense, Chrys," Laurel said. "But when you walk, I can hear it from the other side of the ridge. Asher and I are the scouts. We'll go check it out."

Roshaw took a step forward. "If either of you get caught, they'll kill you on the spot. I can speak their language. It makes sense for me to go in case something happens."

Iriel stepped forward and handed the baby to Chrys. "Can you take him for a minute? My stomach doesn't feel well." Chrys took his son as Iriel walked away from the group, holding her abdomen and waving away his concern.

Alverax raised a hand. "As much as I'd love to help, I don't think this sounds like the right job for Xuçan and me."

"It was my idea," Willow said, eyes bearing down into Chrys. "I'll go. And before you fight me on it, I'm not some old woman you need to protect, Chrys. I have three theoliths. If something happens, I can fly myself out of there."

Chrys clenched his teeth. "It has nothing to do with that. I'm sure that any of you could handle yourselves if you got caught, but we can't get caught. The only advantage we have right now is that they don't know we're here. It's not that we can't get caught. It's that if they even see us, our advantage is lost."

"Then it's settled," Laurel said, raising her hands up. "Asher and I are the least likely to be seen. We'll go."

"I'm going," Chrys said with finality. "One person is less likely to be seen than two. And if it makes you feel better, I'll use a little Sapphire to *drift* as I walk so that I don't make as much noise. I want the rest of you thinking of ideas for how we can stop the army. And try to get some rest while you can."

The others, resigned to his decision, wandered away, back down toward the spot they'd chosen to rest. Chrys handed Aydin over to Willow before she followed the others. He looked in the direction that Iriel had walked. She was beyond his view, the night having grown darker as the clouds over the mountain thickened. Chrys walked back to the ridge, crouched low, and crawled the final stretch. He could hardly see the wastelander camp now. Even the tents had become nothing but blurry splotches on a black canvas.

It was going to be a long night. He would need to wait until well after midnight before making his approach. On the way down, he would need to use as little threadlight as possible. He didn't want his veins glowing, and he didn't want to waste any in case he needed to get out fast. At least until he was a stone's throw from the camp, he would walk. His eyes drifted toward the path he might take, and his heart stopped.

A figure moved stealthily off the beaten path. From his vantage point, he could see clearly. He knew that figure. He knew those shoulders. He knew that gait. There was no question in his mind. He'd been fooled.

Dammit, Iriel.

ADRENALINE COURSED through Iriel's veins as she crept her way through overgrown grass. She knew Chrys well enough to know that he would never let someone else go investigate, so as soon as they'd started to argue, she made her decision. Chrys was a good man, protective, a little too much at times, and he only felt useful when he was sacrificing his own safety for others. But Iriel had always been more suited to stealth work than he was, and she needed this.

While some of her feelings of inadequacy had faded, others had slipped their grimy claws into her skin. For weeks, she'd been the woman in the back, holding the child while the others made the plans. While the others did the *important* work. She was tired of being left behind. She was tired of not helping. And she was tired of hearing Willow talk about the gift of motherhood. It was as though she'd gained one title and lost all others. A mother, and nothing more.

Not tonight.

Tonight, she would prove that Iriel Valerian still had a fire in her chest and threadlight in her veins.

Chrys would be furious, but she didn't care. When she explained how she was feeling and why she did what she did, he would forgive her. He was nothing if not consistent—that's what she loved about him—but she also knew that if she explained beforehand, he still would not have let her go.

As she descended the hill, her foot slipped on a loose rock, creating a small landslide. She reached out, embracing the Emerald in her veins, and *pulled* on each of the falling rocks. One by one, each of the falling pebbles shot through the air and into her hand. By the end, the landslide had stopped, and she had a dozen tiny stones in her palm. She bent down and placed the rocks in a flat place before continuing on.

After several minutes of watchful eyes and careful steps, she reached the bottom of the hill and hid behind a lone pine tree. The captive ataçan were now only a few hundred feet away. With a break in the clouds, she got a better view and counted at least two dozen of the large creatures resting in a pile of limbs. Even at a distance, she noted the difference in size between these and their chief. Xuçan was nearly twice their size.

Iriel looked back up the hill and saw a small head poking out from the vantage point. That meant that Chrys knew, and he hadn't followed her. That was good. He didn't have a reputation for subtlety. As mad as he likely was, he also knew that Iriel was better suited for the job.

A cluster of thick clouds drifted in front of the moon, casting a fog of darkness over the campsite. Iriel took the opportunity and moved. From tree to tree, she weaved her way closer, crouching low behind shrubs and grass until she made her way close to the ataçan.

She hid in a patch of long grass as a pair of wastelanders walked past. She kept silent and still, watching out of the corner of her eye. They came to a stop behind a thick pine tree, and the woman began removing a piece of clothing. Iriel turned away, blushing. At least she knew that they wouldn't be noticing her movements any time soon.

Finally, she reached the cluster of trees closest to the sleeping ataçan and crouched down low behind them. Rather than approaching, she waited patiently. Only a few minutes passed before she saw the wastelander couple return from their late-night escapade.

She'd expected a longer wait...

Iriel looked out over the campsite and was taken aback by how human it all felt. For so long, she'd heard the wastelanders were cannibals, the savages of the east. She'd heard that all they did was eat raw flesh and fight all day. But these people were...people. They may have pointed ear lobes and gills on their backs, but they were still people. She felt guilty for judging Roshaw when the truth of Alverax's origin had come forward. She'd wondered how any man could sleep with a wastelander. Now she saw that, in reality, they were not so different.

As the last vestiges of commotion settled, Iriel moved to take her first step out of cover toward the sleeping ataçan, but just as she did, she saw movement at the entrance to one of the tents in the center of the camp. Out stepped three figures, short and stocky though they were shrouded in the dark of night. An ataçan seemed to appear out of nowhere from the other side of the tent, and one of the wastelanders approached it. Behind them, two taller figures pushed aside the flap and exited the tent. It took only a glance for Iriel to recognize the Heralds' silhouettes. Whatever they had been doing in the tent seemed to be over. Relek's jacket swept back and Lylax's dress trailed behind as the two siblings took to the sky, heading west over the final peak.

The three wastelanders returned to the tent, and the ataçan took a seat outside.

With the Heralds gone, Iriel decided that there would be no better opportunity to approach the collared ataçan. At least if something went wrong, she'd only have an army of wastelanders to deal with.

She stepped out from behind her cover toward the sleeping giants. From what Xuçan had told them, not all ataçan could speak telepathically with humans, but many could. As she approached, watching their massive chests rise and fall with each restful breath, Iriel hoped that—if one of them awoke—it would be one that could hear her.

The closest ataçan had its back to her. Gray hair covered blue-tinted skin, with bright yellow spikes jutting out along its spine. All of the ataçan slept in a pile atop each other, nestled in tightly, limbs entangled in a patchwork of muscle. As Iriel drew closer, she noticed that all of them were sleeping with their hands wrapped around their tusks. It was a small gesture—likely to protect the others—that Iriel found surprisingly compassionate. Xuçan was right; this was a family, and they were captives.

She took the last steps toward the closest ataçan and caught sight of a silver collar wrapped around its neck with gemstones embedded in the metal above the spine. She leaned in, squinting as she tried to get a better look.

Four.

Four gemstones, each a different color.

Iriel cursed as she noticed wet blood beneath the collar. She looked at the others. Every collar was the same. Four gemstones. Blood dripping beneath the silver. What the hell was going on? Xuçan claimed that the Heralds used the collars to control the ataçan because they were not weak-willed like the wastelanders. Aboard the *Pale Urchin*, as they sailed from Felia to Cynosure, Chrys had told her all about his experiences in the Wastelands. He'd told her about the humans that Relek had controlled in the mountains. He'd told her about the lifelight bond that Relek and Lylax had made with the wastelanders. He'd told her about theoliths and what happens when all four are combined.

Stones.

She looked back to the collar.

Green. Blue. Yellow. Black.

Those weren't gemstones; they were theoliths.

She tried to remember everything that Chrys had told her, but all she knew for certain was that, when all four were combined, something changed, which was why Chrys, Willow, and Roshaw still couldn't access lifelight. Which meant if the Heralds were somehow using the power of lifelight to control the ataçan, the collar needed all four theoliths to work. If she could remove one of them, the ataçan would be free.

Slowly, she reached for the collar, leaning over the sleeping ataçan's yellow spikes, extending a single finger toward the silver. A gap in the clouds sent a flicker of moonlight over the tangle of bodies. A nearby ataçan stirred, adjusting its shoulders amidst the mass of gray limbs. Iriel didn't move. She didn't breathe. Her hand hovered in the air like an Alirian statue. A few moments passed, and the clouds blanketed the moon once again.

She breathed and touched the silver, heart pumping as her skin met the binding metal. It was cold, but otherwise felt like any ring she'd ever worn. Still, she knew that the theoliths embedded along its surface were somehow working together to control the ataçan. With her hand still extended, she moved it farther up the collar, reaching for the first theolith, an Emerald like the threadlight running through her own veins. She imagined a similar shard embedded in her heart, feeding the blood that pumped throughout her body.

When her finger brushed against the theolith, she expected a jolt of energy, static, something to denote the power emanating from the stone. But nothing happened. It felt like any other gemstone. Part of her was beginning to wonder if they were theoliths at all, or if there was something else powering the magic of the collars. She stuck a fingernail under the Emerald and tried to lift it out, but it wouldn't budge. She tried again, this time using her thumb. Her arm quivered as she put her weight into it, but it refused to move.

Suddenly, the ataçan rolled over.

She leapt back, barely swooping beneath the giant's thick arm as it flopped down right where she'd been standing. She stood still, frozen, feet spread wide, ready to run. The ataçan's head rolled toward her, eyes closed as it once again wrapped its hands back over its tusks.

Iriel let out a breath and looked at the front of the collar. There was a circular lock embedded in the center. It looked oddly similar to threadlocks she'd seen used in Alchea. If she could get to it, there might be a chance she could open it.

But then the ataçan's eyes opened.

It stared at her, unblinking, dark shadows cast over its pupils from deep set brows.

Iriel didn't move.

It pushed itself up, nostrils flared as it leaned toward her, sniffing, then glancing over at the sleeping wastelanders.

All it would take was one grunt from the ataçan to wake the others. A single call to rouse the entire wastelander army. As she stood frozen, regretting every decision she'd made in the past hour, she lifted a finger to her mouth and whispered the only thing she thought might help. "Xuçan sent me."

The ataçan's thick brows scrunched at the center as it examined her, then a deep voice, female yet gravelly, echoed in her mind. *Xuçan. Alive?*

Iriel nodded enthusiastically, keeping her voice low. "Xuçan is with us beyond the hill. We are here to rescue you."

Cannot, the ataçan said. *Bound. Evil gods.*

"I know," Iriel replied. "I think I can get the collar off, if you'll let me try."

The ataçan eyed Iriel warily, then glanced back over its shoulder at the other sleeping ataçan. Its hand reached up and tugged at the collar, grimacing in pain. *How?*

The single word gave Iriel hope. "There is a piece on the front. Here." She gestured to her own neck, below the jaw. "If I can unlock it, the collar should come off."

Its voice resounded in her mind as it lifted its chin, exposing the silver collar. *Try.*

Iriel stepped forward, slowly, fear swirling through her like a poison. She was lucky that the ataçan had not attacked her, but that luck would not remain forever. If she somehow hurt the ataçan, or if she wasn't able to release the threadlock, the beast was strong enough to kill her in the blink of an eye. She needed to be careful.

As she approached the collar, she smiled. For once, she'd been right. The locking mechanism was a popular—but expensive—style used by many aristocrats with Emerald threadweavers in their employ. A threadlock had no key but was instead unlocked by *pulling* on a small steel disc at the back of the tumbler. Because the disc was the same width as the cylinder, there was no way to engage it without Emerald threadlight, making the lock inaccessible to the majority of the population. Wealthy

Alcheans loved them, because all of the threadweavers worked for them. They were often paired with a more traditional lock for added protection.

But not here. The wastelanders had no threadweavers. No one but Relek and Lylax had the ability to release the lock…until now.

She looked around, checking to make sure no wastelanders were awake and watching, then pulled her collar up and her cuffs down before opening herself to threadlight. Her veins came alive, swirling with veridian power. She leaned forward, trying to find a good angle to see into the lock, but it was too dark.

"Can you turn your neck toward the moon?" she asked. "I need more light."

The ataçan craned its neck to the side cautiously.

Iriel tried again, narrowing her eyes to find the hidden disc. As she stared, the clouds parted for just a fraction of a second, but it was enough to light the cylinder. Iriel *pulled* and felt the weight of the disc shift within the tumbler. The collar clicked, and the section beneath the threadlock split apart. She expected some kind of burst of energy, like when the Convergence had been destroyed, but there was no sign that releasing the lock had done anything.

The ataçan reached back and pulled the collar from around its neck, sneering as it came off. That was when Iriel saw the truth of the design. Four thin needles were built into the collar, embedded on the inside beneath each of the theoliths. Blood dripped from the ends of each as the ataçan brought the collar down and set it on the ground in front of them, staring at it in silence.

"Are you okay?" Iriel asked. "Do you feel different?"

When the ataçan looked up at her, its eyes were filled with tears. Iriel's chest tightened at the sight. She felt a swelling of pride knowing that she'd helped at least one of them, but she also knew that one was not enough. There were many more, and unless she freed them all and helped them get far away, who knew what the Heralds would do.

Please, the ataçan's voice begged. *Help others.*

"We have to be quiet," Iriel said, miming with a finger to her lips. "Can you wake them without making sound?"

A moment later, the entire troupe of ataçan stirred, gray limbs untangling from gray limbs, thick bodies rising from the mass of hair and hide.

Iriel panicked as each of them shifted their dark eyes to her. They moved more gracefully than she would have expected, despite their size. After a short minute, every last one of the sleeping ataçan was awake and looking to Iriel expectantly, and none of the sleeping wastelanders had stirred.

The unbound ataçan nodded to her. *Family. Ready.*

Iriel took a breath and set to work.

One by one, she approached the ataçan, each of which gave her a dubious stare as she worked on the collar's threadlock. But each time, as she completed her work, their expressions shifted to awe and gratitude.

After a dozen had been freed, she heard a shout coming from the camp and whipped her head about to search out the source. A figure stood amidst a throng of sleeping bodies, pointing at Iriel and shouting. The other wastelanders awoke in waves, rising like skeletons in a graveyard, moaning and gesturing wildly one to another.

Stones, Iriel cursed to herself. *We're out of time.*

She moved onto the next ataçan, cursing the darkness for making it so difficult to see the disc in the cylinder. When a shadow fluttered overhead, she startled back, lifting a hand overhead to protect herself. Instead of an attacker, her husband landed beside her, veins glowing with multi-colored threadlight.

"What are you doing here?" she asked, adrenaline coursing through her veins.

"The wastelanders are awake," Chrys said quickly. "Come on. I'll fly us out!"

Iriel took a step back. "Not yet. We need to finish releasing the ataçan." She turned to the first of the freed. "This is my husband. He can help take off the collars. When everyone is free, head over that ridge, and we'll meet up with Xuçan."

The ataçan nodded and grouped up with the others who had been freed.

"Chrys, come on!"

He clenched his jaw but complied.

Together, they worked through the remainder of the threadlocks while the freed ataçan warded off the waking wastelanders. When the last collar fell, Chrys ran to Iriel. She gave one final nod to the first of the freed before Chrys took off into the air. Sapphire and Obsidian shot them into the sky, and Emerald guided their path. When she looked down, the troupe of ataçan were knuckle-running around the edge of the camp while a hoard of wastelanders chased after them.

Iriel's heart dropped when she realized that the entire army was following them toward the ridge...and toward her friends.

BONDS OF CHAOS
30

LAUREL DREAMED OF THE FAIRENWILD. Skyflies fluttering in the canopy. Roses sprouting between rocks alongside a gentle brook. The sound of the waters drifting through the darkness. Her feet wandered of their own accord, forward through familiar paths where shadows danced and bulbous photospores drifted in the staggered wind. She felt drawn to something, a beckoning light in the distance, a silent call.

After her first step, she realized that something was missing. She reached down and felt her pockets, trying to remember what it was. An emptiness. A loneliness. She should not be alone. Never alone. Where was...?

Asher.

She followed the beckoning light, hoping that her companion would be there. She'd made a promise that they would never part, and she would keep that promise no matter the consequence.

As she walked, she felt a tremor in the ground, and she crouched, swiveling on the balls of her feet in search of a source. But there was none; there was only darkness. Still the tremors grew in strength, the ground rattling like an old man's hands.

An odd haze fell over her vision.

She felt something on her shoulder. But when she jerked around to look, there was nothing. The ground shook with greater fervor, and the world blurred even more.

Two invisible hands grabbed her shoulders and shook.

Laurel startled awake, fighting away the dreamland, the home she'd once loved, and breathed in the brisk air of reality. Asher and Willow, with Aydin in her arms, hovered over her, the fear in their eyes laced with a sense of relief. But it wasn't all a dream. Tremors still shook the ground.

She pushed herself to her feet, angry that she'd fallen asleep in the first place. "What's happening?"

Asher nodded to the ridge. *We must move. The army is coming.*

"Gale take me."

"Iriel must have failed," Willow said with a quiver in her lips. "Chrys will find her. We need to go, now."

Alverax and Roshaw stood beside Xuçan, walking toward the ridge. Could they not feel the tremors? Did they not know that an army was coming this way? Laurel had a thousand questions.

"Alverax!" Laurel shouted. "We need to get out of here!"

He looked over to her, a sense of resolution in his eyes. As he walked, something about him looked...taller. His shoulders were thrown back. His chin held high. Even standing beside Xuçan, it seemed like he'd grown in stature. Laurel wondered if it was real, like the green streaks in her hair. Was he changing? Either way, Alverax said nothing as he walked toward the top of the ridge.

"Willow!" Laurel shouted, looking toward the older woman who was already on the move with Aydin in her arms. Whatever Alverax was doing, she couldn't leave him behind. She couldn't leave her pack. "I'm going back!"

Without waiting for a response, she took off toward the others, Asher staying near her side. With her new speed, it only took a few moments for them both to bound across the mountainside and take their place at the top of the ridge beside Alverax, Roshaw, and Xuçan. When she looked out over the ridge and saw knuckle-running ataçan followed by a swarm of wastelanders, with Chrys and Iriel flying in the air above them, her loyalty and bravery withered beneath a mountain of doubt.

"Alverax," she said, hesitantly. "Please tell me there's a plan."

He took a quick glance at Xuçan before turning to her. "There is."

Laurel gave him a look. "A good plan?"

"Could be," he said, his gaze drifting toward the ground.

"And that is?"

Alverax lifted his chin and straightened his jacket. "Xuçan is going to tell them to stop."

Laurel looked over at the massive ataçan, each of its four fists pressing deep into the grassy ridge. The earth shook harder as the army grew closer. The shouts of wastelanders echoed through the canyon as they waved spears and hatchets in the air. Laurel did not like the plan, but they could still escape if something went wrong. Laurel and Asher were fast enough to run, and Roshaw could fly off with Alverax.

Staring at the oncoming army, Laurel decided that if she was going to die, she would do it fighting for those she loved.

Xuçan's words echoed in Alverax's mind. It seemed that, once again, he found himself in a position where he had to convince strangers that he was worth following. But this time, where his role as Watchlord had been mostly symbolic, the wastelanders were just as likely to worship him as a god as they were to send him to an early grave. Fortunately, he had Xuçan, who had already communicated with his family. If nothing else, they would stand beside Alverax as they spoke to the wastelanders.

When the ataçan reached the top of the ridge, they took their place beside Xuçan, eyeing Alverax with curiosity. The chief lifted himself up high, reaching all four arms into the air, and let out a monstrous roar into the night. A spear hurled through the air toward him, and his lower arm snapped down, grabbing it out of the air and crushing it in his massive palm. Again, he leaned forward, lifting his arms high overhead, making himself appear even larger, and bellowed out a roar.

The army hesitated, wastelander men and women slamming to a halt, and the few bonded ataçan in their midst stopped alongside them. The closest of the army fell back, filled with fear. They had worshiped Xuçan for as long as any of them had lived. He was as much a god to them as Relek and Lylax, immortal, a protector. But where the Heralds had bonded the wastelanders, Xuçan had distanced himself. Another spear flung through the air, and Xuçan swatted it aside like a fruit fly. The rest of the army packed in close to their brothers and sisters, staring up at the chief, unsure what to do or how to proceed.

Xuçan brought his arms down, nodded to his family, then turned to Alverax and Roshaw. The next few minutes would decide their fate, and Alverax wasn't sure he was ready for it. His palms started to sweat, and his chest tightened. He was a fraud. The wastelanders would see through his façade as quickly as he presented it.

As all of his doubts surfaced, Laurel's hand slipped under his own, followed by Asher's wet nose rubbing against the back of his arm. He looked to his friends, and they gave him a nod. It was a simple thing—a slight squeeze of his palm—but their support scattered the shadows from his mind.

This *was* going to work.

Xuçan had never shared a bond with anyone in over three-hundred years.

Alverax was the bridge between worlds.

He stepped forward and spoke. "My name is Alverax Blightwood."

Roshaw stood tall beside him, translating his words and speaking them out to the wastelander army in their native tongue. Knowing what he knew now about his mother, it made so much sense how and why his father knew their language so well.

"You do not know me, but I know you. You are the warriors of Kai'Melend. You are the faithful. You are the An'tara!" Alverax waited, letting his father emphasize the words. An agitated curiosity spread throughout the army. "You are also captives, enslaved by those-who-pervert-the-bond. By those who call themselves the Great Anchors. By one who named himself King of the Hive."

When Roshaw finished repeating the words, a buzz grew amidst the wastelanders as they relayed the words to the rest of the army. Alverax watched some of the warriors clutch their weapons tighter. Others spat on the ground, while some stood quietly, looking back and forth between the strangers on the ridge. An ataçan pushed its way through the crowd, a wastelander seated on its back.

"For hundreds of years, Xuçan has waited for the true King of the Hive, the An'tara who would finally bond the chief of the ataçan and lead the people to redemption. Relek tried to bond Xuçan, but the chief of the ataçan refused. I am here to tell you that Relek is not your King." Alverax looked out over the army and nodded. "Xuçan would like to speak to you now."

The chief took a step forward, causing a wave of movement amongst the army as they stepped back. What came next surprised even Alverax. Xuçan opened his mouth and spoke aloud in the wastelander tongue.

Through his bond, Alverax could still understand the ataçan's words. "I am Xuçan, and I have found the true King of the Hive." He stopped and beat at his chest with all four arms, letting out a series of grunts before settling and gesturing with a single finger toward Alverax. "This is the true King of the Hive. He is human *and* he is An'tara. The bond is formed."

The freed ataçan broke out into a roar of approval, beating their chests and slamming fists into the ground. The wastelanders stared in disbelief.

As the ataçan settled, Alverax lifted his hands into the air. "I am the true King of the Hive, chosen by Xuçan himself. The son of two worlds."

He stood tall in front of the wastelander army as he unbuttoned his shirt. Slowly, he turned around and dropped the shirt to the ground, exposing the elixir-healed gills along his spine.

Gasps and murmurs spread throughout the army. With his back turned, he couldn't see them, but he trusted Roshaw and Xuçan to keep him safe if a wastelander decided to hurl another spear. When he finally turned back around, the freed ataçan were bowing and wastelanders were beginning to follow suit, arms held high, crossed, with the tips of their fingers touching. More and more followed the others, bowing down before the true King of the Hive.

Suddenly, his corethread *broke*, and he began to hover in the air, on display for all to see. When he turned to look, his father looked just as surprised to see that Xuçan had Obsidian running through his veins.

As he looked out of the prostrated wastelanders, he felt a swelling of relief.

They had accepted him.

It had worked.

He was the true King of the Hive.

And now the Heralds were going to pay.

BONDS OF CHAOS
31

CHRYS AND IRIEL flew past the others, who stood defiantly at the top of the ridge. By the time they set foot on the ground, Chrys' chest was burning hot, each surge of threadlight flowing in like a drop of magma through his veins. He let go of Iriel and stabilized himself with his hands on his knees while he took in deep breaths.

The Heralds could fly across the entire continent, but Chrys could barely fly up a mountain without feeling on the verge of death. Alchaeus had told them that the power of each additional theolith was exponential, but he'd also said that the Heralds grew stronger with each wastelander they bonded. The implications of such power were frightening.

When he finally caught his breath, he looked to his wife, who was standing with her back to him, staring back at the ridge where the others awaited the oncoming army. Xuçan let out a monstrous roar, arms high overhead.

All of the anger that had been building up inside of Chrys as he'd watched Iriel descend the ridge came pouring out, like a tea kettle reaching its boiling point. "What the hell were you thinking?"

She spun around without an ounce of regret in her eyes. "The plan was to rescue the ataçan. So I rescued the ataçan."

"You sneaking down there *alone* was not the plan."

"No," she agreed. "*You* sneaking down there alone was the plan. I bet you told the others that you should be the one to go down and investigate."

Chrys clenched his jaw.

She continued. "And they probably didn't agree with you—Laurel and Asher are the clear choice—but you made the decision anyway.

Because you can't stand putting someone else in danger, even if they are more capable than you for the job."

His heartbeat quickened. His breaths shortened. Where was all of this animosity coming from? She was mad at him for trying to keep everyone safe? How was that fair?

"Chrys," she said, looking him straight in the eyes. "You don't get to save the world on your own. All of us are in this together, and we're all going to play a part. Ever since Aydin was born, you coddle me as much as you do him. I'm not just a carriage to cart our kid around."

The words landed like a punch to his gut.

He wanted to be mad—the anger seething in his chest demanded it—but she was right, and it nearly broke him. Before she'd become pregnant, Iriel had been one of the most capable Emerald threadweavers in Alchea. Had he forgotten that? In a way, he *had* expected her to cart their child all across the continent, all while he did what he felt had to be done to protect everyone. If the roles had been reversed, how would he have felt? Backgrounded. Standing by as everyone else used their new threadlight abilities and bonds.

Worthless. That's how he would have felt.

That's how his wife had been feeling, and he'd been too stupid to notice.

"Iriel," he said softly. "You're right. I haven't been treating you as a partner, and you deserve better than that. I'm sorry."

Iriel stared at him for a moment before letting out a breath and shaking her head. "You know what the worst part is? I knew you'd forgive me. I knew you'd be mad, and I knew that after I explained myself you'd apologize. After everything you've been through, how are you still such a good man?"

Chrys let out an exasperated sigh. "Being good is all we have left."

"Some people might say that being good is what got us here."

"Some people would be wrong," Chrys replied. "Us trying to be good is the only reason the Heralds haven't won yet."

Iriel's smile faded, and she looked back toward Xuçan and the others. "Speaking of, wasn't there an army coming over that ridge?"

Chrys furrowed his brow and watched as Alverax took his shirt off at the top of the ridge. "What the hell?"

"This night just keeps getting weirder."

A moment later, Roshaw turned, saw Chrys and Iriel, and waved for them to join the others. Chrys spun around, taking another look for his mother in the wild surroundings, but saw only an empty mountainside and the cluster of statue-like wastelanders in the distance. Wherever Willow was hiding, he was certain she would be safe. If nothing else, his mother knew how to protect a child.

Chrys and Iriel walked side-by-side until they reached the top of the ridge where the others stood. Alverax was now hovering in the air with a broken corethread. Whatever they'd done had worked. On the other side of the ridge, the entire wastelander army was bowing to Alverax, making the same odd sign they'd made when Relek had first appeared in Chrys' body and claimed to be the King of the Hive.

A thick wastelander with an unnaturally deep-set brow spoke with Roshaw as an ataçan loomed over them.

The moment was so surreal that it felt like a dream. Chrys was so used to their plans failing that this one victory seemed impossible. With the wastelanders on their side, they might actually be able to beat the Heralds.

But then reality struck. The ataçan had been controlled by the collars, but the wastelanders were still bound to Relek and Lylax. Even if they pledged themselves to Alverax, when the Heralds returned, they could control the wastelanders like Relek had controlled the Alchean soldiers in the mountains. He wondered at the extent of their power. Could they control all of the wastelanders at once? If the ease with which they flew was any indicator, Chrys felt certain that they could. The war was just beginning. And when the Heralds returned, they would bring with them the wrath of centuries.

Unless they didn't know.

Chrys and Iriel stepped up beside Roshaw as the wastelander and his ataçan returned to the army. "Who was that?"

Roshaw ran a hand across his brow. "Rixi. He leads the wastelanders while the Heralds are away. He's bound to that ataçan. Says the wastelanders are willing to defy the false gods but only if there is a plan."

"Tell them to return to the valley and go back to sleep," Chrys said. "They are still bound to the Heralds, which means they can be controlled against their will. If Relek and Lylax return and see this, we'll be dead before a ten count."

Roshaw raised a brow. "Even if they go back down the valley and pretend like nothing happened, won't the Heralds know?"

"I don't think so," Chrys said. "They're not omniscient. When Relek was in my head, he only knew my active thoughts. They could command the wastelanders to tell them what happened. But if they have no reason to ask, they won't be any wiser."

"Even with the wastelanders on our side," Iriel added, "we still don't have a way to kill the Heralds."

"We still have the one option," Laurel said indifferently.

"No," Roshaw said quickly. "Look out there. We are not slaughtering those people."

Laurel shook her head. "We don't have to kill them. Alverax is the King of the Hive. You're the one who told us so enthusiastically about the et'hovon and how the wastelanders see themselves the same. That they are willing to sacrifice themselves for the good of the many."

"Is that a joke?" Roshaw's eyes were bulging. "You can't seriously think that is the same."

"You have a better option?" Laurel asked.

"Enough," Chrys said. "Even if we find a way to get rid of the bonds, the Heralds still have their threadlight. They are still stronger than us. They still have the corespawn. Hell, they could still create new bonds."

"Unless they couldn't," Iriel said. All eyes turned to her. She opened her mouth to continue, then paused, shifting her eyes from Chrys to the others and back to Chrys. "I know we're getting short on ideas, but hear me out. What if we destroy the Provenance? Cut off the source of their power."

Chrys felt his mind reel at the thought. What if? What if they did destroy the Provenance? Could they even destroy it? Would every threadweaver in the world lose their threadlight?

"No way," Roshaw blurted out. "Our threadlight is our best weapon against the Heralds."

"It would hurt them more than us," Iriel said.

Roshaw pursed his lips. "That still hurts us."

"It's worth considering," Chrys said, giving his wife a nod.

"Would it destroy their bond with the wastelanders?" Roshaw asked.

"It should," Iriel said. "We can't know for certain, but I don't see why not."

Roshaw waved his hands in the air. "You realize it wouldn't just be the Heralds, and it wouldn't just be us. Destroying the Provenance would destroy threadlight for every single person in the world. There would be no such thing as a threadweaver anymore. Are we really okay with that?"

Chrys tilted his head. "If the options are death to all mankind or death to threadlight, I think we would go with the latter."

"It's crazy," Iriel said. "But I agree."

Laurel let out a small laugh and mumbled something inaudible to herself.

They all turned to her.

"Alabella always said that the great unfairness of the world was that some people were born with threadlight while others weren't. She wanted to give everyone the chance to be a threadweaver. She wanted 'equality.' Looks like she might get what she wanted, just not in the way she planned."

There was a moment of silence as the idea sank in. Were they really considering the end of threadweaving? It seemed the kind of decision the Lightfather should make, not a group of runaways with everything to lose.

Chrys looked over the sprawling army below the ridge. Their leader, Rixi, spoke to them with his ataçan standing beside him. One by one, then in waves, the wastelanders rose to their feet, a cacophony of emotions rippling through their numbers. Awe. Fear. Curiosity. Doubt. Faith. They were trapped between evil gods and their long-awaited King of the Hive. Chrys couldn't imagine how confusing it must all be for them.

When Alverax finally drifted back to the ground, he turned around to see the group, still without a shirt and the smoky glow of Obsidian threadlight in his veins. He looked to his father first. "Looks like we have ourselves an army!" he said excitedly. When he noticed the thoughtful looks on everyone's faces, he raised a brow. "Did I miss something?"

"We'll explain later," Chrys said. "First things first, we need to figure out what to do with the army. The Heralds could return at any moment, and unless they see a bunch of wastelanders asleep, we'll all be dead before the morning comes."

Roshaw grit his teeth. "I just don't think it will work. Why don't we take them away? Hide them back in the Wastelands or something?"

"As nice as that would be," Iriel said, "where are we going to hide ten thousand wastelanders where the Heralds won't find them? They can fly, and it's not like a marching army won't leave a trail."

"Maybe we can find a cave," Roshaw said, throwing up his hands. "I don't know. There has to be a way we can get these people to safety."

Chrys felt sorry for Roshaw. He knew how much these people mattered to him. How much he cared for them, the last remnant of Alverax's mother. "Roshaw, the truth is that as long as they are bonded to the Heralds, there is nothing we can do."

"He's right," Iriel added. "We should send them all back down and tell them to do everything Relek and Lylax ask. Be perfect subjects. Fight the Alcheans if they have to. When the time is right, we'll have Alverax give them a sign and they can turn on the Heralds."

"I don't like it," Roshaw said. "And I don't think Rixi will like it. But I don't have a better idea."

"Great," Chrys said. "Because you're the only one who can tell them."

Roshaw let out a breathy laugh. "Right."

"And Alverax," Chrys added. "Put a shirt on. You look ridiculous."

Alverax looked down and laughed. "Right."

As soon as he said the word, he and Roshaw looked at each other, but it was Iriel who spoke first. "Like father, like son."

Laurel looked around the group. "What about us? Where are we all going to hide? Xuçan isn't exactly subtle."

Chrys nodded. "No, you're right. Roshaw's comment earlier reminded me. There is a cave not far from here. We can head there and use it for cover."

"Sounds like we have ourselves a plan," Iriel said triumphantly.

Laurel placed a hand on Asher's head and nodded. "The start of one at least."

"Almost," Chrys said, turning around and looking back over the wild mountainside, eyes drifting over the statue-like dead, marked by the *pintalla mox*. "We still need to find my mother."

32. Bonds of Chaos

Willow kept running until she could no longer feel the quaking of the army's approach. Images of the others standing atop the ridge, defiant, flashed like bolts of lightning through her mind. Laurel and Asher. Alverax. Roshaw. Even with Xuçan at their side, there was no way they would survive the assault of an entire army. But what worried her most was Chrys and Iriel. They had both been down there, amidst the sleeping wastelanders and collared ataçan. They could be dead already.

She threw herself under a rocky ledge, ripping at nearby branches and shrubs to build a makeshift wall, a poor attempt at obscuring their location. The child in her arms had not stopped crying since she'd fled the ridge. All of the jostling and stumbling had woken him to a world of darkness and hunger, without a mother to succor him. Willow pulled Aydin in close and tucked his swaddle back around to tighten the wrapping and hold down his hands.

With a soft voice and her grandson bouncing in her arms, she sang an old Zeda lullaby that she'd once sung to her own son so many years before.

> *When the lights fade out, and the faithful doubt,*
> *You should know there's calm in the shadow.*
> *In the darkest days, when the faithless prays,*
> *Close your eyes, find calm in the shadow.*

Willow closed her eyes, sending up a plea to the Father of All. She prayed that Aydin would stop crying. She prayed that her son would be okay, that her daughter-in-law would live to care for her child. She prayed that Roshaw would survive to live out his days with *his* son. He was a good man—so was his son. After all he had been through, Roshaw deserved to retire in peace. She prayed that Laurel and Asher would be safe. And then she prayed for herself, a heart-wrenching plea to a god that felt too distant in a world of living legends. She prayed for courage. For comfort. But above all, she prayed for the strength to accept whatever outcome fell upon her family. Even if that outcome left her alone in the world.

No, she thought. *There is still a chance.*

She wiped away tears and looked down at Aydin, who had fallen back asleep sometime during her prayer. It seemed such a small victory compared to the events around them, but even small victories lend a credence of hope.

As she sat in the dark of night, hiding from the wastelander army, she realized that this was not the first time she had run away with a child. The thought took her not to the Fairenwild or Zedalum, or even to her quiet arrival in Alchea. Instead, it took her to the Convergence. It took her into the warbling mass of threadlight that had expanded to fill the space of the vast cavern. And that, in turn, had taken her to the past.

WILLOW OPENED HER EYES, *standing in a familiar room, in a familiar house on the northeast edge of Zedalum. She saw a new mother sleeping beside the rickety old bassinet her father had made. A newborn child, two days old, who slept as peacefully as Aydin did now, wrapped in the pale blue blanket Rosemary had gifted. The new mother was Willow.*

She had been so young, so beautiful, even though she'd hardly slept since the child had been born. Willow remembered feeling like little Chrys would never wake up if she weren't there watching over him, but she also remembered being too tired to keep her eyes open any longer. And the peach-colored gown that her husband had loved so much looked otherworldly beneath the light of the autumn moon.

She remembered being that woman, asleep in that chair, then waking to see an older version of herself standing above her, a specter sent from the Father of All. Only now she knew the truth: she was no specter at all. She was flesh and blood, sent to the past by a Convergence that had folded the thread of time. She pictured Alchaeus' string, one end brought to the other.

The young Willow awoke, and the elder Willow told her that she needed to take Chrys away from Zedalum. A storm was coming, and the Fairenwild would not be safe.

The memory faded, and Willow returned to her hovel in the Everstone Mountains. She feared that the son she had sacrificed so much to protect might be gone, that the mother of the child she held in her arms might be dead, that the man she...

Breath fled from her lungs, and her heart swelled. Could she? No. Thirty years of pushing away every man who'd come to her, fearing the consequences should they discover the Zeda tattoo on her back. But that was over, and she couldn't deny the feelings any longer. The truth of her past was out in the world. She was free to love however and whomever she wanted.

Despite a dozen reasons why she shouldn't, her heart had chosen that bear of a man who'd traveled across the world with her. His thick arms and coarse hair. His foul mouth and the way he looked at his son, so protective, an echo of herself. A weight seemed to lift from her chest as she admitted to herself, once and for all, that Willow Valerian was falling for Roshaw Blightwood.

The slightest smile touched her lips.

But it might not matter. The last she saw him, he was standing atop a ridge with a wastelander army rushing toward him. And even if he did survive that and if she did find them again, what then? The world was still on the verge of collapse.

One step at a time.

Settling in against the rocks, she tucked in a handful of wheatgrass where the stones were sharpest and watched as the clouds drifted through the night sky. There was still no sign of the wastelander army, and she wondered if she had waited long enough to leave her shelter. She needed to know what had happened to Chrys and the others. But if she was the only one left, then she had to stay alive. She needed to get to Alchea to warn Malachus and Eleandra.

She pushed herself up with one arm, careful to keep her movements smooth so as not to wake the child, and peeked up and over the rocky ledge.

Nothing.

No wastelander warriors, dead or alive.

No Heralds lurking in the sky.

No family.

Willow continued to watch, refusing to accept that her son would not walk around the bend at any moment. There was still a chance.

Time passed, and no one came. A slight breeze fluttered through the grass and brushed through the leaves of the trees, an earthy scent lingering in the air. Still, she watched, threadlight trickling through her veins to offset the chill in the air. She couldn't wait forever; Aydin would need food soon.

She sat back on the dirt and rock, the remnants of her once strong hope streaming away. This couldn't be the end. Not after all they'd been through. She should have stayed with them. If they were going to die, they should die together. But she knew that wasn't true. Aydin needed to grow up. He needed to live a full life. If Willow's sacrifice was being the one who lived so that Aydin might too, then, Lightfather-be-damned, she would not die on that mountain that day.

She stood, lifted her chin, and stepped out from her rocky hiding place.

33

Chrys stopped at the mouth of the cave as the others stepped inside. Ghosts flashed in his mind, figures standing in a line, terrified as they watched their comrade slit his own throat. Chaos. Sorrow.

The memory faded, but the feelings remained. What had at the time seemed such inconsequential violence from the Apogee, Chrys now understood as the beginning. The introduction to the Heralds' grim rule and disregard for human life.

And yet, worse than the memories was finding specks of dried blood crusted to the cave wall.

He breathed, uncertain whether the smell of death was real or his mind clinging to the past, then stepped in after the others. A few paces into the cave, they found a collection of abandoned equipment, pickaxes, dead torches, a small cart with a broken wheel, and hemp sacks. Chrys was certain that none of that had been there before. He wondered if the equipment belonged to Alchea—likely under the continued direction of Henna—or if it belonged to the Heralds.

The others stood around the remains of an old fire pit while Roshaw worked it to life, chipping away at a piece of flint. They were all there except for Xuçan, who was too large to fit in the cave. His bond with Alverax allowed them to communicate, even at a short distance, and he'd already sent word that he'd found a gully not far away where he could hide.

When a shadow flickered over the mouth of the cave, Chrys expected to see Xuçan's looming silhouette. Instead, Laurel and Asher had returned.

With Willow and Aydin.

Iriel sprinted forward, grabbing Aydin from Willow's arms, pulling him in tight and kissing his head. Chrys joined her as they looked down at their son. He thought he'd convinced himself that Aydin was safe. But seeing them now, he realized that the doubt had never quite left.

He turned to his mother and wrapped her in a tight embrace. "I'm so glad you're safe."

"I thought I'd lost you," Willow replied.

Beside them, Iriel unwrapped Aydin and checked every inch of his body before finally taking a breath. She then excused herself and stepped away to give the child an overdue feeding.

Beside the fire, Roshaw and Alverax stood watching, hands stretched toward the flames, smiling at their friends' reunion. And there it was. At first, Chrys hadn't seen the resemblance. But looking at them now, smiles as wide as a river...they were two gems cut from the same stone.

"Come," Roshaw said to Willow, gesturing toward the fire. "I saved a space for you."

Chrys turned and saw Willow fighting back a smile.

They migrated toward the warmth, Laurel and Asher arriving first. The big chromawolf stretched out on the rocks a few feet from the fire. Alverax took a seat on the hard stone next to Laurel and ran a hand down Asher's thick, green fur, laughing over some quiet joke shared between them. On the other side of the fire, Roshaw unpacked a blanket and wrapped it around Willow's shoulders, rubbing his hands in front of the flickering flames.

Silently, Chrys watched them with a sense of wonder stirring in his chest. These people weren't just traveling companions anymore—they weren't soldiers or smiths or butchers with a job to perform that Chrys would soon forget. These people were family.

When Iriel finally returned with a sleeping Aydin bundled in her arms, she stopped beside Chrys. "What did I miss?"

They all turned to her with a blank look.

"You've been discussing the plan, right?" Iriel added.

Nothing.

"We're hiding in a cave," she said flatly. "There's an army outside. Gods who want to kill us. Impending war. And we're not discussing a plan?"

Roshaw shifted in his boots. "I wanted to hear about what happened to Willow. She wanted to hear about the army."

Alverax pointed to Laurel. "She was telling me more about her bond with Asher."

Iriel turned to Chrys. "And you were just watching?"

"Actually, yes."

Iriel let out a clipped laugh and shook her head. "The world deserves better heroes than us."

"Who said we were heroes?" Roshaw said. "I see us more as the world's toilet stick, and the Heralds are just diamond crusted shit stains."

Alverax burst out in laughter. His lively response ushered in an outpouring of giggles from the others. Even Iriel joined in, unable to fight the wit and charm of the older man.

"You are quite the oddity," Willow said, shaking her head at Roshaw.

"I am what I am," he replied with a grin.

Chrys cleared his throat, and everyone turned to him. "Shit stains or not, Iriel is right. We need to figure out a plan. I had an idea, but it might not work."

"What is it?" Willow said excitedly.

"The caves." Chrys gestured down the dark corridor. "It's possible these caves connect with the others. If they do and we have a path to Alchaeus' cave, then we should seriously consider destroying the Provenance."

"Wait," Willow said, shaking her head. "Did I miss something?"

"Ah," Roshaw groaned. "We all discussed it earlier."

Alverax pointed to Iriel. "It was her idea."

Willow slowly looked around the room, settling on Chrys, but it was clear that her mind was mostly within itself. "Destroy the Provenance. Destroy threadlight. Cut off their power. They can't fly. They can't fight. The bonds would be broken. They would be mortal..."

"That's the hope," Iriel said proudly.

Willow's eyes grew wider. "It's brilliant. And terrifying. But if it works, brilliant."

Laurel jumped to her feet. "Asher and I can go check the cave. We're faster and see better in the dark. I'll find some photospores, and we'll be back in no time."

"I can go with you," Alverax said. "My bond with Xuçan is already making me faster. I'm keen to try it out."

"Hold on," Chrys said. He was surprised by the speed with which everyone agreed, despite the glaring reality that such an action would create. A world without threadlight. Were they so willing to offer such a sacrifice? Was *he* willing to offer such a sacrifice? A threadweaver was what Chrys had always been. Since he was a child, he'd always had the power and respect that came with his Sapphire eyes. And now, he had the strength of three theoliths, power beyond even Great Lord Malachus. "Are we certain?"

Their faces grew a little more somber as they remembered the truth. Iriel looked to Aydin. Alverax and Roshaw looked at their own veins. Laurel looked to Asher.

Willow gave a slow nod. "I lived without threadweaving for thirty years. It was difficult at first—I won't lie to you. But as time went by, the sky was still as blue. The sun was still as warm. And the flowers still smelled as lovely as ever. As long as the people of Arasin have each other, alive, healthy, and free of the bonds the Heralds have placed on the world, it will be enough. Take people away from magic, and the power is lost. Take magic away from people, and their power remains. The world will move on."

"The world will move on," Roshaw repeated.

"*We* will move on," Iriel added.

Alverax looked down at the black veins visible on the top of his hands. "In my experience, threadlight brings nothing but pain. We'll all be better off without it."

Laurel nodded but remained quiet.

"Okay," Chrys said. "Then let's hope this cave leads to the tunnels."

A raucous noise rolled up the hill and into the mouth of the cave, thousands of voices cheering in unison. Chrys and the others turned, looking out where the morning sunlight had begun to illuminate the Everstone Mountains.

"Laurel and Alverax," Chrys said. "Check the tunnel. We're running out of time."

The Zeda girl and Asher took off without question, Alverax following closely behind as they darted into the depths of the cave. Chrys ran toward the entrance, his breath ragged with worry for the people of Alchea. As he exited the cave, he could see the valley in the distance, filled with wastelanders standing, staring up at two figures that hovered in the air.

His heart pounded in his chest. This was the moment of truth. If the wastelanders turned on them, letting their fear of Relek and Lylax outweigh their belief in the King of the Hive—their trust in Xuçan—then this could be their last day. If they hid in the caves, the Heralds might create another coreseal. But it was more likely that the Heralds would put a definitive end to the mosquitos that had been nipping at their skin for too long.

As Iriel and the others joined Chrys, the Heralds spun in the air, turning toward the cave. Iriel was the first to hit the ground, but Chrys and the others followed suit with urgency. Together, they lay on the dew-glazed grass, the sun rising behind them, blood pumping through their veins as they waited to see what the Heralds would do. Iriel's hand slid over Chrys' and squeezed.

Another rowdy cheer exploded from the wastelander army. The earth shook as they stomped on the ground, slamming their spears into the dirt. The ataçan—with collars back in place— stood beside them like mythic sentries.

Eventually, the noise died, and the Heralds flew back toward the west. The army immediately began taking down the tents and packing up their belongings. It seemed the wastelanders had held to their promise. Whatever the King of the Hive was to them, it held more weight than their fear.

"Damn," Roshaw said, rolling over onto his back and running his hands over his face. "It actually worked."

"Alverax must have made quite the speech," Willow added.

"You should have seen it," Roshaw said. "Xuçan *broke* Al's corethread, and he hovered in front of them like a god."

"Xuçan broke his corethread?" Willow asked.

"The bond goes both ways." Roshaw said, as if it were obvious. "And you should have seen when Xuçan named him King of the Hive. The entire army bowed down."

Willow smiled. "You have quite the kid."

Chrys pushed himself to his feet and looked back down the cave. Wherever Laurel and Alverax were, they needed to work fast.

With the wastelanders on the move, they were running out of time.

34: Bonds of Chaos

ALVERAX RAN through the dark tunnel, holding a cluster of photospores in one hand. With each step, he could feel Xuçan's strength flowing through his body, muscles expanding against his skin, Obsidian veins oozing with power. Even still, Laurel and Asher were faster. Every so often, they would glance over their shoulder to make sure he was keeping up. He knew he shouldn't be annoyed by it, but he was.

They passed a narrow section of the tunnel with rocks piled up to the ceiling where the tunnel must have been blocked at one time. From the look of it, the recent quakes from the coreseal and the destruction of the Convergence must have opened it. Carefully, they climbed up the pile, rubble falling down the mountain of rocks as they slipped through a narrow opening at the top.

As they moved farther into the cave, he thought about the Provenance, and what life would be like without threadlight. No Masked Guard with their glowing eyes. No Jelium fixing necrolyte races. No acrobats performing wondrous feats at the docks of Felia. The inequalities brought about by threadweaver birthright would be gone. But Alverax wasn't a fool either. He knew people well enough to know that if one reason for lording over others disappeared, another would wriggle its way in. Still, he believed that—maybe, eventually—if enough of those reasons were removed, the world would become just a little better each time.

Suddenly, Laurel and Asher stopped at an intersection.

"Gale take me," Laurel muttered.

"What?" Alverax said, running up behind them. He looked down each corridor, seeing nothing but darkness and the flickering light of distant photospores. "What is it? Which way do we go?"

Laurel silently stepped over to the wall. "Look." She gestured toward a white stain along the stone. "One of Alchaeus' markings."

"That means if we follow the marked tunnel"—Alverax felt a buzz of excitement flow through him—"it will lead all the way back to the Provenance!"

"That's what we came for," Laurel said. "We should go tell Chrys."

Without another word, they backtracked down the tunnel the way they'd come. Alverax felt alive, running even faster on the return than he had on the way down. It surprised him how even his endurance had improved so quickly. Laurel and Asher trailed close behind him, letting him take the lead. He knew it was stupid, but being in front gave him a sense of purpose that he hadn't felt when following. It was silly—he knew that—but still he appreciated that they'd allowed him that small win.

When they reached the narrow opening in the tunnel, Alverax scrambled up and over the pile of fallen rock, squeezing his way through the crevice. He slid down on both feet, smiling as he leapt off the bottom. He took a few steps forward, preparing to continue the run, but paused when he realized he couldn't hear the others.

He turned and saw Laurel standing in the narrow opening, looking down from a mountain of rocks with a boulder in her arms that seemed too large for her frame, Asher's bond fueling her strength.

"What are you doing?" Alverax called out to her.

Her teeth were clenched, and there was a strange look in her eyes. A dark feeling grew in the pit of Alverax's stomach.

"Why are you holding that?"

Her lip quivered. "I have to do this."

"What?" Alverax furrowed his brow and shook his head. "What are you talking about?"

"I'm doing this for the pack," she said flatly.

Before he could speak, Laurel slammed the boulder against the wall so hard that the tunnel shook. Rocks and dust rained down from the ceiling, filling parts of the narrow gap in the tunnel. A thin crack split along the ceiling just above the opening.

"Laurel!" Alverax screamed.

As her name left his mouth, understanding settled over him. When Iriel had touched the Provenance, she'd been blown back by some unseen force. If their plan was to destroy it, whoever volunteered was going to die in the process. Laurel was offering herself.

But if anyone deserved to die, it should be him. Alverax wasn't even supposed to be alive. Time and time again, he'd evaded death's sting. But for what? So he could destroy the coreseal, unleashing the corespawn? So he could release the Heralds from their prison? So he could watch the woman he loved die? If justice demanded recompense from anyone, it was Alverax.

"Laurel!" he shouted again. "This is not your choice to make!"

She stopped after slamming the boulder against the wall once more, the narrow opening already half-filled with rubble so that he could only see her torso. The cracked veins in the ceiling grew larger. "It has to be me."

"You have family!" he said. "A brother in Felia, right? He's ill, isn't he? Laurel, don't do this!"

The words gave her pause, but still she slammed the boulder into the wall once more. "You have your father and your grandfather. Chrys has his family. All I have is Asher, and we made a promise to each other. When the Provenance is destroyed, it will destroy our bond. We would rather die together, so that you all can live your lives with the people you love."

"We can find another way!" Alverax said.

"Just...do me one favor," she added. "When the light goes out, make sure the Heralds pay for what they've done."

"Laurel, stop! There has to be another—"

With one final thud, Laurel heaved the boulder up, throwing it with Asher-enhanced strength toward the ceiling. It struck with such force that the entire cave vibrated. Cracks along the ceiling splintered, rippling down the tunnel. Rubble rained down like hail, and the ceiling above the narrow opening collapsed, causing a landslide of dust and stone to fill the gap.

Alverax threw himself back, narrowly avoiding a massive chunk of stone that fell from the ceiling where he'd been standing.

When the dust settled, she was gone.

Alverax stood, alone, tears in his eyes, angry, heartbroken at the thought of losing Laurel, the one who had sat by his side for weeks while he coped with the death of Jisenna and the return of his father. And yet, the longer he stared, the more he understood. Her words echoed in his mind.

I'm going to do my part to make it better if it's the last thing I do.

He walked over to the mountain of stone and slammed his boot into it, Xuçan's bond sending a wave of force through the rocks. "I'm your family, too!" he screamed, tears flooding down his cheeks, unsure if she could even hear through the wall of rubble. Again, he kicked, as if some kid from Cynosure was strong enough to fight the earth itself. "I'm your family, too!"

She was selfish and impulsive. And if she failed, the whole world would burn. With the tunnel closed, they wouldn't get another chance. On top of that, she didn't even give the others a chance to say goodbye. Willow had treated her like a daughter. Chrys like a little sister. Roshaw and Iriel. They deserved a chance to say goodbye. But, now...she was gone.

Alverax turned around and let himself fall, his back sliding against the cold stone as he closed his eyes. He was just so tired. Of running. Of fighting. Most of all, he was tired of losing everyone he cared about.

"We were all your family," he whispered to himself.

BONDS OF CHAOS
35

CHRYS GLANCED BACK down the cave. They needed to leave...now.

Since the Heralds had left, the entire wastelander army had packed up and begun its ascent over the final peak. Soon, they would drop into the southeastern countryside of Alchea. Chrys was beginning to worry that the only plan they'd come up with wasn't going to work. If the tunnels didn't connect, the cave outside of Kai'Melend was too far, even for Laurel and Asher. And even if the caves did connect, it still might be too far.

From deep in the tunnel, footsteps echoed, growing louder and louder as a lone figure came into view. Alverax, clothes covered in a new layer of dust, slowed to a walk as soon as he saw the others. He held his head high, but the droop in his shoulders was enough for Chrys to recognize that something was wrong.

"Alverax," Chrys said, running over to the younger man. "What happened? Where's Laurel?"

"They stayed behind," Alverax said quietly.

By then, the others had joined. Willow looked over his shoulder. "What do you mean? Stayed behind? Where?"

"She's gone!" Alverax shouted, the façade cracking. His lips quivered, and his breathing grew more frantic.

"Father of All," Willow whispered as she turned away. "The tunnels connect."

Iriel's eyes grew wide. "She's going to destroy the Provenance."

"She'll die," Roshaw added.

Alverax closed his eyes. "She and Asher didn't want to live without their bond. She said to make sure the Heralds pay when the light goes out."

Emotions swirled in Chrys, a stinging in his chest, a pain in his heart that belonged to that young girl he'd met in the Bloodthief warehouse. The girl who'd saved his family from the chromawolves and from Jurius' soldiers. No matter what he may claim, a man's heart never truly grows accustomed to loss. He may believe it has, but it's not the loss that has grown dull. It is the depth of his love, driven by fear, which has grown shallow. Chrys loved Laurel. He loved who she'd become, her strength and gallant resolve. Her loss would weigh on his heart forever.

But...she had given them a gift. The world was in danger, and her sacrifice would lend them their best chance at stopping the Heralds. He would not let her loss be for naught. They needed to be ready when the Provenance was destroyed.

They needed to leave...now.

"The army is on the move," Chrys said softly. "If we want to make sure the world never forgets the sacrifice that Laurel made today, we need to get to Endin Keep before the wastelanders get over the mountain."

Iriel looked toward the cave. "Shouldn't we—I don't know—*try* to stop her?"

"Her course is set," Willow said, nodding her head thoughtfully. "Besides, Laurel and Asher are faster than any of us. If they're on their way to the Provenance, there's nothing we can do to stop them."

"She's right," Chrys said. "We need to be ready when the Provenance is destroyed and threadlight disappears."

"*If* it disappears," Willow added.

"If?" Roshaw repeated. "I thought we were certain here."

Willow's eyes seemed tired. "As certain as we can be. Unfortunately, when you do something that has never been done, there can be no certainty. For all we know, that wasn't the Provenance, and destroying it will do nothing. There is a real chance that our plan will fail, and we'll be left with no way to stop the Heralds. Still, even if all we have is uncertainty, we have to try. If there is any chance that we can make a difference, that's all we can do."

Chrys smiled as he looked to his mother. She'd given him a similar speech a dozen times when he was younger. Whenever a task was too difficult, or a project too overwhelming in scope, Willow would look him in the eyes and tell him that "Valerians never give up." When the world needed them most, that same spirit burned within her. Now, Chrys could see the same flames burning in the eyes of each of the others. No matter the outcome, they were all in this together.

"Damn," Roshaw said softly, looking at Willow with admiration. "You sure you don't have some of that Heraldic mind control stuff? Because I'm pretty sure I'd jump off this mountain right now if you asked me to."

"Not the time," Willow said.

Chrys' eyes lit up. "That actually gives me an idea..."

AN HOUR LATER, after meeting up with Xuçan and trudging through the wild growth of the mountains, they arrived at a peak overlooking the city of Alchea. To the south, they could see the wastelanders preparing to descend the mountain pass like a swarm of ants scuttling down a cobblestone path. It wasn't until Chrys looked west that an icy cold surged through his chest.

At such a height, Chrys could see an army sprawled out on the western border of Alchea. And there was only one nation large enough to march an army of that size. If the city was already under siege from the west, the wastelanders would obliterate them from the east, like an arrow loosed at their back.

That was exactly what the Heralds wanted.

They wanted to stand back, smiling, while Felia, Alchea, and the wastelanders tore each other apart. And if he had to guess, the corespawn would arrive just in time to finish the job. If this war wasn't stopped, there would be no one left alive.

Iriel stepped up beside him. "Chrys, is that—"

"It is," he said.

"How did they get here so quickly?" she asked.

Chrys' nostrils flared as he looked over the countryside. "It's been a long time since we left Felia. The Heralds must have sent them after we departed."

Iriel's chest rose up and down, Aydin cooing against her breast. "Are we too late?"

"No," Chrys said quickly. "But we're running out of time."

Multi-colored threadlight came to life, swirling in the veins of his neck and hands. Willow and Roshaw walked up beside him, their own eyes glowing with otherworldly light.

"Wait," Alverax said.

They all turned to the young man, who gazed over the countryside toward the surrounding army.

"I'll be no use to you in Alchea," Alverax continued. "But if I can get to the Felian army, maybe I can talk them out of the war."

Willow raised a brow. "That doesn't seem like—"

"They'll gut you like a sandhog!" Roshaw blurted out. "You're a traitor there. If you walk into that camp, you'll be dead the second they recognize you."

"I still have a few friends inside," Alverax said.

"Had," Roshaw said. "They've been waiting hundreds of years for the Heralds to return. It would take a hell of a friendship to win over that kind of zealotry."

Though he tried to hide it, Chrys caught a flicker of sorrow in Alverax's eyes, which surprised him. He'd expected to see anger or annoyance toward Roshaw. But instead, the young man held an air of sadness.

"Alverax," Chrys said, placing a hand on the younger man's shoulder. "Each of us will walk a critical path in the coming days or hours, and all of these paths will lead to sacrifice of some kind. But not all will lead to self-sacrifice. Laurel's path is not yours."

"Stop!" Alverax shouted, throwing Chrys' hand away with surprising force. "I know what I'm saying. Stop treating me like a child. If we do nothing, the Felians will kill who knows how many Alcheans, and speaking to the Alcheans isn't going to stop that. We need to consider every angle. For you, that's speaking to your friends in Alchea. For me, it's speaking to mine. One of the highest generals in Felia is a friend, and he's a good man. If I can talk to him, maybe I can delay the army until Laurel can destroy the Provenance."

Roshaw puckered his lips. "It's not worth the risk. They'll—"

"He's right," Chrys said, feeling a measure of guilt as he cut off Roshaw. "If Alverax can delay the army—even for a few hours—it would make all the difference. It could save thousands of lives on both sides of the war."

"But...it's...my..." Roshaw's voice fell to a whisper as his lips quivered and his chest convulsed. He turned away to hide the tears in his eyes.

Chrys felt tears form in his own eyes as he watched the big bear of a man break down. They all knew what Roshaw was thinking, and they could imagine what he was feeling. But imagining pain and feeling it for yourself are not the same. No matter how hard a man may try, he never truly understands hurt beyond what he has experienced himself. Roshaw, a man who had already lost his child once, was faced with the real possibility of losing him again. Chrys looked over to Aydin and felt a swelling of pain in his own heart.

"I know you're scared," Alverax said. "You don't think I am? But like Chrys said, we all have our path to walk, something that only we can do to help. I'm not a hybrid threadweaver like you. Until the Provenance is destroyed, I can't lead the wastelanders. There's too much at stake for me to sit around waiting for that to happen, especially if there's a chance I can help."

Roshaw's breathing steadied, and he looked to his son with bloodshot eyes. "How the hell did you turn out to be such a good man?"

Alverax let out a small laugh. "Sometimes the bad examples help more than the good."

"I'm coming with you," Roshaw said with a sense of resolve. "I can fly you close and watch your back since Xuçan won't be able to come to the camp."

Alverax nodded. "Let's do this."

Clouds had gathered over the mountain range, blanketing the city in a dreary darkness that brought with it an icy chill. The few rays that made their way through the gray felt muted as they reached toward the high stone walls.

Chrys and Iriel took off toward Endin Keep, flying faster than they ever had before with Willow and Aydin beside them. If Laurel managed to destroy the Provenance in that very moment, they would tumble through the sky to their deaths. If they were going to fly at all, they needed to get it over with quickly.

As they drifted toward the keep, memories flooded through him. Toward the base, he saw the room where he and his mother had once lived thanks to Eleandra's kindness. Beside it, he saw the window he'd once shattered while playing as a young boy. Higher up, he saw Jurius' study, where he'd spent countless hours in conversation before the Bloodthieves had compromised the high general. And higher still, he saw the window that his mother had used with Laz and Laurel to break into the keep in order to save Chrys' uncle, Pandan. It seemed an eternity ago. So much had changed since then. The world. The dangers. The people most of all.

Chrys shook his head, trying not to be distracted by the past. Alchea was at war, and while they were not likely expecting an aerial attack from the mountains, soldiers would be out in force. He was a hybrid threadweaver, filled with otherworldly power and fast-acting healing, but a single, well-placed arrow could still take him—or his family—out of the sky as quickly as a crow.

They began their descent, shooting down as the cold wind bit at their skin. While there was no entrance on the top of the keep's highest towers, it was still the best place to touch down and regroup. Chrys glanced back to check on Willow and Aydin, then let out another surge of Emerald to speed up the descent. Surprisingly, two guards stood atop each of the towers, looking out toward the Felian army to the west. He'd never heard of guards posted there before, but it took only a moment of thought to realize that Malachus was smarter than he was. If the Heralds had been as cavalier about flight as they had been in Felia, Cynosure, or even the Everstone Mountains, then the Great Lord knew that he needed to watch the skies. What better way than to station a few Emeralds on the highest point of the city.

Unfortunately, Malachus' wisdom made Chrys' job just a little bit more difficult.

Chrys *pushed* off the stone as he landed, hitting the ground with a louder thud than he'd anticipated. The two guards—one male, one female—spun around in unison, veins flared with Emerald threadlight.

"Soldiers," Chrys said with a nod.

The woman, her thin frame accentuated by the baggy uniform, opened her mouth to speak, but nothing came out.

Chrys offered a sly smile. "Last I heard, your uncle was feeling much better. Is he back in the smithy yet?"

A small grin formed in the corner of her mouth. "He is, sir."

"Good." Chrys looked to the other guard. "I know I did not leave on the best of terms, and you likely have orders to capture me—"

"Sir," the woman interjected. "You—"

"Please," Chrys cut her off. "We are here to speak with Great Lord Malachus, to share information that will aid Alchea in the war. There is no need for us to fight, and it would only go poorly for you, I promise. I would much rather this visit be peaceful."

"High General," the woman said with force. "You were pardoned by the Great Lord months ago. You're free to come and go as you please. No one in Alchea will stand in your way."

Chrys was taken aback. Malachus had pardoned him? Why? Surely defiling the Temple of Alchaeus, colluding with a spy, and directly leading to the death of a dozen soldiers on the edge of the Fairenwild couldn't be so lightly forgiven. But then he remembered what his mother and Laurel had told him about their failed attempt to rescue Pandan. They'd also told him about High General Henna's role in exposing Jurius. The nation needed someone to blame and, where once Chrys Valerian—the butcher of the valley—stood, Jurius had taken his rightful place as traitor.

The revelation gave Chrys a measure of hope, but he knew the truth. There is nothing more dangerous than a measure of hope when the meal is war.

"Good," Chrys said, feeling a weight lighten from his broad shoulders. "I would have hated to kill you." He smirked as the second soldier, a man with bags under his eyes, clutched his sword a little more tightly.

"Chrys," Iriel said beside him. "We need to go."

He nodded, then looked to the soldiers once more. "When this is all over, I'll see to it personally that the both of you are rewarded for your diligence. Keep your eyes in the sky, and watch the mountains. A wastelander army is coming."

With that, Chrys, Iriel, and Willow stepped over the edge of the tallest tower, flaring Emerald threadlight as they walked down the wall, defying gravity. A single skyfly drifted in the air below them, translucent wings fluttering at an impossible speed. It dropped lower as they walked down, taunting them to approach. For a moment, Chrys' heart dropped as he remembered his son. He turned to look and saw the child safely wrapped up and held securely against his grandmother's chest.

Finally, they reached the window to Malachus' study. It looked the same as it always had. For some reason, Chrys had expected a change, as if the darkness that had come over the world would have rusted the hinges or clouded the glass. He paused, remembering his conversations with Malachus as they sat opposite each other. With a glance below to ensure no one would be hurt, he used the pommel of his dagger to shatter the glass, then launched himself inside with an unfocused surge of Sapphire.

The room was empty.

Chrys walked in, smelling the familiar scent of leather books and mahogany shelves. Broken shards of glass dotted the rug near the window, and Chrys felt a hint of guilt knowing how difficult it would be to pick up every piece. Iriel entered next, leaping down off the sill and steadying herself with a hand on the desk. Willow came in last, floating down gracefully with a combination of Emerald, Sapphire, and Obsidian.

Iriel straightened her hair and checked her side for her dangling palmguards. "So far so good."

"Should we wait for him here?" Willow asked.

Chrys shook his head. "No time."

Iriel was already moving toward the door. "He'll have sent Henna up to the front lines to manage the defenses. Too dangerous for him to be there with the Heralds around."

Willow raised a brow. "You think he's hiding?"

"Definitely not," Chrys said quickly. "He's too proud for that. I bet he's in the keep though. Somewhere visible but safe. Like the briefing room." They both turned to him. "It was built for wartime safety of the Great Lord and his family. Reinforced walls. Metal-framed windows with multiple panes. And a collection of bolts and latches for the only door that leads in. The perfect place for him to communicate with his generals safely without fear of the Heralds or the Felian army."

"Sounds like hiding," Willow mumbled.

Chrys gave his mother an unamused look.

"What?" she said. "How is that *not* hiding?"

"He's not hiding," Chrys repeated.

Iriel cocked her head to the side. "It does sound like hiding."

"It doesn't matter," Chrys said, annoyed at both women. "We know where he is, which means we know where we need to go."

"Ready when you are," Willow said.

Iriel gestured toward the entrance of the study. "Lead the way."

Chrys grit his teeth.

"But to be clear," Iriel said with no small hint of levity in her voice, "it's definitely hiding."

Until that moment, Chrys had never questioned his marriage.

He opened the door.

36

NEARLY EVERY PERSON they passed in the halls of Endin Keep recognized them, though Chrys only recognized half in return. Still, it did not stop their flight as they raced down marble stairs, ignoring whispers and quizzical looks, turning around familiar corners until they reached the hall leading to the briefing room where they hoped Malachus would be. Five sentries stood at attention guarding the thick mahogany door.

A promising sign.

Chrys took a step forward, raising a hand to greet the guards when footsteps sounded behind them. Before he could make a move, Iriel had already turned around, lifting a hand and shouting as threadlight flowed through her body. A small, steel dagger flipped through the air from the other end of the hall, flying directly toward Chrys' back. As it flew, its trajectory shifted, drawn toward Iriel and her Emerald threadlight. The dagger finished its arc, landing point-first in the center of her palmguard. Everyone stood still as the sound of metal on metal rang through the air.

The guard who'd thrown it stood slack-jawed as he took in the intruders. "Stones! High General, I'm so sorry. I didn't recognize you! I never would have thrown it if I'd known it was you."

Chrys didn't know the young man, but he did recognize his sincerity. "You are in the middle of a war, and I have been away. I won't hold that against you. But you *are* lucky that my wife was here. If I had a knife in my back, I would not be so forgiving." He turned to the guards at the door. "I need to speak with the Great Lord."

One of the guards looked familiar, a Sapphire with a birthmark on his left cheek and hair to his shoulders. "Of course, High General." He turned and knocked in a specific pattern, and, when he finished, the door swung open from the inside.

The guards stepped aside, and Chrys entered with Iriel, Willow, and the baby.

The inside of the room was dim and windowless, lit by a collection of small lanterns that heated the space to an uncomfortable level. In the center, men and women sat around a circular table with a map sprawled out, filling the entire surface. Small figures and tokens lay strewn across the parchment. Chrys recognized each of the guests, though a few stood out. A surprisingly solemn Tyberius Di'Fier. Stone-faced General Rynan. And the white-haired High General Henna. On the far end, with wavy dark hair that framed his bichromic gaze, Great Lord Malachus Endin rose to his feet.

"Chrys?" Malachus said with a hint of surprise. "You're alive? And with Willow. Come in, old friends. Where have you been?"

A dozen images flashed through Chrys' mind. From the Fairenwild to the Wastelands, the caves below the Endless Well, the Convergence, the Provenance, Felia, Cynosure, and back. "It's a long story."

Malachus gave a sly grin. "With a beard like that, I can only imagine. Now the real question is why have you returned, and why now? I cannot imagine it a coincidence that the Apogee has returned when we are on the precipice of war. Have you come to turn the tide once again?"

"That," Chrys said raising his brows, "is also a long story. But there is no time for that. We are here because Alchea is surrounded." He let the words sink in, puzzled looks passing from person to person around the table. "Your focus is to the west, toward the army on your doorstep and the so-called Heralds. But that is not your only threat. Do you not find it odd that they have traveled all this way and have yet to attack? Almost as if they were waiting for something?"

The Emerald-eyed General Rynan huffed. "They haven't attacked, because they've seen our new weapons."

"New weapons?" Iriel asked, taking a step up to stand beside Chrys.

High General Henna smiled. "We found more thread-dead obsidian. A lot more. Enough to make ten thousand arrowheads."

"Enough to take those damn Heralds out of the sky if they fly too close," Rynan added.

Chrys' mind flooded with thoughts. With an arsenal of thread-dead obsidian arrows, they could wipe out thousands of unexpecting Felians. It would win any ordinary war. Unfortunately, this war was anything but ordinary, and there was more than just Felia to deal with. "It's not enough."

Malachus leaned onto the table, knuckles down, staring into Chrys' eyes. "They *are* different," he said. "I thought it was a trick of the light, but your irises have changed hue. Where have you really been, Chrys?"

Quietly, Chrys pulled out a blowgun from Kai'Melend and set it on the table. "We've been in the Wastelands. The Heralds are in reality wastelander gods, and their army is traveling over the pass as we speak. Soon, you will be attacked from both sides." Chrys slid the blowgun across the table, knocking over tokens and figurines until it stopped at Malachus' hand.

The Great Lord lifted it and turned it over in his hands. "We would know if there was an army coming over the mountains."

Chrys paused, cocking his head to the side. "Would you?"

An uncomfortable silence settled over the Alchean leaders. Chrys could see it in the slump of their shoulders, the heavy breath in their chests. They knew it was true. The mountains at their back were safe. The wastelanders had never led an offensive attack, always content with keeping the outsiders away. They had always stayed on their side of the divide.

Rynan broke the silence, his gruff voice littered with frustration. "Why would the wastelanders attack now? To take advantage of the war? How would they even know there was a war? I don't buy it. Not until I see the wastelanders for myself."

"By then it would be too late," Henna said, turning to Chrys. "If we're going to redirect forces, we need to do it before the wastelanders enter the valley."

Malachus continued to stare into Chrys' multi-colored eyes. "Still doesn't answer how you know all of this."

Chrys turned to Iriel and Willow, who each gave him a nod. "I'll try to make this brief, and it may sound unbelievable, but I promise you that it is all true, with my wife and mother as witnesses."

With that, Chrys told them about the Apogee. He told them about the Wastelands and Alchaeus, the coreseal, Felia and the corespawn. Then he finished with their failed plan to create a new coreseal to capture the Heralds, ending with their escape and the wastelander army. By the end, each of the leaders looked at him as if he were completely mad. Even Malachus, who had known Chrys since he was a young boy, closed his eyes with flared nostrils as he considered the words.

"If you want proof, look at my eyes," Chrys said. "When I left Alchea, I was a Sapphire. Now, I am a Sapphire, an Emerald, and an Obsidian. My mother as well. A gift from Alchaeus himself." With that, Chrys *broke* the corethread of every leader sitting around the table and watched their eyes gape open as they began to float, gripping their chairs to stay down. "Give it a moment, and your corethreads will reappear. Until then, listen carefully. If you do not delay the wastelander army from joining the war, Alchea will be destroyed within the week."

As if on cue, the leaders all fell back into their seats. Rynan took the opportunity to stand and draw a serrated dagger from his belt, holding it out toward Chrys.

Tension built like a boiling kettle, until Tyberius lifted the lid with a fit of boisterous laughter. The large man stood to his feet and pressed on Rynan's arm, forcing it down. "Invisible creatures, flying gods, now blessings from Alchaeus... What a time to be alive!" He turned and addressed the rest of the room. "We all know Chrys, many of us since he was a boy. He has never been one to lie or even stretch the truth. With all that we've seen in the past months, I'm keen to believe his story. I vote that we redirect some troops immediately to the east, even if just to disable the bridge over the Jupyter River."

Rynan crossed his arms, the dagger still in his hand. "And what if he's working for Felia? Trying to thin the troops on the front lines?"

"We still have the thread-dead arrowheads," Henna said. "Even if we redirect troops, the Felians would take a heavy loss if they attacked."

"I would not use those arrows quite yet," Willow said, raising a hand. "You're going to want to save them."

Malachus rubbed at his forehead. "Willow, speak straight. Why should we split our troops and not use our greatest weapon?"

She raised a finger. "First off, Chrys and I are now your greatest weapons. Secondly, the Heralds control the corespawn, and we suspect they will be returning to Alchea as well."

"Dammit!" Malachus shouted, slamming a fist down on the table, tokens and figures tumbling around from the quake. "The wastelanders are coming. The corespawn are coming. The Heralds are coming. How the hell are we supposed to deal with all of this?"

"We have a plan." Chrys turned again to his wife for strength. Iriel gave him a nod, standing tall and strong beside him. "We found the Provenance of threadlight. And we're going to destroy it."

"Destroy—" Henna's eyes grew wide.

"The Provenance?" Tyberius blurted out. "Ha! This just keeps getting better!"

"Quiet!" Malachus scowled. "The Provenance is real?"

Chrys nodded.

"And you want to destroy it?"

"That's correct, sir."

Malachus' eyes looked up and to the left, toward a blank section of the wall. "I don't see how destroying all threadlight would help us. It would do exactly the opposite. It would completely cripple our army and even the playing field for Felia."

"It's not about the army," Chrys continued. "The best war is no war, and that starts with the Heralds. The problem is that they're immortal due to their unique connection with threadlight. We believe that if we can remove that connection, then they can be killed. If the Heralds are dead, we can try for peace with Felia. And we're confident that we can convince the wastelanders to leave as well."

"No," Malachus said flatly.

Chrys' brow twitched. "Malachus..."

The Great Lord leaned forward. "You will not destroy the Provenance."

"Malachus," Chrys said. "If we don't do this, thousands of people are going to die."

"Tens of thousands," Iriel added.

Malachus loomed over the table. "Threadlight is power. And not only that, it is our way of life, woven into the fabric of each and every day. We will find another way, without destroying threadlight, even if that means war with Felia."

Chrys clenched his jaw. "I understand your hesitation. We all had our doubts. But there is no other way to fight the Heralds. Trust me; we've tried. Besides, the plan is already in motion. We have someone traveling to destroy the Provenance as we speak. The only remaining question is if Alchea will be ready for it."

"Dammit, Chrys!" Malachus spat. "That was not your decision to make!"

"I know," Chrys said calmly, hoping to cool the rising heat. "But there was no time and no other way."

Willow put a hand on Chrys' shoulder. "If there was another path, Malachus, we would have taken it. The Provenance could be destroyed at any moment. Today. Tomorrow. We don't know. But we need your help to buy time. We can take it from there."

"You make it sound so simple," Malachus said, his chest still rising and falling with fury. "Stop two armies—three if you count the corespawn—and two immortal beings, for an indeterminate length of time. Are you sure there's nothing else?"

The sarcastic tone gave Chrys an odd sense of reassurance. "There is one other thing."

Malachus frowned. "Dear god, what is it?"

"Your watch broke." Chrys pulled out the pocket watch and held it up. "But that...is an even longer story."

BONDS OF CHAOS
37

THE WASTELANDERS WERE such tiny people.

Laz watched them cross the valley and thought they looked an awful lot like ants. Holding up his thumb and index finger, fitting the army between, he pretended to squish them. Sometimes just one, sometimes a dozen or more. The game made the waiting go faster.

"What are you doing?" Reina looked at him with the same goofy look she often gave, as if she were too dumb to understand what he was doing. Laz still liked her, even if she was simpleminded. She also looked quite silly on that big, white-haired horse. It looked like it could be her cousin.

"Is too hard to explain," he said.

Laz still couldn't believe that Chrys had returned. Now *that* was a man who was not so simpleminded. He always had a plan. Laz missed that. Ever since Chrys had left, Laz had had nothing much to do but boring patrol routes. It did give him an excuse to visit Luther once. That was nice.

On the other side of the river, the wastelander army grew closer, and Laz noticed the other soldiers glancing back toward Endin Keep more and more frequently. But their orders were clear: destroy the bridge. They were also supposed to wait. Don't destroy it until the army was close. That way the army would waste more time finding a new path. There wasn't another bridge across the wide, rushing river for miles.

Just in case, there was a battalion of soldiers with Laz. And not just any battalion...*his* battalion. It was the first time Laz had ever been in charge, but Chrys said he needed someone he trusted, who he knew wouldn't be afraid of the wastelander army. They were so small, Laz wasn't sure why anyone would be afraid. He lifted his fingers up and squished the army one more time for good measure.

"We should do it now," one of the soldiers said. A pretty man, thin frame, nice long hair. Laz did not think he should be a soldier.

"Is not time," Laz said.

The soldier gestured toward the army. "But they'll be on top of us in less than five minutes!"

Laz gave the man his hardest look. "Then we wait four."

The soldier cowered back quietly.

Reina still sat on her horse beside Laz, but she waited for the soldier to step away before speaking. "We really should probably do it soon."

"Soon," Laz said, offering her a toothy grin, "is last chance. If you want to swing the axe, I will let you."

"No, no, no. I think you're definitely the right person for the job."

Laz rubbed his hands together. "Good. This thing will be very fun!"

With Reina trailing behind, Laz walked toward the bridge with a satchel at his side and a skip in his step.

"Hold!"

High General Henna crouched and held a thick shield over her head alongside thousands of Alcheans. If she closed her eyes, it sounded like a wild hailstorm beating against the small cottage she'd grown up in. Only those storms weren't broken by the screams of unlucky soldiers being struck by arrows that her Emeralds were unable to redirect.

"Rise!" she screamed.

As her words were repeated down the line, soldiers rose to their feet, keeping their shields overhead and a careful eye on the outlying army. The Felians had continued their sporadic barrage of arrows for several days, but they had yet to launch a full offensive. Unfortunately, something had changed that day. Whether they were running low on arrows or supplies, the Felians had begun a slow advance. And with the troops recalled to prepare the eastern walls for the wastelander army, there were more Felian soldiers than Alchean on the western front.

One of her captains rushed up beside her, an older man named Kith who'd seen war before and had taken it personally that the Felians had forced him into it once more. "High General," he said respectfully. "The Great Lord needs to reconsider. They're too reliant on their Emerald shields. A single barrage of thread-dead arrows would devastate their ranks and stop their advance. They wouldn't know what hit them."

Henna glared at him. "For the last time, keep the arrows ready, but do not fire them until I give the order."

"We're just going to let the dark-skinned bastards walk right up and slaughter us when we have a way to stop them?"

Henna stepped forward and struck Kith in his face, quite sure she felt something crack in the process. Whether it was her own knuckle or his cheek, she didn't care. "We have men and women of Felian blood fighting in our army. Speak like that again and you'll find out just how sharp those arrows are."

The older man stepped away, rubbing his cheek and grumbling. If Kith had not been hand-selected as a battalion leader by Malachus himself, Henna would have sent him to the front lines. But she would need men like him, who held the respect of the other soldiers. When fighting begins, strength and respect are the only currencies.

One by one, messengers approached, detailing the advancement of the Felian lines. The other generals saw the slow approach as a sign of weakness, as if the Felians were afraid of a full-scale clash. Some even thought a spy had tipped them off about the thread-dead arrows, but Henna wasn't convinced. She knew the Felian generals personally, and she knew they were not fools. If they were moving slowly, then they were waiting for something.

Another messenger—a scrawny man with thick scruff and shaggy brown hair—came sprinting down the line, shoving a younger soldier out of the way and waving his hand in the air. When he finally arrived, out of breath, panting, fear in his eyes, Henna finally discovered what the Felians had been waiting for.

Chrys was right.

"Corespawn!" the messenger shouted. "Coming from the Fairenwild!"

Henna looked to Kith, the older general she'd sent away. "And that's why we saved the arrows."

THE WASTELANDERS still looked like children the closer they came to the bridge, but the swamp gorillas were another story. Laz wagered they were twice his size, which lined up with Chrys' warning, but even still, something about their movements gave Laz the strange desire to wrestle them. But they also had spikes on their backs, which would make wrestling slightly less fun.

Maybe another time.

Laz stood at the end of a twenty-foot-wide bridge that spanned the nearly one-hundred-foot-wide river. They'd sabotaged the whole thing, rigging it to collapse with a few swings of his lucky axe. Reina had tried to convince him not to let any of the wastelanders onto the bridge before he collapsed it, just in case they were able to somehow make it across, but Chrys wanted the army as close as possible. Their goal was to slow down the army, and the longer they spent approaching the bridge, the longer it would take them to find another route.

So Laz waited, and Reina stood beside him with a thick shield and Emerald threadlight in her veins. When the first arrow landed on the other end of the bridge, they decided it was time. Laz stepped up to the first thick rope holding the partially-deconstructed bridge together. He lifted the heavy axe and slammed it down. The sharp edge cut through the hemp with ease, snapping the taut rope and sending a tremble through the structure.

Laz turned to Reina and smiled his toothy grin. "See? Is easy!"

He moved to the next rope and lifted his axe. In a way, it brought with it a sense of nostalgia. Growing up in the farmlands outside of Alchea, he'd spent many summers cutting wood with that very same axe. The grip felt as though his calloused hands had rubbed their way into the wood, leaving perfect indentations for each of his fingers.

With a burst of strength, Laz let the axe fall. Again, the rope snapped, shooting forward at the bridge in a wild arc. The entire structure teetered, tipping onto one side as the second of the four anchors released its hold.

Laz and Reina quickly made their way to the third rope, eyeing the oncoming army which, despite the developments of the bridge, still hurled forward at surprising speed. When they reached the rope, Laz lifted his axe.

Thud.

He looked up and saw an arrow sticking out of Reina's shield and Emerald threadlight glowing through her veins. The look she gave him was enough for him to swing hard and fast. The third rope blasted away as it split in two. The bridge shuddered, the final rope groaning under the weight of the tipping bridge. Laz was surprised that the thick rope held and smiled as he thought of cutting it loose.

Thud. Thud. Thud. Thud.

Laz ignored the incoming flurry of arrows, grateful that he had someone beside him that he trusted, even if she was simpleminded. With adrenaline coursing through his veins, Laz lifted his lucky axe one final time, swinging it down with as much force as he could muster. As soon as the blade hit the rope, the axehead snapped off of the handle, leaving him holding nothing more than a jagged piece of wood.

He looked to Reina.

She looked to him.

They both looked at the wastelander army as the first warrior reached the other end of the bridge. Another flurry of arrows and darts loosed from their front line, drawn to Reina's shield as she *pulled* on a dozen fast-moving threads.

Keeping her eyes on the next wave, Reina screamed, "Do something!"

Laz looked down at the broken axe shaft.

Stones.

"Hold!"

High General Henna stood behind a legion of archers, all equipped with thread-dead obsidian arrows. She felt an overwhelming gratitude for Chrys Valerian, the man she'd once believed to be a traitor, but who had proven himself to be the most important ally that Alchea had. If he hadn't warned them about the wastelanders, they would have been blindsided. And if he hadn't warned them about the corespawn horde, teaching them that thread-dead obsidian is the only weapon against the creatures, then they would have wasted their arrows on the Felians. They would have been left with no way to fight them. They would have been torn apart.

Instead, it was their turn to do the devastation.

"Loose!" she screamed, her voice carrying through the legion, her message relayed until every man and woman holding a bow heard.

The sky darkened as a storm of obsidian rose into the air, falling like a hailstorm of shadows. Thousands of arrows fell, crashing into the unseen horde. General Kith stood beside her, Emerald veins glowing beneath his uniform, eyes fixed on the fields to the north. Henna had no way to know if their arrows would truly work on the corespawn, only Chrys' word that they would.

Her heart skipped a beat as the first arrows touched the ground. When Kith's Emerald eyes doubled in size, a dark cloud swirled in the pit of her stomach. If the thread-dead arrows didn't work, today would be the day Alchea fell. For a moment, she wished that they still had transfusers left over from the Bloodthieves, or anything that would let her see the corespawn and know if their plan was working. Instead, she was left standing still with a rampaging heart as she awaited verdict from the threadweavers around her.

A choir of guttural roars flooded the battlefield mixed with shrill squeals that harmonized like children's screams in a thunderstorm. The ground shook. Henna looked to Kith beside her, whose mouth was left agape at whatever demonic sight he'd seen in the realm of threadlight.

"What the hell is happening?" Henna shouted.

Kith turned, but his eyes seemed fixed to the battlefield. "It's...beautiful."

"Tell me."

Kith shook his head. "The corespawn hit with the arrows burst apart, like popping a bubble. The sky filled with beads of threadlight that quickly faded."

"So it's working?" Henna clarified.

Finally, he turned to Henna with a smile. "Hell yes, it is."

A few cheers rang out from amongst the infantrymen, but only long enough for them to remember that one volley does not win a war. They scrambled to prepare their next thread-dead arrows and aimed with guidance from threadweavers evenly spread throughout the legion.

With the corespawn under control, Henna turned to keep an eye on the approaching Felian army, Emerald-led shields spread through the ranks like life-saving magnets. Regular arrows would do nothing to stop their advance, and Henna worried what would happen when the larger force clashed with her own.

From the back of the Felian army, two figures streaked through the sky, passing their soldiers and slamming onto the ground between the opposing forces, snarling as they looked at the dying corespawn. The Felian lines halted their advance, and a cold stillness rippled through the Alcheans.

The male Herald, thick-armed with hair like fire in the blinding sunlight, wore a long, black robe with gold trim that shuddered in the wind. The woman was dark-haired and shorter than the man and wore a white robe also trimmed with gold. Side by side, there was no doubting who they were. They looked oddly familiar to Henna, but she couldn't place from where.

When the male Herald finally spoke, his words rang out in the open air.

"CHRYS VALERIAN!"

LAZ SCRAMBLED FORWARD and grabbed the broken axehead off of the grassy ledge, nicking the side of his smallest finger as he lifted himself back up to his feet. With great urgency, he slammed down the axehead on the final rope. It bit into the hemp, but not nearly enough to break the overwhelming tension. He slammed it down again and the axehead slipped, twisting and cutting his wrist with the jagged bottom.

He made the mistake of looking up and seeing a swarm of wastelanders throwing themselves across the tilted bridge. They were still tiny, but now he could see why people might be afraid of them. He lifted the axehead once more, ignoring the pain in his wrist, and swung down with every ounce of anger boiling inside him. For the wastelanders and the friends that had died at their hands during the war. For the pain in his wrist. And for his lucky axe. The metal head cut down into the rope, strands snapping off and flying toward the river.

Almost.

"Now would be a good time to finish!" Reina screamed while another volley of arrows and darts rained down toward them.

Laz lifted the axehead a dozen more times, slamming it down on the rope, blood dripping from his hands and wrist, rage flooding his mind and body. He felt like a butcher hacking a boar. Again, he swung. And again, the tension refused to break. The front-line wastelanders were halfway across the bridge now, and more were joining, their eyes fixed to the creaking wood and taut ropes.

Finally, the rope snapped, flinging up and over the bridge, landing in the middle of the confused wastelanders, but the bridge did not collapse.

Laz stared, wide-eyed, counting the cut ropes. One. Two. Three. Four. That was the plan. That was supposed to cause the sabotaged bridge to collapse. Instead, some unseen force kept the bridge from falling.

"Reina." Laz swallowed hard.

Reina strapped the shield on her back, turned from the bridge, and set her feet as she screamed, "Get to the horses!"

Laz slipped the lucky axehead in his pocket and ran, but he only made it two steps before the ground trembled and the bridge behind groaned like an angry whale. When he turned, he saw the end scene of the bridge collapsing under the weight of the wastelander army. Thick beams snapped in half, tumbling into the rushing river that pulled them downstream to the west. A dozen wastelanders fell into the water, rope and wood collapsing atop them as they disappeared into the depths.

In a matter of seconds, the bridge was in shambles, ripped apart by the fast-moving current, boards floating down the river by the dozens. The rest of the wastelanders stood on the far edge of the river, staring with their beady eyes across the water that rippled with refracting beams of mid-day sun.

Laz's lips curled up into a grin. "Ha!" He lifted his hands high overhead.

Beside him, Reina glanced back and forth between the wastelander army and their small battalion, particularly their horses.

"Relax," Laz said. "We won!"

As soon as the words left his mouth, a resounding thud sounded on the shoreline. Laz swiveled around and cursed as he saw one of the swamp gorillas soaring through the air over the rushing river to land beside another. Each of them had a wastelander straddling the back of their necks, like a child on their father's shoulders. By the time the first curse left his mouth, another ataçan had knuckle-run with incredible speed, then launched itself over the river, joining the others. At the same time, the wastelander army huddled in close, linking arms, and walked calmly into the river until the water covered them completely. Line by line, the army disappeared below the water, moving in unison through the rushing river as if it were nothing but a babbling brook.

Laz looked to Reina. "I do not think we won."

38 · BONDS OF CHAOS

ALVERAX COULD FEEL Xuçan's rage along the edges of his soul. On the one hand, he'd wanted to bring the ataçan for protection, but traveling with a creature four times the size of a man wasn't much in the spirit of stealth. So instead, he'd left a very upset—to put it lightly—Xuçan in a valley at the base of the Everstone Mountains.

He gripped his father's wrist with both hands as they flew just a few feet over the ground. The cold wind found its way through every opening in his clothing, reaching its tendrils up his arms and down his chest.

As Roshaw's chest grew hot, they landed and continued their trek on foot. They could already see the Felian camp, and they hoped that—because of their Felian heritage—they wouldn't be attacked preemptively. Still, they knew there would be guards, and it would not be so easy to get in.

When they finished their approach, a host of guards converged on them, and Alverax's mind flashed back to his time in Felia. Guards lining the path to the rose throne when he'd first met Empress Chailani with the elders. Guards floating in the air in the same room while Alverax bartered his life for the Zeda people. And he would never forget the two guards, like opaque shadows, trailing Jisenna wherever she went. In fact...

"Innix?" he said.

One of the guards stepped forward, bringing a hand up over his brow to block out the ambient sunlight. It was one of Jisenna's guards, a man who'd shadowed their walks on many occasions. And though the man had given Alverax many dubious looks over that time, Innix had always been respectful to him as an outsider. "Watchlord?"

The others shifted in their boots, palms placed over the hilts of the swords dangling at their side. A few even unsheathed their weapons. As they looked back and forth at each other, Alverax could tell they were unsure how to react to his return. Which meant that there was likely a bounty of some kind on his head. More than likely, the Heralds had called for his death. Fortunately, he'd built up a bit of a reputation for himself, particularly with the whole becoming a watchlord and using his Obsidian powers to fight off the corespawn from destroying the city ordeal. They knew what he was capable of, and they saw the Midnight Watcher at his side.

Alverax stood tall and walked forward, letting Obsidian threadlight radiate in his eyes. He looked at the guards, one by one, meeting their gazes with his own until he'd reached the end of the line. Seventeen. But from the corner of his vision, he could see more were coming.

Finally, he spoke. "It is good to see you again, Innix." He gestured to Roshaw. "This is my father. As you can see, he is also an Obsidian threadweaver, though his power is beyond my own. We are not here to fight you. We are here to speak with General Thallin regarding an urgent matter."

"*Watchlord* Thallin," Innix said, emphasizing the new title. "Shortly after you left, the Heralds... Well, he became their right hand. I do not think it would be wise for you to speak with him."

Alverax nodded, taking in the information. If Thallin was Watchlord, that was good news. His word alone could stop the war. "Thank you, Innix. The Mistress of Mercy looks down on you kindly from the stars."

At the reference to Jisenna, Innix's composure faltered, and Alverax saw a subtle twitch in one eye and a shiver across his lower lip. It was clear that the man had cared for his charge. The two of them shared a nod of mutual understanding.

"Are we good here?" Roshaw asked with a deep, resounding voice. He looked to the guards with his head held high, multi-colored eyes shining with threadlight.

The guards parted, opening a gap for Alverax and Roshaw to enter the makeshift Felian war camp.

If there was a single word to describe the camp, it would be "muddy." Ten thousand soldiers walking through half-dead grass after a morning of dew—the entire camp had transformed into a cesspool of congealed dirt, made all the more clear thanks to Felia's penchant for white fabric. Tents were stained. Clothes were mottled. And strips of fabric—old clothes and bandages—lay half-buried in the tar-like substance that coated the field. Every step felt like Alverax was back in the Wastelands, trudging through the swamps surrounding Kai'Melend.

Fortunately, the rest of the camp was not as diligent as the outer guards. Alverax and Roshaw, in their own muddied clothes, blended into the bustle as if they'd been there since the beginning. Alverax tried to keep his head down, especially after spotting several familiar faces in the crowd, including General Hish, the older man who'd pissed and moaned when Alverax had first become Watchlord—although Alverax couldn't fault the man for the sentiment.

After another ten minutes of wandering around and keeping their heads down, they finally found the black and gold tent of the Watchlord. Alverax felt his chest tighten and his pulse quicken as he glanced at the guards standing sentry in front. It was now or never. And if he failed, thousands of lives would be wasted, including his own.

Roshaw leaned over and whispered, "Last chance to go back."

For a moment, Alverax considered it. Even though Thallin was the greatest swordsman in all of Felia, Alverax was an Obsidian, and his father was even more. If all else failed, they could *break* Thallin's corethread and walk away. The danger wouldn't be Thallin, it would be getting out of the camp. But then again, they could fly...

"No," Alverax said with a healthy air of resolve in his voice. "If we can save lives, we have to try." He turned to his father. "You don't have to come."

Roshaw looked to Alverax with surprising intensity. "Yes, I do."

Alverax turned away, understanding that his father was still trying to make up for years of absence. But if Alverax was being honest with himself, he did want his father there. Even if it put them both in danger, he wanted him by his side.

Without a word, they approached the Watchlord's tent. The sentries stepped forward to meet them, swords drawn, eyes gleaming with Emerald threadlight. Alverax noted that they each wore a palmguard on their offhand, which he'd never noticed before seeing Iriel's. He almost *broke* their corethreads but didn't want to cause a scene.

"Gentleman," Alverax said, keeping both his pitch and volume low and steady. "If you have not already recognized me, I am former Watchlord Alverax Blightwood. This is my father, a threadweaver with access to Obsidian, Sapphire, *and* Emerald. We have come to speak with Watchlord Thallin. We mean him no harm. When I am finished speaking, you will step aside, and my father and I will enter. If you try to impede our progress in any way, you will regret it."

The confident shoulders and stoic eyes of the guards seemed to vanish while he spoke. By the end, they were nervously looking to each other for guidance. From the corner of his eye, Alverax caught the slightest smirk curl over Roshaw's lip.

"Gentlemen," Alverax repeated as he stepped forward with his head held high. He opened himself to threadlight, allowing the ghostly glow of Obsidian to radiate from the pit of his eyes. Hesitantly, the guards stepped aside.

Roshaw pushed back the flap and allowed Alverax to enter first, keeping an eye on the guards until they were both inside.

As soon as Alverax entered, he saw Thallin, but the man had changed. He seemed thinner, frail despite the bulging veins in his neck that peeked through the black watchlord garb. Golden tassels hung from his shoulders, and a sword hung at his side. When their eyes met, his face was a torrent of emotion, swirling through tides of fury, joy, and sorrow. In the end, a strangely cool calm settled over him.

Thallin unstrapped his sheath and placed it on a thin wooden table. "I am surprised to see you," he said, walking over to a side table and bending down to retrieve a bottle of whiskey.

Alverax felt relief wash over him. "Thallin, it is so good to see you. To be honest, I wasn't sure how you would react."

The Watchlord turned his back, pouring a bit of whiskey into three cups. "I'm not sure how I should react either. The people of Felia are quite torn about you." He turned around and carried two of the cups over to Alverax and Roshaw. "Your heroism against the corespawn hasn't been forgotten, but abandoning the Heralds? There are those who believe you should be killed for such a thing."

Alverax took the cup. "And where do you stand?"

"Please, drink, relax." Thallin stepped over to the table and lifted his own cup to his mouth, drinking a hearty amount. "I stand ready to listen, if you are willing to share."

Something about the way Thallin looked at him both calmed him and sent a chill through his spine, but he couldn't have asked for a better opportunity. If Thallin was willing to hear them out, then Alverax was going to do what he came to do. He lifted his cup and took a drink, cringing at the potency that burned as it slid down his throat.

"First things first," Alverax said, glancing over to Roshaw, "I guess I should introduce you. Remember when I told you that Blightwoods don't die easy? Turns out, I was right. Thallin, meet my father, Roshaw Blightwood."

Thallin stared for an uncomfortable length of time at Roshaw. Straight-backed, his hand rested on the table beside him. His eyes seemed almost lifeless, as if he were seeing something beyond the world.

Finally, Thallin set his hand on the grip of his sword and pulled it from its sheath. "Did you really think you could just walk back into our world as if you had not abandoned our gods?" Each word was spoken with crisp enunciation, blades in and of themselves.

"Brother," Alverax said, lifting his hands. His heart quickened, and his mind raced with the sudden shift.

"I am not your brother." Thallin's eyes burned fire.

"Thallin, please, let me explain."

"No!" Thallin screamed, switching the point of his sword back and forth between the two intruders. "You are a heretic! A black-hearted traitor to your gods! I should cut you down where you stand!"

Alverax's chest compressed. His heart was a clay pot, and each of Thallin's words sent a tremor along its surface. Hope leaked from a dozen cracks. Pain echoed in the emptiness.

"You know me," Alverax said with no more than a whisper. "Look me in the eyes and tell me what kind of man I am."

"It doesn't matter what I think," Thallin said, blade shaking in his outstretched hand. "My perception of truth is nothing compared to the wisdom of the gods."

"Bull shit," Alverax spat.

Roshaw gave him a nervous glance. "Careful, Al."

"No," Alverax continued. He took two steps forward until the point of Thallin's blade pressed against his chest. Head held high, he looked into Thallin's eyes. "Did they tell you what happened to Jisenna? Because I was there. When the Heralds arrived, they called the two of us into the throne room. They said they were going to test our loyalty. But then they —" Alverax choked on the final words, tears swelling up in his eyes. His chest heaved with the blade still pressed against it. "Relek took the Midnight Watcher. He lifted it up. And he drove it into her neck. And do you want to know why? Because I told him she was a merciful ruler. You want to talk about the *wisdom of the gods*? Tell me, Thallin. What kind of a god fears mercy?"

His heart raced. Tears streaked his cheeks. But he saw it. A flicker of apprehension. Thallin didn't want to kill him. And somewhere, deep beneath the walls he'd built, doubts scraped against their coffins. But faith isn't a weed that can be plucked out. Its roots run deep through the soil, latching onto every part of a man's life, *affecting* every part of a man's life. Expanding until there is little room for anything else. They become so entangled that it becomes difficult to see where a man's faith starts and his own mind begins.

Thallin's hand remained outstretched, a slight tremble in the blade. "I could tell something was different when you walked in. Is that it? Are you so filled with pride that you think yourself equal to the Heralds? I remember you pissing yourself at the top of the tower, and now what? You're wiser than the gods?"

Alverax breathed, letting the words pass over him like a cool breeze. "No, Thallin. I don't think I'm wiser than the gods. I just don't believe that the two you call Heralds are gods at all."

With a scream, Thallin slashed his sword across Alverax's chest. The blade cut through fabric and skin, leaving a streak of blood from shoulder to hip. Pain rippled through his body. All the way from the valley, he could feel Xuçan's rage-filled response.

Roshaw charged forward, launching a thick boot directly into Thallin's chest, knocking the Watchlord back. Alverax grabbed his father, throwing all of his weight into restraining the bear of a man.

"LET ME GO!" Roshaw roared.

Alverax, with the strength of an ataçan flowing through him, shoved Roshaw back toward the entrance. "This is not your fight!"

Roshaw growled. "When a man draws my son's blood, it becomes my fight."

"Not this time." Alverax turned around and looked at Thallin. The Watchlord stood with his back against the black tent, sword hanging like a natural extension of his arm. "Thallin, I understand what you must be going through. But you have to see that faith for the sake of faith is worth nothing. It doesn't matter *that* you believe. It matters *what* you believe. And a god that chooses to slaughter innocent women does not deserve your devotion."

The final words seemed to crash into Thallin like a tidal wave, as if they'd been hurled with the weight of a thousand regrets. The Watchlord stumbled back against the wall, eyes closed, clutching his sword so tightly that his knuckles whitened. Alverax finally felt a trickle of hope return.

Thallin shook his head violently, then sent a chair flying across the room with a swift boot. He brought his sword up with both hands, screaming as he slammed it down onto the thin table. The wood split and collapsed with a crash. He shoved the halves apart and sent them crashing to the ground.

The enraged Watchlord lifted his sword once more toward Alverax, heaving with each breath. "No more lies."

"Shit," Roshaw cursed, panic laced in his tone.

Alverax turned to him. "What is it?"

"My threadlight is gone."

Alverax opened himself to the otherworldly energy, sending a horrible burning sensation through his veins. He groaned and cut it off.

Roshaw grit his teeth. "Laurel has the worst timing."

"This isn't Laurel," Alverax said, glancing at his black veins. When he looked back up, Thallin tilted his chin up just the slightest. "The whiskey."

"The Heralds said it would take quickly," Thallin said. "A wastelander herb, I'm told. Now, raise your blade, Alverax Blightwood. No tricks will save you this time."

Alverax grabbed the hilt of the Midnight Watcher. Thallin was the greatest swordsman in all of Felia, and Alverax had sparred with him dozens of times. He knew first-hand that his own ability was no match, at least not before. Now, because of Xuçan's bond, he was faster and stronger.

"Thallin, we don't have to do this," Alverax said, clutching the hilt of the blade in its sheath.

"Yes, we do." Thallin lifted his own sword into a dueling stance. "And this time, I will not hold back."

Bonds of Chaos — 39

A<small>LONE IN THE</small> darkness of the cavern tunnels, everything looked the same. Wet rock, a patch of malformed photospores, stalactites dangling from the ceiling like nature's knives, and more wet rock. If not for Alchaeus' markings, Laurel would have been lost. At each intersection, he'd marked the way home. Between each, they ran faster than they'd ever run before.

A chromawolf's eyes are accustomed to the dark of the Fairenwild, and Laurel found her own eyes adjusting in quite the same way. After a while, she'd dropped the bunch of photospores she held—which had done nothing but slow her down—and ran, fueled by her unique bond with Asher.

What she hadn't considered was how much time she would have to reconsider her decision. For endless hours on end, they did nothing but run. Even when they stopped to rest, she couldn't rid herself of her own thoughts. She found herself missing the annoyingly idle chatter of the others. Without it, she had nothing but her own thoughts to haunt her. And she couldn't stop picturing her younger brother. How had she forgotten Bay so easily? She tried to repeat the lie to herself that Asher was the only family she had left, but the words did nothing but curdle in her stomach.

But it didn't matter. She'd set her course. She'd even caved in the tunnel, which was as close to burning a bridge as she could get. There was no turning back. The others were counting on her. Unless the Provenance was destroyed, there would be no way to stop the Heralds. Maybe —she hoped—by sacrificing herself for the greater good, she could pay back the myriad mistakes she'd left scattered along the road.

As they continued forward, a bright light shone in the distant tunnel.

Laurel and Asher raced on, increasing their pace for what they hoped would be the final stretch. When they rounded the bend, she felt a weight lift.

Alchaeus' cave.

She saw the rose-colored table, broken in two. The storage room filled with corespawn statues. And more importantly, just above the far side of the shimmering, golden elixir pool, was the fracture in the wall, the earthquake-wrought crevice leading to the Provenance.

Laurel stepped forward, eyeing the fracture as if it were an enemy. It was, in a way. A sentry standing guard at the entrance to the Heralds' home. Once she passed the fracture, there was nothing left to stop her but the Provenance itself.

Something touched her foot, and she leapt back with a growl. When she looked, there was nothing but cold cavern air. But when she took another step, she felt movement skittering up her leg. She swatted at it, still unable to see whatever it was that molested her. Tapping into her bond with Asher, like she'd done many times before, she reintroduced the world of threadlight to her achromic eyes. A small, lizard-like shape clutched the side of her thigh, its head moving back and forth as it looked up at her.

Laurel raised a brow, no longer afraid of any real danger. "Are you...Chitt?"

Its head cocked to the side, looking at her with curiosity.

She reached down, and it scuttled into her hand, crawling up her arm and resting on her shoulder. It shifted its feet again and again until it found just the right position. Laurel smiled before she could stop herself. As she craned her neck to stare at the little corespawn, a question she'd not considered surfaced in her mind. A question with consequences far greater than for Chitt alone.

"What's going to happen to you?"

If it truly was the source of all threadlight, and the corespawn creatures were made of threadlight, what would happen to them when the Provenance was destroyed? Would they react as they did to the obsidian dagger? Or would they be more like a person's corethread, which seemed to have been unaffected by the previous disturbance? Looking down at the friendly little creature, Laurel wasn't sure which answer she hoped would be right.

"Come on," she said. Whether to Asher, Chitt, or herself, she wasn't sure. Either way, whatever happened at the Provenance would affect more than just the three of them.

Laurel stepped over to the edge of the elixir pool and gazed up at the fracture in the wall. It looked too narrow to fit through, but if Roshaw had done it with his broad shoulders, then Laurel and Asher ought to be able to fit as well. Slowly, she stepped into the elixir, letting the healing waters rise up to her chest by the time she reached the opening. One step at a time, she scaled the wall, slipping her hands into breaks in the stone and locking her feet atop jutting rocks. With lithe muscles reinforced by her bond with Asher, she quickly reached the fracture, placed two hands atop the ledge, and lifted herself the rest of the way.

She pushed herself to her feet and looked down at Asher, who still stood on the edge of the elixir pool. His voice echoed in her mind. *I will need you to catch me.*

The large chromawolf took off at a sprint along the border of the elixir pool. Just before he reached the end, he leapt up onto the stone, using his speed to run horizontally along the wall toward the fracture. Laurel's eyes widened, and she steadied her feet. A moment later, Asher vaulted across the fracture, paws outstretched. Laurel lunged forward, grabbing his torso and yanking him into the opening, throwing them both into the wall of rock.

Laurel rubbed at her arm where a jagged rock had bit into her skin. "A little more warning next time," she said.

I am sorry.

"No, you're not."

Tiny feet skittered along Laurel's back as Chitt found his way back onto her shoulder. She reached up and touched the little corespawn's head, which was much more solid than she'd expected. Being made of threadlight, she'd assumed its body would be more like a thick mist.

Laurel slid her way through the rest of the fracture until she reached the end, where Iriel had hammered away a section of the wall. Ahead of her, a lake of golden elixir shimmered in a cavern so vast it could have fit the entirety of Zedalum. Stalactites the size of men hung from the ceiling in sporadic intervals, glimmering from the golden light that filled the expanse. And there, in the center of the cavern, far away from where she stood, was the island Iriel and Willow had described.

Asher nuzzled up behind her, peeking his green-furred head from under her armpit to look out into the cavern. *It is time.*

Laurel grit her teeth. "I don't know how to swim."

It is easy.

"Not for a human."

Asher said nothing.

Laurel looked down at the water. "Just make sure I don't drown."

You will not die in the water.

Whether intended or not, the grim humor lingered in the air like a noxious fog. They were one cold swim away from death. A few shivering strokes from destroying threadlight for the entire world.

Laurel couldn't think about that. Not now.

One step at a time.

This was one decision she couldn't allow herself to walk back on. If she did, Chrys and the others didn't stand a chance against the Heralds. This was the path she had to walk, no matter how wet the road.

She scratched Asher's head. "Let's go."

With that, they leapt together from the fracture, sending waves tumbling through the lake of elixir. Cold heat tingled across her body as she sank below the surface. For a moment, she did nothing but float. Specks of light shimmered all around her like sparks of lightning that flashed in and out of existence. On the lakebed, broken stalactites lay scattered like fallen soldiers with clusters of transparent fern-like plants that grew on the crystals, wavering to and fro. Laurel kicked her feet until her head poked back out above the surface and drank in the cavern air.

She turned and reached toward the center of the lake, Asher following beside her. As she awkwardly kicked her way along, she thought of Alverax. Even after seeing the gills along his spine, the idea of a man being able to breath underwater seemed impossible. But her own hair was tinted with green now, and she'd seen an ataçan-bonded wastelander with a spike growing from the base of his skull.

As they swam in eerie silence, she realized that swimming wasn't so difficult after all, at least with Asher-enhanced strength and endurance to aid her. As they came closer to the island's shore, a dark feeling pricked at her skin. She turned and saw a ripple in the water not far away, moving quickly toward her. Adrenaline pumped through her veins. Any enjoyment she'd felt turned to an overwhelming sense of vulnerability. If there was something in the water, what could she do? Wolves are not meant to fight in water.

Opening herself to the bond, threadlight flooded her vision. She saw little Chitt, skittering across the top of the elixir water like a pilliwick on hot sand. Fear washed away as she remembered the friendly corespawn, happy to have him joining them for their final journey.

Suddenly, an explosion of water blossomed from the surface of the lake as a massive creature, hewn of pure threadlight and with a jaw that could swallow a man whole, enveloped the little corespawn as if it were no more than a grain of feyrice. The creature let out a deep, whistling groan that filled the vaulted expanse.

"SWIM!"

Laurel and Asher took off toward the island, moving with as much speed as their paddling arms and flailing legs could give them. Whatever that creature was—some kind of aquatic corespawn monstrosity—Laurel wasn't going to sit around and let it eat them before they had a chance to destroy the Provenance.

The island grew closer, and Laurel swam harder, Asher keeping pace beside her. Just before they reached the sheer edge of the shore, Asher's body disappeared below the surface, Laurel's heart sinking along with the chromawolf.

She dove down, reaching for the dagger strapped to her thigh, its black blade glistening in the golden light of the elixir. When she opened her eyes, she saw Asher thrashing back and forth. One leg was trapped in the massive maw of the corespawn while the others swiped their deadly claws to no effect. Laurel stuck the dagger in her mouth and swam as hard as she could toward the light-wrought beast. It saw her and turned, opening its jaw and releasing Asher, while its tail fins sent it torpedoing directly toward Laurel.

It was too big. Too fast.

Her eyes grew wide as she watched the monstrous corespawn swim toward her. Fear threatened to take hold, but if she was going to die, she was going to die fighting.

Laurel grabbed the obsidian dagger from between her teeth and kicked her feet until she was aimed directly for its open mouth. Just before it reached her, the creature twisted back and forth, a deep groan emanating from its throat. It thrashed its tail, and Asher went flying through the water with a chunk of corespawn flesh glowing in his jaws. Laurel didn't hesitate; there was no time. She kicked forward, reaching her hand back with the dagger high overhead, and slammed it down into the creature's body. The dagger shook in her grasp, fighting the considerable amount of raw threadlight powering the corespawn. She squeezed the hilt with every ounce of strength she had, now grabbing hold with both hands and screaming under the elixir water as bubbles shot up toward the surface. Finally, the massive beast exploded into thousands of beads of threadlight that glittered in the lake like stars in a glowing sky.

Suddenly aware of her need to breathe, Laurel kicked up to the surface and drank in the cold cavern air. With the dagger secured back on her thigh, she spun around, looking for Asher and feeling a sense of dread. Only a moment passed—though it felt much longer—before his green-furred snout broke the surface of the lake. She swam to him and wrapped her friend in an embrace, which submerged them both.

They quickly swam the rest of the way to the island, and when they reached the edge, she pulled herself up and flopped down on the jagged stone, dripping from head to toe and laughing. The longer she lay, the more she laughed, until her voice filled the cavern.

Asher shook out his fur and looked at her. *I do not understand.*

Laurel stared up at the man-sized stalactites hanging high overhead. "Sometimes it feels like the world wants me dead, but it doesn't want me to choose the time and place." She pushed herself up to her feet and looked out over the vastness of the cavern. "GALE TAKE YOU, WORLD! I CHOOSE WHEN I DIE!"

The chromawolf understood well enough and howled beside her. She laughed again—only this time a hint of sorrow found its way into her tone—and rubbed a hand along Asher's wet back. One of his legs was bleeding, but the glowing water congealed around the wound already worked its healing magic.

"We're so close," she whispered.

Can you feel it? Asher asked.

Laurel closed her eyes. In the cavern, there was no breeze. No scent beyond the freshness of the cold air. No sound but their own. And yet, as she reached out through her bond to the world around her, she could feel a buzz, like the rustle of a morning wind through autumn leaves. A song, quiet but alive, calling to her from the center of the island. An instrument begging to be played.

"Is that the Provenance?" she asked.

I think yes.

"Asher," she said, suddenly feeling the weight of reality. "I...I've never been good with words. But I just need you to know. When Elder Rosemary showed up to tell Bay and me that our parents were dead, I felt like my entire world had been ripped away from me. I cried for days, and it felt like this thick cloud of darkness surrounded me. One day my eyes just went dry. I remember staring at a wall for hours and feeling like only a moment had passed. I started to think that maybe *I* should just pass. Ride the winds with my parents. At least then we'd be together again. I just...I missed them so much. But then my grandfather brought me down to Cara's nursery, and I met you. You climbed up onto my lap and fell asleep. I remember feeling so warm. So loved. It was a little thing, but that was all it took. Suddenly, where there had only been a dark emptiness, there was this spark of warmth.

"I will never forget what you did for me, and I just want you to know how grateful I am. You were my spark of warmth, Asher. You saved me."

The big chromawolf, still drenched in cold elixir, approached Laurel and nuzzled his head under her arm. His deep voice filled her mind. *It has been worth every moment.*

They held each other for some time in silence, knowing full well the fate that awaited them, then stepped toward the Provenance.

40
BONDS OF CHAOS

IN THE HIGH towers of Endin Keep, Willow felt like a child staring out the window in the middle of a thunderstorm. From the west, the Felian army advanced. From the north, the corespawn. To the south, the wastelanders finished their trek through the river and made their way to the edge of the Alchean border. The world was growing smaller, compressing, a bubble waiting to burst as pressure squeezed from every side.

Willow stood quietly beside a child swaddled in a sky-blue blanket, who slept as though he could not hear the storm. And all she could do was wait.

The skirmish between the two human armies seemed to have ceased. Whether that was good or bad, Willow did not know. She only hoped that Laurel would act quickly.

"You know," she said aloud, mostly to herself, though her eyes looked down at the sleeping child. "When this all began, we thought that you were going to save the world."

A knock came at the door, and Willow saw a familiar face enter. A beautiful woman with golden skin to match her golden hair and wrinkles along her eyes that told the story of a life filled with joy and comfort. Lady Eleandra Orion-Endin, the Gem of Alchea and wife to the Great Lord, looked older than Willow remembered.

"May I come in?"

Willow offered a weak smile. "Not much to see here. Just the end of the world."

Eleandra rushed inside and threw her arms around Willow, squeezing with the strength of thirty years of friendship. Willow wanted to say something pithy, but Eleandra had always had a way of disarming her. So, instead, she found herself weeping while her old friend held her tight.

Her mind returned to the day she'd first stepped foot in Endin Keep. She remembered being introduced to Eleandra. She remembered lying to her about where they'd come from. And she remembered the unreserved generosity. Willow had cried in her friend's arms that day, just as she did now.

Eleandra pulled away and looked into Willow's eyes. "I have missed you." She stopped, mouth agape. "Malachus told me, but your eyes. They're astounding."

"Oh," Willow said with a hint of color flushing her cheeks. "I suppose they are."

"And your skin!" Eleandra's brows shot up. "Is that part of the magic? You look ten years younger than last I saw you. Is there any way you could share a bit? I wouldn't mind..." She paused and let out a simple laugh. "I'm sorry. You were never one for such conversations. Regardless, you needn't worry. Everything is going to work out just fine. You'll see."

Willow wiped away a tear from her cheek and smiled. "It's so good to see you, even if I don't quite share your optimism."

"It's not optimism," Eleandra said, shaking her head. "It's that I know who fights on our side. I've never met a man as cunning as Malachus and no one as tenacious as your son. Together, there is nothing in this world that can stop them."

Willow looked at the regal woman, surprised to see such sincerity, such deep faith that they would emerge victorious. But Eleandra had never been through true defeat. She'd never had people she loved ripped away from her. She'd never seen the real darkness of the world. Hell, as an achromat, she'd never even seen the corespawn, let alone the immortal Heralds. The more Willow thought about it, the more hollow Eleandra's words became.

"I'm not so sure."

Eleandra walked over to the window and looked over the chaos enfolding. "I know you think I am weak."

Willow felt her stomach drop.

"Everyone does," Eleandra said quietly. "And they've every right to believe that. But not you. I don't want you to see a pampered woman who has never suffered. I don't want you to see a wealthy woman with no foot in reality. Not you. Not now." She paused and turned to Willow. "The truth is that I was never in love with him."

Willow furrowed her brow. "What do you mean?"

"Malachus," she said flatly. "If there is one truth that I hold above all others, it is that the world cannot be made better without sacrifice. But I'm not a warrior. I'm not even a threadweaver. If I wanted to make the world a better place, I had to sacrifice my life in a different way. I remember the day I first met Malachus. He was handsome, brilliant, and dangerous. I saw a cold darkness inside of him, leaking through. With those bichromic eyes, I knew that he would become Great Lord someday. I knew what I had to do. I finally knew what my sacrifice would be. What I could do to make the world a better place. So, I married him.

"I've never told anyone that before. I suppose some truths are too sacred to share. But I just—in case you're right—I wanted someone to see me."

"Eleandra," Willow whispered, staring at the woman she'd known for so long and misunderstood so thoroughly. A veil lifted. And behind it, Willow saw a woman who had given her whole life to shelter the world from one man's darkness. She saw a woman who had seen a grim future and offered her own happiness to prevent it. A woman bearing the weight of a nation with no one to witness. Willow didn't know what to say—what could she? Instead, she pulled her friend into an embrace and whispered, "I see you."

Eleandra's chest constricted as she fought back tears. "That's all I've ever wanted."

As they pulled back, Eleandra rested her head on Willow's shoulder. Together, with a warm sun bathing the chaos, they watched the greatest war the world had ever seen.

41 — Bonds of Chaos

Chrys stepped through the legion of Alchean soldiers, hands instinctively touching the waterskin of elixir at his side. Iriel walked beside him.

Across the way, Relek and Lylax stood in their resplendent robes, sunlight flickering over their wavering forms, paragons of godhood. With each step, Chrys prayed for the destruction of the Provenance. There were no more tricks, no traps, and nowhere to hide. This time, one of them was going to die.

They entered the trampled grass between armies, weaving between broken arrow shafts and littered cloth until they arrived a short distance from the Heralds.

"Chrysanthemum," Relek said with a sadistic smile.

"Relek," Chrys said. "And here I thought you were supposed to be all-powerful gods. What kind of a god needs an army to fight their wars for them. Let alone three."

Lylax lifted her chin and snarled, speaking with a cold, calculating voice. "When this is over, I am going to carve out the eyes from your corpse and feed them to your orphaned child."

Iriel squeezed her fists until her knuckles went white. As she leaned forward, ready to fight, Chrys put a hand on her arm. The last thing they needed was to expedite the fight. The only real chance they had was to delay and pray that Laurel could make the Heralds mortal again.

"What I don't understand," Chrys said loudly, "is why? If you succeed and everyone dies, then what? You'll have no more souls to bind. No one to play god to. You had hundreds of years to plan your triumphant return, and this is the best you came up with?"

Lylax took a step forward, but Relek held her back. For a moment, Chrys saw a grim reflection of him and Iriel. He wondered if Relek and Lylax had always been so cruel, or if time had simply stripped them bare. Before the elixir, before lifelight, had they been more like Alchaeus?

"You assume too much." Relek's eyes grew cold, as if he'd grown tired of the game. "Step forward, old friend, and let the world watch. I have been looking forward to this for quite some time."

They couldn't wait any longer.

Chrys pulled out two newly minted thread-dead daggers, gifted to him by Henna. Beside him, Iriel slipped off her palmguards, letting them drop to the ground as she unsheathed her own black blades.

The Heralds were waiting.

Come on, Laurel.

ALVERAX STUMBLED out of the tent, swinging the Midnight Watcher in wild arcs as he parried a host of lunges and thrusts. Were it not for the speed and strength Xuçan's bond provided, Alverax knew he would not have lasted five seconds against Thallin. Even so, he nearly took a blade to the shoulder from a clever feint at the start.

Thallin followed him out of the tent, dragging his sword along the dirt. "The Midnight Watcher does not belong to you," he said. His eyes seemed darker, shrouded by shadows cast from the midday sun. He strode forward with such confidence and pride that Alverax considered trying to lunge forward to catch him off guard, but he didn't want to fight. He still held out hope that Thallin would see reason.

Alverax tried his plea once more. "I don't want to fight you."

"Neither do I," Thallin said without thinking. His hand squeezed the hilt of his blade. "But it doesn't matter what I want. My faith compels me."

"Quit using your faith as an excuse!" Alverax shouted. "If you don't want to fight, then don't. Faith isn't a living creature with the strength to compel you. Only you have that power."

"Enough!" Thallin shouted, throwing himself forward. His blade came high overhead, but Alverax parried with ease. At the same time,

Thallin threw a kick at Alverax's knee, but he wasn't fast enough. Every move was fueled by so much rage that the Watchlord was nearly foaming at the mouth.

For a moment, Alverax felt a surge of confidence. He swatted away the next lunge and leapt forward, throwing a hard boot into Thallin's chest, hurling the Watchlord back. A crowd began to grow, weapons drawn, shouting. A guard ran forward, but Thallin screamed for him to step back.

"I'm not asking you to give up your faith," Alverax said, lifting his hands. "It's one of the things I admire most about you. All I want is for you to find something more worthy of your devotion." He pointed toward the east where the war was raging between the two armies. "Relek and Lylax. They do not deserve the faith of a man as good as you." He gestured to the growing crowd. "The Heralds do not deserve the faith of any of you!"

"You don't understand," Thallin said, shaking his head with flared nostrils, lower lip quivering. "You don't know what I've done."

"Thallin," Alverax whispered. He looked to his friend and watched the veil fade away, revealing the skeleton of a man, a corpse barely standing as the last remnant of his soul drifted into his blade. A man whose faith had consumed him. Every piece of Alverax's soul wanted to help him, wanted to *save* him. The Heralds had already taken Jisenna. They could not have another.

Tears fell from Thallin's eyes. "My faith is all I have left."

"Brother," Alverax said, feeling the weight of his friend's burden. A weight filled with loneliness and doubt. A weight that Alverax longed to help Thallin bear. "You have me."

THE PROVENANCE WAS different than Laurel had expected, nothing like the warbling mass of threadlight that formed the Convergence. Instead, it was a physical structure, a helix of three twisted, diamond stalagmites twice her height in the center of a deserted island. Something deep inside her yearned to touch it, to embrace the power she could feel emanating from its surface.

Asher whimpered beside her. *I do not like this.*

"I know," she said.

Back in the Fairenwild, when the coreseal was still just the wonderstone, the chromawolves had avoided that place like a poisoned well. Now, Asher was willingly approaching something infinitely more powerful and dangerous. Laurel felt a surge of gratitude for her friend. If this was to be her last day before she rode the wind, she was glad she would spend it with Asher.

Laurel gripped the obsidian dagger. She remembered her first experience with it, sitting beside a feytree and trying to cut her own corethread. She'd felt so embarrassed for thinking that such a thing could be possible. But now, after meeting Alverax and spending time with Chrys, Willow, and Roshaw, she understood how close she'd been to the truth. What worried her now was that the same dagger that was unable to *break* a corethread would be unable to destroy the Provenance.

They strode forward, step for step, as energy poured into them. Laurel felt more alive than she'd ever felt, like the bones beneath her skin were buzzing with power.

The Provenance was so close.

Raw energy sizzled like static across her arms.

It was so beautiful. Hypnotizing. Powerful.

It was power.

She was power.

Infinite.

Free.

Laurel was no longer in a cave.

She was in the clouds.

A bird.

A skyfly.

No, she was the wind itself.

Freedom incarnate.

The world belonged to her and she to it.

As she drifted through the sky, she wondered where she should go. She thought, perhaps, that there was something she was supposed to do.

But she could not remember what.

CHRYS RAN FORWARD and crashed into Relek, both thread-dead daggers ripping into the wastelander god's body like a butcher. Again and again, he thrust into Relek's chest, blades sinking hilt-deep into thick flesh. Every ounce of bottled-up enmity came flooding out of him like a broken dam. Relek was the Apogee. The Apogee was the darkness within. If he could kill Relek, Chrys would be free.

Beside him, he caught glimpses of Iriel, her own dagger biting through snow white robes and staining them with the red blood of Lylax's stolen body. Iriel was a whirlwind, a torrent of lethal grace.

When Chrys finally pulled back, Iriel did the same.

Relek and Lylax stood tall, red blood leaking from dozens of gashes, dripping onto the dry grass. Despite their outward appearance, the wastelander gods smiled. A ghostly light glowed from their myriad wounds, weaving in and out like a surgeon's thread, knitting their injuries back together with borrowed lifelight.

Somewhere in the valley south of Endin Keep, Chrys imagined a wastelander falling to the earth, their life forfeit for Relek's immortality.

Relek breathed in the stolen life, then brushed his hands down his shredded robe. "You cannot win."

"Who said I wanted to win?" Chrys said, spinning a dagger in his hand. "I just want to see you suffer."

Relek snarled. "Perhaps you would like to see your wife suffer."

Iriel gasped.

Before Chrys could react, Lylax reached a hand out as if gripping Chrys' neck from a distance. A ghostly tendril stretched forward, reaching into Chrys' chest, reaching into his very soul, his lifelight. Chrys fought the energy, throwing up a wall, a mental barrier to protect against Lylax's control. Still, it battered against the barricade, slithering around in search of a single crack to worm its viral energy inside.

Let me in, her voice shivered in his mind.

Chrys screamed, and the tendril shattered.

"Give in!" Lylax shouted as she walked forward with fury in her eyes. She lifted her hands, and dozens of rocks rose into the air. She hurled her arms forward, and the rocks launched toward Chrys. He crossed his arms and surged Emerald and Sapphire, bringing the stones together then blocking them with a threadlight barrier.

Lylax rushed him, sullied robes flowing behind her. She launched a flurry of reckless strikes that Chrys narrowly dodged. He lunged in beneath her arm and drove a dagger up toward her neck. She deflected it at the last moment, but the edge caught on a thin chain necklace beneath her robes. The force of it ripped the necklace free and launched it to the ground.

She snarled and reached for the necklace just as a black spear struck her in the chest, sending her stumbling back, barely able to keep her footing.

Chrys turned to see Great Lord Malachus Endin striding forward with a second black spear in his hand. "You shouldn't be here," Chrys said.

"You're right," Malachus said, taking his place beside Chrys. "But neither should they. This is *my* empire. My people. My home. Not theirs. And you were right before. Threadlight is not my legacy. My legacy is what happens right here, this day. Life or death. If we have to destroy threadlight to make it happen, so be it."

A thrill of energy danced within Chrys' heart as he remembered Malachus' old words. "Let's burn the world."

ALVERAX'S HEART pounded so powerfully in his chest that he swore he could feel each beat down to his boots. The crowd had grown quiet, all eyes turned to Thallin, who stood opposite Alverax with a gleaming blade still in his hand. But Thallin had grown quieter still. His head was down, fixed to the dirt near his feet. Alverax held his tongue, though he nearly spoke a dozen times as he waited. But he'd learned from Laurel that sometimes silence is more powerful than words.

Finally, Thallin lifted his head. His eyes were bloodshot, wet and weary. Alverax wasn't sure if it was acceptance of the truth—that the Heralds were no heroes to be worshiped—or if they were tears of submission to the faith that had so fully engulfed him. When Thallin took his first step toward Alverax, he reckoned he would soon find out.

Thallin said nothing until he stood only an arm's length away. "Alverax Blightwood," he said, his head held high, "the Heralds have sentenced you to death."

A shiver ran through Alverax, and he glanced at the sword in Thallin's hand. He wanted to make a plea one final time—his friend *would* see reason. Surely, the truth would prevail.

"For blasphemy and treason, you are condemned by Felian law." Thallin lifted the sword slowly with both hands. "As is our custom, you have had your opportunity to address the people."

From the corner of his eye, Alverax could see Roshaw's chest heaving up and down from the edge of the crowd as his gaze darted back and forth between the soldiers, Thallin, and Alverax.

There, again, Alverax felt a tremble in the ground, a rhythmic beating. It wasn't his heart. It was something different. Something big.

Thallin's eyes grew cold. "As Watchlord—as the right hand of the Heralds themselves—I find you guilty."

Alverax closed his eyes, embracing his failure. If nothing else, he had tried. Perhaps the distraction, small as it was, would be enough. If Laurel could destroy the Provenance soon, maybe Chrys and the others could still stop the Heralds.

"As a man," Thallin continued, standing motionless. "No, as a friend to one who has brought me hope in the darkness, I offer my life for yours."

Thallin tossed his sword to the ground and fell to his knees, smiling with tears in his eyes. The image was a ray of light to Alverax's soul. A heavy rain on the parched earth where his hope was planted. His grandfather's words about chosen burdens echoed in his mind. Thallin had finally accepted that his faith in the Heralds was not worth the weight on his soul.

And now, with his support, they just might be able to stop the war.

The thought gave him pause.

Alverax turned and looked at the soldiers encircled about them. Some looked confused. Others looked angry, unsure how to respond to their Watchlord's betrayal. Roshaw looked stressed out of his mind.

Suddenly, with the sound of an awl punching through leather, an arrow soared through the air. Alverax ducked, but the arrow was not meant for him. It struck Thallin in the neck, just below his chin, knocking him off his knees onto his back.

"No!" Alverax screamed. He dove forward, grabbing hold of the spear, ready to pull it out until Thallin grabbed his hand.

"Stop…" Thallin coughed up a thick gob of blood as he tried to speak.

Alverax again felt the rhythmic beating of the earth beneath him, but all he saw was Thallin. "We can fix this. You're strong. You can pull through it!"

"B…" Thallin wheezed, blood oozing down his chin. "Brother." He looked up into Alverax's eyes, and his lips curled into a smile. His lips moved, but no words came out. And yet, somehow, Alverax understood. *It is better to die free of guilt than to live shrouded in its shadow.*

Thallin's head tilted back, the trembling in his chest growing still as his body relaxed into the grass.

For a moment, Alverax felt like the sky was falling, as if every star in the night was tumbling toward him and all he had were his hands to stop them. He let go of the arrow, staring at the bright blood on his hands. *Lightfather, please. Not again.*

"Al!" a voice shouted.

His father.

Alverax turned and saw Roshaw standing with his hands raised, using an upturned table as a barricade. Dozens of arrows thudded into the wood, some breaking through, some nearly striking his father as they found their way through the openings.

"We need to go!" his father yelled.

Alverax looked around, but they were surrounded. A host of Felian soldiers contained them, weapons in hand, though many seemed nearly as confused as he was.

An arrow slammed through the table and cut across Roshaw's cheek. "Al!"

Thud. Thud.

Again, the rhythmic beating shook the ground, stronger now, like the earth's heart was thudding through the dirt.

The arrows stopped, and the soldiers ran forward.

Roshaw threw the table down and grabbed Alverax as if he was going to fly up into the sky, but their powers had not yet returned. There was no threadlight to save them. No words to convince the soldiers to stop. No tricks to escape.

But there was…

Boom.

The earth groaned as Xuçan landed beside Alverax.

Black veins glowed throughout the ataçan's body, his eyes oozing mists of darkness. Obsidian threadlight surged off of him, spreading over the field like a black wave and *breaking* the corethread of every soldier within fifty paces.

Xuçan opened his mouth and roared.

42

Shrieks swirled together in a storm of chaos as the armies finally clashed on the battlefield. Faithful Felians threw themselves at the Alcheans. The largest of the corespawn monstrosities trampled through the frontlines with Obsidian arrows stuck in their bodies like tiny thorns.

Chrys reached down and grabbed the necklace. It looked familiar, and he remembered seeing it when they fought in the Wastelands. But it wasn't until he saw it up close that he understood what it was. On the end of the chain, wrapped in wire mesh, was a small shard of Amber.

Before he could think, Lylax ripped the spear from her chest, lifelight filling the hole, and lunged back in, swiping for the necklace as she attacked. Malachus stepped in, jabbing with his thread-dead spear, forcing the Herald back. She was faster than either one of them, but it took more than speed to deal with two hybrid threadweavers at the same time.

That's when Chrys saw her.

Iriel stood beside Relek with tears dripping from her chin, but her eyes had gone cold, emotionless, submissive.

Relek turned to look at Chrys. "Kill your husband."

No, Chrys thought.

He knew what she was feeling, how difficult it was to fight, like a battering ram against a city wall, except the ram knew the weakest points in your defenses. But Iriel was strong, and her will was iron. If anyone could rebuke Relek's touch, it was her.

She had to.

She wouldn't...

Iriel reached down and picked up her thread-dead daggers, then turned to Chrys. With cold eyes, she stepped toward him.

Chrys had to do something. He couldn't fight Iriel. He *wouldn't* fight the woman he loved. He needed to break Relek's bond. But how? Dammit, where was Laurel? Was she even still alive? What if they were waiting for a miracle that would never come? No, he couldn't wait for her. He needed to do something now.

An idea blossomed in his mind.

"Malachus," Chrys said.

The Great Lord glanced at him while keeping an eye on Lylax, Relek, and Iriel.

"Keep them occupied," Chrys added.

Before he could convince himself otherwise, Chrys slammed his dagger into the shard of Amber, breaking it into a dozen pieces, then grabbed the smallest sliver of the shattered theolith. In one swift motion, he turned the dagger on himself, ramming it into his chest, deep into his heart, gasping as the pain rippled through his veins. He pulled it out, choking on his breath, and shoved in the sliver of Amber as deep as his bloody fingers could manage, moaning as he dropped to his knees from the pain. He fell to his back, struggling to breathe, frantically clutching at the grass beneath him, a thousand daggers cutting him from the inside. He slapped at his side, grasping his waterskin and undoing the drawstring. With a frantic jerk, he dumped half of the elixir into his open wound.

His chest sizzled from the inside.

Lylax's raging form appeared over him, driving a sword toward his chest. But Malachus *pushed* her steel blade away and countered with his own flurry of strikes. He was taller, with long arms and a longer spear. He stood above Chrys like an angel of death, swinging his thread-dead weapon in wide arcs, forcing Lylax and Iriel back while Chrys lay on the ground in blurry agony.

If any moment would leave a legacy for Malachus, it was this glorious clash of titans. Lylax raged, and he swatted her hands away with the tip of his spear. Iriel reached, and the butt of his weapon whipped out at her.

But the truth was...the Great Lord was no match for a god.

Malachus lunged wide, and Lylax stepped in with inhuman speed. Her hand reached up for his neck, continuing until she grasped the Great Lord's jaw and ripped. A loud crack popped as his head jerked to the left. Lylax spun on her heels, swinging the steel blade around until it cut through Malachus' neck. A clean slice through tendon and bone, muscle and sinew.

The world seemed to slow as Lylax turned to Chrys.

Malachus' head toppled to the ground.

In that moment, the world seemed to shift. A flickering spark of red energy glowed inside of Iriel. Two sparks danced in Lylax. And a dim, fading light flickered within Malachus.

Iriel stepped forward, standing over Chrys with thread-dead daggers in her hand. But even as she lifted the blade to strike, her arm trembled, and her jaw clenched tight. The blade inched forward, reaching, but she fought it with everything she had. Chrys could see the struggle in her eyes.

And that was when he saw it. There, surrounding the flickering spark in her chest, a clear thread, like a rope lassoed around it. Chrys remembered Alchaeus' words, his description of lifelight, and realized what he was seeing. Without thought, he let Obsidian flood his veins, reached out to the transparent thread with the last remnants of lucidity in his mind, and *broke* it.

Iriel gasped, and Relek roared.

Chrys caught Iriel as she collapsed.

Amber threadlight swirled in his veins like liquid gold. He could feel the full strength of a fused theolith in his heart, pounding, surging, expanding within him. His chest burned, a raging fire of power.

When he turned to Relek, for the first time he saw fear in the god's eyes.

Laurel was the wind.

A god.

Drifting in a sea of endless power.

She *was* the sea.

Wavering. Rising. Static creeping along her arms, sizzling like water on a fire. A fire that burned within her, around her, consuming. Eating. Taking. Inviting.

A single tone rang in her skull. Buzzing. Beckoning.

She closed her eyes and listened.

The tone vibrated through her, echoing in her bones, reverberating through her veins.

It grabbed hold of her, and she was the stream feeding the ocean.

Music flowed from her, adding to the chorus.

Art.

Beauty.

Euphoria.

She was alive.

She was power.

She was...

LAUREL!

Asher's voice broke through the dissonance, shattering the false reality that clouded her mind. Suddenly, she was back in the cavern, golden light shimmering up from the ends of the island, blinding threadlight beaming from the helix. She fell to her knees, dazed and scared, feeling like every muscle inside of her had been ripped from her body.

So weak.

So tired.

Perhaps, she would simply lie down and sleep. Is that not what she had come to do? What *had* she come to do? Her mind was so fuzzy, her thoughts so fleeting. It had something to do with the helix. Or was it the elixir? The world was too bright.

She closed her eyes to shut it all out.

Laurel!

Her eyes snapped open, and her memory returned.

The Provenance.

She had to destroy the Provenance.

Laurel felt a nudge from behind and turned to see Asher pressing his nose against her back, pushing her forward as he whimpered from his own pain. She looked to the helix and took a step. Her limbs felt so heavy, her bones on the edge of shattering. But she was so close.

Just. One. More. Step.

She lifted the obsidian dagger.

Her arm shook from shoulder to fingertip.

Asher, she thought.

His voice came through, shaky and pained. *I am here.*

Laurel turned to him, the blade quivering in her hand. *May the winds guide you.*

Asher rubbed his cheek against her side. A single tear fell from the chromawolf's eye as his voice filled her mind. *And carry you gently home.*

Laurel slammed the dagger into the helix.

The earth shook.

Bright light enveloped the cavern.

Endless pain scorched through Laurel's body.

Burning.

Devouring.

Together, Laurel and Asher howled one final time as the light consumed them.

43

Endin Keep shook as if the world had unleashed its wrath. Walls trembled. Buildings groaned. Books fell from shelves and art leapt from walls. Oil splashed against glass as lamps rattled in their metal cages. Outside the room, screams echoed through the halls as a quake unlike the world had ever felt rippled through the earth.

Willow acted fast, swooping down and lifting Aydin from the bassinet. He cried as if he knew just how dangerous it was to be in the tower. She cradled the child close to her chest as she hid beneath a desk. Across from her, Eleandra sat with her back against the wall, knees clutched to her chest.

For a full minute, Willow sat huddled there, eyes shut tight, holding her grandson in her arms and praying that the walls would hold.

But then, realization struck her, and she opened herself to threadlight.

She stood, carefully, and moved to the window, eyes wide as she strained to look out over the battlefield. In the distance, she could see the horde of corespawn. Massive monstrosities dwarfed their companions as they trampled through the warring armies.

Suddenly, a wave of force rippled through the air like a tidal wave washing over the land. Pain erupted in Willow's chest as she clutched the bedpost, gasping as her eyes took in their last glimpse of the battlefield. The force enveloped the corespawn, and they exploded, blossoming like a mushroom that reached up to the clouds.

Eleandra dove out from the wall and caught Aydin from Willow's shaky grasp. The child's piercing cries filled the tower.

"Willow," she said, eyes filled with worry. "Are you okay? What is happening?"

The room grew quiet as the quaking ceased and the pain faded.

Eleandra gasped, and her eyes grew wide. "Your eyes."

After a moment of confusion, Willow understood. She opened herself to threadlight, but none came. No warmth. No power. No pain. Where once there had been a fire burning inside of her, there was only cold nothingness.

She looked down at Aydin, searching his eyes.

Eyes that had sparked the return of the Heralds.

Eyes they once believed would save the world.

And now, their Amber sheen was gone.

44

THREADWEAVERS CRIED out in pain as the earthquake wreaked havoc across the battlefield.

Corespawn screeched and roared as their bodies burst.

Agony.

Like a tidal wave, it crashed into them, then faded away.

Sprawled on his back, Chrys drank in heavy gulps of air, feeling empty, lifeless, hollow. He rubbed at his chest, terrified that the pain would return. When he looked at his wife, he saw tears in her eyes as she stared up into the sky.

Then he remembered the Heralds.

Chrys pushed himself to his feet, finally ready to unleash the full force of his retribution. Relek would pay for all the pain he'd caused. The death. The sorrow. And he would pay for reaching his grimy hands into Iriel's lifelight.

Taking in a deep breath, Chrys opened himself to threadlight.

But none came.

His heart shivered as he waited for threads to appear, for the world to grow chaotic with a myriad of otherworldly connections. But nothing happened. Threadlight never came.

Not now.

He knew what it meant—Laurel had succeeded—but why did it have to be now? He could still feel the raw power like a phantom swimming through his veins. He wanted it back. He needed it to fight the Heralds! He had become a god himself! He could still imagine the flickering sparks of lifelight.

But it also meant...

"Iriel!" Chrys said, crouching by his wife. "Threadlight is gone. The Heralds are mortal."

Iriel clenched her teeth, pain written in her eyes. "I can't," she said, pointing toward the Heralds. "It has to be you."

Chrys rose from the dirt, turning to face the Heralds. For a brief moment, the fighting had stopped as both sides recovered from the quakes. An eerie silence settled over the battlefield. Pain and confusion as men and women realized that their greatest strength, their blessing from the Lightfather himself, had been stripped away.

Relek stood, chest heaving up and down as he looked to Chrys. "What have you done?"

Chrys kept his focus. Every advantage the Heralds held was gone. Chrys may have failed at many things, but if there was one thing he knew, one thing he understood above all else, it was how to kill a man.

He ripped a spear from a dead soldier's hands and hurled it with every ounce of strength in his body, years of martial training flowing through his form, extending back and lunging forward, stretched to full extension as the spear soared toward its target. Time seemed to slow as Relek reached out his hand to *push* the spear away. His eyes went wide as the bladed tip continued forward, blasting into his chest, launching him backward, sliding across the grass and dirt.

Lylax snarled, then screamed a smattering of unintelligible syllables as she dashed toward Chrys. He pulled out a dagger and focused on the fight. Her white robes moved like the wind as she countered his every movement. She pressed harder, redirecting his hands, driving a fist into his ribs and another into his kidney. Chrys' shoulder throbbed. No matter how fast he moved, she moved faster. He pushed forward, trying to stay close so his dagger would keep its advantage, but with every step forward, she slipped back. Finally, she slid beneath his arm and threw a punch into his stomach that sent him doubling over.

Her hand reached out and gripped his neck.

She was strong.

Impossibly strong.

Though she was not tall, Lylax lifted Chrys off the ground, squeezing against his throat, choking his breath. He tried to move, but his body was too tired. And all his mind could think about was how impossibly strong she was. She shouldn't be that strong. She was mortal.

Chrys reached out with his dagger, choking as his mind and vision blurred. With his last clear thought, he rammed the dagger into the side of Lylax's neck.

She stumbled back, dropping Chrys to the ground, pressing a hand against the open wound. Blood gushed down her white robes, dripping through her hand.

Chrys gasped for air, coughing, wheezing, and watching the Herald bleed.

"Try to survive that without threadlight," he spat.

A smoky essence swirled along the curves of her neck and into the wound, glowing, stitching the gash shut piece by piece, skin growing until it stretched across the gaping hole. Lylax turned her gaze to Chrys as a vile fit of laughter rose up behind her. Relek pushed himself to his feet, the spear still lodged in his chest, blood dripping down his black robes. With both hands on the shaft, he pulled it out, coughing and laughing in equal measure as both armies watched in horror. Swirling mist gathered in the fatal wound, filling it with healing energy.

Finally, Relek lifted the bloody spear and pointed to Chrys with a horrid smile. "Threadlight is not lifelight."

Chrys felt his world come crashing down.

Destroying the Provenance had only destroyed their threadlight, but the Heralds' bond with the wastelanders remained.

They were still immortal.

And Chrys was powerless.

BONDS OF CHAOS

45

ALVERAX AND ROSHAW leapt atop Xuçan's back, preparing to flee as fifty soldiers floated in the air around them. Then the quakes hit. Xuçan steadied himself against the ground with all six of his limbs, but Alverax could still feel the trembling ground shaking the great ataçan. A sudden gust of force washed over them, nearly knocking Alverax and Roshaw off of Xuçan's back.

Pain tore through Alverax's body, hot fire filling his veins. He clutched one of Xuçan's spikes, squeezing as if doing so would ease the pain. His father beside him did the same, groaning in agony. Around them, Felian soldiers collapsed to their knees, their screams and cries filling the air.

But as soon as the pain came, it was gone, and all of the floating soldiers came tumbling back toward the ground.

"Go!" Alverax shouted.

Xuçan grunted, then threw himself forward, knuckle-running out of the circle of soldiers as small men leapt out of the way of the massive ataçan. Alverax clutched with all his strength, feeling much like how he expected the necrolyte racers would feel.

That's when he realized his veins were no longer black.

"Laurel," he said aloud.

Roshaw turned to him, still rubbing a hand over his heart. "What?"

"She destroyed the Provenance!" Alverax said. "Xuçan, we need to get to the wastelanders, now!"

In what seemed the blink of an eye, Xuçan bounded out of the Felian war camp and into the southern plains where they could see the amassed wastelander army. They advanced on Alchea like a swarm of shadows. Spears. Daggers. Bows and darts. All mixed in with the wild clothing of the wastelander people and their bonded ataçan. A few lone arrows rained down from the Alchean walls, but not nearly enough to slow the advancing army.

The chief of the ataçan picked up speed, and Alverax held on for dear life, wishing—if only for the briefest moment—that he could use Jelium's trick and bind himself to Xuçan with Amber threads.

As soon as the wastelanders spotted their approach, whispers rippled through their ranks, and they stopped their advance. Xuçan came to a halt in front of the army, and Alverax leapt off of his back, stepping up to the wastelanders.

"The bond is broken!" he shouted.

They stared.

Roshaw strode up beside him and repeated the words in the wastelander tongue. Cheers rose up, filling the air with excitement and joy. Some lifted their hands high overhead. Others fell to their knees, weeping, or embraced those near to them.

But not all were cheerful. Their leader, Rixi, who had spoken with Roshaw in the mountain valley, walked forward with his ataçan beside him. The other warriors stepped aside to make room as he continued until he stood just two paces away from Alverax. He spattered off a collection of unintelligible words in Roshaw's direction.

"What's he saying?" Alverax asked.

Roshaw furrowed his brow. "He says that the bond is *not* broken."

Alverax looked at the wastelander. Rixi was short and stout, his arms as thick as any man Alverax had ever seen and his brows set so unnaturally deep his eyes were shrouded in shadow. The hunch of his shoulders gave him the look of one who had spent more time with ataçan than his own people. It was then that Alverax realized that his bond with Xuçan had not been broken. And if his had not been broken, and Rixi's had not, then it was likely that no bonds had been broken at all.

"It didn't work..." he whispered.

Roshaw turned fully to Alverax, giving a quick glance up at Xuçan. "What are you talking about? Our threadlight is gone, and not just from Thallin's poison. I can feel the emptiness in my chest. She definitely did it. It worked."

"She did," Alverax repeated, realizing the implication.

Laurel was dead.

His friend...

He blinked away the tears before they surfaced and shook the thought aside. "It must have only destroyed the threadlight but not the bonds."

Roshaw stepped in closer. "So, the Heralds are still immortal?"

"Most likely."

"Most likely?" Roshaw repeated, raising his voice. "What the hell are we supposed to do now? As long as the bond is in place, there's nothing we can do!"

"There has to be another way," Alverax said.

"There's not!" Roshaw exploded. "I *knew* this was a stupid plan! We don't have threadlight anymore, which was our greatest weapon. We're all split up. Gods know where Willow is. Chrys and the others, too. And Laurel..."

"Stop!" Alverax shouted, closing his eyes and breathing. "There *is* another way. Just let me think."

It only took a brief moment for Alverax to realize the truth: if there was another way, they would have thought of it already. He wasn't as smart as Chrys or Willow. If they couldn't come up with an alternative, then there wasn't one. Destroying the Provenance was all they had. No threadlight, no bonds. No other way. Not unless they were going to...

Xuçan understood his thought before he finished it. The ataçan's booming voice echoed in Alverax's mind, *I will not.*

"I didn't ask you to," Alverax said, turning to Xuçan.

You did not have to.

Roshaw looked confused. "What are you talking about?"

"It's..." Alverax didn't want to say it aloud, but if there truly was no other way...

"Al, what is it?"

Alverax glanced at the wastelander army, each of the warriors watching with interest. "There is another way."

Roshaw looked at him skeptically. "What is it?"

Alverax kept his father's gaze.

For a moment, Roshaw was silent, but then it hit, and every grain of joy in his eyes turned to red-hot anger. "No. Absolutely not."

"Do you have any other ideas?" Alverax asked.

Roshaw exploded. "We are not killing off an entire race of people!"

"I didn't ask *you* to either," Alverax said defensively. Roshaw and Xuçan shared a glance, as if his father finally understood the previous exchange. "The problem is the bond. Think of it like a moldy loaf of bread. You can either cut off the mold or throw out the bread."

"These are people!" Roshaw said with a look of disappointment. "They're not something you can just discard. Especially when there's still a chance we can cut out the mold."

"That's the thing." Alverax looked to the wastelanders, to their young and old, their men and women. "It's no longer a matter of if; it's a matter of when. If the bond doesn't kill them today, the war will kill them tomorrow."

"Doesn't matter. It's not our decision to make." Roshaw pointed to the army. "If this is really the only path forward, they might have something to say about it. Rixi might have something to say."

"You're right," Alverax agreed, annoyed that his father was insinuating that he didn't care about the wastelander's opinion on the matter. "They should know the truth. Can you translate for me?"

Roshaw reluctantly nodded, and Xuçan's voice entered Alverax's mind. *Be careful, King of the Hive. Your words carry weight now, and it is you who must live with their consequence.*

Alverax opened his mouth to respond, then realized the wisdom in Xuçan's words. If he asked the wastelanders to lay down their lives, and they did, would he be strong enough to live the rest of his life knowing what he'd done? He wanted to bring people hope, not death. Light, not infinite darkness.

The real question was: did he have any other choice?

Alverax remembered his father's words on the path to Kai'Melend, teaching him about the wastelanders and their reverence for the Wasteland bees, the et'hovon. How, like the bees, the wastelanders believed they were a hive, each individual adding to the greater whole. One heart and one mind. Each willing to sacrifice for the benefit of the hive.

If this was the only way, he would give the wastelanders the choice.

Xuçan roared, beating at his chest, then settled and let Alverax begin.

"Our plan failed," Alverax said, loud enough for them all to hear though they could not understand. "You have watched your brothers and sisters die to give life to the false gods and, because we failed, your lives are still bound. There is no breaking the bond. There is no fighting the gods. In the coming days, each of us will die, whether by the blade or by the bond. There is no stopping it. It is inevitable. As long as you live, Relek and Lylax will win."

He paused, letting the wastelanders absorb his words as his father translated. In their eyes, Alverax could see that they already knew. Many hung their heads, others gave a nod of understanding, and others stood tall, trying to be strong in the face of defeat. Rixi watched with intense focus.

"Though our plan failed, it did not fail completely," Alverax continued. "Relek and Lylax are no longer threadweavers. The bond is their last advantage. There is only one way now to stop the false gods, but it is a dark path. And it is a path that only the An'tara can walk."

Rixi stepped forward and spoke.

Alverax turned to his father.

"He said they are not afraid." Roshaw stepped closer to Alverax. "This doesn't feel right. We can't do this. There is no way in hell the Alcheans would do the same. There has to be another way."

"You know there's not," Alverax said. "But you're right that we can't do this. It needs to come from one of them." He looked to Rixi, and his father translated for him. "The false gods cannot create new bonds, but their bond with the An'tara still gives them power. There is no way to stop them so long as the An'tara live."

Rixi looked to Alverax, the tattoos along his nose shifting as he furrowed his brow and replied.

"What of the children who are unbound?" Roshaw translated.

"They would be cared for," Alverax promised. "The choice is yours. The Hive will follow you."

Rixi nodded, taking a minute to consider the request. Finally he turned to the army of wastelanders, his head held high. "An'tara!" he called out. "Look around. See our brothers and sisters, friends and children. We are the et'hovon, and this is our Hive!" When Roshaw finished relaying the words to Alverax, they watched as wastelanders nodded, gripping arms with their neighbors, quiet but empowered. Rixi continued. "There is only one way to stop the false gods, and only the An'tara have the power. But only if we are undivided."

Alverax looked at Roshaw as he translated with tears swelling in his eyes. He loved these people, despite all he had been through, and the truth sent a flood of emotion through Alverax's chest. The wastelanders reminded Roshaw of the woman he loved, the woman he'd lost. Alverax looked up and imagined how he would feel if the Moon's Little Sister suddenly vanished from the sky, and his heart broke for his father.

"If we surrender our spirits," Rixi continued, "the false gods will lose their power. The choice is ours. Let the false gods live. Be their anchor and die tomorrow. Or give our lives today, and take the false gods with us."

The entire wastelander army stood stunned. Not a word was spoken, only the cool breeze fluttering through the grass and the distant sounds of the rushing river. Their eyes all seemed to focus on the ground, as if looking at each other would bring them shame.

Finally, Rixi turned and looked at the rest of the army. He lifted his spear into the air. "If we are to die, I say we die of our own choosing, and for our own purpose! We are the sacrifice. We are the Hive. We are the An'tara!"

The wastelanders stood a little taller, nodding as the Hive made their decision.

Tears fell from Alverax's brown eyes, both for the wastelanders and for his father. And because he knew what was to come.

46

Chrys fell to his knees and felt every last vestige of hope trickle from his pores. Even still, he was not empty. Familiar words expanded within him, lies that choked his bones like a weed. They laughed at him, echoing, mocking him for ever having believed their vitriolic message.

I am in control.

The truth was that Relek had always been in control. Even when he was no more than the Apogee, whispering in Chrys' mind, he'd set the stage for his release. And now, kneeling in a grassy field in the midst of two armies, staring at the gods he'd failed to stop, Chrys finally accepted the truth. He had failed, and the world would suffer because of it.

"Get up."

He turned and saw Iriel walking forward, strapping a palmguard onto her left hand, holding a dagger in her right. Dried blood congealed beneath her nostrils, and mud covered her clothes. Her hair was a ratty mess. And she was ready to fight.

"Get up," she repeated, though her eyes remained fixed on the Heralds. "It's not over until we're dead."

"It didn't work," Chrys said.

Iriel looked to her husband, somehow offering disappointment and rage with the same look. "Then we will make them suffer."

"That's enough for me," he said, pushing himself up.

"Besides," she added. "There are only so many wastelanders. The bonds will run out eventually."

"There are thousands," Chrys said.

Iriel hit the hilt of her dagger on her palmguard, a metallic thud echoing out from the strike. "Then we have a lot of stabbing to do."

Chrys felt a surge of strength flow through him. Iriel was right. If they were going to die, they would go down fighting. Relek was going to regret not killing Chrys in the Wastelands.

He clutched tightly to his daggers as he looked to Iriel. "If this is the end, I want you to know—"

"It's not," she said quickly.

He had a whole speech that he wanted to give about how she was the strongest woman he'd ever known and a better mother to their child than he could have ever asked for. A better wife than he deserved. That she made him a better man. But she already knew, and that truth filled his soul. Even if he'd failed everywhere else, at least he had not failed the woman he loved.

Together, they stepped toward the Heralds.

Chrys made eye contact with Relek, whose prismatic eyes had faded to a deep brown, so dark they nearly matched his torn black robes. Beside him, Lylax's white robes were stained with a hundred streaks of red. For the briefest moment, as Lylax watched their advance, Chrys saw a glimpse of Autelle again. Perhaps, it was the brown in her eyes, but Chrys wondered if she was still inside, crying to be released, or silently watching with no hope of return.

Between the earthquakes, the corespawn, and the loss of threadlight, none of the soldiers knew what to do. So, both armies stood still as the Heralds, Chrys, and Iriel, all circled each other in the center of the field. They watched with reverence, scared to come between gods and legends, wondering what other dark tidings the day would bring.

Chrys and Iriel stood across from Relek and Lylax, each holding a thread-dead blade, though it no longer made a difference. Wind rustled through the grass. Silence swirled through the open air. Fate drifted down on warm rays.

"I should thank you." Relek looked at Chrys with dead eyes. "All of this is because of you. When there is no more left in this world but death and decay, it will be because you were unfit to protect your family. Because you needed me. Because *you* let me out. Tell me, old friend. Was it worth it?"

Chrys' blood boiled beneath his skin, rage sizzling through vein and sinew. His hands shook and his nostrils flared as he fought back his urge to attack. It was what Relek wanted. It was what Chrys came to do. But he would fight when he was damn well ready. Instead, Chrys decided to try another avenue.

"Your brother loved you," Chrys said, waiting for a reaction. Relek gave nothing away, but Lylax, on the other hand, trembled at the mention of the third sibling. "He never wanted to live forever. He did it because he loved you both. He wanted to help you hold onto your humanity. I want you to know that he died helping us. Because in the end, Alchaeus saw what you had become, and it broke his heart."

"Say his name again, and I will cut out your tongue," Relek growled.

Chrys gripped his blade. "If I die today, I will die fighting for the same cause your brother died for. If anyone has a right to speak his name, it's me. When *Alchaeus* died, he was no longer your brother. He was mine."

Relek and Lylax lunged like ravenous wolves.

"Lightfather be damned," Roshaw said, stepping away from Rixi.

"What is it?" Alverax asked. "What did he say?"

Roshaw ran both hands over his face. "*Pintalla mox*... We were so wrong."

"The plague?"

"It's not a plague." Roshaw shook his head. "It's protection from a plague. The translation is literal. The wastelanders can surrender their spirit to protect the Hive. The dead wastelanders we saw didn't die of a disease. They knew that the gods were using them. They saw their brothers and sisters dying to the bond. But they couldn't convince the rest of the Hive to fight back. So they surrendered their lives in protest. First at the Endless Well, and again in the mountains. They sacrificed their own lives. The wastelanders have been preparing for this moment since the gods returned."

Alverax's mind swirled. Confusion. Awe. Disbelief. Even beyond the shock of the revelation, the implications gripped Alverax from the inside. He pictured the wastelanders who had given their lives through the *pintalla mox*, kneeling, skin blackened, statues gathered together in protest against the false gods. The solemn image took on a whole new meaning as tears formed in his eyes. He pictured Thallin, also kneeling as he too gave up his life to protest the Heralds.

He closed his eyes. In the darkness, free of the surrounding world, free of reality, free of the truth, he could almost forget the path he'd set for the wastelanders. He could almost revel in the beauty of it without letting the crushing weight take hold. Just because the wastelanders would, did not mean they should.

He turned to Xuçan, craning his neck to look up into the ataçan's shadowed eyes. "Are we doing the right thing?"

Xuçan let out a huff. *You wish me to justify your path.*

"No," Alverax said, knowing it was a lie. "It's our only choice—which I guess makes it the right choice—but that won't make it any easier to live with."

You are truly he-who-doubts-his-path. The chief of the ataçan bent down low, nostrils flaring with each breath. *If you cannot trust the path you tread, you are already lost.* With that, Xuçan rose up and stepped back, settling on a bed of grass and dirt beside a group of the other ataçan.

Alverax repeated the words in his mind as he looked out over the wastelander army, their Hive. He thought about what they were going to do, and he felt a strange sense of pride. These were his people as much as the people of Felia. But the selflessness they displayed in such abundance was something no human civilization could ever accomplish. They may have a different lifestyle, but they had grown beyond the men of the west in a way that mattered so much more. Thinking of his time in Felia, sacrificing himself for the Zeda people, he wondered if the wastelanders would be proud of him, too.

Trust the path, he thought once more.

Alverax stepped over to Rixi, and, without a word, he wrapped the short man in an embrace. Rixi hesitated, then returned the gesture. Warmth and kinship flowed through them until Alverax let go, grabbing Rixi by the shoulders. "May the true gods embrace the Hive."

As Alverax let him go, Roshaw translated the words. Rixi gave Alverax a final nod and stepped over to the wastelander army, who awaited his command. Quietly, calmly, Rixi and his ataçan companion fell in line with the others, as if they were just any other warrior and ataçan pair. He got down on his knees and the entire army followed, a wave of reverence rippling through their ranks. He set down his spear and lifted his hands overhead, crossing them at the wrist and curling his fingers back so the tips were touching. Every last warrior of the Wastelands followed his lead. Finally, he dropped his hands and bowed to the earth.

The wastelanders—these beautiful, selfless people—did not deserve such an end. But sometimes life does not give the most to the deserving. Sometimes, life takes, and it takes until the once-filled well runs dry. Sometimes, it is cruelest to the kindest and coldest to those already bitten by the frost. It is brutal, callous, and most of all, unfair. And so, it becomes the work of men to bring balance. To fill the empty wells. To warm the shivering shoulders. To sacrifice for the greater good. The wastelanders understood that, and Alverax would never forget.

Without a sound—so calmly that Alverax would have missed it had he not been watching carefully—Rixi's gray skin turned black, an onyx statue in a veridian field. His bonded ataçan collapsed beside him.

Alverax choked back tears. His lips trembled, and his chest convulsed. Roshaw turned away, tears streaming down his face, no longer able to watch. Alverax stepped over to his father and wrapped him in a fierce embrace. But he did not turn away—he had to watch. This was his path, his responsibility to bear.

One by one, each of the wastelanders grew still, their skin fading to black.

Alverax watched them all, still clutching tightly to his weeping father, but now, he no longer fought back the tears. Instead, Alverax embraced the sorrow and welcomed the pain. Men and women, families, side-by-side, holding hands as they surrendered their spirits. What started with Rixi spread through the wastelanders, until the field of grass had transformed into a steppe of statues.

When all that was left was the sound of small children crying, Alverax closed his eyes and dropped his head onto his father's shoulder.

So much death.

No matter how many times Chrys' dagger connected with Relek's body, the Herald continued his attack. Blow after blow, strike after strike, an endless barrage of power and strength. After several minutes of fighting,

Chrys could barely move either arm, and Iriel wasn't faring much better. She had a dozen cuts across her arms and a slash across her cheek that had nearly taken her ear. When she fell back to the ground near Chrys, he knew it was over.

He could feel it in his bones.

He could smell death in the air.

Relek stepped over him, sword in hand, eyes alight with claimed victory. "Good bye, old friend."

He lifted the blade high into the air, holding tight with both hands.

Then his eyes went wide.

Relek's body convulsed. His mouth opened, and he gasped as his limbs trembled. The sword fell from his shaking hands. Lylax groaned beside him, gulping in ragged breaths. In the shadow of a moment, they both collapsed to the ground, clutching at their chests.

Chrys watched in awe.

Something was happening.

Had Laurel found another way?

Whatever it was, he had to act. If there was any chance that their bond with the wastelanders had been severed, he had to take it.

Chrys stepped forward, straining with every movement, fighting limbs that had already given in to defeat. The world seemed to tilt around him. He shut his eyes for a moment, the Heralds still groaning only a few paces away, and took in a steady breath. When he opened his eyes, he saw Iriel on her knees, crying as blood trickled from a dozen wounds. He stepped over and grabbed her hand.

"One more fight."

"I..." Iriel wrestled with her tears. "I think this might be it for me."

"One more fight," he repeated, shoving a dagger into one of her hands and pulling her to her feet.

They were a mess, dirt and blood splattered across their bodies, open wounds peeking through torn clothing. But as terrible as they looked, the Heralds looked worse. Their black and white robes, speckled with red, lay draped across the grass as both Relek and Lylax stared up into the sky, mumbling to themselves.

Chrys and Iriel stumbled over, daggers in hand, and stood over them. All of the power and primacy that had once emanated from these so-called gods had faded, leaving nothing but cracked vessels. These two beings had caused so much pain, so much death and destruction. For centuries, they had cast their poisoned shadows over the earth.

But they failed.

And now, standing over their broken bodies, Chrys was finally in control.

The Heralds' lips quivered, each breath a choking battle. For a moment, as tears swelled in Relek's eyes, Chrys saw vestiges of humanity in the dying man. Perhaps, now that his powers were gone, he could be redeemed. Perhaps, he would atone. Use his centuries of accumulated knowledge for the betterment of mankind. Alchaeus had once believed his brother had goodness left in him.

But Alchaeus was dead, and so were countless others.

Chrys leaned down close to Relek's ear, dagger in hand. "Who's in control now?"

Together, Chrys and Iriel Valerian slammed their daggers into the hearts of the Heralds.

47

BONDS OF CHAOS

ALVERAX GRIPPED his father as he watched mourning children wander through a field of statues. Though the wind blew, all he could hear were the cries of those too young to understand. Too young to join the sacrifice. The unbound few. Alverax looked to Xuçan, hoping to glean a bit of strength from the chief, but he found only sorrow. It was not just wastelanders who had died that day. Bonded ataçan lay scattered throughout the lifeless throng.

Leaving his father, Alverax stepped into the graveyard. Men. Women. Young and old. United. One in heart and purpose. For the greater good. To defy the gods. Not for the benefit of their own people, but for the world itself. Alverax had once felt shame for being a wastelander. Now, he felt nothing but pride and sorrow.

Pintalla mox.

Surrendered spirit.

He touched them as he walked, a hand placed on stiff shoulders, fingers brushing against crisp hair. Part of him wondered if he had the ability as well. If he knelt beside them, could he surrender his own spirit? Should not the King of the Hive be with his people? Perhaps the only way to kill a Blightwood was if he gave up his own life.

Before he knew it, Alverax was on his knees.

It felt so natural, the grass beneath him, the odd scent of the wastelanders drifting in the wind beside him. Even the oppressive sun seemed to cool as he knelt. A chill ran along his spine where the scar had once been before the elixir had opened his wastelander heritage once again.

Heritage.

The word swirled in his mind. The physical differences were not his only inheritance. His heritage was one of sacrifice. A heritage of surrender, a spiritual offering.

Alverax closed his eyes, breathed the air, and communed with his birthright. He looked inside himself, searching for the power of *pintalla mox*. His mind swerved in and out of memories, through canals of strength and endowment. Somewhere inside him, he would find his true ancestry. Hidden. Waiting. A snake in the sand.

But the longer he looked, the more he understood the truth. He had not inherited the power of *pintalla mox*. His sacrifice was not to die but to live with the consequences of that day. He would live so the memory of their sacrifice would endure.

As he knelt, he thought he could hear Laurel's words riding on the wind.

People are like trees, remember? The least we can do is stand.

Alverax picked himself up, slowly, legs bearing countless burdens, but still he stood.

Not far away, his father had made his way to the children, whispering comfort and embracing their pain as his own. They were young; perhaps they would forget. But Alverax and Roshaw would not.

Xuçan suddenly grunted and rose, huffing out a blast of warm air through his wide nostrils. A slight tremble in the ground caused Alverax to turn. From the base of the mountain, a troupe of ataçan knuckle-ran through dirt and grass, slamming their massive fists against the ground, skirting around the field of statues until they came to a stop in front of Xuçan.

One by one, they walked forward and fell under the massive arms of their chief. Xuçan squeezed with all his might before looking to Alverax with approval. *Do not doubt the path*, his voice bellowed in Alverax's mind. *No matter how dark the way may seem, there is always light beyond the bend, if you will take the steps to find it.*

Alverax looked up into the midday sky, searching for a star he could not find. Somewhere, hidden behind the blinding light, drifting through an infinite universe, the Moon's Little Sister stared back at him.

He would not soon forget what happened to these people.

Their blackened skin would haunt his dreams.

Hard as the path forward would be, he would not be alone.

And that was enough for him to take the next step.

48 · BONDS OF CHAOS

THE HERALDS ARE DEAD.

Chrys awoke in a padded leather arm chair. A thick fog rolled along the edges of his vision, remnants of the herbs he'd been given to aid in his recovery. He pushed himself to his feet, groaning at the stitches in his side and the bruises decorating every other part of his body.

He was in the Great Lord's study, and though he was alone, he could still feel the ghost of Malachus watching him, judging him, perhaps even letting slip the slightest smile as he often did when he approved of Chrys' choices. But the truth was that Malachus was gone—and even if he were there, his bichromic gaze would have been replaced by achromic brown. Still, Chrys could feel his mentor's presence, and he hoped the Great Lord would be proud of all they'd accomplished.

The Heralds are dead.

Only a single day had passed, but it seemed an eternity had come and gone. Chrys remembered the shrieks of the corespawn being destroyed. He remembered standing over Relek and driving the blade through his chest. He remembered falling to the ground beside Iriel as the two armies backed away from each other. And yet, it still did not feel real. He was certain that at any moment, the Apogee would return, echoing in his skull or claiming the body of another man.

It would take time—he knew that. It would take help—he could not do it alone. But he *would* move on. With his wife and son at his side, they would find peace.

A knock at the door startled him, and he stood, his hand instinctively reaching for a blade that was not there. The door opened to reveal the two women he had been waiting for, surrounded by a host of blue-clad Alchean guards. High General Henna offered a nod as she entered, her white Alirian hair freshly cropped above her ears. Entering behind her, in a long black dress with an intricate swirling pattern of golden brocade, was Eleandra Orion-Endin.

The night before, after the death of Malachus and the Heralds, the war had ceased, and Chrys and Iriel had been carried to Endin Keep. A council of Alchean officials had approached Chrys, despite his weak state, and asked him to take up the mantle of Great Lord, to establish peace with Felia and lead the people to a safe and prosperous future. But a war-time general was not what Alchea needed. The nation needed a healer, someone who would inspire them to rise up, come together, and rebuild. When the council disagreed, Chrys had an idea.

So, he took up the mantle, becoming Malachus' successor, becoming Great Lord Chrys Valerian. As soon as it was made official, as his first order of business, Chrys named a new Great Lord, one who had cared for Alchea for decades, putting the needs of the many above their own. And so, despite the council's previous objections, Eleandra Orion-Endin, the Mother of Alchea, became the new Great Lord.

"Chrystopher," she said with a gleam in her eye.

He gave her a friendly smile, though his pain still lingered, then crossed the room and offered his hand. "Great Lord."

She shook her head and wrapped him in a warm embrace. "Eleandra," she corrected.

"Only if you call me Chrys."

She laughed and gestured for him to take a seat. As he did, she walked around the desk and took her place on the other end. In the flickering lamplight, she looked older than Chrys remembered. A long night of negotiations and the loss of her husband had taken their toll. Still, she looked strong and graceful, far more ready to take on the Great Lord's responsibilities than Chrys would have been.

"Have you heard the news?" High General Henna asked as she took a seat beside him.

"That's why I'm here," Chrys said. "Did the negotiations with Felia go well?"

Eleandra smiled. "They've agreed to fifty years of peace and open trade. There are, of course, conditions from both sides, but the events of yesterday have brought us all together in unexpected ways. Even the religious institutions of Felia and Alchea have been meeting. They plan to bring together their truths based on the information you've shared, including some of the changes you've requested."

Chrys felt a spark of joy in his chest. "The priests?"

"As Great Lord, I am the head of the Order, and changes have already been instituted, even if there are many traditionalists who are furious with me. The priests will no longer be blinded, and joining will be voluntary. No more conscripting infants or limiting the number of children a family may have."

"That's wonderful." Chrys reached down and touched the waterskin at his side. "And the caves?"

Henna nodded. "We have soldiers headed up the pass as we speak to ensure that the passage is sealed for good. An exploratory party will be accompanying the ataçan on their return to Kai'Melend. They have been ordered to seal the cave entrance and bring back whatever is left of the wastelander culture, including sketches of the city and lifestyle."

"Good," Chrys said, recalling the story Alverax had shared the night before. "They deserve to be remembered."

"The southern field will become a monument to the wastelanders," Eleandra said. "And the children have been taken in by the Order of Alchaeus. They will be cared for, as will the statues of their heritage. As for your final request, of course your friends are welcome in Alchea should they return."

Chrys took a deep breath. Everything he'd asked for—changes to the Order of Alchaeus, peace with Felia, destruction of the paths leading to the Provenance and elixir, a pardon for a friend. With Eleandra in charge of Alchea, Chrys could step away with confidence that the nation would be well cared for.

His mind turned to his family. They were already home, resting, Willow helping with Aydin while Iriel recovered from her many wounds. Chrys yearned to go to them, to lie in bed beside Iriel and sleep until the world returned to some semblance of normal.

But he had one last thing he needed to do.

He thanked Eleandra and Henna, left Endin Keep, and jumped in a carriage headed west.

. . .

After a long, uncomfortable journey, during which his many stitches seemed constantly on the verge of splitting—the carriage did not do well on the army-trampled roads—Chrys finally spotted the farmhouse. It was exactly as it had been described to him: two sprawling barns with fenced-in hogs between them, fields of barley, green pastures with a dozen grazing cows, and a home complex of small, interconnected structures. Enough space for several families.

Chrys stepped down from the carriage and walked toward the center farmhouse. A few paces from the front door, a half-finished bull was carved into the stump of a tree. As he approached, he could hear the sound of children playing inside. Singing, stomping, laughter that was so close to a scream that Chrys wasn't sure which it was. He stepped forward and knocked.

A big man with red hair and a dubious look in his eyes opened the door. "Who are you?" he said with a deep, Laz-like accent.

Chrys raised his hands to show that he was unarmed. "I'm a friend of your cousin. Laz and I worked together. My name is Chrys Valerian."

The man's eyes grew wide. "Is really you? Laz talks about you! Good things, mostly. Come, come. I am Jeshua. You must share drink!"

"Thank you," Chrys said, seeing so much of his old friend in this cousin. "But I can't stay long. I just came to drop off a gift for Luther. I was told he is staying here with his family."

"Yes. Come, come." Jeshua threw open the door and gestured for Chrys to enter. "Is here in back. The kids are so loud, but I love them."

As they entered, Chrys caught sight of Luther's children peeking from around the corner. When they saw him, wide grins spread across their faces and they rushed forward, nearly tackling him with their excited embrace. He was quite certain that one of them tore the stitches in his side.

"Uncle Chrys!"

Despite the pain, he couldn't help but smile. Over the five years that he had worked with Luther—the Emerald to his Sapphire—Chrys had grown very close with his family. Once upon a time, they had hoped that Chrys' child and Luther's third would grow up to be best friends. Two little threadweavers growing up side by side. The Rite of Revelation for Luther's son had changed everything.

While the young girls clung tightly to Chrys' legs, begging him to drag them through the house, Luther and Emory stepped through the hallway. The last time Chrys had seen Luther was days after their son had been taken into the Order, and he'd been a mess. Drinking, threadweaving, and certainly not sleeping, Luther had not dealt well with the outcome. But now, on the outskirts of Alchea, hidden away on a remote farm with nothing but his family and Laz's strange cousin, Luther looked truly happy. Bright-eyed and clean-shaven—head and face—this was the friend who'd stood beside him for so many years.

Next to him, Emory held their infant son, barely older than Aydin but noticeably larger.

"Stones," Luther cursed as he recognized his friend. Emory nudged him for cursing—cut from the same cloth as Iriel. He ignored the comment and walked over, peeling both children off of Chrys' legs and throwing his arms around his friend. "I thought you were dead," he said quietly. "I mean, you don't look far from it, though the beard works, somehow. And, is that blood on your shirt?"

Chrys looked down and noticed that a bit of red had bled through his beige shirt just over the stitches in his abdomen. "Turns out that killing gods isn't as easy as it sounds."

"Is that..." Luther paused and looked at his kids. "News travels slowly out here. All we know is that the Felian army was leaving. Why don't we take a walk? I want to know everything."

"There will be time for that," Chrys said quite seriously. "But there's another reason I came. First, Great Lord Eleandra has pardoned you and your family. If you want to, you are welcome to return to Alchea, no questions asked."

Luther turned to Emory, and they gave each other a knowing look. "Great Lord Eleandra? That's... Thank you, Chrys. I don't know what we'll do, but thank you."

Chrys smiled at them both. "You seem happy."

"A bit of solitude has a way of helping you remember what's important," Luther said. "You know, in the last months, I've spent more time with my children than I had the entire rest of their lives. And it turns out, I even like them. Who would have guessed?" He winked at his oldest. "It's been really nice being able to help out more with the newest member of the family."

"Actually," Chrys said, looking down at the bundle in Emory's arms.

"That's the other reason I came. There have been a lot of incredible things that have happened over the past few months, and I'll tell you all about those, I promise. But I picked up a souvenir for you along the way." He reached down and grabbed the waterskin at this side. Even though he had checked it a hundred times already for holes and leaks, he still felt for the slushing weight of what remained.

Luther gave him a confused look. "What is it?"

"I think about your son's Rite of Revelation a lot," Chrys said, untying the drawstrings of the pouch. "Between what happened to you and what happened to Iriel, that day changed both of our lives. But those times are over. The Order of Alchaeus is dissolving, Luther. No more rites, no more revelations, and no more blinding children." He paused and opened the pouch, a soft golden light emanating from within. "No one can take away the pain of what you went through, but I found a way to make it just a little better."

"I don't understand," Luther said.

"Two threads; one bond," Chrys said. "Do you trust me?"

Luther nodded. "Of course, with my life."

"Emory," Chrys said, though he looked to the bundled child in her arms, "do *you* trust me?"

A flicker of hesitation danced in her eyes, but she, too, nodded.

Chrys stepped forward and stood in front of Emory, cupping the waterskin in his hand. "The wastelanders call this *oka'thal*, or life water. Others have called it elixir. But the name doesn't matter. What matters is what it can do."

Chrys held the waterskin over their son's face and let the remaining liquid pour down. The child squirmed, squeezing his eyes shut as the elixir puddled over them, glimmering in the daylight. For a moment, Chrys felt like he was a priest of the Order of Alchaeus. But where they had hurt, he would heal. The child calmed as the magic seeped into him, relaxing into the warmth of his mother's arms.

But then, the child's eyes opened, and the white haze that had clouded them only moments before was gone. For the first time in his short life, he saw his parents.

Luther and Emory wept for their son.

Chrys wept for his friends.

And at last, Chrys Valerian looked forward to what the future held.

~ EPILOGUE ~

~ SIX MONTHS LATER ~

WILLOW HELD up her grandson so he could see out the window of their carriage. It was late morning, and the green hills were filled with dandelions that danced beneath the summer sun. As a sparrow darted past the window, Aydin slapped his palms against the sill, grunting and gasping with excitement. She couldn't help but smile at the boy's enthusiasm for life.

Shortly after, the carriage came to a stop, and Willow stepped outside. She barely jumped out of the way as a horse lumbered past pulling carts filled with kiln-dried, white clay bricks. Dozens of men moved back and forth, hauling lumber and wheelbarrows of sand and lime. Despite all of the nearby activity, the majority of the noise came from farther west. It was there that she spotted Chrys and Iriel.

She wandered over, avoiding the line of traffic between the newly arrived carts and the half-built brick structure. As they approached, Willow pointed out Iriel and Chrys, and Aydin's eyes lit up. When Iriel turned and saw them, she waved them over with a wide smile.

"Thank you so much for watching him this morning," Iriel said, taking the young boy in her arms. She kissed him and let his bottom settle into the crook of her arm. "Chrys is great with ideas, but he needed some help in coordinating all of the moving parts."

"He's always been like that," Willow said. "Thinks he can do everything himself. It's even worse now. No one wants to correct one of the...godslayers."

"Oh, stop it!" Iriel said, blushing. "You know I hate that."

Willow laughed. "Actions have consequences, and sometimes they come with nicknames. Either way, I'm glad Chrys has you beside him. Someone has to tell him when he's being a fool."

"That, I can do." Iriel smirked. "The others are around here somewhere. I think they're helping mix the mortar. Let me grab Chrys, and we'll meet you over there."

Willow nodded and stepped away, walking past a handful of men cautiously guiding an ataçan as it pulled on a thick rope attached to a pulley at the top of the structure. A crate filled with bricks made its way up to a few workers at the top who slathered them and set them in place. With her arms now empty, Willow felt the urge to reach down and lay some bricks herself, to help in whatever way she could. But she also knew that Iriel had clearly laid out assignments to each of the workers, and whatever Willow did to help was more likely to create an imbalance in their plans. And if she was honest, Willow was getting older, and Aydin was getting bigger. Her arms could use a break.

As she walked around the brick-wrought structure, she found men and women dumping loads of sand and lime into buckets, mixing it up, then adding in water until the mortar came out to just the right consistency. The buckets were then taken by others and brought to the bricklayers. In the far station, Willow spotted two handsome men with their shirts off, wrestling with a barrel of freshly separated lime from the kilns back in Alchea. Sweat glistened off their hardened bodies, even if one was a little more hardened than the other.

She stepped through the other mortar makers and stood with her arms crossed until the two men noticed her.

"Willow!" Roshaw said, smiling as wide as the sea. He wiped his forehead with the back of his hand, then slapped that on his pant leg before walking over and throwing his arms around her.

"Roshaw!" Willow said as she pushed him away. "You're disgusting right now."

"Right now?" He smirked as he lifted her up and planted a sweaty kiss on her lips. He set her back down and turned to Alverax. "Sorry. Can't help myself sometimes."

Alverax shook his head with a grin. "You're not sorry."

"No," Roshaw said, looking back to Willow. "No, I'm not."

Just then, Chrys and Iriel—holding Aydin—came walking around the corner. Even though more than half a year had passed, Willow still saw glimpses of the dirty, frightened couple who had taken their child across the world to stop the gods. Now, Chrys' beard was trimmed close, his clothes well-pressed, and he seemed to stand a little bit taller than he once had. Iriel, on the other hand, seemed another woman entirely. She'd hired a night nurse to care for Aydin and had restarted her rigorous training regimen. Despite her hair now being cut above the shoulder, the biggest change was the fire in her eyes.

When they approached, Chrys gave his mother an embrace. "Could use your thoughts on the designs for the new trails. Want to make sure they're safe and that they'll last. Not convinced about the latter yet."

"Classic Chrys," Alverax said, giving them both a wave. "Right to business."

Roshaw let out a clipped laugh. "I thought you were going to say 'Classic Chrys...needs his mum to save his ass.'"

Willow gave him a look. "And what's wrong with that?"

"Oh, it has nothing to do with Chrys," Roshaw said quickly. "Has much more to do with how badass his mother is."

Willow rolled her eyes and turned to Iriel. "He thinks he's quite clever."

"They all do," Iriel said.

Chrys folded his arms. "Every time I get you all together, you turn on me. I'm going to have to start sabotaging these reunions." He paused before letting the slightest smile creep across his lips. "Why don't we all take a break and show Willow the progress."

Roshaw and Alverax cleaned off their hands and followed as Chrys led the others away from the mortar station. Willow noted the sidelong glances from workers across the field as their group passed. After a life of relative anonymity, Willow had still not adjusted to the fact that everyone in Alchea knew who she was, knew all of them. Except Laurel.

But that was going to change.

When they rounded the corner, Willow looked up at the stairway. Even incomplete, it was a marvel. White bricks laid twenty feet wide, as high as a feytree, jutting forth out of the grassy field and reaching up to the top of the Fairenwild. Some had taken to calling it Heaven's Gate, but that wasn't what mattered. What mattered was where it led.

Willow turned to Chrys as they stared up at the enormous structure. "It's brilliant."

Chrys clenched his jaw. "It will be. There is still a lot of work to be done."

"You know," Willow said, "you don't have to wait for the work to be done to revel in the beauty of it. But more importantly, we received word from Felia this morning. They've already broken ground on their own staircase. They've provided supplies to the Zeda people and workers to help. Zedalum is being rebuilt, bigger and more resilient. A year from now, it'll be a thriving trade route between the two nations."

Chrys took a deep breath and nodded. "I wish Laurel could see it."

"We all do," Willow said quietly. "Her brother most of all. Bay is quite the architect, I've heard. Which is great, because it's going to take some real ingenuity to build a proper trade center on the top of the Fairenwild. Ah, speaking of. Felia also agreed to change the name! They loved your suggestion and are already updating their maps. From now on, it will officially be known as the Laurelwood."

He closed his eyes, and Willow thought she saw a quiver in his lower lip. The stairway. The new name. They had both been his idea, a way for the world to remember the heroism of a young woman who had sacrificed everything. Willow thought it a beautiful gesture.

A handsome young woman with white grime covering her hands called out from the far end of the stairway, gesturing toward a cart filled with fresh bricks. Alverax stepped away with Chrys and Iriel to go help, and Willow watched them go. She was surprised when the young woman stepped up to Alverax, blocking his path, and grinned. He looked down at her with the Blightwood smile, leaned in, and planted a soft kiss on her lips.

"Did he just—?"

"He did," Roshaw said. "It's good for him. She's a sweet girl."

"He looks so happy," Willow added.

Alone, Willow and Roshaw clasped hands and stared up at what would surely become one of the great wonders of the world. It was nearly finished, or so it seemed. Though it was difficult to tell when the higher it rose, the more bricks were required. Still, they could stop at that very moment, and it would still stand through the centuries as a testament to peace and sacrifice.

She placed a hand on Roshaw's shoulder and set her head atop it, her other hand wrapped around his forearm. "On the way here, I was thinking."

"Uh oh," Roshaw teased.

She ignored him. "I was thinking about how, when this started, we all thought Chrys and Iriel's child was going to save the world. The Amber-eyed baby, the chosen one, destined to stop the Heralds, to create a core-seal. But that was all wrong."

Roshaw leaned his head against hers. "What do you mean?"

"It wasn't their children that saved the world, Roshaw." She looked up into his dark eyes and squeezed his arm. "It was ours."

THE END

ABOUT THE AUTHOR

Zack Argyle lives just outside of Seattle, WA, USA, with his wife and two children. He has a degree in Electrical Engineering and works fulltime as a software engineer. He is the winner of the Indies Today Best Fantasy Award and a finalist in Mark Lawrence's Self-Published Fantasy Blog-Off. Zack and his wife are the founders of the Indie Fantasy Fund, a non-profit that provides cash grants to help with the cost of self-publishing.

Join Zack Argyle's monthly newsletter to receive early updates on upcoming releases. Or follow along on social media.

news.zackargyle.com
twitter.com/SFFAuthor
instagram.com/ZackArgyleAuthor

Printed in the USA
CPSIA information can be obtained
at www.ICGtesting.com
CBHW020829150924
14059CB00150B/1389

9 798988 482604